RUSSELL KIRKPATRICK

ACROSS *the* FACE *of the* WORLD

FIRE OF HEAVEN
BOOK ONE

www.orbitbooks.co.uk

ORBIT

First published in Australia in 2002 by Voyager,
HarperCollins*Publishers* Pty Limited

First published in Great Britain in May 2006 by Orbit

A CIP catalogue record for this book
is available from the British Library.

ISBN-13: 978-1-84149-463-0
ISBN-10: 1-84149-463-1

Typeset in Goudy by Palimpsest Book Production Limited,
Polmont, Stirlingshire

Printed and bound in Great Britain by
Mackays of Chatham plc, Chatham, Kent

Orbit
An imprint of
Time Warner Book Group UK
Brettenham House
Lancaster Place
London WC2E 7EN

www.orbitbooks.co.uk

*This volume is dedicated
to the memory of my maternal grandparents,
Geordie and Hazel Larsen.*

CONTENTS

MAP 1: THE SIXTEEN KINGDOMS OF FALTHA

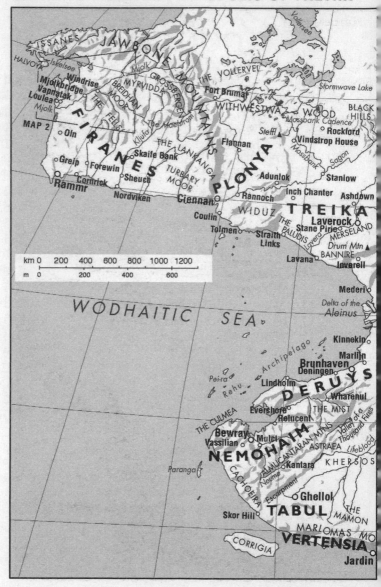

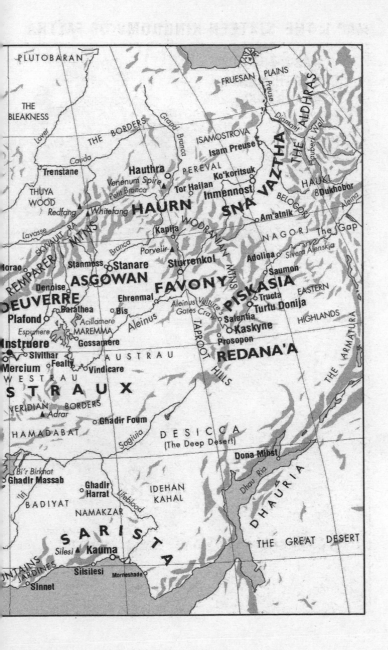

PLUTOBARAN

THE
BLEAKNESS

Lover

THE BORDERS

Grand Branca

FRUESAN PLAINS

Preuse

Diamant

THE ANDHRAS

Hqubert Wall

ISAMOSTROVA

Isam Preuse

PEREVAL

Cauda

Trenstane

Hauthra

Venenum Spire
Petit Branca

Tor Hailan

Ko'koritsuk

Inmennost

SNA VAZTHA

HAUKL

Dukhobor

BELOGOR

Aleina

THUYA
WOOD

Redfang

Whitefang

HAURN

Am'atnik

Kapija

WODRANIAN MTNS

NAGORJ

The Gap

Lavasse

SKYVAULT RA

REMPARER MTNS

Idrao

Stanmoss

Stanare

Branca

Porvelir

Sturrenkol

Adolina

Sivera Alenskja

DEUVERRE

Denoise

ASGOWAN

Ehrenmal

FAVONY

Saumon

PISKASIA

EASTERN

Barathea

Bis

Aleinus
Gates

Vultures
Crag

Tructa

Turtu Donija

Plafond

Acillamere

Aleinus

Salentia

HIGHLANDS

Espunere

MAREMMA

Gossamere

Kaskyne

Instruere

Sivithar

Fealty

Prosopon

REDANA'A

THE ARMATURA

Mercium

Vindicare

AUSTRAU

WESTRAU

STRAUX

VERIDIAN

BORDERS

Adrar

Ghadir Foum

TAPROOT HILLS

DESICCA
(The Deep Desert)

HAMADABAT

Sogiuia

Dona Mihst

Dhau Ria

Bi'r Birkhat

Ghadir Massab

'iri

BADIYAT

Ghadir
Harrat

Lifeblood

IDEHAN
KAHAL

DHAURIA

NAMAKZAR

SARISTA

Silesi

Kauma

THE GREAT DESERT

NTAINS
JARDINES

Silsilesi

Morneshade

Sinnet

MAP 2: THE NORTH MARCH OF FIRANES

MAP 3: LOULEA AND ENVIRONS

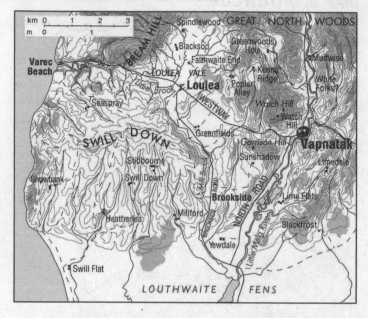

MAP 4: MOSSBANK CADENCE

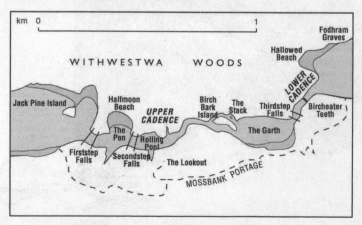

MAP 5: ADUNLOK

CROSS-SECTION

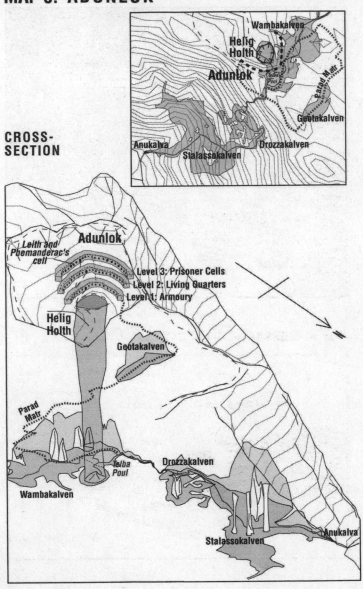

PROLOGUE

THE UNDYING MAN STUDIED the charts and documents laid out on the vast black marble table, searching patiently for the flaw in his long-laid plans. The Hall of Voices, buried deep in the Keep of Andratan, echoed to the sound of steel-shod boots as the gaunt, grey-cloaked figure turned from the table and strode its length, deep in thought. From long experience he knew that the flaw would be there. From longer experience still he knew that, however hard he looked, he would be fortunate indeed to find it.

No matter. His great advantage – his insurmountable advantage – over his ignorant enemies was the knowledge he had amassed from the enduring centuries of his life. Their earthly lives were so brief! They died before realising more than a fraction of their potential, unable from their short-lived perspective to encompass the recurrent patterns of an Age, doomed to repeat the foolish mistakes of their predecessors, while he had distilled a bedrock of wisdom from two thousand years of unbroken success. This was how he knew that the flaw would be there. It would manifest itself some time during his campaign – sooner rather than later, if he was lucky – and he would adapt to it. His wisdom would be sufficient, and he would turn the flaw in his plan to his benefit. His enemies would be destroyed in the moment of their seeming victory. So it had always been.

Indeed, he had an inkling as to what the flaw might be. So helpful, the young Dhaurian had been, in the days it had taken

1

him to die. Oh, he hadn't wanted to help, not at first, but the Undying Man was a man of leisure and had taken time over the long centuries to perfect the art of persuasion. At the end the young scholar had choked to death trying to deliver the information he hoped would satisfy his inquisitor, unable to draw breath in his haste to speak, to say something that might ease the agony. What else could he expect, the fool, when he had the temerity to try to infiltrate the very Keep of Andratan? The Dhaurians had risked much to find out what was happening in Bhrudwo, and they had failed. If this was the best of them, they would continue to fail.

So there was a prophecy. Well, there always was. The Most High could be depended upon to broadcast his plans to his minions. How could the Great Fool be so out of touch with his followers? Did he not understand the power of the spoken word? Now they would be constrained to walk along the road that had been laid before them, losing the one advantage they had: the randomness generated by ignorant mortals which made one's own plans so hard to formulate. He, the legendary Destroyer feared by all Falthans, the immortal Undying Man, Lord of Andratan, was bound by no such path. Not even the Most High could predict what he would do.

And now the prophecy had fallen into his hand, as it was bound to do. There was no doubting its veracity. He had a well-tested feel for these things. Years he had spent, high in his Tower of Farsight, wrestling over the inspired words uttered by the fools pledged to serve the Most High, and they all carried the same aroma. He could smell them, these inspired words; their sharp tang offended him. Foolish restrictions designed to keep the sheep in their pens. But not him! The Undying Man had faced down the Most High himself and emerged victorious, with the secret of eternal life his and his alone. The words of the Most High on that ancient day still burned in his mind. This prophecy had the same sharp aroma as those words, like *jujune* with too much spice.

It was just like the Most High to raise someone to oppose him. Just like him, and doomed to fail. The Undying Man had spent two thousand years learning all about the human soul, and knew how vulnerable this naive saviour would be to corruption. When he found this Right Hand – when, not if – he would *not* destroy him. No! The Destroyer epithet was not among his favourites. He did not destroy; he remade. That is what he would do with the Right Hand that was prophesied. He would find him, foster him, corrupt him, remake him. The prophecy said that Faltha would be ruled by the Right Hand, which suited the Undying Man perfectly. What a delightful irony there would be in presenting the Right Hand of the Most High as the saviour of Faltha, a saviour made in his own dark image.

Yes, perhaps the Right Hand was the flaw in his plan, the random element as yet unaccounted for. But, the Undying Man reflected as he gazed dispassionately at the stump where his own right hand used to be, the simple elegance was so compelling.

CHAPTER 1

LOULEA

THE GREAT OAK STOOD autumn-tinged and alone under a troubled sky. Gnarled limbs spread arthritic fingers out over the sodden common, stretching towards snug, lamp-lit houses. Passing squalls shook the browning leaves, soaking the rich bronze canopy. The stout oaken heart brushed away the autumn rains with little effort; there was undoubtedly much worse in store, even if the coming winter proved to be mild. This far north the snow could lie for weeks, even months at a time in the worst years, but the giant tree would survive. It always did.

Underneath the protective mantle a boy sheltered, shaking with the cold. Occasional drops fell from the branches above him, finding the back of his neck with unerring accuracy. *It was not supposed to turn out like this*, he thought angrily. Cold and wet and miserable, he pressed himself back against the bony trunk. Why had he ever thought to ask her here? What foolish idea had taken hold of him? The others would be laughing at him, he knew it, and the thought of their taunting smiles bit into him more than the icy wind, more than the knowledge that she was not coming, that she had never intended to come.

The wind drove another squall of rain across the common. A gust idly flicked a cold, wet arm under the shelter of the big tree and stung the boy's eyes with the ends of his blond hair. Invisible fingers snapped at a golden leaf, which gave up its struggle and fell swirling to the ground. The youth shuffled forward and peered

4

at the brown dead thing. Why couldn't it be left alone? It was dead anyway; why bother with it further? His eyes glazed over and he sank back against the oak tree. He wasn't leaving, wasn't moving until she came, even if she never came, even if they found him wet and cold and maybe dead.

It would pay them all back.

The sharp north wind seemed to be bringing in darkness as well as rain. Noises of doors closing and bolts being drawn filtered across the common. House lamps stretched pale fingers towards the oak tree, pointing accusingly at the shivering figure beneath it. From somewhere behind him came the shrill voice of a woman scolding a barking dog. Above the tired village the wind rolled the clouds away, exposing the steel-grey sky, darkening towards night. The boy hugged himself and moved from foot to foot to ward off the cold, while he stared up at the stars. Everybody would know by now that she wasn't coming to meet him. She was probably telling them in her low, quiet voice. They would all be watching the oak tree from their windows, talking, laughing, pointing. He could imagine it! Druin's blockish scorn, laced with obscenities, Hermesa's trilling mockery, Lonie's smirk, and Stella's eloquent silence.

Stella! She was as unreachable as the merrily twinkling stars.

The wind died and for a few still seconds the boy could hear a familiar voice calling his name. Then a blast of frigid air from the north carried the voice away. Sighing, he eased himself away from the rough trunk and, with a reluctant stoop, began to shuffle across the rain-soaked turf towards the figure of his brother holding a guttering lantern.

'She didn't come, then.'

'I don't want to talk about it.' The boy's voice was laced with embarrassment and shame.

'Just because she didn't come doesn't mean she hates you.'

'I said I didn't want to talk about it!'

His brother ignored the waspish tone. 'She would have met you, but she's afraid of the other girls, of what they would say.'

'She would never have come. She thinks I'm weak, a spring twig in a snowstorm, they all do. Well, I don't care.' He glared across the room at his older brother. 'She'll tell them all that I asked her to go walking down by the lake. They won't say anything to me, but they'll all be talking about it, especially Druin. You know how he never leaves me alone. Asking Stella to go walking is the most stupid thing I have ever done.'

A frown flickered across his brother's face. He shifted slightly in his bed.

'Stella doesn't think you are weak, Leith. She's just fearful of all the talk. It will take her some time to overcome her fear.'

'And in the meantime?'

'In the meantime, be patient with her. Stella keeps herself to herself. She doesn't give anything away easily. Not only that, she's under enormous pressure at the moment. You'll need to be patient if you wish her to trust you with her companionship.'

Good old Hal. Never criticising him, never telling him to forget about her, never telling him to grow up like his mother always said. Leith sighed. Be patient? By then it would be too late, someone else was bound to have claimed her. What was the use? She was destined for someone else, so why should he get upset? There would always be someone else older, stronger; he would always be second, always the baby, never taken seriously . . .

'Why should I have to wait? By the time she notices me, I'll be too old or someone like Druin will have beaten me to it. She's just not interested, and she never will be interested. I'm too young and I'm not clever enough for her.' He turned his head away from Hal.

'Not clever enough? Leith, everyone else here is in your shade. For the sake of the Most High, don't listen to their nonsense. You *are* clever, you *are* intelligent; you just take your time because you're afraid of making a mistake. There's nothing wrong with that.'

'I don't know . . .' Leith liked to hear Hal saying things like this. He lay there a moment, wondering how he could get his brother to say it again, but Hal spoke first.

'Did you stay under the tree all afternoon?'

'Yes. Clever, aren't I?'

Hal said nothing.

'I asked her to meet me there at two o'clock, so I waited a while and then came home. What was for dinner?'

'A roast, to mark the first day of winter. Here,' said Hal, stretching awkwardly down and feeling beside the bed with his good hand, 'I saved you some.' He handed a cloth-covered plate to Leith.

'Why did Mother have to be so angry? She knew I would be all right. She never worries about you, even when you stay out all night.'

Hal pursed his lips, but remained silent. Leith knew his words were unfair. Hal had never needed any looking after, not even as a young child. Early one morning, nearly seventeen years ago now, Leith's parents had found an infant boy playing happily in an ice-rimmed puddle on the outskirts of the village, a child who couldn't tell them where he came from or where his parents were. A toddler of perhaps two winters, no more; sorely twisted and deformed down his right side, obviously unwanted, discarded, abandoned. The young couple picked up the dirt-laden waif and took him home, where he soon became the child they had longed for, the boy they had needed, the son that kept them together. From that time on, it seemed the petty jealousies and trivial arguments that had darkened the house of Mahnum and Indrett were no longer important, and a year later the barren woman bore a child of her own.

From the day Hal had been found, it was apparent that he was an unusual child. Though he had a crippled arm and leg, he was constantly on the move, never retreating to some sanctuary of self-pity, but always on his feet, playing, visiting, walking in the woods. A faery child, an elfin child, a child unlike others born and raised in the stern, harsh northlands. He did what he wished and went where he willed, unfettered by the restrictions placed on the other children, who were bound to the village by ties of work in the summer and of safety in the winter. Hal the cripple was always welcome in the thatched-roof houses of the village, and a sort of mutual unspoken consent saw him allowed to amble unchecked across the fenced-off farmlands of the Vale, asking permission of no one. Yet though he spent many hours alone, he was in no way deceitful or uncaring of his adopted mother's feelings. He seemed so vulnerable, yet he lacked nothing, had no need that cried out to be met. It was fortunate for his parents that in Hal's character there was little room for self-pity, making it all the more easy to give him love unselfishly, untainted with the need to be loved in return. Leith, their own child, had been so different, crying incessantly as a baby, self-centred and demanding as a toddler; and for a while his parents thought that there must have been something wrong with him. Finally they realised that Leith was a normal boy, and there was something indefinably *right* about Hal.

They had all been very lucky, Leith knew. So very lucky. Only he didn't feel lucky.

'I didn't know that the north wind would come today,' Leith said stubbornly. 'I wouldn't have stayed out there if I had known.'

Again his older brother said nothing. Feeling angry, hurt, and guilty about the irrational resentment that always seized him when he tried to talk things over with Hal, Leith turned away and drew the bedclothes over his head. His cold food fell to the floor.

'Good night, Leith,' came the earnest voice of his brother.

Leith had an uncomfortable night. His body felt hot and cold all at once and his legs and back ached. For most of the night he lay unmoving, waiting for morning to come, trying to think of the snows ahead, of the exploring he would do, of Midwinter's Day and the Play that would be performed. Of anything but Stella. Of anything but the achingly embarrassing thing he had done. *Oh, Most High, why did I do it? Please, let me go to sleep and wake up to find that it never happened.* Finally, as dawn approached, he slid exhausted into a fitful doze.

That morning Hal awoke to find his brother tossing feverishly. He dressed as quickly as he could and made his way quietly into the kitchen. His mother made to greet him, but Hal cut her short.

'Leith isn't well. A touch of Icewind fever, I think.'

'Oh,' she sighed. 'What on earth was that boy doing yesterday? He knows what the autumn wind can do.'

'He wouldn't give up waiting for Stella. Do we have any wintergreen leaves in the cupboard?'

'No, and you're not going out to get any today. It snowed most of the night. We do have birch bark, but it's a little old. Here, you look after the drop-scones while I go out and see what I can find in the wood.'

'You should be able to find a few near the big fir that fell last spring.' Hal knelt down beside the hearth on his crooked right knee and picked up some kindling wood for the cooking fire. 'One light snowfall shouldn't have buried them.'

His mother put on a fur-lined oilskin coat, leather boots and woollen gloves. She smiled at Hal as she pulled the hood over her shining black hair. 'Every year someone in the village catches Icewind fever, and every year they come to you for help. At least this patient doesn't have far to come.'

She opened the stout wooden door and looked out at the morning. Clear, crisp and bracing, it waited to wrap its chilling arms around her in that familiar embrace. The woman turned and looked with affection at her elder son. 'The old enemy is here early this year,' she said ruefully, then stepped out into the cold air and shut the door behind her.

When she returned she found Leith lying blanketed and shivering in front of a banked fire, sipping a thick broth. Hal had more of the soup simmering on the fire, and the aroma thickened the air in the small wooden house. The crippled youth busied himself with more scones on the skillet, but left them when his mother came through the door, slapping and stamping with the cold.

'Did you find many good leaves?' Hal asked over his shoulder as he put more water on to boil.

'Enough. There aren't many about. Will you need much of a supply this winter?'

'Yes; but there's no point in collecting it all just yet. This could be a long winter, and it will be better in the ground for now than

9

drying in the cupboard. Coming, Leith,' he called, and poured more soup into a bowl.

'I'll take it to him.'

The small but strong woman kicked off her boots and padded quietly across the warm rugs covering the polished wooden floor. Her son stirred and reached out a weak arm as she knelt down and offered him the steaming bowl, shaking her head at him. 'Men!' she jibed good-naturedly, hiding her concern at the sight of his too-bright eyes and fevered brow. 'They're so tough. A bit of a cold and they think they're dying.'

'It's not just the Icewind fever.' Hal spoke quietly to his mother, out of earshot of the patient. 'He was hurt yesterday. He feels let down. Mostly, though, he misses his father.'

'Don't we all.' The woman turned away.

'I don't think he wants to get well. Someone needs to spend time with him, but he doesn't want to wait around for a crippled brother all the time. His friends always seem to be doing something else now, chasing girls, spending their afternoons down by the lake, diving from the rock, hiding in the woods, you know the places they go. Leith feels he's not welcome, so he's been playing with some of the younger boys. He gets teased a lot because of it. And when he asked Stella to go out to the lake . . .'

'Pell and Herza's daughter?'

Hal nodded. 'She's the popular one at the moment. All the boys want to be seen with her. They ridiculed Leith when they heard that he had asked her out, and they'll ridicule him even more because she didn't show up.'

'How old is she?'

'Fifteen, sixteen, something like that. Sixteen, I think.'

Indrett sighed. Why did adolescents make things so complicated? How did these fortunate ones contrive to make themselves so unhappy? She remembered her own teenage years . . .

'Leith's been out of sorts since his father left,' Hal said. He pursed his lips thoughtfully and turned back to the skillet.

His mother sat down on her favourite high-backed chair, head in hands. *Leith is not the only one,* she thought. *How much longer? If ever?*

The next few days dawned crisp and clear, with bright mild afternoons. No one in the village was the least bit fooled by their great enemy: he always tempted them with false hope, as if he thought he could convince them that spring was just around the corner. Even though his ruse was obvious, there were those who wished that they could trust the good weather that was offered in the balmy days of autumn.

The world of the North March of Firanes was ruled by the weather. Near the coast, cold northerlies and warmer southerlies fought all winter, and when snow fell it fell heavily but melted quickly. The inhabitants of coastal towns like Loulea and Vapnatak lived in an in-between world of soft white snow and sodden slush. Further inland, up on the Fells where the southerlies did not penetrate, only four months separated last spring and first autumn snow. Though the snow fell inland no more heavily than on the coast, the bitter cold prevented it from melting, and so it steadily accumulated until the spring thaw. The people of northern Firanes could be distinguished by the winters they endured: the few hardy and fierce inlanders holding the 'softer', less adventurous coasters in contempt. Winter controlled much of the lives of all northern Firanese people, wherever they lived, but the northerners had come to understand him. So when five days of fine weather were followed by a bitter north wind and an overnight blanket of white embracing the village, no one in the village was surprised. Driving sleet, a frost and a day of low cloud and chilling temperatures followed. This year the villagers had at least finished gathering the harvest when he arrived.

One villager didn't even see this onslaught, this precursor of winter. Icewind fever was seldom serious; those who suffered it usually spent two or three days with a cold, a sore chest and a headache. Leith, however, could not shake it off. The cough broke after three days, the fever dissipated, but still he stayed in bed. He seemed not to hear the often-expressed concern of his mother and,

11

as his lassitude grew, answered conversation more and more seldom. For most of the time he lay quietly in front of the fire, eyes closed. The village Haufuth called in on organisational matters for the Midwinter festival, but even he failed to get a response from the youth.

'It isn't natural!' the stout headman puffed, leaning on his staff, a recent affectation. 'He should be out and about, helping you get the house ready for winter, not lying about in bed. It looks like a long and hard winter this year. Had I known, I would have sent one of the young men around to give you a hand.'

'Thank you, Haufuth,' the woman replied carefully. In the North March the elected village headman was always known as the Haufuth, for reasons long forgotten, and his birth-name was seldom used. 'To tell you the truth, Leith hasn't been the same since his father left. I'm sure he will be all right when Mahnum returns home.'

The Haufuth frowned. 'But how long will that be? You have work to do before winter's heart. Your boy won't be able to lie about when the snow sits heavy on your unrepaired roof. And Kurr came in to see me yesterday. He tells me that Mahnum owes him a few days on the farm – I forget how many exactly – and asked me if Leith would do in his stead.'

She stared at him, eyes cold, the familiar anger stirring within.

'I've already agreed, Indrett,' he said, his forehead furrowed and his troubled eyes pleading with her. 'Please don't cause any trouble with old Kurr just now. You know how I need him for Midwinter. Without his mutton we just couldn't have a Midwinter. Please get Leith to go and work for him this week. For all our sakes.'

Indrett nodded reluctantly. It was past time for stern words. She wasn't worried about Kurr; the old man was all smoke but no fire. In fact, she rather liked his hard-bitten manner. Better than the polite standoffishness she encountered daily at the market. But the village Haufuth could cause Leith a great deal of trouble if he desired. Perhaps the Haufuth was right. Perhaps she had been too soft on the boy. If only Mahnum was here . . .

'He'll be there,' she said flatly.

'Good, good. Now, about Midwinter. The council have decided that this year we will have new masks. Would you be so good as to make the Snowmask and the Flowermask? You always do such good work.'

'What about the *Sumar?*' Indrett believed in giving them their proper names: *Snaer* and *Falla*, not Snowmask and Flowermask. *Sumar*, not Sunmask. Strange, she reflected, that a woman from the civilised south would want to hold on to traditions the uncouth northerners seemed so careless about. Still, she would make no comment; it would be wise not to antagonise the village headman.

'Herza is making the Sunmask this time. We thought that with Mahnum away, you wouldn't have time . . .'

'Of course I'll do it.' Indrett's quick answer covered his awkwardness.

'Excellent, excellent!' the big man beamed. 'And we would so much like to see the reappearance of your honey cakes. They went so fast last year I never got to try even one.'

In spite of herself, Indrett smiled. The appetite of the Haufuth of Loulea was legendary. Other villages could boast the quickest runner, the strongest woman or the fastest woodchopper, and these claims were put to the test when the villages gathered for Midsummer at Vapnatak. But Loulea was famous for the culinary capacity of its Haufuth, and this distinction had never been seriously challenged. At the table, if nowhere else, the Haufuth truly led his people.

'Why, you should have said!' she replied with a flourish. 'I could make you a batch this week – in fact, I'll send Hal over with a basket tomorrow.'

The Haufuth rubbed his hands together, then frowned. 'Merin put me on a diet yesterday,' he muttered pensively. He thought a moment, and his face brightened. 'She loves your baking. Maybe we could postpone this diet to next week. Yes, that's the answer!' he said, pleased with himself. 'She told me about those cakes. Crisp wheat. Honey centres! Tomorrow, you said?'

'They'll be there,' Indrett said laughingly. 'Off with you now, before you promise me out of provisions.'

'I'll pay for the cakes,' the Haufuth protested.

'Don't be ridiculous.'

The large man laughed out loud: a heavy, laboured laugh. Then his round face grew more serious, and he hitched up the belt around his huge girth, a sure sign he was nervous. 'Look, Indrett, let me pay for the cakes. Some of us are concerned about you. You put on a brave face, but tell me, how are you going to make it through the winter? The council think that maybe if a few of the men of the village donated a day each—'

'We'll make it!' the short woman snapped, her anger rising. 'My family made it through last winter on our own and we'll do it again, with no favours. And who's to say Mahnum won't be back before Midwinter?' Her face lifted proudly, daring the Haufuth to gainsay her.

Wearily, the big man sighed and sat down. 'Look, I didn't want to start on this. We miss your husband in the fields, in the village, on the council. We need him – well, not as much as you do, to be sure,' he said cautiously, noting her icy expression, 'but ours is a small village and even the lack of one man is keenly felt. Your son, now—'

'If it's hands you are short of, I have two to give! I won't have this family beholden to the village!'

'You know that's not possible, Indrett. Women have their tasks, their place, and we need them there . . .'

All thought of not antagonising this man evaporated with those words. 'May all stubborn northerners perish in the snows along with their backward peasant ideas! If only you would think, really think, for just one minute! Mahnum is gone who knows where on some foolish errand for the dead King. Leith is not yet seventeen, and he isn't ready. Hal does the work of three men but no one ever notices. Just women's work, all a cripple's fit for. And all the while we're treated as though we don't exist! No say on the Village Council, a council made up of the leader of every house – if he's a man. People feel we've deliberately hurt them by depriving the village of manpower – as though Mahnum leaving was my fault – and they simply ignore me at the market. All we're good for is masks and cakes at Midwinter! Yet none of those who resent us refuse Hal's ministrations when Icewind fever strikes! Can't you see that if I and the other widows in the village were allowed to work with the men and sit on the council, we could hold our heads high? That no one would have to despise us? That we wouldn't have to be treated like beggars? Can't you see?'

She paused, red-faced and out of breath, anger flickering dangerously in her dark eyes. The Haufuth leaned forward in his gently protesting chair, and softened his expression still further.

'Indrett, we can't let this go on. Already you work yourself to exhaustion caring for your boys. I watched you in the market the other day. Remember when that silly woman from Vapnatak tried to set up her sweetmeat stall in opposition to you? I was proud of how you stood up for yourself without becoming rude or offensive. Honestly, could you do more? Those villagers who scorn you, well, maybe they are scared and ignorant, fearing a foul winter and the loss of their own husbands. And maybe they might even help you, but for your proud independence.'

Indrett shook her head, more to keep the tears from her eyes than to disagree.

'Come to the next council meeting and voice your grievance,' he said gently. 'The council will listen.'

She nodded her head dumbly, unable to speak through the hurt and loss that seemed suddenly to well up within her. Watching her with sympathetic eyes, the Haufuth relaxed tense muscles and looked towards the door. He wasn't much good when it came to crying.

'Now, don't forget about Kurr, will you?'

'No, Haufuth, I won't.'

The sweaty man raised himself from the chair with a groan and walked slowly to the door. 'I'd better be going. It's nearly lunchtime!' he said lightly, in an effort to break the tension. 'I should be just in time for Herza's table. Good day to you.' He touched her shoulder on the way out.

Indrett shook her head as the door closed. She sighed and turned towards the figure sleeping in front of the fire. Time for tears later.

This was not going to be easy; if she didn't handle it right she might lose her son's heart forever.

The wind that blew straight off the snow-cloaked mountains to the northeast rattled the gnarled branches of the oaks and bent the tall, leafless poplars towards the sea. A blond-headed boy with a knapsack on his back trudged down a frosted road, stamping irritably on any ice-covered puddles in his path and only occasionally glancing up at the wispy clouds scudding across the pale blue sky. Around him the rolling hills sparkled silver in the early morning light, speckled here and there with farm animals grazing or lying asleep, their breath steaming around cold nostrils. The road on which he walked led to a farm, where the boy was going to work for the day.

The name of the farm was chiselled on the mossy, slatted farm gate, and on his mind. For a long time the boy rested there, leaning against the half-opened gate, running his fingers absently over the name carved in the splintering wood. Heaving a vast sigh, he straightened and looked beyond the gate and down the rutted track that disappeared over a grassy ridge in the distance.

Better get it over with, Leith thought. Kurr was a legend to the children of the village, the old man who caught boys and girls and locked them in his dark, cold barn. What he did with them then no one knew for sure, though many of the young boys claimed to have escaped from his clutches. Leith himself had once stolen some apples from the bottom paddocks, and had hidden in fear under a hedge while the irate farmer scoured the area for the thief. It had only been for a dare. He didn't really believe all the stories told about the old man – at least, he hadn't believed them last night as he lay in bed – but he would rather have been at home in front of the fire than shivering in the crisp morning air. He thought of what his mother had said, how angry she had been. Rather the old farmer than more of that. Shutting the gate to Stibbourne Farm behind him, he walked slowly down the narrow road.

How could she have thought that he was betraying his father? Would his father really have been hurt by his behaviour? Would he have thought it childish? *Well, if he had been here, things would have been different,* he thought angrily. *It's not my fault!* Where was his father? When would he come home? If he had really loved them, if he had really loved Leith, he would never have gone away.

Leith vividly remembered the day his father had left them. It was at the end of a back-breaking afternoon of seed planting, and the family were sitting quietly together on freshly cut, upturned logs in front of their small house, backs to the reddening sun. A group of finely clad men rode up on tall horses, mail-shirted and armed with glittering swords menacingly drawn, the children of the village trailing excitedly behind them. The men dismounted and hailed his father. Leith could remember how frightened he had felt then. There had been a discussion that rapidly heated into a quarrel, ending with the men abruptly mounting their horses and riding noisily, arrogantly off down the road through the village. Hermesa's little brother had been knocked over, he remembered that. The soldiers never stopped to check if the small boy had been hurt, they just rode off as though they owned the world. Then his father had tried to explain things to them, his mother crying already and Leith wanting to run away or to knock someone down but not knowing where or who.

'The King is dying,' his father had said, 'and he sends me to my death.'

That night he had held them close, and then he had gone away.

An image came unbidden to his mind, an image of a tall man stooping over a log, trying to pull an axe from it. The muscles of his unshirted torso strained with effort. With a grunt the axe came free; then down it came, again and again, until the log was split in two.

Leith knew it was his father, but try as he might, he could not see the face.

He shook his head to clear it of the image, and forced himself back to reality, shivering as the cold wind whipped around him. If growing up meant having to do things he didn't want to, things like walking down the narrow, rutted path leading to the house of Kurr the farmer, then he wasn't sure he wanted to grow up. He

17

wanted to be exploring with his friends, talking with Hal, walking with Stella, working the fields with his father.

He could see the farm buildings now. They nestled below him in a small defile, surrounded by trees bravely fluttering their few remaining autumn flags against the winter wind. Behind the ochres and golds rose another cattle-grazed hill, stretching lazily away towards the sea.

The old man was watching the road from the door of his barn. He saw the silhouetted figure shuffle slowly into view, with head down and hands in pockets, reluctance clearly showing in his demeanour. *Good. He still remembers Kurr the farmer. Well, Kurr still remembers a little episode concerning an apple or two. There's nothing like fear to make a boy work harder.*

He waited until the youth had trudged up the steps to the house and had knocked lightly on the door, as if he didn't really want an answer. Then he eased open the barn door.

'You! Boy! Over here!'

The white-faced boy started, then looked in the direction of the barn. He stood where he was, irresolute.

'Quickly, if you know what's good for you!'

The voice was definitely coming from the barn. More than anything Leith wanted to run, but he forced himself to walk nervously towards the old building.

The farmer waited until the boy was in the shadow of the barn, then stepped out, thrusting a stick before him.

'Mahnum's boy, eh?' the old man bellowed. 'I thought Mahnum's boy was at least fifteen by now. How old are you, boy?'

'Sixteen, sir,' Leith stammered.

'Come now, boy, you're not yet twelve if I'm any judge. I'll have a word or two to say to that fool of a Haufuth if he's sent me the wrong boy. You are Mahnum's boy?'

'Y-yes, sir.'

The old man laughed uproariously, wagging the stick in all directions. 'A cripple and a runt. He got what he deserved, taking up with the fancy woman from the city. A cripple and a runt! Well now, runt, do you know what you'll be doing for me this week?'

'No, sir.'

The old farmer was close to him now, pointing his willow cane at Leith's chest. Leith could see the lines etched into the sharpness of his face, surrounding clear and lively eyes. Eyes full of malice.

'It's in my barn,' he chuckled. 'I want you inside my barn.'

By now Leith was too angry to be frightened. *A twelve-year-old runt?* He took a deep breath and strode past the farmer.

The old man smiled. Fear and anger would make good taskmasters.

Morning gave way to afternoon, and the afternoon dragged on. The air in the barn was thick with animal smells, and as Leith worked at undoing rotted stitching on a canvas awning, the sound of horses in their stalls came to his ears. The noises seemed to be coming from the rear of the dimly lit building. Horses were the main measure of wealth in the north of Firanes. There were a few horses in Loulea, and the council even kept an elderly mare for the children to ride, but Leith had never heard of any of the farmers owning more than one. Leith wondered how such an insignificant old man came to have horses in his barn. Perhaps they were stolen! He could hear them moving about in their stalls, eating their feed and occasionally nickering softly to each other. After listening for a while he decided that there were four of them. Four! A fortune. However he had come by them, the old farmer was a wealthy man by North March standards.

It became harder and harder for Leith to see what he was doing. At first the youth imagined that it was the onset of evening and he would soon be allowed to go home, but after a while he heard the wind rise and then rain began to drum on the wooden roof high above. The weather was closing in. It was definitely getting colder. With the gloom and the chill he was having difficulty in undoing the stitching; his fingers wouldn't work and his eyes began to swim. Time seemed suspended. Leith was having trouble with a particularly stubborn piece of stitching and his frustrations boiled near the surface. He was cold and he had a headache and he just couldn't get this thing undone, and he didn't want to be here at all. Grinding his teeth together didn't seem to help any.

A sudden powerful gust of wind shook the barn and snuffed out the torch by which he was working, leaving the building in semi-darkness. Leith shouted out in fright and jumped to his feet, and there was the old farmer at the door, lamp in hand.

'Better get inside the house, boy,' he said quietly in between gusts, then set the lamp down on a rough wooden table and extinguished it. 'The weather's coming in from the sea at present, but the Icewind is out there just waiting for a chance to blow. Leave the awning there for now and come inside. No telling when the *Iskelwen* might come to try its strength against this old barn.' He clapped himself on the shoulders, folding his arms across his chest, gnarled hands on threadbare cotton.

Iskelwen, Leith thought. *The Icewind*. It had been a long time since he had heard words in the old language from anyone but his mother. No one bothered with the old tongue any more.

Outside the rain leaned in from the southwest, driven before a persistent sea breeze. Leith could taste the salt in the air, and even though he knew the sea was more than two leagues distant he imagined he could hear the booming of huge white breakers on pale sands. It was getting quite dark. He wondered how he was going to find his way home.

'Quickly, now!' he heard the farmer call from somewhere in front of him, and he scurried through the rain towards the patch of yellow light.

Inside he found hot tea waiting for him. He drank it with relief, warming his numbed hands on the mug and his insides with its contents. He thought he heard someone coughing in another room and looked questioningly at the farmer, who returned his word-less inquiry with a flinty stare. After a moment the old man got up and left the room, leaving Leith alone with his thoughts.

As soon as some warmth had returned to his body and he could once again think straight, Leith put his mug down and looked around the room with frank curiosity. Not the sort of house a man who owned four horses might be expected to live in! It seemed large enough – there was a hall leading to what were obviously separate bedrooms – but it was untidy, run-down, a little ragged around the edges. Pale whitewash, yellowing slightly and peeling in the cobwebbed corners, lent a shabby, neglected feel to the room. It was obviously some sort of sitting room, not often used; musty-smelling, cluttered with fragile ornaments placed carelessly on sharp-edged tables, it was not the sort of room a person lived in.

Leith's musings were interrupted by the old farmer returning with another mug, seemingly empty.

'Better get you home, boy. Sounds like the weather's easing off a little, but we won't have much time before it comes down again, and from the north this time. Ready?'

Leith nodded, though he wasn't sure what was meant. Was the old man going to walk home with him? He followed the farmer outside. It was noticeably lighter and the rain sifted straight down, swirled about only occasionally by the wind. Through the barn they went, pausing for a moment to relight the torch. Another torch at the far end of the barn illuminated the stalls, and in the flickering light the farmer busied himself finding saddle and bridle. The horses began to stamp and chafe, seemingly realising that their master wished to ride. Leith felt warm breath on the back of his neck, then a nuzzling from behind. He turned around to see a long face towering above him. With surprise and pleasure, he caressed the horse's head.

The old man led out a bay mare from the hindmost stall, patting her muzzle and whispering to her all the while. Outside in the late afternoon calmness the farmer mounted easily, pulled the boy up behind him and set the mare off at a brisk walk. Leith was going to arrive home in style.

The excited youth travelled in an unreal world high above the turf. The horse trotted much faster than Leith could run, and for a long time he watched the ground moving backwards underneath him. Glancing to the left, he noticed that dusk was spreading from the north with alarming rapidity. Onto the Westway they rode, turning athwart the breeze that grew stronger moment by moment.

A mile or so east to the village, thought Leith. *Maybe five minutes more before we arrive home*.

'Tell me, boy,' the old man shouted over his shoulder, 'why do they call it the Westway when it only goes east?' and he laughed as he drew his hood over his face. Peering out from behind the thin, hunched figure, Leith felt the cutting wind and saw the inky blackness to his right before he heard the howling in the air.

'Head down, boy!' the farmer grated, pushing him back roughly. 'The Icewind is here.'

They arrived at the village in the face of the *Iskelwen* storm. Here and there a chink of light showed through shuttered windows. The wind whipped down empty streets, snatching at dead leaves and piling them against bolted doors, howling its displeasure at being shut out of warm rooms. Up the muddy road came a horse hard ridden, with two figures crouching low on its back. The larger figure reined in the sweat-lathered mare in front of a small house at the end of the lane, dismounted and helped the smaller figure to the ground. While the man led the horse round to the lee of the building and tended it, the boy banged a few times on the door. Soon it swung open and the sudden light swallowed the two figures. The wind gathered, then sprang down the lane a fraction too late, succeeding only in slamming the door shut behind them.

Inside, cloaks came off and cold hands and feet were stretched out close to the crackling fire. The man and the boy leaned towards the flames, for the moment oblivious to the others in the room.

'Get them something hot, please,' Indrett said to Hal. As the cripple limped away, his mother walked slowly towards the fire. She waited for the warmth to do its work.

'You're not going home tonight,' she said firmly to the old man.

'No, girl, I'm not. I'll just be off to the Haufuth's house for the night, and in the morning . . .'

'Oh no, you're not. You'll stay right here in this room near the fire. If this is a real Deep White, then you might never make it to the other end of the lane.'

He turned on her with a scowl. 'So you're giving me advice, are you now? I suppose you learned snowcraft in the streets of

Rammr, did you? You wouldn't have known what snow was until you came here, girl. I've survived nights in the open, rounded up my herd in a blizzard . . .' The old man spluttered to a stop.

Indrett put on her most contrite expression. 'You're right, and I'm sorry. I don't have your experience. But I would worry if you left now, I wouldn't sleep,' she said artlessly. 'Here, I'll get Leith to bring the spare mattress in for you,' and she sent her son scurrying off before the bewildered, badly outmanoeuvred farmer could raise any objection.

It was still dark when the old man woke. For a moment he could not pinpoint what had caused him to awaken so suddenly; but, being a landsman, he knew something was amiss. Then he heard it: the shuddering moan of the wind, a soft, unsettling sound from far off, profoundly disturbing to the old man. He had not heard this particular sound for maybe twenty years or more, not since the night he lost his old barn, the barn built by the Haufuth's grandfather. In a moment he was up and dressed, searching for his cloak. Another moment and he was peering outside.

A light snow filtered down in a calm air. It lay undisturbed, inches thick on the ground. But behind the calm came the sound of approaching violence, a low moaning that set the farmer's teeth on edge.

After venturing outside to make sure his horse was adequately sheltered, he closed the door softly and sat heavily on a wooden chair, lines of concern etched on his expressive face. If he were at home, he would have secured the outbuildings of Stibbourne Farm, bolted all the doors and shutters of his house, moved all the furniture over to the walls, and sat the storm out. Well, as long as Tinei kept herself safe, he wouldn't worry about his buildings. *Please, Most High, don't let that headstrong woman go outside to try to secure the farm!* There was no chance of his making it home before the wind hit. But what should he do here? His hands fidgeted as he thought. *The girl Indrett has probably never seen a real Iskelwen storm before. Will she know what to do? That fool Mahnum! Plenty of girls in the village to choose from! It was just as well that Modahl hadn't lived to see it. His only son marrying a southerner!*

23

He laughed. After all these years, he found himself thinking like a northerner far too often.

He took a deep breath and stood up, grimacing as the ominous sound seemed to mix itself up somewhere in his vitals. He had to do something. Just then the boy Leith came through from the bedroom, rubbing the sleep from heavy eyes. 'What's the noise? Sounds a bit like tomcats . . .' He faltered to a stop at the sight of the farmer's worried frown.

'A real storm! Not the sort of wind you villagers call an Icewind, boy – this is a full-blown *Iskelwen* howler. Haven't seen one for years. This sort doesn't bring snow, it just picks it up from the ground where it lies and hurls it at you. Is your mother awake?'

Leith shook his head. 'Don't think so,' he mumbled sleepily.

The farmer grunted. 'Wake her. We need to get this place ready.'

As they began moving furniture, first Indrett and then Hal came into the room. The farmer explained what they were doing, and soon Leith was busy bolting the storm shutters while the others cleared the room of anything that the wind might be able to throw about should it manage to break into the cabin. The farmer instructed them to extinguish the fire, and set Hal to work damping the embers in the grate. A single candle flickered in the middle of the bare floor. As they laboured the dreadful noise drew closer, and the people in the cabin had to shout to each other in order to be heard. It developed into a shrieking wail; the sound someone might make, Leith imagined, were they being slowly torn limb from limb. Now the roar was overhead, but still no wind.

'Where's the wind?' Leith shouted to the old man. Strangely, the farmer's red-rimmed eyes were lit up with something that looked like excitement.

'Comes with a big cloud,' returned the farmer. Leith could barely hear him. 'Like a breaking wave – sucks air up into it – wind drives the cloud ahead—' but Leith lost the rest. For a moment the shrieking tailed off, then a rumbling, rasping noise like the stampeding of a thousand hills beat at them and the wind struck. Leith thought he could see the northern wall of the cabin beginning to bend. Suddenly a sharp banging noise came from behind them.

Across the Face of the World

The farmer shouted something at Leith, waving wildly in the direction of the bedroom. Leith nodded and ran off. He could feel air rushing past him as he ran. A shutter had come loose in the bedroom. As he went to close it, the wind slammed it shut in front of him, nearly taking off his hand. He struggled to push the rusty old bolt properly closed, hammering it home finally using Hal's staff.

The people in the room settled in to a tense wait. Conversation was all but impossible as the wind howled about them and the timber of the cabin protested with groaning and, more ominously, cracking noises. It was as though some giant had snatched up the cabin and was shaking it with a series of random jerks calculated to catch those inside off guard. Leith wondered how the other families in the village were coping with this monster wind. He wished it was light outside so he could see the storm; what stories he could tell the others! For a moment he began to think about Stella in her cabin at the northern end of the village, at the edge of the forest. Her gossipy, shrewish mother, her dour father, her brother the drunkard. How were they coping with the Icewind?

Then he forgot all about Stella as he saw a corner-post bend slowly, fractionally inwards. Such was the roar from the wind that none of the others seemed to have noticed.

With a loud report it broke in two.

The wind roared in like a wall of water and snuffed out the candle, throwing everything into confusion. The noise was overpowering. A voice shouted 'Out!' in his ear, a strong hand grabbed him by the shoulder and propelled him towards the bedroom door. In a moment they were all in the bedroom with the door bolted. The same hand then pushed Leith down into a sitting position with his back to the door, and someone sat down heavily beside him. Somehow, probably by the smell of tilled earth, Leith knew it was the farmer.

The door buffeted his back with every gust. It felt like a living being, a beast of prey, communicating fear through the wood and into the muscles in his back and shoulders. Leith began to feel the insane desire of the wind to break through the door and get at them; it seemed that a malevolent force had launched an irrational assault on the house and its occupants. Maybe the Fenni, the mountain gods of the northern wastes, were real after all. Stick people, the Fenni were supposed to be, nine feet tall with claws for hands; a hateful, violent race, slaying intruders who dared venture into the mountainous heartland of Firanes, a race of gods who used lightning bolts to kill and who wielded the weather as a weapon. As freezing gusts whipped under the door and snaked around his legs, sending a chill climbing up his spine, the stories telling of the Fenni seemed believable. The pressing darkness settled close about him, while all around the howling, creaking, groaning, whistling of the wind battered his ears and his brain. And in the noise and the darkness a cocoon of weariness enveloped Leith, and everything else save the warmth at his shoulder receded into the distance.

Some time near morning the old farmer shook him awake.

'Move your legs, boy!' he rasped. 'You don't move your legs, you won't walk for days.'

Leith stretched his legs and felt pain in his knees. After rubbing them for a moment, he pulled them up to his chin and clasped his arms around them. He wondered how his mother and Hal were feeling, only a few feet away in the darkness, and hoped they had managed to find sleep in this cauldron of noise and violence. He thought about the village caught in the storm and tried to imagine what it was like outside, with trees bending and breaking, snow piling up in drifts and people inside, clenched up against the wind and the cold. He hoped no one was caught outdoors in the storm. In his mind he pictured himself high in the Common Tree, looking down on the houses, seeing through the thatched roofs and watching people moving about; then, craning his neck to see Stella's house, he watched her sitting by the fire. Secure and warm, needing nothing. Unbidden, a lone figure leading a horse came striding through his imaginary snowdrifts. Leith recognised the broad back and the set of the shoulders, and angrily tried to blank the picture out of his mind. Slowly it faded until all that could be seen was swirling snow, specks of white on a black, empty background.

Finally he could bear the inner silence no longer. He turned to where he knew the old farmer to be sitting, and asked in a brittle voice: 'Do you know where my father is?'

He felt the man beside him turn and imagined the farmer's old, hard face staring into his.

'Nobody knows, boy, nobody knows for sure. He's been gone too long; he should have been back by now. One of the best men in the North March, Mahnum was. Never should have taken two years over a journey to the east.'

'What's he been doing?'

'Following the King's supposed orders, that's what. Hasn't your mother told you anything of this?'

'No,' said Leith. *Of what?*

The old man grunted. 'No, well, she wouldn't. The fools at the Firanes Court are afraid of him; they know he's every bit the son of his own father, Modahl your grandfather. *She* knows all about the Firanes Court, your mother does. Something's up in Rammr, we don't know what, and I'll wager the King doesn't know either. Someone at the Court wanted your father out of the way.'

Leith felt confused. It seemed as if the farmer was talking about someone else. The Court of the Firanes King? What threat could a northern woodsman be to the King? Then he remembered the knights and the horses and the regalia and the swords shining in the sun. He remembered his father's anger, and his hasty departure. But the farmer was still talking, and Leith had to concentrate to prevent the wind snatching the words away.

'He came to see me before he left. Seems that rumours had come to the ears of the King's Court in Rammr, saying that Bhrudwo, the ancient enemy of Firanes, of all Faltha, had grown strong again, and that a new invasion was planned. That rumours of war were being whispered around the Courts of the Sixteen Kingdoms of Faltha, from the cities of Kauma to Inmennost, and that even Firanes was within reach of Bhrudwo's new power. They're even reviving the old tales of the Destroyer. Heard of him, boy? Mahnum said the King was worried about what was happening in the Sixteen Kingdoms. He spoke of treason, of betrayal, of violent death in the Courts of the West. The King was frightened by these tales, and so wanted someone to travel east to gain news. To Instruere first, then to Bhrudwo itself if necessary. Well, the great Modahl is no more, so naturally the King turned to your father, forgetting that whatever he was in his youth, Mahnum retired to the north some years ago. Lost his nerve, some said. The King's men were nervous, your father told me. Men with swords, nervous. Talk of the Destroyer makes anyone nervous. It makes me nervous. Do you know what I mean, boy?'

Leith nodded, then felt foolish as he realised the old farmer could not see him.

The ancient tales of the invasion of the Bhrudwan hordes were well known to Leith. A thousand years ago a hungry army from the east, led by a cruel lord they called the Destroyer, overran the unprepared people of Faltha. Even Firanes, the westernmost and therefore most isolated kingdom, had not escaped. The stories told of the long sieges, of cities taken by treachery from within, of Falthans reduced to eating their dead, of people promised mercy but given lingering deaths. They told how the Destroyer had ridden through the gates of Instruere, the Falthan seat of power, astride a death-pale horse, come to set up his throne and demand tithes and worship from all of Faltha. And they told how the common people had risen against their harsh ruler, causing the armies of Bhrudwo to hate the land they had coveted, and how the Bhrudwans were eventually driven out through the courage and boldness of Conal Greatheart and his band of followers, the Knights of Fealty.

Nowadays everyone knew that the story had been romanticised. The numberless Bhrudwan hordes of legend had undoubtedly been invented to cover Falthan shame at having been conquered so easily. The Destroyer, the legendary one-handed Undying Man, had more likely been a group of commanders than a single person. The Haufuth had taught Leith and the other village children that the Bhrudwan army had been defeated, not by resistance, but by intermarriage. That saddened Leith, who found the tales of Conal and his knights exciting, and often imagined his rude quarterstaff, designed to keep off the few wild animals that ventured into Loulea Vale, was a sharp sword with a name and a history, and that the bushes were Bhrudwan warriors. He knew the Lay of Fealty by heart, but the magic in its verses had somehow evaporated in the face of the Haufuth's logic. It was true that many southerners had mixed blood, and were much darker than northerners, so perhaps they had intermarried with Bhrudwans. And it was also true that the Undying Man had never existed. Still, Leith could imagine Conal bravely facing the Bhrudwan Lord, just as the Lay of Fealty said.

The old farmer was still talking. 'The Watchers have heard tales of a great king rising in the east, of the revival of soldierly arts, of the massing of warriors. But such stories have always been whispered, and only an insecure Court would have heeded them. None other of the Sixteen Kingdoms has reacted to these tales with anything but contempt. However, the command was given and Mahnum had to obey. Your father is a real Trader, boy, and he should have been back by now.'

Leith waited, but the old man said nothing more. So he asked, 'Why my father?'

The old man was silent a while, and Leith could hear the sounds of the wind outside, softer now. Then he spoke. 'A real Trader, boy, has access anywhere. People are the same wherever you go. Even Bhrudwo. They all want what they don't have. That's what a Trader offers them. A Trader travels anywhere, paying bribes, wearing disguises, running and riding and selling his way to a profit. It's a good way to find things out. That's what your grandfather did – and Mahnum too, for a few years. It's the oldest cover in the business. Probably more spies than honest Traders around, though most of them mix patriotism and profit. The art's been lost in Firanes, and that's why they said they wanted your father. Poor fool. When he met your mother he gave up the Trader's life. Hadn't been out of the district since. A real Trader needs to practise his craft continually. He probably never got to Bhrudwo.'

Sadness seemed to flow like a river out of the darkness towards Leith. The old man's talk had made his father seem real again for a moment, but Leith knew that nothing was real save the old ache. His father was gone. But for a while, just hearing his name from the lips of a stranger, he had seemed close by.

The old farmer thought pityingly of the boy beside him. What sort of apathy had brought them all so low? For a moment his own heart misgave him. *Was there really something happening in Bhrudwo? Where was Mahnum?* He sighed and shrugged his shoulders.

The soft light of a silent dawn found a tousle-headed boy resting on a gnarled man's shoulder, together in sleep.

CHAPTER 2

MIDWINTER'S DAY

'WELL, I THINK IT was inconsiderate of him!' Herza said.

'Do you?' replied Indrett wearily.

'Yes, I do. Fancy him promising to cull out his best hogget and mutton, and us planning the feast and all, thinking that he was going to supply the meat just as he always does!' The thin, waspish woman manoeuvred her foot inside the door and a defeated Indrett waved her towards a seat.

'Well, he never turns up to the feasts himself, you know. Oh, no! Too high and mighty for the common folk, he is. There's no excuse for behaviour like that, not even for a *foreigner*.' She laced the word with scorn, perhaps forgetting that Indrett herself was from the far south of Firanes. 'That's what he is, though no one seems to remember. And Tinei, the poor dear, is kept locked up at home, never allowed to see anyone. It's only right that a man like that should have to provide the food for Midwinter's Feast. Never does anything else for the good of the Vale. And now what does he go and do?'

Indrett waited. She wouldn't make the expected response.

But Herza didn't need it. 'Well, it's obvious, isn't it? Can't stand other folks having a good time, so he tells the Haufuth that there'll be no meat this year.'

Indrett raised her eyebrows.

'Well, what do you think? Am I right? Isn't the feast going to be an absolute disaster?'

31

From his seat by the fire, Leith watched his mother smile wanly at the older woman. Stella's mother had always intimidated him with her sharp tongue and mean spirit. The talk in the village was that Herza was the reason Pell, her husband, kept up an active interest in the Village Council, keeping the meetings going long after everyone else wanted to go home. The woman was like autumn drizzle: once she set in, she was there for the day. Leith shook his head and went back to his whittling.

Indrett was now having it carefully explained to her why all the men of the village should get together and go out to Kurr's farm. 'He'll never change his mind after listening to the Haufuth. He's got that fat fool wrapped around his little finger, you know. Mark me, Indrett, we won't get even a single tough old ewe from that man unless we go out there and take it!'

Indrett raised her tired eyes to meet those of her guest, and spoke quietly. 'Herza, he's not the only farmer in the Vale. We could get our meat from any one of them, if one of them would offer.'

'But why should they? It's Kurr's job!'

'Now, Herza—'

'Don't you "now Herza" me, young lady!' the woman stormed. 'I've had enough of that sort of talk from the others. If any of you cared a whit for the feast, if anyone had an ounce of compassion for me while I'm trying to organise this celebration—'

'The Haufuth and his wife are organising it, Herza,' Indrett said quietly, but the other woman did not appear to have heard.

'—then I wouldn't be worked up into an absolute state like I am! Really, dear, feasts don't just magically appear. Everyone needs to help if we're to enjoy a good Midwinter! But there are folks who leave it all to others. Come to think of it,' she said pointedly, 'we haven't seen you out and about much of late, Indrett. I do hope that you're feeling better by now; really, it's been so long!'

She didn't seem to expect an answer, and Indrett didn't offer her one.

Hal came hobbling in on a stick, neatly balancing two cups of tea in his good hand. 'Tea, Herza? Chamomile today, with a hint of something else thrown in. See if you can guess what it is.' He turned and winked at his mother.

After tea and bread the two women began talking again; or, more accurately, one began talking and the other made what she hoped were polite noises at seemingly appropriate places. After a while Indrett grew careless, and had to ask Herza to repeat herself – occasionally at first, then more and more often, a task that even that indefatigable woman began to find onerous. Finally she threw her arms into the air and shouted, 'You're not listening to a word I'm saying!'

Leith started, dropping the carving he had been working on. Hal came in from the kitchen with more tea. Indrett's face reddened, but she said nothing.

'Poor dear,' Herza said softly. 'How rude of me to prattle on about silly little things, what with you and all your worries. Why, just last night Pell and I were talking about Mahnum and where his poor body might be and whether we should maybe organise a memorial service or help look after your children, but then Pell told me about Stella and that splendid boy Druin and I forgot everything else.' She paused, took a short breath, then continued, 'Have you heard? You have heard, haven't you? They say he might be the next Haufuth! And what if they were to announce their engagement? Wouldn't I be so fortunate to have such a boy for a son?'

Leith looked wide-eyed at the old woman. *Stella and Druin, betrothed?* He had seen them together, skating on the lake, but had thought nothing of it. Surely not! But wild images of Stella and Druin together came hot into his mind, and as though his imaginings somehow made it real, he saw them in their own house, with children. He looked down at his carving, but his hand was not steady enough to resume his work. Herza began talking about something else, but Leith paid no attention. And when the woman finally left, hours later, Leith was still sitting by the fire, knife in one hand and carving in the other.

The weather – the whole world – spiralled towards Midwinter. The villagers, so free to wander abroad in field, forest and town during the precious summer months, now found themselves locked inside fragile homes, tempers fraying, able to venture out only in clement weather. Darkness pressed in on them like shadowy, snow-laden trees stooping over a dusky road, an ever-darkening tunnel through which the villagers of Loulea travelled towards the shortest day of the year.

To Indrett, this time of the year was particularly oppressive. Her two boys bustled about amusing themselves in various ways, while she slowly withdrew into herself. Winters were not like this in Rammr, far to the south. There the snow settled only occasionally on wide, paved streets, and was welcomed as a playful friend. But here it stole colour and life, smothering everything in a sterile, cold weight, just as it had smothered her heart. Her hopes of ever seeing Mahnum again faded into a creeping numbness.

Leith did not notice his mother's decline. He was going to show everyone that things were all right, that Stella didn't matter to him. So every opportunity saw him out with the sledge his father had made him, riding the snow-covered downs below Kurr's farm with his friends. He had packed a great deal into the last two months – learning how to repair a roof and succeeding in repairing their own, collecting and chopping wood, working another week for Kurr, then days on the snow of the downs and evenings indoors, close to the fire, working away at his birch carving. It was this carving that occupied him during the solitary, indoor days; a carving of a tall, unshirted man pulling an axe from a log. He had long finished the rough outlining, but was having trouble with the detail, particularly the face. For long periods he would stare into space, and afterwards could never remember what it was he had been thinking about.

Soon the week before Midwinter was upon them. Activity on the cold, snow-lined streets increased, regardless of the weather, as preparations for Midwinter's Day gained momentum. This year's celebrations were to be held at Falthwaite End, a special place on a low hill half a league north of the village. The farm there was recent, but the name was from antiquity. It meant 'cultivated land',

and was the older form of Faltha, the name given by the First Men to the whole of the Western World. Tradition said that the tree-crowned hill was the furthest north ever tilled by the hands of the First Men, but many thought this dubious in the light of old farms still occupied at least ten leagues to the north of Loulea. The feast would be held under a group of magnificent oak trees, and tarred canvas would shield the villagers from the weather. Should the heavy snows come, or the wind rise, there was a small, cramped barn on the far side of the hill they could retreat to. Wherever they were held, the Celebrations would last most of the day and on into the night, with the culmination, the Midwinter Play and the Haufuth's invocation of summer, coming at midnight.

Tradition might point to the invocation as being the highlight of Midwinter's Day, but for most of the revellers the true highlight would be trying to eat as much of the vast amount of food as possible. As a rule winter fare was bland and soon became unappetising, and many villagers consoled themselves throughout autumn and winter with dreams of the Midwinter Feast. And what a feast it would be! Although for some unexplained reason the old farmer Kurr would not be providing the mutton this year, meat from various farms had been promised. Hogget from the downs, hare from the coastal clifflands, and tasty venison from the borders of the deep woods miles to the north. Sweets came from the cupboards and pans of the women of the village: light scones, crunchy biscuits sparingly seasoned with precious spices bought from the Vapnatak market, honey cakes, sticky sweetmeats, toffee and dried fruit.

The drink, supplied ostensibly to aid in digestion of the food, was traditionally laid down in the autumn of the previous year. It was considered bad luck if one lapsed into unconsciousness during the celebrations, so few people became offensively drunk. On the other hand, wine and ale were not regular parts of the villagers' diets, so little would be left over at the end of the night.

Music was an important part of the festival. This year, as well as the regular musicians from the Vale, a well-known family of singers from Oln in the faraway south were wintering over with

Prester up at Longacre, and had promised to put in an appearance if the weather permitted. As the evening progressed, people would join the musicians in song and dance. The stately dances of the North March allowed even those who had overindulged to participate, and eventually all present would be coaxed or cajoled into singing and dancing right up to the time of the Play and the Speech.

Midwinter had been celebrated from time immemorial. The custom probably had its origins as some simple, spontaneous celebration of the turning of the tide, an acknowledgement that from here on the days would get longer, even though the worst of the winter was yet to come; an expression of faith in summer in spite of the evidence all around. Like all such things it had become a tradition, unquestioned by those who took part in it. All over the northlands of Firanes, and in cold, dark places throughout northern Faltha, the custom was played out on the shortest day of the year. In ways such as these winter was made bearable.

The observances at Midwinter and Midsummer were the nearest the northerners of Firanes came to participating in organised religion. They all knew that the Most High had chosen them from all the races of the world many thousands of years ago, and had given them Faltha as a mark of His favour. But it was said by those who thought deeply about these things that the Most High now had little to do with the world of men. Certainly, if He was interested in anyone, it would hardly be in a few northern farmers. And for that the farmers and their families were thankful: wrestling with nature was difficult enough without involving the Most High. Midsummer and Midwinter were really symbols of the victory of humanity over nature, a demonstration of how stubborn persistence could blunt the sharp edge of the wilderness. The Most High – if indeed He existed at all – had obviously left the people of the north to their own devices. And they had made a good fist of things without Him.

The morning before Midwinter found Leith up early. It was his turn to prepare breakfast, and he was busy frying bread dipped in eggs when he heard a knock on the door. Frowning, he took the pan off the heat and went to answer it.

Out in the moonlit yard waited the lightly clad figure of Kurr. When the door opened, he stepped boldly inside and stamped up and down to rid his legs of their numbness.

'Where's your mother, boy?' he asked harshly. 'Get her up, lad; I've got a favour to ask her.' The farmer moved stiffly over to the fire, not even looking to see whether Leith carried out his instructions.

Indrett dressed and followed her younger son out to where the old farmer stood rubbing some feeling back into his hands. 'Isn't it a little early to be making social calls?' she said shortly.

Kurr grunted an acknowledgement. 'I need your boy for the day,' he grated. 'Got some sheep to shift. I'll put in a day around the house after Midwinter. Most High knows you need it,' he said, gesturing towards the corner-post. 'That'll never stand up to another strong wind. I can replace it. Do we have an agreement?'

The woman put her hands on her hips. What sort of a man would refuse to help with Midwinter and then seek assistance moving a few sheep about? Maybe Herza was right. 'It's up to the boy.'

The farmer narrowed his eyes. 'You know where I live,' he said to Leith. 'Be there soon, boy. There's a lot of work to do.' He nodded again, but as he turned away Leith thought he saw a troubled look in the proud man's eye. Indrett gently closed the door behind the departing farmer.

She looked at her son, who sat in a chair and stared into the fire. Eventually he sighed and turned to his mother. 'Will you take care of the breakfast? I think I'll go and help Kurr.'

'You haven't forgotten about the Play?' It was an unnecessary question. She could tell he had not forgotten.

The day before Midwinter was the day when the Haufuth selected the Players for the Midwinter Play. Indrett knew that all of the young people of the village would stay home today, waiting for that knock at the door which heralded the Haufuth's invitation to play Snaer, Sumar or Falla. Her thoughts drifted as she remembered that special Midwinter in Rammr when she had been chosen to play the Falla, the harbinger of spring, the part traditionally played by a young woman. Rammr, the capital city of Firanes, the seat of the King's Court, celebrated Midwinter just like anywhere else in Firanes. It had been Ansula, the most senior of the King's officials, who had knocked on the door of her father's house and who had placed the delicate Flowermask in her trembling young hands. An honour for any young woman, an especial honour for one not born to the noble houses, but that year Indrett had been the flower of the Firanes Court. An honour for the most presentable young virgin of the land, as the tradition said. An invocation of fertility. So Ansula had chosen her.

Ansula had not known about her father.

That Midwinter's night had been special; she had indeed been the centre of the huge celebration, beside which Midwinter in Loulea seemed pale and mundane. Dancing on the marble floor of the Great Hall, heady wine, the murmured compliments of many a lord, a smile from the King himself, gossip and laughter, the handsome, stone-chiselled face of a softly spoken Trader from the north . . . and the unbelievable, never-to-be-expected sensation of falling in love. Her breath still caught in her throat whenever she thought of that night.

Leith shook his head. 'I haven't forgotten,' he said wryly. 'But what can I do? Not much chance I'll be chosen, anyway.'

As he went to get his boots and overcoat, he asked himself what he was doing. Of all the days of the year, why today? Of all the people of the Vale, why him? He peered through the shutters. The weather was cold but clear, and Leith could clearly see the treacherous layer of ice that had formed overnight. A dangerous day to be outside.

Leith hurried through the dark village and on to the Westway, being careful to run on the crackling grass rather than on the icy, rutted road. The youth could feel the cold rising from the ground, biting through his furs, his woollen hat and mittens, and his snug straw-filled felt boots. He shuddered and pressed on. A pale light spread slowly from the mountains behind him, lending a faint glow to the downs before him.

Across the Face of the World

The road to Stibbourne Farm crested over Swill Down, a few hundred feet above the Vale of Loulea. At times like these, when he found himself all alone in the quiet beauty of the Vale, Leith liked to swagger down the road as the owner of the world. But today, as he hurried past darkened hedgerows and snow-laden groves of trees, he felt uneasy. He saw the snow and ice around him take on a rosy glow, noticed the occasional load of snow sigh and slough off a pine branch, listened to the faint hum of a myriad of faraway sounds brought to him on the crisp morning air. But this morning it failed to move him.

At the top of the first ridge he turned and looked to the east, back over the Vale and the flickering points of light that made up his village, towards the seat of the dawn. Though the sun was still shy of the horizon, the reddish glow in the eastern sky threw the outline of the distant Fells into sharp relief. But to Leith the morning just didn't feel right. He deliberately turned his back on the unfolding scene and made his way towards Kurr's farm.

Leith caught up with the farmer on the last slope down to the farmhouse. At the sound of panting breath and crunching gravel the farmer waited, and grunted an indecipherable greeting to the youth when he finally arrived at his side. Without another word, the old man and the youth made their way past the outbuildings to the place where twenty or so long-haired sheep were penned.

To the relief of the embarrassed youth none of his friends witnessed the strange sight of Leith and Kurr driving a flock of cantankerous sheep through the middle of the village. *Probably all still in bed*, Leith thought ruefully. The hard winter had its benefits; it was too harsh to do much outdoors work, the bulk of which was done in the short summer. This meant that, for the youngsters at least, winter was a time of leisure, apart from two afternoons a week learning from the Haufuth. But Leith was finding that as he grew older there were more demands made on him, like working for this cranky old farmer, and less time remained to pursue his own interests. And he knew that if his father ever returned, the job of teaching him a skill would begin in earnest. Leith hadn't thought much about that. He didn't know much about being a Trader, and he didn't know if he wanted to find out.

A grunt of command snapped the youth out of his thoughts.

'Pardon?'

'I said turn them left here, boy.' The old man pointed with his stick down a rutted path towards a tree-crowned hillock.

'Here? I thought you weren't – I mean, aren't you—'

'Yes?' There was menace in the voice. Leith knew he was in trouble. He took a deep breath.

'Someone said that you weren't sending any sheep to Midwinter this year.'

'Oh? Where did you think we were going then, boy?'

Leith mumbled something in answer. He never should have asked the old man questions. He should have stayed in bed.

'Who said I wasn't bringing the sheep? Who said? I'll wager that it was useless old villagers with nothing better to do than flap their tongues like swallows flying south for winter!' The farmer stabbed his stick repeatedly into the ground to punctuate his words. 'None of 'em with the gumption to come and ask why, and just as well for them! And none of 'em with the decency to come and lend a hand! I'll tell you why I wasn't going to bring the sheep. No one offered to help round them up!' The old man swore, then struck the gate a fearsome blow with his closed fist. 'Tinei and me out in the snow! I never should have listened to her. Out in the snow rounding them up, and now she's in bed again, stretched out by the fever. And I've got Mahnum's boy helping bring the sheep to Midwinter. And no thanks will I receive – you'll see! A few polite words, or maybe not so polite, and then back to their work, glad to see the back of an irritable old farmer.' He lifted his face to Watch Hill, the highest land in the North March, a few miles to their right. 'They're not worth it, they're not worth it! No matter what you say!' He stared at the forested hill as though he expected it to answer.

Leith shook his head, unable to follow the meaning of the old man's words.

*   *   *

When Kurr handed the sheep over he received a perfunctory thanks and a few sharp glances. He patted Leith on the head and made his way back down the path towards the road. Leith looked after him until he was out of sight, a pathetic figure, a despised outcast. Perhaps a picture of himself in fifty years.

'Leith! Leith!' came a shout from behind him. The boy turned sharply at the sound of the voice. A group of village elders walked over to where he stood.

'You'll be pleased!' said a smallish, tousle-headed man.

'Congratulations!' another said, and a third slapped him heartily on the back.

'Did you hear who the Falla is?'

'I suppose you know that Lanka from Brookside is the Snaer this year?'

'You'll have to wear stilts to drive that one out!'

'Have you tried the mask on yet?' The questions all came at once.

The confusion on Leith's face made itself obvious to the men. 'Oh!' said Malos, the small man. 'We thought—'

'You'd better go home,' said another kindly. It was Rauth, a member of the Village Council. 'You should make it back home in time. The Haufuth's gone to Brookside to tell Lanka that he's the Snaer tomorrow. You know you have to be home to receive the mask. If you're not there he'll go to the house of the chosen alternate.'

For a moment Leith remained rooted to the spot. He was the *Sumar*! Marked for life! The prized central character of the Midwinter Play!

'Go home! What are you waiting for? Hurry!'

Leith took to his heels.

'There you are! I was hoping you'd be home soon!' Hal greeted him excitedly as he burst through the door. 'Have you heard? The Haufuth came here soon after dawn, and that can only mean one thing!'

'Oh,' said Leith. So the Haufuth had already called. The disappointment would come later; he could still feel nothing as yet.

Hal could read his brother's face. 'No, no!' he said. 'He'll call back. He was upset that you weren't here – he thinks highly of you, you know – and when Mother told him that you were out working for Kurr, he nodded and walked out. But I've been watching from the window – here, come and look – see, he's been walking up and down the road waiting for you. There he is, talking with Herza.'

Leith looked. He could see the fat headman leaning over his staff, listening to the old woman. He imagined he could almost hear her voice.

'Go out the front and stand around. He'll notice you and come over, I'm sure of it.'

Leith went outside. After what seemed a long time, the Haufuth glanced in his direction, struggled to free himself from the garrulous woman, then began a slow walk in the general direction of the house. Leith hurried back into the house, relief pumping inside his chest.

'I'm pleased they picked you,' his older brother said. 'Another year and you'll be too old.'

Leith studied his brother's face. There seemed no trace of resentment or animosity. Hal was genuinely happy for his younger brother. Crippled Hal had never been chosen to play the Sumar or the Snaer. What other things would he never do? Leith had not thought about it. What else would he not be able to participate in? Would he marry? Would he hunt? How could he work?

A knock came at the door. Leith forgot about his brother.

Midwinter's Day began early throughout the northern lands. Lamp after lamp was lit, child after child climbed sleepily out of bed, family after family rushed about busily dressing, feeding and milking animals, gathering food and donning boots and coats for the journey to the celebrations. The few who lived in the interior would often travel great distances for Midwinter, and these people were already at the site of the feast, having taken advantage of whatever clear weather their lands had offered over past weeks. No one stayed at home unless they were ill or otherwise incapacitated; northerners took otherwise unconscionable risks with the weather in order to be with their friends for Midwinter. And each year a few never made it back home.

Well before dawn the inhabitants of the Vale began gathering at Falthwaite End. Men and women bustled about under the canvas readying soup while children played, huddling together in little groups or running about between the tent posts. Finally, as the sun came up on another ice-blue morning, children served the nourishing broth to their parents and elders, then took some for themselves. The whole group moved outside and acknowledged the life-giving power of the sun as it began its brief Midwinter journey through the sky. A cold wind whipped down the valley from the north, its chill making the simple ceremony an act of faith.

For the three hours between the sun's rise and its zenith, the villagers were occupied in preparing the food. Everyone was supposed to be involved in slicing, spicing, stuffing, plucking, stoking, cooking and table-setting. One or two of the younger villagers, of course, managed to find ways of escaping the work and also escaping detection, while others had to be restrained from throwing food or hitting each other with pots and pans. Eventually, but not soon enough for their appetites, midday arrived and everyone was seated under canvas either side of three huge tables, gazing upon a sea of food of every description, waiting with gathering impatience for the headman of Loulea to bid them begin.

The Haufuth stood to speak. The villagers relaxed a little in the knowledge that their leader would give them a head start on most of the other Midwinter gatherings in the north: they could see him trembling with eagerness to do battle at the table, and knew that once again the speech would be mercifully short.

'Thank you all for coming,' he began. 'We stand at the turning of another year, with this feast the evidence of all we have been given, all we have worked for. Let us rise and acknowledge our blessing.' Chairs scraped and feet scuffled as all present rose to their feet. 'We give thanks!' the Haufuth boomed. 'We give thanks,' came the hurriedly intoned echo, then more scraping and shuffling, followed by the earnest clinking of table weapons and muttered requests for food to be passed round. The people were very satisfied. Crazy old Kurr had provided mutton after all, and the speech was the shortest ever.

The villagers sang and danced and ate and drank their way through the afternoon and evening. It was the time of year when grievances were forgotten and feuds were settled early on, as spending a day in close proximity to an enemy did not make for enjoyment of the celebrations. The festival brought together people who worked side by side every day, as well as farmers from the downs and hunters from the borders of the woods who maybe never saw their fellow northerners from one year to the next. Old friendships were renewed and new friendships were made. There were a few quiet corners in the vast marquee, away from the smell of the food and the noise of the musicians, and small groups of people drifted in and out of them, talking, laughing, planning, bartering or courting. It was a scene of delight to warm the heart, as villagers wearing their brightest festive garments enjoyed themselves together.

A light snow began falling late in the evening. By now things had slowed down, the bulk of the food was eaten and the sides of the tent were littered with the bodies of those sleeping it off. The cooking fires had gone out, but the warmth given off by the people under the canvas was enough to ward off the cold. The musicians now began playing a number of slow, sentimental northern ballads, and people began dancing in the heavy atmosphere. More and more joined in, moving together in time to the gentle blandishments of the balladeers, singing of life and death in the legendary days of the First Men.

Midnight drew near, the zenith of darkness and cold. The Haufuth, now in his ceremonial dark green robe edged in gold, motioned to the minstrels, who laid down their instruments. The villagers drifted to the sides of the tent, nudging awake those who had fallen asleep. Tables were shifted away and a space cleared in the centre. The Haufuth waddled forward and raised his hands, making ready to introduce the Play.

To everyone's surprise, the nuggety old farmer Kurr pushed his way into the open space, interrupting the headman as he prepared to speak.

'Are we not forgetting something?' he said in a quiet but penetrating voice.

'Sit down, sit down!' the Haufuth wheezed, red-faced. 'What are you doing?'

'It is customary for the oldest man at Midwinter to speak before the Play!' the gaunt farmer announced above the murmurs in the crowd. 'You will recall that Aldha was buried last spring. I am now the oldest here, and I claim the right to honour tradition.'

The Haufuth tried to respond, but had to wait until a woman whose voice sounded remarkably like Herza's was silenced by those around her.

'Very well, but don't take long. Remember, the Play must be over by midnight.' The village headman retired, frowning his anger at the thin old man.

The old farmer cleared his throat, then spoke in a clear voice.

'We've had many good years, here in Loulea. It's been a long time since we had any real problems. Well, there was that boy from Vapnatak lighting fires in our hay barns, but the worst thing that's happened of late was the Black Winter ten years gone. Crops are good, the weather's been – well, we're surviving. More than surviving, by the look of the feast we had today.' He cast his eye over the crowd, daring any of them to disagree.

'But something is wrong,' Kurr growled at them. 'We've grown complacent. Soft. We live here as though our future is assured, as though no evil thing could ever touch us.'

He paused for breath, and everyone present clearly heard a strident voice at the rear of the group say, 'What's 'e talking about?'

'I don't know if I can tell you what is wrong here, with us,' the old man said earnestly. 'But just think for a moment. For most of the last thousand years people have been at war with each other. The towns of Mjolkbridge and Windrise just up the Westway have been at each other's throats for generations. The Fenni raid the coastlands around Iskelfjorth. Further afield the Lankangas, a loose alliance of ten cities, has ceceded from the King of Firanes. There's a war going on a few hundred leagues away. People are dying. Women. Children. But here all is peace. Do you think the present peace will last? Think about what happened a thousand years ago. Bhrudwo is just a word to frighten infants with, but maybe one day the world will once again be threatened from the east. How will we be prepared for it? I'll tell you how. We won't! It will catch us unawares, because no one ever listens to crazy old men, no one ever listens to the Watchers. Don't think that we of Loulea will remain untouched by war. War is a devouring animal, demanding your sons and your daughters. I've seen it. I have a feeling I'll see it again. Now I've finished. I've said what I had to say. Let the watchman blow the trumpet when he sees the enemy coming, or the blood of the people will be on his head. You can't say you weren't warned. My conscience is clear.'

The laughter when he sat down was audible above the buzz of puzzled conversation.

'Ah, th-thank you, Kurr,' the Haufuth said. 'It's good to have the Midwinter Speech revived. But now it is time for the Play.'

Leith took a deep breath. He felt a little sick, probably as a result of eating too much, he told himself. Or perhaps it was that elderberry wine. Time to move. Both he and Lanka, a tall boy whom he vaguely recognised, went to get their masks. There was no sign of the girl playing the Falla.

His nervousness was not about remembering his part in the Play. Any teenager living in the northern lands of Firanes, Plonya, Asgowan or Sna Vaztha would be able to step into Leith's shoes. Each year they watched the Play, knowing that one day they might be asked to perform one of the roles. There were two male characters: the Snaer, the symbol of deep winter snow; and the Sumar of high summer, whose task it was to defeat Snaer and set the third character free. This third character, Falla, the symbol of spring, was the most revered of the three, and was always played by a female. The defeat of Snaer and the freeing of Falla had become an intricate combination of spontaneous acting within the boundaries of a time-hallowed plot, institutionalised by yearly repetition. Leith had watched many portrayals of the Sumar in the past, and he knew what he wanted to do.

He was nervous about how the Play would turn out. It was believed by many of the more superstitious villagers that the success of the Play as a dramatic spectacle would influence the arrival of warmer weather. Some said that a badly acted Play would delay spring by weeks or even months. The Haufuth said that this was a lot of nonsense, but Leith remembered hearing about the year when the Snaer fell over and broke his wrist soon after the start. The thaw didn't arrive for three months after Midwinter that year, the Black Winter of 1016. The boy who had played the Snaer had gone to live in Vapnatak. Leith licked his lips worriedly as he thought about Lanka, who was supposed to be clumsy. He would be absolutely no help in the Play.

The two youths moved to opposite ends of the open space. Leith's Sunmask was made of oak, sanded, finely polished and stained a deep ochre. The large eyes were bright yellow, and the mouth was set in a fierce snarl. The Snowmask at the other side of the tent was black, fashioned from pine and impregnated with pitch, with tiny slits for eyes and mouth. The impression given was one of implacable power and evil. Leith had spent a lot of time wondering what he would do were he to wear one or other of these masks.

The Falla moved into the cleared circle from somewhere near the other end. Her mask was different in kind from the male masks, for, instead of being solid wood, it was made from slender sticks of birch and alder tied together and painted to look as though they were budding. Compared to the heaviness of Snow and Summer, the Springmask was delicate and fragile. It had taken his mother a long time to make. Leith studied the mask; he had to incorporate that fragile character into his own acting if he were to woo her from the Snaer.

Then his breath caught in his throat as he recognised the girl behind the mask. The Falla was being played by Stella.

Everything happened too quickly for Leith to think. All his plans evaporated in the face of the dark feeling in the pit of his stomach.

47

Lanka in his Snaer mask reached out for the Falla in a cumbersome embrace, then began to move woodenly across the circle towards her. She fluttered about in a series of quick movements, darting in a seemingly random pattern about the circle, always contriving to stay just out of the reach of the black figure. The fragile Falla brushed past the tall Snaer, who stooped and missed. Leith forgot all about acting in that moment. His head went white and black at the same time; he could neither think nor feel. In a crazed departure from the traditional story, he began to circle around the Snaer and Falla even before winter had made spring his captive. He went to grab Stella but missed as she spun to avoid him, a spin that put her in the path of the black hulk of winter. In a moment the tall frame of the boy from Brookside swallowed her up, and Leith went sprawling to the ground on the other side of the circle. The crowd cheered loudly. The capture of spring and the humiliation of summer could not have been more perfectly choreographed.

Leith got to his feet. The fall had brought him to his senses. It was the sheerest luck that had prevented disaster. Now he began to move slowly around behind the black figure and his captive. His character did not have the strength to wrest the Falla from the powerful Snaer by force, so he had to use guile. Usually this was accomplished by simple stealth, sneaking her away while the snow-figure pretended not to look. Leith began to think. How could he show up this Snaer? After his humiliating fall, mere victory would not do.

He made it to the edge of the circle directly behind the Snaer without being noticed. Leith was not sure whether it was good acting by the tall youth, or whether he genuinely did not see the masked Sumar, but the narrow eyes of the black mask had not made any attempt to follow his progress. Stella was expecting the traditional end to the Play, and began gently to free herself from the grip of the Snaer. Leith went towards her but, instead of making to steal her away, threw himself to the ground in front of the tall figure of winter.

The villagers gasped. The Sumar was face down in the dirt, arms extended, pleading for the release of the Falla.

The move obviously caught the Snaer by surprise, as moments passed with no response. Leith lay prostrate on the ground, hoping the youth in black would react the way he expected. Slowly the Snaer raised a black-booted foot and placed it on Leith's neck, uttering a great cry of triumph. The humiliation of the Sumar was complete.

But it was the move Leith had been looking for. He shot an arm out, grabbed the Snaer's other foot and pulled it hard towards him. The huge figure tottered, then fell backwards, scattering a group of villagers and crashing into the side of the tent. The alert Falla had pushed against the tall frame as soon as she felt the boy overbalancing, and had sprung free before she, too, was carried to the ground. Leith gathered her tenderly in his right arm and moved over to where the Snaer lay struggling to rise. The Sumar placed a boot on the figure's neck, and gestured for the Falla to do the same. Spring and summer had combined in a totally unexpected way to defeat winter.

Leith cleared his throat, then shouted the ritual words: 'Winter is on the wane; a new year is at hand!'

For a moment there was silence, then the tent erupted as the inhabitants of the Vale cheered and clapped their approval.

Leith was in a daze as he and Stella, still at his side, found themselves surrounded by villagers. They even applauded Lanka as he got to his feet, ruefully rubbing bruised elbows. Leith could hear the Haufuth's booming voice over the crowd: 'If I hadn't checked myself that all three were kept apart, I would have sworn they arranged the whole thing.'

'You took liberties with the story, boy,' a familiar voice rasped at his side. In spite of his blunt words, even Kurr seemed to approve. Everyone seemed to have something good to say.

Leith and Stella took off their masks and looked at each other. There was something of laughter in her gaze, as though she knew what he had tried to do and thought it foolish. They both knew that it was she who had saved him from embarrassment and earned the plaudits of the crowd. Even so, he had to fight for control of his voice.

'Thank you,' he said. It was the first time he had spoken to her since the day, months ago now, when he had invited her to walk by the lake with him. She nodded and turned away. The look she gave him could have meant anything.

The youth wandered slowly back to the corner where his mother and brother were sitting. He could see a third person there, hooded and cloaked, in earnest conversation with his mother. The set of the shoulders should have told him, but it did not. He approached, expecting more of the compliments that had made his head spin, but instead his mother motioned for him to sit with them in the dark corner of the vast tent, silencing him with a gesture when he made to speak.

The cloaked figure turned towards him and let the hood fall away momentarily. For a moment Leith could only think of a birch bark carving, then he let out a strangled cry.

It was his father.

CHAPTER 3

FALTHA AND BHRUDWO

'DON'T SAY A WORD!' Leith's mother hissed at him. 'Come now, we're going home. You'll hear all about it on the way.'

They drifted out of the marquee through a side flap, and found themselves in a light snow.

'I've left my coat inside!' Leith exclaimed.

'You can go and get it tomorrow,' his mother said. 'Right now, we need to get home.'

The hooded figure walked beside Leith, putting an arm around his shoulder. 'How have you been, son?'

'All right.' The answer meant nothing, he hadn't been all right, but what else could he say? How could he tell his father about feelings he didn't understand himself?

They made their way slowly down the side of the hillock and found the path to the main road. Mahnum ignored the path, taking them on a short cut through the fields.

'We can't use the roads. I cannot afford to be seen by anyone else on their way home,' he whispered. 'We must hurry.'

'Why can't you be seen? Why did we have to leave the tent?' Leith asked, puzzled.

'I don't want anyone knowing I've come back. I'll explain when we get home.' Laced with strain, his voice sounded wearier than Leith ever remembered hearing.

The snow filtered down a little more heavily now. The smell of it was in the air, a crisp smell, not the dampness associated with a heavy fall. The gelid moon sat low on the horizon ahead of them, its fullness occulted by passing cloud streamers. The dull reflected gleam on the snow proved enough light for the small group to find their way across the fields and over the low stone walls to the village.

Mahnum grunted as he climbed over the last fence.

'You're hurt!' Indrett cried.

'Mmmm. A few days ago. It'll be all right with a bit of rest. Not that there's much of that in the offing.' He rubbed his right leg behind the knee. 'This cold's no good for it. You don't realise how cold it gets here until you've been away.'

'Remind me to go away some time, then,' Indrett retorted.

'Almost there,' Hal said gently.

They sat around the low fire and looked at each other for a while. Leith studied the lined, careworn face of his father in the flickering firelight, the face missing from his birch bark carving.

Eventually Hal broke the silence. 'Will you let me look at that leg?'

'Later,' came the reply.

'What happened to it?' Leith asked.

'I was being chased.' Mahnum let out an exhausted sigh. 'For the best part of a year I've been chased from place to place in Faltha and Bhrudwo. Sometimes I thought I'd shaken them off, but they always ended up back on my trail. A week ago they closed in on me as I crossed the borders of Firanes. I set my horse free on the bank of the Fonndelva, then swam it and threw my tunic in from the other side. I ran for the cover of trees but tripped in a rabbit burrow and ricked my knee.' He laughed shortly. 'It probably saved my life. They rode out of the forest just after I fell. I watched them argue for a minute or two, then they heeled their horses and headed off after my mount.'

'Who were these people chasing you?' Indrett asked her husband.

Mahnum sighed. 'I should tell you the whole story. The problem is, we don't really have the time. Look,' the tired man said earnestly, 'we're going to have to leave this place. It's not safe here any more. It'll probably never be safe around me from now on.'

'Leave?' A chorus of voices rang out.

'Yes. They won't have given up looking for me, and they're sure to find me if I stay here. In fact, they probably already know roughly where I live, but it will have taken them some time to run down my horse. I should be safe for a couple of days at least.'

'Leave Loulea?' his wife asked quietly.

'Maybe even Firanes. We might be able to live in a place like Windrise, or in one of the small hamlets in the far north, but I think we would be safest in a country like Plonya or maybe even Treika.'

Leith's head spun. *Leave?* His mind was still in the great tent at Falthwaite End, enjoying the accolades of the crowd, watching Stella make her way arrogantly from family to family with her mother Herza beaming proudly in the background. *Leave Loulea?* He couldn't leave. Not when people were finally noticing him.

'Traders are always going on journeys,' his father was saying. 'I've just decided to take my family with me this time. After all, I have been away the best part of two years.'

'They'll never understand such a hasty departure,' Indrett replied. 'The story will spread throughout the district. Surely if your pursuers follow you here they will find a hundred willing guides to direct them to us.'

'We've no time to say goodbye to the village. In fact, it would be dangerous if the villagers knew. It will be dangerous anyway for anyone remaining here, but I can't do anything about that. Perhaps you can bid a few friends farewell early in the morning – those you know will keep their mouths closed for a while at least – while I wait on the North Road for you. Eventually the story will get out, but by then we'll be well on the road. We won't be found.'

Indrett cast an earnest look at her husband. 'But why flee at all? Why not tell the village what has happened? They'll set these strangers right! And if need be the men from Vapnatak would come and help. Then, when we've sent these people packing, we can settle into a quiet life.' There was no mistaking the hope in her voice.

'You don't understand. I tell you, we must go! Not just for our own sakes, but because the village is in danger. You don't know these people. They are relentless, remorseless. They'll dispose of anyone in their way. There aren't enough men in Vapnatak to keep them at bay. I'd leave tonight if we weren't all so tired.'

'These men who follow you, how many are there?' Hal asked.

'Four,' Mahnum stated quietly.

'Only four!' Indrett looked puzzled. 'What could four do against a hundred?'

'Kill them very swiftly,' the tall man said grimly. 'Or kill them slowly, or any way they chose. I've seen them do it. These four could take a city. They would go through this village and leave no one alive if they thought it would get them closer to me. It didn't take me a year to get here because I lost my way. No, I tried to lead them anywhere else but here. However, I couldn't shake them off and here I am. And I don't mind telling you, the sooner we leave this village the better I'll feel.'

'Who are these four pursuers?' Leith asked.

'They are Bhrudwan warriors, *Maghdi Dasht*. In our language, Heart of the Desert. We know them better by their Falthan name: Lords of Fear. A thousand years ago the Maghdi were in the vanguard of the Bhrudwan armies that conquered Faltha. They are a secret society, a sort of brotherhood dedicated to violence. Ordinary Bhrudwans are petrified of them.'

'Mahnum,' Indrett inquired worriedly, 'what makes you so important that four killers would track you across the northern world for a year? What do they want with you? If you've got something they want, why not give it to them?'

'Because what I have, what they want, is inside my head. It wouldn't do me any good to give it to them. They'd kill me anyway. It's what I know that makes me dangerous, and they want me dead before I can tell anyone else. You remember that I was sent on a mission to Bhrudwo by the Court of Firanes. It seems that some vague rumours had come to the attention of the King, rumours of the rise of Bhrudwan power. He wanted them investigated and so sent for me. In his dotage, he had forgotten I had given up trading and moved back north to start a new life with the jewel of his Court.' He smiled at Indrett, but she did not respond. 'You remember the day: the envoys would not listen to reason. You remember how I felt. It seemed like some half-baked story had been fabricated in order to send me to certain death, based on some petty jealousy at the Court, and the senile old fool of a king had signed the orders. Only it wasn't a half-baked story,' Mahnum said, lowering his voice. 'The rumours are true. Bhrudwo is preparing for war. That knowledge alone is enough to mark me for death in the minds of those who pursue me. But I know more, much more; more than my pursuers know themselves. And this knowledge must be delivered to the King. Though what he'll do with it . . .' The Trader shook his head.

'The old King is dead, Mahnum. He died a month ago. The Prince is not yet old enough to claim the throne, and Wisula has acceded as Regent. The news arrived at the village not three weeks since.'

Mahnum stared at his wife, aghast. 'Wisula? How could they?' He heaved a long, drawn-out sigh. 'Wisula! Oh Lord Most High! This changes everything.'

Hal stood up and approached his foster father. 'What did you find out in Bhrudwo? Whatever it is, you've suffered for it. Tell us. Let us share the burden.'

For a long time the tall Trader struggled for words; and when they finally came, they were brought forth in a low, measured monotone that Leith struggled to hear even in the quiet of Midwinter's Night.

'The fireside stories are true. Bhrudwo is the ancient enemy. I still have to remind myself of that. I was there for a year, I lived among people just like us. Fathers and mothers who love their sons and daughters. Neighbours who do kind things for each other. Villages, cities and even whole countries who try to resist the worst of what the Destroyer seeks to impose on them. Good people, decent people, in the wrong place at the wrong time. They are our enemy not because they are evil, but because a fire is being lit under these good people that will send them surging across Faltha's green fields. The brown-cloaked hordes are set to return, along with the Maghdi killers and, eventually, the Destroyer himself.

'I was taught – you were taught – that the fabled Invasion from the east a thousand years ago could never happen again. I remember my father teaching me that a thousand years of peace bore witness that never again would Bhrudwo rise above its own internal problems to unite in an invasion of Faltha. That all we had to worry about were the greed and pride of the petty kings and lords of Faltha, and next winter's weather, with the latter far more important than the former. But my father was wrong.

'We've grown complacent, we provincials living at the west end of the world. While we squabble over problems as weighty as who will hold next year's Midsummer celebrations, Bhrudwo is amassing a mighty army that will be pointed at the heart of Faltha. And I am the only loyal Falthan who knows their plans.

'I journeyed to Bhrudwo in anger, believing it to be a futile and empty mission. Spy out the land, ascertain whether Bhrudwo threatens the peace of Faltha, and report back to the King. There seemed little hope of completing such a task. I might wander the land for years without seeing such evidence, yet not disprove its existence. Bhrudwo is such a vast land, stretching from ice through desert to jungle, and the paths a Falthan Trader may legally take are few. Nevertheless, I thought myself relatively safe on my journey, because no matter how ancient the hatred, people must live and Traders are needed. As I made my way into the huge land of Birinjh, I knew I was being watched closely. I expected that, but as long as I was careful, I anticipated no danger.

'I was careful, but not careful enough. A few innocent questions in a few obscure villages, with no one able to connect them to me – or so I thought. Had anyone been approached about joining the army? Were people making more tradeable weapons? Did the Bhrudwan army need Falthan provisions? Questions of that sort. I made sure I spoke to nobody who might be part of the Bhrudwan spy network.

'Then late one night came a knock at the door and I was led

away to a damp wooden hut, Trader's Rights or no Trader's Rights. Three men, servants to the Lords of Fear, took turns putting me to the question. What was my mission? Who was my king? I think they already knew the answers because they were gentle by Bhrudwan standards. When I didn't tell them, they tied my hands behind my back. Again they asked me questions, and whenever I answered they did things to my hands. I couldn't see what they were doing, and it drove me wild. It didn't seem to matter whether I gave them a good answer or just babbled nonsense; they burned or pierced or crushed my hands and asked me again. I can't remember much about it, thankfully. Just pain. I don't know what I told them in the end.'

The fire flickered in the grate as Hal placed another log on the embers.

'I came to in a wooden case with three small airholes in it. I was taken on a long journey – probably three or four weeks, I lost track of time – and was let out once a day to relieve myself. They gave me just enough food and water to stay alive. I used to sob with the pain from the cramps in my arms and legs. It was worse than being beaten with sticks. I think they were trying to break me down, softening me for what was ahead.

'I know I spent the last two days of my journey at sea. I had no idea where I was going. But when I was finally freed from my tiny prison I found myself on the island called Andratan.'

The silence around them deepened at the mention of that name, as though a dark spell had been invoked. Outside, the falling snow deadened any sound there might have been; inside, the four people sat absolutely still. A name of power, a name of fear. Andratan.

Andratan? Leith shook his head disbelievingly. Andratan was the legendary island home of the Destroyer, the lair of the ancient Enemy of Faltha, the Cruel One, wielder of the blue fire. From Andratan he would emerge like a fat black spider to ensnare the careless, the lazy, the disobedient, and feed on their souls . . . No, those were just children's tales to be repeated in the dark, a delicious horror to be savoured as families sat safely around a fire.

But was the Destroyer just a children's tale? Leith tried to remember the Haufuth's teaching. It was written in *Domaz Skreud*, the Scroll of Doom, that the Destroyer was named Kannwar at his birth, one of the First Men, born at the dawn of history. Like all the First Men, Kannwar was raised in the city of Dona Mihst, the jewelled city of the Vale of Youth. Like them, Kannwar was granted intimate knowledge of and contact with the Most High, who had given the First Men the Fire of Life and separated them from the animals, dedicated to His service. Like them, Kannwar's gift and his fate was not to die but to be translated, to disappear from the Vale of Youth, to be with the Most High. But unlike other First Men Kannwar rejected the gift, seeking instead immortality on earth and thus control of his own destiny. He used his knowledge of the Way of the Fire, the *Fuirfad*, to further his own interests. Eventually his scheming led to factions within the First Men, rebellion against the Most High and bloodshed before the Rock of the Fountain in the centre of Dona Mihst.

The Scroll of Doom recounted how the Most High judged the First Men for this bloodshed, banishing them from His city and scattering them throughout Faltha. He then covered the Vale in a vast flood, putting an end to all its glory, and the forsaken land was renamed Dhauria, the Drowned Land. To Kannwar the Most High gave a severe punishment. The curse of immortality was laid upon him, and he would never be translated into the presence of the Most High. He was renamed the Destroyer, and was banished from the west. From his island of Andratan in the eastern sea, so the legends said, the Destroyer is ever occupied plotting revenge against the Most High and the Falthans, direct descendants of the First Men.

Legends, Leith reminded himself. *Only legends*.

Mahnum drew a deep breath, then continued slowly, as though unwilling for the words to leave his lips. 'For some days I was imprisoned in a dungeon somewhere under the island fortress. I shared a cell with ordinary Bhrudwans, decent people like you and I, most of them, people who worried about their families and what would happen to them now they were gone. None had any hope of escape. Their crimes—' he faltered for a moment – 'their crimes usually involved asking too many questions of their village councils. For this they were to die, but not immediately. Not until they had been made to betray everyone else who thought as they did.'

The words came even more slowly now, haltingly, as the Trader sought strength to continue in the face of his memories.

'The cells all faced inwards to a true Bhrudwan torture chamber. Most High grant that you never see one. Day and night we were forced to watch men and women taken from their cells and – and questioned. Guards in red robes asked them the same things again and again, sometimes writing down the answers, but mostly not even listening, not even when they were begged. The torturers competed with one another. The loudest scream. The longest – these jailers were not people. They had— there were dogs, trained to – to – oh, Most High, I saw it. I saw it! I felt so ashamed, as though I was one of the guards, as though I pulled the levers, unleashed the dogs, cheered them on. As though I was responsible.'

Mahnum's face looked pinched and small in the firelight, and just as Leith decided to go to his father, to offer him comfort, Hal stretched out his good hand and laid it on the Trader's shaking shoulders. Leith remained where he was.

'Finally my door was opened and I was led out past the eager dogs and the stretched-out figures and the glowing coals, up a winding staircase, and left on the cold stone floor of a lightless room.

'There was a voice in the room, and it asked me questions. The power of it pinned me to the ground, and peeled my mind open like bark off a sapling. It – wanted to know things . . . I don't remember all of it. There was power and authority behind that voice, a great malice, but also a great weariness. The questions seemed like knives laying my mind open, slicing through my memories, whittling me down to the nub, searching for a secret I didn't have. It was agony. I couldn't resist. I couldn't even begin to formulate the desire to resist. All I could do was feel the pain, and know that the pain was my only future.

'The voice knew all about my mission. It knew the name of my

King and my country. It knew everything I knew. It taunted me with the knowledge that an invincible army was being prepared to destroy Faltha utterly. It spread out before me a vast plan, one in which there was no fault. In this plan the power of dark magic and the force of men were embellished by treason and betrayal. Name after name it spoke, names of men and women in places of power, poised to betray Faltha into Bhrudwan hands. The air seemed thick with laughter, with gloating. I was offered a place in this plan if – if I would take a blood-binding oath to seek the "Right Hand". The voice always came back to this. What did I know of the Right Hand? Again and again it asked, as though I could have kept anything from it. Eventually it became convinced that I knew nothing, and gave up in disgust. The moment it released me was the sweetest moment in my life.

'I was taken from the room and brought back to the torture chamber. Then – I can't remember. I can't remember. Blackness, pain, threats, taunts – then I woke in another room with a man bent over me, dressing these wounds.'

Here Mahnum broke off his narrative, threw off his cloak and unbuttoned his tunic. As he turned around, his family saw a raised mass of angry scars on his back. Indrett cried out, while Hal wept quietly. Leith's mind was numb, in a sort of stasis, and he could not react.

The Trader pulled his cloak back around his shoulders. 'The scars still give a little pain; I cannot sleep facing the sky. I was fortunate, for I escaped before I was introduced to many of the instruments prepared for me.

'By chance, it seemed, a Bhrudwan Trader whom I had befriended earlier on the journey had arranged business on Andratan. He later told me that he was courting the daughter of a soldier who had temporarily been assigned to the island. On his way to a secret tryst with his beloved, he said, he came across my cell. He never told me how he gained admittance to the heavily guarded dungeon, but I suspect his beloved was working as a servant somewhere in the keep. Whatever his method of entry, he told of happening upon my inert form on the stone floor of an empty room. Immediately (he said) he forgot his beloved and set to work tending my wounds.

'It was a long time before I could stand unaided, but the Trader never left my side save to bring me meals of bread and gruel. As soon as I could walk again, he led me to another room, similar to the first except that the floor was lined with straw. No one ever came into the room except Vaniyo, my Trader friend. My body healed quickly, but it was many days before my mind was clear again and I could talk with him.

'It turned out that my friend was in league with a number of the guards, for he told me that my death had been reported to the Masters, as he called them. He described to me how he had bribed the guards to keep them from revealing my whereabouts. I was tired and did not wonder at that time why he told and retold this story to me, emphasising the heroic part he had played in my escape from death.

"You will be the first ever to escape these walls of no return," he would say to me.

"How can I ever repay you?" I would reply.

'Then he would favour me with a knowing look, and say, "You'll think of a way."

'Late one night Vaniyo led me from my room, past sleeping guards and some who were not asleep but looked the other way. It was a long, slow journey, ever upwards, avoiding areas where my friend's money had not reached, but it ended suddenly when we found ourselves outside the fortress and running down a steep bare slope to the seashore. That moment has remained with me ever since. Out in the real world again, with a moonlit sky above and the breakers booming against the shore, and in the distance the evil silhouette of the fortress rising up rampart upon battlement from a high bare hill. As I looked at that hateful place it seemed that the remembrance of what had happened inside those walls faded into a dream. If it weren't for the scars I carry, and the names burned into my memory, I'd be sure I had dreamed it all.

'We hauled a little scow from its hiding place behind some rocks and launched it into the sea. Vaniyo rowed out towards the dark shape of a large sailing ship anchored in the harbour. At any other time the shape of a Bhrudwan galleon would have filled me with dread, but now I felt only joy. We pulled alongside and my friend whistled a signal. We were allowed to board and a member of the crew hid me below decks.' Mahnum laughed grimly. 'He did not have to be bribed. It seems that there is little love even in Bhrudwo for what takes place on that island. As Vaniyo parted from me, he assured me we would meet again.

'The ship sailed the next day, and eventually we made land at a city called Malayu. It was here that I was left to fend for myself, with no friend, food, transport or shelter and only a Trader's wits to guide me. I knew that if I was seen by anyone who knew of my arrest I would become a wanted man, for I carried the potential undoing of Bhrudwo's carefully laid plans, and although this seemed highly unlikely, I decided to keep myself hidden. Yet with the knowledge of Faltha's danger locked in my mind I also knew that there was not a moment to spare. I had to return to the Court of Firanes.

'By degrees I made my way to a village high in the coastal mountains to the south. I felt certain I would not be recognised here, expecting pursuit, if it came, to focus on the direct trading routes westward. I sought refuge in order to recover fully from my ordeal, and I intended to use the time to uncover the extent of the preparations for war.

'Up in the high, snowless mountains live people who try to maintain a fierce independence. Yet after living with them for a few weeks I learned that many of their sons had been conscripted into the army. The village was busy producing weaponry – to be used in a local conflict, they assured me – for which they were paid handsomely by Traders of the lowlands. Believing me to be a barbarian from the northern parts of Bhrudwo, with whom they were presently at peace, they were open and honest in their dealings with me, so I can only assume they believed what they told me. None of them had ever heard of Faltha, but it seems that local teachers and officials had recently begun warning about an "enemy afar off" that threatened even their little highland province. I listened to one of these officials pouring out invective against this unnamed enemy, and guessed that serious recruitment was under way. I had by then learned all these good-natured people could tell me, and prepared to make the risky journey home.'

Mahnum looked into the shocked, disbelieving eyes of his family. 'The armies of Bhrudwo will be some time in the preparation. Even were they to be readied within the year, their officers still must determine the best route for the long march. They will obviously attack Faltha through The Gap, just as they did a thousand years ago, but getting there might be difficult. No people will put up with such a huge and hungry army cutting a path across their land, and the Bhrudwan warriors may be forced to fight even before they reach Faltha. Thus it may be a year or even more before the eastern army stands at the portals of the west. But how long will it take us to prepare a response?

'The day before I was to leave, Vaniyo the Trader arrived unlooked for in the village. He told me that he had arranged for me to be followed from the time I had left the ship at Malayu. He reminded me of all that he had done for me, and pointed out how his care for me had cost him much money and the loss of possible earnings. Then he asked for a share of the fabulous wealth I had carried with me from Faltha. I was grateful for all he had done, I told him, and I would gladly give him any possessions I could spare, but there was no wealth.

'"You are lying to me!" he hissed through his teeth. "All the villages in the north spoke of your wealth."

'I argued with him. "A necessary deceit. I pretended to be wealthy in order to learn from the villagers," I said. "Really, I have very little."

'I could not convince him of the truth, and he left me in anger. In a short while he returned, bringing with him two grey-cloaked men. Maghdi Dasht, they were, Lords of Fear. As they approached the house where I was staying, I made my escape from the back window. I stole a horse – the least of my crimes, yet in itself punishable by death – and began the long journey back to Faltha and home.

'It was a journey filled with adventures, for I could not risk travelling the main trading routes. I assumed Vaniyo had betrayed me to the authorities, and I was anxious to avoid another interrogation on Andratan. Twice I became lost, once in the wide inland steppes of Kanabar and once searching for the headwaters of the Aleinus. But well before I reached the borders of the westlands I became aware that I was being pursued. Four Bhrudwan warriors disguised as Traders followed me on horseback, asking for news of me in villages and trailing me on the open road. I tried every ruse I knew to shake them off – and sometimes thought I had succeeded – but somehow they always regained my trail.

'Once through The Gap and into Faltha, I was convinced my superior knowledge of the land would enable me to be rid of my unwanted fellow travellers, but again I was mistaken. I took the disused East Bank Road and followed the Aleinus into Piskasia, and my pursuers gained on me. Even through the trackless paths of the Wodranian Mountains they were never more than a day behind. I set traps for them; they avoided every one. Finally, in Favony, I stopped at a small village and bartered everything I had for a fresh horse, in the hope that I could outrun them. It was a tragic mistake. While I watched from the trees, the warriors destroyed the village in search of me, and took four fresh horses. I watched the inhuman things they did to the inhabitants in their quest for knowledge of me. I would have given myself up to stop those horrible scenes, yet I left that charred village behind and pressed on, knowing that only the knowledge I possessed could possibly prevent that scene being repeated in every village throughout Faltha.'

The Trader paused to rub callused hands over his tired face. 'So much suffering, so much pain!' he said wearily. 'I've seen so many terrible things, and never once was I able to intervene. In my dark days I began to believe we are all powerless against concerted evil.'

He sighed deeply. 'By the use of a little-known route through Favony I gained enough time to press my case before the King of that country. His name was not one of those seared into my mind as a traitor, but I had not counted on the treachery of his officials. He would not see me, I was told. I was delayed, and soldiers tried to prevent my departure. There my pursuers caught up with me and almost captured me. It was as though someone in the King's employ had betrayed me to them, and I was reminded of the taunts of the voice of Andratan. I barely escaped with my life.

'They kept close behind me after that, forcing me away from cities and pressing me ever northwards. I played my last trick on the borders of Firanes, as I told you, and it cost me my horse. I toyed with the idea of travelling to Rammr, but your news about the King's death convinces me that I chose correctly in coming home. Mark well! Horrible danger nips at my heels, and we must flee quickly. We must hide in another land, and I must find there some powerful ally or design some sort of plan to convince Falthans of the perils they face. If I do not succeed, there will be nowhere in Faltha for anyone to hide. Bhrudwo has had a thousand years to reflect on the mistakes made in the first Invasion. They are coming, thousands upon thousands of them, armed with steel and worse. If they succeed in occupying Faltha, they will never be driven out.'

In the quietness that followed this narrative Leith could hear a rising breeze rattling tree branches outside. The world seemed to be at peace, at odds with what his father had just finished saying. For a while no one spoke; then Hal stood and hobbled over to his father.

'How long since you slept?' he asked gently.

'Three days,' came the reply.

'Then you need rest. If we are to leave in the morning, we need you to lead us.'

Hal pressed the palm of his crippled right hand against the Trader's throbbing temple, and said, 'Sleep the sleep of a victor tonight. We'll prepare for the morning, and wake you when we're ready to leave.'

Indrett nodded at her son's last words. Anxiety wrestled with joy for mastery of her features: the joy of an unlooked-for Midwinter's gift revealed in the tent at Falthwaite End, the anxiety evoked by this outlandish tale told beside the very bricks of her own hearth, as though the evil power of Andratan loomed just outside the cottage. She looked nervously at the stout oak wood of the front door, as if she expected the Bhrudwan army to come pouring through, then studied the weary face of the one she loved and allowed its familiar lines and contours to smooth away the ripples of alarm within her.

Leith sat to the left of the hearth, not daring to meet his father's gaze, considering whether to pursue the idea lodged firmly in his mind. Hesitantly, as though controlled by some other will, his hand searched pocket after pocket until it located what it sought; then that same will brought Leith to his feet, guided him across the hearth, and opened his palm. In it rested a birch bark carving.

Mahnum reached out a tentative hand. With reverent fingers he turned the carving over until its subject became apparent.

'Thank you, son,' he said simply.

Leith waited for the embrace with which Mahnum invariably favoured him but, perhaps aware of the changes within his son, or maybe a little wary of his reception, Mahnum hesitated a moment too long. He was about to reach out when Leith turned and stumbled back to his place by the hearth.

Hal helped his father to his feet and massaged his injured knee. Father and son moved slowly towards the bedroom, leaving Indrett and Leith looking to each other for reassurance. The decision had been made. This place was no longer home.

Sleep took a long time coming to the troubled youth. He could hear Hal lurching about in his characteristic way, preparing food for the morning's journey. Hal always seemed to have hidden reserves of energy he could call on, while Leith found that a crisis left him drained and defenceless. Tonight, in his bed, Leith felt in danger of falling victim to his overstimulated mind. The world-wide conspiracy his father had described seemed unreal and, try as he might, Leith could not make his father's return seem real either. The real events of the day, the Midwinter celebrations and the Play, filled his mind.

Across the Face of the World

As he tossed and turned on the borders of sleep, the happenings of this, the shortest of days, passed before him like a Midsummer pageant. The walk to Falthwaite End, the singing, the eating, the dancing, the speeches, the Play, Kurr, Stella; a day filled with long hours that were already dissolving into misty, half-formed memories in Leith's whirling consciousness. Yet as he relived the day a tall, cloaked figure was with him in every activity: walking down a snow-covered road in the soft pre-dawn light; joking with the Haufuth over the laden feast table; applauding proudly as his son defeated the black-masked Snaer and set the land free from the grip of the enemy. Only this time the enemy was not Winter, but was a Bhrudwan warrior cloaked in grey, mounted on horseback and wielding a shining steel blade. And Leith was running, running, with the howling wind at his back and the old farmer ahead of him, shouting encouragement, while his family trailed behind. Ahead, on a moonlit hill in the distance, rose a huge fortress. The wind picked him up and blew him towards it, and he was helpless in its grip.

Leith awoke with a start, drenched with sweat. He could hear a muffled banging. Tension subsided with the realisation that Hal must still be up and about. The banging stopped. As he settled towards sleep he imagined he could hear Hal making his way back towards the bedroom. No, not Hal: the soft click of booted feet was regular. He looked across the room. The bed beside his was occupied. Not Hal. His mother, then. Or perhaps his father! For the first time his heart thrilled with the knowledge of his father's unexpected return. Leaving Loulea didn't seem to matter as long as he never lost his father again.

His thoughts were interrupted by more footsteps. More than one pair of feet, padding with a measured, regular tread across the kitchen floor. Leith began to entertain disquieting thoughts.

His father also had a limp. *Who, then . . . ?*

He held himself rigid and strained his ears to hear more closely. Then, in an instant of terror, sound welled up from somewhere on the other side of the bedroom door – banging and crashing and shouting and screaming. For a moment he froze, then he threw himself out of bed and scrambled towards the door. Hal got there before him and flung the door open.

Dim figures struggled with each other in the hallway. Leith heard his mother shouting his father's name, and hurled himself in the direction of the sound. Strange voices barked things at each other. Again he heard his mother's voice, this time behind him. A dark figure stood in his way and he threw himself at it, only to be brushed off against the wall. Winded, he tried to struggle to his feet.

All was confusion and noise, then light flared inside the house. In a brief second Leith glimpsed Hal with a burning torch confronting a swarthy figure, while a second strange man grappled madly with his father on the floor. His white-faced mother was being pulled outside, through the broken-down front door, by a third figure that had a gloved hand firmly clamped over her mouth. As he watched in horror, a fourth man burst in, armed with a staff. Leith shouted a warning, but before Hal could react the staff was swung across his brother's legs. Body and torch crashed to the floor. The staff swung again, and his father collapsed limply into the arms of his adversary. They began to drag him away.

'No!' Leith shouted, and flung himself at the invaders. Almost contemptuously, one of the figures drew a curved sword from its scabbard and struck the youth an easy blow across the forehead. The house seemed to collapse inwards at Leith, his eyes rolled back and he sank to the floor beside the inert form of his brother. The figure grunted with satisfaction, then picked up the smouldering torch and casually set fire to the thatched roof. Outside he joined his fellows as they mounted their horses smoothly and made off with their captives.

The soft wind coming from the sea bunted at the front door of the house, moving it slightly on broken hinges. It drifted a thin snow a few feet inside the kitchen, and flicked at the sandy hair of the boy lying bleeding on the floor. It sussurrated unimpeded through the whole house, blowing past shattered furniture and scattered possessions. And gently it caressed the tiny red flames as they spread slowly but hungrily across the thatch and down the walls.

CHAPTER 4

THE FARMER

THE MORNING SUN SHONE bright and clear, supervising a roguish westerly breeze. The wind caressed the freshly fallen snow, rattled the bones of the tall poplars and ruffled the dark tunics of the mourners gathered around the two open graves. Around them swirled the glory and bitterness of life: the heartswelling sound of songbirds, the cheeky glint of the sun on the swift-running brook, the crisp wind on downcast faces, the pungent smell of freshly turned earth; the salty taste of sadness and death on such a morning as this filled the hearts of the people grouped together at the graveside. The Haufuth spoke deliberately and with restraint, his measured words reminding the village of the uncertainty of life and the strength of the earth to which they would all one day return. After a time of quiet reflection, four young men stepped up. They lifted and lowered first one casket, then the other into the graves. Then they took up spades and, as the villagers watched, buried their friends.

The gathering broke up into smaller knots of people, some seeking comfort, others giving it. A lone piper played a mournful tune. People began filing down the narrow brick path that led back to the village. Two men, one old and stooped, the other large and short of breath, went aside from the others and stood together in a corner of the small graveyard.

The Haufuth laid a hand on the shoulder of his companion. Kurr glanced up at the fat headman with steely eyes.

'Two funerals in two days!' the big man sighed, shaking his head. 'I would have spoken to you yesterday, but . . .' He groped for words. 'I'm so sorry about Tinei.'

'Nothing anyone could have done,' said Kurr shortly. 'Once the fever took hold it was only a matter of time.' He lifted his chin and gave the village headman a hard-eyed stare, as though trying to prove the loss of his wife was not capable of moving him. But his red-rimmed eyes gave him the lie.

The Haufuth was no good at times like these. He was torn between trying to say something comforting or placing a consoling arm around the old man, so did neither.

'Do you know what finally finished her? Mustering those sheep on the morning of Midwinter's Eve – the sheep on which you and I and the whole village feasted just three days ago – that's what did it. I'm getting old and I can't move that many sheep on my own. She knew that.' He swallowed, and when he resumed speaking his voice came out thinly, as though being forced past a constriction in his throat.

'Haufuth, I asked the men of the village for help but no one came. The only one to lend a hand was Mahnum's boy.' He pointed back over his shoulder to the mounds of fresh earth.

'Tinei found out that no one was coming to my aid. Then foolishly I told her that the villagers were gossiping about me. She insisted on getting out of bed and helping. Stubborn woman! While I was in the village, she rounded up the sheep by herself. By the time Mahnum's boy and I arrived she had finished and gone back to her bed.' His voice lowered. 'She never got up again.'

'Kurr, I'm sorry,' came the lame reply.

'Sorry? The villagers weren't sorry! They only came to the funeral to see if I'd turn up. Only came to gloat, to mock the old fool. Some of 'em probably thought I'd done her in!' He turned and spat on the ground. 'At least these two boys today were given some respect.'

The Haufuth beckoned the old farmer towards the shadow of a tall, dark hedge. 'I must talk with you about those boys. I need your help.'

Kurr laughed bitterly in reply, the shrug of his shoulders shaking his skeletal frame.

'No, listen to me!' the Haufuth continued. 'I am in earnest. No one else can help me. Please! I listened to your little Midwinter speech, but thought nothing of it until the next morning when I heard something that – if it is true – is more important than you, or I, or even this whole village. I trust no one else to keep this knowledge safe. Please listen.' His eyes pleaded with the old man.

Kurr heard the concern in the Haufuth's voice. He grunted and nodded his head ungraciously.

'Good!' Grinning weakly with relief, the Haufuth wiped the palms of his hands on his tunic, then led the farmer behind the hedge to a low tree stump. There was just enough room for both of them to be seated.

The big man took a deep breath. 'The villagers believe that a group of brigands descended upon the village the morning after Midwinter, kidnapped Indrett for some foul purpose and burned down the house, killing the boys. At least, that is what I told them. But there is much more to it than that.

'I don't sleep very well, on account of – well, you know, men my size find it difficult. On the morning after Midwinter, about an hour before dawn, I was woken by the sound of horses being ridden hard down the lane. I heard their riding gear, you understand. I mean, horses don't make much noise in the snow. Still, I suppose you would know that, having horses. Well, I rose to find out what was happening. I had just opened my front door when four horsemen swept past, riding like a gale through the village and off along the Westway.'

Kurr closed his eyes. He ached to be walking the hills of Swill Down, not listening to the Haufuth's gossip. But in spite of himself he stayed where he was.

'Anyway, I followed their tracks back through the village to see where they had been. When I got to the end of the lane, I found Mahnum and Indrett's house ablaze, with the front door broken down and everything a mess. I rushed inside. It was still hard to see, you understand, in the half-light and with the smoke, so I didn't notice the boys for some time. When I found them I pulled them out, but I couldn't find Indrett. Anyway, the fire was taking hold, and I searched as long as I could, but I had to stop eventually for fear of the flames.

'I shouted for help but no one heard. Of all the times for something like this to happen, it had to be the morning after Midwinter, when everyone was sleeping off their excesses of the night before. Anyway, I finally ran out of the house and went over to the boys. Leith was as still as death, bleeding from a blow to the forehead. Hal, however, was conscious, and began to talk to me.'

'What?' the farmer exclaimed, forgetting about all else. 'Hal was alive?' The Haufuth motioned for him to be silent.

'Hal told me that his father had returned the previous night. At first I thought he was delirious, but then I recalled seeing a caped figure over near Indrett after the Play, and she and her boys left with him almost immediately.'

'Yes, I saw him,' said Kurr, scratching his chin. 'I thought . . . I can't remember what I thought.' The memories of that night had been washed away by the discovery he had made on his return home.

The Haufuth continued: 'I remember thinking at the time that it was odd! Anyway, Hal told me that Mahnum had been pursued all the way from Bhrudwo by evil men because he had learned something that placed all Falthans in peril. He said that these men had broken into the house and abducted his parents. Then these men had set fire to the house and left the boys for dead. It was these horsemen with their captives that I heard riding through our village that morning.'

'And the boys,' Kurr asked, now wide-eyed and alert, 'how did they die?'

'They didn't,' the Haufuth replied simply. 'They're still alive.'

'Alive? Then who . . . ?' He glanced confusedly in the direction of the twin graves.

'No one. A necessary fiction. Hal convinced me that Mahnum knew something important, important enough for killers to come halfway across the world to try to snuff out that knowledge. If the horsemen learned that Hal and Leith were still alive, they might come back and kill them, and the entire village along with them, to preserve whatever secret Mahnum had discovered. So I decided that their deaths should be feigned, for the sake of the village. It would be easy enough to pretend that the boys had been killed and their bodies consumed in the fire. For a while I thought of pretending that Indrett had also perished in the blaze, but I was afraid that someone else might have seen the horsemen, and might ask difficult questions. So I decided to tell at least some of the truth.'

'And the secret? What did Mahnum find out in Bhrudwo?' the old man asked impatiently.

'Why don't you ask the boys? I took them home, and there they have remained, recovering from their wounds. Come to my house. Hal has a story that you must hear. And, in return, you have some horses that we may have need of.'

'You're asking *my* help? After all that's been done to me?'

'Yes,' came the simple reply. 'Because of your Midwinter speech. Would you warn us of danger and then pull back when that danger threatens?'

'Why should I help anyone in this village?' the old man repeated stubbornly.

'Because you're a good man. A man with a past, perhaps – no, I don't want to know what it is,' he added hastily as Kurr made to reply. 'I don't care about that. You're a fair man, one who won't stand for any nonsense. One who will act to see that right wins out. I've heard what the men around these parts say about you, and it's not what you think. Stubborn, yes; because you won't let go of something until you've bent it to your will. If some people mistake determination for fierceness, that's their lookout. I know better.

'Now, I've entrusted you with a secret that no one else in the village knows. Will you trust me, and come and hear the boys' story?'

The farmer stood up and looked down at the Haufuth, the deadness banished to the corners of his eyes. 'Let's hear what the boys have to say. It may be that I can supply something even more valuable than horses.'

They found Leith and Hal engrossed in a spirited game of Stickslap, a simple but rather exhausting amusement. Leith appeared to be winning, but Hal was making a good fist of it even though he had to sit awkwardly. Looking the brothers over, Kurr saw that Leith's head wound had subsided to little more than a nasty bruise and some broken skin: he had likely been caught with the flat of a blade. *Hmmm. That was deliberate, a blow to stun, not to kill. They must have wanted him to suffer, so they could taunt Mahnum and Indrett with the knowledge that their boys had been burned alive.* Hal was able to stand unaided, though the bruising on his leg was an ugly blue-brown, and must be giving him pain.

Kurr drew a couple of ragged breaths. It was a strange feeling to see alive two people who, he had supposed, had only just been laid to rest. He looked at Hal, and for a dizzying moment he thought of Tinei: his eyes darted left and right, half hoping that she, too, was somewhere in the house.

'They look much better now than they did yesterday,' rumbled the Haufuth. 'Leith and Hal,' he said, turning to the boys, 'Kurr has agreed to help us. Tell him your story, then we will discuss what can be done.'

Hal looked into the eyes of the farmer. 'I was sorry to hear of your wife's passing,' he said, 'and sorrier that none of our family could honour Tinei at her funeral.'

The old man grunted and sat down. 'What's past is past, boy,' he answered. 'Nothing to be done about it now. Other things, I am told, may prove to be of more importance than an old man's sorrow.'

Heartless, thought Leith. *What a cruel man. Why would the Haufuth involve him?*

The village headman opened the shutters of a window facing away from the street, and the four of them settled down in the pallid sunshine to talk.

* * *

The story Kurr heard that afternoon surprised even the worldly-wise farmer. When Hal related Mahnum's adventures in Andratan, the old man's eyes widened. He nodded grimly as Hal told him of Bhrudwo's preparations for war, as though the news confirmed something he had suspected. He grunted, frowning over steepled fingers as he heard how the Trader had been pursued and of the ruthlessness of the horsemen. Merin, the Haufuth's wife, came in with refreshments as Leith and Hal tried to describe the moments of terror as their parents were taken. As the boys related the improbable tale, Kurr found the words reawakening long-dead parts of his mind, as though the years were being stripped away and he was young again, sword arm aching with exhaustion, rallying his men, shouts echoing in the narrow streets, himself in the forefront . . . The clatter of Merin's tray broke the spell.

'Time for something to eat!' the Haufuth said cheerfully, leaning over towards the food. 'You'd better be quick,' he added unnecessarily.

'Time to decide what to do,' corrected Kurr. 'Now, it seems to me—'

'Wait a moment!' complained the Haufuth, talking through a mouthful of bread. 'Sensible decisions come after stomachs are satisfied! Pass the bread around. What's in the jug?'

Kurr muttered something inaudible and gave the man a hard stare.

A few minutes later the Haufuth looked up. 'Now, Kurr, you were saying?'

'Are you sure you are quite comfortable?' growled the old farmer.

'Yes,' replied the headman innocently.

'Very well. You have asked me here, taken me into your confidence, because you think I can aid you. And you were wise to do so, for I can offer you both advice and practical help.'

'So you believe their story?' the headman inquired gently, arching his eyebrows. 'I thought you would take some persuading.'

'Of course I believe it!' the old farmer snapped, with a touch of his normal asperity. 'It fits with the little I have been able to

76

glean about events in the outside world. I have spent the past two years wondering why Mahnum was sent east, and now I know. It explains a great deal. Kroptur will need to be told.'

'Explains what?' The Haufuth leaned forward, wiping his mouth with the back of his hand.

'I thought Mahnum had been sent on a wild goose chase but, strangely, the King's fears have turned out to be true. I have heard of dark and murderous deeds in Rammr. Just rumours, mind, but rumours that may nevertheless prove to be true. Loyal subjects of the old King have disappeared. Who is behind all this? To my mind, it had to be one with the ear of the King, albeit a king in his dotage. One who has just now acceded to Regent, ruling in the place of an admittedly under-age Prince.'

'Wisula!' exclaimed the Haufuth.

'Exactly. A nastier man I have never heard of, if even half of what is said is true. He's been waiting his chance for years now, trying to steer Firanes into outright war against the Lankangas, so Kroptur says. It is more certain than sheep grow wool that Wisula was one of the names given to Mahnum by the Voice of Andratan. We can expect no help from the Firanes Court. Wisula will be in no hurry to rescue someone who he imagines is a threat. More likely he would clap the lot of us in irons and leave us to rot in his deepest dungeon.'

Leith stared hard at the farmer, puzzled. The old man's slurred North March drawl seemed to be dissolving as he spoke, to be replaced by the clipped tones of someone accustomed to wielding power. *What is going on?* No one else appeared to notice.

'But the Firanes Court sent Mahnum in the first place. Why would they not give his story credence now?' The Haufuth scratched his head.

'The Firanes Court which sent Mahnum to Bhrudwo is different from the Firanes Court of today. Wisula has seen to that. If he is a Bhrudwan puppet, he would not want talk of invasion being whispered about the palace.'

Hal spoke: 'Father warned me that he was told in Andratan of Bhrudwan spies at every Court in Faltha. His interrogator gloated that every king in the land would soon be in the palm of his hand. We must choose our confidants with care.'

The old farmer grunted his agreement. 'So no help will come from the King. But what about the villagers? How long would it take to raise an army from Vapnatak and the surrounding districts?'

The Haufuth laughed in his throat. 'I'll tell you how long. Never! Mahnum and Indrett are somebody else's problem, not theirs. And as for the Bhrudwan threat – well, they simply would not believe it. I'm not sure I believe it! We teach our villagers that all the "Destroyer" stories are fables. Is Bhrudwo a serious threat? None of the village Haufuths will think so. I wouldn't have thought so either, but how else do I explain a man being pursued across the face of the world?'

'Believe me when I say that Bhrudwo is no fable,' Kurr stated gravely.

The Haufuth shook his head sadly. 'I don't know what to believe any more,' he concluded.

The old farmer ground his teeth in frustration. 'For the love of the Most High! You came to me with the story, and now you don't believe it? It really doesn't matter what you think; someone has carried away two people from your village. What are you going to do about it? And there is talk of an invasion. We should tell someone about it. So we still have things to do, no matter what we believe. We still have decisions to make.'

'Like, exactly what we are supposed to do now,' said the Haufuth.

Merin came into the room and closed the shutters against the oncoming twilight. She smiled fondly at her husband, lit the lamps and then went out.

'One moment!' the Haufuth stood and called after her. 'Do we have any cheese? Cheese helps me think.'

'None in the house,' came the reply. 'I'll send someone over to Herza's for it.'

The big man resumed his seat, grinning. 'Got to think ahead!' he explained, shrugging his shoulders.

Kurr stood to speak. By now there was no doubt: his deep-set grey eyes burned with a fire which none of those present had noticed in their previous dealings with the farmer. The old man had undergone some sort of transformation. No longer a grumpy landsman, he was now a sharp-witted adviser.

'Well, it seems obvious to me that we are faced with a choice between doing two impossible things.' He stretched forth a bony hand and counted them off as he spoke. 'On the one hand we have to convince the kings of northern and southern Faltha, sixteen sovereign states in all, to take seriously a threat from the Destroyer. Who are we, northern provincials, that they would consent to hear us, let alone believe us? We have not a shred of proof to strengthen our hand. Yet I guess that we have less than twelve months to do it.

'On the other hand Mahnum and his wife have been adbucted by a band of killers whose only conceivable objective is to ascertain what they know, then kill them and return to Bhrudwo without being apprehended. The Trader and his wife face certain death unless they are rescued.

'So here is our cruel dilemma! Do we rescue our friends or warn the kings of Faltha? We need to do both. We have the power to do neither. Yet we must attempt something or wait here and let our doom, Faltha's doom, roll towards us, eventually to overwhelm us.'

A deep silence followed his words.

'I am sure we are agreed that something must be attempted?' he prompted eventually.

The other three nodded slowly in answer.

'So which one to attempt?' asked the farmer. 'How to choose?'

'If we chose to warn the kings,' the Haufuth said, thinking carefully, 'how would we do it? Travel around the sixteen kingdoms?'

'That would take a lifetime,' Kurr responded. 'But perhaps there is a better way. Ever since the Bhrudwan invasion a thousand years ago, each of the sixteen kings has posted an ambassador to Instruere, the great City of Faltha. The Haufuth knows what I'm talking about. Either of you boys heard of it?' He turned to the brothers.

Hal nodded his head slowly.

'Instruere?' Leith said. 'No . . .'

'You would have, if you had attended to your lessons,' the Haufuth growled at him. 'It was the capital of the world even before the Bhrudwans invaded a thousand years ago. The Destroyer was said to have made his palace there. I told you all about it.'

Leith frowned in concentration. He liked learning; he had shown a flair for it when he was younger, enough to be teased for it, anyway. But these days he never seemed able to focus on his lessons.

'Those sixteen ambassadors make up the Council of Faltha,' Kurr continued impatiently. 'They have the authority to make decisions on behalf of their kings. The reality is that the Council of Faltha governs Instruere, and whoever governs Instruere governs the world. They have more power in Faltha than any of the kings. All we need to do is to go and see them.'

'Hundreds of leagues or more in the middle of winter? We'd never make it.' The fat headman shook his head.

'Over a thousand leagues, actually. But what else can we do? Invite them to come here?'

There was a short silence. Leith sensed that Kurr's patience might not last much longer.

'How to choose?' said the Haufuth nervously, his smallish eyes flicking from one person to another, never resting on anyone. 'In my view, the choice we have is between swift death and slow death. Should we pursue these foul rogues and fall into their hands, our lives will be ended quickly. I'm not really in favour of that outcome. All very well for the heroes of story and legend. If any of you are Conal Greatheart in disguise, or even one of his band, time to speak up. No? Well, taking on the Bhrudwan warriors is not realistic. On the other hand, if we fail to persuade this Council of Faltha that Bhrudwo threatens us all, they won't kill us, but death is no less certain – for many others, if not for us. The Falthans I know could not long resist the likes of those who have taken Mahnum captive. Even if the waves of war do not wash up this far, our crops and our sons will be required of us. Certainly everything we treasure will wither and die.

'Now I, for one, favour the enterprise which provides the greater chance of success. The time it will take us to reach Instruere and summon the council may allow further evidence to surface of Bhrudwo's intentions. If the knowledge of these intentions dies with us in some lonely hollow, nothing will remain to stop the Destroyer catching Faltha off guard for a second time.

'And even more important than the threat of invasion itself is the knowledge that some of the kings of the Sixteen Kingdoms are traitors to Faltha. If we can get that information to the council, they may be able to act to depose the Bhrudwan pawns, so that we can get a united army together to face our ancient enemy.

'I'm sorry, boys,' he said, licking his lips nervously, turning to Leith and his brother, 'but when I put two people against thousands, even though they are two people I love, I can make only one choice. I believe that by now your mother and father truly are dead.' The Haufuth spread his hands wide. 'I'm sorry! I choose the sensible path. I choose to try to save Faltha.'

It was out, it had been said. They were dead. Leith put his head in his hands.

The old farmer stood and strode over to the door, hands behind his back. 'Now is the time to give up dreams of heroic destiny. Politics, not heroics, will save Faltha from the murderous armies. Yes, we should travel to Instruere and tell our story. But not to the council; not yet. We will need to find a sponsor, someone with influence on the council, someone to plead our cause and convince Faltha to investigate our claims. Someone not corrupted by Bhrudwo's taint. For all we know, there may be traitors even on the council! Without a sponsor we will not get past the Iron Door of the Outer Chamber.'

He took a step forward, and lowered his voice. 'I know such a sponsor.'

'Someone with power and influence in Instruere?' The Haufuth's voice was laced with disbelief. 'Who?'

'I'll explain in a moment,' the old farmer rasped, clearly annoyed at the interruption to his argument. 'As for the fate of Mahnum and Indrett, I agree with the Haufuth. They are dead. Why should the Bhrudwans keep them alive, since it is their knowledge that is dangerous? My reasoning says: forget them! I do not wish to die on a foolish expedition without direction or hope. I appreciate how this must make you feel,' he said to the boys, trying to soften his voice but not succeeding. 'He was a good man, and she was kind, for a southerner. But we cannot allow sentiment to interfere with sense.'

'Then it is settled!' boomed the Haufuth. 'As soon as we can gather—'

The scraping of a chair interrupted the big man. Hal struggled to his feet. He faced the older men, leaning on the arm of a chair, his face like stone. The Haufuth lapsed into silence.

'Nothing has been settled.' Hal spoke softly. 'I have listened carefully to you both, without interrupting. Now be quiet and listen to me.' He held them with adamant eyes. 'There are others here who have not yet had their say. It is their turn. Then we will speak of decisions.'

The Haufuth's face burned. What the youth said was true; Kurr and he had dominated the discussion, forgetting about the boys. As the host, he was keenly aware of his lack of manners.

The old farmer, however, would have none of it. Striding back from the door, he stood facing Hal, though a head higher, staring down into the cripple's clear brown eyes, his own hard eyes holding dark fury. 'What could you possibly add to the discussion?' he rasped. 'Are you going to bring your decades of experience to bear on the problem? Does your wide travelling in the North Woods give you insight into how the Council of Faltha will treat our news? Or perhaps some of the foxes and squirrels you talk to have told you which way the Bhrudwan warriors went?' He raised his stick, then jabbed Hal in the stomach with it. 'Face the facts! Your elders have decided what to do. Now sit down, cripple, before I sit you down.'

'Whether I sit or stand, you will listen to logic,' Hal shot right back. The old farmer's eyes opened wide; he had obviously not expected defiance. He opened his mouth to speak, but Hal beat him to it: 'Logic.' His voice stayed firm, his words clipped. 'You speak of our dilemma, a choice between two courses of action. This is not the only way to view the problem. Rather, I believe we have only one course of action with two objectives, and by pursuing this course both of these objectives will be met.'

Leith could hear the anger in his brother's voice. Hal was slow to anger, but when roused he was immovable. Leith had seen it with villagers, with his parents, with himself. Hal did not get angry with the person, exactly; it was as though he took offence at the idea he disagreed with, and sought to bring it down. Leith could truly say he had never won an argument with his brother. And if Kurr thought to rile Hal by name-calling, he'd better think of something more insulting than calling him a cripple. His brother had experienced a lifetime of abuse, both crude and subtle, and had learned how to cope.

'Really?' Kurr replied sarcastically. 'And perhaps the great scholar would share the results of his logic?'

The Haufuth groaned, obviously aware that he should interfere, but just as obviously incapable of it.

Hal would not be deterred. 'Listen. We need to rescue Mahnum and Indrett, and we need to warn the Council of Faltha of the coming Bhrudwan attack. Whether or not we can achieve them both, those are our objectives. Do you agree?' he asked, turning to the Haufuth, who nodded.

'The one thing we lack in achieving our second objective is proof,' Hal said quietly. 'Without evidence, our story is just a fairy-tale. We need evidence. Is that correct?'

Again, the Haufuth's head nodded in agreement. Kurr remained perfectly still.

'Think, now: would a captured enemy soldier, a man from Bhrudwo who has been caught well inside Falthan territory, constitute such evidence? If he could be persuaded to talk, that is?'

The head nodded again, then the Haufuth spoke cautiously: 'If I understand what you are getting at . . . you want us to go after your parents and, in the act of freeing them, capture one of the warriors and present him to the Falthan council?'

'That's right,' said Hal evenly.

They thought about it for a moment. 'Well,' said the Haufuth, 'we might as well add another impossibility to the list. Not that I don't see the sense of what you say. We need evidence, and evidence is fleeing from us at this very moment. But I would have thought it difficult enough to rescue your parents, let alone capture one of the killers. These people are inhuman! What they did at the Favonian village – I don't like the sound of that.'

Hal looked him straight in the eye. 'Neither do I. But I can think of no riskless method of doing what we need to do. I can think of no others to take our place. And I can think of no way to avoid our responsibility, both to Faltha and to two people from this village, without dying an inner death long before the Bhrudwan army gets here.'

Even Kurr looked thoughtful now, though he had not backed away one inch.

'And there is one other matter.' Hal spoke carefully, so there would be no mistaking his meaning. 'There is still one here who has not been heard, and his heart may speak more clearly than our most carefully considered counsels. If he wishes to abandon his father and his mother, so be it. But can you take a heart that longs for the love of a father and kill it, crushing it by cold words of reason, ending hope and sowing seeds of guilt and betrayal? Which of you would give up your family to a cruel fate without suffering doubt – at the least – for the rest of your life? Would you not at least make an attempt to rescue them, vain though that attempt may be? If you do not value hearts like this one, then I tell you truly that it does not matter whether Faltha or Bhrudwo rules, for we have fallen into corruption. Listen to the heart of a son. Let it decide our course.'

The attention shifted to Leith. He felt every eye on him, and he wished he had some eloquent words to deliver. Once or twice he ventured to speak, but nothing emerged from his dry mouth.

'Well, boy?' Kurr inquired gently.

'I – I don't know,' Leith stammered at last. 'At least – I do know what I want.' He dropped his head. 'I don't know about Bhrudwo and armies and wars and councils. I just want my mother and father back.' His voice dropped to a whisper; the others struggled to hear him as he continued, 'I don't want them hurt. I keep thinking about what might be happening to them. I keep waiting for somebody to do something. Can't we do something? Can't we get my parents back?' Suddenly his face was too hot and the tears he had been holding back began to make their way down his cheeks.

Kurr bit his lip. How far would he travel for a chance to see Tinei again? What wouldn't he dare for a chance to wrestle her back from the grip of death? Devoted and true-hearted she had been, strong like the ice of Iskelfjorth, never complaining about her ruination as a young woman but bearing up against the constant pain until the years of harsh living had brought her to an untimely end. And now, if by some miracle he was to be offered a chance of having her back, would he not beg, cajole or even force others to give him aid? Would he not tear down the very vaults of Andratan to set her free? He made his way to his seat and sat down, his red-rimmed eyes betraying nothing.

The Haufuth sat on the edge of his chair, watching helplessly as the boy cried. Once again he was powerless to give comfort to one of his villagers. Why did he always fail them? Lines from the Oath of Leadership, that piece of doggerel all Haufuths knew by heart, came unbidden into his mind:

> To discharge duties great and small,
> A village servant first of all.

What was his duty? To save Faltha, or to help this stricken family? He was reminded of wise words heard long ago from Jarel, the old Haufuth: *If you take care of the small things, the large things take care of themselves.* Perhaps this was the clue he was looking for. Faltha was not his responsibility, but this village certainly was. Maybe in rescuing Mahnum and Indrett, Faltha could also be rescued. But Faltha was not his immediate concern; he could see that now. Perhaps he could take Hayne into his confidence, the youngster he was training to be the next Haufuth. Hayne could look after the village while he was gone. His duty was to these two boys in need, and to two other villagers held against their will somewhere out there in the snow.

Lost in their thoughts, the two men did not notice Hal as he quietly made his way to where his brother was sitting and began to speak softly to him. At intervals Leith nodded his head. Finally the room lapsed back into silence.

Hal cleared his throat and spoke.

'Leith and I have come to a decision. We are going to pursue our parents. We ask you for help but we do not expect it: your duty may make different demands of you than ours does of us. All we ask is that our departure be kept secret, and that you aid us with provisions for our journey.'

The Haufuth spoke quickly: 'I will accompany you on the road.'

'The four of us will journey together,' Kurr corrected.

The big man shook his head. 'Madness!' he muttered to himself. 'But what else can we do?'

'Isn't there anyone who can help us?' asked Leith, an urgent edge to his voice. The night was drawing near, they must leave soon or abandon any faint hope of catching the Bhrudwans, and much still remained to be said.

The Haufuth leaned forward and put his head in his hands. 'Not unless you have a private army hidden away somewhere! Whatever needs to be done will be done by us, or not at all.'

For a moment everyone sat silent, listening to the soft noises of a village preparing for the evening meal.

Kurr straightened himself in his seat and took a deep breath. When he had everyone's attention, he asked, 'Have any of you heard of the Watchers?'

Two headshakes signalled the negative. Leith spoke tentatively: 'You said something about them once, I think . . .'

'Good to find that you remember something, boy,' growled the farmer in his old familiar voice. 'Listen, now. The Watchers were once very influential in Falthan affairs. Long ago, after the Bhrudwan invasion had been repelled, a number of wealthy noblemen from Instruere met together with the determination to ensure Faltha was never again caught by surprise. They formed a small group to watch the borders of Bhrudwo and keep an eye on Falthan politics, reasoning that if they could keep Faltha strong and keep Bhrudwo out, their own interests would be safe. This group became known as the Watchers.

'Eventually their preoccupation with the borders waned in favour of involvement in Falthan politics. These men soon found themselves snared in struggles for power behind the thrones of many Falthan countries. They infiltrated the Council of Faltha. Soon they controlled the movement of goods, the policies of nations and, with these things, thousands of lives. They were invisible men, working where they would not be noticed. They forgot their reason for existence – the strengthening of Faltha – and the Watchers became a name hated by the people of the Sixteen Kingdoms.'

'All very interesting,' the Haufuth puffed, 'but what—'

'Be patient and listen to what I have to say!' Kurr shot back, his grey eyes flashing. 'The Watchers were outlawed throughout Faltha, and many who were accused of belonging to the group were tried and imprisoned, or simply murdered. The idea of moving against the corrupt Watchers found favour with king after king, who had long resented their interference. Their lands were confiscated, enriching the royal coffers. Many kings were extremely zealous in their persecution of the Watchers, using their existence as an excuse to separate many an honest landowner, unconnected with the group, from his lands. This only increased the hatred that people felt against the Watchers.

'But not all the Watchers were killed, or even dispossessed. True Watchers continued to do what they could, albeit tenuously for a while, to protect Faltha from the rapaciousness of others and from her own complacency. The irony was that success in the former meant failure in the latter. No one prepares for war during long periods of peace. Indeed, the Watchers spent most of their time trying to keep Sna Vaztha in check. They could not save Haurn from being overrun in 1006, but they were instrumental in saving

87

Asgowan from Sna Vazthan expansion three years later. And by this time no one even suspected their continued existence. As far as most people knew, the Watchers had perished four hundred years earlier.'

The Haufuth began to look at Kurr intently.

'But to this day our group has continued to exist. We do what we can in the name of stability and peace. We have horses, we have messengers, and we have a network of people whose business it is to know what is going on and to keep us informed of it. We had heard vague rumours that something was happening in Bhrudwo, and the general feeling was that it was just another internal struggle. But I felt uneasy. We also knew about the tumult at the Court of Firanes, and it seems that Firanes was not the only court at which strange goings-on have been reported. But none of us had put things together. Even Kroptur himself does not suspect that Bhrudwo is behind the power struggles in palaces around Faltha. However, he knew something was amiss. Remember what I said at the Midwinter celebration? How I warned that no peace lasts forever? That we had grown sleepy, and were unprepared for war? Those were his words—'

The Haufuth was now leaning forward, pointing a finger at Kurr.

'So you're one of them?'

Kurr ignored the interruption. 'We can help! Horses, supplies on the journey, eyes and ears! All I need to do is send a message, and Watchers in Firanes, Plonya and beyond will aid us in our search for these Bhrudwan killers. What hope have we alone? And when we reach Instruere they will aid us in gaining the ear of the Council of Faltha. These Watchers, I promise you, are men of integrity. They can help us!'

'How many are there?' asked the Haufuth suspiciously. 'What are their ages? Can they fight?'

Kurr looked a little shamefaced. 'I didn't say they were an army. Unfortunately, the Watchers are few and far between in this part of the world. We are so far from the borders of Bhrudwo, you see. We are few and we are old, but we still have eyes and ears and wits to use them. How else will you track the killers? We can watch every eastward trail. Do you have influence with kings and governments? Some of us have.'

'But will even the Watchers believe that Faltha is threatened? It's been such a long time...'

'I don't know,' said the old farmer. 'I truly don't know. They might, and they might not. Kroptur will know. But the word of an old man from the edge of the world, even one such as Kroptur, may not carry much weight. However, we can only try.'

'All right, all right,' the Haufuth moaned. All this talk, all this responsibility, all these new revelations, were gnawing away at his fragile confidence like rats at the autumn harvest. Andratan, the Destroyer, the Council of Faltha, and now the Watchers. What did it all mean to a headman from lowly Firanes? What next? Would the Most High appear before him in a cloud of smoke and charge him with the safety of the west?

He laughed out loud. It was all so improbable and yet it was happening. It was all he could do to keep himself from giggling nervously, a habit he had rid himself of in childhood.

'All right then. Let's say for now that we ask the Watchers to help us. Any real help will be a relief.' He sank back into his chair.

In the stillness they heard the sounds of people moving up and down the lane, then quick footsteps on the terrace outside. A girl's voice could be heard: then, before anyone could react, the door burst open and Stella bustled in.

'Here's the cheese you wanted, Merin!' she called; then, seeing the brothers, she stopped abruptly. The tray dropped from her nerveless fingers with a clatter. Stella took a step backwards, and her hand went to her mouth. The Haufuth put his head in his hands. Merin came in from the kitchen and stood at the doorway, shaking her head. For a long moment no one spoke.

Kurr was the first to recover. 'Sit down, girl,' he said quietly.

She sat in an empty chair, not once taking her wide-open eyes away from Leith and Hal. Four fingers were now stuffed in her mouth. Behind her, Merin walked over to the front door and pushed it firmly closed. She drew the bolt.

'No, they're not ghosts,' the farmer assured the frightened girl. 'They are very much alive.'

Stella drew her hand away from her face, took a couple of steadying breaths, and said, 'Then who . . .'

'We buried no one,' the Haufuth said in answer. 'Not that day, anyway,' he added, glancing sideways at Kurr.

Suddenly the old farmer stood up. 'I have a few errands to run,' he grated, then turned to the Haufuth. 'Back in a while. I'll leave the explanation to you.'

'Of course. Take as much time as you need. But it looks as though we'll need to talk as soon as you return.'

Kurr grunted, then strode out through the back door. 'Keep the door locked!' he threw back over his shoulder.

The Haufuth nodded, then turned to the white-faced girl sitting nervously on the edge of her chair.

'I – I want to go now,' she said.

'You'll stay where you are for the moment. I'm not having you rushing around the village telling everyone what you've seen.'

'My mother is expecting me home. She'll come looking for me soon. You can't keep me here!' Her voice skirled towards panic.

The Haufuth thought frantically for a second, then relaxed.

'Your parents will be told that you're visiting us for a few hours. I was supposed to drop in and see you later this week, to talk with you about announcing your betrothal to Druin. Let's just say that I have taken the opportunity to talk with you now.' He turned to his wife. 'Merin,' he said, 'will you go and see Pell and Herza? Stella will be joining us for the evening meal, at least.'

He paused for a moment while Merin left the room.

'Now,' he continued, 'don't you want to hear about Hal and Leith?'

Knowing she was cornered for the moment, the girl nodded her head cautiously, then cast a glance at the two youths as though she expected them suddenly to disappear. Hal returned her gaze calmly; Leith, however, was anything but relaxed. Of all the people to uncover their ruse! The daughter of the village gossip, the girl who had spurned him, Stella Pellwen! And what was this about announcing betrothal? As she turned to face the Haufuth, Leith risked a glance or two in her direction. She wore a simple fur-lined garment fashioned from brown leather, on to which cascaded her lustrous black hair. Her skin was dark for one of the northern lands, unusual but not unique. But it was the wonder of her eyes that had attracted Leith: pools of mystery behind which anything might swim, and in which anyone might drown. It had been a long time since Leith had dared to look in those eyes, for fear of reading further rejection there, or worse, indifference. He did not dare now.

What next? he thought. *Well, at least the secrecy will be over. No one could keep Stella's mother quiet.* Now at least he could say goodbye to a few friends.

Stella sat in her chair, half listening to the Haufuth as he gave her an abridged version of events. For a moment she had been truly frightened by seeing the brothers she had supposed dead, but then she realised that they were just the same two boys, Hal with his twisted side and Leith with his blushes and clumsiness. Now her fear drained away, anger rushing in to take its place. They were not allowing her to leave! How dare they! What right did they have to keep her here? She tried to keep her hands from shaking as she listened to the headman.

Kurr was away for the best part of an hour. He returned looking thoughtful, and called the Haufuth aside into an adjoining room. While they were away Leith endured an uncomfortable few minutes, not quite knowing where to look, trying to ignore the burning feeling in his chest and the butterflies in his stomach. Why was it, he wondered, that he wanted so much to be near her but couldn't stand being around her?

After what seemed hours the kitchen door opened and in filed Kurr, Merin and the Haufuth. The big man sat opposite Stella, while Kurr drew up a chair to his immediate right and Merin occupied the one to his left. Hal shifted closer to the girl, with Leith a short distance away, so that the seats now formed two lines; one of adults, one of teenagers. The village headman pulled his chair slightly forward and manoeuvred his bulk until he sat on its edge.

'Listen, Stella,' he said kindly, 'you've seen something you weren't supposed to see. Now that wasn't your fault; we should have made sure that no one could disturb us. For that I take the blame.' He looked at Kurr. 'And now you know why we have hidden Leith and Hal. We considered that they were in danger if the village knew they had survived. Well, we've talked it over and our views have not changed. There could be a risk not only to Leith and Hal, but also to the entire village, if outsiders heard about this. We can't take the chance that these raiders might return. Soon the boys will leave here and go somewhere else to live, at least until their parents are found. In the meantime, no one else must find out that they are still alive. That secret must remain amongst the six of us here. Do you understand?'

Stella nodded.

Kurr leaned forward and fixed a stern eye on the girl.

'Do you promise to keep secret everything you have seen and heard here, telling no one, not even your friends, not even your parents?'

'I promise,' she said, but even Leith saw the flash of excitement in her eyes. *She might mean it now*, thought Leith, *but how long could she hold out against the temptation?* The Haufuth exchanged glances with the farmer.

It was sharp-eyed Merin who spoke, in that low, intense voice that compelled everyone who ridiculed her husband to take her very seriously. 'Young lady, you are not fooling anyone. The first chance you get, you will tell your story to anyone who will listen.' She continued, overriding the girl's protests, 'First your family, then your friends, then it doesn't matter who else. Not an ounce of consideration for the concerns of others. Tell me, have you even been listening?'

The girl dropped her head in the face of this attack.

'It's no use. We can't risk it,' Kurr said. 'We have no middle course. Either we take the whole village into our confidence, and trust that the story spreads no further, or we ensure that this girl has no chance to betray us.'

Leith jerked his head up. *Ensure it? How? What was the old man contemplating?* He looked at Stella, and saw that she had begun to cry. Anger against the farmer rose within him. He wanted to reach out to Stella, but even as he thought it, he realised that he would never dare. As he watched, Hal put an arm on her shaking shoulder.

The Haufuth spoke. 'Who will take her? And how far out of our way can we afford to go? We have to tell the village.'

'I don't agree,' said his wife firmly. 'Take her with you.'

The headman began to protest but Kurr cut in: 'Merin is right. It is the safest way. Now that we have gone this far with our deception, we must go all the way.'

'But Stella's parents! What will we tell them?'

Kurr stared at the big man with eyes like flint. 'Nothing. We will only be away a few weeks at the most. Leave a note or something. But we must make a start now, tonight, before anyone else discovers our secret.'

Hal spoke: 'There has been much falsehood already. We should deceive the village no longer. I am sure that once they know how serious things are, they could be trusted to keep quiet.'

'But this is just what we are talking about! Here we have a villager who cannot be trusted, and you counsel us to allow not only her, but also others like her, to spread this strange tale abroad? No, Hal, your advice is too risky. The girl comes with us, at least far enough away from this village to remove the danger of her tongue. Should the riders return, or should any of their sympathisers get wind of the truth, they would not hesitate to put the village to the question. Like the Favonian village.'

'What do you mean, take me with you? Where are we going?' Stella asked desperately. 'I won't tell anyone about this! Can't you trust me?'

The Haufuth sighed. 'It's not a matter of trust. Even with the best will in the world, you will probably let something slip. We need to go after Mahnum and Indrett – tonight – and we haven't got time to explain things to the village. Now stop worrying about yourself and try to do what is best for Loulea!'

'We have a lot to do in the next few hours,' Kurr interrupted, as Stella was about to reply. 'Most important of all, we need to decide where we are going. Do any of you have a guess as to where these brigands might have gone?'

'Down the North Road to Oln, then the Coast Road towards Rammr, no doubt.'

'But are you sure?'

The Haufuth shook his head. There was much he was not sure about.

'No mind,' continued the farmer. 'We'll find out soon enough. Let's get all the equipment together. What you don't have here I can probably find at my house, including clothes for the girl. She is about the same size . . .' his voice tailed off.

Stella brushed the tears away from her face as she began to think, really think. Maybe she could shout or scream and attract the attention of a passer-by. Or she could make a run at the door and perhaps get it unbolted before anyone could stop her. *But do I want to go home?* she asked herself, thinking hard. *If I go home now, there will be another scene.* She could hear her parents scolding her again, trying to convince her that announcing her betrothal to Druin would be anything other than a total disaster. That ill-mannered, thick-headed brute! She shuddered at the memory of his coarse attentions. Perhaps a few weeks away from the village would be a good idea. She really did not want one more day of Druin's hateful company.

Later that evening the group regathered, minus Stella who was talking with Merin in another room, and Hal who had gone to the kitchen to prepare food. Six piles on the floor in the middle of the room, one for each traveller and one pile of general equipment, signified almost everything they were to leave with. It was, of course, quite the wrong time of year for any serious travelling, so they needed to be equipped for adverse weather conditions, even though their journey was to be southwards in the main. However, success depended on their pursuing and catching horsemen who had three days' head start, so equipment had to be kept to a minimum. They would avail themselves of the hospitality of others and live off the land itself where necessary.

Now they were almost ready to leave, but Leith still had no idea of where they were going, or how they would catch so fearsome a quarry. As if in answer to his unspoken question, the Haufuth sat down with the farmer and began to discuss their journey.

'Are you sure your friend at Watch Hill will know?' asked the big man.

'Bound to. Nothing gets past his gaze. Hayne should be back within the hour.'

'Know what?' interrupted Leith boldly.

Two faces turned towards him, one gentler than the other.

'Yes, of course,' the Haufuth said, 'I should have said something. A while ago Kurr dispatched Hayne to ride over to a friend of his who lives on the hill overlooking Vapnatak. From there he can see both the North Road and the Westway. Kurr assures me that this man will have noticed any horsemen in the last week, and when Hayne returns we shall know for sure which direction they have taken.'

'But is there any doubt?' Leith replied. 'The Westway leads into the interior, and no one would travel that road at this time of year.'

'I'm sure you are right,' answered the farmer, 'but it is always best to be certain. There is another reason for contacting Kroptur. He is a Watcher – indeed, he holds command of the North March – and has horses faster than mine. These he will put to good use, sending messages to others further along the road who can report on any strange horsemen who have passed their way. We may be some distance behind them, but as long as they keep to the roads – as they must, at this time of year – we should be able to track them. Our only concern, of course, is what they might have done in the meantime.'

Leith turned away. *What might they have done in the meantime?* He was determined not to think about it.

The world smeared past Mahnum's eyes. His head was on fire; his body ached past knowledge. The stones of the road, the snow-shrouded fields and the occasional bush flashed past, distracting him as he tried to remember what had happened. Things had still not shaken themselves into focus when his head slammed against the rump of the horse and the sickening pain forced him to screw both eyes tightly shut. *Focus, focus,* he told himself. He tried to fight his way back past the bouncing and jerking of the horse, back through the pain, past the lights flashing in his head. He forced his good eye open; the lights danced still, and he fought back the nausea as everything lurched violently around him.

Think! He remembered the beating, when the four men had tied him to a tree and taken turns punching and kicking him, while Indrett wept quietly in the background. Thump, thump, thump, the sound of blows crashing in on him, part of his mind somehow detached from the pain and the fear, the blows sounding like the pounding of an axe on a block of wood. How could something like that sound so impersonal? Then he had been cut loose, and had fallen to the ground in a pool of warm, sticky liquid – his own blood. *No, that was not where the pain came from. Think!* He had tried to pull himself up, but had been kicked back to the ground. Then the question had come again, repeated by one after another of their captors, always the same unanswerable question. Where is the Right Hand? Where is the Right Hand? He had tried to answer, but could think of nothing convincing to say. Then the four Bhrudwans had dragged Indrett to the tree and tied her there – *Oh Most High, that was the source of the pain! Please, please, let her go! I could tell even the Voice of Andratan nothing about the Right Hand! Please!* He had cried out again and again, his cries louder than hers as they had brutally beaten her, fists and sticks and the flat of a sword. And finally the red haze had taken him, and he had not seen the end of it.

He twisted and stretched, trying to catch a glimpse of Indrett, but could see nothing of her. His hands were tied behind his back and he lay face down, lashed to the back of a black Bhrudwan horse. As he struggled, pain roared mercilessly in his brain. It hurt to lift his head, it hurt to do anything, it hurt when he did nothing. *What had they done to her? Did she hurt like this? Was she still alive?*

He tried to imagine his tough girl from the south lying cold and dead in some ditch, her pretty face bloodied and pale, her sparkling eyes unseeing, but he couldn't. *She must be alive.* He gritted his teeth. *She must be alive!* Then he thought of his boys, remembering their cries and then the silence and the fire, and he realised with faltering heart that they were certainly dead. And soon, perhaps very soon, he would be wishing he could join them. He knew these Bhrudwans. *Why, oh why, did I lead them straight to the ones I love the most?*

He tried again to lift himself high enough to see the others, but he was too tightly bound. He could hear their voices ahead of him, shouting to each other above the rushing of the wind, the sounds of efficient cruelty. His struggles finally attracted their attention, and a voice just in front of him hissed words he could not understand, a warning to keep still. But he would not give up; he had to see Indrett, had to know she was alive. The voice came again, the warning unmistakable even if the words were in a foreign tongue.

He sensed rather than saw the blow coming, but could not duck. For an instant the helpless terror choked him again, then something crashed into the back of his head and the redness exploded within. His head slumped against the rump of the horse; his body went limp, and moved only with the movement of the mount beneath him.

Satisfied, the Bhrudwan warrior slung his staff back across his shoulders.

Finally the Company of five travellers were ready for their journey. Hayne had returned and Kurr had gone outside to speak with him. The news was puzzling. Kroptur had indeed seen four horsemen, early on the morning after Midwinter, riding eastwards along the Westway. As much as it didn't make sense, this was the road that the Company would be forced to take in their pursuit of the brigands.

The Westway! That road would lead them into the cold continental interior, away from the towns and villages of coastal Firanes.

The Westway was once the main route between Firanes and the rest of Faltha, having been built in the days of the First Men as the link between the fabled northern city of Astora – the capital of Firanes until it was taken by the sea over a thousand years ago, so the stories said – and Instruere. Travellers and trade now went south to Rammr, the main city of Firanes, and then by ship to the ports of the Wodhaitic Sea.

The Westway was a tortuous road even in summer, and during winter was not used save in the most extreme necessity. People travelled short distances along those parts of the road that ran between settlements, but for months at a stretch the road saw no horseman or foot-bound traveller. In some places it was paved, but for the most part the Westway was a rutted track or forest path, now in the grip of the cruel northern winter.

'At least we know where they've headed,' the Haufuth grumbled. 'One thing about it, we won't lose them in that country. They'll stick to the road, and so will we.'

'But how will we catch them?' asked Leith.

'Their horses won't be much use to them on Breidhan Moor, not this time of year. They'll have to walk, same as us.' The village headman shook his head bemusedly. 'I don't understand it! Had they ridden to the south they could have been well on their way to Rammr by now, and be taking ship to Instruere, or Lavana at least.'

'There are any number of reasons why someone might take the Westway,' responded Kurr. 'Think. Would such people be granted ship's passage without question, especially when they had unwilling companions? The Most High grant that Firanese have not yet fallen so far. The Westway is the most direct route to The Gap, and they have to go through The Gap to get back to Bhrudwo. Why should they go south?'

'Yes, but in the winter? Surely the Westway, though the shorter, will prove the slower?'

'I'm sure you are right. But do they know that? They are foreigners in this land. Might they not simply retrace their steps to Bhrudwo, not knowing any other route?'

'That is far more likely,' the headman admitted.

'It is my hope that they are forcing Mahnum to act as their guide. He may have chosen the Westway for them, knowing it will slow them down. The horsemen will not know about winters behind the Fells, a fact that may be our first piece of good fortune.'

It was time to leave. Stella emerged from another room, her arm firmly held by Merin. Leith felt light-headed; whether from fear of the unknown, the excitement of imminent departure, worry about his parents, or sheer nervous exhaustion, he could not tell.

A hand ruffled his hair. 'Best we get moving,' Kurr said. 'You'll be all right, boy. Plenty of your father in you.'

As they filed out the back door of the headman's house and strode off into the night, Leith looked within himself for whatever bravery his father might have passed on to him. He found only fear.

CHAPTER 5

UNDER WATCH HILL

FURTIVE SHADOWS FLICKERED ACROSS the flank of the ridge overlooking Loulea. Below them the night lights went out one by one, and slowly the village sank into sleep. The moon picked out the figures – one, two, three, four, five, all but the last leading a horse – as they paused to look across the small northern valley that contained their lives. Tree groves were dark smudges on the shimmering snow-dappled valley bottom ground, silver where the snow lay on last year's fields, charcoal-grey over scrubby hillslopes. Through the valley wound the gossamer thread of Lime Brook, which flowed into the Vale from under the Great North Woods in the far distance, then turned west just short of Loulea and funnelled between Swill Down and Bream Hill to the sea.

As beguiling as this midwinter view was, the eyes of those on the ridge were drawn to the east. There they could see the line of Brookside Road, marked by the shadows of tall hedges. Beyond the road the ground rose into Garrison Hill, around and behind which snaked the Westway on its journey inland from Loulea and the sea. Only three leagues away, hidden by the bulk of the hill, lay Vapnatak, the largest town in the North March of Firanes. On the far side of the Westway they could make out the upper slopes of Watch Hill, the highest point in the region. A single point of light burned near its summit.

Stella desperately wanted to leave this valley tonight. The men had made her follow them out of the village, and the path they chose had taken them so close to her own house she felt sure that a shout would have brought her father running. But she had not shouted. Even though they were going into danger and perhaps death, she had decided to follow. Better death than a life with Druin.

Kurr pointed to the light atop Watch Hill. 'There are our beds,' he commented. 'Now I have settled my mind that the farm is secure, we can go on to Kroptur's house. Two hours and we can rest!'

'I hope Kroptur is ready for us,' the Haufuth breathed nervously. 'I've never met the man.'

'He will be ready. Do you think he keeps his lamp burning this late every night? And don't worry. Legend and rumour make a man more than he is in reality.'

The Haufuth grunted, then turned and walked away. They were off down the hill, away from the moonlit vista, heading towards the Westway, away from Loulea.

As they walked, Leith ran the last few hours through his mind. They had embarked on a journey that might well change their lives. They were headed into Fell country, through Breidhan Moor and maybe beyond, travelling at the wrong time of year. Of the five, only Stella and he could be described as young, fit and healthy. Kurr looked old and thin, walking there up the front with the aid of his stick; the Haufuth puffed behind him in a sort of shuffling waddle, though he had left his walking stick behind; and Hal – well, Hal had perfected a spidery walk that saw his good left leg shoot out and his withered leg trail behind, acting only as a balance. It was almost comical to look at, but Leith didn't laugh. His older brother was nothing if not courageous, and had spent years learning to adapt to his disability. Leith grunted inwardly. *I haven't adapted to being normal*, he thought wryly.

He adjusted his pack. 'Sit your pack high up on your shoulders,' Kurr had said. 'Do the belt up tight around your waist. Lean forward – let the weight sit above you, not behind you. Let it push you forward, not pull you back!' Fortunately, he reflected, they were going to load most of this stuff on to the horses once they arrived at Watch Hill.

Sometime late in the evening the Bhrudwans reined in their steeds and made camp. Rough hands jerked Mahnum from his horse and he fell to the ground, the fall serving to wake him. Still bound hand and foot, he was dragged across bare ground and propped, half dazed, in a sitting position against the rough trunk of a pine tree. He cast frantic glances around the little wooded copse until finally he saw what he most wanted to see. There, across the small clearing, set against a Y-shaped tree and with a broken limb over-shadowing her, was Indrett.

He looked more closely, and he was cut to the quick. Her face was caked with blood, her eyes were swollen shut, her face a mass of welts and her hair straggled lank and filthy over her bent shoulders. *Bent but not broken*, Mahnum thought. They would kill her before they broke her spirit. Fear rose within him at the thought. Was she still alive? The flush of her cheeks, the rise and fall of her breast – she lived yet. *Oh Most High!* He sat against the base of the tree, unable to do more than watch her from afar, while around him the Bhrudwans set up camp. They pitched a curious, round-shaped tent, tethered their horses next to Mahnum's pine tree and set about cooking a meal, but the Trader hardly noticed. He was heartsick with longing for his Indrett, he was frustrated with his inability to help her, and stricken by the certain knowledge of what these murderers could and would do to her.

Later that night hunger awoke him from a fitful dozing that had been filled with dark shapes, questions, threats and blows. The Bhrudwans had not fed their captives, nor had they been given anything to drink. *It is unlikely anything could have gotten past these swollen lips*, though Mahnum bitterly. Next to him a horse nickered softly, then nuzzled him. These beasts were not evil like their masters. Such evil! He had learned much about these Bhrudwans in the last year; how they combined a frightening singleminded-ness with great strength and discipline; their absolute obedience to their leader; their lack of any moral inhibition; their love of violence. How could he have led them home to Loulea? What was he thinking? He felt the horse nuzzle him again, half-apologetically, as if concerned for his wellbeing.

Then the germ of an idea began to take shape in his mind. Farfetched, but possible. Right out of the legend of Cowyn the Hunter it came. *Nothing to lose. Why not?* But would he have the strength? *No time to wonder*, he thought. *Do it now!* He rolled to the right and fell away from the tree to lie prone on the bare, stony ground. The breath was knocked out of him and he lay there for a long time, exhausted. Then slowly, painfully, he forced his stiff body around in circles as his hands scrabbled behind his back for the stone he was looking for. There were a few stones loosely embedded in the soil, but after feeling them he discarded them one at a time. *Be patient*, he told himself. *You've got all night. Stay awake. Wait for the right one.* His fingernails filled with dirt as he scrabbled sightlessly in the soil.

Finally he found what he was looking for: a perfect sliver of stone, small but razor-sharp. For a moment he thought of trying to cut his bonds, of freeing Indrett, of escaping these cruel men. *How far would we get?* he mocked himself. *Probably not even out of these woods.* He sighed. His first idea was probably his best – and if it didn't work, probably his last.

Slowly, carefully, he wriggled back to the tree trunk. Now he made low murmuring noises, sounds he hoped were reassuring to the animals nearby. Again he had to find something, and again he would have to use his hands, bound tightly behind him. The moonlight shone through the trees, but was of little use. He groped until he found it: a horse's leg. Now sure of himself, he deftly pulled the leg up, speaking soothingly to the horse as its breath ruffled his hair. He held the sliver of stone between thumb and forefinger, took a deep breath – he would have only one chance – then felt for that dull, gristly spot between hoof and shoe. With all the strength he could muster, he drove the stone shard up into the gristle. The horse neighed and shook his head, that was all, at the slight pain in its hoof. But it was enough. Immediately those in the tent stirred, and someone came out to see what the matter was. Mahnum had only a moment. With all his remaining strength he twisted across the ground until he felt the tree behind him, then pulled himself against it. The horse neighed again and stamped its leg, forcing the sliver deeper into the hoof. *It will be only an annoyance at first*, Mahnum thought absently as he slumped against the trunk, trying to quieten his ragged breathing. Now one of the Bhrudwans strode across the open space to check on the horses. Surely he would see that his captive had been up to something? A wave of pain and nausea washed over Mahnum. *I must not be sick*, he thought. Where was the Bhrudwan? Would he notice the disturbed ground? Light-headed and giddy, Mahnum had lapsed into unconsciousness by the time the warrior got to him.

The Bhrudwan gave a grunt. These Falthans were soft, and he felt nothing but contempt for even the best of them. He kicked his captive expertly in the ribs, and heard the satisfying crack of leather against bone. *This one is in no condition to cause trouble*, he mused. *But he will provide us with much entertainment before he tells us what we want to know. He'll tell us, of that there can be no doubt. By the time we've finished, he'll be begging us to listen.* Content, he wandered back to the tent, while behind him one of the horses stamped his right foreleg, trying to rid himself of an irritation in his hoof.

It was well into the early hours when the Company finally tracked under Watch Hill.

Perhaps it was the lateness of the hour, or maybe the excitement and tension of their mission had taken something out of them, but the determination to stride out quickly, to make up time on the Bhrudwans, had somehow dissolved into tired stumbling as they made their way along the Westway towards the outskirts of Vapnatak. At least, Leith hoped there was some sensible reason for their slowness, a reason other than that they were unfit, cruelly unsuited for such a journey. The stony road crunched under their boots, a sound so loud that Leith was sure it would drive away any animals, or lead to their discovery should anyone come looking for them. On either side of the road stood tall hedges, against which were piled high drifts of snow. The moon hovered just above the horizon, and the shadows cast by the hedges made it difficult to see.

Behind the hedges to the left rose the shadowy bulk of Watch Hill, Magic Mountain as the children of Loulea knew it. Every once in a while some child claimed to have climbed Watch Hill, but none could prove it. Watch Hill had always been off limits to the children of Loulea Vale. The Haufuth said it was because a remnant of the Great North Wood covered its slopes, a haven for wild animals, but the children knew better. It was Magic Mountain, the place where the Sorcerer lived. Leith made a point of never looking at it on his way to and from Vapnatak, the few times he had been there. The Westway passed right underneath it.

I don't believe in the Sorcerer, Leith told himself, then grimaced. *I didn't believe in Bhrudwans, either, until a few days ago.*

Over the brow of a low saddle they crunched. Looking back from his position behind Hal, Leith could see a small part of the Vale of Loulea. Ahead, around the next bend, they would see the lights of Vapnatak. The horses began down the slope.

Kurr barked a sudden command. 'Stop!'

Immediately the horses were reined in; and in the cold silence that followed they could all hear the sound of footsteps coming from somewhere ahead of them.

'No sense in hiding,' said the old farmer in a low voice. 'If we can hear him, he can hear us.'

'Why do we need to hide, anyway?' Leith breathed to his brother.

'Night travellers out on midwinter roads would make a great story in these parts,' Hal replied. 'Someone in Loulea might work out who the travellers were, and come out after us.'

'Oh! And what—'

'Shhh!' breathed the Haufuth.

At that moment a tall, stooped figure emerged from between hedges beside the road, some way ahead of the Company. He had a lantern in his hand.

105

Kurr breathed out his relief as a sigh. 'Master!' he exclaimed. 'What are you doing on the road?'

'More to th' point, what are you people doin' out here so late?' crackled the reply in a voice like fire. 'You should have been here hours since!' He paused, counting the Company. 'Five? Why five?'

'When I explain why we are late, you will understand why we are five and not four,' said Kurr. 'But why don't we talk inside? It's cold out here, and we're making a lot of noise.'

The shadow in front of them grunted a reply that Leith did not catch.

They picked their way slowly down the stony road, then abruptly turned to the left and ascended a steep and narrow path that edged its way up a bush-clad slope. The higher they climbed, the more Leith could see, until Vapnatak was spread out before him. A few lights flickered insistently behind the city walls, but otherwise that town too was asleep.

Looking back, he imagined he could make out the Vale and the lights of his home village. One last glimpse and they were gone, swallowed in the dark tree shadows of Watch Hill.

Near the crown of the hill was a large house. Their ascent, by a narrow, winding path through a forest of tall pine trees, had taken the best part of an hour. For a while during the climb Leith had peered uneasily left and right into the darkness under the forest eaves, half expecting the denizens of Magic Mountain to appear – perhaps the Sorcerer himself leading a party of goblins and fairies, all with blazing green eyes and flames coming out of their mouths – but eventually the long climb and the sleepless nights caught up with him, and his eyes dropped to the ground in front of him. The rest of that night was a waking dream, with stables and smells, strange faces with names he did not catch, bowls of hot water, warm towels and a soft bed in a musty room with a high ceiling.

The next morning Leith rose with the sun. On awakening he caught his breath, memory failing to remind him for a moment why he lay in a strange room. Absently he fingered the sheets: they were made of some soft, slippery fabric, not the rough cotton of home. To his left, on a three-legged stand, sat a bowl of steaming water, no doubt for him to wash in. Did his mother and father have such comforts? Instantly he felt a pang of guilt: why had he spent the night in selfish ease instead of riding through the darkness in search of them? His mind told him he was being foolish. He was not the leader of this expedition; it had not been his decision to halt here. But no matter how hard he exercised his mind, the feeling of guilt would not leave him.

The youth washed away the remnants of sleep and towelled himself dry, then dressed quickly in yesterday's clothes. The room he had slept in was huge, the polished wooden floorboards partially covered by an ornate tasselled rug. In one corner an enormous dresser rose perhaps ten feet, though still falling a yard short of the ceiling. Apart from his bed, the basin stand and the dresser, the room was entirely bare; yet the impression it communicated was not one of poverty, but of austere wealth. Leith furrowed his brow. Perhaps it was in how the furniture was positioned, or maybe the attention to detail shown by the delicate carvings on the legs of the basin stand and the colours worked into the door of the dresser. He had never seen furniture like it. Who would spend so much time over bedroom furniture? And once someone had done so, why would they then consign it to what was obviously a spare room?

The bedroom opened into a long, narrow hallway. Leith looked along it to his right and counted six doors similar to his own, all closed; to his left the hall ended in a door which, judging by the amount of light filtering under it, led outside. Not knowing quite why, he closed his door quietly behind him and crept down the hall to the outside door, eased it open, then stepped into the morning light.

A small green lawn, completely cleared of snow, gave way to a narrow stony path which led upwards through the forest to the crown of Watch Hill. Finding himself a helpless victim of the desire to climb to high places, Leith scurried up the path. As he climbed, the trees gave way to low macrocarpa bushes and then to a small rocky promontory. The crown of Magic Mountain.

And it was just as he had always imagined it. The world was spread out beneath him like a crumpled blanket at the end of a picnic, patchwork on the plains and downs, hills thrown into sharp relief by the morning sun, dark forests brooding on the steeper slopes. To his left – to the west – lay the Vale of Loulea, smaller but more perfectly displayed than he had ever seen it from Swill Down or Bream Hill. Directly beneath him the forest spread towards the Vale, merging with the ordered fields just short of his home village. And there lay Loulea, houses tiny but distinguishable in the crisp morning light. The people were invisible at this distance, but probably getting on with the tasks of the day, having no doubt already forgotten about the funerals of Leith and his brother, the last chapter of the story of Mahnum's unfortunate family.

He swung left again – southwest – towards Swill Down. In his mind he ticked off the landmarks: Stibbourne Farm just over the brow of the hill, Seaspray Farm, Millford Farm, then the Down gave out to the Brookside Valley. Brookside where Lanka lived, the boy he had defeated in the Midwinter Play. *Did he come to my funeral?* Directly south the view was partly obscured by Garrison Hill, thinly forested like a middle-aged man not yet ready to admit to baldness. To the left again – now turning towards the east – lay the confused tangle of limestone ridges that separated the coastlands from Louthwaite Fens, the huge marsh that sat astride the lower reaches of the Mjolk River. Mist hung like hazy smoke in the folded valleys. He recited the farms on the ridges: Lime Flats, Limedale, White Forks, Under The Wood Farm, Mudwise Farm. Next, almost due east, Vapnatak should have lain, but it was hidden by a spur of Watch Hill: a disappointment. The high wall and huge arched gates of the North March's biggest town would surely have looked impressive from this height. Never mind: to the northeast lay the upper valley of the Little Melg, which snaked across its narrow floodplain, accompanied by the North Road. Someone was up early, as testified to by a lazy spiral of smoke signifying a burn-off. Some farmer no doubt ridding his paddock of plough-wrecking tree stumps. Watch Ridge was to the north, thickly forested, hiding Greenwoods Hole and the strange limestone formations on the border of the Great North Woods. And there they were, on the horizon, outlined in black, a vast dark army marching across his field of vision. Now swinging towards the west again, Loulea Vale came back into view. Spindlewood Farm, Blacksod, Falthwaite End, Poplar Alley, all backed by the bulk of Bream Hill, which separated Loulea Vale from the sea.

Now that he had completed the full sweep of the vista before him, he raised his eyes to the distant places he had avoided, perhaps without realising it. To the west, the sea. To the east, the Fells. The two features that determined the shape of the North March. The sea, some five leagues away, stretching into the unfathomable distance, glittering in the morning sun, beguiling, deceptive. The people of the North March were not sailors, and seldom ventured far from the shore. To them the sea was unfamiliar and frightening, something not to be trifled with. Adding to their fear was the legend of Astora, the Drowned City. It was said that somewhere off the coast, perhaps even opposite the mouth of Lime Brook, lay the ruins of a great city built by the First Men. The story told of a city on the Downs, high above the sea, the westernmost great settlement of the First Men; of how the cliffs gradually retreated, cutting back towards the city; of a series of great storms, each larger than the one before; and of a final cataclysmic night when the hillside collapsed and Astora slid into the sea. 'Just off Varec Beach,' the fishermen had told him, nodding fiercely; but every fishing village along the coast of northern Firanes made the same claim for their stretch of coast. 'Ah yes, but none of the others have the Westway finishing by their shores. Must mean something, must that.' Which was also true.

Other legends of the sea, probably equally fanciful, included a fierce race of men who lived on ice floes to the far north, and who had raided the North March centuries ago, forcing the farmers to take shelter in the dark northern woods; and a story about a giant sea-dragon washed ashore near the mouth of the Mjolk River. That last, at least, was possibly true. Leith had met an old man in Vapnatak who claimed to have seen a tentacle from the dragon that measured fifty feet.

But it was to the east his eyes finally turned, to the Fells, the mountain range that fenced the habitable coastlands from the fierce interior. Sharp-spiked mountains glittering in the sun, peaks separated from their foothills by low cloud. The Fells in turn were but the footsoldiers of the Jawbone Mountains, the spine of Firanes. For a measureless time he stood riveted to the spot, staring to the east without really seeing. Somewhere out there, alive or dead in the snowbound distance, were his parents. The Westway pointed towards the Fells, and so did their journey.

Hal, who had risen earlier, limped his way up the path to fetch Leith for breakfast. The morning meal turned out to be a sumptuous affair, pancakes and syrup, brought to the table by a maidservant. As the brothers began their breakfast, Kurr and the Haufuth came in from the next room, herded to the table by one of the most unusual-looking men Leith had ever seen.

Kroptur was tall even for a northlander, tall though he walked with a stoop: the men and women of the North March were considered of above-average height amongst Firanese, but even Kurr, one of the tallest men in the Vale, stood a head shorter than this strange-looking man. Tall and solidly built, but this on its own did not mark him down as odd. It was his face, his head: Leith could not stop looking at him. He had a long, narrow face, lined with age if not so old as Kurr's, with a wide moustache and thick, dark eyebrows – and was otherwise completely bald. Where his hair should have been, shiny skin reflected the morning sunlight. All in all he gave the appearance of great physical power, for all his age, reminding Leith of the wrestlers he had seen the summer before last in the circus troupe that had passed through Vapnatak. Or perhaps, with those sharp eyes under beetling brows, more like a huge bird of prey. *If he really is one of the Watchers*, Leith thought, *he certainly looks the part.*

'The girl, she is a mistake,' Kroptur growled in a rough country voice as the three men took seats at the breakfast table. 'Admit it, y' fool farmer; you panicked.'

The farmer's eyes flashed in reply, but he held his tongue. Immediately the status of Kroptur was raised in Leith's mind. Whoever could talk to Kurr in such a manner without rebuke was a strong man indeed.

'It's still not too late to let 'er go. Leave her 'ere; I'll make sure she gits home.'

'And within days the whole of the North March will know about Leith and Hal,' replied the Haufuth.

'So? How will the horsemen hear about it? You goin' t' run after them shoutin' the news? It's miles ahead of you they are. Past Mjolkbridge, if not in the Fells already!'

'That's not the point, Master,' Kurr insisted. 'We've been warned of treachery and spies. We know that Rammr is infested with trai- tors. What if they come to hear of it? What if there is a Bhrudwan agent down in the Firanese Court? Or even one in the town?' He jerked his thumb towards the eastern windows, where the sun glinted from the roofs of Vapnatak, partly visible round the spur of Watch Hill. 'Should our enemies hear that someone knows their plans, do you think they will just wander into Loulea and ask politely for news of their whereabouts?'

Kroptur stopped to consider this for a moment, scratching his moustache as he thought.

'Are ye sure she would talk?' he asked.

'Her mother has a ready tongue! We can't take the risk.'

'That mebbe so, but have y' taken thought as t' how much she'll slow you down out there in the Fells? That land is no place for those as without experience.'

'We won't be taking her that far,' replied the Haufuth. 'Hopefully we won't have to go that far ourselves. If we do, then we'll leave her in Windrise; surely the village headman there will look after her until we get back.'

'Another matter,' Kroptur continued, pressing them. 'How were you thinkin' to explain the sudden vanishment of three people? Don't you think the villagers down below may wonder a little?'

The Haufuth stood up, and spoke with deference. 'Stella was supposedly at my house to talk about announcing her betrothal to a local boy. My wife Merin will tell her parents that we refused her permission. She will say that Stella rose in anger and ran from the house. Kurr and I followed after her, worried about her state of mind. That will be the last anyone has seen of us. They will probably conclude we stumbled into Lime Brook or some such other misadventure.'

'Six deaths in a week,' Kurr growled under his breath. 'Never so many at once before. The village may not recover.'

The Haufuth looked squarely at the old farmer. 'The tally may yet be accurate,' he said dryly.

'Are you sure you won't come?' Kurr said, swinging round to face Kroptur. 'Your knowledge might be the thing which keeps us alive, and we could benefit from your strength. Will you not reconsider?'

'Ye know I cannot,' said Kroptur gently, and again the flames crackled in his voice. 'I am werebound t' this place as surely as the forest is to the hill; my roots go down deep. Far too late it is for me t' leave it now. You'll not need my strength, or my thinkin', such as it is, for what you face.' He looked up, momentarily startled as the door opened and Stella walked in. 'Ah now, the girl,' he said. 'Come and sit down, lass. Have you some pancakes. A little syrup remains in th' bowl, despite your Haufuth's thievin' hands.'

The Haufuth went to laugh, but ended up looking just a little shamefaced.

Stella's eyes narrowed somewhat as she gazed at the speaker. In her weariness she had taken notice of very little last night. His tone she considered little more than patronising, his accent strange and his face downright ugly, but unaccountably she was in a good mood this morning, so she let it pass. On second thought, perhaps she did know why her mood was good. A night's sleep untroubled by dreams of Druin's jowlish face leering at her.

'So, here y' all are,' Kroptur said, quite unnecessarily in Stella's opinion. 'Five foolish travellers ready to risk everythin' for the sake of their friends and family. How can such as that fail t' attract th' approbation of the Most High? Five daft travellers! Not the five I would have chosen, mind, but then, thankfully, I'm not the Most High, and the choice was not mine. For He has chosen ye, be sure of what I say. Listen now as I tell you plain: He will add to your number those marked for this task, for you five are the fingers of a gatherin' hand. I'm tellin' you, so listen! You five are His chosen instrument t' bring salvation to Faltha, if ye prove equal t' the task.' His eyebrows knitted together into a fearsome scowl, a sight which did nothing to encourage Stella. *Not the five I would have chosen? What does it have to do with you, old man?*

The tall Watcher continued: 'I am utmost convinced that danger lies ahead. Hold on to this, now, what I'm tellin'. You do not go on a journey without hope; though I can't see the end of your adventures, or guarantee the safety of any one of you, I full believe you have a high chance of success. The Most High still has His compassionate eyes on poor old Faltha.

'Do not disremember the Watchers. They may prove helpful on your travels, if only as a fount of encouragement. Don't worry 'bout tryin' to seek them out. They will be watching, and are trained to spot the unusual, and that you are. Unless they have wholly forsaken their calling, they will find you and offer you succour. But be careful! Not everyone who offers you aid will turn out t' be your friend, and not everyone who opposes you will be your enemy. One thing I know, this from experience, so listen now as I tell you plain: you will meet both friend and foe unlooked for on the road appointed you. Keep your eyes open! Do not give up hope!'

Then the big man stood, pushing back his chair with a flourish to make room for his frame, and raised his arms over the five gathered at his table like a giant bird of prey unfurling its wings. Suddenly Stella was reminded of the childish stories, and for a moment she could almost see lightning flashing from under those dark brows. The Sorcerer of Magic Mountain. Her breath caught in sudden fright.

'Heed my words as I declare the wisdom of a Watcher of the

seventh rank. You are simple villagers living at the edge of the world. You don't know what the real world is like. Don't make the mistake of thinkin' that your world is the real world. If I could show you just three of the real world's wonders, you would call me a trickster to my face. You are ignorant. Unwise. Raw. Blind. Mark me! As soon as you think you know everythin', your doom is sealed. Put on humbleness like a ridin' cloak, put it on every morning, and be ready t' learn.'

Stella bristled as this oafish man lectured her and her friends, and glanced over at Kurr, waiting for the explosion of anger from the old farmer. Yet Kurr's eyes were attentive, and his manner, if not exactly humble, was at least charitable to Kroptur. Her own eyes widened a little in wonder.

The tall man with the stooped frame – he really did look like the Sorcerer of Magic Mountain – kept his upraised hands hovering over the five travellers, and continued to speak. 'As you leave this little valley, you'll be leavin' the realm you know, the realm of your own eyes and ears, of your own doings, the realm of the flesh, and you'll be drawn into the Realm of Fire. The Realm of Fire is where th' most important things happen, things you maybe can't see and hear, things you won't understand with your fleshly Loulea minds. I'm not rebukin' you! It's just that farming 'n' courtin' by the lake isn't the best trainin' for a journey into the Realm of Fire. A life in Loulea Vale teaches you t' read the signs in the sky, in the soil, in your stock, and to figure out what's going to happen to your crops. But it doesn't teach you how to read the signs in the Fiery Realm. Miracles there are in the Realm of Fire, and illusion, and dreams, and prophecy to bind and to loose, and dark magic. Beware of magic, and the binding of the dark, but look for the miracles of the Most High.

'Yet, despite my best warnin', you travellers will disbelieve in the Realm of Fire. You are too long in the flesh. Whatever realm you believe in, that realm is the most real t' you. Nonetheless, I foresee that the Most High will be trainin' you in the ways of the Fiery Realm. Don't yet be stubborn. Weigh the evidence if y' must, but don't forget your humble cloak.'

All the while during this speech the Haufuth had sat with a puzzled expression on his face, which now stretched towards chagrin. 'What are you talking about?' he interrupted. 'Flesh and fire realms? I thought we were chasing a group of Bhrudwan warriors, trying to rescue Leith and Hal's mother and father. What about giving us some of your wisdom about that?' Kurr spluttered in the background. 'And while you're at it, how about telling us how to win over the Council of Faltha! We haven't got time to listen to lectures on magical kingdoms.' His voice finished on a slightly petulant note, but he kept his eyes raised, staring into those of the stooped man. *You're braver than I*, Stella thought wryly. *But those are the words I would have said.*

'So it's plain-spoken advice you want, is it? You want wisdom cut up and served on a plate?' Kroptur growled, and Stella shivered at the steel that rang through the words. The broad country accent seemed to melt away as he spoke, leaving a sharpness that cut like knives; an almost visible menace seemed to hang about his shoulders like a cloak as he leaned towards the village headman. 'I've heard your name, and know you to be a newly raised Haufuth, younger than most, a man of logic and sense, but the full extent of your foolishness has been hidden from me. Listen to me, you fool man, and listen to me plain. Two thousand years the Destroyer has had, two thousand years and more, t' search out the dark secrets of the Realm of Fire and bend them to his use. Generation after generation is born and dies, and their knowledge and experience is lost, and mistakes have t' be made again and again. But not the Destroyer. Not the Undying Man. Cursed of the Most High is he! For the blessing of death has been taken from him, and he must live in the world forever, troubling the lives of men and women, findin' neither rest nor reward, never to be taken t' be with the Most High. Yet he has turned this curse into strength, and has harnessed the Realm of Fire to be his servant. Illusions he can weave to empty your bowels, words he can twist like knives in your belly, and the dark magic serves him like a slave! You fat fool! He could appear before you clothed in the disguise of a Watcher like me, and with his power he could force you to your knees, and you would beg to worship him!' The voice of the Watcher roared, and the Haufuth slipped from his chair, as though he was indeed about to fall to his knees. To Stella the man suddenly seemed the Sorcerer incarnate, ten feet tall with dark clouds wreathed about his beetling brows and lightning at his fingertips. She waited for the killing blow that would surely come, as the great Sorcerer destroyed the foolish one who dared to question him. Yet the tall, stooped man just laughed, and the spell broke.

'I forget that ye are indeed children, even thou, Kurr my valiant friend. Do you not see? I am just an old man, not the Sorcerer of Magic Mountain. Oh yes,' he laughed again, 'I know what they all say. Yet if the merest amount of illusion serves t' cow you, how will you defend yourselves against the dark servants of the Destroyer, who are equipped more mightily than I? Do you not see? This journey is a requirement of your training. Why have Mahnum and Indrett been taken? How else can the Most High draw you out of your ignorance and set your feet on His ordained path? And how can you learn what you need to know unless first you are told the class is in session? So why do you not listen?'

'I – I . . .' the Haufuth stuttered. 'How did you do that? I thought for a moment . . .'

'You are a very suggestible man, despite your logic and your sense,' said Kroptur, with a wry smile on his face. 'The legend of the Sorcerer who lives up Magic Mountain is known throughout the North March. I should know: the Watchers of Watch Hill have cultivated it like a box hedge for generations. It helps t' keep nosy people away. So all I had to do was put on a certain expression, stand in a particular way, and change my voice a little. All of a sudden, it was the Sorcerer who stood before you. You all saw it?'

Five heads nodded.

'Is that all there was to it?' the Haufuth said faintly, licking his lips.

'Well, perhaps not, but I am old and experienced and ye are young and suggestible.'

'Is that how all the scary stories start?' Leith asked. 'Just clever suggestion and people's imaginations running away with them?'

Kroptur turned and stared at him, and Leith thought he saw something odd in the man's eyes for a moment, something . . . he could not say what it was. 'No. Illusion is only one of th' flames of the Realm of Fire, and it is the least of them. There are three flames of Fire: Illusion, Word and Power. Which is enough for you to know, though before this is all finished I'm thinkin' you'll know more than Kroptur the Watcher, and more than you care to know.

'Now, of course I'm goin' to help you get Mahnum and Indrett back. And I will do what little I can to help you with the council behind the Iron Door, though what I can do beyond prattlin' on, giving advice –' here he turned his sharp dark eyes on the Haufuth – 'I do not know, because I've heard nothin' from the Watchers of Instruere for years now, nigh on a decade. Still, I can send messages, and pray that the people I send them to are still alive, and still have their wits about 'em.'

The tall man turned back to Leith and Hal. 'As for your parents, I have already acted. While you slept last night, I 'quipped and sent a rider along the road, a Watcher of the third rank, a man under my command, a man who can be trusted with secrets. He knows somethin' of the Realm of Fire, and will not be caught in th' first snare laid across his path. As soon as he receives news of the Bhrudwans he will return down the Westway. When you meet him, he will tell you his news. May he travel swiftly!'

Kroptur turned his face towards the door. 'It is time for you to leave. I have given you horses, the best I have. Kurr will teach you how to look after them. In the saddlebags you'll find food for your journey, and extra clothes for the Fells, on the evil chance that the chase should take you there. While you have been break-fastin', my servants have placed ridin' gear in your rooms. The horsemen are at least three days ahead of you, and you'll find it difficult to gain on them. Expect to be in the saddle many days an' you'll not be disappointed. Go now, and prepare for your journey. You do not have much time.'

*　*　*

Preparations for their departure took a little longer than expected. Kroptur's servants had laid out a set of clothes each for them, grey clothes of an old style, which he assured them would provide better protection against the winter winds than anything else they might have. He reminded them that the journey was to take them inland, through country far colder than anywhere on the coast. Then, when they had packed these clothes, they had some trouble organising their horses. The Haufuth, of course, required a mount of his own, while initially Kurr was to share a horse with Hal, and Leith with Stella, while the fourth horse was to be a pack animal. Embarrassed, Leith had asked to ride with his brother, but would provide no reason when pressed. The others had given in to his wishes, a little puzzled, but only Hal guessed the reason for Leith's reluctance.

A few minutes before the Travellers were to leave, the Watcher of Watch Hill drew Leith and Hal aside. 'My heart tells me that you two are goin' t' face hard times ahead,' he said. His voice was not stern or commanding, yet Leith felt unable to draw his attention away from the words. 'This is not a foretelling, just a feelin'. Still, somedays I'm not assured of the difference.'

'Tell us more of this Realm of Fire,' Leith said. 'Can it help us get my parents back?'

'Well, now, son, the Realm of Fire isn't like that. Ye mustn't reach out and twist the Fire to suit yourself. That's the way of the dark. All ye can do is be in the place where the Fire of the Most High strikes the earth, and see how it might aid ye. Leastwise, that's how I think of it. Other people have different ways of expressin' it, perhaps.

'Now, I know this sounds mystical, which perhaps isn't all that surprisin', considerin' who's doin' the telling. It's just a way of thinkin' about things, useful if you see it, useless if ye don't. Listen as I speak plain. The Realm of Fire has many aspects, some of which are hidden from the world of men. But three of them we Watchers know well, and you will encounter them on your road, should ye have eyes to see. The first is Illusion. One skilled in the shaping of Illusions can make suggestions to the gullible minds of others, causin' them to see what is not there, or hidin' what is. The strength of an illusion depends on the belief of those who see it, and on the subtlety of the one weavin' the web. The walkers in both the dark and the light can make use of it, though it needs a canny and creative mind, attributes not usually cultivated by dark-dwellers.

'The second aspect is the Word. Usin' the Word requires strength of purpose and an iron will. There are some who can weave the real meanin' of their mind into their ordinary speech, sayin' one thing and communicatin' another. This is not really my area, you might be surprised t' learn,' and he grinned at them. 'This enchantment is called the "wordweave", and is most amenable to the corruption of the dark, bein' mostwise based on deception. Another manifestation of the Word is Prophecy, where fancy words are used to cloak messages about the future in mystery. Now there's a good reason why we do this. Were we always t' speak plain, the hearers might understand the message too soon, and change their actions thereby.

'The third and highest aspect of the Realm of Fire is Power, but it goes by two names. To the unholy it is magic, and is wrapped in darkness, the stuff that fills our folk tales. It is the dark part of the realm, and only followers of the shadowed path use it. Now here's why. Magic is the binding of others through the will of the user, takin' flames from the Fire and using 'em like ropes. That's the nearest I c'n get to it. It's not like Illusion, because it actually changes things. But unbeknown to the servants of the dark, the power of magic is mostwise drawn from the souls of those who practise it. And they wonder why magicians die young, many from a wasting disease, which eats 'em out from the inside. Fools! Scars they get, I've seem 'em, gruesome they are, on their face and hands, the mark of a magician. The high priests of the dark, the Lords of Fear, they know about it. I don't want to talk about it. The Most High forbids the use of magic, even for good.

'The second name of this aspect is Miracle. Now listen to me plain: this is the sole preserve of the light. Darkness cannot touch it. Ye take a step of faith, a risk, and trigger the power of the Most

High. His power, not yours. But there is one rule. Miracles only happen when y' have done all ye can, not before. Ye can ask for them, but ye might not get. But sometimes ye do. Sometimes they come without askin'. Oftentimes they can be explained by natural happenings, which perhaps they are, though timed just right. Above all, they are rare. Now, mark me! There's one name for the man who claims to do miracles regularly, and that name is liar. Run from such a man.

'All three aspects ye will encounter on your journeys, this I foretell,' said Kroptur, staring at them intently all the while. 'Illusion, Word and Power. But will ye really see them? More to the purpose, will you be ready to do what is necessary? On their own, these powers cannot rescue your parents. But you can, and maybe you will need to use them. I think you will need to use them.

'Oh, yes,' said the Sorcerer of Watch Hill, seemingly as an afterthought. His gaze seemed to narrow to two bright points of light. 'One thing more. Answer me this question. Do ye two boys love each other?'

'What?' Leith started with surprise, and began to blush before he could settle himself. *Love? Of course I love Hal, it's just that . . .*

'No, don't answer me out loud, not now, not yet. Wait until you know the answer for certain. Then give the answer to each other.'

Hal said nothing, an unreadable expression on his face.

The big man put a burly arm around each boy's shoulder and drew them together. 'You're going t' have to answer that question some time, boys. The most important question of all, is that. It lies at the root of everything. See that you find an answer. Make sure that it is the right one.'

It was midmorning before they were ready to leave. To Leith something indefinable hung under the shadowed eaves of the House on Watch Hill. *Probably the Realm of Fire*, he thought, only half-mockingly.

The vulture-like figure of Kroptur emerged just as they mounted

120

their horses. *Just like the Sorcerer of Magic Mountain*, Leith thought wonderingly. As if he wasn't confused enough, Kroptur chose just that moment to wink at him.

The Watcher stood in front of the assembled group and spoke in a commanding voice: 'I have done all I can for you. Now I will go inside and pray, and I will not cease prayin' until I hear that you are dead, or that Faltha is once again safe from the lust of the Destroyer. I will delay you no longer.'

Kroptur stood tall, all traces of a stoop gone, raised his right hand in a farewell blessing, and on his fingers many-faceted rings flashed with fire. The Sorcerer of Magic Mountain, beyond any shadow of doubt. *'Fuir af Himmin!* Go with the blessing of the Most High!' he called after them, as they shook the reins of their horses, then turned and made their way towards the dark forest eaves of Watch Hill.

CHAPTER 6

MJOLKBRIDGE

THE PATH THE COMPANY took on their way down Watch Hill
was not the one they had taken on their way up. Judging the
chance of recognition on the Westway too great this close to
Vapnatak, they decided to head east, taking a seldom-used path
through the forest, one which would bring them to the North
Road and the Little Melg River a few miles north of the walled
town.

Leith turned from the receding figure of Kroptur and glanced
around him. The forest seemed to breathe cold air at them, and
under its eaves lurked a perpetual twilight. Southern outlier of the
Great North Woods, these ancient trees stood defiantly on a slope
too steep to have warranted the woodsman's axe. Ancient,
brooding trees.

'Who was that man?' Leith asked his brother. 'I've never heard
of him, yet here he is living in riches only a few miles away from
the Vale.'

'Kroptur is a Watcher like Kurr,' replied the Haufuth, over-
hearing the conversation. 'Certainly he is wealthy, but I wouldn't
say he lives in riches. He has very little to do with anyone in these
parts, apparently, and is considered to be a recluse by his neighbours. Obviously, the children of the Vale have another theory to
explain Kroptur of Watch Hill.'

'He is more than a Watcher,' Kurr added. 'He is what we
Watchers call a Cerner – a seer in the modern tongue. I have

known him a long time. A real man of the North March, boy. He is my elder in the Watch, of the highest rank.'

'A seer?' interrupted Leith. 'Is that part of the Realm of Fire? If it's true, how come we weren't taught it?' He turned to the Haufuth for support. In Kroptur's house, under the spell of the deep, rich voice, the Realm of Fire had seemed close around them. Even here, amongst the ancient trees, the Fiery Realm seemed a possibility, but the power of Kroptur's words faded as they rode. Miracles, magic, illusion. Just the words of a strange old man.

'There is little magical about him, boy,' insisted the old farmer with a trace of asperity. 'He is old and wise, knowing from experience how unexpected events can bring out the best in good people. He believes that good people are better equipped to deal with the hardness of life than are bad people. He does not see into the future like a true prophet, if there are any such left in the world. Shrewdness and common sense give him insight into the hearts of those he encounters. If that's magic, then he's magical.'

'That's not quite how he explained it,' muttered Leith. *He did not see into my heart.*

'Sounds more like wishful thinking to me,' the Haufuth commented. 'Still, I was impressed with what he had to say this morning.'

'He has great faith in the memory of the Most High,' Kurr continued, 'so he believes that our journey will ultimately be successful. I'm not so sure myself. I think the Most High has forgotten about Faltha. What would a few peasants on horseback mean to him?' The old farmer laughed grimly. 'I'm not a mystic like my master, who seems to see more of the Realm of Fire than he does of the real world. Comes of spending all his time in that house of his, gazing out over the affairs of the North March like some demigod. I'm not saying that the Most High himself is only a fable. I've heard foolish talk like that, and I'll have none of it. But it's my guess that we'll make our own future, with precious little divine assistance. Still, it is encouraging to have the confidence of someone like Kroptur. And his messengers may do some good.'

A few minutes later the Company emerged from under the firs and pines of the Great North Wood. Before them was the narrow valley of the Little Melg, and to their right stood the town of Vapnatak. Tufts of sodden grass poked here and there through the thin snow cover, which seemed to have melted somewhat overnight as a warmer breeze from the south brought fine weather. In the flat mile that stretched between them and the North Road lay paddocks which normally held sheep, but which were devoid of stock at this time of year. Beyond the road, hidden behind a single hedgeline, lay the Little Melg River. Beyond that again lay a series of low, tree-cloaked limestone ridges stretching towards the horizon.

Kurr glanced up at the sun, now well above the hills and shining on the walled town just to the south.

'Time to make a dash for it, before the road gets too busy,' he said.

The travellers picked their way over a low gorse fence, then cantered quietly across the gently sloping paddock, being careful where possible to keep cover between themselves and the town on their right. They reached the road and scurried across, apparently without being seen. On the opposite side of the road they found a gap in the high hedge, and made their way through a stand of oak and willow trees down to the river.

'The water will be cold,' the old farmer called over his shoulder. 'Don't dally in the river!'

Kurr spurred his reluctant horse across the narrow, stony stream, Stella clinging to his back like a burr in his britches. Halfway across he reined in his mount and waited for the others. As he waited, he observed their horsemanship. The big headman seemed competent enough, but would obviously never make an agile rider. Hal was surprisingly adept at manoeuvring his mount, in spite of his clumsy left side and the encumbrance of his younger brother pressing close in behind him. Shaking his head, the farmer tried not to think of how these people might cope with the journey in front of them.

Low, misty clouds began to blow in from the south, moisture

drawn inland from the sea. The small Company made their way up the bank on the far side of the river, then trotted hurriedly across the open fields. On their right the Westway snaked towards them, curving north then west as it emerged from the Water-gate of Vapnatak. Kurr led them slightly north of west to avoid being seen from the road, although few people appeared to be abroad on this winter's morning.

A hundred feet of gentle climbing and the horses were at the top of the first of a series of broken ridges. They did not pause, dipping immediately into White Forks Valley and leaving the Little Melg, and their little world, behind.

By midmorning the mount of the Bhrudwan leader was lame, hobbling painfully along the road. In spite of their obvious hurry, the raiders dismounted and clustered around the stricken animal, concern on their faces and in their voices. While they were not watching, Mahnum turned and twisted, ignoring the agony in his ribs, until he could see Indrett, similarly strapped to another horse. She was looking at him! She smiled! She was all right! *Well, maybe not all right*, he thought as he looked at her injuries. *When we get out of this, then she'll be all right.* But the eye contact worked on his battered body in a way no medicine could.

After a few minutes of puzzled conversation, the riders remounted, only to stop again after a further hour's riding, dismounting this time in a belt of trees beside a river, a large river if Mahnum was any judge. He could hear it flowing away to the right, out of his sight. *It has to be the Mjolk*, he reasoned. *No other river this big around here. But we've been riding for days – how can this be the Mjolk? Unless . . . unless this is the Westway!* He began to piece together the fragments he had seen since Midwinter's Day: cobbled road, waving grasses, pine trees, large river. *This has to be the Westway. But why? If they're taking us back east to Bhrudwo, why go this way in the middle of winter?* It still hurt his head to think.

At the end of this second short delay, the riders set off once more.

Ahead the lead mount entered the water, then stumbled, its

leg collapsing under it. Mahnum heard a cry and a splash as the rider fell into the stony river. Then came a confusion of sounds: a horse squealing in obvious distress, angry voices shouting, more splashing and curses from the direction of the river. Then the noise ceased, and for a minute low voices hissed in urgent discussion. Finally some kind of agreement was reached, and the steed on which Mahnum was an unwilling passenger was coaxed down to the water's edge, the beast acting skittish as they passed an obviously distressed horse lying on its side, its right foreleg bent at an impossible angle. For a moment the Trader felt a twinge of regret, but it passed as he remembered the horrors of Favony and the terror of what had been done to Indrett. The beatings. The fire. The screams. The smell of death. He would never forget what he had seen; he would do all he could to save others – and himself – from such a fate. He cursed the Bhrudwans under his breath for all they had done, and blessed a sharp stone and the name of Cowyn the Hunter.

In the background two riders clattered across a wooden bridge. Hearing this, Mahnum breathed a sigh of satisfaction as the final piece of his puzzle fell into place. *Things are turning a little in my favour. The enemy has been slowed down, and that sound tells me exactly where we are.*

The five travellers, with Kurr in the lead, spent the rest of the day trailing up and down ridges that cut at right angles across their path. Progressing at no more than walking pace, they kept the Westway well to their right. Just before suppertime it began to rain, a steady drizzle from the sea.

Finally they surmounted a last ridge and looked out over a wide plain in the hazy half-darkness of twilight. To their right the Louthwaite Fens spread southwards towards the horizon. A hundred feet below them the Westway wound around the base of the ridge and struck out across the northern corner of the wetlands. In the murky distance a large river wound lazily through the marshy lands: the Mjolkelva, or Milk River as it was known to foreigners, which rose far away in the Jawbone Mountains and travelled hundreds of leagues to the sea, draining much of northern Firanes. Leith had heard much about this river, particularly from the fishermen of Varec Beach, but had never before seen it. His eyes followed the path of the river upstream through a broad valley to the grey horizon. At some point in the rain-softened distance the Westway seemed to merge with the river.

'Tomorrow we must risk the road,' Kurr said, turning to the others. 'We must begin to make haste, and the chances of anyone recognising us on this side of the Downs are slim. Today's travel was slow of necessity. I wanted to give the horses time to get used to their riders before we try them at more than a walk, and I was worried that we might exhaust them prematurely by pushing them too hard over the treacherous limestone ridges. But by now the Bhrudwans are possibly four days' ride ahead of us. We will take a night's rest here, then we will ride!'

Gratefully Leith eased himself off his horse. Like most of the other Vale children, he had ridden around the village on Salopa, the horse kept by the Loulea Village Council. But riding for a whole day was another matter entirely. His arm and leg muscles ached horribly, and he considered himself fortunate that his lower back was numb. He never would have guessed that merely sitting on a horse would be so exhausting. But, sore as he was, he was better off than the Haufuth, who lay on the ground, twitching uncontrollably as his back spasmed. Leith and Hal took turns rubbing the big man's back, trying to ease his pain.

Each of the Company took water from a flask, and set about eating a little bread and honey. While they ate the drizzle slackened, then stopped. As the veil lifted, the Fells could be seen on the horizon ahead of them, their snow-covered summits gleaming in the pale sunset. A day closer, a day more forbidding. Behind their stern slopes, Leith knew, lay Breidhan Moor and the Company's likely path.

The next morning they picked their way carefully down the slope to the Westway. The horses clattered on to the empty road, grateful to be away from boggy fields. The old farmer pulled his woollen hat down over his ears, turned up the collar of his coat, then motioned to the others to do likewise. He then wheeled his horse around and, spurring it on, began to ride swiftly up the road. For a moment the others did not react, apart from the Haufuth, who groaned as he knuckled the small of his back, seeking to lessen the agony. Then they, too, urged their mounts forward.

During the afternoon the wind came in from the north and rolled the low clouds away, exposing a pale blue sky streaked by wispy horsetails. The north wind continued to blow in from the forest-cloaked Noyan Hills to the left, cutting through their protective clothes and chilling their hands and faces. The road beneath them was stone and gravel tightly packed, and it made a straight course through the marshes. It appeared to be a significant engineering feat warranting regular and heavy traffic, but apart from the occasional stone fence and farm gate there was no sign of human habitation. Although they were still close to Vapnatak, humanity seemed to have been swallowed up in the wildness of the landscape.

But though it was wild, to these northern dwellers the landscape was far from empty. Their passing disturbed a number of creatures, and Leith was delighted to see a covey of ptarmigan rise noisily from a belt of trees to their left. Though there were few other animals to be seen, apart from wheeling gulls off to their right, the marshes harboured a wide variety of wildlife. Fieldmice, rabbits, weasels, stoats and the beautiful mink, the red fox and maybe the occasional white fox; all would be going about their business unconcerned about a few humans riding down the road.

By late afternoon the countryside had become discernibly wetter, and no more farm gates bordered the Westway. Raised on its own stony bank, the road divided a seemingly endless sea of rushes, still running straight ahead in far too much of a hurry to be mistaken for anything natural. They reined in to let Kurr swap places with Stella, and Hal swap with Leith. As Leith remounted he could hear the wind in the marsh-grass. From somewhere to his left came the plaintive piping of a bird. Then they were off again, the wind roaring in his ears, and sensation receded save the numbing pain in his buttocks and lower back.

128

Across the Face of the World

The world had descended into twilight by the time the travellers stopped for their evening meal. Still the marshes stretched out on both sides of the Westway, though the hills to the left, after having all but petered out during the afternoon, had drawn in closer again.

'We must travel further tonight,' the farmer told them, 'and take advantage of the moon. It has been a long time since I have ridden this far, and distances are difficult to judge in such a featureless land, but my guess is that it is still another ten miles before the fens fail and we can leave the road to find a place to spend the night. We cannot sleep here on the road, where the exposure to night winds would freeze us. And we must go more slowly. I do not want to risk injury to any of the horses. They have had a hard day.'

The weary Company walked their mounts for the next four hours. Dusk slowly turned to night, and for an hour or so it was quite dark, the stars giving the only light. Then the moon rose over the reeds to their right, and they could see again. Nothing had changed; the road continued on its course straight for the distant and now invisible Fells. Leith found his eyes growing heavy, and he struggled to stay awake. After a time he noticed that the shadowy ground was slowly rising to left and right, and the marsh-grasses were thinning out. Then, to his relief, he heard Kurr's voice: 'Over to the left, in the shadow of those trees. We'll spend the night there.'

The Company pulled aside from the road into a stand of pines, dismounted and tethered the horses to the trunks of tall trees. The branches, hanging almost to the ground, would provide enough shelter from the wind. Kurr set a fire in an old hearth while the others cleared a space to sleep amongst the pine needles. One by one the five members of the Company wrapped blankets around themselves and settled down to sleep.

As if to help the Company make maximum progress, the next two days dawned fine, windless and frosty, with the warmth of the afternoon sun melting the last of the remaining snow on the road verges. The three horses were ridden steadily during the third day and walked during the moonlit hours. The third night found them sheltering under another stand of trees not more than a mile short of the Troldale Road, marked by a strange Y-shaped pine. In this fashion the Company arrived at the Alvaspan, the last bridge over the Mjolkelva, at dusk on the fourth day since they had left Watch Hill.

The bridge was no more than a series of wide planks set on wooden piles, but it was the one dry crossing of the river between here and its source. The only other safe way of crossing the wide expanse of slow-moving water was by ferry at Windrise, two days further up the road, though crossings could be hazarded at times of low water at a number of places between the Alvaspan and Windrise. The Haufuth let out a shout of joy as they approached the bridge, for beyond the crossing lay the lights of the town of Mjolkbridge, and the possibility of ale and a comfortable lodging. The Company clattered across the bridge at the close of a long, wearying day.

At the far end of the bridge, they were met by a man holding a staff across his chest. He shouted something that Leith did not catch, and motioned for them to dismount. While the rest of the Company did as they were asked, Kurr remained astride his horse.

'What is the problem?' the old farmer asked gruffly.

The man laid down his staff, then drew a gleaming sword. 'Please, sir,' he said politely but firmly, 'get down from your horse.'

'Since when is the Alvaspan held against men of the North March?' Kurr demanded.

The man relaxed visibly at the mention of the March. 'If you will dismount, we might be able to explain ourselves.'

As Kurr dismounted he caught sight of other men in the shadows, armed with axes, staves and knives. He held out his hands, palms up, in the Firanese sign of goodwill.

'Why is our way barred? We mean no harm!'

'What is the nature of your journey?' the man asked in reply.

'We are travelling to Windrise,' Kurr said carefully. 'One of our number is the Haufuth of Loulea, who is taking his niece to visit some of their relations. The others of our Company wish to see the beauty of the Torrelstrommen valley, of which we have heard much.'

Half-suppressed laughter came from the shadows. Evidently the name of the Haufuth of Loulea was known in Mjolkbridge.

'The valley of the Torrelstrommen is indeed beautiful, but you have chosen the wrong time of year to see it.' The man sheathed his sword, but still barred their path. 'That valley is an autumn wonder, but will now be locked up in the winter snows.' He looked at the Company with suspicion. 'This is not the season for travelling on the Westway!'

The situation was beginning to get out of hand. 'We agree with you!' Kurr replied, with an attempt at heartiness. 'However, we have heard that the uncle of our Haufuth is very ill, perhaps near to death, and we cannot wait until spring. We have ridden hard these last four days, and will continue to do so until we arrive in Windrise – if we are allowed to pass this bridge!'

'Wait there a moment!' the man commanded, then withdrew to talk with the other men in the shadows. A few moments later he stepped forward again. 'You may pass,' he said, 'and then you must come with us.'

'Must?' muttered the Haufuth. *I wonder what has gotten into these people?* He shuffled after the small knot of men towards a lightless lodge at the far end of the bridge. *Whatever it is, I hope it hasn't affected the quality of their ale.*

Shutters were drawn, lamps were lit and chairs were pulled up for the five travellers. Leith found himself sitting behind the bulk of his village headman. Across a bare table sat a youngish man with greying hair and a worried frown, his companions hidden away out of the flickering lamplight.

'Now, then,' began the young man, whom Leith recognised as the man who had talked to them on the bridge, 'I'm sorry you haven't paid us the courtesy of telling the truth about your travels.' He smiled wryly. 'But that is your business. Had we not known the Haufuth of Loulea, at least by reputation if not by sight, we might have been a little more insistent in our questioning. However, let me reassure you that we are confident of your trustworthiness. Whatever your business, the people of Mjolkbridge will be glad to help you where we can.'

The Haufuth muttered his thanks.

'Why the guard on the bridge?' Kurr persisted.

Some of the men in the shadows began muttering in response to the stranger's show of bad manners. *Accept the offer*, Leith willed. *Don't get us into trouble.*

'Quiet!' barked the young man, turning on his countrymen. 'Please continue,' he said to the old farmer, but the politeness was forced.

'I've lived in these lands for many years, good and bad, and I've never heard of bridges being barred to men of the North March before. Where is the legendary hospitality of the Mjolk valley?'

The frown on the young man's face deepened. 'I have said we will help you, oldling, and help you we will. In many parts of the world that alone would be hospitality enough for legend. But since you have insisted on uncovering that which we obviously wish to conceal, I will explain our behaviour. Food, drink and a soft bed, those things will have to wait a while.' He paused and looked over his shoulder, as though seeking support from the men behind him. 'As for the reception on the bridge . . . three days ago, two strangers rode over the Alvaspan and into our village. One of our men, a farmer from the slopes of Vinkullen, was in the village collecting supplies. He was about to leave when the strangers approached. The two men ran him down and attacked him with their swords, then took his horse and rode off upvalley.

'By the time we discovered what had happened they had made off. Poor Storr told us what happened before he died of his wounds. We have few horses here, but such as we have were mounted and pressed into a pursuit. A little distance up the Westway we came across three men at the side of the road, standing around a shallow grave, conducting some kind of ceremony. They were burying a horse.

'As we rode up, filled with anger and thoughts of revenge, the three men walked out into the road brandishing swords.' The young man licked his lips nervously. 'We of Mjolkbridge are brave of heart, never taking a backward step when challenged. At least that's what we like to think. But it has been many years since last we rode to battle, and that only against the land-grabbing Windrisians. But we ... Suddenly we could see nothing but the sharp edges of their swords, and read our deaths on the faces of these strangers, so we retreated and set up watch at both ends of the village, lest they return. I can put it no more clearly than to say we were bewitched. Wiser heads may say that we were afraid, yet it did not feel like fear at the time, just common sense. I know not how to explain it, save to say we were under the spell of enchanters.'

The Haufuth nodded and said quietly, 'Brothers, we do not judge you. Believe me.'

'You people are the first travellers on the road since then. To be honest, we thought you were the riders returning, clattering over the Alvaspan in the twilight. I hope you understand the precautions.' The young man sat back, his shrewd eyes watching the Company.

Kurr stood up. 'We won't deny it, since you have guessed already. We know of these horsemen, and are following them along the Westway.'

Angry murmurs came from the flickering shadows.

'Don't misunderstand me! They are our foes and we pursue them. More than that I cannot say. They are a dangerous enemy, as you have learned. My attempt to deceive you was for your safety.'

'What hope have you against such as they?' came a voice from the back of the room.

'Faint hope at best,' replied the old farmer frankly. 'But we make do without hope. Now, I have something to ask you. Are there any here who saw those horsemen?'

A few men spoke up.

'Did any of you see a man and a woman with them? Did these horsemen have any captives?'

A hubbub of voices ruled for a few moments, then all was quiet.

Apparently no one had seen anything but the riders and their weaponry.

'So! It becomes a little clearer!' said the young man. 'Perhaps the relatives you wish to visit are travelling with these men?' His gaze searched the faces of the Company, reading assent. 'If so, they must have parted. We saw three men only.'

'Then we have hope!' The Haufuth of Loulea stood. 'When these men paid a similar visit to my village, there were four of them. You did not see their whole party. Could others have passed here unnoticed?'

'It's possible,' conceded the young man. 'A little way upstream there are rapids, and above them the river can be forded if the water is low, as it is now in midwinter. The others may have crossed there.' He looked inquiringly at the members of the Company. 'So they have taken captives! A strange thing for death-dealers such as these!'

The Haufuth was still standing. 'We can say little more, other than to express sorrow at your news. While it brings grief to your village, it brings hope to us. We started our pursuit four days behind these men, and now it appears that they are only three days ahead of us. If we make all speed, we may catch them before they reach the moors.'

'Breidhan Moor?' The young man was incredulous. 'They would take horses up on to the moor at this time of year? And you would follow them?'

'Only in greatest need. But these men, while more ruthless than you could imagine, do not know the depth of a Firanese winter. Such knowledge is our advantage.'

The young man stood and extended a hand towards the Company. 'I would like to talk further about these things, but you and your friends must be hungry and thirsty. It is time for the hospitality you have heard about. Come, perhaps we will talk some more at the village inn. Then you may have beds for the night – unless, of course, you intend to ride these men down without resting!'

The Haufuth laughed. 'I was hoping you would get to the part about food and drink. Travelling rations are fine for some, but I could do with some real food!'

The young man held out his hand in greeting. 'I am the Haufuth of Mjolkbridge. I am sorry we have met under such circumstances. Let us talk for a while of more pleasant things over a glass of the finest ale in the North March.'

After the meal, the Haufuths of Loulea and Mjolkbridge retired with Kurr to a back room of the pleasant and well-appointed Waybridge Inn. Left to themselves, the others, prompted by Hal, went outside to escape the smoke-filled air.

A cold wind funnelled down the valley towards them as the brothers, with Stella between them, walked slowly up the street. Pale light shone from houses sitting back on either side of the cobbled road. Mjolkbridge was a village of maybe thirty or forty houses straddling the Westway, providing for farmers making a living at the northern extremity of civilisation. The houses seemed a little smaller than those of Loulea, as though they were hunched up against the cold. The trees, too, seemed shorter than those at home, and their silhouettes leaned downvalley away from the prevailing wind. *Perhaps*, thought Leith, *it is an illusion*. High hills clustered close on both sides of the valley, and their ominous shadowy presence dwarfed house and tree alike. Overhead low clouds streamed downvalley, silver against the darkness of the night sky. The crescent moon sat low on the horizon, its pale light sparkling on the evening dew. The wind grew perceptibly colder.

The three of them walked some way along the road in silence. *Here I am, walking with Stella*, thought Leith bitterly. *At any other time I would be delighted. If only Hal were somewhere else . . .*

Hal stopped abruptly, interrupting Leith's musings. 'I'm sorry,' he said, 'but my leg is sore from all that hard riding. I can't walk any further. I'll wait for you here.'

Leith was about to protest when Stella spoke up. 'Thank you, Hal; we won't be long. Come on, Leith,' she added, as the boy gave no sign of continuing up the road. He managed to get his legs to move, and started up the road with a burning in his stomach. He dared not look at her.

As soon as they were out of earshot, Stella turned to Leith. 'Is it true?' she asked. 'Did you wait for me by the Common Oak all afternoon?'

'Yes,' replied Leith, embarrassed beyond measure by the bluntness of the question. Tears lurked dangerously close to the surface. That pitiful afternoon under the oak tree was a symbol of all that had happened to him since. Of his loneliness, of his foolishness.

'What happened to you? How come you didn't turn up?' he blurted out.

'I'm sorry,' she replied blandly.

Leith's anger rose at her words, so few in number, delivered with such ease. Did the whole thing mean so little to her?

She continued, 'I said I'd come with you because I wanted to annoy Druin. But when he found out he became angry, and wouldn't let me go to meet you. Believe me, Leith, I couldn't have got away from him even if I'd tried.'

'Then why didn't you tell me this earlier? The next day, the next week – some time before now, at least!' The rage, the tears, seemed to close in on him.

Stella shrugged her shoulders helplessly. How could she explain it? All the other girls had ridiculed this boy who had waited for her. He had been their joke. How could she have gone and apologised to him? Could he not understand that some of the ridicule would have rubbed off on her? To have the others laughing at her, the way they had laughed at him – she couldn't have stood it.

That gesture by Stella sealed it for Leith. He took a deep breath and, just as though he was stuffing rags into a bottle, forced his ragged emotions down through his chest and buried them deep inside himself. The effort cut into him like a knife.

The two tormented teenagers continued walking.

'Is it true about you and Druin?' Leith suddenly asked, the words being forced through clenched teeth. 'Are you going to announce your betrothal?'

Stella did not reply for so long that Leith thought she hadn't heard him.

'Yes,' she said eventually. 'Our parents have planned it for a long time.'

He heard the despair in her voice, and it puzzled him. 'Your parents? What about you? Isn't it what you want?'

Stella stopped walking. Her hair hung lankly over her down-cast face; it shone in the moon's silver light. For some time she said nothing, as if weighing whether or not to speak her mind. Leith could think of no prompting words. He moved ahead in order better to see her face, but she started walking too, as though she didn't want him to look at her. She walked faster and faster as they approached the end of the village. Suddenly she stopped.

'Oh, Leith, I hate him so much!' Her voice was thinner, more vulnerable than he had ever heard it. 'Druin has been after me ever since he heard about our parents' plans. He forces himself on me. He never lets me out of his sight! All the others think he is wonderful, but he isn't! For a while I tried to like him, but every day brings some new thing to loathe him for. I'm not going back, Leith; I'm not! No matter what!' Then she began to cry.

Leith had never seen a woman cry before, except his mother. He wanted to reassure her, to hug her like he hugged his mother, but he could not force himself to take the risk. The fear of her rejection, as real as a physical pain, almost buckled him over.

'We'd better go back,' she said aloud.

'Yes,' Leith replied lamely. He knew he had let himself down, but he was powerless to tell her how he felt.

'I'm sorry about the Midwinter Play,' he said eventually.

Stella laughed bitterly. 'It was perfect! I've never seen Druin so angry! If you hadn't been killed – I mean, if you hadn't pretended to be killed . . . Anyway, I was going to warn you if I could. Druin was so jealous, I'm sure he would have come after you the next day. His was the only happy face at your funeral.'

'He wouldn't have done that, would he?' Leith asked uncertainly.

'You don't know him,' Stella replied simply. 'He has two faces. Well spoken and well mannered in public, but uncouth and abusive in private. I hope he dies before I get back!' The vehemence in her voice was frightening.

Leith did not answer. It seemed to him that he was losing himself, falling, falling down a deep well into darkness.

Kurr stared across the table at the Haufuth of Mjolkbridge. 'Now you know something about these riders and their captives. Is there any way you might be able to help us, or that we might be able to help you?'

'You can help us very simply,' came the reply. 'Kill these riders. Let no mercy be shown to the unmerciful! Or if you do not wish to kill them, bring them back to Mjolkbridge where they will stand trial for what they have done!'

'A neat trick if we could do it,' muttered the Haufuth of Loulea.

'What you ask is also what we wish,' the old farmer responded. 'Is there anyone here who could help us do it?'

'No one in their right mind would come with you,' replied the Mjolkbridge headman. 'Vengeance aside, it is the wrong time of year for such a venture, if there ever is a right time for the pursuit of such fearsome men. However, we have two young men who have not been in their right minds since their father was killed. We were hard pressed to stop them stealing horses and setting off in pursuit and into certain death. But by now, unfortunately, they will hear that there is a party of strangers riding after these men, and will not be denied their revenge. They will seek to join you. To let them even speak to you is against my better judgment, for they are young and foolhardy, but I don't think I can stop them. Do you wish to see them?'

The Haufuth leaned over to Kurr. 'What's to be gained from talking to them? We don't need more people getting in our way.'

'I agree with you,' Kurr whispered in reply. 'If we rely on strength of numbers we haven't a hope of rescuing Mahnum and Indrett, let alone taking one of the Bhrudwans alive. And yet . . .'

'What?'

'If these youngsters know the moors, they might be invaluable. On the other hand, we're already taking three children into danger.'

The Haufuth nodded, then turned to his Mjolkbridge counterpart. 'What about yourself? Would you come with us?' he asked his fellow headman.

At that moment the door crashed open and two men burst in, drowning out the reply. 'Where are they?' one shouted, knocking a chair to the floor with a loud clatter. Other people crowded around the door to the inn's main room, but were careful not to be seen by their village Haufuth. No one wanted to appear too inquisitive.

'Where are they?' the man repeated, looking wildly around the room.

The Haufuth of Mjolkbridge sighed, then turned to face the intruders.

'Sit down, Farr,' he said, pushing a chair towards him. 'There's another chair over in that corner,' he said to the second man. Then, wearily, he got to his feet and went to the door.

'Sorry, boys,' he said cheerfully. 'Private business.' And he shut the door.

'Well?' demanded the first man, a thin, angular fellow with a beaked nose and a perpetual scowl. 'Are these the ones? Is this all? I thought there were five. Where are the others?'

The man sat down reluctantly when it became obvious that he was not going to get immediate answers to his questions. His brother, who had not yet said anything, was already seated.

The young Haufuth sat back in his seat. 'I apologise for the intrusion,' he said, addressing the men of Loulea. Then he turned on the newcomers. 'You were told to wait outside,' he scolded, but his voice was too gentle to carry much of a rebuke. 'Could you not have waited? What will the men of Loulea think of you? Will they believe that you would respond with obedience and maturity in a time of crisis?'

The first man tried to reply but was interrupted by his headman.

139

'Farr, be patient. These men have had a long and tiring day, and will not be well disposed towards youngsters who come between them and their well-earned rest.'

The younger brother stood. Shorter than Farr, this man's wide shoulders bespoke strength. 'My name is Wira Storrsen,' he said to Kurr and the Haufuth of Loulea. 'Please forgive our impatience. We are eager to hear of your plans for the horsemen who killed our father.'

The stout Haufuth of Loulea struggled to his feet, smiling at the younger man. 'If we were to make youthful enthusiasm a subject for forgiveness, the world would eventually become a sterile place!' he said, holding out his hands to Wira in the Firanese gesture of peace. 'I am the Haufuth of Loulea, and this is Kurr, one of my companions. Together with three others we are pursuing the riders who attacked your father. Please sit down; it is our pleasure to talk with you.'

The Haufuth of Mjolkbridge sighed his relief. But Farr was not to be denied.

'So what did they do to your village?' he snapped at the Loulea headman.

Kurr's eyes narrowed. 'Much the same as with yours,' he snapped back, forestalling the softer answer of the Haufuth. 'Only they captured rather than killed. Two of our villagers have been taken and we want them returned to us.'

'No deaths in your village?'

'No deaths. At least, we hope that our friends are still alive.'

Farr kept pressing. 'The other three – your companions – they are fighting men?' He looked at Kurr with blazing eyes.

The Haufuth cleared his throat. 'Not exactly,' he admitted. 'In fact, if it comes to a fight I suspect we will be dispatched very quickly. But we will rely—'

'Then you need us!' Farr exclaimed triumphantly. 'We Storrsens are good with sword and stave. We are mountain men of Vinkullen, not soft coastlanders. Mountain men are more than a match for any southern horsemen! When do we leave?'

That was enough for Kurr, who drew in his breath sharply. *Who did this boy think he was?* He was about to answer back when, to his disbelief, his Haufuth began to laugh.

'You two men are just what we need! We leave tomorrow morning, one hour before dawn. Will you be ready?'

A wolf-like grin appeared on the thin features of the older Storrsen. 'We are ready!' he shouted, then stood, knocking his chair backwards. His brother stood beside him. With a swift motion Farr drew a knife from his belt and held it aloft in front of him, point aimed upvalley. 'Let our enemies beware!'

At that moment Stella came through the open door, followed by Leith and a limping Hal. Two men, one brandishing a knife, stood confronting the men of Loulea. Were these men two of the riders? The three youngsters froze.

Farr turned on them in amazement. 'Are these the rest of your companions? But they are mere children!' He let slip the knife, and it dropped to his side. 'Do we go as fighters or as nursemaids?'

Wira clapped him on the shoulder. 'Children? No, brother; take a closer look! I see two determined young men, and—' here his eyes opened a little wider – 'a woman of rare beauty!'

Stella blushed at the frank look of admiration on the man's face.

'Farr,' the younger brother continued, 'it may be you who needs a nursemaid, since you cannot restrain yourself. Don't let grief rob you of good sense! They have accepted us, and we have a chance to avenge the death of our father. What else do you want?'

Farr mumbled something, picked up his knife and sat down. His brother followed, eyes resting for a moment on the Loulea girl. Her eyes sparkled at the attention. Deep inside himself Leith took hold of the bottle and pressed hard down on the cork.

The Company eventually tumbled into beds in musty rooms at the end of a long, dark corridor. But Leith could not sleep, and he listened through the wall as Kurr talked with the Haufuth.

'Why did you accept the offer? What do we want with a couple of hotheads?' The old farmer was angry.

'Only one of them is a hothead,' the Haufuth replied languidly, already drifting towards sleep. 'Those boys would have gone after the riders, whether with us or on their own. You could see that for yourself! This way, there will be no surprises. We can keep an eye on them. I'd rather have them with us, knowing where they are, than have them getting in our way.'

Kurr grunted. 'Something in that,' he acknowledged.

'And now we have two fighters,' the Haufuth reminded him.

'If their boasts can be believed,' Kurr said doubtfully. 'According to Kroptur, no Firanese could call himself a fighter in comparison with these Bhrudwans.'

'Perhaps. But it may yet come to swordplay, and what use would you or I be – or the others, for that matter?'

'Slim chance that these mountain boys could defeat four battle-trained Bhrudwans!'

'Slim chance is better than no chance,' replied the Haufuth.

As Leith lay there it seemed that he was a detached observer, watching another young boy called Leith lying in a strange bed. The young boy looked small, weary and powerless. *Go to sleep*, he told the young boy. *Don't think about it. Think about something else.*

The young boy took his advice, and eventually drifted off to sleep.

Surely this was too real to be a dream.

Leith could see his mother sitting trussed to a horse ridden by a grey-cloaked rider. She jerked from side to side as the horse scrambled up an ice-covered path that wound through dark, snow-laden trees. Ahead were two more horses, a smaller northern steed and a large Bhrudwan stallion, both carrying heavy-booted warriors. Further ahead still another horse bearing his father and a fourth Bhrudwan picked its way cautiously up the path.

The fourth rider held a sword against his father's shoulder blades. A deep wound defiled Mahnum's cheek, and his father raised his hand to touch it, as though it gave him pain. The horseman barked orders in a strange tongue. In response his father pointed ahead into the murky forest. Leith seemed to keep pace with them easily as they rode on up the tree-covered slope. Then they came to a level place and a circular clearing, in the centre of which lay a small blue-green pool. Leith watched as his father was pushed roughly from his horse and forced to gather sticks for a fire. It was cruel work, scrabbling in the snow for wood. His mother they left tied to the horse. She shivered as she sat there, too far away from the warmth of the fire, her face bruised and swollen, her eyes dull with pain and fatigue.

What have you done to her? Leith asked. *Are you going to let her freeze to death?*

The men seemed to hear him. They drew their swords and rushed towards him. Blue light pulsed like a spreading bruise around and between the warriors. *Mother! Father! Run! Run!* he shouted as the Bhrudwans came at him. Then with a cry the men were upon him, everything went black, and Leith jerked himself awake.

He had still not shaken off the dread of his dream as the travellers, now seven strong, assembled in front of the Waybridge Inn. The Haufuth of Mjolkbridge stood in the half-light of the pre-dawn morning to see them off. Kurr stamped his fur-lined boots on the frosted street and grumbled about the cold. His stamping and the sound of the horses nickering and blowing were the only sounds in the world.

Above them the tiny stars were beginning to fade, their light swallowed by the hazy pink of a mountain valley dawn. The cloud had cleared away, but Farr warned them about this kind of weather. 'Never stays calm for long,' he commented in his trenchant fashion. 'We'll ride into a wind for most of the day. Be hard pressed to make Windrise by nightfall tomorrow. We should've left earlier!'

As they made final preparations, Leith recalled the comical scene a half-hour ago at the inn. The Haufuth of Mjolkbridge had offered them weapons from the village cache. Each of the Louleans had selected a sword from a pile of rusted and broken relics. The Haufuth was first. He chose a long, curving blade but could not get the belt of the scabbard to fit around his ample waist. 'Oh well, no sword for me,' he'd said, a good deal more cheerfully than he ought. 'Oh no, we can't have that,' his Mjolkbridge counterpart had replied, and found for him a length of rope with which to fasten the scabbard. When the sword was tied around his waist, it would not sit flush against his side. 'A smaller sword!' the big man cried, and finally he settled on a squat little blade not much bigger than a knife. As he wielded it in clumsy fashion it almost disappeared in his huge hands. Kurr could not help it; he started to laugh.

'All very well for you,' huffed his Haufuth. 'I'll have my revenge up on the moors, nice and warm while you freeze to death.'

Kurr chose a sturdy sword, one that looked recently made. It had two notches near the hilt. Stella pulled a long blade from the table but could hardly lift it. 'Don't worry,' Wira said to her amid the laughter that ensued. 'None of them could wield it either. It's an ornament, not a proper sword.'

Stella looked at the young valley man with grateful eyes.

Hal dug deeper into the pile, finding some old, rusted blades. 'These will do,' he cried, forcing one into its scabbard. He took another and passed it to Leith. Even with all the rust, it felt very light.

'You don't want to bother with rusty old blades like those!' the Haufuth of Loulea told the boys.

'On the contrary,' corrected the Mjolkbridge Haufuth. 'Those blades were fashioned for use in the war against Bhrudwo, and they saw service in old border disputes between Mjolkbridge and Windrise.'

'You mean . . .' began Leith.

'Yes, they're over a thousand years old.'

Leith looked at the pitted surface of his sword: he could well believe it.

'Surely it would be better to have new blades?'

'No,' the young headman countered. 'We can't make them like these now. They are true blades, and have a history.'

Then the farce began, as one by one the five coastlanders engaged in mock swordplay. The Haufuth of Mjolkbridge had a smile on his face as he watched, and Farr laughed outright.

'The horsemen are in danger all right,' he said. 'One look at you fools and they'll die laughing!'

'Then I'll give my sword a name,' said Hal lightly, holding his blade aloft, deflecting the thoughtless words of the elder Storrsen. 'I name this weapon Ribtickler!'

This remark had occasioned still more laughter, which Leith did not join in. He wished he had thought of a clever name for his blade.

Now, out in the cold morning air, Leith fingered the hilt of his unnamed sword as it hung uncomfortably against his leg. Up until now this adventure had been like a dream, an unreal series of events, but now the cold weapon at his side spoke of danger and death. He hardened inside as he thought: *Perhaps that is the best way of all.*

Everything was set. The coastlanders mounted their horses in the accustomed arrangement, while Farr and Wira each had a steed. Farr shouted; the Haufuth of Mjolkbridge waved them off; and with a clash of hoof on icy stone the Company rode through the village and off up the Westway.

CHAPTER 7

WINDRISE

THE MORNING PASSED QUICKLY. Mile after steady mile was eaten up by the greedy hoofs of their horses as the Company made their way through the scattered farmlands north of Mjolkbridge. The land sloped steeply on either side of an increasingly narrow valley shared by road and river. To their left rose the squat hills of the Vinkullen, flat-topped highlands between the Mjolkelva and the ever-frozen Iskelsee far to the north. On their right Starfjell, the northernmost of the Fells, heaved its balding snowpate crown into the pale blue sky.

Here in the upper Mjolkelva valley, near the borders of civilisation, the land seemed somehow older. It wasn't just the moss-draped fences enclosing dilapidated farms and stony pastures, or the increasingly unkempt nature of the Westway itself, now little more than a grassy path; it was as though human influence here had only a tenuous hold – or perhaps the wilds were fighting domestication, attempting to reclaim land long tamed. Certainly the effect was unnerving, combined as it was with a landscape of rearing hills and snow-capped mountain peaks.

Ahead, appearing first as a black smudge on the horizon, then as a dark green band, lay the Great North Woods, drawing ever nearer. Leith could not escape the sensation that his horse stood still in the centre of a moving landscape – grassland, hills, mountains, clouds and sky rolling past him like a series of breakers at Varec Beach. Then, suddenly, the dark green border flashed up in front of them and they reached the woods, the true wilderness. The boundary of the forest was as clear as the mark of high tide, as though the woods had flowed down the valley to this point and were now lapping against the open country.

The Great North Woods stretched unbroken across the North March of Firanes. Like a great green wave, the trees washed across the landscape, over the roots and up the sides of the Jawbone Mountains far to the east, the eastern margin of Firanes. In the sterile heights of those far-off peaks the woods ended, but began anew on their far side, the same forest with a new name flowing unbroken − save for the thousands of still blue lakes and a few village clearings − right across northern Faltha. The Great North Wood of Firanes was but the western division of a vast army of trees, millions upon millions of them, standing to attention, always alert, as though they were guarding some hidden northern secret. The wood that extended green fingers into the Vale of Loulea, and which overshadowed the Westway, also marched to the margins of Bhrudwo thousands of leagues to the east. To Leith it felt like a direct link to the Destroyer himself.

The trees were giants, much larger than those Leith knew from the woods at home. Spruce and larch, fir and giant pine all towered above the travellers as they followed the Westway under the wood. Overhead the canopy admitted very little light, leaving them straining their eyes in the semi-darkness. What they could see caused them to take care, as the forest floor was littered with fallen tree trunks, covered, like everything else, in a thick blanket of moss and pine needles that swallowed sound, leaving an eerie silence. Moreover, the ground itself was strangely uneven, a tangle of man-high ridges, shallow, waterlogged depressions and occasional erratic boulders that made travel difficult, reducing the Westway to a forest path that could be taken only in single file. There was little undergrowth in the forest; the same semi-darkness that encouraged the enveloping moss prevented the growth of flowering plants. Strangely to those used to the woods of Loulea Vale, there was no sign of animal life, save the intermittent sound of birdsong high above and the middens of squirrels, made up of discarded cones, lying at the bases of the largest spruce trees. Occasionally the travellers came across a clearing, where one or two forest giants had fallen. Here they saw signs of new growth: lush meadows of wild grasses, blueberry bushes (not yet in fruit, of course) and a number of saplings seeking to usurp their elders. In one such glade the travellers stopped to camp for the night.

'What must this be like in spring,' Hal wondered aloud, 'if in winter there is so much beauty?'

All Leith could see were the surrounding trees, dark and sinister in the light of a winter's afternoon. *Beauty?*

Wira answered Hal. 'It is beautiful, and I am pleased you can see it. We have had a mild winter thus far in the Mjolkelva Valley. I've seen gorse start to flower, and some of our fields are covered with snowdrops. It is beautiful, but I feel sorry for the flowers. They have been tricked; winter is not yet finished. In the north, winter can hit late and hard. Is it not so in your land?'

'Yes,' Hal replied. 'But our coastlands get more of the seasnow than do the uplands. Perhaps this year will be mild. Come, Wira,' he beckoned the younger brother, 'show me some of your trees!' The two young men walked off together, one tall and broad-shouldered, the other crippled, animated by a common interest.

Mahnum fingered the cut to his face. *That'll teach me for remaining silent when they ask me a question.* The man he identified as the Bhrudwan leader – he who issued the commands and to whom the others deferred, the tallest of the tall warriors, raw-featured and with recessed eyes – had asked him *that* question again.

'Where is the Right Hand? Take us to the Right Hand!'

The Trader couldn't stand it any longer, had taken enough, so simply turned away as though he hadn't heard. A quick movement, a deft flick of his curved sword – such skill was frightening – and Mahnum's face bled for some time. Indrett hadn't seen it; she was still asleep, trussed up on the back of a horse. *Just as well. Much more of this . . .*

The Trader turned his attention to his task. Gathering sticks for a fire was difficult when the deadfall was covered with snow, but he knew that no excuse would be accepted. The pain in his ribs reminded him that these men were ruthless, not hesitating to beat him as he lay helpless. Still, he had slowed them for a while. Perhaps someone would come to rescue the captives, perhaps the Haufuth had been able to organise a pursuit, perhaps deliverance was at hand – if a pursuit had indeed been raised, if there were enough in the party, if they had fast horses and had ridden them hard, if they had picked the right road, if, if, if . . . Mahnum sighed. *Forget it. No one is coming.* He would have to find a way out of this before the Bhrudwans decided their captives were too much trouble, or that they were telling the truth and really didn't know anything about this Right Hand.

But why were they asking? Hadn't he told the Voice of Andratan all he knew?

In his search for firewood he drew close to a small blue-green pool, gamely reflecting the pale sunlight in a world of shadows. Behind him the trees of the Great North Wood stood placidly, uninterested in humans and their quarrels. *No escape that way,* thought Mahnum. *The wood would swallow me, or the warriors would find me, or they would do things to Indrett until I begged them to stop.* He watched the Bhrudwans prepare the camp. Two were younger, learning the ropes. The leader and his lieutenant were older, more experienced warriors, bearing the scars of battle. The Trader had learned of their skill this last year, as he had been pursued across Faltha. The two young Bhrudwans would be adding tracking and survival skills to their already formidable fighting prowess. These warriors could fight effectively armed and unarmed, with sticks or club, axe or sword; superbly fit, they showed few effects of their arduous journey through the Falthan winter. And now they were learning to torture and kill, to extract information from their enemies. Mere efficiency would not be enough for their leader; he would expect them to enjoy the terror of their captives, to develop a taste for blood, to savour the hunt and the kill. And by the time they reached the age of their leader, they would be ruthlessly efficient fighting machines. True Lords of Fear.

Mahnum shuddered. *Had these men ever been children?*

Vulnerable, needing their mother and father, crying, admitting weakness? He tried to imagine it, but failed. How could something so innocent be made over into something so evil? *Concentrate on your task*, he told himself. *Gather the wood, keep them happy, make them complacent, then . . . Just keep yourself alive until they present you with an opportunity.*

He was about to hurry back to the camp, arms filled with wood, when he heard the sound of a horse, muffled by the intervening trees. Someone coming along the road! Before he had time to react the Bhrudwans had drawn swords and spread out around the clearing, finding hiding places under the trees, waiting for the appearance of the rider. The very air began to pulse with an ominous blue cast, laden with violence and power. The approaching noise became louder and louder, then suddenly the rider was upon them, bursting into the clearing. A stab of disappointment shot through the Trader: one rider only, and not of Loulea. Hardly a rescue party.

Would they let him pass? *Keep riding, keep riding,* willed Mahnum. *Don't stop!* But the rider reined his horse in, looking more closely at the campsite, and that was his undoing. Before Mahnum could muster a warning shout, the Bhrudwans had rushed from their concealment and surrounded the hapless rider. No questions were asked, no mercy was given. A sword flashed, a swathe of blue light, and the horse was down and thrashing about on the cold ground, making a pitiful noise in its agony. The rider, pale with fright, stumbled away from the death throes of his mount and fumbled with his sword, making ready to defend himself. *Leave him alone!* Mahnum wanted to shout. *He's little more than a boy!* But the bloodlust was on them now; they would not have heard him, let alone taken any notice. The warriors stood motionless and watched the intruder clumsily heft his broadsword, then look from one grey-robed figure to the next, seeking a way of escape. Panic turned to terror in his eyes as he looked on the faces of his implacable executioners. His face settled into the look of one who knows he is about to die.

The leader struck first, a blow that even Mahnum did not see coming. The flash of steel took both sword and hand, severing them from the arm of the shrieking youth. It was as good as over, and Mahnum wanted to turn away but could not. He had seen this at the Favonian village, and the memories flooded back into his consciousness like bile into his gorge as the second Bhrudwan struck at the luckless rider who had merely been using the Westway. Now blows rained fast, swords biting into flesh, blows designed to wound but not to kill, and still the fear-frozen youth did not move to defend himself, hopeless though it would have been. Finally they hacked him to the ground where he lay twitching, making small sounds that cut at Mahnum like swords. *Finish it! Finish it! Don't leave him to suffer!* As the Trader watched, the four evil faces turned to him as one, their smiles communicating an unmistakable message. *This demonstration is for you! Tell us what we want!*

What could he do? He didn't have answers to satisfy them.

Mahnum gazed sadly on the twitching form of the young rider. They hadn't asked him for answers, and soon they would no longer ask Mahnum and Indrett.

Dispassionately the Bhrudwans watched the rider's life ebb away, as though judging the last possible moment to deliver the final blow. Enjoying the pain, feeding on it. Finally, at a nod from the leader, one of the younger warriors took a knife and plunged it into the youth's back. A few more twitches, then stillness. It was over.

The Company found themselves travelling more slowly during their second day out from Mjolkbridge. The road took a tortuous path through the forest, and care was needed to avoid tree roots that had grown across the rutted soil. Above them a thin line of blue sky mimicked the turns of the Westway, and all else was forest. Deep, dark, sombre, silent. As the Company rode they were enveloped by the muted gloom of the woods. One or two of them nodded towards sleep.

The Westway occasionally emerged from the woods to overlook the Mjolkelva, so the Company gained intermittent respite from the oppression of the trees. As they rode towards its source they saw the river in its youth: it was now a collection of braided ribbons lying in a wide gravel bed, fringed with broom, birch and willow, hemmed in by the feet of mountains whose heights were hidden in cloud. The road was now perceptibly uphill, running along a narrow terrace between the river on their left and the Fells on their right. Swift, cold streams crossed their path. A thin rind of transparent ice clung to their banks and thickened over any backwaters or pools. The Company marked the vanishing of the sun below the horizon, even though they had not seen it for hours, by an intensification of the forest gloom and a sharp drop in the temperature.

As they made their final dash to Windrise, a cold wind sprang up to meet them. It set the forest creaking and groaning, the branches clashing overhead in a sort of slow dance, in which the trees grappled drunkenly with each other like old men too far in their cups. A broad shingle fan came down from the right, and the road made a long, slow ascent across its width. The line of trees on either side gave the travellers the feeling of riding through a roofless hallway. At the end of the hallway they could see the outline of a flat-topped mountain, fringed in delicate pink cloud, but as they rode towards it, the mountain shrank until it disappeared altogether.

'Where did the mountain go?' Stella asked the old farmer, who shrugged his shoulders tiredly in reply.

Wira rode up beside them. 'That's the Capstone; Windrise is at its foot. It didn't really disappear. We're climbing quite steeply here, and it has dropped below the level of the road. This is called the Hall of the Disappearing Mountain. Not far now!' He grinned cheerfully, then let his horse drop back behind them. As much as she wanted to, Stella resisted the temptation to turn and talk some more.

A minute or two later he pulled in beside them again. 'This is the Torrelstrommen fan,' he said to Kurr, but his eyes were on Stella. 'Windrise sits at the joining place of the Torrelstrommen and the Mjolkelva. In a moment we will see it!' Sure enough, as though at his bidding, they came over the midpoint of the shingle fan, the forest drew back, and in the gloaming of evening they beheld the twinkling lights of a village. Wira rode ahead to join his brother and did not look back. He didn't need to; he could feel her admiring eyes on him.

It was quite dark when the Company finally rode into Windrise. The stars were out but the moon was not yet up, and shutters on the windows selfishly kept the light indoors, away from the dark streets. Farr rode next to the Haufuth, saying nothing, a grimace fixed on his face which might have curdled milk. The Loulea headman thought twice about asking the Mjolkbridge man about lodgings for the night, turning to his brother instead.

'There are two inns to choose from,' Wira replied. 'The Aspen Grange is quiet, and the beer is properly aged. But the Briar and Thistle is more popular. Do you have a preference?'

Farr growled something indistinct.

The Haufuth frowned at the older brother for a moment, but he might as well have been frowning at the night sky for all the acknowledgement he got. 'I know neither place: I have never been here before. Kurr,' he called, turning in the saddle to face the older man, 'do you know this village?'

'I haven't been here for twenty years. There was only one inn in my day, the old Windrise Manor. Didn't something happen to it?'

'Burned down,' Farr replied roughly. 'Sparks from a forest fire got into the thatch. Took everyone with it.' There was no escaping the hint of satisfaction in his voice.

Wira spoke. 'Why don't we try the Briar and Thistle? It may be in Windrise, but at least it has some life! Good company and a great warm fire. Take my advice!' He rubbed his hands together in anticipation.

'That settles it!' the Haufuth said. 'As much as I would like merriment, what we need now is rest and privacy, with the fewer questions about our journey the better. The Aspen Grange it is!'

Wira turned to the big man. 'Do we not require news of the

horsemen?' he reminded them. 'I, at least, should spend some time at the hearth of the Briar and Thistle, asking a few subtle questions.'

'Go ahead,' the Haufuth decided, 'but be careful!'

Farr scowled darkly after his brother as he vanished into the night.

The grand-sounding Aspen Grange was a small, slightly seedy one-roomed bar, with a scarcely larger sitting-room and six tiny rooms out the back; but the beer served there was wet, the fire threw out a great heat and the mattresses promised to be soft, so the travellers minded but little. The younger members of the Company turned in early, while Kurr and the Haufuth waited up with Farr for Wira. One or two locals filtered into the tavern, eyed the strangers suspiciously over their mugs of warm ale, talked together for a while and then left.

'Unfriendly place,' Kurr remarked.

'Don't know how the publican makes a living,' the Haufuth replied. 'Perhaps he takes advantage of the summer traffic on the Westway.'

'Too far back from the road for that. Most people would miss it. Besides, the other inn is much nearer the village gate, so it stands to reason that it would attract the travellers.'

'If there are any.' The Haufuth shook his head. 'This doesn't feel like a village many people would want to visit.'

Kurr nodded in agreement, then took another deep draught from his mug. 'At least the ale's good.'

The Haufuth turned to Farr, who supped his beer like it was poison. 'I didn't get the straight of it, but from what your Haufuth said there's been trouble between Mjolkbridge and Windrise. What do you know about it?'

The young man laid his beer aside, sat back on his stool and folded his arms. 'I'll tell you what I know about it,' he said deliberately, in a voice designed to carry. 'People here are arrogant, ill-tempered half-breeds. You can feel it, right enough. Well, I can put a name to it. *Losian.*'

'Not a word to use lightly,' the Haufuth said quickly, glancing around the room to see if anyone had heard Farr's insult. The barman had his back to them, cleaning mugs at the other end of the bar, and gave no indication that he was listening to the conversation.

'No, but accurate all the same,' came the retort. 'You know nothing of the history of this valley. Nothing! We've been at odds with the Windrisians for as long as we can remember, and sometimes it comes to fighting, as it did in my grandfather's day. Call themselves true Falthans, they do, but they trade with the hidden kingdom and with the beasts of the *vidda*. Nothing good can come of that. I'm not a religious man, but I cannot abide the thought of trafficking with half-men. Save your dealings for descendants of the First Men, and keep yourself pure.'

'Half-men?' The Haufuth was puzzled. 'Hidden kingdom? I've not heard of such things.'

'I just told you about that, if you'd listened.'

Kurr stirred angrily, but the Haufuth restrained him with a hand on his arm. 'So help us, then. What's this about half-men?'

But Farr was not to be sidetracked. 'Windrise is surrounded by barbarian lands. You'd think that with the road to Mjolkbridge being their only link to civilisation, they'd be a little friendlier, instead of burning our farms and trying to take our lands.'

'The half-men?' Kurr tried to keep the anger out of his voice.

'It's simple, old man. Up above the Mjolkelva gorge, perhaps three days' walk upriver from here, the land opens out into a wide valley, so wide that in the centre the mountains cannot be seen, where the air is warm and things grow that will not grow anywhere else in Firanes. At least, that's what they say; I've never been there, and I never want to. There the Scymrians live, *losian* to a man, misfits who rejected the Way of Fire. Everyone knows that to have any kind of contact with *losian* sullies the soul. Yet Windrise makes much profit from trading with the hidden kingdom of Scymria.'

'So what's wrong with that?' Kurr interjected, angry at the 'old man' jibe.

'No self-respecting Falthan should have anything to do with

155

the *losian!*' Farr snapped. 'No matter how well made their goods, or how lissome their females. Oh yes, the men of Windrise have done more than trade. Hardly a pure-breed amongst them now. Tainted, they are; sullied with the blood of half-breeds. They are now half-breeds themselves!'

The Haufuth glanced over his shoulder. The barman had turned to face them, and his granite-set face indicated that he was not happy with the direction of their talk.

'Can't you keep your voice down?' Kurr snapped. 'Do you want to continue the feud between Mjolkbridge and Windrise single-handed? Young idiot,' he finished. Farr turned to stare at him, his face not at all repentant. The two men looked ready to trade blows.

'You still haven't told us what started the troubles in Mjolkelva valley,' the Haufuth said in little more than a whisper. 'Surely you didn't go to war with Windrise just because they have dealings with strangers?'

'What would you soft coastlanders understand about—'

With a bang, the inn door opened and Wira burst excitedly into the room. 'There's someone outside you must talk to,' the younger Mjolkbridge man said urgently. 'Come quickly!'

The Haufuth put down his pint and struggled after the other two. Out in the cold breath of a mountain night stood a shortish, unshaven man, a parcel under one arm. He looked the strangers over shrewdly from beneath bushy eyebrows.

'Lookin' for news of strange horsemen, are you?' he rasped, spitting as he spoke. 'I can tell 'e a thing or two about strange horsemen!' and he spat again.

Kurr stared at the man with distaste. 'On with it, then! What do you know?'

The man pretended to look hurt, then turned one of his pockets inside out with a knowing gesture. The Haufuth sighed, then pulled some coins from his wallet. The unshaven man made a great show of counting them. 'That all?'

'All until you tell us something of some use, at any rate! Now, what do you know?'

'The local gravedigger, that's me,' announced the slovenly man. 'Yesterday a man was found on the west road, a few miles up yon Torrel valley,' and he pointed away into the darkness. 'Dead he was, cut with swords an' knifed in the back. Never seen a body more ready for my services.' The man spat prodigiously into a puddle, and gave a short barking laugh like the slamming of a coffin lid. 'He was wearin' strange clothes, like them coastlanders wear, like you is wearin'. One of the locals brought him down. Afore I buried him, I took 'is clothes – or what's left of 'em – and kept 'em. This young feller here was talkin' in yonder inn, and his storymakin' has remembered me of them, so I gone and got them. 'Ere they are.' He produced the parcel from under his arm with all the drama of a conjuror.

Kurr reached out for the parcel, but the man pulled it away. 'If you want these clothes, you're goin' to have t' pay for 'em,' he stated.

'How much?' the farmer asked, trying to keep the anger out of his voice.

The man looked at the coins in his hand. 'Don't want no fretas,' he said. 'I want ten pending.' He looked slyly at the strangers and their nice neat clothes. He had seen their horses. They could afford ten pending.

The Haufuth was about to agree, albeit reluctantly, when Wira interrupted. 'Ten pending?' he replied, sounding incredulous. 'We haven't got that much between us. I told you that at the Briar and Thistle. Besides, we have all the clothes we need. Good night, sir!' Turning on his heel, he beckoned the others to follow him.

The uncouth man squirmed for a moment. He had seen that the fat man was ready to pay the money, but had also heard the determination in the youngster's voice. 'All right,' he said at length. 'Five pending.'

'Three.'

'Three?' It was the unshaven man's turn to look outraged. 'I went to all the trouble of tellin' you about them clothes, and going home to fetch 'em, and you want to rob me? Four.'

'Four it is,' replied Wira, wearying of the debate. 'Wait there; we have to fetch the money.'

'What was that about?' the Haufuth asked Wira when they were inside the inn.

'I didn't want the man to think we were wealthy,' Wira replied. 'I don't trust him. He and his friends might think that wealthy travellers could be easily parted from their money.'

The three men went outside again and gave the man his four pending. After another exaggerated show of counting, he handed them the parcel as reluctantly as a man bidding farewell to his beloved. He made to walk away.

'Wait!' Wira barked. 'You don't leave until we are sure we have our money's worth!'

Inside the greasy cloth was a bloodsoaked woollen tunic, shredded by swords, but unremarkable in colour or style. 'Could be anyone's! Certainly not one of the horsemen,' the Haufuth said with disappointment.

'Somebody died violently, at any rate,' said Wira thoughtfully. 'Do you think we should get Leith and Hal to look at the body? It could be their father.'

'Not in that tunic,' the Haufuth responded. 'I'd be willing to swear Mahnum doesn't own anything like that. Of course,' he continued in a less certain voice, 'he might have picked up all manner of clothing in the course of his journeys.'

'Look!' Kurr turned the tunic over and emblazoned on the left breast was a white star. The uncouth man leaned close, his beady eyes full of inquisitiveness.

'What is it?' the Haufuth and Wira asked together.

The old farmer rolled the tunic up, then wrapped it in the cloth and turned to the gravedigger. 'Thank you,' he said dismissively. 'That will be all.'

The ruffian scurried away into the night, muttering as he went, and the sound of hawking and spitting came to them on the cold mountain wind.

'Inside!' Kurr commanded. The others followed him into the Grange, and the three of them huddled around the glowing embers of the fire. The old farmer unwrapped the tunic again and held it up for the others to see. The star was sewn to the tunic with a silver filament.

'This is Kroptur's sign, the token of the Firanese Watchers,' Kurr said quietly. 'Remember, Kroptur sent a messenger up the Westway to gather news of the Bhrudwans.'

'It looks like he got too close to them.' Wira pursed his lips.

'How do we know that this messenger was killed by the Bhrudwan horsemen?' the Haufuth asked. 'Perhaps some robber did him in! Maybe even that repulsive fellow did it himself!'

Wira shook his head. 'No, it was the riders all right.' The others turned to face him, surprised at the hatred in his voice. 'That's how they killed my father, hacking at him with swords until he could no longer resist, then stabbing him in the back as he lay on the ground. The cowards! He didn't stand a chance.' He turned the tunic around, and they could all see the jagged, red-stained tear in the middle. 'Look here! See the mark of a fair fight!'

No one said anything. For a moment each was left to his own thoughts. Somehow the find had made their quest all the more real. The Haufuth could almost feel the swords at his own flesh, biting, biting.

'That ruffian said that the body was found up beyond the village. It must have been where the Westway winds through the Torrelstrommen valley.' Kurr looked thoughtful. 'The messenger of Kroptur left Watch Hill five days ago, three days behind the Bhrudwan killers. So how did this messenger catch the riders so easily?'

The Haufuth spoke with excitement. 'Perhaps the riders have met with some misfortune, something that slowed them down!'

Perhaps they stopped to dispose of their prisoners, the old farmer thought, but he said nothing aloud.

'Whatever the reason, they are within reach,' said Wira with a smile on his face, but locked behind that smile was intense pain. The Haufuth could see it.

'So the messenger's body was found yesterday. But who knows

how long he has been dead? And the Bhrudwans may have taken their horses up on to Breidhan Moor, which will increase the distance between them and us – in the short term at least.' Kurr considered for a moment. 'I do not yet know whether we ought to take horses up there. If it fell to snowing, the horses would never make it through the drifts. Even if the weather stays fine, it will be rough going. We may have to walk.'

The Haufuth sighed and looked down in the direction of his feet, which were hidden by his huge girth. 'I'm not sure which I look forward to less: another day in the saddle, or taking to my feet! Either way, let us get a good night's rest,' he said. 'From what people say about the moors, we'll need it.'

Kurr roused the Company early the next morning. After a hearty breakfast, they assembled in the Great Hall of the Lodge – surely named in jest, though judging by the Windrisians they had met, perhaps not. The Haufuth then sent Wira and Kurr on errands: the old farmer to gather provisions for the days ahead, and Wira to hire a guide.

'I've made up my mind,' he declared, over the protests of the Storrsens. 'We can do with as much help as we can get. The last thing we want is to get lost on the moors – and, no matter how well you think you know Breidhan Moor, a local is bound to know it better.

'I have made another decision,' he continued. 'We are probably only two days behind these riders now, and we stand a good chance of catching them before we even reach the moors. However, if we leave our horses here, they will outdistance us up the Torrelstrommen valley. So we will take the horses as far up the valley as possible, and if the weather is fine, we ride across the moors. Should the weather turn against us, we will find a sheltered spot for them, and leave them there until we come back. That way we will save another day, and we will be able to carry Mahnum and Indrett out more easily – especially if they have sustained any sort of injury.'

Kurr returned first from his errand, laden with biscuits, dried meat and cooking fat. These extra provisions entailed a complete repacking of the Company's supplies, which took nearly an hour. Even so, the travellers were packed and ready to leave when Wira returned with a thin-looking man in tow.

'I'm sorry about the delay,' he apologised to the Haufuth. 'I had great difficulty in persuading anyone to guide us over the moors at this time of year. A few agreed, but wanted such an exorbitant sum of money that I turned them down. This man, on the other hand, has agreed to take us as far as a mountain range called The Brethren, on the far side of Breidhan Moor, for twenty pending. He can ride our packhorse—'

'Twenty pending?' The Haufuth choked. 'That's a month's wages!'

'Nothing to the seventy or eighty pending some of the other men wanted. You can make do with what I have secured for you, or you can take our advice and let the Storrsens guide you over the moors.'

The thin man sneered. 'You wouldn't get a mile past the Snowfence without getting lost, coastlanders!'

The Haufuth turned aside to the farmer. 'I had heard the Windrisians were a proud people, but I would not have believed this! No wonder few people come to see the wonder of the Torrelstrommen valley, even in summer!'

'All right,' Kurr replied. 'I don't like it either, but don't forget why we're doing this. Bad manners will be forgotten once we have rescued Mahnum and Indrett, and taken one of these Bhrudwan riders captive.'

'What is your name?' the Haufuth asked the thin man.

'Kaupa,' he replied.

'Are you ready to start?'

'At the minute. But are you?'

'Insolence!' Kurr hissed.

The thin man cocked his head at the old farmer. 'Sounds like he doesn't want a guide!' He made to walk off.

Farr stepped in front of him. 'As a matter of fact, it was his idea. Some of us are not so sure that it was good one. Now, we're leaving. If it's not too much trouble, get on this horse and at least look like a guide!'

Kaupa sneered again, less convincingly this time. He ran a nervous eye over the Storrsen brothers: broad shoulders, mean eyes, swords hanging loosely around their waists as though they knew how to use them, and heavy staves strapped to their packs. No one would carry such an array of weapons unless they were proficient with them. Mjolkbridge men, if he did not miss his guess, and such as they would not hesitate to do harm to such as he. Kaupa mounted the horse proffered him.

The eight travellers finally left Windrise an hour after dawn. 'Good riddance!' Farr shouted as they left the last hut behind. His voice echoed back from the hills in the distance. Kaupa glowered at him, but passed no comment.

'There's a lot of ill feeling in the Mjolkelva valley,' said Kurr to the Haufuth. 'For hundreds of years the people of Mjolkbridge and Windrise feuded, and many battles were fought. In fact, Wira tells me that for a time Mjolkbridge was quite a powerful town, as far as things go here in the valley, and Windrise was forced to pay tribute. But about a hundred years ago the coastlanders – as all foreigners are called – were driven out. Now there is an uneasy peace.'

Leith looked around him. They were a mile or so out of Windrise, and the straggling, stony fields were already petering out. To their right the forest loomed, behind which rose the ramparts of the Fells. To their left was the river, and up ahead the flatlands ended abruptly in a sheer drop, from the bottom of which came the sound of rushing water. The far cliff was visible in the clear morning air, fluted and scoured by many rains, and seemingly just beyond this cliff rose the Capstone, now much taller than it had appeared in the Hall of the Disappearing Mountain. There was sign neither of human nor of animal.

'Not much to fight about, if you ask me,' Leith observed.

After a short while they met the woods again, and spent the morning with their heads down, following the Westway as it wound through the trees. Here the forest was not as tall as that nearer Mjolkbridge, whether because of the chill wind or through some past natural calamity, Leith could not tell. Clouds gathered overhead, grey and numinous with edges smeared on the sky, the unfriendly snow-bearing clouds of winter. Leith found himself squinting to see the road ahead.

A melancholy mood settled over the travellers. Even the Storrsens seemed affected. Whenever anyone spoke, it was in hushed whispers. The realisation settled on Leith that he was an alien in a land that did not seem to care for his presence. The morning's ride had taken him over some invisible line dividing the land of humans from the land of – well, of gods perhaps, of monsters, of raw, untamed nature, a wilderness which could not be controlled, in which people needed skill, strength and luck to survive.

Finally he could stand it no longer. 'What is wrong with this place?' he asked, directing his question to no one in particular. Seven heads turned to face him.

The Haufuth laughed somewhat nervously, breaking the tension that had been building throughout the morning. The shadows seemed to draw back a little.

'It does feel a little uncomfortable, doesn't it! I've been telling myself that above these trees the sun is still shining, but it doesn't seem to be working. Still, the trees don't go on forever.'

'This is Vithrain Gloum, the Valley of Gloom, the lowest of the three Torrelstrommen valleys,' Farr informed them solemnly. 'A few miles further on from here we come to the place where the Aigelstrommen joins the Torrelstrommen, and just above are the rapids of the Gloum Stair. Then comes the Valley of Respite, where the going is a lot easier. We'll be riding in the sunlight again today, mark my words.' *There*, his words were saying. *I told you we didn't need a guide.*

'Of course, you haven't told them everything you know about this place, have you, Mjolkbridge boy?'

Farr spun around to face the thin Windrisian.

Kaupa spread his arms wide. 'What my friend conveniently

forgot to tell you is that Vithrain Gloum was once open farmland. Then the men from Mjolkbridge, not satisfied with their own lands, came to raid ours. It was here in this valley – the valley we once named Tilthan Vale, the Valley of Plenty – that the courageous men of Mjolkbridge rode in without warning and cut down our defenceless men, women and children as they harvested the crops.' The thin man spat in the general direction of the Storrsen brothers. 'And now they want peace. Peace! There are bones buried here that once belonged to people who begged for peace, and who received only death. And these coastland heroes want us to forget!' He sawed at the reins, spinning his mount around to face the men from Vinkullen.

Immediately, the Haufuth rode in between them. 'That's enough,' he said, with all the authority he could muster. 'Perhaps tonight we can have a retelling of the old stories, but not now, not here. Our task is to write another story, one which may be every whit as bitter as the Valley of Gloom.'

Kaupa pulled away, visibly upset. For a while he rode a little distance ahead of the others.

Wira shook his head. 'I've never heard it told like that before,' he said quietly.

CHAPTER 8

THE VALLEY OF RESPITE

EARLY IN THE AFTERNOON the travellers reached the Aigelstrommen. A narrower, swifter river, it leapt capriciously from bank to bank, finally plunging over a cataract and into its bigger brother, the Torrelstrommen. There was no place to cross the foaming Aigel near the meeting of the two streams, so the Westway edged back up the side of the hills until it found a fording place.

The road had risen barely a hundred feet, yet the difference in temperature was noticeable. Ice clung to the banks of the Aigelstrommen, which was much reduced in size from its spring torrent if the bare, boulder-strewn slopes between the road and the river were any guide. Here and there snow patches lay, hardened to ice by the continual freeze and melt of cloudless days and nights. Again Leith noted the absence of animals and birds. Some of the birds he had seen flying over Loulea on their way south, he realised, could have been from this forest. The springtime would undoubtedly see them overhead again, in small wedges or in huge black croaking clouds. He shivered. Spring seemed a distant memory in the midst of this cold.

The road continued to wind up a narrow shelf. From somewhere ahead came a muted roaring, like autumn thunder playing on the Fells as heard from Swill Down. The sound grew louder as they climbed. The travellers were now some three hundred feet above the Valley of Gloom, and at intervals Leith caught glimpses of the lower Torrelstrommen valley. The wide, saucer-shaped vale was carpeted in a sombre green – the trees they had ridden under – split by a cliff-lined river winding off into the murky distance, back towards Windrise. Above them mists swirled about the tree tops; the weather, which had threatened all morning, seemed to be closing in around them. They were climbing a north-facing slope, and ice covered the rocky path under their feet. Soon they had to dismount and were slowed to less than a walk, watching their step all the way. It began to rain, a fine, soaking drizzle.

Finally the path levelled out and they could remount. They came to a clearing, in the centre of which lay a small blue-green pool. Beyond the pool lay the remains of a fire, and Kurr stopped to poke around in the embers. Something about the place nagged at the edge of Leith's consciousness, but he couldn't retrieve the memory.

'This is where I found the coastlander,' Kaupa said.

'What?' exclaimed Kurr and the Haufuth together. '*You* found him?'

Immediately the Windrisian was subjected to a barrage of questions. How long ago? Had he been able to tell how long the man had been dead? Where exactly had he found the body? But the thin man clammed shut under the questioning and would say nothing further. The Haufuth groaned with exasperation.

Kurr went back to the remains of the fire, then spent some time looking around the clearing. 'Horses have been here,' he announced, 'and their riders set a fire here some time ago. Could have been two, maybe three nights ago. Can't really tell. They slept the night over there—' he pointed to a rocky ledge '—and extinguished the fire the following morning. The fire could have been set by anyone, but there's a good possibility that the Bhrudwan riders came this way.'

'What of their prisoners?' asked the Haufuth.

'Impossible to say,' Kurr replied. 'But if they are unencumbered by prisoners, why are they not making better time? My guess is that Mahnum and Indrett are still alive.'

Kurr remounted and the Company went on, plunging back into the forest gloom, heading towards the source of the now-thunderous noise. A few minutes later the travellers emerged from the trees. Ahead and slightly above them the Torrelstrommen roared down the Gloum Stair, foaming and churning as it leapt from rock to precipice. As they drew nearer Leith realised that the mists and rain actually came from the waterfall. The Westway, now only a narrow path over rocky outcrops, was slick with spray blown towards them on a wind generated by the falling torrent. Dominating all else, the noise of the waters beat at the travellers, the trees, the very rocks of the earth. Leith clutched at his neck in something approaching fear; the sound had set the cords in his throat vibrating.

Kaupa walked sure-footedly to the very edge of the cascade and looked down.

'Not much water even for this time of year,' he said laconically, as if dismissing the power of the sight to move him. 'The river upstream will be locked up. Must be cold on the moors.'

Were the Gloum Stair within walking distance of Loulea, Leith speculated, it would surely be regarded as one of the wonders of the world; yet the Company could not spare even a few moments to appreciate its raw power. They hurried up the path, which abruptly turned right and funnelled through a natural cutting in a granite ridge, emerging at the bottom of a treeless valley. The absence of trees caused the Company's spirits to rise, as though an oppressive weight had been lifted from them. The mists drew back and the roaring behind them faded to a dull rumble that was felt rather than heard; and as they progressed even that fell away into silence.

'Vithrain Uftan,' Kaupa announced, his voice cutting a swathe through the tranquillity. 'The Valley of Respite.' Leith shook his head. The thin man had managed to frame even this welcome announcement with a sneer.

The wide-open valley encouraged them to ride their mounts hard. Fresh after a morning's slow ride through the forest, the horses responded willingly, kicking their heels as though in their foals' paddock again, glad to be rid of the menacing Vithrain Gloum.

'At this rate we'll make it to the Kilthen Stair before nightfall!' Wira shouted happily to his brother, who grunted an unintelligible reply.

Up in Vithrain Uftan the hills were brown and bare, with slopes of loose rock spawned from seemingly every high place about them. The valley cut a trough straight and true between the maze of hills to their left and right. Leith could see snowdrifts even on their lower slopes. The browns, greys and ochres of the mountain rocks and grasses seemed much brighter than the morose woods they had left behind. But not wholly left behind; in some sheltered spots stunted spruce trees held tenuously to the soil, while dwarf willows – some not much bigger than knee height – huddled together on the lee side of boulder piles like wounded soldiers left behind by a defeated army.

'The weather's not going to last much longer,' Kurr observed. 'From the smell of those clouds, we're bound to have snow soon.'

Other, smaller valleys poured their collected water into the Valley of Respite. Leith looked down the first of twin valleys on their right. There, sheltered from the downvalley wind, stood a copse of fir trees. But as the clouds lowered the wind picked up, driving into their faces, and it became difficult to think of anything else but the cold tearing through his clothes, seeping into his bones. He pulled his cloak more tightly around his face, so that as little as possible was exposed to the wind. His view was that of someone peeping through a crack in a door. Even Kaupa, their guide, apparently felt the cold, or at least his horse did, as he began to drift back through the Company. Leith risked a glance to his right. They were about to pass the second of the twin valleys.

Horses!

Leith's mount came to an abrupt halt with the others as Kurr reined him in. From the opening to their right issued one, two, three, four horsemen, riding hard. Now they could hear cries coming from the lead rider, who lifted his arm and brandished a sword. Fear gripped the Company.

Hal slid to the ground, the first of the Company to react. Leith could not move. 'The riders! The riders!' the Haufuth shouted. 'The Bhrudwan riders!'

Farr instantly took command of the situation. 'Dismount! Get down from your horses!' he barked. 'Make a circle around them! Face outwards towards your enemy!'

More shouts, this time from behind! Leith whirled around, to see another four riders come galloping out of the fir trees behind them. Surrounded!

A hand pulled him roughly from his horse. Leith started with fright, but it was Wira. 'Draw your sword! Face your enemy!' he shouted. 'Didn't you hear my brother? Don't you want to live?'

In that moment fear overwhelmed him, but instead of cowering behind his horse, he found anger and desperation rising to meet his fear. The emotions bottled up inside him broke open. Here was something he could attack, something he could pay back. He threw back his hood and pulled out his sword, his knuckles white on the hilt.

The Haufuth grabbed Stella and placed her behind him, then drew his own weapon. Hal and Kurr had theirs at the ready. The Storrsen brothers, one at the front of the Company, the other at the back, held a sword lightly in one hand and a stave in the other.

In a few moments the riders were upon them. But instead of attacking immediately, they began riding around the Company in a circle.

'These are not the Bhrudwan warriors!' Kurr grated. 'Look, they wear Windrisian garments! And there is the man who sold us the clothes last night!' Sure enough, the unkempt Windrisian rode along with the others.

'What do you want?' the old farmer shouted. 'Let us pass! We're leaving your lands!'

The riders laughed among themselves, mocking the travellers. They slowed their horses to a walk. 'Leaving our lands?' one replied. 'Not likely!'

169

'This is where you'll stay!' another crowed. 'Planted in the tree-less valley! Maybe coastlanders will grow where trees will not!' The others laughed uproariously at the joke.

'You die in the Valley of Respite,' called another, 'because we would not sully Tilthan Vale with such carrion!' His friends roared their agreement, clashing swords on bucklers.

The unkempt man drew a little closer. 'I want that one there,' he said, pointing his short sword at Wira. He spat in the direction of the young Storrsen, who returned his gaze unflinchingly. Then he pulled his horse back and joined the others as they began to gallop around the Company, moving closer, then further away.

'What are they doing?' the Haufuth asked over his shoulder.

'Trying to intimidate us, to break our spirit,' replied Farr. 'When they think we're sufficiently cowed, they'll attack. I don't think this was their original plan. They wouldn't have expected us to make a stand like this.'

'What do they want?'

'Sport,' came the reply. 'And revenge on Mjolkbridge. But they'll not get it. When I raise my staff, make a rush for the rider on the black palfrey. Ready?'

But matters were taken out of their hands before the signal could be given. Suddenly, with a bloodthirsty roar, the men of Windrise descended on the Company. Immediately the Storrsen brothers leapt forward, swinging their staves, and in an instant two of the enemy were knocked from their horses. The other ruffians drew back, startled.

Another yell and the men dismounted, then came running towards Wira. Out of the corner of his eye Leith saw movement, then turned to see a figure raise a dagger ready to strike at Farr's unprotected back. Kaupa! Leith shouted a warning, then slashed in the general direction with his sword. There was a cry, and a body fell to the ground at his feet.

Then the attackers were upon them. Swords flashed, staves swung and for a few moments all seemed lost. One of the Storrsens was down with a Windrisian on top of him, Kurr and another rider were locked together, the old farmer fighting with surprising energy. Leith found himself fighting beside his brother. He feinted at one of the men, who ducked into Hal's sword. Then Leith heard a girl scream. It was Stella, crying out not in fear but in anger. Stepping in front of the Haufuth, blood streaming from a cut to her arm, Stella fought off the unkempt Windrisian with a flurry of energetic if untutored thrusts, which he was quite unable to counter. Her face changed slowly from a look of helpless terror to a fierce joy, as she realised beyond expectation that she would survive, even win, this fight. The panic grew on his face as the possibility he might die turned to a certainty, and that panic robbed the man of any ability he might have had. She dispatched him with a blow to the head before he had a chance to beg for mercy.

It was over as quickly as it had begun. The three Windrisians who remained uninjured had no further stomach for the fight and fled to their horses, pursued by Wira and Farr. They galloped off back down the valley, shouting defiance once they were far enough away. Farr made for his horse, but Wira growled, 'Let them go!'

The Company looked down on the bodies of their enemies. One of the riders knocked off his horse by the Storrsen brothers had cracked his skull. Another had fallen at the hands of Stella. Still another had met death at the end of Hal's sword. The eighth they found trying to crawl away, uninjured except for a broken leg. Kurr stood over him, sword drawn. Kaupa was nearby, still alive but bleeding badly from a wound to the back.

The other members of the Company stood looking at each other, breathing hard. Then, one by one, relief broke out on their faces.

Leith felt a wild exhilaration. He had done it! But his delight was tempered somewhat by the memory of the paralysing fear, and the sight of the dead Windrisians. He took a deep breath and wiped his sweaty palms on his cloak. Then he found he no longer had the strength to stand, so he sat down on the stony ground, and for a while all went black.

Stella sat down also, allowing Hal to tend her injured arm. He staunched the bleeding with a cloth dampened from a nearby stream. 'It's not serious,' he reassured her. She smiled weakly, but

Hal saw that the smile was meant for the young Vinkullen man, who strode towards her with concern and admiration fighting for control of his fair face.

Leaving Stella in the care of Wira, Hal hobbled over to their treacherous guide. Kaupa had rolled over on to his side, but his wide-eyed face was pallid and his hands clammy. He was trying to speak, but could only cough.

'He's dead,' said the Windrisian with the broken leg, who under the watchful gaze of Kurr had dragged himself to his companion. 'Or at least he soon will be.' He turned to Kurr. 'Are you going to let him suffer?'

'It's what he deserves,' Kurr replied.

'No one deserves to die,' Hal said, and stretched his arm towards the dying man.

At that moment the other Windrisian whipped out a knife and plunged it into Kaupa's breast. Kurr made a lunge at him, but Hal held him back.

'Now he can die with dignity,' the Windrisian said, and laid his knife down beside the still form of their guide.

The travellers took stones from a nearby ridge and covered the bodies. 'They don't merit a burial,' Kurr said, 'but we need to cover them so that wolves aren't attracted to this valley.' The last remaining Windrisian asked that he be left with his dead companions, so they built a fire for him and left him there with his sword and his knife. No doubt his friends would be back to set his leg and help him home.

The Company took the Windrisian horses, so that each member had a mount, and rode on, more slowly now and with little cheer. For a long time not a word was said, as everyone was preoccupied with thoughts they were not able to share. The clouds lowered still further and snow began to drift across the valley.

Evening camp was made in the lee of a huge boulder ridge. Leith and Hal gathered wood for the fire; they found a large quantity a little way up the slope of a shingle fan, some distance from

172

the Torrelstrommen, enough not only for the fire but also to build a rude shelter from the snow.

'That's the level of the spring flood,' Wira told them. Leith could make out another line of driftwood on the other side of the valley, and tried to imagine the sights and sounds of a river so large that it could fill the space between. Then his thoughts went to the Gloum Stair, and what it might be like in the midst of a great flood.

After the evening meal, the Company tried to piece together the meaning of the day's events. 'It seems like the ruffians decided that four pending wasn't enough, and that we were wealthy but defenceless,' the Haufuth offered.

Wira shook his head. 'No – our goods and horses would have been a bonus. It was the old hatred that brought them to this valley. It was my brother and I they were after. They wanted to strike a blow against Mjolkbridge. You people of Loulea just happened to be in the way.'

'I wonder,' Farr added, 'if in their hatred these Windrisians can no longer distinguish between foreigners. Perhaps all coastlanders are their enemy.'

'Better to think of it as just a few malcontents,' Hal put in. 'I'm sure that most Windrisians, like most people of Mjolkbridge, don't carry grievances over the past.'

'But how did the men get to the valley before us?' Leith asked. 'We didn't see them on the road.'

'They followed us, I think,' Wira replied, 'but my guess is they continued up the Aigelstrommen instead of following the Westway into the Valley of Respite. There is probably a low pass between the Aigel valley and the two ravines they ambushed us from.'

'Will they be back?' The Haufuth shuddered. 'Perhaps bringing others with them?'

'No,' Kurr decided at length. 'I don't think so. If there were more of their ilk in Windrise, they would have attacked us with the others. Besides, I think they have learned to fear the mighty warriors of Loulea!' and he laughed. The Storrsens laughed with him.

The conversation settled into mundane talk, but Leith could not join in. He watched and listened as a detached observer, once again outside events. And time and again throughout the firelit evening he saw the gaze of Stella stray towards the shadows where the Storrsens sat.

The morning dawned grey and cold, with dry snow falling lightly. The Company quickly broke camp. On the advice of Kurr they loaded up the horses, and every spare space in their packs, with driftwood, against cold nights on the exposed moors.

'We'll be out in the open all day, and for some days to come,' Wira warned them. 'The horses will make only ten or fifteen miles in such weather. We will be able to do little more than walk them.'

'The snow looks like it's stopping,' Stella said helpfully.

Kurr muttered under his breath, wondering how far they were falling behind the Bhrudwan riders. 'Curse this Vithrain Uftan, this so-called Valley of Respite!' he shouted angrily.

'I give it a new name,' said Farr. 'This is now Gealla Dalen – the Valley of Spite.'

The members of the Company took one last look at the valley where they had fought the Windrisians; then they set their faces to the southeast, towards the moors, where their quarry lay.

CHAPTER 9

BREIDHAN MOOR

IN THE LATE AFTERNOON the Company halted in the lee of the Kilthen Stair. Here the youthful Torrelstrommen surged down a hundred feet of stony steps, framed by steep snow-striped hills. Though not a true waterfall, and though carrying perhaps half the volume of water that thundered over the Gloum Stair, the Kilthen Stair still acted as a tangible barrier between one section of the Torrelstrommen and the next. The ever-variable flow formed ephemeral shapes of foam, so to Leith's eye a face, mouth wide open, was replaced by the outline of an outstretched hand on the face of the Stair. Thickening ice clung to the banks of the river, unable as yet to squeeze the life out of the racing torrent.

While the youngsters unpacked the horses, the Haufuth and the old farmer clambered up a notched but slippery rock and stared over the upper lip of the waterfall into the maw of the desolate upper valley. To reach that valley the Company would have to brave the Westway, a thin white line winding precariously up a near-vertical cliff face between them and the top of the Stair.

'Listen!' Kurr shouted above the sound of the foaming water.

A strong wind whipped around the mountain shoulders above them, making a noise uncannily like a human cry. Now and again, as the wind died momentarily, the men could hear the boom and clatter of falling scree, sometimes near, sometimes further away. The Haufuth wiped his suddenly sweaty hands on his cloak.

175

'Does the wind always blow like this?' he asked, cupping his hand near Kurr's ear.

'Always, so Wira told me. The people of Windrise don't come here except in great need. They have another path to the moors.'

'Can we take that path?' the Haufuth asked hopefully.

'It would take us far to the north, into the *vidda* proper, of which Breidhan Moor is only the southern outlier. There the deep snow would be the least of our worries; it is a land where wild men and wild beasts would see us as easy prey. Besides, if the Bhrudwans came this way, this is the way we must go.'

A strong sense of foreboding flowed towards the two men, borne on the cold wind.

'What's that noise?' Stella asked. She had clambered unnoticed up to the rock platform.

'Kilth Keening, it is called,' Kurr said, 'the Valley of the Lost Soul.' The wind, angry at the disclosure, whipped his words away.

The weak sun went down behind the hills as they watched. The air grew noticeably colder and shadows crept across the valley below them, eating away what little colour and life remained.

'Let's get down from here,' the Haufuth called. 'We'd better find a place to sleep – a place out of the cold, where we can't hear that sound!'

'We'll be fortunate to find either,' countered Kurr glumly.

The travellers spent a miserable night under the shadow of Kilth Keening. They had found an overhang of hard blue stone to shelter under, but it proved a mistake, as the cave collected water from Kilthen Stair, and no one could keep dry. One by one they gave up trying to sleep and the whole Company was assembled well before dawn.

The ascent of Kilthen Stair had to wait until sunrise, but the sunrise was slow to come. In the hour before dawn, Leith watched silver fingers of mist pour like a slow-breaking wave over the heights to his left. Gradually the valley filled with a cold fog, draping like a shroud over the travellers. Soon it was impossible to see more than a few yards in any direction.

Tired, wet and irritable, the Company made its ascent of the treacherously narrow Stair. The horses were nervous and had to be coaxed up by degrees. The Haufuth demonstrated a surprising gift in encouraging the horses to follow him up the path. It took more than an hour for everyone to negotiate the climb. Finally, however, they were at the top.

Here, the mist was if anything more intense, a cold cocoon muting all sound. The babbling of the Torrelstrommen receded into silence, the only noise the slow, measured plod of the horses' hoofs on the ill-formed road. Soaked inside and out, from sweat as well as moisture, Leith shivered uncontrollably. His jaw ached from clenching his teeth against the chill.

'This is no good!' Kurr exclaimed at last. 'We have to get dry. We will stop and build a fire.'

'I have a better idea,' Wira responded. 'The fog came down from the moorland above us. Often in the Vinkullen such a thing happens, and while the valleys are filled with foul weather such as this—' he indicated the dankness around them with a sweep of a half-visible arm, '—the heights are clear, warm and sunny.'

To Leith and the others such words were like the promise of a banquet to one who was starving. Could such a thing be? Leith tried to speak, but could hardly move his jaw.

'We're two days from the Snaerfence, three if this weather continues,' Kurr argued. 'We'll be frozen into blocks of ice well before we get to the moors!'

'Then why don't we find a path that will take us above this fog now?'

'And get ourselves lost? Or fall down a hole, or off the end of some bluff?'

'You have obviously never lived in the mountains, old man,' Farr interjected. 'We might only have to climb a few hundred feet. Maybe even less.'

Hal held up his hand. 'Wait a moment! Can you feel it?'

'Feel what?' came a chorus of voices.

'The wind!' And as he spoke, the others felt the breeze on their

177

faces. In a moment it ruffled the edges of their cloaks. And as they looked up, they saw that the fog was thinning.

Just in time, the Haufuth reflected. *If the argument had progressed much further it might have come to blows.* Kurr and Farr would bear watching; they seemed to strike sparks off each other.

After stopping to build a fire and dry out their sodden clothes, the Company continued their trek up the Torrelstrommen valley. A bleak and forbidding landscape unfolded around them as they rode. The last wisps of mist fluttered away in the mounting wind, revealing the winter face of Kilth Keening. Soft, dry snow all but covered the hardy mountain grasses; the exposed turf looked brown and scorched, as if the snow had somehow burned it. There was no other visible vegetation. In place of trees lay boulders, the huge *wacke* of the northern Fells, many larger than the travellers who passed them. They were strewn about the valley floor, seemingly the result of some recent gigantic hailstorm or rockfall. When the travellers passed close to one of the great *wacke* they noticed moss and lichens growing on its sides. Many of the rocks were cracked open, revealing an orange rind, as though they rusted where they lay.

The Torrelstrommen, ice-rimmed and narrow, chattered in its steep-sided bed, while silent ice-locked streams lay suspended in their side valleys. On either side of the narrow defile of the Valley of the Lost Soul rose grey, snow-streaked hills, their outlines now emerging from, now receding into, the leaden sky. Into the midst of this desperate country the Westway continued without complaint, now a snow-covered path distinguished from its surroundings only by the absence of boulders and the provision of marker poles planted in the earth every few hundred yards.

The downvalley wind rose in intensity and the dreadful, high-pitched cry returned to oppress them like a mourner's threnody. The Haufuth rode with his hands clapped on the sides of his head, while Leith took a handful of down from the lining of his cloak and stuffed it in his ears. But nothing could keep out either the sharpness or the sound of the wind. By late afternoon all exposed skin was red and raw from the abrasive blast. Leith again found his jaw clamped tightly shut, this time against the chilling wind and its equally chilling sound.

The Lost Soul of Kilth Keening tortured the Company all day. Her cries seemed to seep into their spirits in the way that a sick infant's wails tunnel their way into a mother's heart, sapping strength and wearing down resolve. Snow slanted in, rain sheeted down, a pallid sun shone amidst scruffy clouds and hail pounded them, but the travellers hardly noticed the weather. The clean-picked bones of some large animal – probably a horse – lay just to the side of their path. No doubt it had lingered in the valley too long. The bones seemed entirely in keeping with the frightful wind. Perhaps the wind had separated the flesh from the bone unaided; it seemed capable of anything.

The travellers found talking next to impossible, as the Lost Soul raged up and down the canyon. No one felt like discussing Bhrudwan riders or Windrisians or what might be happening back in Mjolkbridge or Loulea, where things were warm and the winds were still. Emotions were as raw as hands and faces. Even during meals no one attempted conversation.

Sleep was especially difficult. Partially sheltered from the cold and warmed by the fire, there was still no escape from the cries of Kilth Keening's tormented soul; her shrieks continued all night. At one point everyone was awake, either sitting by the fire or pacing around the rock ledge of their shelter, watching the *Kleitaf Northr*, the Northern Lights, in their familiar dance across the sky.

Mid-morning on the second day in Kilth Keening saw them reach the Snaerfence, the path to Breidhan Moor. Here the road turned away from the Torrelstrommen and into a small valley to their left, using the lesser slopes of this valley to scale the walls of Kilth Keening. The high moors were only a few miles away. The Company dismounted and stretched their stiff limbs.

'We have endured Kilth Keening,' Wira said wearily, 'and soon we will be out of earshot of her cursed voice. The experience was even worse than I'd been told.'

Farr agreed with his brother. 'I thought the description of this

179

foul valley was put about to justify the fears of cowardly travellers, yet I would rather spend a week without food on the summit of Vinbrenna in the season of the Pollerne gales than another day in Kilth Keening.'

'Yet what awaits us on Breidhan Moor may make us wish for the safety of this valley,' said the Haufuth querulously. 'I had hoped we would catch the Bhrudwans before they reached the moors. Breidhan Moor has an evil reputation.'

'But we did not catch them, and so up on to the moors we must climb,' Kurr snapped. 'Now let's get on. We're wasting precious time!' Leith shook his head doubtfully, but mounted his horse and followed the old farmer towards the sheer snowgrey wall rearing in front of them. The Westway left the valley floor and crawled upwards across the sheer southern side of the Snaerfence itself. Their eyes followed it until it disappeared into the gloom.

This is the closest yet I have been to her, Mahnum thought ruefully as he lay face down on the snow. Beside him, not three yards away, lay Indrett. Standing between them, curved sword drawn and ready, a Bhrudwan warrior ensured their silence. They lay on the edge of a ridge overlooking a wide valley of white. Snow-cloaked hillocks and ridges dominated the view in every direction. They were on the high moors, that Mahnum knew, the Westway buried under feet of snow.

In the peaceful valley below a terrible drama unfolded.

Earlier that day the Bhrudwans had found footprints in the snow. Immediately Mahnum and Indrett had been led off to a sheltered hollow to wait, while two of the Bhrudwans had gone on ahead to scout the road. In less than an hour the warriors returned and in haste led the horses forward through the treacherous snow. Now the captives waited on the ridge while the Bhrudwans stalked their prey.

Unaware of their peril, four men warmed themselves by a fire while a woman packed the last of the meat they had hunted into a leather bag. Mahnum could see the three Bhrudwans striding down the slope, taking little effort to conceal themselves. Their prey stood by the fire, backs to the ridge, weapons some distance away beside their packs. Mahnum wanted to cry out a warning, but knew that any cry would bring swift death to both him and Indrett. Besides, there was nothing he could do. These unfortunates were dead already. They had been dead since the moment their footprints had been discovered, and now the Bhrudwans would simply turn certainty into fact.

The Trader closed his eyes to shut out the scene below, but another scene replayed itself behind his closed lids; another open place, a village far to the south and east, a small fishing community on the banks of the Aleinus River. As he hid in the trees at the edge of the clearing, he had watched the merciless warriors going from hut to hut, dragging people out and butchering them on the street, or killing them in their homes. The screams were terrible, terrible; mothers pleaded in vain for the lives of their children, who were slaughtered in front of their eyes just before they themselves were slain. As Mahnum had watched in helpless frustration, the villagers had simply been wiped out. Pointlessly. None of the villagers could tell their tormentors anything about him; few were given the chance. Finally the huts were set on fire and the village razed to the ground.

Shouts of warning drew his attention back to the present. He shut his eyes, but he couldn't close his ears, and the sounds that came from below were every bit as dreadful as he remembered.

The woman was not killed. Instead, she was knocked unconscious by a blow to the head and carried up the slope to where Mahnum and Indrett lay. For some reason the Bhrudwans had taken another captive. Mahnum was too sickened to wonder why. Too often now he had been forced to watch helplessly while others suffered as the result of his own choices, and though he told himself that it wasn't his fault, he could not fight the guilt settling on him. Each wound inflicted by the warriors he had drawn westwards created another debt he had to repay; each death at their hands was an added burden he had to bear. He would do all within his power to see that the Bhrudwan invasion was thwarted. Somehow he must escape and warn the Falthan kingdoms, somehow he must make them believe him. He could not bear to think of these atrocities being repeated in every village in Faltha, in his own sleepy village of Loulea.

It took the Company all morning to climb the Snaerfence. In parts the path could be taken at a pleasant walking pace; other parts were boulder-strewn and broken, or had been washed out by swift spring meltwaters, now locked up in icy prisons on the heights above. In three places the path became a stair; twice the steps were stone-hewn, the third made from sawn timber. The riders were forced to dismount and lead the horses over the worst parts.

'Who made these steps?' Leith asked as they puffed their way up the second stair. 'And who keeps the road in repair?'

The Haufuth did not have the breath to answer. Kurr began a reply, but his attention was taken by the sight of Hal labouring up the stone steps just above him. He could see that the youth's legs were shaking with the effort.

'Perhaps we'd better call a halt for a while,' the old farmer declared. 'I'm running short of breath.'

Then, abruptly, he turned and sniffed the sky. 'What is that?' he exclaimed. 'Can you smell it?'

'What?' Wira asked.

'Seasnow! The air is thick with it!'

'We're too far inland for seasnow,' Farr commented. 'We must be two hundred miles from the coast.'

'I know seasnow when I smell it!'

'I've been inland many times before, many more times than you, old man,' Farr argued, 'and when it snows here, the flakes are dry and light.'

Kurr held the sleeve of his cloak up to his face. 'Unless, of course,' he laughed, 'the smell is on these clothes.' He laughed again, sheepishly. 'Yes, that's what it is. Kroptur probably had these clothes stored in his barn last winter.'

'I told you it wasn't seasnow.'

'Yes, yes, thank you, Farr,' the farmer said, embarrassed by his mistake.

Across the Face of the World

By now the Haufuth had recovered his breath, and cast about for something to steer the conversation away from the possibility of conflict. 'Who made this road, you ask?' he said, turning to Leith. The boy nodded.

'It was made by the First Men, in the days before ships. Many years they spent building the road, the only link between Firanes and the rest of Faltha. Once it was well maintained, with people employed to collect tolls and repair the road, but with the advent of ships the road traffic fell away, and the tolls did not pay for the repair. So, gradually, the Westway fell into ruin. The villages along the road – like Loulea, Vapnatak and Mjolkbridge – do the best they can to look after it, but it is not what it was.'

'Remember the poles back down in Kilth Keening?' Kurr added. His mistake now forgotten, he joined the lesson. 'They were placed there by the First Men to help travellers keep to the road in times of heavy snow. My guess is that the Windrisians maintain them still, though they do not often use the Westway to ascend to the moors. That accounts for why this section of the road is in such a state of disrepair.'

'Haufuth,' Leith said timidly, 'you speak as though the First Men were real. But didn't you teach us that they were only legends?'

Kurr barked a laugh. 'Caught out by a child! What sort of nonsense have you been teaching our children? There is no such thing as *only* a legend!'

'Just because I find out that something is true doesn't make it any easier to believe,' grumbled the big man. 'I didn't want the children to grow up believing every fairy tale people told them. Open, inquiring minds, that's what they need.'

'When the fairy tale comes riding into their village and makes off with their parents, I'd say it was time to believe,' Farr said flatly.

'For most people the First Men are figures of legend,' Kurr said solemnly, 'but the great stories from the *Domaz Skreud*, the Scroll of Doom, are known amongst the Watchers. I learned them in my youth, when I . . . never mind.'

'What stories?' Stella asked, filled with curiosity.

Kurr glanced at Hal, who still breathed heavily. 'We have a moment,' the old farmer said. 'In fact, it might be an idea if we ate lunch now. We still have some way to climb. During the meal I will tell you about the First Men, since aspects of the stories relate to our own predicament.'

'We know how the Most High made the world and all that is contained within it,' Kurr began, lapsing into the formal story-telling idiom common to all Falthan people. The Company settled comfortably beside the path, sharing bread and cheese. 'But this was not the only world He made. Throughout the fields of time and space He scattered countless worlds and made many creatures to live on these worlds. He then travelled across the field of space and chose some of these creatures to be His servants.

'On our world the Most High chose to anoint only one creature, the race of men, who in their primeval state were as the beasts around them. He set then a whisper in their hearts, drawing those who would listen across the wilderness and the desert to a bountiful vale in the north, and He followed them as a great thundercloud. On the lofty rim of the vale the Chosen waited, and the towering cloud drew swiftly up behind them. Down a narrow trail into the virgin land they went; in terror of the rearing cloud and in fear of the tortuous path they trod, yet they went in obedience to the voice that called them on, and they walked in hope. On a hill in the centre of the vale they rested, with the great cloud high above them. It was there, in the Vale of the North, that the Most High came with fire upon the race of men.

'From the overshadowing presence of the Most High descended flaming pillars of lightning, and each of the chosen was enveloped in fire. In the midst of the flaming pillars another, greater, column of fire formed, as the Most High joined with men. Fiery filaments sprung from His presence, joining the pillars of flame, and in that moment was Man touched with the Fire of Life, imparting fellowship with the Most High, and for a while glory burned on a hill in the Vale.

'With His Right Hand the Most High touched a rock. From

the heart of the rock sprung forth a Fountain of quintessential Water, with a potency sufficient to douse the pillars of fire. Then in a great cloud the Presence vanished from amongst them, going they knew not where, yet leaving something in the heart of each one present. And as the spray from the fountain sprinkled their upturned faces, the Chosen fancied they heard a Voice speak within their minds.

'At that time the Most High entered into a covenant with men, saying: "I am the One, the Most High God. I have given you life and set Fire to your hearts, a Fire which will grow if nurtured with reverence and fear and love. My Presence remains with all who seek to dwell within the Fire of Life, and in the mist of the morning and in the cool of the evening I will walk with anyone who earnestly desires fullness of life. You cannot grow without My touch; you cannot sustain the flame by your own deeds, however praiseworthy. Yet by My touch your works shall endure and have merit, and shall add strength and beauty to My creation. For this end I have gifted you Life, that you might live for My glory, adding perfection to that which is already Perfect.

'"I will walk with your sons and your daughters, and when their hearts burn for Me, I will share with them of the fire. Should any choose to reject the fire for which they were made they shall leave the Vale of the Chosen, and they will wander the world in search of truth but will not find it.

'"Fire I have given unto you, and fire shall be your sustenance. You shall walk the vale of your birth, eating and drinking of the Fire of Life, and you shall not die. Fellowship you will have, one with another and each with the Most High, and by this fellowship will your flame grow, becoming strong and pure. When the flame has reached maturity I will come for you and translate you beyond the walls of time to a place you know not. As a token and a promise of this I have set amongst you a spring, the Fountain of Eternal Life, from which none may drink. Yet the fountain shall seal my covenant in you, and I will constantly refresh your spirits by its waters.

185

"'I am the Most High; I am the Fountain in your midst, the Flame in the centre of your being. Rejoice and fear not! My words cannot fail of their fruition."

'As darkness after light was the cessation of His words, and all the people mourned His departure, yet rejoiced at the grace shown to them. And in the Vale of the North they went about their lives outwardly unchanged, but inwardly transformed by the gifts of the Most High.'

'We must not tarry on this road,' Farr said after a while. 'There is no shelter here were it to rain or snow.' He looked pointedly at the old farmer.

One by one the travellers arose, groaning and stretching weary limbs, then led the horses slowly up the remainder of the climb. The air was still and bitterly cold; and with the keenness of sight common at this altitude, they could now gaze across Kilth Keening below them to the heights opposite. Around a corner they went, and a wider vista opened behind them: snow and ice wreathed the upper slopes of the fells across the Torrelstrommen valley. Further up their eyes were drawn, to where the mountain peaks jutted into the clouds. Further up still Leith looked, and then gasped: an immense grey cloud towered over the mountains, dwarfing them. Dirty black at the bottom, puffy and white near its top, the cloud leaned menacingly towards them.

At that moment the path levelled out. They had climbed the Snaerfence, crossing the threshold into Breidhan Moor. Ahead the land was open, a wild wasteland of rolling, snow-covered hills, into which the Westway disappeared without trace. But the Company had eyes only for the cloud behind them. Leith thought of the cloud that had shepherded the First Men into the Vale of the North. Had it looked like this? As he gazed on the towering cloud, rising rampart upon rampart into the sky, he could feel awe settling upon him, awe edged with fear.

'Seasnow!' Farr breathed, in spite of himself.

'Yes, and headed our way,' the old farmer grated.

'There are few places to hide from storms on Breidhan Moor,'

Wira said. 'We'd better move on, and hope that the snow stays away.'

The travellers turned their backs on the approaching cloud and hurried on into the moors.

It grew dark as they stopped to eat their evening meal. 'We can go no further,' the farmer warned them. 'It is now two weeks from the full moon of Midwinter's Night and, even if the storm passes, there'll be no moon tonight. We cannot risk travelling in the dark.'

A little way ahead of them Farr let out a cry. 'A fire site!' he called to them. 'Someone has built a fire here in the last few days. Come quickly and see!' The others hurried after him.

Just to the left of the road the land dipped into a bowl-shaped dell, sheltered from the east and west by limestone walls. Snow lay deep around the perimeter of the bowl, but at the centre it was only a thin wispy covering. 'Look!' Farr called, brushing aside the snow.

The Company scrabbled around in the deepening gloom. 'Definitely a fire site,' Kurr agreed. 'A group of people spent the night here two – no, probably three – days ago.'

From the darkness beside him came a cry. Kurr wheeled around: it was Leith.

'What's wrong?'

Leith could not answer. Instead, he held out his hand. There was something small in his palm. Kurr bent over, peering through the murk. It was a birch bark carving.

The farmer held the carved figure up against the pale eastern sky. 'What is it?' he asked.

Hal answered him. 'I've seen it before. It is a carving of my father. Leith himself made it.'

Beside him Leith stared into the distance, his expression as blank and unchanging as that on the carving in the farmer's hand.

'Well, there's no doubt about it, then,' the Haufuth breathed. 'The captives were here, and had wits enough to leave a sign behind.'

* * *

187

The fire burned brightly and soup simmered in the pot. While Hal tended the meal, the others set up a shelter against the threat of seasnow. They arranged their packs in a semicircle around the fire and used their staves to make a frame, the opening to the east. Spare cloaks and some of the wood they had brought up from the valley lined the frame; in this fashion the shelter was completed. Wira tethered the horses to a limestone outcrop some way up the far side of the dell, then made his way back to the shelter.

And not a moment too soon. From their seats around the fire, the Company watched dim grey snowflakes filter down past the doorway and settle on the ground. Before long the snow fell heavily, swirling and slanting from right to left across the blackness in front of them. A few flakes backed into their shelter; heavy snow, wet from its journey across the sea, the sort that fell on the coast. The wind gusted above them, but the shelter was exposed only to the eddies, being spared the full force of the gale because it was at the bottom of the dell. Outside the white blanket deepened.

'It never snows like this on the moors,' Wira said.

'Open your eyes,' his brother commented.

Again the Haufuth moved to quell a potential argument, turning to the figure of the old farmer outlined in the flickering fire. 'I'm glad you advised us to bring wood up on the moors. It would be a cold night otherwise.'

Kurr grunted his thanks for the acknowledgement.

Time passed slowly. Hal stirred the embers of the fire. Outside, the snow continued to fall in a pale curtain, and now lay inches thick on the ground. The others saw the reflected flames dancing in the eyes of the old farmer. He began to speak again and Leith closed his eyes, letting the rich, deep voice wash over him.

'Now I will tell you the story of the leaving of the Vale. It is called *Dhaur Bitan*, The Poisoning.' After clearing his throat, he began.

'On a fair spring day a boy child was born to parents of high rank in the House of Leuktom, a child exceedingly beautiful to behold. His features seemed to all to be perfectly formed, and in his countenance the dullest could read a destiny of greatness and lordship. At the foot of the fountain in the Square of Rainbows, his parents gave thanks publicly for their firstborn son, a gift to them and to the Vale from the hands of the Most High.

'Many watched the antics of the small but growing boy with amusement and love; for in those days, a thousand years after the settlement of the Vale, the play of children in the streets near the fountain had become rare. Only those who were of the families of clan leaders now lived in the streets from where the Rock of the Fountain could be descried. Saurga, the younger brother of the leader of the Kerd Clan, had long been held in high esteem for his wisdom and compassion. Now, with the birth of such a son, he was further exalted among the people of the Vale.

'On the morning of his third birthday the young boy escaped the vigilance of his mother and was gone from the city a while. When he returned the people of the Vale marvelled, for the child had met with the Most High and received from Him the Fire of Life at an age younger than any other. In but a little while he surpassed his parents in knowledge of the *Fuirfad*, the Way of Fire; and even Weid his instructor was amazed at the depth of understanding the boy demonstrated. His naming day was moved forward from his fifth birthday, and he was named Kannwar, the Guardian of Knowledge.

'The years of maturing were marked in Kannwar by wisdom and insight, and he was ever desirous of justice and fierce in its defence. Much time he spent in the Hall of Lore, debating with the elders and poring over scrolls written by scholars of centuries gone by. Seldom did he join in play with those his own age, and his peers, though in awe of him, did not understand his disposition. The Council of Leaders often discussed the young man, some seeking to appoint him to a position of responsibility so as to test him. Yet the wisest among them counselled patience, divining that knowledge alone would not suffice to make the youth a leader of men. And so they waited and watched; and some noted that Kannwar had no close friend.

'When Kannwar was eighteen years of age Raedh, the leader of the Kerd Clan, departed from among them and all knew he had been translated. The Council of Leaders assembled and selected Garadh son of Raedh, a man of gentle demeanour, to assume leadership of the clan. All applauded the choice save Kannwar son of Saurga, who saw the rejection of the claims of his father to leadership as an injustice and a slight to his family. His own wish to become a leader of men seemed thwarted; for now, instead of being the son of a clan leader, Kannwar was merely cousin to a leader to whom might conceivably be given lordship of the House of Leuktom. Saurga dismissed the grievance of his son and worked to support Garadh his nephew. In heaviness of spirit Kannwar spent much time alone in the Hall of Lore among the scrolls, but these could not console him for the loss of his destiny. He took to wandering alone; seldom thereafter was the young man seen in Dona Mihst. His cousin Garadh sought him out and attempted to heal his wounds with words of conciliation, but the bitterness within Kannwar turned to pride and, after words of scorn, he smote his clan leader a blow to the head, knocking him senseless to the ground. Before Garadh could recover, he fled, and not until the end did he return to the City of the Fountain.

'For three years Kannwar kept his own counsel, walking in ways none other had ever trod, travelling far from Dona Mihst and gathering knowledge of the world. His parents despaired of his whereabouts. Some guessed that he had met with an accident, not unheard of even in those days of joy, while others speculated that he had been translated by the Most High. Garadh did not reveal what had taken place between himself and his cousin, for fear of besmirching the name of the family of Saurga.

'At about this time a tall, gaunt figure began speaking in the outer villages to such as would listen. In ringing tones he spoke of justice and fairness for all; with subtle words he placed questions and doubts in the hearts of men. The villagers lived far from the fountain, and suddenly this began to trouble some among them, who began to wonder why they were excluded from the great city where only leaders and their families lived. With great command of the *Fuirfad*, the stranger reminded them of the founding of the

Vale, when all were as one; and of the settlement of Dona Mihst, in which all had been given a place close to the Water of Eternal Life. He told them of his many travels, of a vast, rich world waiting outside the walls of their small valley; of a world of promise in need of ordering, a world of bounty ripe for possession. Men had lived in timidity and fear long enough, he said; it was time they matured and broke out of the womb in which they had long been imprisoned. This thinking men adopted as their own and, becoming discontent, amplified the arguments of the grey-cloaked stranger. He would then move on, seeking new audiences to sway, new hearts to poison, and soon he had a sizeable following.

'The hearts of some misgave them and they reported these words to the Council of Leaders. Weid of the House of Wenta covertly attended a number of meetings held by the mysterious stranger, and discerned that in this man the Fire of Life had gone out. The mark of the fire he definitely bore, and his knowledge of the *Fuirfad* was considerable; but his words were not the words of the Most High and his agreeable manner hid a disfigurement of spirit. Then Weid remembered his former pupil, and for a while would not accept that this sower of rebellion was Kannwar, the child of promise. But soon this could no longer be doubted.

'A group of discontented villagers sought an audience with the Council of Leaders. At their head strode the stranger who, though professing reluctance, had been persuaded to lead the delegation. The Council of Leaders discussed the grievances, but being pure themselves could not understand the minds of those led by Kannwar. The youth they had once known frightened them, for they could see an unnatural change in him, and dire threats were written on his brow. None but Weid perceived that the Most High had withdrawn the fire from Kannwar, for none but Weid conceived that such a thing might be possible. After the angry group had departed from the hall, the Council of Leaders debated over a course of action but could not agree upon what should be done. They decided therefore to observe only, in spite of the warnings of Weid of the House of Wenta.

'Emissaries Kannwar now set in the city itself to disseminate his ideas, but he himself remained hidden. Many there were who listened to and believed words of anger and hate spoken in those days, though fewer openly joined the ranks of the disaffected. Few in the city, however, opposed Kannwar in word or in deed, for many felt guilty of the privileged positions which (as it now seemed to them) they had occupied in the stead of their fellow men; and others found they did not have the courage to publicly denounce the purposeful young man, silenced as they were by threat and intimidation.

'Early one morning, during the first stages of the conflict, the city awoke to find an arrow embedded in the Square of Rainbows between the Tower of Worship and the Rock of the Fountain. Its iron shaft glowed red-hot; it was tipped with gold and bore *mariswan* feathers that moved gently in the morning breeze. To the crowd that gathered in the square it seemed that a voice spoke, fraught with warning. None could remember the exact words, yet all felt a presage of doom. Some then repented, and not a few forsook the society of Kannwar. The arrow then vanished; only the mark of its landing remained. It seemed then that disaster could be averted, but with words of blandishment and guile Kannwar bound people to himself with promises of freedom from innocence and exhortations selectively quoted from the *Fuirfad*. Thus he claimed that his followers alone did the will of the Most High, for only they saw the need to use the gifts they had been given to rule the whole world; only they saw the need to abandon the Vale. It was at this time that Kannwar openly advocated in public speech the breaking of the prohibition imposed by the Most High.

'He stood in front of a great crowd of men, saying: "The Most High has purposed that on the day you drink of the fountain the eyes of your spirit will be opened and you will be like Him, possessing all knowledge and power. These are the gifts we need to possess the whole world, and they can be obtained only through the partaking of the Water of Eternal Life. The fountain is pleasing to the eye, will feed our bodies and will enrich our spirits; how can the Most High mean for us never to drink of it? For His plan is that we should drink of the fountain, and on that day we shall break free of the restraints of childhood and become men indeed, no longer dependent on the Most High for every gift but able to give and receive pleasure from our own hands. He is but waiting for the time when His children grow into this understanding. Our task is to persuade all those who dwell in the city of their need to partake of the fountain."

'In the midst of a heated debate in the Square of Rainbows a second flaming arrow landed, throwing the factions into disarray. Again the warning and the premonition were felt, accompanied by a command: rebellion must cease and the leaders tried in the Hall of Lore. The supporters of Kannwar then made their escape from Dona Mihst, and not a hand was laid upon them. The rumour of the words of the Most High spread throughout the city, and many who had considered rebellion in their hearts were afraid and hid, fearing the judgement to come. The Council of Leaders met and decided that the words of the Most High had ended the rebellion, for none of the rebels were abroad in the city. Yet some opposed this, saying that the council was bound to place the leaders of the trouble on trial. Dissension among members led to open quarrel, and no decision could be made.

'Just before noon on the day following the second arrow, Kannwar returned to the Square of Rainbows with the force of his followers behind him. In the hundreds it numbered, men and women, and all were armed with sharp sticks, clubs or rocks. There Kannwar issued a challenge to the Council of Leaders, calling them to be present as witnesses to what he was about to do. As word of the challenge became general knowledge, the people of Dona Mihst and those from all other villages in the Vale slowly gathered in the square. The two factions of First Men, the group led by the council hardly outnumbering those who acknowledged Kannwar as their lord, opposed each other in silence; the splash of the Fountain between them the only source of noise. Then one of the council, Sthane of the House of Saiwiz, the least of the clan leaders, stepped out and stood before the tall, grey-robed rebel and said: "Son of Saurga, will you not return to the path of wisdom from which you have strayed? The deed you purpose to do may not be done by men, for of the Fountain of Eternal Life none may drink, lest they drink of the judgement of the Most High. I call you, with the people of the Vale as my witnesses, to reconsider your action. But if you do not, I at least will oppose you." And the old man folded his arms across his chest and stood grimly, feet apart, facing the grey figure. None in the city went to his aid.

'Kannwar answered Sthane by raising his huge club and, with one fell blow, slaying the old man where he stood. With a cry, he leapt over the body of the clan leader and ran unopposed to the fountain. Stooping beneath the great jet of pure water, he cupped his hands and put them to the fountain. In utter silence, with the eyes of Dona Mihst upon him, he raised his hands to his lips and drank.

'Kannwar turned to his followers with blazing eyes and shouted in triumph, a shout suddenly cut off by the appearance of a shadow looming over the Square of Rainbows; a shadow formed as a giant Figure stepped in front of the sun. His feet were planted on either side of the town, and His white-robed body and jewel-crowned head towered above the stricken city. In His left hand He carried a bow and in His right hand a flaming arrow. His countenance was terrible to behold. Men shrank in terror from that gaze, yet none could flee; all were transfixed as though time itself were frozen. Slowly, in silence, the Figure nocked the arrow to the bow, drew the string back and raised it to His shoulder. With a swift movement he loosed the flaming arrow at Kannwar, and its gold tip hewed off his still-cupped right hand and buried itself in the side of the Rock of the Fountain. Then Kannwar cried aloud for the third time, a cry of anguish and fear. A tremor shook the city, throwing many to the ground. Cracks appeared in the marble flagstones of the Square of Rainbows, and all around was a noise as of groaning, which slowly died away into silence.

'Then did the Most High speak to the doomed city, saying: "What is this you have done? You have neglected the gifts I have given you, regarding them as worthless, and have sought after the one gift I have forbidden you. Foolishly you seek your own dominion: which one of you, by his own hand, created any world or the hosts within it? You have sought to take eternal life by force when it was freely available at My Right Hand. Fools! Did you not know that the very air of the Vale is laden with the spray of the fountain I set amongst you? Every day you breathe eternal life: it is this fountain that has preserved you thus far. Your bodies cannot yet contain the undiluted Water of Life. He who drank of the fountain, he whom I now name the Destroyer, will surely now never die. I shall not withhold the gift of the fountain from him. He will be tormented for the rest of time by the power in his body, a power he cannot control, a power that will destroy his spirit and his soul and his mind while preserving his body forever. The gift is thus his punishment: he has his wish, he is free of My dominion, and he will lose the gifts I gave to him and keep only the one he stole from Me.

"'But now, you men of the Vale, heed My judgment. My complaint against the Council of Leaders is this: why did you not obey Me? And My grievance against the city is this: why did you not heed My words? You did not call the leaders of rebellion to account, being concerned only with your own opinions. Though you yourselves did not rebel, in your disobedience you set yourselves against My Face. Thus you have forfeited your right to the water of the fountain, and the Fire of Life will die within you, to be given to another generation. You shall be banished from the Vale, and for many years will have to survive alone in the world ere I visit you again with My Presence. You shall take nothing with you, no relic or scroll or treasure to remind you of joys past, for the Vale and all things within it I shall utterly destroy. One thing only shall you bear on your journeys, to remind you that I have not forsaken you. The symbol of unity among your clans and houses shall be the symbol of My wrath against all evil: the flaming arrow which I now name the *Jugom Ark*, the Arrow of Yoke. If at any time it is produced before the Council of Leaders, be assured that conflict is at hand. Without the unity it represents, you will not survive to see the day of your deliverance. I give it now into the hand of the Arkhos of Landam, who shall select a suitable guardian for the arrow.

'"One Clan only retains My favour; in memory of the right-eousness and courage of Sthane of the House of Saiwiz, the Rehtal Clan shall be the prophets of My words in the days to come.

'"Now, unto those of the Vale who followed the Destroyer into rebellion of the heart, I raise My Right Hand in judgement. Those who set their face against the will of the Most High shall die."

'The Figure in white raised His Hand above His Head, and a great earthquake rocked the Vale, splitting the Square of Rainbows in two. And He pointed a finger of His Right Hand towards the Council of Leaders on the far side of the smoking chasm, and spoke sorrowfully: "Now go! Flee for your lives, for hardly shall you escape the destruction to come." And from those cowering in fear at His feet the Most High turned His face and vanished from the world.

'The council and their followers turned then and ran from that awful place, leaving Kannwar and the others to their fate. Each one made his way to the sheer wall of the Vale northeast of the city. As they ran, great tremors and shakings of the earth over-took them, throwing many to the ground. Huge fissures opened in the earth and fire and smoke belched forth from them, flowing over the land about them. In their terror some cast themselves into these fiery chasms or stumbled unseeing into the rivers of fire. Accompanied by the noise of tortured earth and the smell of sulphur, they ascended the Vale wall by a narrow path, and those who still lived assembled at the rim of the valley and watched its destruction.

'All was a haze of smoke and steam and the world roared about their ears. Those with keenest sight then descried a vast wall of water advancing along the Vale from the south. As they watched, it covered the mighty city of Dona Mihst, and the Tower of Worship and the Hall of Lore were no more. The waters divided in two below them and flowed up the arms of the valley to their left and to their right. The hill upon which the refugees stood shook from the battering of the wave as it swept past. As the water engulfed the fissures in the earth, a roaring and a mist rose up out of the Vale, billowing higher than where they stood, and in mercy hid the final destruction from their sight. Though muted now by the fog, the noise of it continued for several hours, slowly subsiding into a bleak silence.

'Thus the First Men were cast adrift, abandoned in a desert land. For months they wandered along the rim of the Vale without purpose, following the northward branch of the now-dead valley. When the mist finally dissipated they could see that the valley was drowned, filled with water released from the south by a terrible violence. Among the survivors were the members of the Council of Leaders, who attempted to order the lives of the people along lines they had known in the Vale, but most were too dispirited to do more than merely exist. The Jugom Ark they had, but it offered them no comfort, only a reminder of what they had lost and the manner in which they had lost it. Already some among the leaders had begun quarrelling over the bearing of it, and during the second month of the journey north Furist, Arkhos of Landam, and Raupa, Arkhos of Leuktom, came to blows over the still-warm arrow.

'It was Reynir of the House of Wenta who first suggested that they should try to find the pasture lands said to be to the north. The Council of Leaders adopted his idea, and after six months of travel they crossed the upper reaches of the valley, beyond the furthest extent of the water. In the dim light of a dull evening the refugees saw a tall, grey-robed figure hurrying up the valley ahead of them. He turned towards them with a shrill cry and lifted a threatening, handless arm. Furist then held the Jugom Ark aloft and when the figure saw it he quailed, then turned and fled from their path, towards the east.

'Finally the forlorn group escaped from the desert and came to greener lands, but not before death had visited some among them. All saw it and were ashamed. A remnant only remained alive to reach the Aleinus, the life-giving river of the north. On the banks of that broad river Furist and Raupa again contended one with another for possession of the Jugom Ark, and the council consigned the care of the arrow to Bewray of the House of Saiwiz. There on the greensward the survivors of the destruction parted company, for some clan leaders aligned themselves with Furist and others with Raupa over the issue of the arrow. The greater body crossed the river in driftwood rafts and travelled north out of knowledge. With Furist as their leader, and with the Jugom Ark accompanying them, the remainder travelled slowly west along the south bank of the great river.

'Generations of men have passed and those born in the Vale died, one by one. They settled in fair countries, though few of those who had dwelt in Dona Mihst could see their beauty. Children were born to them, sons and daughters without knowledge of the Way of Fire, never to be called to that secret meeting with the Most High.'

Sorrow hung cloyingly around the voice of the farmer. He took a deep breath.

'There is little else to tell of the years of joy, for only fragments of old songs remain; much has been lost in the destruction that laid waste the Vale of man's youth. Swift is the passing of a peaceful age, and uneventful tales are short in the telling. Pause and reflect upon the grace of the Most High and the folly of men.'

'Is that all?' Leith asked, incredulous. 'Didn't the Most High rescue them? Did he just ignore the First Men?'

'Most of the Watchers believe that the Most High has washed His hands of men. Others, like Kroptur, argue that He still involves Himself in our affairs. Personally, I have never seen any evidence of it.'

Outside, the deep wet snow packed down hard. The blizzard howled as strongly as ever, but the Company sheltered in an eerie calm, thinking about the First Men, their own forefathers. There, in a snow-filled hollow on Breidhan Moor, a few lonely people sheltered against the elemental forces of the world, seemingly protected by nothing but their own resourcefulness. One by one they fell asleep by the fire, under the shadow of the cloud.

CHAPTER 10

THE FENNI

THERE WAS TO BE no travelling for the next two days. During that time the storm relented only slowly, and the Company anxiously waited it out in their makeshift shelter. They kept surprisingly warm, with their body heat enough to maintain the air at a comfortable temperature. To keep occupied, they repaired various rips and tears in their clothing and packs, talked about their home villages, and listened as Kurr told them more about the First Men.

Wira re-emerged from peering out of the airhole early on the third morning, and reported: 'The storm seems to have blown itself out. Now, perhaps, we can be on our way!'

Slowly, carefully, the travellers dug themselves out of their snow-lined cocoon. This was a much more difficult task than they had imagined, because they had to free their packs and cloaks from the grip of the heavy blanket that pressed down on them. It was not until mid-morning that the travellers stood silently on the surface of a cold carpet stretching unbroken in every direction.

Their first concern was for the horses. This was compounded when they discovered that their mounts were no longer where they had been tethered. A frantic search was begun, with everyone scratching around in the snow in ever-widening circles. Finally Hal let out a shout: wisely, the horses had taken shelter on the far side of the limestone wall at the eastern end of the dell, and had received only a light dusting of snow.

The next problem was far greater. The Westway had completely disappeared under the seasnow. Because of the frequent gales that swept over the area, there were no poles on Breidhan Moor. Farr told them that the road was marked by a line of boulders, but these had been covered without trace by the billowing drifts. With mounting despair, Kurr looked out over the moors. The view was much the same in every direction, white mounds, blue sky and hard, dazzling light.

'We should make for the highest point, then fix a course on a landmark on the horizon,' Farr suggested. 'There's no sense in charging off in the general direction without any reference point.'

So the travellers loaded up their horses and began the long, slow slog across country. But the next serious problem immediately became evident: although the surface of the snow was hard, having frozen overnight, it was soft underneath, and the horses kept breaking through and getting stuck. Time after time the travellers had to stop and free them, and after a while their legs began to bleed below the fetlock, where they rubbed against the crusty surface of the snow. Their progress was painfully slow, marked by a series of blood-rimmed holes. After a stop to unload the horses, the Company carried the packs themselves, and the horses broke through the hard snow crust less frequently. In this fashion the Company crawled up the nearest ridge.

The sun was near its zenith when finally they made the summit of the low ridge. Looking back, they could still see the dell and the remains of their three-day camp, a grey smudge in a rolling sea of white. A brisk east wind blew dry and cold across the exposed bones of the moors, blowing the softer snow away from their compacted footprints, leaving a raised trail to indicate their morning's tortuous progress.

Away to the east a line of hills raised themselves above the snowy sea. 'The Brethren,' Farr pointed, 'maybe thirty leagues away. The Westway goes in that direction.'

Leith looked back over his shoulder at the site of their shelter, then ahead into the distance, the hills seemingly floating above the snow, painfully white. *At this rate*, he thought, *it'll take forever to get there.*

'We can't take too much of this,' the Haufuth groaned. 'I can't feel my feet!'

'We should light a fire,' added Wira.

'But not here,' his brother put in. 'Not on this ridge. We need to get out of the wind.'

Kurr grunted, then moved off, leading his horse towards firmer snow.

Lunch was eaten under the shadow of shoulder-high spruce trees which had found a sheltered gully to grow in. The fire burned the last of their fuel as they huddled together, trying to stay warm. As each log went into the flames, an unspoken realisation grew. They were not going to make it across the moors. While Hal rubbed a salve into the abrasions on the horses' legs, the others sat there, seemingly drained of energy, while the afternoon passed slowly by.

Stella stared at the fire with glazed eyes. Her front was warm but her back was freezing, and her bones ached with the cold. They had been much warmer in the shelter, where the company had been cheerful and she didn't have to worry about going home. *Home*, she sighed. She realised that they were about to turn for home, beaten by the snow. The moment her feet turned for home, her life would begin to end . . . Across the fire sat Wira. Stella tried to catch his eyes with hers, but his face was downcast, his features set grimly as if drained of energy. Casting her gaze upwards, she watched the smoke from their fire curl lazily up out of the gully, then move off behind them in the wind. Everything here was stark and sharply defined: the marble whiteness of the snow, the icy blueness of the cold afternoon sky, the crispness of the line that separated snow and sky. She looked again, tried to clear her eyes, then gasped.

The shapes of men stood above them, looking into the gully.

The others turned to Stella, then followed her gaze upwards. Four men stood there silently, black figures outlined against the pale blue sky already purpling with the twilight. The smoke of their camp drifted up past them, a message for anyone to read. As one, the travellers jumped up and went for their weapons, but they were too late. There was a shout, and the menacing figures had drawn bows. Another shout, and an arrow flew between Farr and Wira, stopping the Company in their tracks.

Down the gully came the four black figures. Leith looked towards the Storrsen brothers, whose faces were white, drained of blood. No one moved. No one spoke.

'*Fenni dach?*' asked the first of the figures. '*Fenni dach?*'

The travellers looked at each other, but made no reply.

'*Hasteval! Forlin du andach!*' the lead figure called to one of his fellows.

Leith waited. A tall figure crunched through the silence and approached the campfire.

'Not speak Fenni?' the man asked.

'No, we don't speak Fenni,' Kurr replied hoarsely. 'What is Fenni?'

'Us Fenni!' the tall man replied sharply, pointing to his own chest, then at his companions. 'Why you on Myrvidda?'

'We're travelling on the Westway,' Kurr replied cautiously.

'What you speak?' the man responded, eyes narrowing. 'What you say?'

'Ah – we are going on the road,' said Kurr.

The tall man laughed so hard his cap fell from his head, revealing long blond locks. He turned to the others. '*Descray oyval, descray oyval!*' he repeated, and the others laughed too, the sound rattling around in the narrow gully.

'No *oyval*, no road, only *anvar* snow! Where you go?'

'Following other men,' the Haufuth blurted out before anyone could stop him.

'Other men? Horses men?' There was a silence. The figures drew a little closer in the fading light.

'Yes,' Kurr replied eventually.

'*Iglindin descray du tendar!*' the leader called, and swiftly the Company was surrounded by the four tall warriors. Ropes were produced with which to bind the travellers.

'You come with us!' the tall interpreter commanded. One of

the men began to tie Farr's hands together. The ashen-faced Vinkullen man did not resist.

Three more figures strode down into the gully, one dressed in red. The others all bowed to him as he approached. Sharp words were exchanged between him and their questioner, who deferred to him with a low, sweeping bow. '*Undin descray!*' he commanded, and Farr's ropes were removed. The red man nodded as they fell to the ground.

At the prompting of the bowmen, the travellers packed up the remains of their meal and reloaded their footsore horses. Then, at a command, they were marched up out of the gully by the escort, with the red-clad man bringing up the rear.

'Are these the Bhrudwan riders?' whispered Leith nervously to his brother. Hal was about to reply but Wira, who was immediately behind them, interrupted.

'No, these people are Fenni.' Leith turned and almost stumbled. The warrior nearest him growled; Leith kept walking.

'Fenni? The only Fenni I've heard of are the cruel northern mountain gods who— oh . . .'

Wira began a reply, but was cut off by another growl from their guard.

The captors and their captives struggled up out of the gully and struck across the snow-cloaked moor. There were no landmarks to tell the Company where they were being taken, or whether they had been on this stretch of moor before. The setting sun provided the only clue. They were travelling towards the northeast, with the sun at their backs – away, Leith was sure, from the Westway. For a while there was no sound except the soft shuffle of feet and hoofs on crusty snow; then the younger Storrsen, who had increased his pace slightly, drew level with Leith and Hal.

'Haven't you heard about the Fenni?' Wira whispered.

Leith shook his head slightly without turning around, for fear of the guard. 'At home we tell stories about them, the stick-men of the snowfields, cruel and fierce, with a deep hatred of outsiders. If Breidhan Moor is their land, why didn't you tell us about them?'

'They're not supposed to live here. Further inland lies a plateau called the Myrvidda; that's where they are said to live. Anyway, the stories we told were just that – stories. I never dreamed that the Fenni were a real people! No one in Mjolkbridge believes in them.'

'Are you sure that these people are the Fenni?'

'They said so, didn't they? No, there's no mistake. Our stories tell of the red-cloaked man.'

'Who is he?' Leith asked. He was beginning to shake, not only from the cold.

'A priest.'

No more was forthcoming, so Leith risked a sideways glance. Wira stared straight ahead, lips pursed, brow furrowed, face drained of colour.

'Wira,' Leith asked quietly, knowing the answer as he did so, 'are we in danger?'

'Danger?' Wira replied, his voice strangely flat. 'Danger? If our stories are true, we're already dead.'

Up ahead the Haufuth let out a cry as he broke through the snow crust. The horse beside him also sank into the snow, bringing the procession up short. The black figures converged on the trapped man and horse, struggling to free them in the gathering gloom, all the time urged on by the man in the red cloak. Eventually the horse was freed and the Haufuth climbed out of the hole and dusted himself off, but he became stuck again almost immediately.

The man in red cried out. Instantly one of the figures darted away into the distance. The other Fenni gathered around the priest, save one bow-wielding guard who was left to watch over the prisoners. Wira and Farr wasted no time telling the others of their desperate position. Farr suggested that they attempt to escape immediately, with only one guard to overpower, but Kurr was against it. 'He would take two of us with his bow before we got to him, and then we would be at the mercy of the others. No; I'd rather find out what they want and settle this peacefully. See to it that no one makes any move that could be interpreted as aggressive,' he said, gazing with meaning at the hotheaded older Storrsen.

Farr was about to argue further when a barked command, the sort that is intelligible in any language, cut him short.

The Fenni made their prisoners stand in a line. Leith swallowed hard and tried to be brave. Perhaps his time had come to die, but he would not cry or plead for mercy. Beside him his brother appeared calm, and Leith took some comfort from that. If Hal was not afraid, perhaps there was nothing to fear.

The figure who had been sent away now returned, carrying a pack. It was opened, and flat, paddle-shaped objects were handed out amongst the Fenni. What sort of weapons were these? Leith wondered. Pieces of leather stretched out over a wooden frame? The members of the Company braced themselves as the figures approached.

'*Kunlun in*,' their interpreter said. 'Put on *snershil*!' And he showed them how to attach the paddle-like objects to their feet.

This the Company did, to their puzzlement. 'These are special snow shoes!' Kurr cried, but the others did not understand him until they took several awkward steps forward. Instead of breaking through the snow, the wide-framed shoes spread their weight over a wider area, and they could walk in safety upon it. Similar shoes were fitted to the horses and, after some delay while the horses were coaxed forward, they moved off, slowly at first, then more sure-footedly, into the darkening sky.

They reached the Fenni campsite at the edge of darkness. About a dozen tents made a circle in an open, flat area of moorland from which the snow had been cleared. The waxing half-moon lit the snow-covered hills around them with a silver sheen, against which stood the black silhouettes of the tents, animals and other possessions of the Fenni. Several huge cattle-like beasts stood at the far edge of the Fenni camp. *Aurochs! They must be aurochs!* Leith marvelled, his danger forgotten for the moment. Even he had heard the fanciful tales of the aurochs, cattle taller than men, which had once roamed freely across the length and breadth of Firanes. He shook his head in wonder. Surely they walked in another world, another place and time, in which fireside tales rose up out of the ground and mixed themselves up in the lives of ordinary people.

But, he reminded himself, *this is no ordinary journey.*

In a clearing at the centre of the camp a bright bonfire burned, surrounded by dozens of people sitting and talking. They pulled back as the strangers approached, making room for them at the fireside. Mothers hurried their children away; others joined the circle around the fire, emerging from their low-slung tents. All wore the same black garb – all save the old man dressed in red, and an even older man clad in chiefly white, sitting silently in the shadows. The priest beckoned his prisoners to be seated, then stood amidst a profound silence interrupted only by the crackling of flames eagerly devouring dry wood.

The travellers looked into the many faces on the opposite side of the fire. On some they read hostility, others merely idle curiosity, still others showed indifference, boredom or tiredness. But every face came awake when the red-cloaked man began to speak.

He addressed them for quite some time, his words unintelligible to the members of the Company. But his meaning became clearer when he raised his voice, then snatched a blazing firebrand from the flames and pointed it at the prisoners, then at the Fenni themselves. Angry murmurs broke out amongst the gathering.

Kurr leaned over to the Haufuth. 'We're on trial here,' he whispered, 'and we don't even know what the charge is.'

Now the man in red pointed to another man at the far edge of the fire, indicating for him to stand. Gasps came from the Storrsen brothers as he stepped forward into the light.

'Perdu!' cried Farr. 'Is that you?'

The man gasped in turn, his hand going to his mouth in shock and surprise. After a long moment he turned to the red-cloaked priest. A short but animated conversation passed between them, then the man came over to the travellers.

'Farr Storrsen!' he cried. 'My clan chief wishes me to ask: what have you done with our food? What have you done with our dead?'

'Perdu! It *is* you!' Farr replied, rising to his feet. 'What are you doing here? We thought you were dead!'

Across the Face of the World

The man called Perdu glanced back towards the man in red. 'Please!' he pleaded with them, speaking clearly, enunciating every word as though grappling with a seldom-used tongue. 'We will talk later, if things go well. For now, answer my clan chief. What have you done with our food? What have you done with our dead? Answer with care, I beg of you.'

Farr was in no mood to answer questions, having too many of his own. Sensing this, his brother pulled him down, then rose to take his place. Farr cried out angrily, but Kurr gripped his arm tightly. 'Be still, you young fool!' the farmer hissed in the ear of the mountain man. 'Your brother has sense enough for both of you; leave it to him!'

Wira faced Perdu. 'We are sorry if our conduct has offended your clan chief,' he said amiably, putting as much quiet authority into his voice as he could muster. 'We know nothing of Fenni food or Fenni dead, though it grieves us to hear of your loss.'

Perdu smiled his relief, then turned to his chief. A long conversation followed, in which Perdu pointed to himself, the travellers and back across the moonlit moors. Finally he returned his attention to the travellers, his face impassive, his eyes solemn.

'My clan chief is sorry, but he must know the truth. He believes that two days ago your party waylaid a group of our people, killing four Fenni and stealing their food. You took a Fenni woman as prisoner. Fenni from another camp saw the attackers, and will be here soon. They will identify you. My clan chief asks: where is your prisoner? Where is our food?

'I personally do not believe that the sons of Storr would do such a thing, and I have told him so,' Perdu continued. 'Nevertheless, Fenni have been killed by strangers riding on the moor in winter, and he awaits an explanation of your purpose.'

'Tell your clan chief that we are not the people he seeks!' Wira replied boldly. 'Two days ago we were huddled in a shelter against this snowfall. We did not emerge until today, and our tracks will verify my tale. We met no other people on the moor.

'As to our purpose,' Wira continued, 'we travel over the highlands not by choice, but because it is the route taken by the enemy

207

we pursue. This enemy is a group of four fearsome Bhrudwan warriors, men who have done the same to us as they have evidently done to you. On Midwinter's Night these riders entered the town of Loulea and took two prisoners, the parents of these young men' – he indicated Leith and Hal – 'and three days later they attacked and killed Storr of Vinkullen as he stood defenceless in the main street of Mjolkbridge. It is for no light reason that we attempt the winter passage of Breidhan Moor. It is my belief that the men you seek are the men we also seek.'

Perdu stood dumbfounded before them. 'They killed Storr? My uncle is dead?' He spread his arms wide, as though trying to encompass the news, and tears began to fall from his cheeks.

A sudden command from behind turned him around. The man in red saw Perdu weeping, and placed an arm on his shoulder. The two men walked over to where the man in white sat, and all three talked at length in the Fenni language, on and on as the fire burned down and the moonshadows deepened. Leith's legs began to ache, and he was light-headed from hunger and tiredness.

At last Perdu turned and faced them again. 'My clan chief welcomes you into his tent,' he said, indicating the whole camp-site with a sweeping gesture. 'This is a great honour, reserved for true friends of the Fenni. He does so because he fears he has made a mistake in accusing you of the deaths of his people. He now believes that you are not the people he seeks, and wishes to hear more of the ones you pursue. That is my wish also. Will you come into his tent?'

The Haufuth, standing tall and straight with regal bearing, replied: 'Yes, we will come into your tent!' When Perdu conveyed this answer, the old man in white smiled and nodded his head.

Drink followed food as the travellers took their ease inside the huge aurochs-skin tent of the clan chief. Leith marvelled at the colourful weavings and tapestries adorning the walls, but his breath was taken away by the huge variety of foods presented to them. The Fenni were traders, and their skill at making goods for sale was complemented by their ability to make a good trade, so their larders were well stocked. Leith certainly had not expected a few short hours ago to be supping at the table of the fabled Fenni of the North. 'Friends unlooked for,' Kroptur had said, and certainly the Fenni had been unlooked for. Leith shook his head in wonderment: Kroptur himself had turned from legend into friend, and now the Fenni had done the same. Perhaps it was not foolish to harbour hopes of success after all. Perhaps he would see his mother and his father again.

During the meal a man and a woman were led in and presented to the travellers. They quickly shook their heads and left. 'The Fenni who saw the Bhrudwan assailants,' Perdu informed them. 'They have told the clan chief that you were not the ones.'

'That's a relief,' Farr responded. 'What would have happened to us had we been found guilty?'

Perdu shook his head. 'You don't want to know. Fenni have great hearts, quick to compassion, quick to anger. Suffice it to say that you would not have seen the morning – if you were fortunate.'

'What are you doing amongst them?' Wira finally asked the question that the brothers were keenest to have answered. 'All we knew was that you went missing on a journey to the Iskelsee. How did you end up here?'

'I was bringing home furs from Fanajokull, on the far side of the Plains of Pollerne, but I miscalculated the thaw and the sea ice broke up around me as I crossed Mudvaerks. I lost everything – my dogs, my furs and Jona, my friend. Remember Jona? He was from Hustad under Vinkullen, experienced in the icelands, and I often accompanied him north. The Fenni found me lying on a beached ice floe on the shores of Iskelsee. They nursed me back from the threshold of death; and when I came to myself again I learned that I was a captive of the Fenni, high up in the trackless wastes of the Myrvidda.

'They gave me a stark choice: become one of the Fenni, or die. They would not let me go, for fear I would tell others the true extent of Fenni hunting lands. But I had grown to respect these people, so the choice was no choice, and I stayed with them. I serve as interpreter whenever the Fenni wish to trade with outsiders. I work with them, I live with them, I am Fenni. I have nothing – except everything I ever wanted.'

'There are people back in Mjolkbridge who still grieve for you,' Wira replied gently, 'who still place flowers on your memorial stone. Could you not have contacted your mother and father, your brothers and sisters? Your cousins?'

'Once or twice I tried to get messages out,' Perdu responded, 'but obviously they were not received. I myself can never return to Mjolkbridge, not even for the love of my family. For now I have another family,' he added and, turning behind him, grasped the hand of a young woman, who smiled shyly. 'My boys are asleep. Perhaps you will meet them tomorrow.'

'Well, well!' Farr shook his head, unable to contain himself. 'Who would have believed it! The Wild Man of Vinkullen tamed by the wild men – or should I say wild woman – of the north! And you've had children on her!' His voice clearly communicated his distaste.

'Don't listen to him,' Wira said. 'I'm glad to hear that you are alive, and that you are happy. With your permission, that is what I will tell your parents, sparing them the details. Is that all right?'

'Sparing the details? Wild woman of the north? What is this?' Perdu leaned towards the Storrsen brothers, eyes narrowing. 'You boys have been too long feuding with your neighbours. The *vidda*'s too big for your petty provincialism. So you would spare my parents the details of my new life? How dare you! Don't despise what you don't understand! These people are not animals, no matter what the First Men say. The Fenni are a noble people, a proud people, who survive in lands no others can endure. They make the men of Vinkullen look soft by comparison.' Farr sneered disbelievingly at this last statement.

'But they are not of the First Men,' Kurr said. 'They are the outcasts, the *losian* who did not receive the Fire from the Most High.'

This Perdu was like his fellow Mjolkbridgers in spirit, even though he did not share their looks. 'And who puts that *losian* nonsense about?' he said. 'Is it not the so-called First Men? Don't you think it's a self-serving way of thinking about the world?'

'You call us self-serving?' Farr bridled. 'Look at you! Couldn't find a woman who would even look at you back home, so you end up making half-breeds with some slattern from the moors! Aren't you better than that?'

Both Kurr and the Haufuth had been trying to restrain the elder Storrsen, and both groaned in frustration. Perdu rocked back on his heels as though he had been struck a blow.

'You had better think carefully, cousin, before you say any more,' he said quietly, 'or I might have to repeat the lesson I gave you the last time you set foot in our house. Remember the black eye?'

'All I remember is a bully who enjoyed picking on those younger than himself,' Farr ground out between gritted teeth. 'But maybe things have changed. Maybe you've grown soft while I've grown up. Maybe I could black *your* eye!' And before he could be restrained he stood abruptly, then threw himself at the older man.

Chaos erupted. Up until this moment the chief and his retinue had been unaware of the building tension, but now they scattered, uttering cries of dismay, as the two men wrestled on the thick woollen rugs. Food splattered everywhere. Kurr tried to intervene, and received a blow on the cheek from a stray elbow as a reward for his efforts. Cursing, he staggered dazedly into the fur-lined wall.

As quickly as that, the situation moved beyond redemption. The hitherto silent clan chief barked out orders and two stocky, broad-shouldered men strode into the tent. At the sound of his clan chief's voice, Perdu's shoulders slumped ashamedly and he surrendered himself to a brutal one-handed grasp from one of the men. For a moment Farr struggled on, throwing a couple of ineffectual roundarms at the Fenni man who had grasped him on the shoulder, then without warning he found himself face down on the floor, with his right arm forced up behind his back. He ceased struggling, but was not allowed to his feet. The only sound in the tent was Farr's heavy breathing.

The Company bowed their heads as knowledge of their perilous position came home to them. To have been invited into the clan chief's tent, and then to have abused his hospitality with their foolish fighting, would undoubtedly call dire consequences down on their heads. These were the Fenni. The grace they had extended to the Company would not extend so far as to excuse this insult. Confirmation was all too clear on the clan chief's grim face.

Moments later, everyone stood outside around the fire. News of the underworlders' indiscretion drew the Fenni clan from their warm tents, some curious, some indignant at what they had heard. The foreigners had somehow escaped justice earlier in the evening, but now they would be made to pay. There they were, hunched together over in the shadows just outside the clan chief's tent, flanked by the dark silhouettes of the *chillan*, the clan chief's personal bodyguard.

And there stood Perdu, beside the clan chief, who was seated on a simple wooden chair. The adopted Fenni was obviously in disgrace, though the ignorant underworlders probably had no idea. He would be required to interpret the decision of the clan chief. Everyone leaned forward as the *chillan* prodded their charges into the firelight.

'The Fenni do not lightly offer hospitality to strangers,' said the clan chief in a surprisingly mild voice, as a white-faced Perdu interpreted. 'The First Men of Faltha have not endeared themselves to the Fenni. We who once ruled the world of Qali have been herded into the *vidda* like wild animals. Yet it is not we who behave like animals in the tents of our hosts.

'If like animals you wish to behave, then like animals you will be treated, and thus the balance the Fenni seek will have been met. So hear my judgement and marvel at the fairness of the Fenni. We withdraw our welcome to you, and shame you thereby. You will be put out of the tents of the Fenni, and must leave the *vidda* tonight. Your horses and weapons will remain with us, lest you are tempted to do us any injury. Should any of our people see you on the *vidda* after this night, they have the right to put you to death.'

Kurr groaned and shook his head in frustration, then shot a

venomous glare like a poisoned dart at Farr Storrsen. Worse, however, was to come.

'The man Perdu is no longer Fenni. I name him *intika*, anathema to the Fenni, and close the doors of our tents to him. He may never again sit at our fires or join us on our hunts. His wife and his children remain Fenni, but become the property of the priest, to serve in the temple of Qali.' A cry, suddenly bitten off, came from somewhere around the fireside. Perdu faltered at this point, deathly pale and with blood trickling unregarded from a lip bitten in shock, and could not continue.

Into the silence strode the red-cloaked priest, with arms upraised and the faintest of smiles on his lips. 'I pronounce you *intika*,' he intoned. 'You are Fenni no longer.' He lowered his arms to point at the distraught man. 'All ties are severed. Begone from among us, underworlder.' Though the priest's words were not translated, the Company knew exactly what had just happened.

Leith waited for the Haufuth or Kurr to say something to put things right, but the two men remained silent. He glanced at his brother, half expecting him to intervene, but Hal gazed steadily in the direction of the clan chief, his eyes hooded, his expression unreadable. As the foreign words came rumbling from the clan chief's mouth, Leith fought to keep down a rising panic.

'What are you talking about?' came a shrill voice from immediately behind him. 'What nonsense is this?' Leith turned, and was shouldered aside by Stella, who marched determinedly forward until she stood opposite the white-cloaked chief.

'No, Stella, no!' the Haufuth cried hoarsely, but his words were choked and came out thinly, and the girl did not hear him.

'Why are you talking about punishing this man?' she challenged, pointing at Perdu. 'What did he do? He only defended himself. It is that man there who should be punished!' She spun on the balls of her feet and pointed straight at Farr. 'What happened here is his fault, nobody else's, and if you can't see that, then your people need another leader! Punish him, and let the rest of us go!' She folded her arms and stood her ground, staring straight at the clan chief.

One of the *chillan* stood directly behind Perdu, as though holding

213

him up, which perhaps he was, Leith thought. The shocked man made no move to translate what Stella had said, which was just as well – they were in enough trouble already – but apparently her intent had been understood, for the clan chief rose out of his chair and stepped forward until there was only a few feet between them.

'You will be silent until I have delivered my judgement,' he said quietly, but in a voice that carried over the crackling and popping of the fire. Perdu translated automatically in a monotone which matched the mood entirely. 'The underworlder who has offended us with his fighting in the tents of the Fenni has forfeited his life to us. We offer him this choice. Either he serves us as a slave on the *vidda* for the rest of his life, or he will be put to death at sunrise in a manner of his choosing. He will now be taken to the place of waiting, where he will make his choice. Hear the judgement of the Fenni and be glad, for it restores balance to the *vidda*.'

'We hear and are glad!' thundered the reply from a hundred throats.

Several things happened at once. Farr sprang forward, but was seized by one of the *chillan* and dragged away shouting. Stella went deathly white and fell to her knees, her hands on her head and her wide, frightened gaze fixed as much on herself as on the struggling figure disappearing towards the tents. But most piteous was the reaction of Wira, who fell to the ground in what seemed like mortal anguish.

Rough hands were laid on the Company and they were dragged to the outskirts of the tented camp. Both Kurr and the Haufuth tried to reason with the Fenni clan chief, but Perdu, overcome with grief, could not translate for them. In a scene of confusion, Leith found himself trying to argue with three men who could obviously not understand him as they half pushed, half dragged him to the top of a steep, snow-covered slope. He continued to struggle until the moment they pushed him over the edge, where he fell, rolled, tumbled and then slithered to the base of the slope to join the others. Their last glimpse of the Fenni was of a line of figures, backlit by the moon, turning and receding from sight.

*　　*　　*

214

'You played your part well,' the white-robed clan chief told his red-robed priest. 'I am pleased you guessed my intent.'

'They will return to free their comrade?'

'Undoubtedly. They will attack before dawn, believing that their friend will choose death rather than a life of servitude. Our actions have served their purpose – our people still have faith in us, and will continue to respect our leadership – but we have not harmed the underworlders.'

'But surely they cannot now pursue their enemies? To do that would have required our help!'

'Be at peace. I have made provision for this. Warn the guards to be alert. There must be no injury incurred in what is to come, or I will have little option but to carry out the substance of my decision.'

'We have two choices only,' the Haufuth said wearily. 'We can abandon the pursuit and return home, or we can try to take back what is ours.'

'What we forfeited, you fat buffoon,' snarled Kurr, who was seemingly in the grip of an uncontrollable anger. 'Remember that. Focus on that! Remember who it is we have to thank for our present situation! And I refuse to go on some death-cursed venture to rescue him from his just punishment!'

'Perhaps we could consider—' began Wira in a conciliatory tone, but the old farmer cut him off.

'The Storrsens have no right to speak here. I do not want to hear your considerations! What right you had to speak was lost when you could not restrain your loudmouthed fool of a brother!'

'Kurr, that's hardly fair—'

'You are right! It is manifestly unfair! But not as unfair as the situation we now find ourselves in!'

'A situation which you are only inflaming with your talk, my friend.' The Haufuth took a deep, settling breath, and faced the ruin of his expedition squarely and realistically. 'The problem, you see, is that we would probably not survive the journey back to Windrise without food and horses. And even if we did, what help could we expect from the inhabitants of that cursed town? More than likely, those we bested down in the Valley of Respite would seek us out and attempt to take their revenge on us. I do not think we could prevent them.'

The travellers huddled together behind a snowdrift at the bottom of the valley, trying to keep out the cruel night wind. The shock of the events of the last hour rendered the three teenagers silent, leaving the conversation to the four older men, at least one of whom was finding it difficult to think rationally.

'There are plenty of other ways back home. We don't have to go through Windrise.' Kurr's fierce gaze and unrelenting attack wore at the Haufuth's thin patience, and he took another deep breath to steady himself.

'Do you know of any? Have you travelled any other route, even in summer? Do you really, honestly think we could strike out into the wilderness and survive?'

'We should at least make the attempt—'

'I don't know why I'm reasoning with you, old man,' said the Haufuth, whose patience had given out. 'I don't want anger and blame. I want someone to help me think of a way to stay alive long enough to complete our quest. And you, Kurr, are not helping.' He leaned forward and stuck a chubby finger in the old farmer's bony chest. 'You are not the leader of this expedition. I am. So you will abide by my decision, and unless you have something helpful to say, I expect you to remain quiet.'

'You can't talk to me like that! You're only a village headman, while I'm a Watcher of the sixth rank!'

'You are a dead man in the company of dead men, unless you or one of us comes up with a good idea. Don't you understand that?'

Kurr said nothing in reply, though he remained coiled like an overwound spring held together by last year's twine.

'Haufuth, surely the nature of our quest has changed.' Wira spoke quickly, insistently, as though expecting to be interrupted at any moment. 'Farr is – was – one of our party. Surely he is your responsibility still, no matter how foolish he has been? Do we not have an obligation to attempt his rescue?'

216

'I'm not sure whether we do have an obligation to your brother,' the headman answered. 'That's the problem I'm wrestling with. What he did may have cost at least a handful of lives, possibly many thousands if we are prevented from warning Falthans about the Bhrudwan plans.'

'What he did was lose his temper in an unfamiliar situation. Farr's never been much good at those. But even he would have held his tongue had he been aware of the consequences!'

'Are you sure, cousin?' Perdu's voice was redolent with bitterness. 'Farr has always been a hothead. You remember when he got you into trouble with the Vatnoyans over the business of the eggs? Did he ever tell you that his cloak was found up near Vinbrenna, and that it was covered with chicken feathers? You took the punishment for him then. How many times since? Isn't it time he faced up to his wrongdoing and took his own punishment?'

'Not when the punishment is death or a life of slavery!' Wira shot back. 'Not when the punishment is out of proportion to the crime! I've just lost my father. Is it your opinion that I should lose my brother also?'

'You've lost? *You've* lost! What have *I* lost? I have just lost my wife, my children, and my people. Am I supposed to risk my life to rescue the one responsible?'

For a moment there was silence, more from frustration and exhaustion than a lack of things to say. *The quest is flying apart like dry clay on the wheel*, the Haufuth realised. *No one wants to do what we must do. Yes, must. We can't go back. Our quest is no less right just because it has become more difficult. Our only route to survival lies through the tents of the Fenni. Whoever wishes to remain part of our Company must ready themselves for danger and death. Whoever does not wish to face this can leave and find death somewhere on the road home. There are no other choices!*

'I choose to come with you,' Stella said firmly, rising and linking her arm to that of the Haufuth. The big headman realised that he must have spoken at least some of his half-formed thoughts aloud. Wira followed her, linking his arm with hers, with a defiant gaze directed at Kurr and Perdu.

Leith and Hal looked at each other. There really was no choice, not if they wanted to see their parents again. Hal raised an eyebrow, Leith nodded; and they joined Wira, Stella and the Haufuth, who shook his head in sorrow at the risk they were being forced to take.

'You are a fool, Haufuth, and a disgrace to the name,' Kurr ground out as heads turned towards him. 'But you are right. Most High curse you, you are right! We have to go on. Just don't expect me to like it!'

Perdu looked on the forlorn coastlanders for a moment, then laughed bitterly. 'Look at you,' he said. 'You can't begin to understand what you're up against. If the Fenni hold a captive, no one can set him free. Eager as you might be for death, and inevitable as it is whether you go forward or back, death at the hands of the Fenni is a truly awful thing. Last summer I saw them boil alive a Scymrian trader who had short-weighted them. You must understand that the Fenni know no mercy, only the harsh justice of the *vidda*. It is not cruelty by their standards, merely the balance of life and death. But I must make this clear to you: if you go back to the Fenni camp, they will kill you cruelly.'

'Nevertheless,' said the Haufuth.

It was perhaps two hours shy of dawn, as far as Leith could tell. Back home in Loulea the farmers would be well up, and most others in the village would soon begin the business of the day. Ahead, however, the Fenni camp lay in darkness. Ahead lay danger and death.

'This way!' a voice hissed from the blackness to his left. It was Perdu, calling the main group forward. That left Leith and Wira to approach from behind the tent Perdu had identified as Farr's likely holding place. There was little in the way of a plan beyond the hope that the Fenni were not expecting a rescue attempt, and for weapons the Company had nothing more than a few sticks they had found by a frozen stream before the moon had set.

Leith crept forward, following in Wira's footsteps. He had always

218

prided himself on his ability to move quietly, but now his life depended on it. He would soon know if his skill was sufficient.

'Listen to the noise,' one of the *chillan* guards remarked to the other. 'Are all underworlders truly so talentless?'

'Their food falls from the sky on to their plates,' his fellow replied. 'Why should they learn anything about the hunting arts?'

'It's time,' said the first, more quietly now as the two groups of underworlders approached the tent.

Wira stretched out an arm towards the tentskin, keeping his weight evenly distributed on both feet to ensure that his joints made no sound. With all the care of a man tickling a trout, he raised the skin a fraction, just enough for Leith, who was lying prone, to look inside. After a moment the boy signalled with a slight movement of his hand, and Wira let down the skin.

'Guards by the front of the tent, looking the other way,' Leith whispered into Wira's ear. 'They're gambling, doing something with dice. Farr is awake, in the back of the tent only a few feet to the left, bound hand and foot with ropes.' Wira nodded his understanding, then lifted the flap again.

This time Leith pushed a stick into the hole, in the direction of Farr. He had overestimated the distance between Farr and the back of the tent, so rather than the merest touch, Leith managed to jab Farr in his neck. Farr let out a shout, Leith dropped the stick and Wira let go the tent flap; but amazingly there was no movement from the guards, whose silhouettes remained near the front of the tent. Wira looked at Leith, who was taking great gulps of air in an attempt to calm himself, shrugged his shoulders, and lifted the tent flap again.

Farr had spun himself around so that he could see the back of the tent, and so when Leith's face appeared in the hole, he was ready for it. Hands reached for him as he scrabbled towards his rescuers and the tent frame groaned as Wira made the opening wider; surely they were making far too much noise. But still the guards did not turn, seemingly engrossed in their gambling.

After what seemed to Leith like an hour or a mere moment – he couldn't be sure which – Farr's bound shape was outside the tent, and Wira, with Leith's help, picked him up and carried him off.

When the noise had finally receded into the distance, the *chillan* turned to each other and shared a quiet laugh, then went on with their dicing.

'We have him, we have him!' Leith whispered exultantly as they met up with the remainder of the Company. Wira, with Farr on his back, was completely out of breath. 'Did you get the horses?' he managed to ask.

The Haufuth shook his head in reply, and pointed down a short slope to where the animals were kept. Leith could see nothing but shadows among shadows.

Then there was a movement from his left, and to his horror a dark-cloaked figure stepped out from between two tents and stood in front of the Company, arms raised in a pronouncement of doom. It was the priest of the Fenni.

In the pre-dawn darkness, with his doom assured, Leith noticed the most trivial of details. Beside him Wira coughed, and his breath clouded in the cold night air. Away to the east the sky lightened, and the starlight faded in response. A faint breeze ruffled his cloak, then died away again. The priest's robe hung down from his shoulders, unaffected by the breeze, making the man look like some bird of prey, a circling falcon ready to swoop upon the helpless rabbits caught in its gaze.

But were the rabbits helpless? Wira turned to Kurr, both with the same thought: *One of him, many of us*. Beside Leith, Stella coiled herself as though readying to spring upon their adversary.

Then the world changed as the priest lowered his arms and put a finger to his lips, begging them for silence. The Company were shocked into stillness, unable to keep up with the twists and turns of this strangest of nights. Perdu stepped forward into the stillness and exchanged quiet words with the priest.

'It's all right,' Perdu breathed. 'The clan chief plays his own game. Follow me. And make no noise!'

Leith followed, as did the others, wondering how being captured by the Fenni could possibly be all right. The priest led them away from the tents, over a low hill and down a defile until they were well out of sight of the encampment. There stood half a dozen men with torches, including the two guards from the tent where Farr had been held captive. With them was the clan chief.

The man in white came forward and beckoned Perdu to his side. He slipped something into the outcast's hand, then stood back with his arms folded as Perdu approached the still-bound form of Farr, took the knife he had been given and cut the cords binding him.

'Cousin,' he said quietly as Farr rubbed his arms, 'for my part in what happened last night I am sorry. I did not intend to offend you. Can we make peace?'

'Yes, cousin, we could make peace,' came the proud reply. 'But with whom am I making peace? A strong Vinkullen man, or a Fenni of the wild wastes?'

'A dead man,' was the prompt reply. 'And you are a dead man too, unless we make peace right here, right now. Can you do it? Can you control your infernal pride long enough for us to survive this? Come on, man. Take my hand and at least act like you're sorry! If not sorry for what you said to me, at least sorry for breaking Fenni protocol!' And, having said this, Perdu held his hand out to Farr.

The mountain man paused, just long enough for fear to again grip Leith; then he stepped forward and clasped Perdu in a tight embrace. 'Does this priest person understand our language?'

'He does not.'

'Then I declare that I'm not sorry at all. You've turned your back on us and taken up with *losian*. You are *losian* yourself. I will not speak to you again until you repent and embrace once again the ways of the Most High.' He released Perdu, stepped back and gave the man a broad smile. 'I am a man of principle.'

Expressions guarded, betraying nothing, the Company watched

as the clan chief came over to them. He began to speak, and Perdu interpreted for him.

'I regret our rough treatment of you yesterday, both when you first set foot on Fenni lands, and when you fought in our tents. I have been assured that you are trustworthy, and that you had no part in Fenni deaths. So, although it is not Fenni custom, we gave you our hospitality.

'It is a grave matter to offend the Fenni, especially when we have set aside our rules to accommodate you. This is why I brought a harsh judgement against you. My people expected it. Had I shown you mercy, their displeasure would have had me unseated as clan chief before next summer's clan gathering. Worse, it would have sown doubt amongst our people, who must remain singleminded in order to match their strength against that of the *vidda*.

'But it is in our best interests for you to be on your way. There are matters of which I must be mindful, but about which you know nothing. Perdu tells me that your beliefs do not allow you to consider the courses and counsels of the great heavenly houses, the stars which guide us in our journey through life. You do not know, then, that the sky itself has spoken of you.'

The priest came and stood beside his clan chief. 'The Five Houses of the West have come together for the first time in a thousand years,' he said, as Perdu interpreted. 'They are stretched out across the heavens like a vast hand, and they point to the east, where a great flame has arisen. Behold!' he cried, and pointed to the eastern horizon, where the sun was beginning to rise. 'The West unites in fiery opposition to the Flame of the East. Soon there will be a conflagration, and all will burn as the fire of heaven falls to earth. It is written across the sky in the handwriting of the gods. They have declared it, and so shall it be.'

'You pursue your enemies across the *vidda*,' the clan chief continued. 'Yet my priest tells me that you are part of a much larger plan. The Five Houses of the West hover over you. There is something you must do, something greater than the pursuit of the four horsemen; something in the lands of the underworlders,

222

something that affects the Fenni. Therefore, you see, I must let you go.

'That is why I did not have you killed outright last night, as was my right under Fenni custom. Sometimes it is necessary to break small customs to keep the larger ones, and now is one of those times, I deem. So today I send you to seek those who have done you wrong, and to discover what it is the gods would have you do. You must leave soon, so my people do not discover my deception. Therefore I cannot offer you food to break your fast, but I have filled your packs with provisions enough for many days.

'My fear for you is that you will not survive long on the *vidda*. These moors are no place for underworlders. They are too big for small souls like yours. The snow will eat you within three days.'

Kurr glanced at the Haufuth, and spoke softly out of the corner of his mouth. 'He's right, you know.'

'The snow will also eat your enemies. You could choose to go back to your homes, knowing that they have perished in the *qali* snow of the *vidda*. But because your people are their prisoners, you will continue on to your deaths. No matter. How strangers fare on the *vidda* is not normally the concern of the Fenni.

'But these men, your enemies, they have killed Fenni. They have captured Fenni. They have dared to assault a Fenni outpost on the edge of their winter homeland. We wish to look upon the dead bodies of our enemies. Then the spirits of our dead will be able to rest in peace.

'And there is the matter of the stars. It is beyond the wisdom of the Fenni to know what the stars are saying, for it is not to us they speak. But we would not be responsible for thwarting their plans by failing to give you aid.

'So we suggest a bargain between us. Give us your horses. They will be an encumbrance to you on the snows, and cannot be ridden hard until springmelt. Horses are highly prized among the Fenni. We will become the only Fenni outpost south of Myrvidda to have horses.

'In return, we will give you an *urus*, aurochs in your tongue. This beast can travel even in winter, and will bear a greater burden than all of your horses together could. We will give snowshoes to each of you, and as I have said, we have supplied you with enough provisions to get to the Rotten Lands beyond the mountains, should you need to go that far.

'One further thing we would ask. We wish one of our men to travel with you. Let him look upon the dead faces of those who dared to kill Fenni. Then let him return home with the news that will ease our hearts. He will be your guide across the *vidda*. Look after him well, for without him you are lost. Now, what is your response?'

Kurr and the Haufuth turned to each other with broad smiles wreathing their faces. 'It's everything we could have hoped for,' the Haufuth stated.

'So the enemy is undone by his own violence,' Kurr responded. 'Without their assault on the Fenni, we could not have crossed Breidhan Moor.'

Farr spoke, anger rippling through his voice. 'I don't like it. Vinkullen men at the mercy of some Fenni guide? We need no guide! Take their aurochs, take their food, take their snowshoes by all means, but do not suffer being led by such as them!'

'That settles it, then,' Kurr hissed. 'If you force me to choose between you and the Fenni, then I choose the Fenni, notwithstanding your valiant defence of the Company in the Valley of Respite. We accept their offer or we return home unavenged. What is it to be?'

'We accept,' said the Haufuth. The others concurred, even Wira, who was favoured by a venomous glance from his older brother.

The Haufuth stood up. 'Let the enemies of the Bhrudwan riders join together in their pursuit!' he declared. When this was translated, the clan chief smiled, then lifted his staff into the air in acknowledgement of the agreement.

Perdu grinned his relief. 'I am to be your guide,' he said. 'I will go with you as far as the mountains if necessary, though I doubt we will need to travel that far to find these murderers.'

At this Wira relaxed visibly, as did his brother. 'Oh,' he said, 'you are to be our guide? Why didn't you tell us?' But Perdu did not answer.

'What about your family?' Stella asked. 'Are you still banished? Will they come with us?'

'They cannot come with us,' Perdu replied. 'My boys are not old enough to face the *vidda* yet without the protection of the clan. And I am still outcast, for a year and a day or until I return with the cloak and sword of one of our enemies, whichever comes the soonest. The priest will look after my family while I am gone. He is a good man. Nothing will happen to them.' Perdu's voice carried more hope than certainty, and his eyes were rimmed with sadness.

The aurochs was presented to the Company with a small ceremony. From what Leith could understand, they were being accorded a great honour. Never before, Perdu said, had the pride of the Fenni been given to underworlders. Leith looked in awe at the beast. A grey-brown colour, it stood at least six feet high at the shoulder, with forward-pointing horns that gave it a fearsome aspect. It lowered its head and swished its tail upon hearing that it had new owners.

'His name is Wisent,' Perdu told them, unable to keep the wonder out of his voice. 'He is the clan chief's own *urus*, the strongest and most cunning of his breed. His value is beyond guessing. But the clan chief loved Ostval, one of the dead, like a son. Thus he favours you.'

The Haufuth bowed to the clan chief, who returned the gesture with a nod.

Equipped with snowshoes and fully laden with provisions, the Company was ready to travel. As they were about to leave, the young woman Leith recognised as the wife of Perdu came running down into the valley, tears in her eyes. She was followed by two small boys, upset because their mother was crying. The woman embraced her husband, then stood before him, head bowed. Perdu said something to her, but she was not consoled.

She approached the Company with a jar full of a black

substance, then smeared some on the face of Perdu, making a black mark under each of his eyes. Then she made to do the same for the Haufuth, but stopped, puzzled, when he drew back.

Perdu laughed. 'Have you never seen *mot*? The Fenni wear it whenever they make a long journey in the snow. It protects your eyes from the blindness of Qali.'

'What blindness is this?' Wira asked.

'You have been on the moors a few days now,' Perdu replied. 'Do any of you have pain in your eyes?'

One after another the Company nodded.

'That is the blindness of Qali. The longer you stay on the *vidda*, the worse it gets. Fenni who do not wear the *mot* end up blind. Please, let Haldemar put *mot* on your faces.' So, one by one, the Company allowed the woman to spread the sticky black lotion under their eyes. Only Farr resisted, backing away and waving his hand in angry refusal.

'So be it,' Perdu sighed. 'I hope the days are cloudy, for your sake.'

All was now ready for their departure. Perdu gave Wisent a slap on the rump and the huge beast ambled slowly off, his wife hoofs making hardly a dent in the icy snow. The Company followed Perdu and the aurochs, walking along the defile, away from the white-robed figure of the clan chief and his red-garbed priest. Haldemar and her children walked with them for a while, then stopped and bade them farewell.

They turned a corner, climbed a slope and made their way up to the brow of a low hill, covering in a few minutes the same distance that the previous day had taken them a whole morning. Farr looked ahead at Perdu, who obviously struggled with leaving his family, then whispered to his brother: 'I hope he turns out better than our last guide!' Stella, who with the Haufuth brought up the rear of the Company, marvelled at the two brothers. *How can the one be so hateful, and the other be so – so interesting?*

From the crest of the hill Breidhan Moor extended in every direction, a featureless expanse of snow-covered rolling hills. Even The Brethren, the mountains that the Company had seen on the previous day, were nowhere to be seen. Again the sky was cloudless, the day numbingly cold, the snow offensively bright. Leith was glad of the *mot*, though he was unsure how it would protect him. Was it just a superstition, like all that talk about the stars? *I'll soon know*, he thought grimly. *Surely the Bhrudwans cannot be far ahead!*

CHAPTER 11

MAELSTROM

THE TRAVELLERS SOON NOTICED that Perdu was not leading them in a straight line. Instead, they zig-zagged every few hundred yards, as though they were looking for something. 'I am trying to find the tracks of the Bhrudwans,' their guide explained. 'The clan chief believes they went this way after they attacked— ah, here they are!' he cried. 'Now we have them. Let us ask Qali to withhold his snow for a few days!'

It was a simple matter for the travellers to follow the raised tracks. Even Leith could have done so unaided. What was much more difficult was trying to work out where they were heading. For everyone except Perdu, who knew the secrets of the moorlands, the sun was their only guide. Apparently they were headed east, approximating the path of the Westway buried under feet of snow. During the afternoon huge clouds built up to their left and threatened them for a while, but they were blown away by a warm wind that sprang up from the south.

'I hope this wind does not last,' Perdu muttered. 'The Snoweater will render travel impossible. It is a spring wind; it should not be on the moors at this time of year.'

And soon after, as if in answer to his petition, the wind died down. By nightfall the air was calm and the sky cloudless.

'Right, we are going to have this out here and now,' the Haufuth declared. 'I will not lead a divided Company. Either you cousins

228

patch up your differences, or I will be forced to send one of you away.'

'And I know which one it should be,' Kurr whispered to no one, but loud enough for everyone to hear.

The Company sat around a small fire, set in front of a surprisingly large tent that had been an unexpected gift from the Fenni clan chief. Perdu and Farr sat on opposite sides of the flames, staring at each other with anger in their eyes. The Haufuth stood near Farr, arms folded across his chest.

It was Farr who stood and took up the challenge. 'Very well, then. I've made my feelings clear on the subject of the *losian*, yet no one seems to listen. But it's not just my own personal feelings that are important here. We're chasing four Bhrudwans across the moors, and what are Bhrudwans if they are not enemies of true Falthans and of the Most High? Is not what we are doing a mission from the Most High Himself? And if it is, we must keep ourselves pure, uncontaminated by those who turned their backs on the Most High in the Vale! My fear is that if we associate with the *losian*, or with those who have been in contact with them, we will lose our purity and will no longer be of use to the Most High. Can you not see it? Am I the only true believer amongst us? I say that my cousin needs to repent of his life with the *losian*, to reject his half-breed family and consecrate himself a First Man once again. Or, if he will not, he should leave us and return to his *losian* friends.'

'What sort of religion is that?' Perdu cried, standing and staring at his cousin across the fire. 'Not the sort of religion we were taught as children! Yes, we are the First Men. Yes, we have supposedly been chosen by the Most High as His special people. But what of forgiveness? What of tolerance?'

'Yes, what of it?' Farr shouted back. 'Would you have preached tolerance to the Falthans enslaved by the Destroyer during the Bhrudwan occupation a thousand years ago? Would you have begged the First Men to forgive their oppressors? If you had, you would have been executed as a traitor, and rightly so!'

'Since when have you been religious, anyway?' Perdu countered.

'You never used the name of the Most High as a child, except to blaspheme. Are you sure your religion is not just a cloak for your own petty hatred and fear?'

'Fear? I fear no man! The enemies of the Most High are my enemies also, and my brother and I will hunt them down. And if the blessing and the mandate of the Most High is written in the stars, then I will take that mandate and hunt down all the enemies of the Most High, whether they live in huts or caves or even tents, and I will destroy them!' The threat could not have been more obvious and Farr leapt to his feet, readying himself for a fight.

Suddenly, without seeming to move quickly, Hal stood in their midst. 'Close your eyes for a moment,' he said, addressing the Company. 'Imagine that you are back in the tent of the Fenni clan chief. Take a look around you. There's a mother with her child suckling at her breast. Beside her a young man readies a spear for tomorrow's hunt. A man and a woman clear away food. The clan chief looks around the tent, his heart filled with happiness and pride at the competence of his people. Look closely. What do you see? Do you see animals – or do you see people?' The intensity of his gaze forced each of the travellers to consider the imaginary scene he had painted for them.

'Animals or people?' Hal repeated, drawing the travellers back into his gaze.

'People,' said the Haufuth, eager to settle things down.

'People,' agreed Stella.

'They are people,' Leith stated.

One by one the others agreed, except for Farr, who would not look directly at the crippled youth.

'Then treat them as kinsmen, just as they have treated you,' Hal said. 'Otherwise, by your conduct, you acknowledge them as more human than you are, and all discussions about the First Men and the *losian* are moot.'

Perdu looked gratefully at the crippled youth. 'What is your name?' he asked. Hal told him.

'Are your parents in the hands of the Bhrudwans?' Hal nodded. 'Then I have another reason to desire success in our pursuit.'

The Fenni man smiled warmly. 'If they are as true-hearted as their son, they will be well worth rescuing.'

The following days were a severe strain on the Company. Though they were well clad, certainly wearing much thicker clothing than their hardy guide, they felt warm only in the evenings when they huddled together around the fire. Their feet ached, their eyes ached and their hearts began to ache as day followed day and the tracks continued ahead of them, with no sign of their foe. The weather held fine and clear, and the Company walked in the stillness of a world that seemed empty of life save their own. Not a single animal could be seen: no birds, no deer, no life on four feet or two feet. Just the pale blue sky, the blinding snow, and the endless tracks.

'Does nothing live on the moor?' the Haufuth asked Perdu after a midday meal. 'Surely some animal must live here in the summer? Where do they go when the snows come?'

Perdu answered the headman by leading him over to a nearby bush, actually a stunted fir which had grown no higher than his knee. 'Look,' he said, pointing to a hole in the snow. 'Here is the home of some small animal, probably a vole. Underneath us, at the bottom of the snow blanket, the voles and the other small animals make tunnels. It is warmer down there, and they live there during the winter. They come out only occasionally, because the cold wind would quickly freeze them solid. Or the owls might catch them, or the foxes or the wolves.'

'Wolves? Here on the moors? Why have we not seen them?'

'They will avoid us because of Wisent. But have you not seen their tracks? The *vidda* is covered with animal tracks. Still, you have not yet learned to see as the Fenni see. Or perhaps you have eyes only for the tracks of your enemies?'

The Haufuth nodded wearily. He was beginning to forget what uncovered earth looked like. Where were these Bhrudwans?

Hunger. Tiredness. Pain. Fear. Cold. Mahnum knew that a lethal combination of these factors was killing him. He had energy for little more than the raising of one foot and the placing of it in front of the other. At least the relentless questioning and torment from their captors had ceased, as everyone in the party, captor and captive alike, focused on survival. It seemed to Mahnum that the cold was now a part of his body, that ice shards had replaced his bones, that his flesh was turning to stone. The cruel deaths of hunger and cold beckoned him, and he did not have the will to resist their call.

Day after day they travelled across these white lands of winter on a summer road. The food the Bhrudwans had taken from those they had killed had all but run out, and with it disappeared their chances of surviving on the moors. *Why don't they just kill us and get it over with?* Mahnum wondered. *More food for them, faster travel, a chance to get out of the moors alive. What drives them to keep their captives at the risk of losing their own lives? What was so important about this secret weapon, this Right Hand?* For the hundredth time the Trader turned these matters over in his mind. *I wish I could live long enough to find out!*

What now? Mahnum looked up from his musings. Something was wrong. They had come to a halt in the bowl of a wide, shallow valley, and the Bhrudwans, gaunt-faced and themselves obviously suffering the effects of hunger, began a discussion some distance away from their bound captives. In silent, weary agreement, the three prisoners sank to the ground. The Bhrudwans either didn't notice or were too preoccupied to rebuke them.

The discussion between the Bhrudwans soon became an argument, with menacing voices raised. *Perhaps they are turning on their leader*, Mahnum hoped wildly. *Perhaps it is a mutiny!* Gestures were made in their direction as the argument continued unabated. Behind them the horses, by now mere rags of skin shrouding skeletons, stirred uneasily at the unfamiliar, unsettling sound of the open anger in their masters' voices. Finally a decision was made and, as the three captives watched in horror, the Bhrudwan warriors turned to face them, then eased their wickedly curving swords out of their sheaths. At a signal from their leader, the four grey-robed men began a deliberate walk in the direction of their helpless prisoners.

As the grim-faced Bhrudwans came towards them with swords drawn, the Trader deliberately turned his gaze away, his eyes moving past Parlevaag's frightened, wide-eyed visage and finding the battered face of his beloved Indrett. She couldn't find the strength to smile, but the warmth in her eyes was enough for Mahnum, and again he lost his heart to her. There they sat, drinking in the sight of each other like that very first night at the court of Rammr, as though the intervening years had dropped away, as though their bonds meant nothing, as though they were not about to die at the end of a sword. At this moment, at the end of everything, all he could think of was her, and about how it had all been worthwhile.

On the ninth day out from the Fenni camp the Company came to the end of Breidhan Moor. As they crested a final ridge, they were confronted by the huge bulk of the first of The Brethren. The rolling hills of the moor were replaced by a depression that veered off to the right, funnelling down into a wide, deep defile. The tracks turned in that direction.

'This is the valley of the Thraell River,' Perdu exclaimed. 'The Westway can be found on the far bank of the river. But road and river both are buried under this cursed snow.'

'Look!' Farr said, pointing down into the valley. 'On the far slope. What are those black specks?'

Perdu scanned the valley ahead of them, hands shading his eyes. 'Wolves,' he replied eventually. 'They are stalking something – see, further to the right, at the bottom of the valley. Something is lying on the snow.'

'It could be Mahnum and Indrett!' Kurr cried, voicing everyone's fear. 'We must do something!'

Perdu urged Wisent forward, and the Company pounded down the slope after him. It would be a near thing. On the far slope the wolves moved slowly, stalking their prey, as yet unaware of the commotion on the slope opposite. The Company threw themselves down towards the inert forms on the valley floor, straining every muscle for extra speed. Perdu and the aurochs began to draw

233

away from the others. Perhaps he would get there before the wolves.

But the wolf pack had crept close to their prey. Perdu shouted to attract their attention, but the upvalley wind carried the noise away from the wolves, intent on nothing but their upcoming feast. Behind him the other travellers ran, falling over and picking themselves up again, lungs burning with the cold air. The Haufuth stopped, exhausted. Just in front of him Kurr had also come to a halt. Behind both of them Hal stood watching the race. They could do nothing. Leith and Stella ran towards the bottom of the slope, side by side. Ahead of them the Storrsen brothers flung themselves forward. And now Perdu had almost arrived at the valley floor.

But it was too late. Ahead of them all, the snarling wolves pounced on the bodies lying on the snow. Five, ten, twenty seconds passed. Leith could not watch. Then Perdu and Wisent ran into the scene of death, and the huge animal scattered the wolves in every direction. They drew away up the opposite slope, reluctant to abandon their meal, yet knowing they could not attack the immensely powerful aurochs. Snarling and yapping, they watched as, one by one, the Company arrived to stare at the blood-stained snow. What was left of the wolves' prey lay dead. Leith counted. One, two, three, four. Four Bhrudwan horses.

'They can't be far ahead!' Perdu cried as the others gathered around the carnage. 'These horses haven't been dead long!'

'Perhaps the wolves killed them,' Leith commented.

The Fenni shook his head. 'No – we saw them lying on the snow before the wolves got them.'

By now Kurr had most of his breath back. 'What we don't know is how long they had been lying there before the wolves found them. The Bhrudwans may be miles away by now.'

'Not likely,' Perdu argued.

'Look here,' said Farr, pointing to one of the corpses. 'This wound is not fresh like the others. A sword thrust, perhaps?'

'What does it mean?' two or three voices asked in chorus.

'It looks as if the Bhrudwans killed their own horses. Look, here's a similar wound on another horse.'

'But why would they do that?' Kurr asked, incredulous.

'Take a closer look,' Farr pressed. 'These animals are nothing more than skin and bone. I'm surprised they made it through the moors! But obviously they could go no further. My guess is that these horsemen could not stand the sight of their horses suffering agonisingly slow deaths. So they put them out of their misery.'

'You may have read it right,' Kurr growled. 'Maybe.'

Farr turned to the others. 'The blood is dry and hard on the older wounds. These horses have been dead many hours, perhaps since yesterday.'

'I don't know how they've done it,' the Haufuth remarked, 'but the Bhrudwans have kept ahead of us, even without the benefit of a guide, snowshoes or an aurochs. What sort of magic has sustained them?'

The elder Storrsen laughed. 'Not magic! Remember, we haven't used the snowshoes for the last three days. Like us, they would have had no trouble walking on such hardened snow. They have kept up a strong pace; I hate to think what it will have done to their captives.'

Kurr turned to where Leith and Hal had been standing, but they were no longer there. He saw them some distance away, Hal with a comforting arm around Stella. *Upset about the horses, most probably.*

'We must rest,' the Haufuth said. 'The run down the hill has left me spent.' He sat down on his pack.

Farr threw a hand into the air in exasperation. 'We can't wait! We must go on!' No one replied. His arm dropped to his side. 'Oh, what's the point? How can we ever catch them, a ragged bunch of old men, fat men, cripples and children? Give me half a dozen mountain men – we'd soon overhaul these Bhrudwans!'

'See here,' he continued, earnestness in his voice, 'how much more of this can the children stand? Look over there – the girl is all in. Whoever thought to bring her along was misguided! And look at Hal, the cripple. He says nothing, but he struggles to keep up. And the other boy. He's afraid to wake up in the morning! What use will he be when we finally have the enemy in a corner? If we ever catch them.' He stabbed his stave into the snow, punctuating his words.

'You seem to have forgotten the Valley of Respite,' Kurr muttered darkly, but Farr ignored him.

'I say it is time to send the weak home,' he concluded. 'Let them go back to the Fenni with our guide. Then the warriors can finish this business.'

No one replied. Hot anger deprived Kurr of speech for the moment. The Haufuth, cooler and more thoughtful, recognised the truth in what the mountain man had said. How could the weak, the old and the callow succeed against seasoned fighters like the Bhrudwans? He sighed. All he had were words.

'We're all here because we've had something taken from us: our friends, our family, our pride. Strength alone will not get them back. We cannot hope to overwhelm these men by sheer force. But on old legs walks experience and wisdom, while on young legs walks enthusiasm and desire. If we persevere, these things may overcome mere strength.'

'Fine words,' Farr mocked, 'but they mean nothing.'

'We'll see,' came the reply. 'Now, enough. If you wish to go on ahead and assail your foes alone, so be it. Otherwise, we continue down the road set for us. But not yet!' he added. 'Not until we've had a rest!'

The rest turned into an overnight camp. The travellers moved some distance back up the near slope, wary of the wolves, and during the night could hear them snarling as they argued over the meat. By the morning little of the horses remained.

Leith rose early and went down towards the line of the stream to get some softer snow for melting into drinking water. As he began to dig through the crusty outer layer of hardened snow, he heard voices from the other side of a low ridge.

'Where did you get that?' said one voice.

'None of your business!' snapped the reply.

'Look, you know it's no good for you,' the first voice said. 'Couldn't you survive even a few days without it? I'm disappointed in you.'

'It's nothing!' the second voice protested. 'Just enough to see me right for the day, that's all I need!'

Leith closed his eyes. These voices sounded familiar . . .

'What is that stuff, anyway?'

'Try some!'

'Agh! This is poison! Surely you did not bring this from home?'

'No, I got it from the Fenni. In exchange for my fur hat.'

'You fool!' came the stinging reply.

The Storrsen brothers! Leith remembered their bearskin hats, and realised that they had not been worn since the Torrelstrommen valley. But what were they talking about?

'You know what this does to you!' the rebuke continued. 'I suppose you refilled this flask at Windrise as well?'

No answer came, a mute acknowledgement.

'I thought you had overcome this, but I see I was mistaken. Give me the flask.'

'Leave me alone! I'm all right! I need something now that Father is dead – I'll get over it in a little while! Please, please leave me!'

'I don't want to fight you. But for all your fine words, you'll be no use to anyone if you keep drinking this. Give it up.'

Which voice belonged to which brother? Leith couldn't be sure. He began to edge around to the side of the ridge, hoping for a glimpse, but by the time he made it to where they had been talking, they were gone.

Later that afternoon Farr called for the others to stop. His hands were on his eyes, which streamed with tears. 'I'm sorry,' he said, 'but I can hardly see anything. My eyes hurt.'

Perdu shook his head. '*Mot* would have prevented this,' he said. 'Now you will just have to rest your eyes.' He tore some fabric off one of his shirts and placed a blindfold around Farr's head. The man did not complain; rather, he looked ashamed. Perdu seated him on Wisent's back and for the next two days, until he regained his sight, Farr rode the lumbering beast. Leith watched him as he sat there, unseeing. The others were all sure what it was that had temporarily blinded him, but Leith remembered the blindness of the Loulea village drunkard. *I think Farr has a drinking problem. That's all we need.*

The days that followed were quiet, with no sign of the Bhrudwans. The line of the Westway dropped steeply down into the Thraell valley, a deep gash in the hill country which ran towards the south-east, eventually emptying into the Kljufa. On their right rose the ever-higher fence of Breidhan Moor, while to their left marched the huge, ponderous domes of The Brethren. It took three days to put the first of these hills behind them, only for it to be replaced by another just as large, then yet another. The snow cover gradually thinned, and on the eighth day in the Thraell valley, the Company came abruptly down through the snowline. Behind them all was white and grey; ahead they could see colour again for the first time in weeks. There ran the Thraell River, unlocked from its icy prison, and to its left marched the Westway, not much more than a cutting in the skirts of The Brethren. And there, amid patches of snow and ice, grew grass for Wisent to eat, which he attacked with joy.

The Thraell was a noisy river, leaping energetically from bank to bank as it rushed towards lower lands. The Company, however, could not keep pace with it. Hal's withered leg pained him, and he and the Haufuth alternated on the aurochs' back while the others trudged wearily along beside them. Leith walked on leaden legs, and his back ached from the weight of his pack. Their food ran low, and they could not eat grass like Wisent. *How much further can we go?* Leith wondered.

Eventually they came to a nameless creek which descended from the left, pouring its water into the Thraell. Beyond this creek lay the fourth and last of The Brethren, and ahead Leith could make out the treeline well below where they stood. In the hazy distance the Great North Woods stretched away forever. The Thraell dropped down into the forest in a series of steep rapids and water-falls, a narrow throat through which it had proved impossible to build a road. So the Westway turned here to the left, following the creek on its course between the lower slopes of the third and fourth Brethren.

The travellers spent a further four days stumbling up the boulder-strewn valley. They seemed consistently to be a day behind their enemies: tantalisingly close, but not close enough to set eyes on them. Each night they camped at the site of the Bhrudwans' hearth of the previous night. The weather took a turn for the worse, with first rain and then snow falling mercilessly upon them. The wind blew hard out of the east, cold and cruel. Numb fingers fumbled with cloaks and clasps. Furs were drawn close around faces and hands. Farr brought out his distinctive hat to keep his ears warm. Wira, who did not seem to feel the cold, remained hatless.

Stella's injury, sustained in the skirmish in the Valley of Respite, began to ache with the cold. At first the pain was dull, but it gradually became unbearable and she withdrew within herself. Thoughts of what awaited her on her return home drove her on up the mist-wreathed slopes, while her shoulder ached and her legs trembled with the effort of walking, head down, one foot in front of the other. The repetition numbed her mind, so that at times she couldn't remember why she walked up this valley. Tramp, tramp, tramp. She thought of the hot summer days, two years ago now, sitting in the shade under the Common Oak with her friends, chewing grass, not a care in the world, idling the hours away with inconsequential gossip. Tramp, tramp. Bustling in the kitchen, indoors on a cold northerly winter evening, warming her freezing hands by the skillet. Tramp, tramp, tramp. Waking up in the morning this last terrible summer with that familiar hollow feeling in her stomach as she realised that the weather was fine and Druin was going to come calling. Lying in bed, imagining with dread the knock at the door, the simpering of her parents, the moment when she could delay no longer and had to emerge from her room. Tramp, tramp, tramp, tramp. Held in that vice-like grip, paraded up and down in front of his friends like some new toy . . . *Oh Lord Most High, why couldn't it be Wira?* Ow! Stella turned her ankle on a boulder and collapsed in a heap. Strong hands from behind gently raised her up. She turned, grateful: it was Farr. She thanked him as she brushed herself off, then closed her eyes and imagined that it had been his younger brother.

Again her world narrowed down to the grey path in front of her, but not for much longer. Suddenly she ran into the back of Leith. Everyone had stopped. She lifted her eyes.

They had reached the head of the stone-strewn valley, a wide bowl with steep sides and a level floor. The walls were smooth, except for huge scratch marks that must have been made by some giant with a piece of flint. Rocks were heaped everywhere, like toys discarded when the sun comes out. In the middle of the bowl lay a lake filled with cloudy grey-green water, in which icebergs floated. Some distance behind the lake, at the far end of a wide boulder field, rose a wall of ice. It was the snout of Styggesbreen, the *Iskelelva*, famed ice river of the east. Up, up Stella gazed, following Styggesbreen back to its source, past icefall and moraine into the cloudy distance. There the afternoon mists veiled her view; but as she watched, the clouds parted and for a moment Stella beheld great snow-covered pinnacles, peaks soaring in the air, seemingly detached from the earth: the towering bastions of the Jawbone Mountains. Then the mists swirled again and the majestic sight was hidden.

'I never thought we would come this far,' Kurr said dreamily, to no one in particular. 'Here is the heart of Firanes; here are her bones. But what has happened? I don't remember it like this! In former times Styggesbreen filled this *dalen*, this bowl; he sat right up against the Westway, but now he has withdrawn up the valley and left a lake in his place.'

The Haufuth, eyes full of questions, came over to where the old farmer stood. 'What do you mean, you don't remember this? Have you been this way before?'

Startled out of his thoughts by his headman's voice, Kurr dropped his eyes. 'Actually, I *have* been this way once before.'

'Then why didn't you tell us?'

'I didn't think it would be of any use. It was only once, when I was a young man – more than fifty years ago. I travelled from east to west, from Plonya into Firanes. And it was in the middle of summer, so conditions were much different.'

'But you could have said something! Why keep it secret?'

'It has no bearing on our journey, I tell you!' the old man snapped. 'Don't you think I would have told you if I thought it important?'

By now the whole party had gathered around the two men.

'Yes, but – but here we are, in the middle of nowhere, no one knowing anything about what we have to face – and then we find out that you have been here before! Even if you had told us how many days it takes to travel through this accursed valley, we could have planned our rests and maybe— I don't know,' the Haufuth blustered. 'Kurr, I don't understand!'

'Some things are private,' the old man replied. 'In any case, I can't remember how long it took us to come down this valley in summer – no doubt it was much quicker than climbing up it in the middle of winter. Why the fuss? Don't you trust me?'

'No, it's not that – oh, I don't know! Maybe we've been walking too long. Perhaps it is because I feel responsible for you all, and here we are in the middle of a wasteland, hundreds of miles from home, and I feel useless. I can't protect you. I can't feed you. I can't ease your aches and pains. I can't promise you a successful end to our journey. All I can promise you is a bitter struggle, a violent death and an early grave!'

He sat down on a large boulder and rested his head in his hands.

'Perhaps you should lead the Company,' the Haufuth moaned. He looked up at the old farmer. 'You do, anyway. You know the road, you're quick to think. Take the others with you, go and rescue Mahnum and Indrett. I'll be waiting here when you return.'

Kurr sat down beside his Haufuth, waving the others away with his hand.

'Come on, now. I've known you for years. No one else could lead this group. Look at me!' he laughed harshly. 'I just have to open my mouth to offend someone. I tell you, if you wait here for us, someone will be carrying Farr Storrsen's body back to Mjolkbridge, because I won't be answerable for my actions. You got us over Alvaspan, through Windrise and the Torrelstrommen valley, over Breidhan Moor and past the Fenni. I'll be honest with you. I would have handled each of those incidents differently, and in each case I would have been proved wrong. People would have died. We started this journey because of you, we're here because of you, we will continue because of you, and Mahnum and Indrett will be rescued and Faltha warned of her peril because of you. So take heart! Remember why you became our Haufuth in the first place.'

The big man smiled wanly. 'Thank you,' he said. 'I'm glad you came on this journey. I wouldn't have come without you.'

Kurr grunted, then stood up and walked slowly away.

The travellers were forced to make camp by the grey-green lake that night. The next section of the Westway, Kurr told them, was a steep climb, then down a long slope to the mighty Kljufa River, a greater river than any they had yet seen. 'By then,' he said encouragingly, 'we should have overtaken our quarry.'

The next morning Leith awoke early, well before dawn. It was time for the final push, the great effort they would need to catch the Bhrudwans. The camp was broken with haste and the Company well on its way as the sun began to suffuse the sky with a pale pink light.

'Red sky in the morning, farmer's warning,' intoned Kurr.

From behind him Farr laughed. 'I've seen many a red morning lead into a fine, clear day.'

'No doubt,' the farmer retorted, 'but on days such as these the wise farmer keeps his stock close to shelter.'

Up out of the bowl-shaped valley they climbed. Kurr and Perdu went first, with Perdu leading Wisent, on whom the majority of the load was placed. Behind them came Leith, Hal and Stella, followed by the Haufuth. Protecting the rear were the Storrsen brothers, each brandishing his long stave. Presently the Company reached the rim of the bowl, and immediately ahead the land levelled out for a space. There they halted involuntarily, awestruck, as the glory of Firanes unfolded around them.

The mountains that had been hidden the day before were now revealed. The red dawn set fire to peak after peak, stretching uninterrupted across the horizon. Snow and rock alike glowed with the rising sun. Above, the sky was dark purple, merging into black; below, the foothills of the mountains were shrouded in deep blue shadow, serving only to highlight the power of the great peaks. These were the Grossbergen, the front range of the Jawbone Mountains, the most spectacular if not the highest. To the left towered Thyrtinden Massif, the Cloudpiercer with three peaks taller than any other of the Grossbergen. Directly in front of the Company, a little nearer than the others, rose the upthrust, sheer-sided pinnacle of Manimeria, a single razor-sharp peak that seemed to puncture the very sky, called Moonraker in modern rendering. And stretching away to the right were the flanks of Stravanter, the Stormbringer, its rounded dome burning with a fierce red flame. On either side of these great peaks the Jawbone Mountains marched, summit after summit soaring into the sky. On such a morning as this the First Men had first sighted these mountains and had called this land Firanes, the Cape of Fire.

Each member of the Company stood transfixed as the morning glory slowly faded from the mighty peaks, as blue and white replaced the dawn fire. Already the mists of morning gathered in the valleys, and the rightmost peak of Thyrtinden wrapped itself in a wispy scarf. Soon the sun would suck moisture from the cold valleys and drape it on the mountaintops. It was time to be moving.

The road now turned to the southeast. Across their path lay a range of snow-capped hills, low outliers of the mountains now strung out to their left. When finally the sun rose high enough to shine on their faces, the travellers had negotiated a few boggy miles and found themselves at the feet of the hills. Ahead, just to the left of the road that wound its way up the slope, they could make out a dark vertical line.

'The Chute,' Kurr announced. 'Up there, over the horizon, is a lake. It drains out to the river over there, to the right.' He pointed to a chattering stream some distance away. 'The Westway used to run up the valley of that stream to the lake. You can still get to the lake that way, but the road is in disrepair and it takes you many miles out of your way. A long time ago there was a big earthquake in these parts and a rockslide blocked the outlet to the lake. The water swelled to many times its original size, until finally it found the point of least resistance – the top of the notch you can see in the distance. Then, in a mighty torrent, it came pouring down this hillside and in one afternoon carved a chasm in the rock. For a while afterwards the lake outlet flowed through the Chute, but latterly it has returned to its original riverbed. Now we can walk directly up the Chute to the lake, as long as the weather is fine. When it rains, the Chute becomes an impassable torrent of water once again.'

Farr laughed. 'How old were you when they told you that one? It would have taken years to cut a notch like this, not one afternoon!' He dissolved into laughter.

Kurr clenched and unclenched his fists helplessly. The Haufuth reached out and put a steadying hand on his shoulder. Their eyes made contact. With a supreme effort, Kurr rounded on the elder Storrsen and smiled.

'Yes, you're right,' he said, forcing laughter through unwilling teeth. 'I was a young man when I heard that tale. Still, you never know in the mountains.' The Haufuth sighed with relief and removed his hand.

'That's why you have mountain men with you,' Farr remarked.

All that day and all of the next the Company travelled, trying to go as fast as they could, but though they knew they must be close behind the Bhrudwans, they never caught sight of their quarry. The road ran mostly downwards and to the left, winding down the flanks of the hills, drawing ever closer to the mountains which remained hidden. Here the Westway was broad and travel was easy. During the afternoon of the second day Wisent picked up a stone in his hoof and had to be tended, delaying them somewhat. Now evening drew in around them.

'Should we continue into the night?' the Haufuth asked the old farmer.

'No, I don't think so. We could walk right into their camp without knowing it. A new moon and low cloud means we won't even have starlight by which to see our way.'

The road rounded the flank of a hill on their left. As the Company followed the road, a broad river came into view. At least six hundred yards from bank to bank it stretched, and although the water was low it filled its channel with ease. The water was a deep blue, and moved swiftly and with great force away to their right. Near the banks the water swirled and eddied.

'The Kljufa,' Kurr announced, 'the great river of Firanes. We follow it through the mountains, if indeed we need to go that far.'

Surely not, thought Leith. *Surely it will be over soon.*

They travelled only a little further that day, making their camp some distance away from the road, in a hollow in the side of a low hill. From the camp they could see the river flowing away from them, flowing on its journey out of the mountains, flowing down through the Great North Woods, passing by the vast emptiness of the Lankangas, watering the fertile plains of southern Firanes and emptying into the Wodhaitic Sea near Derkskogen Forest and the port of Nordviken five hundred miles away to the south.

The next day they forded a wide, stony river that came down from the Grossbergen. The hills began to draw in close, pinching the Kljufa from both sides, until the water ran white and turbulent. The day was grey and the height of the mountains on either side could only be guessed. Ahead of them came a roaring that reminded Leith of the Gloum Stair, the waterfall on the Torrelstrommen, only here in the hills the noise echoed all around them.

'This is the Lower Clough, the first of the two gorges of the Kljufa,' Kurr told them. He pointed ahead. 'Look to your left. See the road? The gorge is so narrow, the road had to be cut out of the mountainside itself. See there? The road has a wall and a roof.'

The old farmer had remembered correctly. Leith could see a groove, perhaps four hundred yards in length, cut into the side of a spur that rose vertically from the river. It looked like a tunnel with only one wall, open to the river a hundred feet below but hemmed in by rock everywhere else. Leith could only marvel at the mighty accomplishment of the road-builders.

The Westway began to wind up towards the roofed road. The noise of tortured water grew louder. Leith looked down, startled: the Kljufa seemed to emerge from the very rock, fountaining up from a dry bed! Yet as he lifted his gaze, he could see the river clearly further upstream. What was this?

As they entered the roofed road, the mystery was solved. Leith risked a further glance over the sheer cliff to his right. There he saw the mighty river enter a vast whirlpool, water spinning faster and faster, disappearing down a huge hole only to emerge as a fountain a hundred yards or so further downstream. The rock in between was perfectly dry, so that one could walk across the riverbed without getting wet; though such a journey would gain the traveller nothing, as another vertical wall rose on the other side of the river. The sight was breathtaking, the sound beyond belief; loud enough, it seemed, to split the very rock. He turned to the old farmer.

'The Maelstrom,' the old man shouted. 'One of the wonders of the world.' Leith could hardly drag his eyes away from the sight.

Then came a frantic cry from Perdu at the head of the Company. Two figures in grey stood at the far end of the roofed road! As Leith watched in horror, they drew their swords and advanced towards the Company.

The travellers turned in panic. Trapped! Behind them were two more grey figures, swords menacing. They were cut off, with nowhere to run. The ambush was perfect.

The Bhrudwans were perhaps two hundred yards away, walking faster now. 'Stand back to back!' Farr shouted. 'Draw your swords! Strike the first blow!'

'Shouldn't we charge one of the groups?' Kurr asked, his voice thin and breathless.

'No! That's just what they want us to do! Let them come to us!'

'Join me, Leith!' cried Wira. 'Together we will repay these men for their evil deeds!'

Wide-eyed with panic, Leith did as he was asked. He drew his sword, pitifully small in comparison to the wicked curving blades wielded by the Bhrudwans. Only a hundred yards away now. He could see their faces. They were smiling.

At that moment something brushed past Leith, knocking him to the ground. Wira shouted, then cursed. Leith picked himself up in time to see Wisent, with Stella clinging to his back, charging at the Bhrudwans behind them. 'Run! Run!' Farr shouted. 'After her!'

The warriors in front of them halted in amazement. The Bhrudwans behind stopped their advance, then turned and ran from the charging beast. Stella urged the great animal on. As he drew close to the enemy she rolled to the right, placing herself next to the wall, holding on to the aurochs' mane for all she was worth.

One of the Bhrudwans turned and struck at the beast with his sword. Whether the blow landed, Leith could not tell. Wisent bored straight into the unlucky warrior, knocking him sideways. For a moment the Bhrudwan scrabbled at the edge of the precipice, then he fell into the river with a cry. Almost immediately the Maelstrom pulled at him. Frantic now, he tried to escape the clutches of the vortex, but inexorably it drew him in. Leith saw him disappear into the Maelstrom's maw.

Ahead Wisent gained on the other warrior. The Bhrudwan was now caught in his own trap: there was nowhere for him to run but straight ahead. The huge beast bore down on him. Stella urged the aurochs forward. Faster he went, but not fast enough. With a last effort the Bhrudwan emerged from the roofed road and scrambled up the rocky slope at the side of the spur. A moment later Wisent, with Stella still holding on tightly, flashed past him.

A few seconds after that, the rest of the Company emerged, Leith and the others running as hard as they could. Leith turned and looked up. The Bhrudwan was high up on the slope, foot braced against a large rock. 'Look out!' shouted Leith. The

Company stopped in their tracks as the first rock crashed down on to the Westway.

'Keep going!' Farr shouted. 'There is still danger behind us!' He was right; the other two warriors were close behind, running for all they were worth, having recovered from the shock of seeing one of their fellows taken by the river. Hal and the Haufuth, the last of the Company, scurried past the entrance to the roofed road, dodging rocks as they came.

Ahead, Stella had managed to halt the rampaging charge of the huge aurochs. She turned, ready to repeat the strategy. In a moment Farr and Wira were past her, followed by the others. Leith watched his brother in amazement. Hal used his crippled leg like a staff, throwing his weight forward whenever he landed on the stiff right leg. In this fashion he was little slower than the Haufuth.

The Bhrudwans halted, realising their peril. Then they turned and retreated down the roofed road, rejoined by their fellow warrior, who had scrambled down from the slopes above. In a little over a minute they had vanished from sight.

'Let's go after them!' Farr cried.

'No!' Perdu answered emphatically. 'Wisent is hurt.'

There was a large open wound on the animal's left flank, extending down from his shoulder. The blood flowed freely. Perdu grabbed clothing from his pack and ran to a small freshet at the side of the road. He soaked the clothes in the water, then used them to try to staunch the wound. Wisent appeared not to feel any pain. The light of battle gleamed in his eyes, and his mouth foamed with excitement.

Wira turned on Stella. 'That could have been you!' he said, pointing to the animal's flank.

'But it wasn't,' the young woman replied, a fierce light in her eye. 'We taught them a lesson, Wisent and I.'

Kurr shook his head. 'Amazing!' he said. 'I couldn't believe it when I saw you on the back of that mad beast. I would not like to have been in your way!' He laughed. 'What made you think of doing that?'

'I don't know,' admitted Stella frankly. 'Just an impulse.'

Leith looked at those eyes. They contained the same laughter that he had seen on the night of the Midwinter Play. He could not fathom them then; neither could he now. *Perhaps it is courage*, he thought. *Certainly I would never have attempted such a thing.*

Hal took a sharp needle and some stout cord from his pack. While the others kept a lookout in case the Bhrudwans returned, Hal stitched the gaping wound closed. It took a long time.

'Will he be able to go any further?' Stella asked Perdu.

'It will take more than a sword cut to stop Wisent,' the Fenni replied. 'That was a foolish thing to do,' he added, but there was a smile on his face. 'I wouldn't have believed that anyone who is not Fenni could have ridden an aurochs like that. But he likes you, doesn't he?'

Stella held her hand in front of Wisent's face. The great animal licked her. 'Yes, he does. And I like him.'

The Company once again went forward, this time much more carefully. 'We can't afford to be surprised again,' Farr commented. 'We were lucky this time.'

'Lucky?' his brother said. 'No; we were saved by the pluck of a beautiful woman.' He turned to Stella and smiled. She cocked her head and smiled back. Leith turned away.

The travellers passed through the roofed road without further incident. Beyond they found a straight stretch of road which lay deserted. After a few miles without a bend, the road curved gradually to the left, away from the river. The walls moved further apart, and the river quietened down; they were through the Lower Clough, and the Bhrudwans were nowhere to be seen.

Where are my father and mother? What has been done to them? Now that Leith had seen the enemy face to face, the fate of his parents had turned from vain imaginings to frightful reality. Like the others, the boy from Loulea had brushed against something evil and it had changed him, marking him like the dirt from the bark of the trees beside the Loulea village pond. Just by being close to the Bhrudwans he had become unclean somehow.

Six weeks they had been on the Westway, and finally they had seen the warriors they pursued – though for moments only. They had vanished again, as quickly as they had appeared, to Farr's disappointment. No one else spoke, though no doubt they all wished they could confront the Bhrudwans. Leith tried to act disappointed, tried to hold back the relief that flooded every part of him. Relief, but disappointment too, for now he knew beyond doubt that he was a coward. His fear of death had outweighed the need of his parents.

He tried to feel sorry, but mostly he felt reprieved.

CHAPTER 12

ROLEYSTONE BRIDGE

HEMMED IN BY CRUEL mountains, pressed forward by anxiety for their loved ones but held back by fear of their implacable foes, the Company tracked slowly northeast in wary pursuit of the Bhrudwans. Early each morning Wira or Farr would scout the road ahead, searching for the enemy's abandoned campsite of the previous night, then would return to lead the travellers forward with caution. Three days passed in this fashion, until the crossing of the Jawbone Mountains was nearly complete. It was now late February, and the worst of winter was behind them – or so they reasoned.

On the fourth day out from the Maelstrom the wind turned to the north. Originating above the vast snow-covered wasteland of the Vollervei, the gale whipped icy rains down the mountain-walled valley of the Kljufa. For a while they continued trudging stubbornly into the sleet; then, one by one, the travellers faltered. Hal's crippled leg cramped up, making it difficult for him to keep pace with the others. Kurr's joints were on fire: as he walked his bones rasped together, as though they had been drained dry. Stella lost all feeling in her hands and feet, but clenched her teeth and tried to continue. It was only when she stumbled and fell that the others realised her danger. After seeking shelter in the lee of a south-facing ridge, they discovered that her toes were numb and in danger of being frostbitten. She whimpered with pain as the Haufuth rubbed the circulation back into her feet, while the Storrsen brothers hurriedly set a fire.

251

'We can go no further with the girl like this.' Farr shook his head with frustration. With every moment the Bhrudwans and their captives moved further away. To have come this far only to be beaten by the weather! Worse, the Mjolkbridge man suspected that some of his fellow travellers were not as keen to confront the hated Bhrudwans as they made out.

'I could go no further anyway,' the Haufuth replied. The cold had seeped into his bones, and a deep weariness had settled upon him, dampening his spirits. 'I need a rest. A day's rest here and maybe we can make better time.'

Each member of the Company voiced his or her concern at the delay, but secretly each one was glad. The fear of the road, and what might await them at its end, had been mounting steadily as they had travelled across the highlands of Firanes. Muscles tensed and hearts raced as they approached every bend in the road, the crest of every hill, in anticipation of sighting their quarry. The prospect of any lessening of the tension, even for just one day, seemed like a welcoming fireside at the end of a long journey.

'Chances are the Bhrudwans won't be going far in this murk,' Wira said optimistically. No one believed him. In their heart of hearts, they imagined the raiders forcing Mahnum and Indrett, and Parlevaag the Fenni woman, on through the driving rain. Their suffering must be terrible.

One by one the travellers changed clothes and drew close to the fire. For a while conversation was light-hearted, with talk of the upcoming spring in the lowland vales, but gradually discussion came around to their present situation.

'How much further will we have to go?' Stella asked, her question addressed to no one in particular. The Haufuth continued to work away at her feet, the rubbing relieving most of the pain.

'I don't know,' he said. 'Far enough so they have forgotten about us. Far enough so we can catch them unawares.'

'But close enough so we still have some strength left with which to fight!' Farr added.

Wira laughed. 'You'll always have the strength!' he teased his brother.

'Well, it's what we're here for,' Farr responded, uncomfortable with Wira's comment.

'Will we ever get close enough to do it?' Leith asked.

The Haufuth considered a moment. 'We've caught them once; we can catch them again. But Farr is right, we cannot wait forever. It may be time to take a few risks – but, then again . . .' He tailed off, absorbed in his thoughts.

'Can we catch them before we get over the Jawbone Mountains?' Leith asked again.

'We're nearly through them already,' said Kurr. 'Somewhere close at hand is Roleystone Bridge, where we cross the Kljufa River; from there the Westway follows the south bank until we pass through the Portals—'

'But when do we climb over the mountains?'

'Were you not listening when I explained this yesterday? There is no climb. The river cuts a path right through them. All we have to do is to follow the river.'

'How could the river have cut through these mountains?' Leith waved his arm at the steep hills, their flanks mist-shrouded, their tops buried in cloud. Nothing seemed less likely.

'How would I know?' The Haufuth became irritated by the persistent questioning; he wanted time to think, time to evaluate the options before him.

'The Fenni tell a story about the mountains and the rivers,' Perdu said.

'Well, tell them about it,' the village headman shot back. 'I'm going for a walk.' He got up and stomped off into the sheeting rain.

Perdu raised his eyebrows, looked at Kurr and shrugged his shoulders.

'Go ahead,' the old farmer encouraged. 'The fire is warm and people are ready for stories.'

'It's not really much of a story, especially the way I tell it. What we need is a really good Fenni bard, someone like Parlevaag . . .' He faltered, then recovered. 'Well, we have no bard among us, so here goes.'

A gust of wind whipped over the brow of the low ridge, flattening the flames for a moment. Sparks flew as the fire roared; the Company drew back; then the wind passed and the weary travellers again crept closer to the warmth.

'A long time ago, before the fathers of men walked the earth, the land was flat and featureless, rimmed to the north by ice, to the south by sea. Two proud rivers flowed from the ice to the sea, with nothing to disturb their courses. These rivers ruled the land, and spoke often to each other about the lofty positions they occupied and the privileges they enjoyed. Their vanity was plain for everyone else to see, and of the occupants of the land they were the most hated.

'One day the two rivers called loudly to each other across the land, forcing everyone else to listen to their boasting. The other dwellers in the land had heard enough, and held a gathering.

'"It is time we took action," said one of the large lakes. "Without the rivers, they tell us, we would have no water coming in and no water going out. We would stagnate and die. This might be true, but I am tired of hearing about it."

'A small stream spoke up: "The rivers remind me constantly of their length and breadth, the beauty of their waters, the mystery of their depths. Mere streams are so small, they sneer. As if size is everything!" A number of other streams murmured their agreement.

'A deep, rolling voice came up from the south. "Those rivers never leave me alone!" the sea complained. "Without us you would be empty, with your bones exposed for all to see, they say. They laugh at my waves, and pour scorn on my tides. Something must be done!" the voice boomed. Cheering broke out amongst some of the younger, more excitable members of the gathering.

'"So what do we do?" they asked each other.

'"Perhaps we could ask the ice to withhold its meltwater," said one. "Without the meltwater, where would the rivers be?"

'"The ice won't be coming to the meeting," came the sad reply. "Fast asleep."

'"Can we block the rivers somehow?" someone asked hopefully.

'"How?" they all asked.

'"What about snow and ice? If some of us went and asked Qali, perhaps he would help!"

'This was the best they could come up with, so a deputation was chosen to approach the great snow god Qali.

'"O great Qali," said a particularly deep lake, the leader of the delegation, "we need your help to put a stop to the boasting of the rivers. Will you help us?"

'"Why should I?" the god replied, amused at the rag-tag group.

'"Because the rivers boast that they are the greatest inhabitants of the land," the lake replied.

'"Even greater than the great god Qali?" Qali asked, darkness suddenly appearing on his brow.

'"Oh yes, much greater," lied the lake.

'Then the enraged snow god stormed across the land, scattering all the inhabitants before him. First he tried to melt the ice, but this was too slow for the impatient god, and only served to make the rivers even greater. Then he tried to freeze the rivers over, but found he had power over the rivers for only part of the year. Finally he gave up in disgust and left the land, going on a long journey.

'This made the rivers even louder in their self-praise. Before they had been irritating; now they were unbearable. The members of the delegation to Qali were held responsible by the others for this state of affairs, and found themselves spurned. The land became a very unhappy place.

'One day the great god Qali returned with the fruit of his journey. Hidden in the hollow of his hand was a small bag of seeds, and in his eye was a smug gleam. That night he walked across the land from north to south, at intervals taking a seed from the bag and planting it in the cold earth. His soft laughter fell as autumn snow across the wide plain between the ice and the sea.

'The next morning revealed the work of the great god Qali. Where he had planted seeds, mountains had grown. Steep-sided and tall, the mountains had chased the lakes away and broken up the streams. Most importantly, they blocked the two rivers from flowing out to sea.

'Mjolk, the northern of the two rivers, was sleepy that night, and the mountain-plants took him by surprise. Before he had time to react, his course had been split in two, and he had lost his link to the ice. From that day on Mjolk was a much smaller river, flowing from the mountains to the sea, and his boasting voice was never heard again.

'Kljufa, the southern river, lay awake in his bed, expecting some trick from the snow god. When the mountains began to grow, he gathered up the lakes and streams nearby and flowed with great power between the huge peaks. No matter how fast the mountains grew, the river cut down between them. By the time the mountain-plants had finished growing, Kljufa was bigger and louder than ever. The remaining inhabitants of the valley, those who had not been swallowed by Kljufa or scattered by the mountains, were dismayed. The great god Qali was beside himself with anger.

'While Kljufa celebrated down by the sea, singing his own praises to anyone who would listen, Qali took his seed-bag and crept northwards, intending to plant more mountains. However, when he looked in his bag, all that remained was dust and seed flakes. In disgust he flung the bag on the ground and retired to his eyrie, defeated.

'The next morning, the land awoke to find that the seed-dust had taken root in the north of the land, near the ice. Instead of growing mountains, the dust formed a series of low hills, blocking the outflow of the ice, which ponded into a huge sea to the north. Kljufa began to get thinner and rushed northwards, too late. He was cut off from his headwaters. From that moment his laughter was silenced, and the sound of his waters became the sound of mourning.

'The great god Qali could hardly believe his good fortune. At a single stroke, two of his most powerful rivals had been defeated, the ice was cut off to the north, and the lesser inhabitants of the land had been scattered or cowed. So he assembled all his powers and covered the land with snow. And from that day until this,

Qali has ruled the land with a cold hand, having subdued it to his will.'

When the Haufuth returned from his time alone, he found his travelling companions asleep around the fire. They lay in pairs: Leith and Hal, Farr and Wira, Stella and Kurr, Perdu and the *urus* Wisent. Sleep had smoothed out the lines on their faces, and for a while his friends looked as they had done two months ago, before all this started, untouched by evil. For a long moment the stout headman thought of waking everyone, turning them around and taking them home. The captives were probably lost; realistically, what could they do? Who could blame them if they abandoned their quest?

The Haufuth sighed. What about Faltha? *Let Faltha take care of herself*, thought the bone-weary man. He reached out his arm to tap Kurr on the shoulder, hesitated a moment, then withdrew it. It was too late. Evil had touched them already; they could not go back in time. They had to go on, try to free their friends, and probably perish in the attempt. All that stood between those innocent faces and a horrible end were an old farmer and a fat headman, wisdom enough between them for perhaps one good man and strength for not even that.

For a moment his gaze lingered on the weather-beaten face of his friend the farmer. *Kurr, I am thankful you chose to come on this journey. But perhaps you had no choice. Are you also running, even as I am? You run from the memory of a good woman, as I run from a village which ridicules me even as they use me. What a pair we make.*

But you have more strength than do I. This trek has exhausted me, body and soul; soon I will sink to my knees on the side of this road and you will take over leadership of the Company. He laughed to himself. *You have already taken over. And so you should: you're one of the Watchers, and you are trained to think clearly. Sleep well, my friend.*

The rain continued all afternoon, falling steadily as the travellers slept; in the evening the rain slackened, and as Hal moved quietly about preparing the meal, it turned to a light snow. The wind fell away, and for a while the Upper Clough was quiet, with the mournful sibilance of Kljufa's deep waters the sole sound in the canyon.

Leith awoke refreshed the next morning to find the weather had improved further. Already the clouds were lifting and the day promised to be clear and cold. The others slept on as he stirred the embers into flame, then wandered down to the river's edge to wash.

The deep blue waters of the Kljufa were very, very cold. Behind some ragged bushes Leith undressed and washed, the chilling water serving to fully wake him from the daze of the last twenty-four hours. As he dressed, he heard Farr and Wira come down to the riverbank some distance upstream.

'Well, you drank it,' said one as they came within earshot.

'Are you sure you don't have any? No wine? No ale?' The voice sounded frantic.

'Of course not. I've been watching you, little brother. Yesterday afternoon you went through our things when you thought we were asleep. What were you looking for? Did you think you might have found some liquor in our packs? That there are other sly drinkers among us?'

Leith couldn't help himself. He moved quietly forward until he was sitting among the bushes, looking down upon the Storrsen brothers as they argued by the water's edge.

'Come on,' said Farr, gesticulating at his younger brother. 'Put it out of your mind. Is anything more important than avenging our father?'

Wira kicked at an angular rock. 'You're heartless. We're miles away from anywhere; it could be weeks before I get another drink.'

'Good! What will the others say when they find out? What will the Loulea girl say?'

'They'll never find out. I've been careful!'

'What if I tell them?'

'You wouldn't!'

'If you can't control yourself, I may be forced to tell the fat man. Then what will the coastlanders think of my fair-spoken brother?'

Wira sank to the ground. Even from a distance Leith could see the despair in his eyes, hear the pleading in his voice.

'Please! They don't need to know about this! I'll not mention it again.'

Farr stood above his brother with his arms folded, a satisfied smile on his face.

It was all too much for Leith. It was as though Farr stood over him, gloating over his weakness like the other children had done when Leith was a boy. He pulled back, stumbled over a tree root and slithered away out of sight, making far too much noise. Head down, he ran back to the campsite, not stopping to see if he had been heard.

A few moments later the Storrsens came back into the camp. He tried to control his heavy breathing as he lay pretending to be asleep. The brothers looked around for a minute, then gave up and settled down to make breakfast.

Rejuvenated, the Company made their way through the Upper Clough. While not as precipitous as the Lower Clough, and with no hazards like the Maelstrom and the Roofed Road, the narrow upper gorge of the Kljufa was still spectacular. The river surged over rapid after rapid, white foam beating at snarltoothed shoals, with inaccessible islands encircled by swift blue arms. Above them the hills grew into mountains, stretching up to the roofless sky. The great god Qali had spread his white blanket across the land, but the Kljufa still flowed vigorously. Evidently, whatever the Fenni bards said, the snow god did not have everything his own way.

Later that day, however, the travellers came to an impasse. At the borders of Firanes, where the mountains gave way to the waste-lands of the Vollervei, the Westway crossed the Kljufa by a single stone arch called Roleystone Bridge, then trailed away southwards into the depths of Withwestwa Wood. Leith could see the road on the other side of the river, following the far bank into the distance.

But there was no way of getting to it. The great stone arch of Roleystone had been thrown down.

Farr crawled as far out as he could on the ruined bridge. 'This was done recently,' he said. 'No sign of wear – in fact, the stone has been cut here, and here.' He pointed, but the others were too far away to see.

'That is a pity,' Kurr said sadly. 'The bridge was a thing of beauty, and has been standing here for a thousand years and more.'

'The real pity is that they are over there and we are not,' Farr grumbled. 'Look!'

On the far side of the river, three threatening figures emerged from the shadows. Three Bhrudwan warriors. The sounds of jeering filtered across the expanse of water. As they watched in horror, one of the warriors dragged three further figures, ragged and bound together, out into the light. Hal bit his lip; Leith cried out. Thin, bedraggled, cruelly used, Mahnum and Indrett stood a bridge-span away on the other side of the water, along with Parlevaag the Fenni woman.

'Stand firm,' said Kurr, placing his arm on Leith's shoulder. 'They mean by this display to torture us and their captives both.' Evil laughter echoed around the canyon.

Finally, tiring of their sport, the Bhrudwans drove their captives down the Westway. Slowly they disappeared from sight. The Company could only watch. Leith sobbed with frustration as with every step his heart was torn further in two. As he endured the sight of his life vanishing into the unreachable distance, he learned that there is a pain more fierce than the edge of a sword. His world dissolved into a mist of tears, and for a time he knew nothing but the emptiness inside where his heart had been.

'How did they pull the bridge down? The thing was made of solid stone!'

'I have no idea,' Kurr said wearily in response to his headman's question. 'Perhaps the arch was weak anyway.' *Kroptur, where are your fancy words now?*

'Perhaps if they had stayed around, we might have asked them,'

Farr said bitingly. 'What does it matter? It is over now; there is no crossing this river for weeks in either direction. They are gone.'

'Is there no way of crossing this river?' the Haufuth asked, eyeing the far bank. 'Perhaps we could make a raft . . .'

'Out of what?' Farr turned on the stout man. 'Look around – do you see any wood? Have you seen any trees since the Thraell valley? And even if we had wood and could make a raft, do you suppose it would survive in that?' He pointed down to the powerful currents below, then shook his head. 'Was there not anyone in Loulea with sufficient wit to lead us? Or did the Bhrudwans choose our leaders for us?' He laughed bitterly in the stunned silence that followed his words. 'Who will avenge our father now? The great god Qali?'

'How dare you!' Kurr cried. 'Have you no respect? You would do better to let your brother do the talking! Learn from your betters!'

Farr did not reply. Instead, he walked slowly away, paying no attention to the stares focused in his direction.

'Let him go,' the Haufuth said quietly. 'He's upset – we all are. Take no heed of his words.'

'All the same, we would have done better to have two like Wira on this expedition. Even one like Wira. The older Storrsen is a liability.'

Immersed in his grief, Leith said nothing. He knew the inaccuracy of their opinion, but he didn't have the energy to correct them.

Ten minutes later Farr returned. His time alone had not eased his mood.

'I've had enough,' he announced flatly. 'My brother and I will go on alone. You people are worse than useless. Come on, Wira.'

'To where?' his brother responded. 'The river is uncrossable. We have nowhere to go but home. Are we going to abandon our friends?'

Farr stormed over to Wira and leaned his face close in to his brother's. At first Wira returned his gaze, but then his eyes dropped.

'You and I both know why you have to do what I say!' Farr hissed in his brother's face. The younger Storrsen nodded dumbly.

'What's going on here?' Kurr asked.

'None of your business!' snapped Farr.

This was too much for the old farmer. 'It is our business!' he yelled. 'Here we are in the middle of nowhere, vulnerable to attack – we need each other! Whatever is happening concerns all of us!' He began to walk towards the Storrsens.

The Haufuth rose, arms wide in a calming gesture. 'Come on, let's not fight amongst ourselves—'

Kurr strode up to Farr and Wira, then pushed in between them.

'Come on, old man, watch what you're doing!' Farr warned.

'Show some respect!' Kurr replied, his chin jutting forward. 'You don't have the right to go off on your own!'

'Be careful. I'm warning you!' Farr stepped back, hands twitching.

'Kurr!' the Haufuth shouted.

'When will you learn sense?' pressed the old farmer, irate beyond reason. Emotions rubbed raw by weeks of friction, suppressed for the sake of the Company, were released in the atmosphere of disappointment on the wrong side of the river. 'Keep your mouth closed, and leave the thinking to others!' He reached out a restraining hand towards the elder Storrsen.

'Don't touch me!' Farr screamed. He knocked the farmer's arm aside, jumped back and drew his sword. 'Get away!'

Now things spun out of control, and other members of the Company began to shout. No one heard the Haufuth's vain efforts to calm them down. Farr stood back on his heels, waving his sword threateningly at Kurr. Unnoticed in the tumult, Hal moved behind the elder Storrsen, then darted forward with an agility that belied his deformity and chopped down quickly on Farr's wrist. The sword dropped on to the stony ground with a clatter. Quickly, Hal scooped it up and cast it away. Farr spun around, fists raised, set to strike his attacker. Hal stood firm. And as Farr stared into the eyes of the crippled youth, his anger and frustration drained away. He lowered his fists, took a deep breath and let it out slowly.

Across the Face of the World

For a moment all was quiet, then from behind the Company someone began to clap. 'Bravo! Bravo!' a hearty voice shouted. 'Magnificent! Bravo!'

The travellers turned around, startled. On a ridge to the right of the road, fifty or so yards behind them, stood a small fat man with a huge bushy beard, alternating between cheering, clapping and filling the air with full-throated laughter. Instantly swords were drawn, Farr making an undignified scrabble for his blade.

The fat man raised his arms, palms upwards. 'No swords! No swords!' he called, but his friendly face showed no fear.

'Put your swords away,' Perdu said, in a surprisingly bright voice. 'This man is one of the Fodhram, and is no threat to us. In fact, he might be able to help us.' The Fenni beckoned to the bearded man, who left his perch on the ridge and came bouncing down to them.

Leith stared at the fellow with undisguised curiosity. Of indeterminate age, his long, straggly hair and a full moustache and beard partially hid a weather-beaten face lined with creases that were surely laughter lines. He was short, astonishingly short, and portly, with his stomach hanging over his wide belt.

'What a performance!' the man cried, throwing an arm around a startled Hal. 'Disarming the fighters with one blow! I salute you!' He cast an amused eye over the travellers. 'And what were they fighting about, I wonder? What is worth wasting energy on in such a place as this?' He laughed. 'For that matter, what brings coast-landers into the toughlands?'

No one offered a reply. His appearance had taken them by surprise.

'Perhaps I can guess,' he said, a shrewd gleam in his eyes. 'I have seen another group of people today, not so soft, hurrying through an unfamiliar land. Do you wish to have words with them? More than words, perhaps?' He read their faces as he spoke. 'I thought so. A pity, then, that Roleystone is fallen. You will not speak with them today.'

Perdu bowed from the waist, then clasped the man about the shoulders, much to his delight. 'Fellow travellers,' the Fenni said,

263

'may I introduce to you a member of the Fodhram, whose name is . . .'

He looked expectantly at the rotund man, whose smile only broadened.

'You seem to know the Fodhram,' the man replied, smiling. 'If that is so, you will know that names are not the property of strangers. My name I keep to myself; my hospitality, however, I share. Do you wish for the hospitality of the Fodhram?'

Perdu nodded vigorously. 'We're all in need of a little hospitality right now,' he said ruefully. 'It's been a long road, and we need new strength in order to face its end. The hospitality of the Fodhram would be most welcome.'

'Magnificent! Wonderful news! New faces around the fire! My boys will be proud of me!' The man did a little jig, then turned and cupped his hands around his mouth. 'Boys!' he yelled. 'Guests for dinner!'

In response to his call three bearded faces appeared above the ridge. In a moment they were amongst the Company, three stocky men scarcely taller than their leader, greeting them as if they were long-lost friends. The Storrsens in particular were taken aback by the show of friendliness, so much unlike the Vinkullen Hills where everyone kept to themselves, and strangers were most often ignored.

'It is the Fodhram way,' Perdu said out of the side of his mouth. 'Greet them warmly; any less is an insult.' So shoulders were clasped and bows were exchanged, but no one asked anyone else's name.

All right, Kroptur, thought Kurr. *I'm sorry I doubted you: you were right. 'Friend and foe unlooked for,' you said. Well, we have had both today. I only hope friend helps us triumph over foe.*

That night twelve people sat around a huge campfire sharing salted meats and tall tales. Five there were from Loulea: the Haufuth, Kurr the farmer, Stella, Hal the cripple, and his brother Leith. From the hills of Vinkullen came the Storrsen brothers, Farr and Wira, who sat next to those from Loulea. Perdu of Mjolkbridge, who had adopted the Fenni of Myrvidda as his people, laughed along with the Storrsens; and from wooden cottages deep in

Across the Face of the World

Withwestwa Wood four of the Fodhram sat: all twelve far from home. In the background the outline of Roleystone Bridge flickered in the firelight.

Leith lay quietly on his back a short distance from the fire, content to rest, allowing others to do the talking. He yawned and put his hands behind his head. Above him stretched two tall fir trees, scarce in the valleys of the Jawbone Mountains. Through their boughs Leith could see the sky, lit by the faint glow of a newly hatched moon: ragged clouds fluttered by on a cooling breeze, occulting the northern stars.

Behind him the four Fodhram were making merry. They seemed to have no interest in who the newcomers were, or the business that had brought them so far from home, contenting themselves instead with singing and shouting with great gusto. Most of the songs were new to the Firanese, but even here on the borders of Firanes and Plonya familiar words or snatches of melody could be heard, and the canyon of the Upper Clough echoed to melodies such as the ubiquitous 'My Lady Fair':

> Saw her at the autumn harvest
> Sunlight shining in her hair
> Promised she would not forsake me
> Loved her more than I could bear.
>
> Oh, I adored her
> When I saw her there
> She played my heartstrings
> How I loved my lady fair!
>
> When she stepped across my doorway
> Then she stepped into my life
> Tenderly she gave love to me
> Gladly she became my wife.
>
> Oh, I adored her
> When I saw her there

265

She gave love to me
How I loved my lady fair.

She left me for another lover
One who said he loved her more
Took my knife and ran it through her
Left her lying on the floor.

Oh, I adored her
When I saw her there
She lay there silent
How I loved my lady fair.

They sang the song through again: it was a favourite right across the northern lands, encapsulating lives lived on the edge of the world, far from the moderation offered by civilisation. As they began the last verse, Stella stood quietly, a glow in her fathomless eyes, and walked gracefully around the fire to where Wira was seated. Without a word she sat beside him, then took his hand in hers.

He turned to her, and in a low voice he said: 'Promise you won't forsake me.'

'Never!' she replied, and tightened her hold on his hand.

'That is just as well,' he said. 'I'm no good with a knife.'

Oblivious to what was happening on the other side of the fire, Leith drifted into sleep, lulled into temporary forgetfulness by the melodies around him.

'So, you're trying to catch these Bhrudwan raiders and set their hostages free.' The short man grunted as he pondered the story he had just heard. 'Not only that, you want to capture one of these Bhrudwans and make him tell the Falthan kings all about the coming invasion from the east.' The Fodhram leader laughed long and lazily. 'Perhaps you might also ask them to pull the old town of Astora out of the sea!'

The fire had died down along with the singing; now only the crackling of embers and the low murmur of conversation could be heard. Above, the pale stars glistened in the cold air like snow crystals suspended in the night.

Kurr smiled. 'So what would you advise? That we should go back home to sit on our porches to await the end?'

The short man leaned forward, a new seriousness entering his manner. 'Bhrudwo is an old and not very convincing story, and the Destroyer – well, the Destroyer is simply a tall tale. And here you are telling me that today I saw a man who has been on Andratan, a man held captive by Bhrudwans.' He laughed again; it seemed that this man laughed at everything.

'No, I'm not convinced. My counsel would indeed be to return home and abandon this hopeless quest. So of course you should continue, for in this case your hearts should never yield to counsel, however wise. But how, you are thinking? Roleystone is impassable, and there is no other way for you to cross the river. In that case, you had better come with us.'

'Where are you going?'

'We are making the Southern Run, the first run of the season.'

'How will that help us?' Kurr wanted to ask what the Southern Run was, and where it went, but dared not show his ignorance.

'We will make much better time on the Run than these raiders can make on the Westway. They will be immobilised by the spring thaw which even now approaches Withwestwa Wood from the south. We can wait for them at Vindstrop House.'

The Fodhram man's proposal began to make sense to the old farmer. Vindstrop House was the best part of a thousand miles east of the Jawbone Mountains, a small trading settlement sitting astride the Westway. Between Roleystone Bridge and Vindstrop House a handful of people eked an existence from the deep northern forest, trading in furs and cutting timber for the citizens of Plonya and Treika, countries far to the south of Withwestwa Wood. These people were the Fodhram and the forest was their domain. This Southern Run was probably some trading route known only to the woodcrafty Fodhram.

'The only risk we run is the chance that they may leave the

Westway before Vindstrop House,' Kurr replied. 'Other than that, we'd be delighted to accept your help.'

'And we'd be glad of the company, I won't deny it!' the portly man laughed. 'Five months of winter cooped up with these three animals is quite long enough. But you'll have to pay your way! I'll not disguise the fact that meeting you here is a lucky chance. We've checked the winter traps and found far more pelt than we can easily carry. There are some strong shoulders among you, shoulders that can carry a bale or two along the Southern Run. Agreed?'

Kurr did not hesitate. It was either this or return home. 'Agreed!' he said, with as much passion as he could muster.

This brought another hearty laugh from the Fodhram. 'Tomorrow morning we can tell your headman!' the leader said. 'The food and ale have sent him to sleep!'

'More likely the talking!' another of the Fodhram added. 'We have a saying: "Friends who meet on the road should drink first and ask questions later." I intend to prove the old saying! Come,' he said, beckoning the Storrsen brothers. 'Will anyone join me?' He pulled a flask of liquor from his pack.

'I'll take part in your experiment,' Wira said quickly, too quickly for Farr to protest. The flask was passed around; the laughter became even heartier and the stories more outrageous as the night wore on and the fuel burned low. Some time in the hours before dawn the last of the revellers fell into slumber; for a while after that Wira sat alone by the fire, nursing the remains of the flask.

The next morning the Fodhram leader told them more about the Southern Run. It was the southernmost of three major fur-trading routes: the others were the Northern Run and, far to the north, the Summer Run. This latter run had once been the most rewarding of the three, but the weather had changed for the worse in recent years and in some seasons it could not be attempted. The Southern Run was the first to reopen after the long winter, with the thaw usually coming some time early in March.

The four Fodhram had made an early-season expedition to check the winter traps, hoping the thaw would come early so they could use the maze of lakes and rivers of Withwestwa Wood to canoe the fur pelts down to Treika. They risked a long, hungry wait for the thaw, but the rewards for bringing the first fur of the season to the fashion-conscious Treikan women were very high. So every year a few foolhardy Fodhram took the gamble and set out during the deep winter for the Portals of the Kljufa River, the western terminus of the Southern Run. They footslogged through snow and ice, then waited out the worst storms, living on salted meats and what they could hunt in the woods. And every year a few Fodhram were swallowed by wood or water, never to be seen again.

This year had seen an average winter, the Fodhram leader told the Company. The thaw was not expected for at least four more weeks, even this far south. So they had planned to wait it out in the shelter of the mountains, then take to their birch bark canoes once the waterways were clear. Now, with the advent of the Company, another idea presented itself. They could take advantage of the Southern Run while it was frozen, wait at Midrun for the thaw, and then use their canoes to get to Vindstrop House. Kurr and the bearded Fodhram leader held a long discussion, then approached Perdu.

'Are you determined to continue?' the old farmer asked the adopted Fenni. 'You have already come a long way further than you planned, and your family are many miles behind you.'

'Don't remind me,' Perdu replied morosely. 'I'd give anything to return to my hearth. But the clan chief laid a sacred duty upon me, and I cannot return until I have beheld the dead faces of our enemies, so into the Rotten Lands I must go.'

'The Rotten Lands? Do the Fenni name our rich lands so?' For the first time a hint of anger marred the jovial face of the Fodhram leader.

'Indeed yes; and by what name is the Myrvidda known amongst the noble Fodhram?' inquired Perdu slyly, knowing the answer full well.

'You have a point,' the bearded man replied, laughing again. 'So it is with people whose own lands must be first in their own minds!'

'Well then,' Kurr interrupted, keen to be on his way, 'here is the nub. You need to cross the land of the Fodhram, but Wisent cannot come with you. The aurochs is too large for many of the trails we must follow, and there is no birch bark canoe in existence that could hold his bulk, even if he were persuaded to embark on one. So what are we to do?'

'A rhetorical question, no doubt!' Perdu replied, troubled that in his sadness at travelling ever further away from his loved ones, he had forgotten his clan chief's great gift. 'I'm sure you and the worthy Fodhram here have a suggestion to make!'

The worthy Fodhram laughed until his belly shook with the force of it. 'You are right; and here is the answer. Not far north of the Portals lives a hermit, a man who survives by hunting forest animals. He is an outstanding hunter, and he sells meat to all the Fodhram who pass his way. My thought is this: we need to eat, and he needs a pack animal. Could we not fashion an exchange that will advantage all parties? The alternative is a week's hunting in the depths of the wood, something that we do not like and you would find very uncomfortable. What do you say?'

For a long time Perdu stood silently, considering the problem. At intervals he glanced over to the huge bulk of his shaggy friend, their saviour at the Roofed Road. Indecision was written on his brow.

Kurr spoke. 'Our friend and helper, are you going to return home, or will you come with us? Make your choice!' Kurr was sorry to press the Fenni so hard, but time and the anxious fear of delay were pressing him.

'Give me a moment,' Perdu responded.

'As you wish.'

The adopted Fenni walked off sadly, shoulders slumped forward, seeking a quiet place to think. Unnoticed, another figure followed him.

Kurr watched Perdu leave, then turned to the Fodhram leader. 'If I read him right, he will come with us. We must make preparations to leave. Is the house of this hermit far from our way?'

'No; it is only a mile or so from the beginning of the Southern

Run. I will gather my men, and we will make ready. Fodhram, Fenni and Firanese travelling the Southern Run together! This has the makings of a fireside tale – with appropriate embellishments, of course!' Again the laughter, carefree and happy even in the face of such a risky journey.

A little while later the old farmer turned to the Fodhram leader. 'I have to know,' Kurr said. 'What do the Fodhram call the Myrvidda?'

The bearded man laughed shamefacedly. 'Rakkra,' he said. 'The Land of Sour Smell. Though the word has a literal translation somewhat less presentable than the rendering I have made.'

Kurr strode together with the Fodhram leader at the head of the group, even the pretence that the Haufuth led the Company having been dropped. Indeed, the big man seemed unwell. He walked slowly at the tail of the group, frequently stopping for breath and rubbing at his legs. Although he was trimmer and fitter now than when the journey had begun, the Haufuth was still large of frame and was finding the going hard. But harder still to take was the failure he felt, stemming from his inability to make decisions in times of crisis. He had been right: Kurr was the man to lead them now. Perhaps he would be better off going back home – or, better still, just sitting down and resting, resting . . .

Roleystone Bridge disappeared behind them as they walked the last leagues out of the Upper Clough. Ahead, two low hills marked the Portals, the exit from the mountains. The Westway ran across the foot of the rightmost Portal, while the ill-formed path they were now forced to take led them directly towards the left hill. And beyond the hills lay the dark smudge of Withwestwa Wood stretching away to the horizon.

Stella and Wira walked together, the air about them almost crackling with suppressed energy. *Something has happened*, Leith thought as he followed them. *I've lost her, lost her for good.* He laughed mockingly at himself. *Just another dream melting away in the harsh light of day.*

Perdu walked beside Wisent. Both their heads seemed to droop

271

forwards, as though they shared the sorrow of parting. Stella left Wira and came up beside the Fenni.

'I'm sure he'll be taken good care of,' she said reassuringly.

'I know. I just can't help it. I've known Wisent for years; it seems sad that such a noble animal as he, born and bred for the wide open spaces, should end his days in the forest.' He sighed. Beside him, the aurochs let out a low, piteous moan. 'Come on, Wisent, cheer up; plenty to eat and plenty to do where you're going.' The animal moaned again in response.

'Still,' Perdu continued, glad to talk to someone, 'Hal was right. He told me that Wisent had been gifted to the Company to help us catch the Bhrudwans, and without him – and you – we would probably already be dead. It is time to let the gift go. Wisent has done all he can; now let him serve someone else as faithfully as he has served us.'

Stella nodded her agreement.

'Fine words, but they bring me no comfort,' the Fenni concluded. 'It still feels like losing my best friend.'

Ahead Kurr had stopped, waiting for the others to catch up. 'Come on!' he shouted. 'We still have a job to do!'

Behind them the Haufuth slowly got to his feet. 'I can't go on . . .' he groaned, but no one heard him. He was forced to continue, and though it seemed to him that he had come to the very end of his strength, he managed to stumble forward after the others.

In this fashion the group straggled out of the passage of the Jawbone Mountains, passing the Portals by late afternoon, and at day's end they watched the twilight envelop the rolling woodland country that hid their path deep within.

CHAPTER 13

THE HERMIT UNDER THE HILL

THE WESTERN TERMINUS OF the Southern Run was little more than a clearing in the woods. There were signs that people had once lived in this clearing – here a brick chimney, there some foundation posts – but most of the evidence had been covered by a forest vigorously intent on reclaiming the open land. A thin layer of freshly fallen snow completed the disguising of what had once been a settlement, as though nature wanted no one to know that for a time men had conquered her.

'Welcome to Fort Brumal! Used to be able to buy provisions and equipment here,' one of the Fodhram drawled. 'Even in my father's time a store here sold flour, corn and peas, along with fresh game and dried meat. All gone now.'

Leith waited to hear the reason why the settlement had been abandoned, but the man had finished speaking. A little quieter than the others, this fellow had a huge scar down the left side of his face. 'Swatted by a bear,' he had told them. 'Too close to her young 'uns. Served me right.'

'A generation ago this area was all trapped out,' the Fodhram leader explained. 'They say that once these woods overflowed with beaver and wolverine, racoon and mink, enough furs for everyone. But not enough, seemingly; and the Traders moved away north and east. The big town now is Vindstrop House. You'll see!' He laughed. 'We'll have a time there! Maybe we'll sell our bales right there and have ourselves a party! They pay more in Stanlow, but there is nothing in Stanlow to spend it on.' A chorus of agreement came from the other Fodhram.

'Not much of a fort now,' Farr observed.

'Well, this is the largest town you'll see before we get to Vindstrop House, so make the most of it!' the rotund man chortled at them. 'I'll go and see if the Hermit is home. I do hope he is in a good mood; he can be rather grumpy, and he is not used to company. If I'm not back in a couple of hours, he's probably eaten me!'

'Get on with you!' one of his compatriots growled good-naturedly at him. This man was slimmer but still short, with a stubbly beard and shabby clothes. Even in the cold of late winter his leather jerkin was open. He appeared to be wearing a thin shirt underneath and nothing else, an act of sheer bravado or proof that the Fodhram were born to this land. His trousers were heavily patched, perhaps a sign that someone at home cared for him. The number of unpatched rips and tears suggested that some more caring would be needed when he returned.

The amiable Fodhram leader nodded to Perdu, who sighed and prodded Wisent in the flank. Together they ambled off along a narrow path, and in a moment the forest had swallowed the two men and the great beast.

While he was away his 'boys', as he called them, dragged out from the brush two sleds loaded with huge bales of fur pelts. The tallest of the Fodhram, who still only came up to the shoulders of the Vinkullen men, hefted one of the bales with ease and placed it on the remains of an old stone wall.

'Practice time!' he said. 'Might as well get used to the feel of the pelts.' He beckoned to the members of the Company, inviting them to lift the bale.

Kurr looked around. No one seemed eager to try their strength. He frowned, then stepped forward and approached the bulky object.

There seemed no place to grip the cloth-covered fur bale. He spread his arms wide, bent over and encircled the bale. In this fashion he heaved the bale up from the stone wall. After staggering around with it for a few moments, he dropped it back on the wall.

'Nothing to it,' he declared with a deep breath.

'Excuse me,' Stella said, 'only I can't see how we're to carry all these bales along the path.'

Wira leaned towards her. 'That's what the sleds are for. No one could carry one of those for any length of time. They must weigh a hundred pounds!'

'Only ninety pounds each,' the scar-faced Fodhram said cheerfully. 'The curse, we call them. If we carry two, it's a double curse; three, it's a triple curse and so on.'

'Carry two?' Wira said doubtfully.

'Oh yes,' the shabby Fodhram replied soberly. 'Or more. Of course, we use the canoes mostly, but when the rivers are low or the rapids are too rough we portage the pelts and the canoes to calmer waters.'

'You can't be serious!' Farr muttered, looking at the piled-up sleds.

'Naturally, the fewer trips we make, the quicker we get to market and the higher the price we get for the furs. So sometimes we take on the rapids when maybe we shouldn't. And other times we carry more bales than we should. Our leader holds the record for the number of bales carried over the High Portage – nine miles mostly uphill – which is why he's our leader.'

'How many bales?' Kurr asked, incredulous.

'Let's just say that on that day he laboured under a five-fold curse.'

The members of the Company drew a collective breath. Five bales! Four hundred and fifty pounds! What manner of men were these?

'Let me have a try!' Farr cried. 'We coastlanders are at least as strong as other men!' The Fodhram glanced at each other with amusement in their eyes, then nodded to the mountain man.

The elder Storrsen strode purposefully towards the bale, then with a quick motion bent down, lifted it over his head and placed it on his shoulders. He stood erect in triumph, and said: 'Get another bale!'

The Fodhram nodded to each other, and the shabby man picked up another bale and brought it over to Farr. The young man bent down, and the Fodhram placed the bale on top of the first. With visible effort Farr stood up, his back and shoulders taking the weight. He stepped forward to show them all that he could manage the weight.

The Fodhram applauded, and the shabby one looked quizzically at the brave coastlander. 'Another bale!' Farr commanded, and bent down to further increase his burden. This time his powerful legs struggled to raise the load, but with a supreme effort of will he stood upright, the three bales balanced one upon another.

This time the Fodhram yelled their approval, real respect on their faces. Farr, his own face flushed with the effort, sank to his knees, from where willing hands took his burden from his shoulders.

'Truly remarkable!' Scar-face said. 'Three bales on the shoulder!'

'Three is not five,' Farr responded. 'And a few shaky steps is not nine miles uphill.' His voice left no doubt: he was in awe of these fur traders.

The Fodhram looked at each other again, this time a little guiltily.

'Actually, we have a small confession to make,' the tallest one said.

'What?' Farr cried. 'You were lying to us?'

'No!' they laughed. 'Only we have a little help in carrying our bales, and here it is.' Each man took from his belt a leather strap about a foot long and three inches wide, with holes at each end. As the Company watched, they pulled rope from their pockets and tied lengths of it to each end of their straps. Smaller straps were then produced and tied to the loose ends of the rope, making a sort of cradle.

'This is a tumpline,' Scar-face said, indicating his strap arrangement. 'Here's how we use it.'

He placed the broad strap across his forehead, allowing the ropes to hang down behind him. Shabby then took a bale and placed this at the bottom of the cradle, resting on the small of Scar-face's back. Two further bales were placed on top of the anchoring bale, and the three bales fitted snugly against his back. As he stood, his powerful neck and shoulder muscles easily took the strain.

'With a bit of practice, a man can go a long way with three bales and a tumpline.' The Fodhram laughed together and looked at Farr.

Leith also looked with apprehension at the hot-headed mountain man, waiting for the inevitable explosion. But it didn't come. Instead, a slow smile spread over Farr's features, eating up the tension that invariably locked his face up tight.

'A tumpline, you say it is called?' he said with a grin. 'Will you show me how to make one?'

'Indeed,' Taller replied. 'In fact, we'll make a tumpline for you in honour of three bales lifted without one. That is a feat worth retelling!' The others echoed their approval, and Farr's grin grew wider. Leith had never seen the man look so pleased.

The Fodhram leader returned to find the coastlanders practising enthusiastically with tumplines and bales. All except the Storrsens contented themselves with two bales: while heavy, the weight did not seem unmanageable. They walked bent under the load, as though they were about to topple forward with every step. Once they had got under way, the weight of the bales actually kept them going. Round and round the ruins of Fort Brumal they paraded – all except the Haufuth, who excused himself by patting his huge stomach and complaining that he was already carrying more than the rest of them. So he sat on a slab of stone, saying nothing, seemingly unmoved by the hilarious antics of his countrymen as they jerked about under their loads of pelts.

'Excellent, excellent!' Leader boomed. 'We'll make Fodhram of you before we're finished!' The Fodhram laughed together at the thought of coastlanders working the fur trails, and the Company laughed with them. Then they collapsed on to the snow-covered ground, sloughing off their burdens and laughing for the sheer exhilaration of it all. The good humour of the Fodhram seemed to be infectious; none of the Company really knew why they laughed. But it was some time before the Fodhram leader could continue.

'The Hermit has agreed to the trade,' he reported. 'On one condition. He wants to see our party before he will give us his provisions.'

'Why?' Farr asked, outraged. 'Wasn't giving him Wisent enough?'

'Don't worry,' the Fodhram leader responded quickly. 'We'd all have to help with the provisions anyway, and his abode is hardly out of our way. And,' he added, 'you never know – he might have something to our advantage.'

'What could an old hermit possibly offer us?' Leith whispered to his brother.

'Nobody said he was old,' Leader replied.

The Hermit lived in a cave deep under a tree-crowned hill. In times long forgotten a few intrepid drops of water had found their way into cracks in a great limestone block, dissolving a tiny hole for other drops to follow. Water and ice worked hard, day and night, summer and winter, for year after year in the youth of the world, hollowing out the roots of the limestone hill. Then one day desperate men discovered the cave, exploring the depths of its passages and the heights of its caverns, never guessing that the vast network of caves had been created by drops of water.

For many years the cave was the haunt of robbers, a base for raids on the Westway. The bandits left bones strewn around the Portals, and travellers found other paths from Firanes to the rest of Faltha. Then the peoples of Withwestwa Wood began fur trapping in the area, and fought inconclusive battles with the robbers. Finally Whitebirch of Woodsmancote raised an army which laid siege to the limestone cave. The robbers, under a fierce leader whose name has not survived, held out for months, being well provisioned and having an abundant supply of water. That final charge, with hand-to-hand fighting in the tunnels and caverns of the great hill, became the defining legend of the Fodhram people, the day when the clans of the deep woods forgot their enmity in the face of a common foe. Whitebirch and the bandit leader fought with swords on a stone table in the main cavern, and after a desperate battle the robber king was felled with a sword-thrust; but Whitebirch himself suffered mortal hurt, dying on the road home.

All this the Fodhram leader told Leith and the others as they approached the limestone hill. Ahead it lay, dark in cloud-shadow, as though it brooded over the evil that had fermented in its bowels.

Suddenly the Hermit appeared, blue-robed and shimmering at the base of the dark mass. Leith gasped. From where had he come?

The man beckoned for them to approach. As they drew close, they saw a narrow crack, a line of blackness in the grey of the hillside. It was from here that the Hermit had emerged. The travellers made their way through the opening, at one point having to duck as the roof lowered. 'Watch your heads!' their host growled as he led them into the bowels of the hill.

The Hermit was not at all what Leith had imagined. Scarcely more than forty years of age, the tall, well-built man looked more like a courtier than a hermit. He had a shaven face, long, flowing golden locks, intense eyes and a prominent brow which he employed to scowl at his guests.

'Sit down,' he indicated with a stab of the finger. They stood in a wide, torch-lit chamber. A narrow crack in the roof led upwards to the sunlight and a single shaft of light shone down on to a stone table laden with bread and meat. Around the sandy floor of the cavern were a number of rocks worn smooth by the passage of time. These the Company used as seats. A small fire flickered redly in one corner, sending a spiral of smoke drifting upwards to the crack in the roof.

'Eat your fill,' the Hermit said gruffly. 'I will not join you; I have an experiment I do not care to abandon.' Without waiting for a reply, he stalked away into a separate chamber. Hungry enough to ignore their host's strange manner, the travellers began to sample the more-than-ample fare. Wine, fresh bread and salted meats. Whatever else he was, the Hermit was no ascetic.

He returned just as they finished their meal, and insisted on formal introductions to the Company. As they gave him their names he nodded and whispered them under his breath, as though memorising them. Finally he came over to where Leith sat with his brother.

Hal offered his name and received his perfunctory welcome to Bandits' Cave as though it was a gift. Leith smiled inwardly. Hal lived a lonely life, the only mystic in a farming village. Perhaps he and the Hermit might make friends.

Then the blue-robed man turned his eyes on Leith, and instantly his eyes lit up with recognition. Indifference shrugged off like a discarded cloak, he announced solemnly: 'This is the one I have been waiting for.' He turned to Kurr. 'I must speak with this man.'

The puzzled travellers looked at each other, then at Kurr, who shrugged his shoulders. What could the Hermit possibly want with Leith? How could he have been waiting for him? Surely he had not known Leith was coming? Could this man be a Bhrudwan spy?

The blond-haired man peered closely at the Loulean youth. 'I have been shown aspects of your future. I will tell you what they are, if you wish it.'

'What do you mean, you have been shown?' Leith was cautious.

'I mean that I have seen what is to come.' The Hermit sounded quite certain about it, and seemed unperturbed by the blank look on the boy's face. 'Don't you have prophets in your country?'

Leith shook his head.

'Well, do you want to hear what I have to say?'

Leith shrugged his shoulders, unconsciously echoing Kurr's gesture. *Why not? It can't do any harm.*

Suddenly Hal stood, then pushed his way between the two. 'Answer me this,' he said, facing their host, his voice clipped in what Leith recognised as anger. 'Who gives you permission to speak to my brother?'

'Permission?' the Hermit echoed, taken aback. 'Why should I need permission? What custom is this?'

'You have not told us by what authority you will speak these words. Do you read the future using your own power?'

'Of course not!' the Hermit snapped. 'I hear the words of the Most High and repeat them!'

'So you claim the authority of the Most High for your prophecy?'

'Certainly! I do not speak on my own behalf, but on His.' The Hermit grew increasingly testy. He was experienced in the Realm of Fire. What made this boy think he could question the prophet?

'Hal, Hal!' the Haufuth cried, placing an arm on the cripple's shoulder. 'What is the matter? Why do you treat our host so rudely?'

'Then I rephrase my question. Did you get express permission from the Most High to speak out these words?'

'What possible reason could I have been given the words, other than to share them with the one they are intended for?'

'In other words you presumed. You seek to speak words in public that are better kept private, without asking permission of the owner of the words, and without telling us whose words they are, thereby taking glory for yourself. How do you think the Most High will regard your behaviour?'

'My behaviour?' the Hermit cried. 'It is not my behaviour that is in question here! This is my house; who are you to come here and lecture me on what I can say to my guests?' Spittle sprayed from his mouth at the vehemence of his speech. 'Always there is someone who wants to crush the words of the prophet!'

'I am more concerned for the effect you might have on my brother!' Hal retorted.

'The Most High will be pleased His words were given voice! Your brother needs to hear them!'

Again the Haufuth tried to stop the argument, but he might as well have tried to stop rain falling, for all he achieved.

'Even if correct, your words may ruin everything if their timing is not right,' Hal continued, as though he was a teacher and the Hermit was his pupil. 'Now listen carefully, for I have a word for you. "Rejoice more in the speaker than in the words spoken." Do you understand?'

The Hermit drew himself up to his full height and loomed over Hal as though about to strike him. But before he could respond further, the cripple spun around and looked his fellow travellers in the eye.

'I know you think I am impolite to our host,' he said. 'You wonder how I can object to his words before they are spoken. But it will be too late to object once they have been said!' He grimaced, as though he had finally realised that he was not making a good impression, then made it worse by adding: 'I would not expect you to understand issues of the Realm of Fire.'

With these words the cavern burst into an uproar. Kurr and the Haufuth demanded Hal apologise for his arrogance, and while others tried to calm them down the Hermit stood against a wall, arms folded, a slight smile on his face at the cripple's discomfiture. Eventually Kurr's bellows cut through the noise and the cave fell quiet.

The old farmer took a deep breath. 'I am at a loss for words,' he said, 'though first I must offer the Hermit our apologies for such disgraceful behaviour.' He inclined his head to their host. 'I thought we learned our lesson the last time we accepted the hospitality of others. Did our narrow escape from the Fenni mean nothing to us?' He turned to Hal, ready to dress him down – then snapped his mouth shut. Something invisible flashed between the old farmer and the youth, and Kurr's features softened.

'I – I . . . perhaps we are all tired,' he finished lamely. 'Maybe we will see things differently after a restful night's sleep.'

'Or perhaps you all need to learn something of the Most High,' the Hermit said, disgust in his voice. 'My offer of hospitality is withdrawn. I will not ask you to leave immediately, as I owe my Fodhram friends a debt for finding a pack animal for me; though I would have no qualms about putting you out into the snow. However, I expect you to be gone from my house before I rise tomorrow morning. And be warned, I rise early!'

Within moments Leith had been left alone in the cavern. 'What about my prophecy?' he said softly, but there was no one left to hear him.

*   *   *

Some time later, the Hermit returned to find the young man sitting on the sandy floor by the dying fire. 'Do you not require sleep, youngster?'

'I don't want sleep,' Leith replied. 'I want to know what you were going to say to me.'

'Of course you do,' said the Hermit, and his voice was edged with a compassion that had been absent before. 'Will it cause a problem between you and your brother if I tell you?'

'No!' said Leith quickly. 'Hal's often this way. He sees things so clearly, and never thinks he's wrong about anything.' The bitter words touched the Hermit's heart.

'Very well, then,' the blue-robed man said, squatting down and placing a hand on Leith's shoulder. 'As I said, I have foreseen things about you. The first was in a dream, one that came to me in the late night watches about a week ago. I saw you standing naked at the edge of a vast abyss, a captive of cruel men. Other captives stood to your left and right. Your captors threw them into the chasm, one after another.'

'And what happened to me?' Leith said anxiously, unsure whether he believed what he was being told.

'I did not see. I believe that what will happen to you depends on your remembering the message I have for you.' The Hermit lowered his voice. 'Here is the message: "The only way out is to cling to the fire."'

Leith waited expectantly, but the Hermit had evidently finished.

'Thank you very much,' he said politely. There didn't seem anything else to say. His face reddened as the Hermit's piercing eyes rested on him. He made to stand up.

'I have had more than one vision concerning you,' the Hermit said, pressing down on Leith's shoulder. 'Do you want to hear more?'

Leith nodded.

'This one is much simpler. It is a word that came to me two afternoons ago as I walked the paths of my forest. As I meditated on the dreams and visions I had seen, your face came clearly to me and a voice spoke, saying: "When the flame comes within

283

reach, tell the faithful one: Grasp it without doubt, for only in this fashion will the fire become your servant."'

'Is that it?'

'That's all I was given to tell you.'

Leith pursed his lips. There was an arrogance about the words of this fellow, an unshakable conviction that what he said was right. A dreamer of dreams, a hearer of voices – someone who in the prosaic northlands of Firanes would most likely be made fun of, like Hal had been. Yet he sounded so certain of himself!

'You don't believe me.' A statement, not a question.

Leith shrugged his shoulders.

'Very well then, youngster without faith. Here are two signs to confirm the words I have spoken. Before tomorrow is through you will be soaked to the skin. Only you; none of the others. I feel sorry for you – you'll get very cold. Secondly, within two days you will have the opportunity to tell someone your secret.'

'What secret?' Leith interrupted, puzzled.

'You know something about one of your companions, knowledge you could use to your own advantage, and you don't know what to do about it. Do you understand me? Don't say yes unless you know what I mean.'

An image of Farr and Wira arguing came into Leith's mind. He thought of Stella, of her brother who was a hopeless drunkard, of what she would say if she knew about Wira.

'Yes,' Leith said thoughtfully, 'I know what you mean.'

'Good! Within two days you will be convinced of the truth of my words.'

'But how do you know these things?' Leith wanted to know. 'Whose is the voice you hear?'

'I told you; I hear the voice of the Most High. I have shut myself away from the flesh, and thus it is easy for me to inhabit the Realm of Fire. I have lived twenty years in this cave, dedicated to listening for His voice.' The man's eyes misted over. 'He can be heard in many places: in the trees as they talk with the wind, in the movements of animals, in the rhythms of the seasons. Sometimes, when I have fasted and prayed and gone without sleep for many days, He speaks directly to my mind. Such were the words He gave me concerning you.'

Leith nodded, astonished that a man living in a cave a thousand miles or more from Loulea would have a message just for him.

But what did it mean? He asked the Hermit to explain the prophecies for him, but the man in the blue robe said he did not know. Leith could not tell whether he told the truth – but why would such an obviously holy man lie? And, more to the point, why had Hal, who always spoke of the Most High, resisted the words so strongly? It was not Hal who had been the subject of the prophecies! It had been so totally out of character for him to speak as he had done. He was sure the others felt the same way: Hal had shamed them all.

Then, as though reading his mind, the Hermit questioned Leith about his family. It was clear from the questions that the man regarded Hal with a high degree of suspicion, even going so far as suggesting that the cripple was motivated by jealousy.

'Jealous of what?' Leith said. *If only you knew*, he thought. *I've spent my whole life being jealous of him.*

The blue-robed stranger drew himself up to his full height.

'I see a high and lofty destiny for you,' he proclaimed, eyes blazing with passion. 'This I prophesy: you will rule over men; yes, and even kingdoms will obey your voice. Your deeds will inspire others now and in the ages to come. You have been summoned from your own land for such a time as this.' He lowered his voice for a moment, and his eyes lost their intensity. 'Perhaps your brother, who undoubtedly has foresight, if only in a small measure, sees something of this, and is jealous of what he will never attain.'

'Are you certain of this? A high destiny?'

'I am sure,' the Hermit replied, breathing heavily in the aftermath of prophecy. 'Though it takes me by surprise as much as it does you.'

That night Leith could not sleep.

He had left the Hermit in the main cavern and had found his friends sleeping in several small alcoves near the rear of Bandits'

Cave. Hal lay alone in one alcove, nestled on a smooth rock bench, his bedding neat as always. Leith's bedding had been laid out on another bench a few feet away. As Leith entered the small cave, he realised that Hal was not asleep, but he said nothing as he scrunched his blankets into a less uncomfortable position.

The Hermit *had* taken him by surprise. He had not known how to react as the stranger had given him words of prophecy, nor did he know how to deal with them. The words ran again and again through his mind. A high and lofty destiny. Rule over men and over kingdoms. Inspire others. *High and lofty! This will show them all.*

His ruminations were disturbed by movement on the shelf beside him. Hal, who obviously couldn't sleep either, was rising. *That's unusual! I've never known Hal to do anything other than sleep deeply.* As Hal left the sleeping chamber, Leith rose and followed quietly.

The cripple went directly to the Hermit's room, finding it unerringly although it was almost completely dark in the unfamiliar caves under the hill. Following at a distance, Leith kept bumping into things, taking the skin off his right knee at one point. *Surely Hal must know I am following him,* Leith wondered. *Surely he must hear me.*

Cautiously he peered into the small chamber in which the Hermit slept. Hal stood over the sleeping man.

Do I shout a warning? What is my brother going to do to him?

Then Hal began to speak slowly, quietly, clearly, deliberately.

'You have disobeyed the Most High,' came Hal's voice. 'The prophecy you gave to Leith tonight was given for your benefit, not his, to guide your steps, not his. It was a clear signal to you that the Hermit of Bandits' Cave was to *serve* the instrument of the Most High, not be that instrument himself. The prophecy was to be kept from him until the appointed time. Because of your disobedience, he has heard it too soon, and it will be too great a burden for him to carry. He will suffer doubt, and others will suffer because of it.' He took a deep, shuddering breath, as though he was in pain. 'Now you have ruined the plan, and have made it difficult, if not impossible, for the child to fulfil his calling.'

The figure in the bed made no response. *He must still be asleep*, Leith thought.

'You were supposed to accompany Leith on his journey into the heart of Faltha. You were to be his guide, his teacher. He would have learned from you the things which, in his pride, he will not learn from me. Armed with the prophetic words you have been given, you would have served as his protector. But tonight you have exposed the roots of your own pride, and they run deep. You are not fit to teach him. The Most High must now find another teacher. Beware! Your own soul lies in mortal peril.

'Therefore the Most High requires a hard task of you, teaching you by experience what you would not learn by humility. You will look after the Haufuth and nurse him back to health, restoring his strength and his hope. Know this: the Haufuth started on this journey carrying a great responsibility alone. He knew that unless he acted swiftly and with prudence, all of Faltha might be lost. However, he has since surrendered responsibility and leadership to those who appear swifter, stronger or wiser than he. Now he feels he has no place in our Company, and he believes he is a hindrance to our journey.

'Listen closely, Eremos, for I have a question for you. Are you prepared to do anything for the Most High?'

Without indicating that he was in any way awake, the Hermit nodded his head.

'Anything? You are quick with your answer! Nevertheless, let it be as you say.'

The crippled youth stretched out his right hand and took the hand of the Hermit. As their hands clasped, a line of blue fire spread slowly from Hal's arm to his hand, then to the hand and arm of the Hermit. For a moment both men were swathed in a pale blue light, outlining a pair of shadowy wings on the back of the cripple. Then the fire faded. Hal withdrew his hand, and the Hermit fell from his cot to the floor, gasping for breath.

'Bring him to Instruere when he is well again,' said Hal quietly, and turned to leave.

Stunned at what he had seen and heard, Leith ducked away

from the door and stumbled blindly back to his room. When he finally found his way there, Hal lay fast asleep in his corner.

Leith gazed on the peaceful form of his brother. *Hal! Hal!* his mind screamed. *What are you?*

'Something has happened! Something is wrong with the Hermit!' Perdu came running from the cave, nearly knocking over Hal in his haste. 'Come quickly!'

'What's the matter?' Kurr asked.

'The Hermit is lying on the floor, breathing faintly and in a high fever,' Perdu explained. 'I fear he might be dying.'

The Company, followed by the Fodhram, rushed into the cave where the Hermit lay. Spasms racked the man's frame, his hands were pale and clammy and he was sweating profusely. Hal and Stella rushed off to get cloths and cold water.

An hour later his condition had deteriorated. His heart was beating too fast, the clamminess had spread and his back arched in convulsions. No one had any doubt the Hermit would die.

Hal looked up from the pale, golden-framed face and turned to the others. 'I have never seen this kind of sickness before,' he said. 'Is there any among you who have heard of such a thing?'

Leith wanted to cry out: *Hal! This is your doing! You have cursed him with this sickness!* But he could not speak the words of betrayal, even if his brother had been proved evil.

No one spoke; the horror and helplessness of death was upon them. Finally Perdu stood and came over to where the Hermit lay, then beckoned for the Haufuth to follow.

Together they bent over the man. 'Do you remember the plague of black flies back when Clyma was the King in Rammr?'

'I wasn't born when Clyma was King,' the Haufuth replied quietly.

'Neither was I!' Perdu admitted. 'But surely you have heard about it? Black flies throughout Firanes, dark clouds covering the sky like smoke from forest fires – then the clouds came down to the towns and cities, biting the King in his court and the baby in his cradle. One after another the people took sick and died. My father told me that people in Mjolkbridge came down with a high fever within hours of being bitten, just like this Hermit here. I've been trying to remember what this reminded me of. What do you think?'

The Haufuth sighed. 'Why do you ask me? Surely Kurr would remember it?'

'I've heard about it, of course,' the old farmer said shortly, 'but I wasn't living in Firanes at the time. Now, in the name of the Most High, if you know anything about this plague, please tell us!'

Perdu turned to the Fodhram. 'Didn't you say that Withwestwa Wood has seen a mild winter?'

'Milder than usual,' came the reply. No one was smiling now, not even the Fodhram.

'And what colour clothing does this Hermit wear? Does he always wear blue robes?'

'How would I know?' said the Fodhram leader. 'I've never seen his wardrobe!'

'Have you ever seen him in anything else?'

The Fodhram thought hard. 'No.'

'I thought not. These flies, so the stories go, were most strongly attracted to anything coloured blue.'

The others waited quietly as Perdu thought.

'Turn him over on to his back,' the Fenni man commanded.

'But that might kill him!' Leith protested.

'He'll die if we do nothing! I need to see if he has any bites. Black fly bites are very distinctive – if they get infected, a large carbuncle will develop around the wound. Like those!' he said, as they turned the Hermit over.

Leith gasped as he saw the festering sores. How had the Hermit received such bites?

'They are infected black fly bites,' Perdu pronounced. 'Now, we must work fast! The only salve I know for black fly bite is to make a poultice from the bark of the tamarack tree.'

'The tamarack?' Shabby exclaimed. 'There's a grove a half-hour or so along the Southern Run. But for all I know they could be buried under the snow!'

'You'll have to go and find out,' said his leader.

'Please hurry,' the Haufuth urged. 'He may not have much time remaining.'

Within the hour Shabby had returned, clearly having run all the way. Leith could only imagine the effort this Fodhram must have expended as he ran through the snow. His legs shook with exhaustion as he emptied the contents of his knapsack in front of the Haufuth.

The big headman set to work making a poultice. He called Hal over to help, and together they crushed the tamarack bark. Immediately a brisk, earthy fragrance filled the cavern, the sharpness setting Leith coughing and bringing tears to everyone's eyes. The bark was placed in a light cloth wrapping to form a bag, which was drawn closed by string.

'We'll have to strap it to him,' the Haufuth muttered.

'No need,' Hal whispered back. 'Look.'

The spasms had stopped; a bad sign, Leith thought. The Hermit was fading. The Haufuth placed the poultice on the wounds, which were grouped close together, then Hal soaked a cloth in water, and added a few drops from a vial he carried in his pack. He dabbed the Hermit's lips with the cloth. In a moment, colour returned to his cheeks and his breathing eased.

The Haufuth leaned over the prone body. 'His heart has settled down. What was that you gave him?'

'Just a few herbs in water.'

'Will he live?' Stella asked.

'Perhaps,' the big man replied. 'We'll know better in a few days.'

'We don't have a few days!' Farr's voice rang through the cavern. 'We have to leave now!'

'Too true,' Kurr agreed. An agreement between the farmer and the elder Storrsen was so rare as to occasion comment, but it passed unnoticed.

'But who will look after the Hermit?' Stella pressed. 'What's the point of saving his life only to leave him to die?'

'Someone must remain behind,' said the Haufuth. 'Either that or we must all stay behind.'

'What is the Hermit to us? Our task is to fight, not to nurse-maid!' Farr was unsympathetic.

'You may be right,' Kurr agreed. 'This is not our affair. We have been given the responsibility of Mahnum and Indrett, of rescue and vengeance. We can't afford to wait for this man to heal – if indeed this is not his time anyway.'

'But he'll die if we leave him!' Stella could not believe what she was hearing.

Farr shrugged his shoulders. 'He would have died sooner had we not been here at all. Perhaps it would have been better if he had died.'

Wira stood next to Stella, as if lending her support. 'Don't you think that is being just a little selfish? Can't your revenge wait a few days?'

Farr clenched his fists. 'Who are you to talk to me about self-ishness? How *dare* you!' The elder Storrsen was furious with his brother, his reaction leaving the others mystified.

'I'd leave one of my men with the Hermit,' said Leader, 'as he has been a faithful friend of the Fodhram for many years. But none of my men is an apothecary. We'd just as likely kill him unwit-tingly as nurse him back to health.'

Another dilemma! Leith thought. Perhaps if this had just been a simple matter of pursuing and fighting the Bhrudwans then maybe, just maybe, they might have accomplished it. But the combination of bad weather and bandits, of enemies expected and unexpected, an overall run of bad luck, and now this affair of the Hermit, had conspired against them. Delay after delay, dilemma after dilemma, had led them to the side of a sick Hermit under-neath a hill many miles away from their true road, while the Bhrudwans and their captives drew further and further away at every moment.

Finally Kurr sighed and spoke. 'I have made my decision,' he said. 'We leave immediately, and trust the care of this Hermit into the hands of the Most High. We must pursue our quest. I cannot willingly exchange the lives of Mahnum and Indrett, not to mention Parlevaag, for this Hermit. He has entrusted his life to the solitude of this wood, and I say we should allow the forest and the hill and the cave to nurture him.'

One or two nodded their heads at this speech, Farr shrugged his shoulders, Leith frowned. Stella cried out: 'No!' Then silence settled on the party, punctuated by the shallow breathing of the Hermit.

'I'm staying with him,' the Haufuth said quietly.

'What?' Kurr exploded.

'Kurr, you have made the decision to go on. By so doing you have taken leadership of the Company. No, my friend,' he said, over the old farmer's protestations, 'it was only right and proper that you should do so. I've shown no leadership since we left the North March of Firanes.'

It was no good arguing, the Haufuth explained; his mind was made up. All along he had known that his presence on this expedition was a liability. He was no real leader, he told them; instead he found himself unable to keep up with the Company. He would be no use in a fight. He had been wondering how he could leave them without causing problems, and now this Hermit needed looking after – and no one else (with the exception of Hal) could do it. No, his decision was final. He would stay with the Hermit until his charge had recovered.

Arguments raged back and forth most of the morning, but the Haufuth's decision remained firm. He had been supported by Farr (not surprisingly, thought Leith) and by the Fodhram. There was food enough for three months in the Hermit's larder – three weeks, the Haufuth estimated with a smile – but the Hermit obviously could not feed himself. His poultice would need regular changing. He would need water. Someone would have to stoke the fire. Wild animals had to be kept at bay. Wisent had to be fed and watered. Someone had to stay with him, and the Haufuth was clearly the best choice.

'Keep listing my indispensable talents,' the big man said, 'and you might convince me that I should come with you after all! Now off with you and get ready to leave. I must tend the needs of my patient.'

* * *

292

Stella threw her arms around the big man as they stood at the hidden entrance to the cave. Her tears ran down his neck.

'Look after yourself,' the Haufuth said gruffly.

Stella nodded, not trusting herself to speak.

'You know, it is when I think of you left amongst all these uncaring men that I doubt my decision.'

'Not all the men are uncaring,' she whispered, a blush reddening her complexion.

The Haufuth frowned. 'Now you really have me worried,' he said. 'Be careful! Things with men are not always as they seem!'

The young girl laughed brightly, a little too brightly. 'Don't worry! Anything is better than the fate awaiting me should I return home a single woman!'

Now the Haufuth took a deep breath, ready to reply with heat, but Stella skipped away out of his reach. 'Don't worry about me!' she called, then walked over to where Wira stood. Her hand slipped easily into his. *I'm capable of looking out for myself,* her gesture said eloquently.

Now Hal said his farewell to his village headman. 'You'll take good care of him,' he said with assurance. 'And when he is well, you'll follow us to Instruere. We'll meet again there.'

Kurr nodded his farewell, and shook the Haufuth's huge hand. 'I didn't mean to . . .' he began.

'No need,' the headman replied. 'I know. You wanted to lead the Company as little as I did.'

'Be careful! And make sure you come to Instruere when the Hermit is healed. We'll need you when we speak to the Falthan council.'

'I'll be there,' the Haufuth said. 'Now go, otherwise the Bhrudwans will be at Vindstrop House before you.'

Finally the Company took their leave of the Hermit, of the faithful Wisent, and of the Haufuth. The vast bulk of the headman and the aurochs were specks at the bottom of a small cliff when they waved for the last time, then the trail dipped over a low hill, the specks disappeared from view and the snow-shrouded forest swallowed them again.

The urgency of their journey began to press at them, and the events of the Hermit's cave receded as once again the travellers set out on their road. Kurr now strode unchallenged at their head. But the Haufuth was not forgotten; every now and then, a member of the Company would cast a glance towards the tail of the procession, as though expecting to see him. But he was not there, and somehow they felt incomplete without him.

CHAPTER 14

A NIGHT ON THE ICE

THE AFTERNOON SUN GLOWERED impotently at the Company as they wound their way up a snow-covered ridge. She stretched pale yellow fingers towards the fur bales bobbing on the backs of the heavily laden travellers, but she could not touch them. At this time of year, as the clouds cloaked the land, she did not often see the snow and the trees. And she seldom if ever saw humans abroad in the northern winter, the season when the great god Qali ruled the land and the skies. Never mind, she thought, remembering that there were places far from here over which she held absolute sway. Perhaps one day she would see these humans in the arid lands far to the south. Then she would show them a thing or two.

The Company pulled two laden sleds. Each sled carried eight fur bales and a pile of provisions, while each of the four Fodhram had two bales on his back. The rest of the Company took turns to pull the sleds: two pulled on the ropes, while a third pushed from behind. In this fashion they guided the sleds over the snowy path.

'Couldn't do this in the summer,' Shabby grunted. 'Track is a mess of tree roots, stones and dust after the thaw.'

'Never been on it in the snows,' Taller chipped in. He was the least spoken of the Fodhram, but was their cook and the best singer among them. On both counts he was a valuable member of the group.

'Well, it's easy here,' Leader agreed. 'But that's because we haven't got to the river yet.'

He turned to the others. 'What I mean is that this track doesn't go all the way to Vindstrop House. See, we don't have the time to make tracks like this one in the woods. Even if we did, we'd never use them enough to keep them open. The forest would just close right over them again.'

'Who made this track, then?' asked Stella.

'Not who, but what,' Leader replied. 'This is a bear track, made by the animals to get to the river. They use it all the time; the trees wouldn't dare close this track up!'

'We have bears in Loulea Vale,' Leith said, trying not to appear ignorant. 'Huge ones. I saw one once.'

'What colour was it?' Leader asked him.

'Ah – brown, I think.' Leith already regretted his comment. It hadn't been much more than a glimpse, really.

'You haven't seen a bear until you've seen the black. Massive, they are. Take your head off with one swipe.' Taller sounded quite proud of them.

'From what I hear, we're not missing much,' Farr said. 'Black bears are mean enough to tear a man apart as soon as look at him. Better off without them.'

The Fodhram looked shocked at these words, but their leader merely laughed. 'Maybe some time we'll teach you better! There's nothing grander in the woods than the bear. In fact, the bear and the woods were made for each other! Remind me to tell you about it around the fire tonight. But for now, we'd better stop wasting breath and get on with our walking. River isn't far now!'

They wound their way up an exposed ridge, out under a bright but cold sun, then topped the ridge and took a moment to catch their breath. They were on a high point in the gently rolling, tree-draped land, and for mile after mile on every side the still, white forest stretched away. A long way behind them the Jawbone Mountains stood, mist-covered and grey. Ahead the horizon and everything in between was made of wood and wore a coat of snow. *Behind me lies everything I know*, thought Leith, as he tried to visualise the miles they had travelled. *But somewhere to the south lies everything I love, marching to death at the point of a Bhrudwan sword.* He stood on tiptoes but could not see any sign of the Westway. Feeling foolish, he shot a quick glance at Stella, whose eyes were on Wira. *Well, perhaps the Bhrudwans do not have everything I love. Do I really love her?* He watched her as she walked beside the Vinkullen man. *It doesn't matter whether I do or not. She loves him.*

When did it happen? He tried to think back. *Somewhere in the mountains, some time after I saw him and his brother argue over his drinking . . .* He mentally fingered the knowledge he held as a weapon against Wira. *I could tell Stella at any time*, he thought, *and that would be that. Stella's older brother would be about Wira's age, too.* He shuddered when he thought of the Loulea village idiot, unkempt and filthy, smelling of the drink he always seemed to get from somewhere. *Everyone avoided him – except Hal*, thought Leith with a small pang of guilt. *Hal took care of him when things got really bad.*

Would he tell Stella? Part of him said yes, he wanted to see her cry, to see her angry at Wira, to comfort her . . . but he knew he wouldn't tell her. He knew it would be wrong. *She'll find out soon enough anyway*, he thought.

And what of Hal? Leith still couldn't accept what he had seen: his gentle, wise and good brother had somehow poisoned a defenceless man. It seemed to Leith that just as he was trying to put his world back together in one place, it was coming apart at another. *Was nothing as it seemed?*

He looked up. Lost in thought, he had drifted some way behind the others. He stopped for a moment and adjusted the bale on his back. He had asked for two, like Wira, but the Fodhram had given him only one. Then he sprang forward hurriedly as he saw the others disappear around a bend in the path. His foot caught an exposed tree root and he fell, landing heavily on his side at the very edge of the trail. Helpless because of the weight on his back, he slid from the path and down a slope to the right. At the bottom waited an ice-covered pond, but the ice was not thick enough to support Leith and his bale. Crack! The ice broke open and freezing water enveloped him.

Up ahead the Company walked on, unaware of what had happened behind them. Then Kurr, who had trained himself to look regularly at his companions as a way of assessing their condition, noticed that Leith was missing.

'Hold up a moment!' he cried. 'Where's that fool of a boy?'

The Company pulled up, and eyes were cast anxiously back down the trail. 'He was with us when we stopped last,' Stella offered.

'Follow me!' the Fodhram leader said, taking Wira by the arm. Together they ran back down the trail, retracing their own footprints. A few moments later they came to the scene of Leith's fall and in an instant Leader saw what had happened: the tree root, disturbed snow and the marks of a slide down from the path. He scrambled down the slope, the younger Storrsen following. At the bottom of the slope a bale floated in an icy pool.

'Leith!' Wira shouted. There the youth was, lying on the snow next to the water. Wira tried to lift him: he was soaking wet, and the water was beginning to freeze his clothes to his body.

'Ahhnn . . .' Leith tried to speak. The pain seared his senses as his body stiffened into uselessness. He had managed to scramble out of the pool, but had collapsed from the effort.

'Get his clothes off!' Leader shouted. 'Quickly!' As Wira fumbled to obey, the Fodhram leader set off up the slope to get the others. 'We need a fire! And warm clothes, and a blanket!'

By this time the others had arrived. Scar-face fished the fur bale out of the pool. Waterproofed, it had suffered no harm. Brisk hands dried the naked youth and reclothed him, while others started a fire.

'Keep rubbing his arms and legs,' Leader said. 'He'll be in pain when the feeling returns.'

'We'll go no further today,' Kurr said, and the Fodhram leader nodded.

'Just as well you noticed him missing,' Shabby said. 'Wouldn't have lasted much longer. Funny thing though, sometimes they last longer in the water than out of it. Kind of slows them down, if you know what I mean. We found old Toothless once at the bottom of a lake. Been missing for an hour or more. Cold and dead he was! But we heated him up just the same, and he came back to life. With a bit more grumblin' and complainin' than this lad, mind you!' He laughed at his recollections.

As the preparations for the evening meal went on around him, Leith gradually came to himself. Words spoken to him came to his mind: 'Before tomorrow is through you will be soaked to the skin,' the Hermit had said. 'Only you; none of the others. I feel sorry for you – you'll get very cold.' The first sign. There was another to come – what had been said? He could not make his sluggish brain remember. It didn't matter. Leith was already a believer.

Within an hour of rising the next morning, the Company came to the Kljufa River, near its headwaters hardly any larger than the many streams that drained into it. Taller stared across the frozen water. 'We're in luck. Last night's wind seems to have blown the snow off the river ice. Makes for easier travelling.'

Carefully they guided the sleds out on to the ice. The frigid floor stretched away ahead of them, bright and clean in the morning sun, a smooth platform framed by tree-lined hills. 'It's not really a river, either,' Leader added. 'The Fodhram say that Withwestwa is so beautiful a land that the rivers themselves rush from beauty to beauty, lingering there; thus creating strings of lakes connected by rapids.'

And so it proved. Lake followed lake, long and narrow, fed by rapids that in late winter were crumpled ice over rock. Only the largest of them made any noise, murmuring quietly as water flowed deep under the ice. Their journey was a succession of swift marches across lake ice, interspersed with slow clambering around rapids and ice-bound waterfalls; and as the coastlanders walked through the snowgrey lands a transformation took place within them. Their senses were sharpened; as one who is imprisoned in darkness learns to hear and smell and touch afresh, and then eventually even to see, so the Firanese began to look past the sameness of the forest and to hear and smell and touch the beauty of Withwestwa Wood. By day's end they were entranced, none more so than Farr.

'So that's the tamarack, and there's a jack pine – no, two – three jack pines. And over there a hillside of white spruce.' Farr shook his head in wonder. 'So much more variety than we have back home!'

'There are many trees you have yet to see,' the Fodhram leader said, pleased with his pupil. 'Come back here in the autumn and you'll see the paper birch and the aspen, their leaves golden in the sun. Stay until the spring and smell the muskeg, watch the marigold flower and the juneberry bloom, and hear the loon's cry over the lakes, the thrush and the nuthatch in the trees. And, if you're fortunate and favoured by the forest, you might meet the beaver or the bear.'

'This wood is light somehow, still and clear and timeless. Our forests are nothing like this,' Farr said. 'They are all dark and heavy.'

'Perhaps you have not seen them with the eyes of love,' Leader responded.

'I belong here,' the Vinkullen man said with certainty. 'I wish to be a man of these woods.'

Wira came up behind him. 'Don't forget your revenge, my brother,' he whispered mockingly.

'How are you feeling, boy?' The old farmer walked beside Leith, both of them shouldering a bale easily with the aid of a tumpline. It was the same gruff voice, Leith reflected, but the farmer was not the man who had left Loulea, bowed with age and broken with grief. Far from draining him, the long trek from the North Marches of Firanes had somehow infused the old farmer with strength. His stick had been abandoned weeks ago, somewhere between Vale and *vidda*. Leith no longer feared him.

'I'm well, thank you,' Leith answered politely.

'Good! For a while yesterday I thought we'd lost you. Whatever possessed you to take a swim at this time of the year?'

Leith opened his mouth to reply, then remembered what he had been thinking about when he had tripped over the tree root. Stella and Wira, Wira and his drinking problem. On top of this came the memory of the words of the Hermit: *'Within two days you will have the opportunity to tell someone your secret.'*

'The rest of you were walking so fast I got hot and tired,' he replied. 'I forgot to take my bale off before I dived in.' Leith decided to make the prophecy work for its fulfilment. Why should he blurt out his secret just because he had been told he would?

'Is that so?' Kurr laughed. There was something in this boy, something out of the ordinary, something worthwhile that waited to emerge. But there was some blockage that kept it in and kept others out. *If only I were young again*, Kurr sighed, *training the Watchers like I used to. I could do something with this lad.*

'Tell me,' Kurr said, 'have you noticed anything strange about the Storrsen brothers?'

Oh no, thought Leith. 'Strange? Like what?'

'I'm not sure. But there's something going on between them, of that there can be little doubt.'

'Perhaps Farr is jealous of Wira and Stella,' Leith said ingenuously.

'Maybe that's it. Certainly Farr is worried about his brother. Let me know if you find anything out, won't you.'

'Of course.'

It wasn't until Kurr had left him that Leith thought more carefully about what the Hermit had said. *You fool*, he thought. *He didn't say you would actually tell someone; only that you would get the opportunity to tell someone.* He shook his head.

'All right,' he said aloud. 'You win.'

Their path wound slowly just north of eastward, following a maze of lakes, streams and rapids. Without their guides, the Company would never have found their way through the hills and valleys, bluffs and dead ends that made up the vast Withwestwa Wood. Even with their guides and the best of the late winter weather, they made slow progress.

'Faster than the Bhrudwans, at least,' Kurr reassured them. 'That far south, the thaw will have begun.'

Spring was indeed painting the southern margins of Withwestwa Wood with rich hues. Snow turned to slush as the sun regained her power and banished Qali to the northern marches. Ice rotted in the lakes, dripped down from waterfalls, fell in shards from trees and cracked disconcertingly underfoot. Snow dropped from trees in huge clumps. As it fell on lower branches, many great limbs collapsed under the weight. Trails turned to mud as the world melted. The woodsmen and their families, long experienced in this most difficult time of the year, kept to their huts and waited for the thaw to conclude.

But the Bhrudwans could not wait. They had made good progress along the Westway, finding ample food and shelter in the abundance offered by Withwestwa Wood. This came to an abrupt end when the thaw came. Their untrained eyes, more used to the desert than the wood, did not read the danger signs: the thinning of the ice along the riverbanks, the melting and refreezing of the snow cover, the warmer winds and, above all else, the return of sound to the silent forest.

Mahnum noticed the change. Even in their desperate plight he was heartened by the turn of the season, as though the spring brought new hope. He felt less alone as the birds started singing and the streams began to babble in the forest. Occasionally during those wearisome days he had taken the chance to whisper a few words of encouragement to Indrett, words snatched as they came together during the day or when he dared during the long, dark nights. Invariably she would nod and smile wanly; she was nearing the end of her strength. The flesh had fallen from her, eaten away by the rigours of the road and the privations forced on them by their captors. Mahnum wept to see it. How he wished the Bhrudwans did not keep them apart. How he wished he had something, anything, he could tell them about this 'Right Hand'. He would have done anything to halt the slow, lingering decline of his dear Indrett. He suspected that the

Bhrudwans realised this, and withheld food from her in order to make him talk. But he remained silent, not knowing what they wanted him to say.

The forest around them was no longer silent. While the humans retreated indoors, the animals emerged. Mahnum saw moose, deer and many smaller creatures. All struggled in the bog-like conditions.

Previously they had made fifteen or twenty miles a day; now their progress could sometimes be measured in yards. On two occasions Mahnum was sure they did not move out of sight of their previous night's camp during a whole day's travel. The mud was terrible. It bit at their ankles and clung to their legs. Any straying from the trail only made matters worse, as the forest was full of quagmires into which the unwary would sink to their knees or their waist. It took half an hour to free the Bhrudwan leader one afternoon, after frustration had led him to try his luck away from the flooded trail. None of this improved his temper, and he regularly struck his captives, but Mahnum could no longer be hurt by their blows.

Instead he thought about what he had seen at the bridge in the mountains. With their swords and their bare hands, fuelled by white-hot rage at the death of their fellow warrior, they had dismantled the arch over the Kljufa River. Watching the power of their anger destroying the old stone landmark, he could not imagine anything hurting these efficient killing machines. Yet one of them had vanished, having met with a mishap somewhere near the Maelstrom.

The bridge destroyed, they had waited in the shadows. To his astonishment, figures unmistakable to his eye had come into view across the river. Surely that was the fool of a headman! And here came Kurr! Then he shouted with joy. There were his sons, Hal and Leith. Both alive, both well. Hope rose again in the Trader's breast.

Beside him Indrett had begun to sob with joy. They had thought their boys dead, burned in the fire started by the Bhrudwans. Mahnum put his finger to his lips; best not to give the Bhrudwans any idea that their sons were still alive. Indrett nodded, but a fire had been lit in her eyes.

So there was rescue on the way. If only they came before Indrett gave out! How much longer could she survive this treatment? At least they were travelling slowly now. Perhaps she would recover.

It was now well into the fourth week since they had left the Hermit's cave, and still the Company made slow but steady progress. Their path had turned due east and was now at its northernmost point, but even here the signs of the approaching thaw were visible to the trained eye. They had to be careful when they ventured out on the ice, which had worn thin in places. The Fodhram expertly avoided the rotten ice, invisible to the coastlanders but deadly should they blunder across it. As the ice and snow melted, the Fodhram drove forward with increased urgency.

Shabby pointed to the riverbank, where a telltale black line spoke of thinning ice. In places the ice had broken away and tilted high in the air. 'We have a few days at the most,' he said. 'Perhaps we will have to travel at night.' But that night there was no moon, and a warm breeze blew from the south.

'How far is Midrun?' Kurr asked as they sat around the fire. 'Will we make it in time?'

The plan was to get to Midrun, a small shelter beside a lake at the halfway point of the Southern Run, before the thaw reached its peak. There they could wait out the worst of the conditions and, when the rivers cleared of ice, they could launch the birch bark canoes stored there and make quick time downriver. Leader estimated that the run would take about three weeks from Midrun to Vindstrop House.

'We need to make Midrun tomorrow or it could take us a week. The thaw is hovering just over the horizon, waiting to pounce.'

Kurr grunted in reply.

The next day they climbed up a steep ridge and reached a high plateau devoid of trees. This was the watershed between the Kljufa River system and the Mossbank River, known to locals as the

Fenbeck, itself a tributary of the Sagon, the river which drained much of northern Treika. Here on the watershed the south wind did not penetrate, and the snow was still firm. All morning the Company pressed forward, manhandling the sleds over the ice and crusty snow, with two or even three pushing each sled in spite of the bales on their backs.

Just before midday they reached the far end of the high plateau, and looked out over the northern reaches of Withwestwa Wood. Ahead the ground sloped down to more snow-shrouded trees, with icy lakes glinting in the sun. But to the south the trees were green and the snow absent. The thaw was upon them.

They dared not pause for the noon meal, instead hustling down the side of the hill, trying to beat the sun. The world changed all about them; where previously the greys of winter had dominated, now splashes of green and yellow challenged the grip of Qali. Cinnamon ferns unfolded, spotted amongst the gentle blue of hare-bells and the fiery russet of dogwood. Here and there pussy willows glinted with silver. The unrelenting south wind, the Snoweater, seemed to strip the trees of their white cloak, and beneath their feet the trail turned to water.

All afternoon the travellers battled the thaw. The bales came off the sleds and were distributed on to the backs of the Company, as the runners bit into the slush and mud. All around them spring hummed and sang, but the travellers sweated and groaned as they made their way down past streams that had shaken off their icy shackles. As the waters celebrated by chattering to each other, they came up against ice that had not yet melted and banked up, spreading out behind the temporary dams and flooding low-lying areas. A precious hour was wasted as the Company tried to find a way past one such lake.

As the sun came down blazing red to the horizon, they entered a long valley with steep sides and filled with a lake. Here the ice had not melted, being somewhat out of the sunlight. At the far end sat a small speck. Taller gestured, his face telling all. Midrun hut.

'Do we risk the ice?' Leader asked the other Fodhram. Shabby knelt down on the seemingly solid ice floor; it moved perceptibly under him.

'What's the alternative?' Kurr asked.

'We will have to climb out of this valley and make our way around the ridges to the hut. At least three days, and we'll have to leave the sleds here.'

'How far is the hut across the lake?'

'About an hour. We could make it in less if we hurry. But I don't know if the ice will hold.'

'Two days could make all the difference at the other end,' Kurr said gently.

'To you, yes. But don't forget that our families depend on the money we earn from our furs. We have to get them to market, and one or two days either way will make no difference.'

'Are you serious?' Farr cried, outraged. 'What are furs in comparison to lives?'

The Fodhram leader laughed, and a grouse startled out of a brake behind them. 'Nothing, of course. I was just reminding you of our concerns. Haven't we been pushing on hard? Do you doubt our concern for your friends?'

Scar-face returned from checking the ice. 'It's starting to refreeze, but it is very brittle.' He smiled. 'It's been a tame journey thus far. Time to liven it up! I say we take on the ice.'

'Right, then,' Leader said briskly. 'You lead the way. And you'd better have that nose working.'

Leith tried to ignore the creaking and groaning of the ice as they made their way across the lake. In many places the surface had cracked, and water spread over the rotting ice. Scar-face avoided these areas, even to the point of crossing the width of the narrow lake to avoid one doubtful patch. Finally, as twilight gathered, the worst appeared to be over. Midrun Hut sat ahead of them, a few hundred tantalising yards away in the gloom.

At that moment a loud crack echoed across the valley and the ice shook. A hissing sound came from behind them.

'Forward! Forward!' Scar-face shouted. 'Quickly!'

Leith turned as he ran forward. Behind them a gaping fissure opened in the ice, the snow hissing as the crack snaked towards them. As he watched, it changed direction and headed towards him, then cracked again and shot out sideways. The ice buckled under Wira and Stella, then gave way with a snap.

Wira disappeared.

Stella screamed and threw herself flat on the ice, groping in the water with her arm. She grabbed something and pulled.

'Get off the ice!' Scar-face cried. 'It's ready to go!'

No one moved.

'Help me!' Stella shrieked. She had hold of something but did not have the strength to pull it up.

Ignoring the danger, Perdu and Leith ran across the ice towards her. The others made to help, but the ice cracked and hissed again and they were cut off.

'Get off! Now!' Leader barked. Faced with no option, the others sought the safety of the bank.

Leith lay to Stella's left, Perdu to her right. Together the three of them groped in the icy-cold water for a firm grip.

'I'm losing him!' Stella sobbed through clenched teeth. Her fingers had numbed.

'I've got something!' Leith called. 'Over here! Grab my arm and pull!'

Stella lost her grip and rolled over with a cry of despair.

Perdu and Leith pulled together. Slowly something came to the surface.

It was Wira. They had hold of his ankle.

Behind them, the ice continued to hiss and heave. 'Keep still!' Kurr shouted from the shore. 'You're making it break up!'

Slowly, agonisingly, they pulled Wira above the surface. His bales were still firmly attached to the tumpline. 'Stella! Help us!' Perdu called.

Now Farr came running across the ice. He had found firmer footing and leapt over the ever-widening crack. Four pairs of hands drew the inert form and the dead weight of two fur bales out of the water. Perdu and Leith pulled the tumpline away and the bales tumbled on to the ice, sending the end dipping under the water. A loud crack came from behind them.

Farr bent down and scooped his brother up in his arms, then ran for all he was worth. The others followed, leaving the bales behind. Ahead, Farr cleared the gap in the ice with ease. Stella just made it, but twisted her ankle sharply as she landed. Leith barely missed her prone figure as he jumped the gap. He pulled her to her feet, but she cried out in pain when she set her foot to the ice. He put his shoulder under her arm and set out for the shore.

Farr, Perdu and the body of Wira were now safe on land. Slowly, Leith and Stella drew near.

Then a further loud report echoed across the lake, and another crack opened. This time it came from the direction of the hut, and raced up the lake towards them.

'The whole lake is going!' Scar-face cried.

Leith lunged for the shore, but they were too late. Ahead of them the ice opened: one yard, two yards, three yards, four yards wide. Perhaps Leith could have made it, but not Stella in her condition. The two stood together in horror as the ice widened beyond any possibility of crossing.

On the shore, Kurr gestured helplessly. What now?

'Sit tight,' Leader called across the widening gap. 'Perhaps the ice will settle down. Move away from the edge. We'll see what we can do.' He tried to sound reassuring.

Night was falling and Leith could hardly make out the nature of the activity on the shore, but he could guess. As he and Stella moved back from the edge of the ice, the Company would be busy building a fire. He could just make out Farr, who was vigorously rubbing his brother's legs. *Had Wira survived?* he wondered.

Leith and Stella sat side by side, trying to spread their weight out across the ice. Stella strained her eyesight across the lake, but could not see what was happening on the shore.

'Is Wira all right?' she called, anxiety in her voice.

'We're not sure yet,' came the reply. 'He's alive, but we can't wake him.' Stella heard the concern in Farr's voice.

'Now you just sit still and don't worry,' Kurr called to her. 'We'll get to you soon.'

For a while the night was quiet. High above, the wind blew strips of cloud across a sky awash with stars, but the air was still and cold on the lake.

'We're drifting away,' Stella whispered to Leith. He stared into the darkness. It was true; the fire on the shore was growing smaller.

'Hoy!' she called out. 'We're moving away! Can you hear us?' There was no answer.

'We'll be all right here,' Leith said quietly. 'The lake will probably freeze over again tonight, and in the morning we'll simply walk off.'

'I hope he's all right,' Stella said. Leith did not reply.

After a while the girl beside him stirred, then tried to stand. 'My arm!' she cried. 'I can't move it!'

'What's wrong?' Leith responded in alarm.

'It's the arm I had in the water, trying to raise Wira. I can't feel it.'

Leith turned towards her voice. It was dark now, unrelieved night, and he could not see her face. *Just as well*, he thought. *It means that she can't see mine.* Tentatively, Leith reached out in the darkness and touched her arm. It was icy cold.

'You're freezing,' he said, trying to keep his voice level. Here they were, stuck out in the middle of a lake with the prospect of freezing to death, and all he could think about was this girl sitting next to him. He tried to breathe normally, but his heart was in his throat. He tried to calm down. *Surely she will notice! Surely she will laugh at me!*

Stella tried to rub some feeling back into her arm, but it was no good. Her teeth began to chatter, and she shook uncontrollably.

'I'll help you,' Leith said, but not with his own voice – it seemed another voice, calm and self-possessed, spoke through him. Another youth, a confident, assured youth, reached out to the girl and rubbed her arm with gentle firmness. Then, when the shaking had subsided somewhat, this voice said: 'We had better huddle together and keep warm.' Leith was astonished at what the voice had said.

Stella murmured a reply and moved close to him, her head nestling on his shoulder. Together they huddled under the cold stars, drawing warmth and comfort from each other.

Later that night the south wind rose, and it carried voices to them across the lake. At first they were indistinct, but soon they could be heard all too clearly.

'Wira! Sit down!' That was Farr.

'I need more! Give me another one!' The voice was petulant, demanding.

'You've had enough already. Be quiet or you'll wake the others!'

'Don't care! I'll die without another drink. I know you've got the flask. Now give me another!'

Now the voices gave way to the sound of a struggle.

Stella nudged Leith awake. 'Leith! Leith! Something's happening on the shore!'

They listened further, but the sounds were unclear.

A new voice spoke up. 'What's going on?'

'Nothing. We're just having a little disagreement,' Farr explained.

'Ask him if he's got any more!' Wira bellowed.

'So!' The voice was that of the Fodhram leader. 'This is our sneak thief! I wondered who watered down our ale. Son, why didn't you ask? There's plenty here for everyone!'

'Ask him,' came the sullen reply. 'He won't let me.'

Stella couldn't breathe for fear of what she was hearing.

'I'm afraid you have discovered our little secret,' Farr said. 'But if I had known he was stealing from you, I would have told you. I'm sorry.'

'This is a serious matter,' came the reply. 'Or at least it would be, if there were not more serious things afoot. You may have been saved from drowning, son, but those who risked their lives for you are themselves in danger, marooned out there on the lake. Or do you give them no thought?'

'I – Is Stella out there?'

'Yes she is, and Leith also.' Kurr spoke. 'Now I know what was troubling me about you Storrsens. My fears are confirmed.'

'Was it you who spied on us?' came the angry reply.

'No, not me. I think Leith knew about you from the beginning, but he chose to say nothing. You gave yourself away.'

The voices were silent for so long that Leith began to think the wind had changed.

'Please don't think too harshly of him,' Farr said suddenly, his voice sounding much closer. 'He's been that way since his mother died. It's more my fault, really.'

'He'll sleep well the rest of the night.' This last from Hal.

'That's something,' Kurr said. 'But how are Leith and Stella coping out there on the lake?'

Leith felt something warm and wet soaking into his shoulder. Stella was crying softly. He straightened up and brushed her tears away.

'Sorry,' she said quietly.

'It's all right,' he said, knowing it wasn't. It had happened, she knew about Wira, but he didn't feel any of the joy he expected. Instead he felt only pity and sorrow.

'Did you really know?' she said some time later.

'Yes,' he replied simply.

'You must think I'm such a fool.'

'Why?' he said, and it was as though the other voice spoke again. 'Wira is handsome and strong, and he cares about you. Without him we would never have made it this far. Don't think badly of him. How would you have coped with watching your mother die?'

Stella sighed. 'You sound just like your brother.'

She's right, Leith thought. *I do sound exactly like my brother. Is it his voice I'm hearing? Can he do that?* After the night in the Hermit's cave, Leith was unsure of anything to do with Hal.

'What you say is true,' she continued. 'Wira is nice to me, and I love him – or I think I do, and – and – he's not Druin, and –

311

oh, things are such a mess!' and she cried as he wrapped his arms about her.

Leith said nothing, but continued to hold her throughout the long night and on into the dawn.

Together Kurr and the Fodhram leader scoured the lake from a vantage point high above their campsite. During the pre-dawn hours the two men had sat together, talking about Loulea and Withwestwa Wood, about Faltha and Bhrudwo and the quest of the Company. Now they sought news of Leith and Stella.

As the sun rose and flushed the lake with saffron, two figures standing hand in hand out in the middle of the lake cast shadows that stretched across to the shore.

'They're alive,' Kurr breathed.

'Yes,' his friend agreed, wisdom in his deep eyes. 'Perhaps this morning they are truly alive.'

Out on the lake Leith and Stella searched the shore. 'Perhaps the fire has died down,' she said.

'Let's go and find out,' he said. Was that his voice? He no longer cared.

Together they walked slowly, carefully across the ice, skirting the newly-formed surface, Stella limping on her sore ankle. For a time it seemed as though they were making no progress, but eventually they drew close to the shore. Ahead they could see activity as their companions readied themselves for the journey.

'Do you think they've missed us?' Stella wondered aloud.

'Of course!' he replied. 'I wonder how Wira is.'

The woman beside him did not answer.

They came up to the camp, and Leith realised he was holding her hand. His awkwardness returned and he let her hand drop, not noticing the brief flicker of pain that crossed her face.

'I can't wait to sit by the fire,' she said. 'I feel so cold. I only survived the night because of you.' Embarrassed and with his head averted, Leith did not see the look she gave him, filled with gratitude and friendship.

* * *

312

Their reunion with the rest of the Company was full of relief. The fur-lined cloaks had kept Leith and Stella from the full effects of the cold, and the warm southerly breeze had taken the deep chill from the air. Back at the camp Wira had slept deeply, and was now fully recovered except for his customary morning headache. This morning, he realised, there was no point in disguising that fact.

The journey to Midrun Hut took no more than thirty minutes. They had come so close the previous night before near-tragedy had overtaken them. The travellers kept close to the shore, where the shadows had kept the ice from melting. The hut itself was on a rock shelf some twenty feet above the lake, close to where the rapids drained it. The door was unlocked, opening easily to a push.

Within minutes the tumplines and their loads were deposited in the corner, boots came off and the fire was lit. Breathing a prayer of thanks to the travellers who had left fuel by the fire (then realising with a chuckle it was probably he and his lads), the Fodhram leader called for attention.

'Welcome to the best accommodation west of the hills and east of the mountains!' he proclaimed, with a bow and a sweep of his arm. 'In fact, welcome to the *only* accommodation west of the hills and east of the mountains. It isn't much,' he said ruefully, 'but it is better than sleeping on an ice floe. Depending on the company!' he added, doffing his cap to Leith, who blushed bright red at the laughter of the Fodhram.

'Now then,' Leader continued, 'we have some time to wait until we can travel again. The thaw will make all rivers and portages impassable. No one in the northern lands will be moving. So for the next few days we should make ourselves useful by checking the canoes' – he pointed to the shells in the far corner of the room – 'and repacking our gear. Which should leave us plenty of time for singing and talking around the fire!'

His men roared with delight. This was the kind of speech they approved of! In a very short time hot food and mugs of warm tea were passed around, and the bright spring morning was filled with the raucous sound of singing only those who had come close to disaster could produce.

CHAPTER 15

THE SOUTHERN RUN

'COME WITH US,' WHISPERED Taller, shaking Farr by the shoulder. The afternoon was quiet, and the hot sun coming through the slatted window had sent the Company to sleep. 'Come with us. We're going to watch the Mossbank go out.'

Farr rubbed his eyes clear of sleep and shook his head. Never one for relaxing, he had begun to sleep deeply in the arms of the forest. Something tense ebbed out of him. 'I'm coming,' he said quietly. 'But what about the others?'

'They need their rest. I don't think they realise how much the journey has taxed them.'

The Vinkullen man nodded, pulled on his boots and followed the four Fodhram out into the sunshine.

The chattering stream that drained Midrun Lake emptied into the headwaters of the much bigger Mossbank River a mile or so to the south. It took them half an hour's struggle through the soggy morass of the forest floor to find a suitable site overlooking the confluence of these waters. They came to a high promontory from which they could see a complete panorama of the northern woods, velvet in the afternoon sun as they lay draped over the tortured folds of the wilderness.

About a hundred feet below them lay the ribbon of the Mossbank, still locked by ice. Smaller streams, flowing with steeper gradients and by now ice-free, merrily discharged meltwater from

314

a million trees into the reluctant river. As the water level rose, so the pressure on the ice mounted.

'We're just in time,' Shabby drawled.

'Say nothing, just watch and listen,' Leader advised them.

The Mossbank River went out shortly thereafter. Directly below them the ice buckled up with an unearthly screeching sound, the upper floe overriding the lower. From somewhere upstream came more howls and shrieks as the ice fought free of the riverbank. For a few heart-stopping moments the river paused, as splintering ice from upriver met resistance where the river narrowed; then everything let go.

Floe after floe cascaded down the river, breaking apart on the rocks and on each other. The sound was enormous, and Farr could not be sure whether it was the ice or merely the sound which shook the rocks upon which he sat. At one point an ice jam formed, blocking the river, which simply flowed over the banks and through the trees until the howling ice gave way.

With a rush the trapped ice from upstream roared past them. Huge, jagged floes beat themselves to death on the rocky shores. In various places they overrode the banks, stripping the bark from ancient forest monarchs and shearing off branches and even whole trees as though they were twigs. On one patch of ice an animal – possibly a racoon – crouched in fear: the whirling current took it out of sight in a matter of moments. Death amidst life.

Now fewer chunks of ice came down from the watershed. The river was more water than ice – then nearly all water. Glittering shards were left high on the rocks, on sandy beaches and even in the forest itself as the water returned to its bed. The screeching and wailing of ice upon ice abated, becoming a faint backdrop to the quiet satisfaction of the woods as the breakup continued further downstream.

A change stole over Farr as he watched. He began to see the forest as a living thing waking from a long sleep. As the ice melted, the lifeblood of the forest was once again able to flow down the rivers. He'd watched the grey of winter fall away, he'd seen the forest's green summer coat revealed. Tender new shoots unfurled amid the protection of the dark evergreens, the yearly promise of life renewed.

Since the death of their parents, life had been hard for Wira; no wonder he'd turned to the drink. As Farr listened to the far-off rumble of ice to the south, he acknowledged for the first time that life had been just as hard for him – and he hadn't had an older brother to support him. Since his mother died, he'd put on anger like a grey winter cloak. *Take it off*, the forest whispered to him. *Winter is over*. He let out a long breath.

Beside him the Fodhram exchanged smiles.

The Company began the second leg of the Southern Run well before dawn. The Fodhram made sure that Midrun Hut was shut fast against the elements, as some of the strongest winds in these parts came in the spring. 'Other Fodhram will be here later in the season,' Leader told them. So they supplemented the fuel for the fire by taking fallen branches from around the hut. All four birch bark canoes had been mended, even though the Company would be taking only two. They pulled shut the door of the hut and stepped out into the clear, cold night.

The fragile, twenty-foot-long canoes were lifted over a rocky beach and lowered gently into the water, then packed with fur bales interspersed with members of the Company. With short, powerful strokes of wide-bladed paddles, the Fodhram powered the cumbersome canoes out into the darkness.

The flat-bottomed canoe settled well down in the water. Leith took a deep breath: he could smell the fur bales ahead and behind him, and across the lake drifted the fragrance of spring, the sweetness of pollen and sap. At the prow of his canoe sat Shabby, who seemed to be in command; behind him Perdu and Stella talked quietly. Separated from them by a couple of bales was Hal, who was in turn two bales forward of where Leith crouched uncomfortably. Behind him lay the bulk of the bales, and Taller paddled vigorously at the rear, steering when necessary. Every once in a while Shabby would call out instructions to Taller in a rough, unintelligble tongue.

It was still dark when they reached the stream which drained the lake. The canoes were beached by the stream, and their cargo quickly unloaded. All of the Firanese took up tumplines and at least one bale, while the Fodhram carried the canoes, the bowsman and steersman taking an end each. It was time for their first portage.

Leith could not believe the ability of the Fodhram to see in the dark. They led the travellers confidently along the narrow and boggy path, singing as they walked, avoiding with their bulky canoes trees that Leith blundered into. For a while the trail climbed, then it wound down to the river's edge. When the Company emerged from the depths of the forest, it was to the faint light of dawn under a low overcast. There on the riverbank the pattern that was to dominate the next two weeks was established: the canoes were gently lowered into the water, sterns held by the steersmen, while the Company unburdened themselves of their fur bales and tumplines. These were then placed in the canoes, the travellers clambered on board and the steersmen settled into the sterns as they cast off into the current.

Dawn came and went. The river emptied into a larger body of water than any they had yet seen, announced as Lake Cotyledon by the Fodhram. Out on the lake the south wind blew, raising a chop with foaming whitecaps. The canoes kept to the southern shore, as on the far shore the waves would have pounded the canoes into matchwood. Even so, the ride was slow and uncomfortably rough, and soon Leith began to feel unwell.

'When do we stop for breakfast?' Kurr call out to Leader. His reply was a hearty laugh. 'Be patient! We have a routine we must adhere to.'

'Patient? The Haufuth wouldn't have stood for this, you know,' the old farmer commented, half jokingly.

The Fodhram leader indicated his own ample girth. 'Does it look like we are underfed? Patience! We will have a banquet at the far end of Cotyledon.'

What about the Haufuth? Leith wondered, clutching his upset stomach. *Has he survived the rigours of the late winter and the spring thaw?*

*   *   *

The thaw had not in fact yet come to Bandits' Cave. The limestone hill, in the shadow of the mountains, still lay in Qali's jealous grip. Days of leaden skies gave way to rain and sleet, and it proved impossible to go outside. Not that there was any need. There were plenty of provisions laid on in the cave's cool interior, so the Haufuth reasoned that even he should survive until the thaw.

Wisent, however, was another matter. Much of the food was not suitable for the huge beast, and so eventually the Haufuth had with great reluctance let the animal go to forage for his own food. But what, he wondered, would the aurochs find to eat out in the ice-hardened, snow-covered forest? The big headman shrugged; what could he do?

His other charge was doing much better. The Hermit had remained unconscious for many days, then for two weeks after his eyes opened he had not spoken or acknowledged the Haufuth in any way. The man with the long blond hair was totally dependent on the village headman from northern Firanes, who prepared his meals and fed them to him, who cleaned and bathed him, and who talked to him long into the cheerless nights even though he got no response. The normally gregarious Haufuth was severely taxed by this situation, and couldn't help wondering whether he shouldn't have gone with the others. But one look at the helpless man in his care reminded him that, without his constant attention, he would have died.

For a while the Haufuth assumed that his sickness had affected the Hermit's mind, but gradually he had come to himself. On two nights he had woken, crying, 'The Right Hand! The Right Hand has struck me dead!' The Haufuth did not understand it, but rejoiced to hear at least some words pass the lips of his charge.

Finally the day had come when the Hermit had been able to speak with some coherence. The light was back in his eyes, and he beckoned the Haufuth over to the side of his cot.

'Tell me,' the Loulea headman asked in a gentle voice, 'do you feel well enough to get up for a while? You can't stop in bed forever, you know.'

'How long have I been – asleep?' The voice from the bed was still painfully thin.

'Four weeks.'

'I don't feel able to – I'd better lie here for a while longer. I'll be right in a while. Did they – have the others left?'

'The day you took ill.'

'And you? Why did you not go with them?'

The big man turned away from those alert eyes. 'What else was there to do?'

The Hermit laughed softly. 'Presumably continuing a quest so pressing that it brought a company of dread warriors hustling across the moors and mountains!'

The Haufuth shrugged his shoulders. 'I think the dread warriors will do better without me,' he said quietly.

'Not so! In fact, the quest will not succeed without your continued involvement.'

'What do you know of our quest?'

'Nothing,' the Hermit said evenly. 'I don't have to. You yet have a role to play.'

'You're still not well.'

'True!' The man levered himself up on his elbows, the better to deliver his wisdom, then collapsed in a fit of coughing. After a few minutes, he was able to continue. 'I hear what I hear. Not, mind you, that I always know what to do with what I hear!' He frowned. 'That's why I became sick.'

The Haufuth shook his head. This man seemed a paradox of certitude and confusion. No wonder Leith had looked so bemused after talking with him!

'Now I have a question for you,' the Hermit said, and the Haufuth could hear the eagerness in his voice.

'Yes?'

'When did you first meet the Right Hand?'

'I have never met this "right hand". What is it?'

'But the Right Hand was with you! I spoke to him!' Then, too late, a thought entered his head. 'You don't know!' he said incredulously. 'He hasn't— no one knows!'

319

The Haufuth bent over and patted his patient on the arm. 'Time to eat. I'll get you something.'

The Hermit rubbed his forehead. 'I'm sorry. Perhaps I have underestimated the effects of a month in bed. Forget what I said.'

The Haufuth had already done just that. It was past dinner time.

The fine weather was never going to last for the entire journey to Vindstrop House, but there had always been hope. However, the Fodhram had not expected the late snow that kept them pinned three days beside Mossbank Cadence, unable to attempt the portage.

'Unseasonal,' was all the Fodhram leader would say.

'That's what you said last year. Remember the week at The Neck? Your fault. Some leader!'

Leader laughed and tried to cuff Shabby around the ear, but he was too quick.

'How far are we from Vindstrop House?' Kurr asked.

'Less than two hundred miles as the river runs,' Leader replied. 'Don't ask me how long that will take, because with this weather I can't say.'

'What if it cleared now?'

'At best we'll have to wait another two days. The snow's piled up into drifts out there. We'll not make it through the portage until the snow melts and the meltwater drains away.'

'The thaw will be over down south by now.' A statement, not a question.

'Well over. I'm sorry.'

The snowfall that fell on the lower Mossbank was only the edge of a huge band of storms which had its origin to the far north. The weather over Withwestwa Wood had been good, too good; the southerly winds had died, giving the travellers a week of perfect weather, but also allowing the storms to move in from the north. The huge mass of cold air funnelled down against the Jawbone Mountains, blanketing Bandits' Cave with cloud and finally snow;

it reached frigid fingers out past Midrun and touched the Mossbank River system, trapping the Company. But it reserved its full force for southern Withwestwa Wood, from the Portals to Steffl Mountain. In this tempest of ice and snow, the revenge of Qali for an early thaw, the Bhrudwans and their captives were caught and held fast.

At first the snow was barely a nuisance, nothing to be compared to the weeks of pain and struggle as Mahnum, Indrett and Parlevaag fought through the thaw. But soon it began to mount in drifts, and each hour saw the wind grow sharper. Eventually the Bhrudwan leader called a halt.

Later that afternoon two of the Bhrudwans went ahead on some errand. Mahnum guessed that they were after food; their own meagre rations of flour and water had been halved, and they were not eating enough to survive. This far south, closer to human habitation, there had been few animals even for warriors to catch, grouse and rabbit providing an infrequent supplement to their monotonous diet. One of the warriors, the one Mahnum had come to know as the Acolyte, remained behind to guard them. The Trader had often wondered about this younger man. What had compelled him to become a murderer? What threat, what reward could there be to make a man do things that were so distasteful to him? Or did he truly have an evil soul? Mahnum tried talking to him: he had been snarled at for his pains.

An hour or so later the Bhrudwan veterans returned. Conditions had deteriorated to the point where Mahnum did not see them until they were a few yards away. *We'd call this a blizzard back home – stay inside and stoke the fire.* He hadn't been truly warm for ages, not since before he first set out for Bhrudwo over two years ago. He tried not to think of a warm fireside and a full stomach. And laughter. He especially tried not to think of laughter.

The Bhrudwans made their captives march forward into the blizzard. *What are they doing?* Mahnum puzzled. Ahead of him Indrett coughed; he could hear the pain in it. *She won't live through this.*

It took them nearly an hour to struggle a few hundred yards down what Mahnum supposed was still the Westway. Then they turned off the path and wound their way under a dense canopy of trees where the snow cover was lighter. In a while they came to a glade, in the midst of which was a house surrounded by deep snowdrifts. The front door was open, broken off at the hinges, but there was no sign of life. A deep sense of dread settled on Mahnum.

There on the verandah lay two bodies, savagely mutilated. One was a child.

Indrett began to sob. The Bhrudwans did not acknowledge the sound, and stepped over the larger of the two corpses to gain entrance. The Acolyte forced the captives inside, making them step over the body of a man. Had he been trying to escape, or to protect his family? He had died in obvious agony, knowing that he had failed to protect them.

In the main room lay two more bodies, a woman and her daughter. They had died trying to hide from a force more implacable than their most evil dreams. Their end had undoubtedly been horrible.

At a nod from the Bhrudwan leader, the other warriors carried the bodies outside and threw them on the snow.

Food, warmth and shelter, thought Mahnum later that night, as he lay on the floor where the dead bodies had lain. *I would rather be cold and hungry*. That night he did not sleep.

'No one has ever survived Mossbank Cadence,' Taller said flatly.

The Fodhram leader shrugged his shoulders. 'That's because no one has ever had the opportunity we have. The Southern Run is usually completed in late spring or early autumn. It's barely past thaw now; I've never heard of any other Fodhram taking on the Southern Run this early.'

'True.' This from Shabby, who had not yet made up his mind.

'So there's still plenty of meltwater running down the Mossbank. Especially in the wake of this latest snowfall. In fact, she's very nearly in flood. So here we are – the hand of the Provider, I say – with a chance to shoot the Cadence and sail right into a song.'

'Look, do you know how many graves there are down at the bottom of the rapids?'

'Thirty-three. I've counted them. Do you think they'd sing about our deeds all over Withwestwa if we canoed across Cotyledon on a still morning? We've got to earn fame with brave deeds! And do I have to remind you of Trenstane and Thuya Wood?'

Scar-face spoke up. 'That's right. We came on this trip, knowing all the risks, because we wanted the high early season prices at Stanlow. But if no furs should come out of Withwestwa until the summer, the gold will all be spent at Trenstane. There's nothing those stoat-eaters from Thuya Wood won't do to get a little Treikan money.'

'Maybe the storm will let up,' Taller said defiantly.

'It's already too late for that,' Leader assured him. 'Besides, it's a matter of honour. We agreed to take these Firanese to Vindstrop with all possible swiftness, and we can't let them down now. They're on a mission of mercy. Which of you would not risk the Cadence in order to save your loved ones?'

Reluctantly, Taller nodded his head. He could see which way the vote was going. 'Aye, then,' he concurred. 'We'll shoot the rapids. If even one of us survives it will make a tale worth the telling.'

'We'll make sure it gets told!' Leader laughed. 'And you know what happens to tales repeated around Fodhram campfires. Before the season is out they'll have us dancing on Bircheater Teeth in our stockinged feet.'

One by one the Company emerged from their hastily constructed shelter into the lightly falling snow. The forest canopy was coated like the first snowfall of September, drifts lay deep on the ground, and the chill north wind whistled tunelessly through the tree tops. The sounds of spring were muted now, with the rush of the rapids coming faintly through the forest to their right. Kurr cast a glance up the portage trail, where a deep drift blocked their way.

'This is the only way,' the Fodhram leader said quietly. 'The weather could take a week to clear.'

323

'It has come to this before,' the old farmer replied. 'Time and again, choice has been taken away from us. So be it!'

Leader had assured him that the rapids were nothing to worry about, but this he doubted. Else why the delay in running them before now? The too-eager looks on the faces of the Fodhram did nothing to ease his mounting fear.

The canoes were floated and loaded, and the Company cast off into the green waters of the lake. The two craft turned to the right, floating between the shore from which they had launched and a small island with a solitary jack pine atop it. The Fodhram stopped paddling, but the canoes continued to pick up speed. Ahead the lake disappeared between the trees, and Leith could make out rocky heights far up in the mist. Mossbank Cadence.

Now the paddlers beat against the current, their efforts hardly arresting the progress of the canoes. Leader manoeuvred his canoe to the front, and Leith watched from the second canoe as Leader's craft suddenly disappeared from sight.

In an instant the second canoe came to the edge of a steep fall, a series of steps down a seemingly sheer precipice. Before Leith could catch his breath, the prow dipped down and bit into the foam. He was thrown up in the air, and scrabbled for his seat as the canoe shot down the falls. Ahead and behind the Fodhram stood, using their stout blades to push the canoe away from rocks. Leith found he was shouting unheard at the top of his lungs, the great voice of the Cadence obliterating all other sound. Down they plunged, down the foaming rapids of Firststep Falls. Water and rock flashed past the frightened passengers. Then, suddenly, they shot out into a pool of calmer water. They had been in Mossbank Cadence only a few seconds.

To their left was a sandy beach lightly dusted with snow. Above them sheer walls stretched on both sides. Around them the green-blue water surged. Ahead the first canoe dropped again from sight.

As the trailing canoe approached Secondstep Falls, it struck an unseen snag, spinning the boat sideways. Leith was almost jerked from his seat. Taller thrashed in the water with his broad blade, which promptly snapped in two. The canoe drew closer to the falls, rocking sideways, lurching dangerously over pressure waves. Then, at the last possible moment, Shabby jammed his blade in between two rocks. The canoe twitched, the stern shot forwards and they broached the head of the falls backwards.

Leith tumbled backwards over a bale, striking his head on the side of the canoe. The leaden sky swirled above him, lurching as the canoe bucked uncontrollably down the stair-like rapids. Had the water been lower they would have been wrecked on the rocks; the Mossbank in flood, however, propelled the eggshell canoe over all rocks and obstacles, and spat it out into Roiling Pool. They had a hole above the waterline, but were otherwise undamaged.

Still the current drew them inexorably forwards and downwards through the vortices of the Roiling Pool. Here the gorge narrowed further to a point where all the waters draining east of the watershed many miles behind them passed through a twenty-foot gap between sheer smooth walls. Around a curve they whipped like seeds in a storm. The lead canoe, flicked left by the irresistible current, cracked against an outcrop on the left-hand wall, splintering the bow under the steersman's hand. Immediately the canoe began to take water. Behind them Shabby, now the steersman for the second canoe, frantically thrashed his paddle in the boiling water as he fought to avoid the wall. Closer and closer they came; then the current twitched them left and they glanced off the rock, squeezing past the outcrop by a matter of inches. Leith caught a brief glimpse of the first canoe as it drifted into a widening channel, then the powerful current took them again and threw them straight at the riverbank.

At the last possible instant the canoe found a tiny channel between the sheer wall and an island of white birch trees. For a moment the water quietened, and Leith found he was sitting near the bow, beside Stella and his brother.

'Where are we?' Leith called to Shabby. The Fodhram shrugged his shoulders in reply.

'Never been this far through the Cadence before!'

Taller sat wearily in the stern of the canoe, helpless without his paddle. They were virtually at the mercy of the current.

Ahead of them a large rock divided the channel still further. Straight towards the rock the canoe drifted, again picking up speed as it entered another stretch of white water. For a time it appeared they were going to go to the right, the larger channel, but once again the tearing current took them left, just left of the tall rock. As they passed Leith felt a branch flick his arm, then suddenly the river disappeared as they fell ten feet from a rock platform. The canoe smacked hard into the water, splitting the stitching open.

'Water! Water!' Stella cried as the canoe began to fill.

Shabby ripped a piece of cloth from his shirt and stuffed it in the tear, stemming the flow, but now the canoe wallowed in the river. The bowsman paddled furiously to keep them going forward, and after a minute or so they drifted into a large, still lake.

The Fodhram cheered loudly. Ahead and to their right the first canoe was beached, and already the Fodhram were at work making frantic repairs. A series of strong strokes saw the second canoe up on the beach beside the first.

'We made it!' Stella shouted excitedly.

'Well, not exactly,' the Fodhram leader said. 'This is the Garth; it lies between the Upper and Lower Cadence. We've made it through the Upper Cadence, but the Lower Cadence still awaits us.'

'Still more rapids?' Leith said. 'I don't think I want to try any more rapids.'

'We can't go back, and we can't walk out of here,' Leader said, pointing at the sheer walls either side of the Garth. 'Up there to the right is the portage, but it is out of our reach. Or can you walk up walls with bales and canoes on your back?' He laughed long and full, an incongruous sound in the depths of the grey-walled gorge.

Leith looked more closely. The faces of the Fodhram were flushed with excitement, not fear. Something in their eyes told him that as soon as repairs were completed they would pit their lives against the Lower Cadence.

*   *   *

326

An hour of caulking and restitching restored the second canoe. The lead canoe, however, had suffered severe damage to its bow, and really needed rebuilding. 'No time for that,' Leader said, the fire still burning in his eyes. So makeshift repairs were made, and Taller fashioned another paddle out of driftwood.

It had been easy casting off into the unknown, but this time Leith knew what to expect and fear gripped him as the canoe left the shore. For a few minutes the Fodhram paddled the boat across the lake, then the current grabbed them and the paddlers stood up to steer. The lead canoe was slightly in front of them. Leith heard Leader say: 'The Lower Cadence is much shorter and much wilder,' and the roar of the Thirdstep Falls took the rest.

Thirdstep Falls was a spout followed by a sheer drop into a boiling punchbowl. Down the canoes shot and the cries of the Fodhram rang out, cries of exaltation as they flew amongst the tortured water drops and slammed into the foaming pool. Immediately the canoes jerked forwards, the second shooting ahead of the first as they were drawn down the Lower Cadence. Side to side, spinning, bucking and weaving, the tiny Fodhram canoes battled the immense power of the Mossbank.

Leith began to feel the excitement of the journey as it overcame his fear, but then he noticed a black line ahead stretching across the river from bank to bank. As they drew nearer the line resolved itself into a group of sharp pinnacles dividing the river into a series of narrow slots, all seemingly far too narrow to admit their canoes. 'Bircheater Teeth!' Taller cried with joy, as to a long-lost lover, and he leaned forward as though eager to dash himself to pieces on their sharp edges.

Leith spun around to see the other canoe close behind them. Shabby paddled hard, trying to steer to the right. The teeth came closer, as though the canoe was still and the rocks rushed towards them. The boy from Loulea held on tight as they approached the impassable barrier.

Ordinarily no canoe could pass these voracious teeth, Leith could see that. However, with the rise in the water level, the teeth were partly submerged and the gaps between them were widened. A steersman just had to choose the correct path.

What was that sound coming from the front and the back of the canoe? Louder and louder it grew, louder than the thunderous churning of the Lower Cadence. The same sound came from the canoe behind. For a moment Leith could not place it, then he realised that the Fodhram were laughing.

They laughed as the canoes flashed up to the Bircheater Teeth, and laughed as the current took the canoes out of their control. The laughter continued as the pinnacles flashed past on either side, and they fended off the rocks. Then the boats floated out on to a long, narrow lake, and their laughter echoed throughout the forest. Finally they stood quietly on Hallowed Beach, at the bottom of Mossbank Cadence, and reverently paid their respects to the many graves lining the shore.

The Fodhram leader faced his countrymen, the exhilaration of the rapids still rimming his eyes. 'That won't make much of a fireside tale, after all.'

His three fellow woodsmen nodded, exhausted.

'Why not?' Kurr asked. He had never done anything at once so terrifying and so exciting.

'No one would believe us,' Leader said sadly.

Snow continued to fall the rest of that day, and the travellers took time to repair the canoes and take meat and drink. Later in the evening the snow stopped, the sky cleared and the moon came out, and they launched the canoes in the silver light.

This was the first time they had travelled by canoe at night. Ahead a forest moon quartered low in the sky, laying a pale path across the lake ruffled by a light breeze. The snow gleamed in the clean moonlight. The sky was sprinkled with sharp-edged stars, outlining the darkness of the forest. It was altogether lovely, the image of Withwestwa Wood that Leith carried all his life.

From somewhere on their left came an unearthly voice raised in a howl. For a moment it was silent, then it came again. Another voice joined it, then a third. The voices echoed across the forest, the song of the wolves of Withwestwa Wood.

Leith found himself gripping something tightly as the harmony died away into the silence of deep night. He turned and looked down; he had Stella's hand in his. Immediately he let it slip. 'I'm sorry,' he stuttered. He could see her smile in the moonlight, and it burned a hole in his chest.

'That's the second time,' Stella said, still smiling.

Leith flushed scarlet. 'I— forgive me.'

'Why?' she said, her voice whispered on the breeze.

'I don't know what has come over me,' Leith blurted. 'That night on the ice – I—' He couldn't finish.

'Oh, Leith,' Stella laughed, 'don't spoil it by trying to explain. Can't you be my friend?'

He bit his lip, trying not to cry out with the power of his longing. Stella said nothing more, but reached out and took his hand.

'Thank you,' she said some time later. 'Thank you for explaining to me about Wira. I would have hated him otherwise. I'm glad that you're my friend.'

Leith watched her as her eyes darted across to the other canoe. There a tall, shadowed figure sat in the stern, head bowed, oblivious to the beauty around him. Wira had said very little since the night the ice had nearly taken him.

He still has her heart, Leith thought. *She is my friend; that's all I could ask for.* The illusion lasted for a few moments. *I don't feel this way about any of my other friends!* His overriding impulse was to let her hand go and turn away, but somehow he couldn't. After all, their paths were to be shared for a long time yet.

By the time the weather broke in southern Withwestwa, the snow lay level with the windowsills. For a while Mahnum hoped the Bhrudwans would be discovered, but he remembered the bodies out on the verandah, and did not wish to contemplate what they might do with anyone who stumbled on their hideaway. And after a few days there was so much snow about that the likelihood of discovery receded to almost nothing.

These days were a chance to recuperate after a journey that had taxed the captives to their very limits. The larder of the house contained food and drink to spare, and the Bhrudwans allowed their prisoners to have their fill. The two women were locked in a back room somewhere and Mahnum did not see Indrett during their stay, but he was content, as he knew she would benefit from the rest. Not to have to march all day was bliss, a luxury he had not experienced for over two years. A luxury, however, he would readily exchange for freedom.

In these days the weary Trader was able to think clearly for the first time in months. What was it that the Bhrudwans wanted from him? He was the only one who knew about the imminent invasion from Bhrudwo. So why didn't they make an end of him? It could only be that his supposed knowledge was more valuable than the risk of keeping him alive. Why, then, didn't they torture him? He had seen Bhrudwan torture first-hand, and knew that no matter how strong his resolve, soon he would be pleading for them to listen to him. It could only be that someone else, a superior of theirs, wanted to question him.

So who was it who wanted to speak to him? Surely not the one who had interrogated him on the island of Andratan – unless he was to be questioned about his escape. But would they drag him across the face of the world to ask him about castle security? Mahnum could think of only one answer to the riddle. Someone else, perhaps a rival in the Bhrudwan leadership, sought to gain information from him that he could get nowhere else.

As he thought further about it, he became more convinced he had read the situation correctly. The inquisitor on Andratan had asked many things, but had continually come back to one question: who or what was the 'Right Hand'? It had become obvious to his questioner that the Trader knew nothing, and the questioning had stopped. Now his captors wanted to know the same thing: where was the 'Right Hand'? They could not be working on behalf of the Voice of Andratan.

So who, what, or where was the 'Right Hand'? It all came down to this question. Something to do with the upcoming invasion, he was certain. Some mighty warrior or some secret weapon, some hidden society that threatened the plans of the Undying Man. He reviewed all his acquaintances, all the people he had ever heard of, and every place, organisation or thing he had seen or knew about. He went through his life year by year, place by place. Finally, at the end of a long, exhausting week, he confirmed what he already knew: nothing. He had never heard of or seen anyone or anything that he could possibly construe, by whatever leap of imagination he could conjure up, as being a 'Right Hand'. Although his curiosity remained unsatisfied as to what could be so important that Bhrudwo sought it with such energy, he was thankful that he did not have the knowledge they sought. Should he not manage to escape his captors, he had no doubt he would be questioned with torture. It was better for Faltha that, if there really was some powerful secret hidden deep in the unprepared lands, he did not know anything about it.

During the week they hid in the house, the Bhrudwan warriors said very little. They did not question Mahnum, nor did they talk freely amongst themselves. Instead, they sat perfectly still on chairs, as though they had turned themselves off. Mahnum had seen this already on his travels: Bhrudwan villagers had practised an art they called Mul, involving extended periods of meditation. The Trader had out of necessity learned how to exercise Mul, but found it a waste of time. From what he understood, many Bhrudwans meditated on their knowledge of tides and seasons to make crucial life decisions, such as when to have children, when to marry, and so on. Mul was supposed to restore energy and equanimity, but Mahnum had lived among the Bhrudwan villagers and had his doubts. Perhaps the warriors were better practitioners of the art than those he had seen.

Abruptly one morning the Bhrudwans roused their captives and began the old routine again. Wearily Mahnum dressed and ate the rations given him, obeying mechanically when the Bhrudwan leader barked orders at him. Outside waited Indrett and the Fenni woman. He caught a glimpse of his beloved and noted with satisfaction that she had regained some weight and her bruises had faded a little. *You'll need all your strength, my love,* he thought. *We've a long way to go yet. And one day they'll slip; one day we'll get our chance and the three of us will be off. Or perhaps we'll be rescued.* Hope stretched out as long as the remaining miles of their journey. However many there were.

During the last few days of the Company's journey the weather turned to rain, a moist wind from the east making conditions unpleasant for all but the Fodhram, who seemed thankful for the rain. 'You get either rain or mosquitoes,' Shabby explained. 'We have had the mosquitoes. We choose the rain!' and they all laughed.

They made excellent speed in spite of the weather. The portages, though frequent, were short and, because river levels remained high, many rapids could be run. The Mossbank grew broader and more languid, carving a deep trench in the uplands that underlay Withwestwa Wood. As spring came on many more animals ventured out from winter homes, but in the main the local wildlife avoided the trail. Finally, about a day and a half's travel from Vindstrop House, they met a party of Fodhram travelling north.

Leader spoke to them, clearly explaining the presence of non-woodsmen in their party. At one stage Leith could tell that he was retelling the running of Mossbank Cadence to a disbelieving audience. Though the language he used was unintelligible to the Firanese, his hands told a story unmistakable in its drama – though did that hand motion indicate one of the canoes capsizing? Knowing the Fodhram, Leith thought such exaggeration very likely.

Eventually the fur traders went on their way northwards, canoe blades flashing silver in the afternoon sun. 'No outsiders have been seen at Vindstrop House,' Leader reported, 'as of two days ago, at least. So you may be in luck.'

They hurried on into the dusk, eager to return to civilisation.

Late the next afternoon the forest gave way to pasture. The Mossbank grew slow and wide, brown with sediment, tired after its journey down from the watershed. Houses appeared on grassy slopes that swept down to the shore. As the sun went down on the northern lands the river made another languid turn and drew them towards a small village on the right bank. Vindstrop House.

A few hundred years ago there had indeed been only one house on this site. Surrounded by deep woods, an intrepid forest-dweller began to act as an agent for the burgeoning fur trade, setting aside at first one room in his house as a trading post. Very soon he constructed a separate building for the purpose. Within a few years a small community gathered around Mr Vindstrop's house, all there to profit from the extravagance of fur traders with money in their pockets.

Mr Vindstrop had been killed in a dispute over weights and measures, but the town was still named after him. It became the unofficial 'capital' of the Fodhram communities, though the Fodhram had neither central government nor king. The nearest thing to a leader the Fodhram tolerated was the informal title of 'Warden', bestowed on merit since the days of Whitebirch. Despite living in lands claimed by Plonyans and Treikans, the Fodhram of Withwestwa Wood owed allegiance to no one.

The village was quiet that evening. It was far too early in the season for fur traders, the bulk of whom brought their riches into town after midsummer. There was no one near the bank when the Company lifted their canoes from the water and tied them to the base of a large pine. Tired shoulders bore the burden of fur bales for one last time, and the travellers filed slowly up the slope away from the river and towards the welcoming lights of the village.

CHAPTER 16

THE SLOPES OF STEFFL

AFTER HAVING BATTERED WITHWESTWA Wood, the great storm rolled south over northern Plonya, then slowed and intensified as it encountered the broad uplands known as Clovenhill, Blaenau Law in the old tongue, the home of the Widuz. Lands that seldom saw snow even in winter were smothered by a dry white powder, keeping everyone indoors. The cloud and snow lingered day after day, preventing the hunters of Widuz from finding food for their families. The south of Clovenhill fared much worse than the north, with drifts virtually burying villages and towns. Tolmen, the big city on the coast, froze in Qali's icy grip. In desperation the hunters of Widuz began to venture north into lands they had been forced to leave centuries ago, foraging for food in areas that had escaped the worst of the storm.

The proprietor of Vindstrop's Trading Post was surprised indeed to see a group of fur traders marching up to his door, muddy and tired, with bales on their backs and weary smiles on their faces. His boy had come running in excitedly with the news that the Fodhram have come, the Fodhram have come, and had received a cuff around the ear for telling lies. But here they were, standing on his floor, bales ready to be inspected. *A gift from heaven*, he reflected.

As the bales were unpacked and his assistant began the weighing and measuring, he had a closer look at the travellers who had so fortunately interrupted his lean spring. Indeed a motley collection, he observed. Well, the Warden he knew. Short and stout, Axehaft the Warden came from Fernthicket deep in Withwestwa Wood. It was an honour to have him back in Vindstrop House; every run the Warden had led in the previous two years had ended in Stanlow. And who was this with him? Mulberry, born here in Vindstrop House nearly thirty years ago: a rascal and a thief, he had joined Axehaft after his parents died, improving his character considerably. The only legacy of his former life was his slovenly dress. Aspenlimb of Rockford he had met only once before. Rockford was at the eastern margins of Fodhram lands, on the slopes of the treeless Black Hills, and folk there seldom if ever ventured far from home. The proprietor did not know how the tall eastlander had come to befriend the Warden of Withwestwa Wood. And the fourth man dressed in traditional Fodhram garb? He stepped out of the shadows: Leafholm, the famous scar-faced fur trader, who came from Birch Hill near Fernthicket, the only man to best Axehaft in the autumn quarterstaff tourney. Everyone said he would be the next Warden. The pragmatic proprietor made sure he always paid him the greatest respect.

But what of the others? None of these were Fodhram. A wiry old man, a solid-looking, swarthy man, two taller, fairer youths, obviously brothers; then a lame – no, crippled – youth and a white-faced boy, surely no more than fifteen years of age – and a woman! Where were these people from? Would they need accommodation? Many questions formed in the storekeeper's mind but, in the fashion of all Fodhram, he did not ask their names. Names were reserved for people in whom trust had been established. Definitely not for outsiders. There was some story here, a story he would probably never hear.

The proprietor rubbed his hands in satisfaction as the figures were added up. Quality was excellent, and the furs – beaver, ermine, mink – were eminently saleable in Stanlow. As was the way with these things, the storekeeper would make a greater profit from these bales than those who risked life and limb to collect them. He frowned. Still, they had the life, travelling the wide open spaces, exploring new territory, undertaking deeds of great renown. He got to keep store. His reward, he reasoned, was only fair.

The whole party, it turned out, wanted lodging for the night. They really did appear all in; even the Fodhram seemed overcome with weariness.

The adding completed, the Warden merely nodded when the scrip was handed over. Normally he drove a hard bargain, but tonight he said nothing, prompting the storekeeper to shake his head. What kind of adventures had they been through? Something more than warranted by the season alone, he was sure. He shook his head again, gathered up his weights and measures and showed his guests to their rooms. Talk, if there was to be any, would have to wait for the morning.

'What now?'

Welcome sunlight streamed through the open window. The Company sat around a large table, still half asleep, trying to decide how to approach the nub of their task. Perdu's question hung in the air.

'We continue with our original plan,' Kurr responded. 'Remember? We make our way back down the Westway until we meet the Bhrudwans.'

'Then we hold a little discussion, persuade them to give up their captives, and ask one of them to accompany us to Instruere and tell the council all about their nasty plans.' Perdu was far from convinced.

'We'll have the advantage of surprise,' Farr contended. 'It's up to us to make the advantage pay!'

'An ambush is our best chance,' said the old farmer. 'Trouble is, how do we slay these Bhrudwans without hurting our friends? And how do we capture one of the warriors alive?'

'How do we avoid being killed ourselves?' Leith muttered. Beside him, Stella voiced her agreement.

'In your case, my lady, it will be easy. You'll be staying here in Vindstrop House. It won't help protesting, I've already discussed it with Leader, and he has found a place for you.'

'So you've asked Leader, have you?' Stella was incensed, and made no effort to hide it. 'What about asking me? Don't you think I might have an opinion? Or are you going to continue to treat me as you did when I walked in on Leith and Hal? Dragging me away when it suits, and leaving me behind when I get in the way?'

Nonplussed in the face of this onslaught, Kurr didn't know which charge to answer first. Stella gave him no chance, her arguments carefully marshalled as though she had anticipated this.

'I want you to explain something to me,' she said, words tumbling over each other in their urgency to be heard. 'What would you be doing now if I hadn't been with you on the Roofed Road? Would they have killed you swiftly or slowly? Perhaps you might have had the chance to test your swimming talents against the Maelstrom!'

'I—'

'Do you think Wira would have surfaced yet if I had not been with you on the lake near Midrun Hut? Maybe his body might even now be washed up on some unreachable shore!'

'Perhaps—'

'We are a Company; we live or die together. You might as well kill me as leave me here to await your return. If you don't come back, where would I go?'

'She's right,' Wira said. 'We owe her our lives. Stella is the most courageous member of our party. Who are we to judge her?'

'But – it's not right to send women into battle!' Kurr could not understand the opposition mounting against him.

Hal spoke while Stella spluttered. 'It is not right to send anyone into battle, unless it is necessary. The fate of Faltha may depend on the upcoming conflict. Sheltering anyone from the battle now may expose them – and everyone else – to it later.'

Now Stella had regained her breath. 'Are you saying that I would be less a warrior than – please forgive me – crippled Hal or old Kurr?' The farmer drew in his breath sharply. 'Do you mean to bring me here against my will and then leave me here against my will?'

Kurr was about to insist, but then glanced around the room and thought better of it. The risk of division within the Company was too great; he might lose more than he would gain.

'Very well, then,' he acquiesced. 'You may come with us, to die quickly and unpleasantly, most likely.'

Stella smiled grimly. 'I would have followed you anyway,' she said.

'So how are we going to best these warriors?' Perdu asked.

The Company had left Vindstrop House after breakfast that morning, having bade the Fodhram a final farewell.

'Goodbye, my friends,' Leader had said, embracing each of them in turn. He insisted on paying for their accommodation, provided them with food for their journey and gave them a small bag of money.

'What's this?' Kurr had asked.

'Part payment for your help in getting our furs to market!' the answer had come.

'So how much do we owe you for guiding us through Withwestwa Wood?' Kurr had pressed.

'Nothing,' was the reply. 'Either you are brought through by friends or you don't come at all.'

The kindness and good humour of the Fodhram had been an unlooked-for blessing on their road. Without their kindness, the journey might have ended at Roleystone Bridge. *Who will help us now?* Leith wondered.

The travellers waited for Kurr to answer Perdu, who had spoken for them all, but the old farmer said nothing.

Behind them the day drew to a close. The sun filtered through between tall pines, mottling the path ahead with uncertain shadows and picking out the occasional icy remnant of the previous week's snowfall. A shifting breeze flicked under the high boughs, giving the forest a feel very much like a spring evening in the woods north of Loulea. On such an afternoon of sleepy beauty Leith could not imagine danger and death approaching them, yet it was. He noted that Kurr still had not answered Perdu.

Without warning the track emerged at a cliff edge. The narrow path of the Westway wound down the side of the bluff, falling perhaps two hundred feet to a lower land. From the edge of the cliff Withwestwa spread out before them, a verdant carpet covering hilly ground, yet less folded than that further north. The muted rushing of waters filtered up from the forest below.

Some way ahead a solitary mountain rose from the plain, cutting the horizon. Thus the travellers had their first glimpse of Steffl, the tallest peak in the land of the Fodhram. Forest-clothed but with a bare head, Steffl towered three thousand feet above them, sinister and malevolent although still a long way off. Misty smoke draped the bushy valleys carved into its sides. If the stories told by the Fodhram were to believed (and that was by no means certain), Steffl had at times in the past spouted smoke and burned with fire. Mystery and fear clung to the mountain along with the mist.

Kurr stopped to contemplate the view. Somewhere out there, under the green canopy before them, the Bhrudwans marched, making for this spot. Could they be defeated? Were their captives still alive? He had not forgotten Perdu's question.

He turned to face the Company. 'I have nothing but hope to offer you, and not much of that. For weeks now I have been aware that one day we would have to attack these warriors with nothing but sticks and rusty swords. I have come up with plan after plan, and have rejected them all.' He took a deep breath, and looked at each face in return. *Dear hearts each one*, he thought. *Even Farr.* Against his will he had grown to like this gruff, impatient man.

'We'll need to send a scout ahead who will watch out for the enemy, and return to us when he knows where they are. Obviously we must choose a place suitable for our ambush, settle in and then spring with swiftness upon them when they walk into our trap. Some of us should try to isolate one of the Bhrudwans and take him alive; the others must dispatch the two remaining warriors as quickly as possible. So we will divide into two ranks. Farr will lead one; I will lead the other.

'The first rank, which Farr will command, has the responsibility of taking care of two Bhrudwans, and ensuring the safety of their captives. One of their number should also act as scout. Perdu, Stella and Hal will form the first rank.

'I will command the second rank, made up of Leith and Wira. Our task is to capture one Bhrudwan, preferably without injuring him. Whichever rank accomplishes its task first should offer assistance to the other.

'We'll make camp here tonight, with the first rank taking the first watch. These Bhrudwans could come at any time.'

'Not at night, surely?' Wira asked.

'Any time. We could pay for our assumptions with our lives.'

The Bhrudwans did not come that night. The next evening saw the Company making camp low on the southern slopes of Steffl, just off the Westway. Above and to their right the mountain loomed, its hooded peak and scarred flanks hidden by crusty snow which sent an invisible breath of cold air down into the valley. All around them newly returned birds chirped and cawed as they settled down to roost in their beloved northern lands. A musky scent rose from a bog somewhere nearby.

Leith lay back on his sleeping roll, his head nestling on his pack. *This could be my last night*, he thought. *For so long we have tried to find these Bhrudwans, and now we are near them, I wish we were not. Well, whatever happens, I will see my mother and father again.* He sighed, and a deep fear of the pain of the sword blade and the coldness of death settled on him. From his pack he pulled a birch bark carving and held it close to his chest. *Father! Please help me! I know you need all the courage you have, but lend me some for tonight!* A few cold tears fell on to the unfinished face of the carved figure.

Stella could see Leith on the far side of the clearing, his features distorted by the heat from the flickering fire. *He's beginning to show the strain*, she thought. *Still, he's only a boy.* Her thoughts turned to Wira and the words they had exchanged that afternoon. *I'm sorry I never told you*, he had said, and she had felt her anger melting as he smiled at her. *I know I should have said something.* He had explained how he would never drink again, how not a drop had passed his lips since that night on the lake, how she could help him . . . and she had found herself telling him about her brother and the heartache his drinking had brought into her family, how they had tried talking to him, punishing him, locking him away, but always he had found more drink, and now he was an addled idiot, a shame to them all . . . Tears came to Wira's eyes, and he said that he didn't know, he could see how much he had hurt her, and would she forgive him? She had said yes too quickly, but she could not hold her feelings for him in check. They had embraced right there in the forest as the rest of the Company marched on ahead, and she wondered at a man brave enough to admit he was wrong, to face his weakness and to still have the courage to love her. She could see it in his eyes: he loved her. And these feelings she had – were they love? At least they were not the revulsion she felt whenever she thought of Druin and the fate that awaited her if ever she should return home. *Anything but that.*

Wira lay alone in the shadows, some distance away from the others. To his left Stella sat, staring into the fire. *What is she thinking? Does she believe me? If it comes to that, do I believe myself?* What he had said about not touching the drink was not strictly true; he had found some on a shelf in the store at Vindstrop House, and had left some money as payment. Still, it was not strong drink, and it had not lasted into the second day. He felt dry, so dry, and his hands shook as he lay there hoping that no one – that she – would not see. He thought of her embrace, so tender, so young, so beautiful. *I'll give it up for you, Stella, I will.*

Kurr and Perdu sat together by the fire, their older bones appreciating the heat. *It's all right for the young ones to sleep in the shadows. The sap flows vigorously in their veins,* Kurr thought enviously, casting a glance at where Wira lay. *Too vigorously. But does it run true?* Until the night on the ice he had been certain which of the Storrsen brothers he preferred, but now he wasn't so sure. *At least I know what I am getting with the older brother. And what of this friendship – call it friendship for now – between Wira and Stella? Was this what Kroptur feared?* The whole thing made him uneasy.

Perdu was immersed in thoughts of his own. *Haldemar! And my boys! Are they well? For that matter, how are the Fenni faring up on Myrvidda?* The auguries had suggested a lean winter and a late spring on the high moors and, as much as he enjoyed the companionship of his countrymen by birth, Perdu found he was now irrevocably Fenni, and wished he was back home with his family and his clan. He sighed. *Not until I have witnessed the Bhrudwans' deaths,* he thought. *Or not until I have died myself. Either way, soon now I will be back on the vidda, watching over my family. May the gods be with us!*

Farr got up and added fuel to the fire. *How will the old men fight?* he wondered. *Better than the youngsters, most likely.* Kurr would put up a brave showing, of that he had no doubt. Farr had a grudging respect for the feisty old farmer who had put aside his stick and his sorrow, and now looked years younger than when they had first met. *And Perdu?* He remembered his father's cousin only vaguely, but knew he had been a hunter, not a fighter. Still, perhaps being with the Fenni had toughened him up. He certainly carried a lethal-looking sword. *No, it is the young ones who are the worry. Well, perhaps not the girl,* he admitted. *She is ferocious! Better Wira than I!* But the Mahnumsens – best not to expect anything from them. There was no doubting the older boy's courage, but he was too crippled to be effective in battle, notwithstanding the lucky blow he had landed in the Valley of Respite. *And the younger? Unreliable. Consumed by his own fears. He should have been left at home.*

Ah, but I'm missing the Fodhram, Farr thought sadly. *The forest here is still beautiful, but I miss the laughter, the passion. Maybe I'll seek them out when this is over; maybe I'll stay here a while.*

Near the fire, Hal slept quietly.

'What are you doing out of bed again?'

'The sooner I regain the use of my legs, the sooner we can leave.'

'Leave? It will be weeks before I let you out of this cave!' The Haufuth shook his head. *Really, the man was impossible!*

'Weeks? That will be too late. We need to arrive at Instruere within a fortnight of Midsummer at the latest, so we should leave within the week. Even that will be cutting things a bit fine.' He scowled at his big nursemaid.

'Perhaps you don't understand,' the Haufuth said kindly. 'You've been seriously ill. Going outside is out of the question until you have completely recovered. And travelling to Instruere? Perhaps next year.'

'It is you who do not understand, my friend. My sickness was given to me as a gift. I have unwrapped it and found it pleasing. The weeks of confinement have taught new lessons, and now it is time to put what I have learned into practice. I must go to Instruere.'

The big man sat down wearily. 'Never try to reason with a mystic', the old proverb went. *There is much wisdom in the old proverbs*, the Haufuth reflected.

The Hermit fixed his overbright eyes on his benefactor. 'I left the company of men because I preferred my own, and despaired of finding answers amongst them,' he said. 'I have spent long years listening for the truth, and I have learned that the truth is a Person, that I can hear His voice. In the silence of the years I learned to distinguish the true from the false. I have more answers than I knew questions existed for; I know more than I can live out in practice.'

The Haufuth began to feel uncomfortable under the man's intense gaze.

'So here I am, clean and pure and useless. Years of discipline and singleminded devotion have brought me to the place where I can deny myself anything. A year ago I was content, believing myself holy. But now I am not so sure.'

He *can deny himself anything?* The Haufuth's thoughts currently focused on breakfast, and he hoped for a swift end to this homily.

'I am pure only because I have removed the source of temptation, not because I have faced temptation and overcome it. Now I see that my purity is like the purity of a stone: single but useless. I am no longer bad, but I am no longer good. I know everything but do nothing. I take no risk and so receive no reward. Far from adding, the years of contemplation have stripped goodness from me.'

There was a quiet despair in the voice of the Hermit which prompted the Haufuth to say: 'But what about the truth! Surely knowing the truth is a good thing?' He thought of his own dilemmas; if only he had known the right thing to do!

'It is a curse!' came the vehement reply. 'To know the truth and yet not put it into practice; to gaze into the face of truth and yet remain unchanged; to know what to do and yet not do it – this is the path to guilt and to madness. It is the path I have trodden.'

The Haufuth remained silent.

'And then you and your friends came. I was happy, because I had foreseen your coming and knew much regarding your quest. I thought that I could help you, and that in doing so I might lay my guilt to rest. Instead, you have helped me through my sickness, and made me face my pride.

'Your care for me was a gift beyond price. I know that your self-doubt motivated you to remain with me, but still you gave of yourself to a stranger when your heart was with the others. During the nights I have heard you: *I wonder where they are now? I hope Kurr is leading them well!* Your gift to me has cost you a great deal.

'For years I depended on no one but myself. Now I have had to admit that I need others. That I am of no use out here in this cave. That there is more virtue in one kind act than in years of sterile contemplation. You have taken me down from the shelf, polished me and readied me for future usefulness. I thank you!' The Hermit bowed low, his blond locks brushing the cold stone floor.

'Strange as it may be,' the Haufuth replied, leaning forward in his turn, unwillingly caught up in the conversation, 'your sickness has been good for me also. I arrived here ready to give up and go home, and even that decision seemed beyond my strength. I felt useless, a hindrance to my friends. But in the last month I have learned that this is not so, that there are uses for me yet, if not perhaps the glorious fame of leadership that I imagined for myself. I am content, and ready to rejoin humanity.'

The Hermit laughed. 'We should both thank the Right Hand of the Most High! Perhaps when we get to Instruere we will speak to him about this.'

The Haufuth shook his head. *Perhaps I should be thankful for at least a few minutes' lucidity!* Yet he no longer doubted that soon they would be on their way to the great capital city of the Falthan kingdoms.

The morning dawned late under a low overcast and light drizzle. Leith rose quickly, stretched the stiffness out of his back, rubbed life into his weary legs, dressed and prepared for another day on the road. Except that this might be the day he feared. The last day of all.

'Perhaps the Bhrudwans took the Fiannan Road south to Plonya,' Perdu offered over breakfast.

'If they had wanted to go south to a seaport like Ciennan, why take the Westway in the first place?' Kurr had been through this argument in his own mind many times. 'They obviously intend going home by the shortest possible route.'

'Maybe that was their original intention, I'll grant you,' the Fenni continued, 'but you yourself said that they would have been unfamiliar with the severity of an upland winter. Isn't it possible they abandoned their original path for an easier one? Or that they went south simply to survive?'

'We should have come across them before now,' Wira said.

'Nothing we can do about that now,' Kurr said gruffly. 'If they turned south then we'll turn south too and take the Fiannan Road. If they've boarded a ship, then we'll take ship and follow them. Or perhaps some want to give up?'

'Of course not,' Wira answered. 'We merely question the wisdom of taking the Southern Run, of abandoning the Bhrudwans' trail.'

'Did we have a choice?' his brother countered. 'Or are you forgetting Roleystone Bridge? I don't believe we would have survived Withwestwa Wood without the Fodhram, so even if we had made it over the river we would have died on the road. If you want my opinion, that is the fate that overtook the Bhrudwans and their captives.'

'Whatever path the Bhrudwans took, whatever fate befell them, we are going forward today to find out.' Kurr was tiring of the debate and wanted an end to it.

The road climbed the lower slopes of the mountain and soon Withwestwa Wood lay spread out before them. The forest thinned out in places, and other areas were obviously secondary growth, as though some catastrophe had rolled down from the mountain and destroyed the virgin timber. Occasionally the path wound its way through regions of black, broken rock, upon which nothing grew. Thin, foul-smelling vapours rose from cracks in the rock, and in one place a pool of boiling mud bubbled at the very edge of the path.

Above them the drizzle thickened into a steady rain, and the Company paused to don their cloaks. The ground grew sodden, and the forest leaves dripped their burden down on the travellers. The air filled with mist and moisture and the smell of sulphur. Still the path climbed.

Midmorning the Company halted. The Westway had now levelled out, skirting around the slopes of Steffl at least a thousand feet above the plain, but they could barely see either plain or mountain. Mist clung to the slopes, coating the trees and bushes with a watery film, decorating spiders' webs with pearly beads, and deadening all sound.

'I'm sending out a scout,' Kurr announced. 'At least, Farr will send out a scout from his rank. From now on there is to be no talking, and we must move as quietly as possible. Farr, whom will you send?'

'I will go myself.'

'But who then will take charge? That would defeat the whole purpose!'

Perdu spoke. 'I have acted as scout and tracker in many Fenni hunts. Perhaps I might volunteer?'

Kurr was about to accept, but remembered that he had asked Farr to choose. 'Very well,' Farr said grandly. 'Try to report back every couple of hours or so. And be careful! We don't want to warn them of our presence!'

Perdu smiled at this slight on his ability. *They know nothing of Fenni skill*, he thought. *Still, neither do I, really*, he added ruefully. *They sent me out as scout only after they had hunted enough, and then purely to teach me some skill. Well, we'll soon find out how much I have learned!* He waved to the Company and set off at once.

It had taken a mere two days for the soreness, the deep weariness, the gnawing hunger and the despair to return. During some marches Mahnum had plodded forward only at the prodding insistence of the point of a sword. *There is a limit to what I can endure*, he thought. *How much longer until I sink to the ground and rise no more?* This weariness overwhelmed him, dominating even his desire to escape, his anxiety for Indrett, his concern for Faltha, his will to survive.

He hadn't lifted his head in hours, and when he did, he was greeted by the sight of a single mountainous cone rising in the distance, ahead and to his left. *Have we come this far?* he wondered. *Is that Steffl?* The next time he raised his head, the mountain was much closer, its head and upper slopes shrouded in cloud.

Then something happened to change everything. The Bhrudwans called a halt, stopping to eat the midday meal; dried meat for the captives, stewed rabbit for the warriors. As always, Mahnum had been placed as far away from Indrett as possible, but his brutal captors couldn't stop him gazing on her. This he did, and while they swallowed their tasteless food they held each other's eyes across the forest path. Around them preparations began for recommencing their journey. Then, to his left, on the edge of vision, Mahnum noticed a flicker of movement. He turned his head slowly, keeping an eye on the Bhrudwans, and Indrett followed his gaze. There! There it was again!

It was a hand, deep in the brush. A hand waving. And a face. No one he knew, but a face nonetheless. The hand went to the

347

lips, cautioning silence. Mahnum tried not to look directly at the face. The hand waved again, then it and the face disappeared into the forest.

The Company had just finished a cheerless lunch when Perdu came racing back into the camp.

'I've seen them!' he cried. 'I've seen them!'

Questions arose at once from the travellers, each striving to be heard over the others. Kurr motioned for quiet.

Farr strode forward. 'Make your report!'

Perdu tried to catch his breath. 'I have seen the Bhrudwans,' he said, in between breaths. 'They are coming this way, just like Kurr said they would.'

'Are the captives all right?' Leith asked, unable to contain himself.

'The captives are alive and well, from what I could see.' Leith put his hands to his head in relief.

'That is indeed good news!' Kurr said.

'The Bhrudwan warriors also appear alive and well.'

'That is not such good news, but only to be expected.'

'I saw them break camp and watched them walk along the Westway. Two Bhrudwans lead them, with the captives driven by the third.'

Farr asked for silence. 'Did they see you?'

'I took care not to get too close. I am sure the Bhrudwans saw nothing.'

Kurr rubbed his hands together in satisfaction. 'Well done!' he said.

Farr was doing some quick thinking. 'How long since you left them?'

'About fifteen minutes ago. Between there and here the Westway climbs up the skirts of this hill.'

'So they are perhaps forty minutes away,' Farr estimated. 'That doesn't give us much time to prepare our ambush.'

Perdu spoke again. 'There's a place about five minutes from here that is perfect for an ambush! There a narrow log rope bridge crosses a deep gully cut into the flanks of the mountain, and once on the bridge the Bhrudwans will be vulnerable.'

'Excellent!' Kurr cried. 'Then we must make for this bridge with all speed!'

Within moments the Company sprinted down the road, all weariness forgotten. 'Draw your swords!' Kurr commanded in a hoarse whisper as they ran. 'The first rank will cross the bridge and hide in the trees on the far side. The second rank will remain on this side.' The bridge appeared ahead of them as he spoke: a sixty-foot-long span over perhaps an eighty-foot drop to the riverbed. Huge trees with roots exposed leaned over the edge of the sheer-sided gully as though floodwaters from Steffl had torn away the ground from under them. The stream at the bottom of the chasm flowed a deep, foam-flecked brown, swollen by the rain that still fell on the wide flanks of the mountain hidden somewhere to their right.

Kurr and Farr took a closer look at the bridge, exchanging brief words. Four strong ropes held it together; split logs formed a precarious road over the foaming water.

Kurr beckoned to Leith and Wira. 'Find cover!' he hissed. 'I'll watch for the Bhrudwans. Hopefully they will still be walking in the arrangement Perdu described. We will let the warriors pass and trap them on the bridge. When I give the signal, Leith, Wira and I will leap out and cut the ropes. Farr, take your rank and be ready to free the captives. It will be your task to deal with any remaining Bhrudwans. We'll join you as soon as we can.'

Farr nodded his approval. The first rank scrambled their way across the bridge, which swayed crazily as they passed, one at a time, Farr, Perdu, Hal, Stella. In a moment they had melted into the trees on the far side.

'Shouldn't we cut through the ropes now, leaving them just holding the bridge and no more?' Wira asked. 'That way we can guarantee the bridge will fall with one blow.'

'Good idea. Wait here, Leith. Wira and I will attend to the bridge.'

Leith couldn't help wondering how, once this was all over, they would cross the river without the aid of the bridge.

In a few minutes the other two returned to the shelter of the trees. 'Just as well you suggested weakening the ropes,' Kurr commented. 'We still would have been hacking at it when the Bhrudwans came down on top of us!'

Moments later, Perdu heard footsteps coming up the road. *Now for it!* he thought. The sound was the steady crunch, crunch, crunch of boots on gravel, which to those listening among the trees seemed to herald an army. *I thought there were only three*, he thought nervously. Now someone came into view around the bend in the road.

Tall, grey-cloaked and stern of face, hand hovering above sword-hilt in constant wariness, the lead warrior strode down the Westway. The image burned itself in Perdu's mind. For a moment the warrior was hidden by the swirling mist, which then parted to reveal he had been joined by a fellow Bhrudwan. They shortened stride and followed the path down to the swingbridge. The Fenni held his breath as the warriors passed by.

Leith could see the far end of the bridge from his position in the trees. The roar of the water below him masked all other sound, so the Bhrudwans came into view with no warning. He stiffened, and his thoughts began to flow through his mind far too quickly, as though they were a stream in flood. *What will happen next? Where are my parents? Have the first rank been discovered?*

Perdu watched the first Bhrudwan step on to the bridge. At the same moment the third warrior came into view, driving the captives forward: there was Parlevaag, and the man and woman who must be Hal and Leith's parents. *They look exhausted*, thought Perdu to himself. *I hope they manage to keep out of the way.*

Now the two warriors were halfway across the bridge. *Where are the captives? Are they still alive?* Anxiety for his parents robbed Leith of his fear of battle, so that when Kurr tapped him on the shoulder he jumped up immediately, rusty sword in hand. Kurr, Wira and Leith sprang out of the forest and were at the end of the bridge before the warriors realised what was happening. With a shout they drew their swords and rushed along the bridge. Leith and Wira hacked at the ropes: one, two, then three parted. Together they turned to sever the last rope.

Now the Bhrudwans realised their peril, saw that they would not cross the bridge in time, so turned and ran back in the direction they had come from. Wira made one last swing with his sword and the rope parted. As the Bhrudwan warriors scrambled towards safety, the bridge under them fell towards the river. A despairing hand sought to grasp an overhanging branch but failed: logs and ropes smashed into the rock of the far bank. The bridge was left hanging on by the ropes at one end.

At the first shout, Farr leapt out of his hiding place in the forest with a cry, followed by the rest of his rank. Immediately the three captives threw themselves sideways into the trees, leaving the lone Bhrudwan to face his four attackers. For a moment nobody moved: then, with a cruel grin spreading across his dark face, the Bhrudwan warrior slowly drew his curved scimitar. He stood there, confident in his own strength, waiting for the courage to drain out of his enemies.

'Enough of this!' Farr hissed. 'You killed my father!' He drew his sword and made for the tall warrior, followed by Perdu, Hal and Stella. In his rage the Vinkullen man seemed to have forgotten the others, and did not think to send his rank against the Bhrudwan as a group. He took a wild swing, crying out in fury; but the warrior avoided him with ease, then answered with a slashing blow that cut Farr's sword arm open. With a cry of pain, Farr dropped his sword. The warrior smiled his easy smile.

How can we do this? Stella wondered, strangely calm now that the time had come. *This beast looks like he could take us all on and win.* In the midst of the heat and blood, she was for some reason reminded of that day, years ago, when Anoan, the older brother of Druin, had blocked the path to the lake so the little children couldn't go swimming. He had knocked down the few boys who tried to challenge him, but Stella had forced him to give way. How could she ever forget? Suddenly a chill went up her spine and across her scalp, totally unrelated to the drama unfolding in front of her. *Druin hates his older brother. Is his interest in me, his treatment of me, an attempt to prove that he is stronger than his brother? Am I merely a trophy with which to humiliate Anoan?* The malice in her prospective husband frightened her more than the warrior before her. *How dare he?* Her blood flamed within her. *If he were here, standing on this path, I would bring him down!*

The Bhrudwan stepped towards the elder Storrsen. *Hurry, hurry,* Stella admonished herself as she turned and ran back towards the bridge. *There isn't much time!*

Perdu saw Stella run away, but had little time to consider it as he rushed to Farr's aid. The Bhrudwan slashed downwards; Farr rolled away as the blade bit the ground just behind his head. He groped for his sword. Perdu yelled, hoping to distract the Bhrudwan as he sought to deliver the killing blow, but with his left hand the grey-cloaked warrior drew his staff out from the pack on his back and flicked it at the approaching Fenni. The staff smashed into Perdu's sword hand with surprising ferocity, cracking across his knuckles. Now Perdu too groped on the ground for his weapon.

The Bhrudwan warrior stood over the defenceless Farr, who was at his mercy. Stella gathered four suitable rocks from the stony path. She hefted the first and desperately hoped that her hands had not forgotten the two-stone trick her brother had taught her. One, two, she practised her counting as she had been taught all those years ago. *The first one doesn't have to be accurate,* Stella reminded herself; she had practised and practised this, though she'd not used it since the day she had nearly taken Anoan's eye out.

Now! came a voice into her mind, *One,* she counted, and threw the first stone as hard as she could. It thudded into the Bhrudwan's shoulder and he spun around with terrible swiftness to confront his attacker. *Two,* she counted, and let fly with the second – not quite as hard, but with careful aim. The small rock struck the warrior hard on the temple with a sickening crack. Stella threw her third and fourth stones even before he began to fall. They missed, passing where his head had been an instant before. With a clatter, the warrior's sword and staff struck the path, followed a moment later by the warrior himself.

Farr sprang forward and grabbed the scimitar in his left hand. Stella ran to the fallen figure. 'Do it!' she cried. 'Finish him off before he wakes!' Farr shifted the blade to his right hand, not trusting his left to give a fatal thrust even though it was uninjured and his right hand was not. *Our lives depend on this*, he thought. *Let the strike be clean!* He remembered his father lying dead on the Mjolkbridge road. *This is for you!*

'No!' Hal said, moving in front of Farr. 'Don't do it!'

Farr snarled as his rage consumed him. 'Get out of my way!'

'This is not for your father!' Hal cried. 'You do this for yourself! You want to cut away the pain of a lifetime. Haven't you learned anything in this forest? Isn't it time to let the wounds heal?'

Farr was beyond understanding, and made to strike at Hal.

'Wait!' Perdu shouted. 'Listen! What was the task of our rank? Didn't we have to capture a Bhrudwan alive? Here he is in our hands!'

He walked up to Farr, whose eyes smouldered still. 'Put down the sword. Help me to bind this man. Then let us go and revenge ourselves on the remnants of our enemies.'

Farr began to waver as Perdu's good sense fought with his rage.

'Please,' Hal said. 'I have other things to attend to. Give me the sword!' The cripple held out his twisted right arm.

For a moment no one moved; then, reluctantly, Farr placed the wicked blade in Hal's hand. Behind them Mahnum and Indrett emerged from the trees, followed by Parlevaag. Farr sank to the ground with his head in his hands.

Tears in her eyes, Indrett went to embrace her son, but he turned away. 'Please,' he said, 'there will be a chance for us later. I have already lost too much time!' Hal turned to Stella. 'We need some water to wash these wounds. Would you go up the path and get some from a stream?' Stella nodded wordlessly.

Mahnum took rope from Farr's pack and bound the Bhrudwan, who was beginning to stir. Stella returned with water, to which

Hal added something from his medicine pouch. Then he went over to where the Bhrudwan lay, and began to wash his bleeding temple with a rag soaked in the water.

'What are you doing?' Farr asked, incredulous. 'What about my arm? What of Perdu's hand? Aren't we more worthy of your attention?'

Hal turned and fixed the Vinkullen man with an earnest stare. 'Unless I do this, all our journey is in vain. Be still! I will attend to you soon enough.'

The Bhrudwan warrior had regained consciousness and, though dazed, knew he was in the hands of his enemies; yet he showed no fear, and did not struggle against his bonds. Perhaps he did not care about his fate. Perhaps he knew that the face which hovered over him was not going to order his death. The twisted hand that should have been so clumsy ministered to his broken temple, cleaning and putting ointment on the wound. Then the cripple turned to Farr and Perdu, and made ready to salve and bandage the wounds of battle.

All the while Mahnum stood over the fallen warrior with Farr's sword in his hand, unwilling to trust mere rope to hold his tormentor. *Yet this is only the Acolyte, the least experienced of the three. What of the others? And where is Leith?*

'That turned the tables on them!' Kurr cried in triumph. 'Perhaps now they know the fear we knew on the Roofless Road!'

Beside him Leith pointed. Across the far side of the now-unbridged river the bridge hung uselessly, cut ropes trailing in the water, but on it clung two figures.

'They are still holding on!' Wira shouted, and all three rushed to the edge of the chasm.

One of the Bhrudwan warriors, the higher of the two, clung to a rope with one hand, his other arm hanging by his side, apparently broken. The lower Bhrudwan, however, climbed grimly hand over hand up the rope towards safety.

'What can we do?' Leith asked. 'The others are in danger!'

'Nothing but watch,' Kurr responded.

'No!' Wira cried. 'There must be a way of crossing this river, perhaps further upstream! We can't allow our friends to be overwhelmed!' And with this he set off into the trees.

'Shall we follow him?'

Kurr didn't answer, instead growling in frustration as he watched the warrior climb slowly up the bridge, which was now a ladder up the sheer side of the gorge.

Half a mile upstream, Wira found a crossing place, where the walls of the gorge lowered far enough for him to scramble down a narrow ravine to the stream bed. His chest and throat burned from his sprint; several times he had come close to falling over roots and branches. Now he waded the swift-flowing stream and clambered up the far bank. He was desperate to get there in time; he could think only of Stella, unaware of her danger, defenceless against the ruthless warriors who even now had possibly made the top of the cliff . . .

Ahead of him, on the edge of vision, a light shone which only he could see.

Leith and Kurr remained at the east end of the bridge, helplessly watching events unfold on the far bank. Indistinct figures grappled on the path; whether friend or foe Leith could not tell. There was his brother – he would know that shape anywhere. One figure was down; a curved sword was uplifted. Now the sword bearer was down also. What was happening? This helpless watching was worse, far worse, than any fear of battle. Without a word, he turned and ran after Wira.

'Leith! Come back!' Kurr cried, but the crashing of a body through the forest died away and the old farmer was left alone.

Ah well, there is nothing I can do anyway, he thought as he strained to see across the gorge. The figures on the far side of the chasm were blurred in the misty air, but he could clearly see the two Bhrudwans as they tried to climb up the bridge. The upper figure, the one with the broken arm or shoulder, had not made any progress. As Kurr watched, he tried to use his broken arm, but it would not bear his weight. The lower figure hung immediately below him, having climbed quickly and seemingly with no hurt, but his progress was now blocked by his fellow warrior. For a moment both were still – perhaps they are talking together, Kurr guessed – then the upper figure tried again to climb, but could obviously not manage it. Then, as Kurr watched in disbelief, the lower figure reached up an arm, took hold of a black-booted foot dangling above him, and pulled. The Bhrudwan tried to hold on, but again his fellow pulled at his foot, and he lost his handhold. He floated slowly away from the bridge and fell tumbling to the bottom of the gorge, his body breaking on the rocks below. The remaining Bhrudwan did not waste time looking down, but continued his climb to the top of the cliff.

A fire burned in Wira's leaden frame, and his limbs seemed unwilling to obey him. *If only I had taken better care of myself*, he thought as he ran through the forest. *The drink has robbed me of the strength I should have.* In that moment, as he swerved to avoid yet another tree root, he decided that enough was enough: he would forsake the bottle and prepare for marriage. *For I will propose to Stella*, he told himself, *and she will say 'yes' to me if I put my drunkenness aside.* He grew light-headed. The bright light in front of his eyes made it difficult to see where he was going. Nevertheless, he fought on. He knew only that his beloved was in danger, that she would be slain if he arrived too late.

The Bhrudwan neared the top of the ladder. Only one rung to go. Now he reached a hand up on to the path and began to haul himself up. From the far side of the gorge, Kurr tried to shout a warning, but the distance and the churning water defeated him.

The Bhrudwan heaved his muscled bulk up on to the road. Ahead he could see a group of people surrounding a bound, grey-cloaked figure lying across the road. *I wouldn't have expected anything else*, he thought. *The young fool deserves death, and I will give it to him. But these Falthans, their deaths will come upon them unexpectedly also.* He took a moment to try once again to draw on his dark magic; but, as had been the case since the moment this audacious ambush had begun, his abilities remained out of reach. It was exactly the same effect as when his Master, the Undying Man, swamped his link to the spirit realm by his mere presence – but that could not be possible. There were no magicians worthy of the name in this backward land. No matter; magic would not be necessary. He melted into the trees on the right of the path, and began to move with inhuman stealth towards his unsuspecting victims, of whom a girl bending over a water-pouch was the closest. He drew his sword. The lust of death rang in his ears as it always did.

Wira staggered through a tunnel of light, then slammed into a tree. Or was it a tree? For a moment his vision cleared. Before him a dark figure lay on the ground. He shook his head; the light retreated to the corners of his vision. A Bhrudwan warrior!

Instantly the warrior regained his feet and struck at him. Wira ducked, but too slowly, and the blade laid open a dreadful wound across his shoulder and back. He collapsed in a sea of pain, as the white light closed over him.

The Bhrudwan leader turned back to the path. *Kill them all!* His sword cried out for more blood. There was the girl. He made to strike.

As his arm came down, something crashed into him from behind and his stroke went wide. He regained his feet with a curse.

'Stella! Watch out!' came a cry, and Wira staggered forward. He had found the strength from somewhere to come at the Bhrudwan again, but his effort had taken its toll. As the warrior leapt to his feet to face his attacker, Wira fell into the invisible light and lay still on the ground.

With a cry of anguish, Stella leapt towards her fallen Wira, but Perdu grabbed her arm. The cruel sword came down again, missing Stella by inches. The Fenni pulled her away, but she could not take her eyes off the unmoving figure by the side of the path.

Pure hatred poured from the Bhrudwan, unnerving those who looked into his eyes. One by one the Company began to back away from that sword, those singleminded eyes. Only Hal stood firm.

Mahnum retreated from the horror before him. This was the Bhrudwan leader, a captain of the Lords of Fear, his strength and power revealed. His own son stood there opposing him, yet he could not force his legs to take him to Hal's side. The terror of the Bhrudwan was on him, reinforced by weeks and months of fear. *Don't look at his eyes!* came a voice into his mind. He flicked his eyes beyond the warrior, and saw hope.

For there, creeping quietly out of the forest, came Leith, with his short sword drawn.

The Bhrudwan stepped slowly over the body of Wira and approached the bound figure still lying helplessly on the road.

Leith came up behind him, sword shaking in his hand.

The bound man tried to warn his leader of the danger behind him, but he had barely begun before he was interrupted.

'Save your pleading!' the Bhrudwan said to his fellow warrior in the common tongue. 'Die with praise to the Destroyer on your lips, not begging for mercy like some Falthan animal!' He plainly meant his enemies to hear and to understand, perhaps to gain a foretaste of their own fate. He raised his sword.

Leith closed his eyes and, with all his strength, drove his blade forward into the warrior's shoulder blades. The look of triumph on the evil face changed to one of surprise, then of rage, as his legs stopped going forward in obedience to his will. The Bhrudwan leader tried to cry out, but his own blood choked him. Then he fell backwards on to the hilt of the sword piercing him, driving it through his body. With a groan, his life disappeared.

For the longest moment, no one moved. Above them birds chirped and called to each other, and beyond them the sound of foaming water echoed through the gorge. Still nobody moved.

Finally Hal stepped forward, over the body of the Bhrudwan, to the side of the fallen Wira Storrsen. 'I'm sorry,' he said, tears in his eyes and in his voice. 'I was too late.'

The Company crowded sorrowfully around the body of Wira. Stella sobbed as she touched the golden locks of the one on whom she'd pinned all her hopes. Oblivious to the others, Farr threw himself to the ground and cradled his brother's head in his hands, weeping openly. One by one, the others began to weep also.

Leith thought of Kurr and the anxiety he would be feeling. Numb and in shock, still trying to forget the feel of his sword as it had slipped into flesh, killing another man, Leith turned and headed towards the edge of the gorge. But when he got there he could not see the old farmer. Wearily, with little emotion in spite of their great victory and the prospect of being reunited with his parents, he turned back up the Westway.

Without warning, rough hands grasped him from behind, and something was clamped over his mouth. Unseen by any of the Company, he was carried into the forest, then borne away out of his knowledge.

CHAPTER 17

THE BLUE FIRE

THE SENIOR OFFICIALS OF Malayu waited under a sky slashed with red, the City Factor at their head. He rubbed his sweaty palms down the outside of his silk-clad thighs, realising that the gesture betrayed his anxiety to anyone who cared to look. He hated himself for his lack of control, but knew that no one would be looking, not today. For at least the fifth time since he had arrived at the docks, he tried to turn his head, knowing that he should run a critical eye over the men under his suzerainty, wanting desperately to reassure himself that he was not the only one suffering nerves; but he could not tear his gaze away from the sea. His neck muscles cramped with the strain. Perhaps the Destroyer's magic was already at work, compelling his attention. Cynic though he was, he could believe anything of the Lord of Bhrudwo after that night one short month ago.

All Factors were acquainted with the blue fire, employed for two thousand years to communicate the wishes of the Undying Man, though it hadn't been used in any of the provinces of Malayu in living memory. Truth to tell, none knew how it worked, but at least they knew what it was for. It was early in the third watch of the night that the dull, unemotional voice of some servant or other had woken him, and delivered the news that the fire was flaming blue. The servant's voice had been so casual that he was obviously unaware of the import of his news. The Factor had actually needed to ask the man to repeat himself.

360

Across the Face of the World

He had descended hurriedly to the sacred chamber, wrapped only in his nightshirt, an unbecoming state for the most powerful man in Malayu. But the Factor did not care. His thoughts were already bent towards the flame, and as he entered the room its irresistible power sought him out, reading him, stripping away his remaining dignity, rendering him nothing but a frightened mass of flesh. That it was not the Destroyer himself delivering the message was the only saving grace of the night. The message had not been good news.

And this day one month later, the day of his lord's arrival, had been filled with the sort of minor crises that drive a man to the edge of panic, and it was not getting any better. The royal barge drew close to the wharf a full half-hour earlier than he had been told to expect it. Men cried instructions to each other, each desperate not to make a mistake, each aware of what the occasion meant, every wharfsman knowing what would happen to him – to them all – if they profaned this holy moment. Ropes, expertly handled by men with years of experience, secured the huge vessel to the wharf. A young apprentice boy, whose master should have known better than to have involved him in this, caught a careless slipper on a rope, slipped on the wet timber decking and fell between the barge and the dock. As the lad scrambled for safety, his master rushed to his aid, then drew back . . . as the figure that had filled his dreams for weeks began to walk down the gangplank. The dockmaster clapped his hands to his head in despair, for he could see the barge swing against the wharf, and knew the fool boy would doom them all. Then, just as the boy's dying screams began, a great fanfare blew, heads snapped to face the gangplank, and the dockmaster lived again.

Down the gangplank came the figure in grey, and all present pressed their faces to the rough timber surface of the dock. Down he came; and the Factor of Malayu sought the inner peace of *Mul* to steady his nerves as he rose to greet his master, hoping he had done him sufficient honour. He had thought this day would never come, not in his lifetime or in anyone else's, but here it was, and he could not escape his duty. For the first time in a hundred years,

361

it was said, the Undying Man, Lord of Bhrudwo, had left his dread castle of Andratan. And he had chosen Malayu as the port at which he would come ashore. At this, the moment of moments, in front of thousands of citizens and in the presence of he who commanded the power of life and death, *Mul* proved elusive, and the Factor went to greet the Lord of Darkness in fear of his life.

The figure in grey reached the bottom of the gangplank, then halted. His retinue remained a respectful distance behind. The Factor of Malayu approached, leading the selected group of officials, their fine speeches evaporating in the face of the presence in their midst. They approached; then abruptly the figure made a gesture with his hand, the air rippled, and the Factor and his group froze, unable to move, wholly in the grip of the Undying Man's magic. Something hot and unbearably sharp sliced through his mind, exquisite pain exposing motive and deception, laying his innermost thoughts bare like the innards of some gutted fish flapping on the rough boards of the wharf – then was gone as abruptly as it had started. The Factor would have collapsed had he not been frozen in place.

The figure moved forward again, seeming to glide across the wharf as though propelled by some inhuman device, until he was face to face with the Factor. There could not be a deeper fear than this. His lord's eyes . . . ah, they were shafts carefully sunk into the black pits of the underworld, the unblinking, amused stare of a carrion bird considering how to dismember his prey. Abruptly the compulsion was released and the Factor voided himself unnoticed, as around him a full third of his officials crumpled up and fell to the ground, stone dead.

'Loyalty.' The cruel voice of the Lord of Bhrudwo ripped across the docks and through the city, enhanced by his magic arts, though he had barely whispered the word. 'I demand loyalty.' To some gathered there, the words seemed to stab at them like knives cunningly wielded; to others, the voice was as a winnowing fork, sifting their secret thoughts. None within earshot remained unaffected.

'Loyalty must begin with those who claim to serve me. See! I have tested my servants and found some wanting, harbouring treacherous thoughts in their innermost hearts. In honour of this occasion, the beginning of the war I seek to prosecute against Faltha our enemy, I have granted them a merciful death. It will not always be so.'

The crowd gazed upon the still forms lying in testimony to their lord's mercy, and murmured uneasily.

'Do not be mistaken; I am not deceived. Many of those gathered here doubted my existence. Some doubt still! A hundred years is a long time – for such as you. But it is nothing to me. Nothing! So for the doubters I have one message: *Believe!*' And such was the Wordweave exercised by the Destroyer that many of the weaker-minded among the crowd found their doubts erased without their own volition.

The Undying Man took a step forward, and turned until he faced a section of the assembly perhaps fifty yards away. 'I hear you, my son,' he whispered, a rasp across rough timber, and raising his one hand, pointed into the crowd. 'I hear your thoughts.' People drew away from the unfortunate white-faced man thus confronted, until there was a clear space around him.

'I see the doubt in your heart, my son.' The man looked on the verge of collapse. Perhaps only the magic of the grey figure kept him from falling to the ground. 'So, as a sign to all those who doubt, I call you to me. *Come.*' And he closed his hand into a fist.

As the word was uttered, the man rose struggling into the air and floated over the water, like a feather on the wind, to land in a heap at the feet of the Lord of Bhrudwo.

'Stand up,' came the command, and the words themselves jerked the man to his feet, or so it seemed to the onlookers. In a moment he found himself fixed by the gaze of the Undying Man.

'So, doubter, do you doubt now?' Frantically, the man shook his head, but the figure ignored him, holding out his left hand, palm half-closed. 'I know a way to put an end to doubt in a man's heart. Do you feel my hand within your breast?' The man nodded, his eyes wide with terror. 'To end all doubt, I simply crush the heart lodged within my hand. Like this.' And he squeezed his hand shut.

A second passed, then another, then the man's eyes bulged wide and he threw his arms backwards.

'Be free of your doubt, my son,' came the soft voice, and everyone heard it, everyone saw the man gasping for air, flailing and thrashing as though his fate could be escaped by struggling. He fell to the ground, and his struggling ceased.

'Does anyone still doubt?' The figure swept his gaze across the people gathered there, and the crowd froze wherever the feared gaze fell. 'You! You think this is trickery, that these traitors are paid to act a part. And you! You at least believe in the magic, but still you do not believe I am the Undying One.' Two forms burst suddenly into flame, and although their screams echoed across the harbour, their loved ones dared not rush to their side.

Now the Destroyer's tone became suffused with patient love, like a stern father dealing with recalcitrant offspring. 'My wayward children! I do not wish sorrow on you, but the task set before us demands our whole-hearted effort. My ancient enemy is corrupt, and is rendered vulnerable by that corruption. Riches beyond your ability to imagine await you all as we take back what is rightfully ours. Yet Faltha will not fall to a people weakened by unbelief. I must weed out half-heartedness, corruption and doubt from within your midst, and so must you. Set your heart upon our goal, and do not waver for a moment. If you remain faithful, I can promise you that Faltha will be ours!'

His retinue, primed for this moment, cried out in response: 'Faltha is yours! Faltha is yours!' and it seemed to all gathered there that a mighty multitude gave voice. 'Faltha is yours! Faltha is yours!' They all joined in, until the air rang with the declaration. Then the Lord of Bhrudwo raised his hand, and all fell on their faces and worshipped him, glad to have escaped with their lives.

It might as well have been a mud-daubed hut with an open fire set on the floor as the grand drawing room of the Factor's palace. The Undying Man didn't care. He was focused, his time was at

364

hand, and the playthings of the material world with which he had amused himself through the long dark years of his strengthening meant nothing to him now. Truly he did not notice the tapestries lining the walls, depicting in sequence his triumph over the Most High – here the speech in the Square of Rainbows, there the Water of Life raised to his lips – though had he taken time to notice, he might have remarked on the total absence of dust on the hangings, which spoke either of a fastidious chatelaine or their recent rescue from some storage cellar.

'Set the fire in the grate,' he commanded; and the Factor of Malayu, without equal in his huge province, bent like a servant to obey his lord's will.

'My lord,' ventured one of his aides, 'the sacred flame is set down in—'

'Yet I choose to consecrate the blue fire here,' came the soft reply. 'Here. Do you object? There are others who would take your place.'

'No, lord, I do not object,' came the firm reply. If there was a formula for survival in the retinue of the Lord of Darkness, it was found in the avoidance of overt displays of either weakness or strength. The aide judged that his reply would suffice, though he kept that thought half-formed in the back of his mind, for the Undying Man could scoop out a man's thoughts as easily as skimming scum from the surface of a stagnant pond.

'Bring my pouch. I will conduct the ceremony myself.' In a moment, the pouch lay open in his hand. It was a repository of efficacious chemicals, nothing more, though few apart from himself knew of their origins. There, that pale yellow liquid carefully stoppered in a vial had been extracted from alpine herbs found on the slopes of the Aldhras Mountains, and the only people who knew its secret had died centuries ago. And there, far more sinister, was the pink powder *omat*, a mixture of a mildly hallucinogenic mushroom and dried human blood. It was the manner in which the blood was obtained that made *omat* rare. That secret was still known in many places in Bhrudwo; the Destroyer could not dispose of everyone.

But it was from another vial the Undying Man took a pinch of blue powder, and the provenance of this none but he knew. He had not bothered to give it a name. In truth, it did little more than make the passage of his magic easier. For what these fools who called themselves his servants did not know was that the power to perform magic came from the practitioner himself. Two thousand years ago, the Lord of Bhrudwo had set himself to study magic, and he had learned. He had learned it all. And what he had learned was that down through the ages the great magicians, the true sorcerers, had all died young. They had died because they had drained themselves, ageing before their time. Those who had found out the horrible truth were by that time addicted to the power only a magician can know, and were unable to lay that power aside, even to save their own lives.

Ah, but the greatest discovery of all, the truth that made him who he was, was known to him alone. He alone knew how to perform magic by using the strength of others.

'Come closer, my friend,' the Destroyer said to the Factor of Malayu, in a friendly tone. 'Watch and learn.' And he put an arm around the Factor's shoulder. *Perhaps I have found favour with my lord after all*, the Factor thought in wonder.

The fire burned merrily in the grate. The Undying Man stretched out his hand – into the flame – and sprinkled a tiny amount of the powder into its burning heart. Then the pull – there from his followers, and there from the foolish Factor, who should have ruled his province with a far firmer hand – and the flame seemed to collapse in on itself, feeding on itself – or something – from the inside out. Slowly it turned a dark blue, as though bruised, the colour of used blood.

The faces of his followers turned pale, as they always did when he practised magic, though they never knew why. He was careful to limit his abuse of their strength to very small increments, spread evenly amongst them. But the Factor was another matter.

'Is something wrong?' came the quiet question.

'No, my lord, truly—' but the Factor collapsed on to the hearth, his face drained and newly lined, his lips blue.

366

'The Factor is tired after a long day. See he finds his bed,' the Lord of Bhrudwo commanded one of his servants.

'Yes, lord.' He manhandled the Factor through the arched door and out of the room with little apparent effort, though the truth of it was the day had exhausted him also.

Now the flame had steadied, indicating that the link had been made, and suddenly a disembodied voice spoke from within the blue fire. 'Great Lord, it is your servant Deorc,' it said. 'I stand ready.'

'And where do you stand?' The Destroyer fashioned his Wordweave into something which resembled, metaphorically speaking, a mallet. It did not pay to be subtle with Deorc: a faithful lieutenant, brimming with intelligence and ambition, he would have been a worthy successor to the Undying Man except for the obvious fact of the Destroyer's immortality. Deorc would recognise any attempt at deception and despise it, favouring strength and cruelty over the use of his intellect – which was his strength and his weakness, of course.

'I stand, my lord, above the Aleinus Gates, at the mouth of the Vulture's Craw. I expect to be in Ehrenmal within the fortnight, and will arrive in Instruere a few weeks after midsummer.'

'You have made good time.' The Destroyer allowed a little approbation to seep through the fiery link.

'Yes, my lord. The horses we obtained from the Nagorj have proved their stamina, and can go further yet. They compare favourably with the best in Birinjh. I will arrive in time to do my master's bidding.'

'And my headstrong Lords of Fear? Have you heard any news of them? Have your spies yet found out who ordered them west?'

'I have heard nothing, Great Lord.'

Ah, Deorc, I hear the resonance. You must know I hear it. You are not lying, but you are not telling me all you know. The Destroyer shook his head. Such things genuinely saddened him. Yes, he could ask careful questions until he forced his lieutenant to tell all he knew. Or he could bludgeon the man through the magic of the blue fire, compelling him to reveal all, though Deorc's strength to resist would not be inconsiderable, and he would take some time to break. But either way Deorc would be rendered useless. And strong men must be allowed their secrets, surely? *So you know something about these four warriors, but not where they are? No matter. They can do nothing to hurt me. No one can, not now.*

'I expect you to find out,' he answered pointedly. 'If they are acting on someone else's orders, then I have been betrayed. They are deceived if they believe they do my bidding.'

'Yes, lord.'

I can sense his fear. He is involved somehow. The Undying Man knew he could reach through the blue fire and have his answer, but he withheld his power. *I'll leave you with your little secret. But you will tell it to me someday.*

'Do not fail me, my brave captain,' said the Destroyer, and allowed the faintest filament of mockery to feed into the flame. 'They must be supple for the day I ride through the gates of Instruere in triumph.'

'How can I fail, Great Lord?' came the answer quick as a flash. 'It is your plan I will execute, and your plans are always flawless.'

The Lord of Bhrudwo laughed then, a full and hearty laugh that would have been recognised by those who lived in the latter days of the Vale of Dona Mihst, had any of them been less than two thousand years dead. *He knows I know something – it is the nature of the blue fire to know something of the other person's thoughts – yet he still walks the line with his jests. Ah, Deorc, perhaps I will let you live after all.*

The Factor of Malayu trembled between the silk sheets of his bed. He was ill, that he knew, and he felt worse even than the time his foolish brat of a son had tried to poison him. But here there was no one to strike out against, no carcass to hang from the city gate. Or at least there *was* someone, but this someone was one that no one dared strike out against.

He did something to me, I sensed it. The Factor knew that magic had been performed, and that he had suffered as a result. *He drained me. He sucked something out of me to make his dreadful blue flame.*

He had felt it, a fact only possible because his father's personal apothecary was himself skilled in aspects of rural magic, and for the last six months had been teaching the Factor the rudiments of this powerful art. It had sensitised him.

What if the Destroyer – in his anger the Factor could not call him lord – *what if he calls me to his side once again? Will I obey? Will I wait like a goat on the altar slab for his power to wound me once more?*

Wait. What was it old Freina said? 'Don't make resolutions in the presence of magicians, for they can pick the very thoughts out of your head, the strongest ones first. Don't think about it, slide away from the decision, let your mind deal with it without the interference of your will.'

I'll have to go to him if he calls me, he thought. The alternative would be even worse. The Factor groaned; his body ached, and his head pulsed with pain. *Put the thought aside, just think about sleep. Don't let the word form. Think about something else.*

Revenge.

The Lord of Darkness sat alone in the darkened drawing room, the only light coming from flickering embers in the grate. He did not sleep. He never slept. So it was that he heard the stray thought and followed it to the mind that was trying not to think it.

Ah, now. So the worm squirms under the boot of his master. He smiled, a thin gesture indistinguishable from a snarl. *This will be diverting.*

CHAPTER 18

FIELDS OF MOURNING

TIME PASSED UNNOTICED BY the Company as they stood together, hand in hand, looking upon the still forms in their midst, the grey-cloaked Bhrudwan warrior and the tow-headed youth from Mjolkbridge. Above them the moist grey mist swirled, drawn down the mountainside by a cool, sulphur-tainted breeze, lending a sharpness to the afternoon air on the cruel slopes of Steffl.

They had done it, they had overcome the Lords of Fear, rescued Mahnum and Indrett, and against all odds taken one of the Bhrudwans captive, but no one celebrated. The feeling amongst the Company was closer to shock. Weeks of pursuit had ended suddenly, violently, tragically, leaving pursuers and former captives alike dumbfounded. Where the polite, well-spoken youth from the hills of Vinkullen had been, there was now only a broken body and a dull ache.

Farr broke the mood. He walked over to the bound warrior and prodded him in the ribs with his foot. 'Was it worth it, our fine revenge?' he said quietly, as if to himself, but everyone heard him. 'For this?' No one answered him.

He stepped over the broken body of his brother and knelt down by the dead Bhrudwan. With a sudden violence he rolled the corpse on to its side, grasped the hilt of Leith's sword and pulled, almost falling over as the blade slid free.

'If by stabbing you a hundred times I could bring back my brother, I would!' he shouted, and behind him a bird took flight at the sudden noise. Turning his back on the fallen warrior, he grasped the sword hilt in both hands, disregarding the pain in his lacerated right arm, and raised it above his head. Ignoring the cries of his friends, he drove it into the ground inches away from the head of their captive.

'Let this remain for all time as a memorial to my brother!' he cried, in a voice so desolate that all who heard it were cut to the quick. He then sat on the stony path of the Westway, his head in his hands, and would not be consoled.

Mahnum and Indrett sat together on the trunk of a fallen tree, a few feet apart from the Company, unable to share in their sorrow. She laid her head on his breast, resting quietly, saying nothing, allowing the fears and the pain of weeks of sordid, demeaning captivity to fade from the forefront of her mind. Hal squatted awkwardly next to them, speaking softly and slowly, explaining all that had happened since Midwinter's Day. In turn, they told him of their trials as captives of the Bhrudwans. Somehow the simple act of talking brought a measure of healing: Mahnum and Indrett allowed the tension to drain out of them, and entertained the possibility that after so long they might be together with their family again.

'Where's Leith?' Indrett asked, anxious to see her son.

'Gone to fetch Kurr from across the river,' said Hal. 'Now that the bridge is no more, he may have had to go some distance to find a suitable crossing place. He'll be back soon.'

'Is it really all over?' she whispered to Mahnum.

'Yes,' he answered, running his fingers through her hair. 'At least for us.'

A few paces down the road, Perdu and Parlevaag talked in low tones, their language unintelligible to the others. The adopted Fenni nursed a badly bruised hand: the Bhrudwan warrior's staff had smashed it with surprising force, and already his knuckles had swollen. He knew he ought to wash it in running water, then bandage it, but the hurts of others seemed more immediate.

'How have you been treated?' Perdu asked the woman.

'Not so well,' she replied, fingering the scar on her cheek. 'They were beasts wearing human skin. I wish they had slain me along with Horstaag.' She talked of her dead husband with a hollow voice, frightening in its lack of emotion. 'I did not have a chance to bury him, to prepare him for his meeting with Qali. Who knows where he now walks?'

'Did they – harm you?' Perdu was solicitous in his concern, but also somewhat reserved. He hadn't known the woman at all well; Fenni women were considered their husband's property, and to be seen talking with one unchaperoned was to invite a duel or the judgement of the clan chief. She was young, and from the north of Myrvidda, that was all he knew. Horstaag he had known; they had hunted together on the margins of Scymria, had found the spoor of the legendary *mamoti*, and it grieved him to think of the man's death. But in all their time together they had never talked of their wives or families, which was considered proper Fenni behaviour.

'These men were too single of purpose for that,' she replied. 'They drove us hard, seldom feeding us and not allowing us even to speak. At times the other woman and I tried to communicate, and she explained to me as best she could who these men were and what they were doing.'

'You're safe now,' Perdu said comfortingly.

'Yes,' she replied doubtfully, looking around her at a landscape totally devoid of familiar landmarks, at people she did not know, and at the bound figure of one of her former captors. 'Yes, I'm safe now.'

Stella stood apart from the others, eyes hooded. When Mahnum addressed a comment to her, and when Hal tried to engage her in conversation, she turned towards them, raised her deep brown eyes and stared right through them with a frightening intensity. Her mind was filled with Wira crying out her name in warning, with the *flash* of sunlight on a swinging blade and him falling, falling to the ground, along with all her hopes and dreams . . . *flash* he cries her name, the blade falls and he crumples to the ground, her name on his dying lips . . . *flash* he climbs to his feet and flings himself at the Bhrudwan in a final attempt to save her life . . . *flash* he folds up like a withered flower and the world grows dark and cold, and she hears and sees no more . . . and oh, Most High, her numb, self-betraying heart refuses to weep for him, thinking instead of a life locked up in a small northern village, paraded in public on feast-days by a brute of a husband, his coarse hands . . . his hands . . . She shrieked and shrieked inside her head, but no one heard her, no one came to set her free, and her dread-filled vision of the future seemed all but a certainty.

An hour passed before Kurr finally made his way to where the Company awaited him. He took in the scene with one glance. Two bodies, one Bhrudwan, the other – *Who is it?* – the other Wira, a Bhrudwan captive, the others sitting patiently waiting, no serious injuries. *We've won! We've done it!* Mahnum and Indrett alive and well, smiling at him, but looking right through him as though looking for someone else – *Who?* He did a quick count.

'Where is Leith?'

'We were wondering the same thing,' Farr replied.

'He went running after Wira, heading this way.'

'Yes, we saw him,' said Farr. 'He arrived just after Wira, and cut yonder Bhrudwan down from behind. Then he went back for you. We were too busy with Wira and the remaining Bhrudwan to pay much attention. Did you not see him?'

Kurr shook his head. 'The woods are very thick down by the riverbank. He could have passed within hailing distance and I would not have known.'

Farr stood. 'What now?' he said, indicating the dead with a sweep of the arm. 'We can't wait here forever.'

'Once Leith discovers I have left my place by the bridge, he will return swiftly,' the old farmer replied confidently. 'But first we must dispose of the carrion!' And before anyone could move, he grabbed the Bhrudwan leader's body by an arm and pulled it along the Westway towards the remains of the bridge. As the others watched, he dragged the body to the very edge of the gorge, then rolled it over the cliff with his foot.

'A fitting end for such a one,' he said when he returned, out of breath but with a smile of triumph on his face. 'I saw what you did not; how he pulled his fellow to his death on the wreck of the bridge in order to escape death himself. Now he lies broken beside the one he betrayed.'

'Then let us honour my brother,' Farr said. 'No matter how pressing the task that remains, we must pause and remember him.'

Solemn and silent, the members of the Company filed down the path, bearing the body of Wira above them on a bier of leaves and branches. Without a word, they lowered him on to the pyre, a pile of dry timber hastily gathered and laid out beside the sword embedded in the ground.

Numbly, Farr lit a taper and approached the pyre. *He looks so peaceful, so beautiful,* he thought. *He who will now never grow older. What did you find in the forest? What answer has given you peace in so violent a death? If only you could speak, my brother, you could tell me what you know.*

Reluctantly, Farr touched the taper to the pyre. A small flame took hold, spreading slowly along the branches.

The Company wept as the fire consumed their friend, their saviour. Stella alone could shed no tears; she leaned on Perdu's good arm as, uncomprehending, she watched the pyre burn. As the crackling died down, Kurr called out: 'Farewell, friend! Good speed on your journey!'

'I owe you my life,' spoke Perdu. 'It should have been me. Thank you.'

Hal stepped forward. 'Your death matched your life: valiant and single-hearted. We will meet again in that place where the light burns brightest.' The cripple saluted the flames.

Grief overwhelmed Farr, and he cried out: 'Wira! Wira! I told you to stay home. Oh, my brother! My brother, I'm sorry! Forgive me!' Then his voice broke and he fell to the ground weeping.

* * *

Across the Face of the World

The weather cleared, spring made its first foray north to the dim holds of the Jawbone Mountains, and nothing remained to impede the Hermit and the Haufuth starting their journey to Instruere. They left Bandits' Cave as soon as the snow melted, with Wisent the aurochs laden with supplies, including dried food and pemmican. Finding the Westway quiet this early in the new year, they made good time through Withwestwa Wood. Here the road marked the northern border of Plonya, one of the Sixteen Kingdoms, though in truth it had been a long time since the kingdom extended any sort of sovereignty this far north. For all practical purposes the area was administered by the loose collection of fur trappers and woodsmen known as the Fodhram; stern of face and unwelcoming of outsiders, or so the stories went, though the four men the Company had met belied this description.

Travelling with the Hermit proved a sore trial for the Loulea headman, sorer indeed than that of nursing the man back to health, for the blue-robed man insisted on explaining details of obscure theology to him, whether he wanted to hear them or not. For the first time, the gregarious Haufuth found himself well and truly overmatched in a verbal battle.

Telling the Hermit the details of their quest had probably been a mistake, the Haufuth was ready to concede. Perhaps if he had kept quiet the flow of questions would have been less constant. Or perhaps not; the Hermit seemed willing to examine any subject at length. He recognised no hint that the Haufuth was tired of conversation, and even a comment to this effect, direct to the point of rudeness, did little to dampen his ardour for discussion. *I suppose he has to make up for all those years alone*, the Haufuth reflected. *I just wish it wasn't with me!*

He breathed an exasperated sigh; this latest conversation was faring little better than any of those previous to it.

'So you're trying to tell me that the future of Faltha depends on a shadowy figure of myth?' The Haufuth was perplexed.

'Not shadowy. He's real. The Most High told me this years ago.' The enigmatic Hermit, sitting awkwardly on the back of Wisent, bobbed around above the Haufuth.

'But why he is so important?'

'You need to ask me that?' the Hermit replied. 'You who have told me that even now the Enemy of Faltha plans our destruction? You who have travelled across the northern wilderness, and have seen for yourself the decline of the once-proud First Men of Faltha into squabbling bands of villagers?'

'What could one man do about those things?'

'Not just a man. We speak about the Right Hand of the Most High, the man who the sages said would inherit the earth and all that is in it.'

'So he's got a fancy title. But he's still just one man. What can he do?'

The Hermit smiled, and for a moment he was human again. 'Perhaps he will make some great show of power, something that will mark him out as the one.'

'But will people be watching for him? I for one had never heard of this man until the start of our adventures. None of our sages say anything about him!' The Haufuth did not hide his scepticism. *Not that we have any sages*, he added in the privacy of his own mind.

'Where I come from, the name of the Right Hand has not been forgotten.'

'And where is that?'

'I am from Mercium, a seaport and capital city of Straux. Remember? I told you this yesterday. There we remembered the words of the First Men.'

'Straux? Then how did you end up in a cave on the borders of Firanes, hundreds of miles away?'

'Hundreds of miles away the cave might have been, yet it has proved insufficiently far away to escape from life.' The Hermit laughed. 'Life has found me, and now it bears me away to Instruere on the back of a wild beast. With such momentum, how can it be stopped? Who can avoid the grasp of the Right Hand of God?'

'So what stories do they tell in Mercium of the Right Hand?'

'I know nothing of what they tell now. Twenty years and more it has been since I escaped from the City of Vice and made my way north to Bandits' Cave. Perhaps they still speak of the old prophecies, or perhaps' – here he frowned doubtfully – 'perhaps they have found new ones.

'Half a thousand years ago it was that a man came wandering through our city, a man friendless and without fortune, for he had been banished from Instruere for fomenting rebellion. This last the city fathers did not know at first, or they would not have allowed him to stay, nor would they have provided him a place from which he could address the people of Mercium as they went about their business. But allow him they did; and this stranger from the deep south preached a message of prophecy and hope, naming a deliverer who would save Faltha from her indolence and her many transgressions.

'"For there will come a day when the Most High will again have congress with the First Men," the prophet said. "And this shall be the sign: the Right Hand of the Most High will arise and gather men unto himself from every nation, and will set a table before them. At that table men will feast together in harmony, the First Men and *losian* together. From the east and from the west they will come, and will celebrate together the defeat of the Destroyer, the Undying One of Bhrudwo, and his Lords of Fear.

'"And the Most High Himself shall descend to the world of men once again, and the fire will fall, and the long abandonment will be over. So be ready, watch with all diligence for the coming of the Right Hand, for he brings with him your deliverance." Thus the prophet spoke.

'Mercium was even then named an evil place, a seat of corruption and wickedness, built on the foolishness of speculation and the lure of the flesh, not on the rewards of honest toil. Thus it was that few listened to the prophet, and after a time he was banished from the great marketplace. Nevertheless, the seed had been sown, and in the days following his preaching many frightened ones came to him, seeking to receive an anointing that might protect them from the sins of their neighbours and the judgement to come. Greater and greater the numbers grew, until the authorities sought to disperse them, seeing in their number a threat to

377

public order. The prophet they imprisoned, and some of his followers were struck down and killed by the mobs. But still this revival of hope could not be quenched. Eventually the mayor of Mercium laid hands on the prophet and had him cruelly put to death in a public place, hoping thus to restore order. With his dying breath, the brave prophet bade his followers to forswear violence and to put their trust in the immanence of the Right Hand, who would deliver them.

'Yet his followers did not listen, and pitched battles were fought in the streets. The mayor pleaded with the King of Straux, who in those days had his throne in Instruere, to send his army. When the army came, it drove all before it, whether they were followers of the prophet or no, and many were put to the sword. The Right Hand of the Most High did not arise to save them from their plight, self-inflicted as it was. Thus the movement died, and for many years the memory of the prophet was anathema to the citizens of Mercium, though the name of the Right Hand was not forgotten. And ever since that time, devout men have carried that name in their hearts, awaiting the time of their deliverance.'

'Hmm,' the Haufuth managed in reply. 'And did they say what that name was? It might make our task a little easier if we could hand the hard work over to a miraculous saviour.'

'You misunderstand the story,' said the Hermit patiently. 'His name is the Right Hand; none other was given by the prophet.'

'And from where did this prophet get his information, I wonder? Sounds like a rabble-rouser to me.'

The Hermit glanced sharply at the fat Firanese man. He had told the story as it had been told to him by his father; it had never failed to move him. *Has the man no soul? Am I mistaken in what I see?*

'Got his just deserts, in my opinion,' the Haufuth continued. 'If I'd been the mayor of Mercium, I doubt whether I'd have shown as much patience.'

'You speak flippantly of what you do not understand, my companion,' the Hermit said quietly. 'The coming of the Right Hand is nigh. He is nearer to you than you think. I wait only for

378

permission to speak more plainly of this to you, yet this I can safely reveal: I know who he is, and I have met him.'

'Get many visitors to your cave, do you?' The Haufuth tried unsuccessfully to keep the sarcasm out of his voice. But his attempt to goad the Hermit misfired: the blond-headed man would say no more on the subject.

I suppose I should be grateful for the silence, the big man mused, thinking on the man's story. *All nonsense, without a doubt.* Yet he chose to stifle his memories of Kroptur the Watcher.

Silence again settled over the fastness of Withwestwa Wood. At the rate they were going it would be two, probably three, months before they made it to Instruere, and their food would barely sustain them with minimal rations. The Haufuth sighed and looked down at his belt; not only could he see it for the first time in years, he was appalled to notice that the well-used eyelet that used to measure his girth was now three whole notches too big for him. *I hope the Hermit is right*, he thought ruefully, *when he says that the inhabitants of this wood are friendly. I'm in need of some generous helpings of hospitality right now!*

Eventually his thoughts wandered back to the fate of the Company. Surely by now their quest had succeeded or failed, and some sign on the road would point to their fate. Thus far there had been nothing. The Haufuth had tired of the mysticism of the Hermit, and longed to be back with the others.

Wira was now gone from among the Company, leaving the memory of a quick laugh, a kind word and bravery beyond measure. For a while everyone was left with his or her own thoughts.

As the smoke from the pyre began to die away, Mahnum stood. 'Surely Leith should have been back before now?' he said, not caring to mask the worry in his voice. 'Perhaps we should organise a search.'

'Quiet!' hissed Perdu. 'I hear something in the trees!'

The Company barely had time to stand before sword-wielding figures sprang silently from the forest eaves on all sides. *The Bhrudwans!* But there lay the bound form of their captive, and they reassured themselves they had not simply imagined their victory. All this took place in a moment. Their eyes then returned to those confronting them, and the old farmer relaxed somewhat as he realised that these marauders were Fodhram.

'Don't move!' one of the men called out. There were perhaps thirty of them, short in stature, clothed in forest green. They looked to the coastlanders like close cousins to the fur traders they had so recently befriended. In vain Kurr searched their faces for Leader, Scarface, Shabby or Taller.

'Send for the Warden,' came the order. One of the men, little more than a youth, dashed off into the woods.

The apparent leader of the Fodhram barked another order from the shadows. 'Disarm these intruders!' Stern men strode forward.

'We mean no harm,' Kurr began, arms outstretched with palms upward in a gesture of peace. The men hesitated, then stopped.

'Let us pass,' the old farmer said. 'We are travellers on the Westway, afforded protection by treaty. We have urgent business, and have just fought—'

'Silence!' A serious-looking man, small even for a Fodhram, came forward and addressed Kurr. 'You are not Widuz, that is plain. Who are you, and why do you trespass on Fodhram land?'

Kurr was not impressed by the man's officiousness. 'I am accustomed to more courtesy from the Fodhram,' he replied shortly.

'You are fortunate that I have chosen to speak at all! Raiders from Widuz have attacked, killing Fodhram and taking many captive, as has not happened in many a year. We are pursuing them and came to investigate the smoke from your fire. Now, quickly; we are in great haste. Why should we spare your lives?'

'We were given leave of this land by a Fodhram party whom we accompanied on the Southern Run,' Kurr stated tersely. 'Their true names are not known to us, of course, but they deposited many bales of furs at Vindstrop House. Surely someone here has knowledge of them?'

'You lie,' said the little man, red veins standing out in his neck. 'No one makes the Southern Run this early in the year. By your lies you are betrayed. Bind them!'

380

Three Fodhram, dressed in regulation garb, came forward with rope. The Company drew together, and Farr and Perdu went for their swords. In a blur of motion, steel was drawn around the clearing, and the Fodhram came menacingly closer. Kurr closed his eyes. To have bested the Bhrudwans, only to fall to the Fodhram . . .

'What is this?' came a voice from the trees. A familiar figure strode into the clearing, followed by another armed band of Fodhram.

'My friend!' Kurr cried, relief filling his voice. 'I would ask you another favour as companions along the way. Would you vouch for us?'

'Vouch for you?' laughed Leader as he came over to the old farmer and embraced him in the Fodhram greeting. 'Of course I will vouch for you!' He aimed a level gaze at the small man in charge of the first Fodhram band.

'It appears that I've arrived just in time to stop a war,' Leader exclaimed, and laughed heartily. 'You coastlanders were about to destroy one of our reserve divisions.'

The Fodhram leader turned to the commander of the division. 'I'll speak for these people. They have the freedom of the wood. Perhaps you might consider applying your undoubted skills to tracking the Widuz raiders.' The members of the Fodhram division sheathed their swords, and shuffled off up the Westway after their embarrassed commander.

'Well, my friends,' Leader boomed expansively, 'you appear to have been busy since last we met! I see you have a new, if somewhat unwilling, member of your Company' – he nudged the captive Bhrudwan with his boot – 'and you have rescued your friends. Excellent!'

'But not without cost,' Kurr said, indicating the smouldering pyre.

Leader bowed his head. 'I am sorry. But there is nothing more honourable than death in battle.' The habitual smile was absent now, replaced by a mixture of admiration and concern.

'You must tell me about the battle!' the small man exclaimed.

'Losing only two men against such fierce opponents! By guile you must have bested them, not by strength of arms. Would that I had been here to see it, to be part of it!' He frowned. 'We had planned to bring you aid. Evil men such as those must not roam unchecked in our lands, especially about such foul business. We aimed to apprehend these Bhrudwans ourselves, travelling faster than you were able by the use of paths known only to the Fodhram. But we were drawn away by a band of raiders from Widuz who attacked members of one of our villages as they worked their fields, killing some and taking others captive. Have you seen any other strangers in the wood since you left Vindstrop House?'

'Lost two?' Kurr said, still preoccupied with the first thing the Fodhram leader had said. 'We lost only one fighting man, valiant Wira from the hills of Vinkullen, who was slain while shielding us from a surprise attack. But the young boy, Leith, has gone missing. We think he is on the other side of the river. Have you seen any sign of him?'

Leader was about to reply when one of his fellows whispered something to him. The stout Fodhram nodded, dismissing the young man with a smile and a pat on the shoulder.

'One of my scouts tells me that no more than an hour or two ago he saw a small band of raiders somewhat to the south of here, nowhere near where we believe the main body of Widuz to be. I am sorry to say we could spare none of our men for a pursuit.'

'The timing is right, unfortunately,' Farr commented. 'How else can we explain his disappearance? He ought to have been back long before now.'

The Fodhram leader nodded soberly. 'We know the Widuz came as far north as Meall Gorm, the mountain you know as Steffl. The main group must have passed by to the east, somewhere between here and Vindstrop House, travelling swiftly despite the captives they have taken.' He kicked at a loose stone on the path, a scowl on his laugh-lined features. 'Leith may have been taken by this second group, especially if they came south on this side of yonder stream. But if there were two groups, perhaps there were still others, and more of our villages may have been attacked. We must press on: Fodhram have been taken captive, and my foolish compatriot has led us instead to you, who pose no threat at all. But such a chance has perhaps aided you in your search for your companion.'

'What are they saying?' Indrett asked. 'What has happened to Leith?' Mahnum put his arm around her, but his face was drawn.

'Who are these Widuz, and what do they want with captives?' Perdu asked.

'The Widuz are a barbarian race,' Leader said, with some feeling. 'They live in a land far to the south of here.'

'So why have they come north?'

'We don't know. But every now and then they raid our lands, stealing our crops and animals.'

'Your lands?' Mahnum said. 'They might dispute that! Of old they laid claim to all these lands, and dwelt here long before the First Men came.'

'But we live here now, and they have no right to attack us as they do. Are you excusing their behaviour?' The Fodhram leader looked askance at this new member of the Company, obviously until recently a captive of the Bhrudwans.

'Now is not the time for such a debate,' Mahnum replied carefully. 'If they have my son, my duty is to rescue him. I suggest we search the riverbanks for one hour, then set off after these raiders.'

'And abandon any thought of warning the Falthan council at Instruere?' Farr was incredulous. 'After we've come all this way?'

'Were you going to continue?' Perdu asked him. 'I thought you joined the Company to take revenge on your father's killers.'

'Two of my family have died because the Bhrudwans plan to invade Faltha,' Farr snapped back. 'I won't sit and wait for them to kill the rest of us!'

'Enough, enough!' Kurr groaned. 'What do we do now?' he said. 'If we wait any longer for Leith to turn up, only to find that he has been taken captive, he may be removed beyond our ability to give him aid. But we will not abandon our quest now. We must get to Instruere with all possible speed.'

'We cannot tarry while you make up your mind,' Leader said. 'We must track these Widuz and rescue our people. You don't know these wild men; undoubted harm awaits the captives at the end of their journey, if not before.'

'I'm coming with you,' Mahnum said. 'They have my boy; I'm sure of it.'

'As you wish,' Leader said. 'Another sword will be useful.'

'A sword I do not have,' Mahnum replied. 'But I know the Widuz. Have you been to Clovenhill?'

Leader shook his head.

'Perhaps you might find that a Trader can be of some use to you, then.' Beside him Indrett sighed deeply.

'A Trader!' Leader raised his eyebrows. 'A true Trader would be useful indeed, especially one who knows the unmapped paths of the Widuz.'

'Stay with the others,' Mahnum urged his wife. 'You don't have the strength for such a journey.'

'Neither do you,' she whispered back.

The hour passed quickly, too quickly, and still Leith had not been found. As the Fodhram prepared to leave, Mahnum and Indrett shared a tender embrace.

'Some day soon we shall all be together again,' he told her. 'Then everything will be as it was before.'

She buried her face in his hair. 'I'll never be as I was before,' she said, her eyes filling with tears.

'I'll see you in Instruere,' he promised.

Looking at Indrett his wife and Hal his son, he said to them: 'Take good care of each other.' Then he turned and walked away.

Slung over someone's back like a sack of potatoes, Leith could see very little of what was happening around him. His captors travelled swiftly through the forest, sometimes striding, sometimes jogging, and occasionally he was able to raise his head enough to see thickets of trees, bushes, moss and spring flowers jerk past him.

For a while he had been in shock: one moment he was exhilarated, having slain the Bhrudwan warrior and won a great victory; the next he was picked up off his feet, roughly handled and taken away against his will. His struggling had served only to encourage his captor to grip him more firmly. He could not cry out, as his mouth was covered by cloth tightly wound around the lower half of his face. *Perhaps these people are Fodhram*, Leith thought hopefully. *They might release me when they realise their mistake*. But something told him that the merry Fodhram would not behave like this.

Without warning his captors halted and he was thrown to the ground with a sickening thud. When finally he was able to raise his head, he saw that he was in a wide, mist-filled clearing, surrounded by fighters armed with spears and clubs. Beside him were other captives, pale-faced and scared men, women and children, some bruised and bleeding. *These captives are Fodhram!* he realised with horror. Who, then, were his captors? As he watched, still more people were brought into the clearing, all gagged so they could not cry out. *There must be more than a hundred people held here by these fighters!*

Commands were barked in an unknown tongue, and the fighters moved amongst their captives. Some they made to stand, and hauled them off to one side until there were at least twenty of them, mostly young men. Just when he thought they had finished, one of them hauled Leith to his feet and shepherded him over to the others. He was nearly paralysed with fear. What were they going to do with him?

Their hands were bound together in front of them, then with ropes the captives were linked one to another, in two lines of a dozen or so. They were prodded with spears into a slow, shuffling trot, delayed only slightly when one of the boys in front of Leith fell to the ground. Under the eaves of the trees they shuffled, leaving the other captives in the clearing, surrounded by spear-wielding men.

The late afternoon light was fading and fine, misty rain sifted down when the Fodhram departed. Mahnum took spare clothing from the Company, and the Fodhram found a broadsword for him. Farr looked on enviously as the Fodhram division formed up for the march south. Now Wira was gone, he longed to go with them. With a command from their leader, the Fodhram saluted the Company, wheeled around and set off into the forest at a swift march.

After they had gone, Kurr gathered the dazed members of the Company together and spoke earnestly to them.

'Today has been a day of heartache,' he said. 'We have achieved our task of rescuing Mahnum and Indrett of Loulea, and Parlevaag of the Fenni, but we have laid Wira to rest and Leith is lost. Now we have to consider what to do. Mahnum has chosen to search for his son, aided by the Fodhram. I believe we who remain must travel to Instruere and tell the Council of Faltha about the Bhrudwan invasion. It is time therefore to re-form the Company. Who will come with me?'

Hal stood immediately. 'Our family was drawn into this in the beginning,' he said, 'and we will follow it through until the end. If we can be of any use, let us be part of the Company.'

'Wira's death will be meaningless unless we can prevent the Bhrudwan invasion,' Farr said. 'I must go to Instruere.'

'Of course you must come with us,' Kurr responded. The gruff old man was pleased; he had feared Farr might return to Mjolkbridge after the death of his brother.

Perdu stood, his face mirroring his indecision. 'I have fulfilled the command given me by my clan chief,' he said. 'I have seen the Bhrudwans die, and were it not for the need of the Company, I would demand that the remaining Bhrudwan be made to face Fenni justice. I ought to return to give my report, taking Parlevaag with me. And the gods know I long to see my family again!

'Yet I do not feel comfortable leaving the Company with its task only half complete. I have begun to suspect that there was a purpose in my becoming Fenni, that my joining the Company was no accident. I am undecided as to what to do.

'For her part, Parlevaag wishes to remain with the Company. She has lost her husband to the Bhrudwans, and does not want to go back to the *vidda*. She feels she has a debt to pay the

386

Company, although she does not know how she might discharge it.'

Kurr stood to reply. 'Tell Parlevaag that she has something valuable that we need. The Council of Faltha will listen to an eyewitness account such as hers. She is most welcome to join the Company, but she must not think she has to repay any debt.' He turned and smiled at the Fenni woman, who worked her troubled face into a slight smile in return.

'I must have more time,' Perdu said. 'I will give you my answer in the morning.' He walked over to Parlevaag, sat down beside her and began to explain what had just been said.

As the twilight faded into night and the drizzle intensified into a steady rain, a long silence enveloped the group perched on the slopes of Steffl. The low clouds ensured total darkness, so that no person could see any other, and people were left with their own thoughts. And still Stella had not spoken a word since the battle.

A cold wind blew through Withwestwa Wood. The Fodhram moved surely in the fading light, making swift progress through thicket and thorn until the dark made further travel impossible. Then, after they had made camp, there was a lot of talking, mostly in a language the Trader couldn't understand, but just hearing the conversation began to reawaken something human within him. A fire was lit, hot broth was passed around and laughter shared, warming Mahnum's heart.

That dark night was a series of sounds and smells, a parade of friendship that Mahnum's dry spirit drank in thirstily. Never afterwards was he to forget that night, though he could not remember one word of what had been said. Through the rest of his life, the pungent aroma of leather, the sound of carefree laughter, or the soft whisper of voices in keen debate evoked in him bittersweet memories of the first night he shared with the Fodhram.

His thoughts strayed to his younger son. Images of Leith rose up before him: his awkwardness at the Midwinter Play; bright, intelligent eyes that were so often clouded by fear and self-doubt; a frightened youth with upraised sword, teetering on the edge of courage and fear as he prepared to smite the Bhrudwan leader. An enigma, a boy who had needed his father the most when he had not been there. *Hold firm, Leith; I'm coming for you.*

Farr rose to meet the dawn. The low cloud had been borne away during the night by a stiff easterly breeze, bringing with it the overpowering stench of sulphur from the heights of Steffl. Now the day awoke bright and clear, as though nothing untoward had happened under the cloak of night.

He knelt for a few minutes by a pile of ashes next to the Westway, then picked himself up and spent an hour searching the banks of the river. Some animal had been at the two bodies below the broken bridge; apart from that, it appeared that nothing had stirred along the steep-sided stream. Certainly there was no sign of Leith.

On an impulse, he headed upslope. Soon he found a ridge that rose above the treeline, and on the open ground he was able to increase his pace. Finally, after many minutes of strenuous effort, he turned to survey the wood.

Once again, just as it had when the Mossbank River broke up, the presence of the forest flooded his senses. This time the sensation of vigour, of solidity, of peace and joy, was even stronger than before. He was lost in it beyond recovery. It offered him privacy, a sanctuary he had never found in the raw, exposed slopes of his Vinkullen home. There was a freshness, an honesty, in the wood and in those who dwelt there that offered him hope. Perhaps he could be more than he had been.

There's magic in these woods, he thought as he watched the spring colours brighten below him, picked out by the morning sun and shadow. *There is a song here that one could sing forever; there is a task here that one could give his life to fulfil.* He laughed at himself. *Listen to Farr Storrsen, the great philosopher! Perhaps I should join the Hermit in his cold caves!* But in spite of his feeling of foolishness, there was something all around him, a bright light that would not go away.

Farr turned and glanced at the morning sun; with a shock he

realised that an hour had passed since he had left the river far below. The others would be ready to leave, or perhaps even looking for him, afraid that he too had been taken by an unknown enemy.

As he scanned the horizon a final time, he noticed a smoky haze far to the south. For a moment he strained his eyes, but even the far-sighted vision of a Vinkullen man could not see the source of the smoke. Nevertheless, his skin chilled at what it might signify. With great haste, he abandoned his high seat and scurried down the mountainside towards the others.

What am I going to do now? How will I ever escape my fate? Stella spent the early hours of the morning pacing along the cliff-top, seeking an answer for her dilemma. *I could not bear it if they make me go back to Loulea: no matter what they do, I shall not, I shall not be the wife of such a brute.* Her eyes were continually drawn to that place beside the Westway, beyond the sleeping members of the Company, where Wira had given his death to her. *Why, Wira, why?* she cried in the loneliness of her mind. *Why did you have to die?* She shook as she poured all her passion, all her powers of concentration, into the image of Wira still alive, still with her; but the ashes of the pyre stayed where they were, stirred fitfully by the morning mountain breeze, and her abject solitude rose up as an enemy before her, trapping her in a deathly embrace.

'If you don't want him, give him my name!' Fania had said to her when Stella had finally found the courage to tell someone about Druin's attentions. 'Really, Stell, he can't possibly be that bad. You must take him as your husband; it's your duty. Besides he's so – well, look around! Who else in Loulea Vale compares to Druin?' She ran through the contenders. 'Dammish? All he ever talks about is hunting. Gloan would be all right as long as you never had to get closer than six feet from him. Feerich? Hasn't the wit to remember anyone else's name but his own. Stend? He only has eyes for Anesel – and just as well. Leith? He's far too young. I know he's the same age as you, but really, he's a baby. Hal? Well – is Hal interested in girls? And then there's Lanka from Brookside; his mother would never let him marry someone from Loulea. Apart from Druin, there is no one suitable this side of Vapnatak. Come on, Stell; don't be so proud.'

Proud? Stella snorted. *I'd do anything, endure any kind of public humiliation, marry any of the other boys, or even one of the widowed farmers, anything, anything . . . Oh Wira, I needed you so much! They don't know Druin, none of them do. The perfect outcome would be to return to Loulea and find that he had moved on, or died, or something, please . . . Perhaps he will volunteer for the army when this war they are all talking about finally comes; perhaps he'll be killed . . .*

If we ever return to Loulea, it won't be for some time yet. We're still moving east, we still have a task to complete, one which may take many months – the longer the better. Druin – all of them – will think, probably already think we're dead; perhaps he will marry before we return. Maybe Druin and Fania . . . Hope rose within her so strongly she felt sick, felt dizzy with the pain of it. *Let it be so! If there is any way I can prevent our return to that sorry little valley, I'll do it. Let them marry! Let them forget about me!*

She sat on a fallen tree, overwhelmed by her misfortune, and buried her head in her hands. There was no one she could talk to, she was certain none of the others would understand. If she leaned forward she could see over the edge of the high bank, down into the stream far below. In her misery she could not keep the image of falling from flashing through her mind, the rocks coming ever closer . . .

Mahnum and the Fodhram were up and travelling in the dim pre-dawn light after only a few hours' rest under the rain-soaked eaves. The forest-dwellers had divided into several small groups and fanned out over a wide front, seeking sign of their quarry.

Ahead the air was hazy, as though a mist had blown in from the south. Mahnum found himself coughing and his eyes began to run. *This is no mist,* he thought. *The forest is on fire!* Ahead the Fodhram increased their pace, breaking into a trot.

Where the smoke was at its thickest, they broke out of the forest. There was something burning ahead of them – no, there were fires at several places in the clearing. Flames licked the roots of those young saplings over to the right. Mahnum looked more closely; they were spears, not saplings. Rows of spears. He stared a moment longer, then turned away in horror. The spears were protruding from the burning bodies of men, women and children.

All around the clearing men hid their faces. Others wept openly, the smoke adding to their tears. Grimly, the Warden of Withwestwa Wood walked among his men, comforting the ones who had kin among those the Widuz had taken. Mahnum had thought he was inured to horror, but he was wrong. *How could the world bear such cruelty? Why did men do such things?* It was beyond imagining.

The Warden walked up and down the rows of spears, his face streaked with tears, while the stricken Trader sat on the ground at the edge of the clearing, afraid to look for his son among the charred remains. Time stood still: the morning itself seemed to slow down to take a closer look at the violence committed under its nose.

'Not all the captives lie here,' the Warden said. 'We must go on.'

'We go on!' one of the men shouted hoarsely. His wife lay butchered in the clearing.

No one else spoke, but Mahnum could feel the anger and grief in the thick, smoky atmosphere. These normally jovial people, quick to laugh and ever ready with speech, had been stunned by the scene in the clearing. Soon the shock would turn to anger. *What are these people going to do?*

Did his own son lie in the clearing? The Trader did not want to face the task of searching along the gruesome rows, but he took a steadying breath and forced himself to his feet. *Lord Most High!* he grimaced as he walked through the unnatural thicket. *What terror must have filled this place?* Up and down the rows he went, fighting wave after wave of the dizziness that threatened to overwhelm him as he searched for the face he feared to find. It seemed to take forever to come to the end of the spears, but finally he did, without finding his son. He nearly collapsed from the sudden release of tension.

The Warden posted a few guards to protect the clearing of the spears, then they moved swiftly away to the south, into lands unknown by any of the dwellers of Withwestwa Wood.

Leith and the other captives shuffled on into the forest, past hunger and pain and into numbness. At the end of each day they were allowed a few hours' sleep on the pine-needle-strewn cold ground; well before dawn they rose and were force-marched through the day, with nothing to eat or drink until evening. No one was permitted to talk throughout the long march south. The captives were roped together, but Leith never learned the names of either the boy in front of him or the woman behind. On the seventh day – as near as Leith could tell – a boy near the front of the line collapsed and did not get up again. Within moments he was cut away from the others and pushed against a tree. A little girl – possibly the boy's sister, she had hair the same colour – started to cry. The line jerked forwards and the cruel pace continued, leaving the boy behind. After a while the little girl stopped sobbing and only the sound of feet on the path disturbed the eerie silence of the trees. After a week of this punishment Leith no longer cared whether he lived or died.

The captives were too exhausted to notice the land begin to rise. The trees towered above them, unchanging to all but the most subtle of eyes, but there were changes in the forest as they progressed further south into warmer lands. Trees which in northern lands grew tall and unadorned were in the south draped with vines and climbers, and the undergrowth was much denser. Lianas, ferns and all manner of climbing plants fought with each other to scale the great trees, struggling upwards towards the light hundreds of feet above the dank forest floor. Many of the trees looked as though they were being silently strangled to death. The forest grew darker, thicker and more forbidding as the captives went south into shadow. By various narrow paths they were taken deep into the dark, tree-draped highlands of Clovenhill, the land of the Widuz.

The forest sounds changed also, as though somewhere behind

the captives an invisible line had been crossed. In Withwestwa Wood the sparrows and finches, magpies and kites sang of spring-time and made quiet nesting sounds, but here in the south the birds, invisible in the gloom, made harsh noises. From up in the canopy came a cacophony of croaks, screeches and howls as birds of unknown shape competed with each other for the meagre resources of the semi-darkness. And occasionally other sounds came from the depths of the forest: snarls, growls, moans and once the high-pitched scream of some terrified animal in the throes of death.

For all they could see in this dim, twilight world, the captives might as well have been blindfolded. So it was that Leith did not see the crude poverty of the people who lived near the paths the captives took. The poor soils of Widuz were thinly spread over a bed of limestone and marble, and would not support farming for more than two or three years at a time. Typically, farmers would burn down an area of forest, then farm in the clearing, the soils given some passing fertility by the ashes of the trees. The very rare visitor to these hidden lands was struck by the lushness of the green forest, a fecundity that passed imagination when compared to the pine forests of the north, but was astonished to realise that the same soil that supported the mighty forest would feed only a few thousand people, and that at purely a subsistence level. And the very rare visitor to the hidden lands of Widuz seldom left them.

The Falthans, the descendants of the First Men, had largely forgotten what had made the Widuz such a fierce and insular race. Those who had not dismissed them entirely from their memory merely considered them a barbaric people who would attack their neighbours without provocation. They did not remember the way the children and grandchildren of the First Men treated the Widuz, who were then a numerous race inhabiting the wide plains between the Remparer and the Jawbone Mountains; how they were harried and hounded, driven from their lands with violence, treachery and bloodshed, retreating to the fastness of Clovenhill, the poorest of their vast lands, pursued to the forest's edge by fire and sword. The few survivors of the slaughter swore to rid the land of the First

Men, but had found their energies absorbed by the bitter task of staying alive.

The descendants of the First Men thought no more of the Widuz, assuming they had not survived. They were reminded of their existence, to their cost, when they tried to force a road through Clovenhill in order to connect far-flung Firanes with the rest of Faltha. Hundreds of Falthans died before they learned to leave the Widuz alone. The road-builders found the Widuz ruthless and intractable, expert hunters and setters of devious traps. Eventually the Falthans gave up trying to force a road along the coast and, at great expense and over many years, constructed instead the Westway to the north of Widuz. From that time only those Treikans, Plonyans and Fodhram who lived along their borders had to reckon with the Widuz.

During the second week of the journey south, Leith lived an animal existence. Hunger, weariness and lack of sleep drove all thoughts of Bhrudwo and the Company from his mind. The prisoners fought amongst themselves for the scraps of food tossed them at the end of each day's march, with the stronger taking food from the weak. Leith, who had been exhausted by the months of travel on foot through the northern wastes, was one of the first to weaken, and seldom had the energy to eat. His overriding thought was to lie down and surrender to the darkness, but the merciless rope pulled him on and on. And somehow the days passed.

The climate, which had warmed as they marched south, began to cool again with a gradual rise in elevation as the path they followed wriggled up the spine of Clovenhill. One morning they emerged from the deep woods out into the open, the sunlight blinding captives and captors alike. The grassy slopes upon which they stumbled were at the very crest of the great hill, where huge limestone bluffs protruded from the grass like rotted teeth set loosely in a giant's mouth. Here and there gorse bushes sat in small hollows. The pallid sky seemed to sit low over the place, brooding on a land so ancient that the time when the Widuz had dominion over northern Faltha was a recent memory.

Eventually they reached the summit, and Leith stood seemingly on the very top of the world. On every side the grass fell away to the eaves of the dark forest far below. All around were the contorted shapes of bare rock, exposed by the earth as though flesh had melted away from bone. There was no sign of life, no habitations, no animals or birds, just the bright green grass and the bones of old hills under a wan sun.

Leith felt the familiar tug on the rope as the prisoners ahead of him rose, answering the goads of the Widuz with a shuffling walk. From the bald crown of Clovenhill they descended along a spur and down into a tree-lined valley to the right. A small stream gurgled beside them, an incongruously cheerful sound. Momentarily his mind cleared of despair as he remembered the fallen Bhrudwans and his parents' rescue, and was glad. He could still feel the memory of the sword in his hand, and he wished that he still had it.

Presently they came to a crossroads marked by four huge standing stones, one beside each of the paths. Here their guards stopped and, disregarding their prisoners for a moment, walked into the middle of the crossroads, stood in a circle and touched raised palms in the centre.

'Cepan aith!' they shouted together. 'Andja il robben!' Once more they raised their arms and touched palms. A moment later the strange ceremony was over.

Another league and their journey came to an end. Ahead the stream seemed to run straight into a sheer wall, a wall with small holes in it at regular intervals – Not holes, windows, Leith realised as they approached. Beside him to the right the stream grew noisier as it flowed more steeply downhill. The path wound downward and limestone ridges stood taller on either side, unbroken by any gap. Finally the prisoners stood on a natural rock ledge which jutted out into nothingness, as the stream beside them flowed joyfully into a black abyss, a dark, circular wound in the earth perhaps a hundred yards across. Leith felt his feet tingle with the fear of the depths below, and he tried to edge away from the brink.

'Adunlok!' one of their captors cried. 'Adunlok!'

Then their guards made them all disrobe, and the prisoners

stood, thin, pale and frightened, on the ledge while their clothes were gathered up. With a contemptuous flick, one of their captors threw the pile of rags over the edge. Leith listened for a sound, but heard nothing. '*Adunlok!*' their guards cried again, grim of face, then led the captives up a narrow winding path to a doorway in the rock. One by one, the prisoners filed in, bare feet on cold white stone, and the huge stone door was rolled closed behind them.

CHAPTER 19

PHEMANDERAC

LEITH AWOKE FROM A deep sleep to find himself in a dark, narrow room, not dissimilar to his bedroom back in Loulea. He imagined he could hear his brother shuffling around in the darkness. His bed was harder than he remembered it, and what was this sacking instead of his blanket?

Gradually his mind came back into focus. He recalled the weeks of walking, and his memory wandered along the Westway: through Mjolkbridge, into the Great North Woods, up the Torrelstrommen valley, into the heart of the wilderness, a slow tramp over the moors, down the Thraell, beside the Kljufa, past the Maelstrom, a pause at Bandits' Cave – his thoughts began to move more swiftly – then along the Southern Run, with snowfall and snowmelt and the passage of the rapids, through Vindstrop House and back along the Westway and the horror of facing the Bhrudwans. A pause on the sinister slopes of Steffl, an ambush, a sprint across the river into the face of fear, a triumphant grey figure and the raising of a sword . . . and then nothing.

Nothing except a body that ached as if it had been trampled by an aurochs.

Leith sat bolt upright, casting the pungent sacking aside. The memories of the last two weeks settled on him like snowladen clouds. His capture, the forced march, the cruelty. And now a prisoner in the fortress of an enemy he did not know, hundreds of miles from his family. The deep weariness and hunger that had been demanding his attention since he awoke were suddenly augmented by a desperate hollowness akin to shock, paralysing in its intensity.

'So, you're awake,' said a heavily accented voice from the other end of the room. 'Good! Perhaps you can explain some of the things you said in your sleep.'

'Who's there?' Leith said, snatching at the sacking to cover himself. He could see no one else in the room; perhaps the speaker was hidden in the shadows. Or this might be his jailer, come to make an end of him. The youth remembered his father's tale of cruelties on the island of Andratan, and his insides cringed with fear.

'A fellow prisoner,' came the reply in a deep, sonorous tone. 'They have us two to a cell. Here, have some food. This is yesterday's meal: it is no longer warm, but perhaps it will taste better cold.'

Leith heard someone coming towards him and gradually, out of the darkness, he could make out the tall form of a young man offering him a plate.

The man looked at it for a moment. 'Perhaps not,' he said.

Leith stretched out his hand and took the plate. The food was a fearsome gruel, foul and unappetising, but in his hunger he swallowed it quickly.

The man sat down on the end of Leith's slatted bed. Maybe twenty-five, thirty years of age, Leith thought, slender, almost gaunt-looking, with hollow cheeks, a bulbous nose and a high forehead framed by lank dark hair. Not handsome at all.

'I've waited more than a day for you to wake up.'

'A whole day!' Leith exclaimed. 'I slept for a whole day?'

'You obviously needed it. Though I'd be surprised if the rest has done you any good, with all the struggling, the talking and the shouting in your sleep. What were your dreams about? What do you know about the Bhrudwans?'

'You still haven't told me who you are,' Leith countered warily.

'My name is Phemanderac, though names don't matter much in here,' the tall young man said. 'Like you, I'm a captive of the Widuz.'

'The Widuz?' Leith echoed. *What did Kurr say about them? And why would they want me as a prisoner?* 'Where are we?'

'This place is called Adunlok, high keep of the Widuz. We are a hundred leagues north of Tolmen.'

Leith shrugged his shoulders. The names meant nothing to him; he should have paid more attention to Kurr's maps. Not that the knowledge would do him much good now.

'I guessed you were not from this region,' Phemanderac said. 'What is your name, and where do you come from? I've not heard an accent like yours on my travels.'

'My name is Leith Mahnumsen, and I live . . .' He fumbled to a stop. *Be careful, I know nothing about this man.* But he knew his thoughts for foolishness. The man was a fellow prisoner, not a threat. 'I live a long way away,' he finished lamely.

'As do I,' the thin man replied, sighing. 'As do I. It seems we have two things in common, you and I. We both come from far away, and we've both ended up here, held captive in this prison.'

'How were you captured?' Leith asked.

'Foolishness, utter foolishness. You'd think that after two years travelling I would have known better. But no. The elders warned me of the dangers. I asked villagers down on the Treikan plains whether it was safe to cross the mountains, and they said the land was uninhabited. After I'd played for them, too! I guess they don't like strangers, or at least harpists. So, none the wiser, I followed a game trail into the mountains, and fairly soon I became the game, hunted by the Widuz. A dozen of them with swords took me prisoner and brought me here.'

'Travelling? Why are you travelling?'

'How else can a young man learn?'

'How else can a young man die!' Leith shot back. 'I would have stayed home if I'd been given the choice. Why would someone take their life into their hands when they could be safe at home?'

'Were you safe at home?' Phemanderac stared at him intently.

'Of course! Loulea is a place of peace . . .' His voice tailed off as the image of grey-cloaked warriors wrestling with his family in the darkness of his own house came crashing into his mind. 'Maybe not,' he finished lamely.

'I feel something,' Leith's thin-faced companion pronounced unexpectedly, still staring. 'Something about you, Leith. There's a bond – we have something in common. I don't know what it is. It'll come to me.' He shrugged his bony shoulders.

Feel something? What? Am I trapped here with a madman? Leith's mind raced feverishly, and he stood up slowly to try the stone door.

'Tried it. Many times. Always locked.' Phemanderac smiled. 'You'll try it anyway.'

Leith knew it would be locked, but he had to check . . . the irrational hope that perhaps the guards had forgotten to secure the door, the lure of freedom . . . the door was locked. He stumbled, and a great weight of fatigue settled on him like a dark mantle.

'What do we do now?' he asked faintly.

'In your case, get some rest. Sleep.' Abruptly the thin man's voice seemed to be coming from far away. 'Sleep. You're no use to anyone until you've rested. Then we'll see . . .'

The Warden of Withwestwa Wood did not need to harry his men to pursue the Widuz. In fact, Axehaft had found it was all he could do to restrain them from marching night and day, without sleep or food, so desperate were they to engage their quarry. Prudently, the Warden had held his men back, partly to preserve their strength, and partly because too many of them sought revenge for the deaths of friends and loved ones – *and a man driven by revenge is a man not in control of his judgement*, he reminded himself. *A man vulnerable to ambush*. Axehaft did not want any of his men killed unnecessarily.

The Widuz are driving their captives at a furious pace, he had reflected as early as the third afternoon. From all the signs, they were no closer to their quarry than when they left Fodhram territory two nights earlier. *What cruelty were they using?* he wondered. *My men are resting but seldom, and I hear murmurings of discontent among them already. They expected to have overtaken their enemy by this time. Little do they know the Widuz!* Axehaft knew the Widuz. He had been just a lad when the last Widuz raids had decimated Fernthicket, the place of his birth. He shook his head. *I do not want my warriors to learn about the Widuz in the same fashion I did.*

Axehaft sought out Mahnum, and found him pleasant and informative. He inquired how Mahnum had gained knowledge of Widuz, and learned that the Firanese man had indeed been a Trader, one who made his living by finding markets for goods and then risking money, and often his life, getting the goods to the market – all as a cover for an even more dangerous game, spying for his king. But Widuz? Surely they did not trade with the Falthan world? No, Mahnum laughed; he had posed as a Widuz from the north and had done profitable business in Tolmen, a coastal city many hundreds of miles to the south. In the course of his journeys, Mahnum said, he had learned much of interest about this fierce race, and had grown to appreciate their ways.

Axehaft had been taken aback by this, but remembered that Mahnum had not suffered at their hands. So he listened politely as he was told about their habits and customs, about their sophisticated society and beliefs. 'They were not ignorant savages,' Mahnum had assured him dispassionately, as though his own child was not in their cruel hands. 'They know about conditions in the outside world, but they are fiercely proud and do not forget grudges, and so will not readily entertain outsiders, even in the more liberal areas south of the Sagon River. In the north superstition still rules people's lives, and it may be that the hunting party has come north to take captives in appeasement to some local deity.'

As much as he did not want to admit it, the Warden gradually came to the conclusion that Mahnum was right; the Widuz raiding party had taken prisoners for sacrifice. It was the possibility he feared more than any other. The Fodhram knew what happened to prisoners taken in such circumstances. Should they not overtake the hunting party, their captives would undoubtedly be killed. But what had brought the fearsome Widuz north?

Perhaps it had been the great snowstorm, the storm that had trapped the Company on the Southern Run and forced them to shoot the Mossbank Cadence. It was a similar storm that had triggered the raid on Fernthicket all those years ago. He sighed and shook his head, trying to clear it of unwanted memories. *Perhaps it is time to give my warriors their heads. Four days now and still no sighting of them.*

So he had quickened the pace and shortened the period of rest, but still they seemed to gain no ground. 'Have these men grown wings and flown away with our people?' his men asked. Some, unskilled in tracking, voiced concerns that perhaps the Widuz had disposed of their prisoners and thereby increased their speed, but Axehaft assured them that the signs still spoke of a large group of bound captives – perhaps as many as thirty – being force-marched against their will. And late in the afternoon of the seventh day since the Westway even the most doubtful of the Fodhram received sad proof of the ruthlessness of the Widuz.

'This is my brother's son,' said a man mournfully as they gathered around the body of a boy lying against a tree. It had taken some time to drive the carrion-eaters away, to find that the boy had probably died that very day; in spite of the attentions of the foul birds of prey, he was relatively unmarked. 'He obviously couldn't keep up,' the man concluded bitterly. 'Why? Why would they do this? We leave them alone, and do not interfere when they hunt close to our lands. Why should they treat the defenceless this way?' None of the party supplied the man with an answer.

'At least this means we are not far behind!' said another.

'Aye,' agreed a third. 'We will catch them soon.'

'We must,' their Warden agreed, wiping his eyes. 'Come now, my friends. Put forth all your strength. We must overtake the Widuz before they reach their forest hold.'

So they had raced on into the darkening forest, stopping to sleep only when no light remained to aid them. For the next week they rose before the sun, walking through the day until they could barely see the path before them, yet made no ground on their quarry. And in their heartache and frustration, none of them realised that the reason they could not catch the Widuz was that their foe knew the path well enough to travel at night.

'M'Bilou!'

Leith woke suddenly from a deep sleep as the echoing sound subsided.

'M'Bilou!' came the cry again, from somewhere on the outside of the small barred window.

'M'Bilou! Ou Bregou!'

'What is that?' Leith asked. 'What is happening?' He got up, wrapped the sacking modestly around his nakedness, and went over to the window.

Phemanderac looked up momentarily from his bed at the other end of the cell. 'I've seen it too many times before,' he said simply, and rolled over again.

'M'Bilou!'

Leith pressed his face to the bars and looked down. For a moment he blinked against the sun's harsh light, but then the scene came into focus. Down below was the huge hole he had seen when he had first arrived. It seemed that the window from which he looked was set in the side of the cliff that fell away into the abyss. The solid rock ended in blackness signalling unguessable depths.

'M'Bilou!'

The cry had come from somewhere below and to the right, and Leith craned forward, fighting against his fear of heights. There on the right was the platform from which his clothes had been thrown – and, carved into the cliff on either side of this platform, was a narrow path in fashion like the Roofed Road in the Lower Clough of the Kljufa River. On this path people stood, facing inwards towards the blackness. They were naked.

'M'Bilou! Ou Bregou!'

Leith could not see the person making the noise, as it came from below him, out of his line of sight. Then, to his right, where the path came into view, he saw movement: it was one of the Fodhram captives, a young man about Leith's own age, his hands tied behind his back. His eyes were closed and his face wore a blank expression. Behind him stood a figure wearing a red mask and a grey cloak. The figure raised its arms and the cloak's long sleeves fell to the elbows.

'*M'Bilou!*' it shouted. Then the arms came down and pushed the Fodhram forward, off the path and into the abyss. The young man made no effort to avoid the fall. For a moment Leith saw the body, spinning end over end as it fell, then the black throat swallowed it.

Leith blinked, unable to believe what he had just witnessed.

The figure moved behind the next captive, a girl who had been three places in front of Leith on their long journey south. She had cried when her brother had been discarded on the march to this awful place. Leith could now see that two guards accompanied the masked figure, who raised his bare arms to the sky. Leith pulled away from the window.

'*M'Bilou!*'

The youth from Firanes sat on his bed in numb disbelief. He began to shake uncontrollably.

'They drug them first, you know,' Phemanderac said quietly.

For a long time Leith could not speak. Every shout from outside caused him to shudder. Finally he said: 'Why are they doing this?'

'This is Helig Holth, the Holy Mouth,' Phemanderac said by way of reply. 'The Widuz believe this is the mouth of Mother Earth, their most powerful god. They are feeding their god because they think she is hungry.'

'Don't you care?' snapped Leith, enraged by Phemanderac's seemingly phlegmatic attitude to the horror outside their window.

'Of course I care. But there is nothing I can do from in here. Mother Earth is not the only hungry god in the world. I have seen many evil things on my travels. Have you been to Bhrudwo?'

Leith shook his head in reply.

From behind the door of their cell came the sound of booted feet on solid stone. Someone was coming! Fear snapped tight like an iron band around Leith's chest. The footsteps stopped outside the door. He was paralysed with panic. *Perhaps this is why the Fodhram did not resist*, he found himself thinking.

The door opened, and two plates of food and a jug were thrust into the cell. Then the door slammed shut and the footsteps moved away. Neither prisoner moved.

'They seem to have forgotten about me,' Phemanderac said eventually, 'yet they keep feeding me. Perhaps you should consider yourself lucky to be my cellmate.'

But Leith did not answer. He could hear nothing but the recurring cries: 'M'Bilou!' Long after they stopped echoing around Helig Holth, they continued to echo through his frightened mind, reviving fears long forgotten.

He remembered the time he had climbed the thousand-year pine the week after the big storm. The top fifty feet were so frightening, with the damaged tree shaking at his every movement, but he had kept going. And what about the time when, as an eight-year-old, he had been separated from his parents on the western side of Bream Hill, and had wandered to the very edge of the sea cliffs? Leith could still remember how scared he had felt when he leaned on an old railing and it had given way. Only a desperate clutching at the railing had saved him from plummeting into the sea, so very far below. His father had found him a hundred yards from the cliff, sobbing with fear.

But it's not only the fear of dying, of the pain, of the terror, Leith thought. *I don't want to come to an end. I want to continue forever! I want to achieve something worthwhile, win some renown, prove my worth to those who have mocked me! I want to be with my family – with Hal, with my mother, with my father whose face I still can't remember* – his hand flashed to his breast pocket, where he had kept the birch bark carving. But it had gone, his father had it now ... no, they had found it again, up on Breidhan Moor ... yes, it was gone, along with his clothes, into the black mouth outside his cell window. His father had gone, fallen, pushed by a man in an evil mask, a man who would be coming for him ... His mind spiralled down into fears too deep even for thought, and he drew his knees up to his chest and began to cry.

* * *

The Fodhram war party had finally come out of the dismal forest and into the welcome sunlight. They pressed on to the very top of the highest hill and scanned the horizon in all directions, but could see no sign of their quarry. While the trail had been easy to follow in the detritus of the forest path, even the most experienced tracker could find no sign of Widuz passage in the short-bladed grass that covered the crown of this ominous hill.

There had been signs that as long ago as the previous week the Fodhram party had been close behind their quarry, perhaps as close as a few hours if the scouts had it right. But somewhere in the oppressive forest darkness they had taken a wrong turn. The trail had grown cold. Anger had faded into an energy-sapping despair as the days dragged on.

Now what? thought the Warden as he shielded his eyes from the westering sun. *They are nowhere to be seen: we may have to do circuits in the forest to pick up the trail again. We were so close,* he thought bitterly.

'Warden, someone has set a fire ahead of us. Do you see it?' the man beside him asked, pointing into the setting sun.

'No, you have better eyes than me. What do you see?'

'Down in the forest, perhaps three leagues away, I see a thin column of smoke.'

At that moment one of his men came running up to the hilltop. 'I have found the path at the forest edge,' he said breathlessly, 'and a group has passed over it recently.'

'Point to it,' the weary Warden said. The man pointed in much the same direction as had the man who saw the smoke.

'Time for revenge!' cried someone behind him. Axehaft did not turn to see who had made the comment; he knew that the man spoke for many in the group. *Whatever gives you strength,* he thought.

But what have we come to? he asked himself as they scrambled down the hill. *I have heard no laughter since we left Withwestwa Wood, and a Fodhram without laughter is like a riverbed without water or a tree without leaves. Has the cruelty of the Widuz dried us up? Are we withered like them, seeking to heal ourselves by hurting others?*

He tried to dismiss these thoughts, but they grew within him,

a deep disquiet forming in his mind. He was not ready to fight.
But, ready or not, a fight lay just a few hours ahead.

'I have it now,' Phemanderac told Leith triumphantly.

'Have what?' Leith asked in reply. 'What do you have?'
Already he was becoming used to the thin man's way of
conversing.

'I thought about it while you were asleep. It's just struck me.'

'What has?' Patience was not normally one of Leith's virtues,
and tiredness had undermined the little patience he possessed.

'Where did you say you were from?'

'I didn't, did I? I don't think I told you.'

'I'm sure you did. Never mind; where do you come from?'

'Far to the west of here,' Leith replied carelessly, and at once
he realised that his words had inflamed his cellmate's interest.

'Far to the west?' The thin man rolled the words around on his
tongue, as if savouring their meaning, then he snapped his fingers
with an extraordinarily loud crack. 'I knew it, I knew it. Yes, I am
sure of it now. I know what it is you and I have in common. You
can help me with my quest, I can feel it.' Phemanderac smiled.
'What kingdom do you live in?'

'In a country called Firanes.'

The thin man's smile broadened even further, if that were
possible, and he nodded vigorously. His throat worked as he said:
'Firanes? The Cape of Fire?' His eyes were bright orbs, his face
febrile with excitement, as if he had been struck with madness.

Leith nodded uneasily. 'That's what Firanes means.'

'Then listen to this:

> 'Darkness spreads from coast to coast,
> Blown by Bhrudwo's basest boast.
> Falthans fall on bended knee
> And heaven hears their heartfelt plea.
>
> 'Hand stretched out against the dark,
> He gave to them the Jugom Ark.

Bhrudwo scourged by iron rod
Wielded by the Hand of God.

'*Hand of God is now concealed,*
Soon to stand in strength revealed.
The final fate, our hopes aspire
To lowly vale on Cape of Fire.'

'It is a small part of the *Arminia Skreud*, a saying of one of my countrymen. What do you make of it?'

'Say that last line again,' Leith prompted. His head felt giddy, possibly from the hunger and tiredness.

'"To lowly vale on Cape of Fire",' Phemanderac repeated dutifully.

'What does it all mean?' Leith wanted to know.

'It is a foretelling, a prophecy if you like. It tells how Bhrudwo will launch an attack against Faltha, and how the Hand of God will come to the aid of all Falthans.'

'Why do you tell me this saying? What does the Hand of God have to do with Firanes?'

'I was hoping you might be able to tell me!' said Phemanderac, leaning forward. 'Meeting someone from Firanes cannot be a coincidence.'

'Why not? I had to be from somewhere.'

'Not when I have travelled across the world, the first from my country to do so, in search of the Cape of Fire and the lowly vale. We believe the time for the fulfilment of the *Arminia Skreud* is at hand, and I have come to search for the Hand of God.'

Leith could contain himself no longer.

'Would it help if I told you my home village is named Loulea?'

Leith watched as realisation bloomed on Phemanderac's face. 'That's what I thought you said earlier on!' He nodded his head in satisfaction. 'The old fool Pyrinius was right! He's argued for years that "lowly vale" might be a proper name. You see,' he said to Leith, who didn't see, 'it makes sense if there is a place called Lowly. The Most High has not let me down yet!'

'You mean that you have come from the other side of the world to find Loulea?'

Phemanderac nodded.

'Why? There's nothing special in Loulea!'

'Nothing special? Listen to the saying: The *Hand of God is now concealed*. If the saying is true, that's exactly what I would expect you to say.'

'Wait a moment!' said Leith sceptically. 'Doesn't the saying go on to say something about "soon to be revealed"? If there had been something special in Loulea, that would have proved your argument as well. You couldn't lose!'

Phemanderac laughed. 'Spoken like a true philosopher!' he said. 'Now, tell me, how did your village acquire such a humble name? Why would villagers live in a town called Lowly?'

Now it was Leith's turn to laugh, his predicament all but forgotten in the enthusiasm shown by his companion. 'I'd never thought of it that way!' he exclaimed. 'Actually, the town's name comes from the wide valley it is set in, a sort of low lea, if you know what I mean. Nothing to do with humility at all. Indeed, we're quite proud of our village. Since Astora fell into the sea, Loulea is the last town on the Westway, and some say Falthwaite End, just out of the village, was the furthest north and west the First Men ever ventured.'

'The uttermost end of the earth,' Phemanderac murmured.

'Pardon?'

'Oh, just more doggerel. But I didn't realise that the *Sayings of Hauthius* contained anything about the Hand of God.'

'The sayings of who?' Leith asked.

'Whom. The sayings of whom,' Phemanderac corrected absently, as though he was a Haufuth correcting the village children. 'Now, let's complete the circle. What are you doing in the Death House of the Widuz?'

'The what?' said Leith in alarm. 'Death House? I thought once I got a chance to explain, they'd let me go!'

Phemanderac laughed, a pleasant sound. 'You'll not be given a chance to speak to anyone. The Widuz do not readily speak the tongues of outsiders. But don't worry, we've not been brought together here to add to the pile of bones at the bottom of Helig Holth. Tell me; what are you doing so far from home?'

Behind Phemanderac the sunlight began to creep into the darkness through a small, barred window at the far end of the stone-walled cell. Leith was by no means reassured by the words of this stranger, but he wanted to talk. Two weeks without being allowed to communicate had made him hungry for the sound of something other than the barked commands of guards. And this man Phemanderac was saying some very interesting things.

So he lay back under the sacking and told his cellmate everything that had happened since Midwinter's Night. Phemanderac's eyes grew wider as he heard about Mahnum and his escape from Andratan, how Leith's parents were taken captive by the Bhrudwans, and how the villagers mounted a rescue. He hung on every word as Leith described the final battle with the Bhrudwans on the Westway, and his own part in the outcome. (He tried not to embellish it too much.) Leith explained how he had been snatched away at the very moment of victory and brought to this place, not knowing why. The tale took an age to tell, with Leith often digressing to answer seemingly trivial questions by Phemanderac. ('How old is Kurr? Your older brother is a cripple, you say? Does your Haufuth intend to travel to Instruere?') Finally he finished, and the thin man shook his head in wonder.

'Well, it is obvious why you were taken captive by the Widuz,' he remarked.

'Why?'

'So we could meet, of course! Now, the question is, what do we do about it?' He began to wave his arms about in agitation.

'But the Widuz don't know who I am,' Leith replied, puzzled. 'How could they have arranged our meeting?'

Phemanderac dropped his hands in exasperation. 'You are a descendant of the First Men, that is obvious from your features,' he said. 'But clearly you have forgotten about the Most High. The Widuz just want to kill you, no doubt to appease one of their gods, on whose territory you trespassed. But the Most High has used them to bring us together. Don't you see?'

Leith shook his head. This man reminded him of the Hermit of Bandits' Cave, or perhaps Kroptur of Watch Hill. Full of portentous pronouncements that ultimately turned out to be meaningless. *But what about the Hermit's foretelling of his fall into the pool of icy water?* he remembered. *Is there really a Most High God moving people about like toys?* Leith hoped not; the idea faintly disturbed him. He wanted the freedom to walk his own paths.

'What do you know of the *Fuirfad?*' Phemanderac asked.

Leith shook his head. 'What is it?'

'Well, if you don't know, that answers my question. I was hoping that some knowledge of the Way of Fire would have been retained by those who lived in the country – the very village – of the Hand of God.'

'I'm sorry,' said Leith helplessly. 'I've never heard of this thing you mention, unless,' he added as an idea hit him, 'you mean something about the First Men.'

Phemanderac looked at him with renewed hope.

'Kurr, the farmer I told you about, he told us stories about the First Men. One was about a man who betrayed the First Men. Is that right? Do you know who I mean?'

'Kannwar, the Destroyer.'

'That's right,' said Leith, as he began to remember. 'There was something in the story about the Way of Fire – I can't remember what.'

'Well, at least that's something,' Phemanderac said, more to himself than to Leith. 'They remember the end of the First Men. But do they remember the glory, I wonder?'

Both lapsed into silence, a silence that lasted through the hottest part of the day. *This is as hot as midsummer in Loulea,* Leith thought. *How far south have we come?* He began to feel drowsy with the heat.

Phemanderac awoke with a start. How long had he been asleep? The late afternoon sun streaming through the barred window gave him his answer. He shook his head to clear it, but an unusual dull-ness remained.

Over on the other bench the youth from Firanes lay snoring, mouth wide open. *Poor Leith*, he thought. *The boy has really been knocked around. To what purpose is all this?* he wondered.

He ran a thick tongue over dry lips; the hot sun had dried him out. It was a long stretch from his bench, but he managed to grab the water jar their guards had replenished that morning. For a moment he hesitated; the water had a metallic smell. *Probably from sitting in the sun all day.* He raised the jar to his mouth and took a long draught. *That's better.*

Far from feeling cooler, Phemanderac continued to sweat. *What was the matter?* This climate was not as hot as that of his home. He had travelled across deserts to get here, searing sand and bleak rock ridges that would have killed lesser men. So why did he feel so hot? He licked his lips; they had the same metallic taste as the water. He glanced across at the water jug, then the truth exploded in his mind. He lifted his oh-so-heavy head, blinked his eyes and stared at Leith, who continued to sleep soundly, too soundly. His own head fell forward on to his chest, and he raised it again only with a great effort. Now the room began to swim before him, and he knew it was too late. He just had time to make a small silence within himself before the drug overwhelmed him, and his inert form fell back on to the bench.

The sound of boot on stone came along the corridor. Clack, clack, clack. A key rattled in the lock, then the huge door to the cell opened. Four shaven-headed Widuz came quickly into the room and hauled out the two motionless figures. With a hollow boom the door slammed shut, and the boots clacked their way down the corridor until they faded into silence.

Mahnum listened to the Fodhram planning their assault. He was not much of a swordsman and knew little of war tactics. In truth, he found himself near the limit of his strength and feared that he would get in the way of the warriors. The Warden would have to detail a couple of Fodhram to look after him, which meant his presence might actually weaken their fighting strength.

And what would their priority be? he asked himself. *They are frustrated and angry that they didn't catch the Widuz, and they will be out for revenge. Will they even recognise my sandy-haired son? Or might they think he is one of the Widuz?* His skin chilled as he realised that Leith's life might depend on him.

He glanced at the others, all preoccupied with checking their axes and swords. His decision made, he allowed himself to drift to the back of the small group, then waited until the path turned sharply to the right. Knowing that he would not be missed, the Trader slipped behind a tree. He would search for Leith on his own.

The man with the red mask walked slowly out on to the carven way, the grey cloak the only defence his purified body had against the cool evening breeze rising from the north. He nodded to the guards following him; it was time to begin.

This was the last day of feeding the Earth Mother. She would be satisfied with one more offering, and the snow would not come south to assault them again. Her anger against the northerners had died; she was full, satiated on Falthan blood.

Good. He didn't really enjoy this, though his grinning companions did. If only the Earth Mother would learn to love the taste of other meat, deer perhaps, then the dreadful fear might leave him and the pain around his chest might subside. The Priest of the Earth Mother detested this aspect of his vocation.

He tried not to look at the first sacrifice, but he did notice she was a Fodhram woman. He stepped behind her, then raised his arms.

'M'*Bilou!*' he cried. *For you, Mother!*

He pushed the woman gently and she lurched forward, then fell, spiralling lazily down into the shadow of the yawning abyss.

Another Fodhram was next, a small boy. *Smaller than my own lad*, the priest reflected. *Still, these Fodhram killed our children and took our land. Remember that!*

413

'M'*Bilou!*' His cry echoed harshly around the natural amphitheatre, and he gave the boy a rough shove. Deeply drugged and oblivious to his fate, the young Fodhram fell forward off the carven way and into Helig Holth.

The next sacrifice was a sandy-haired, pale-skinned youth. Certainly no Fodhram, the priest noted with surprise. *How has he been caught up with the others?* He looked further on; the next prisoner was a foreigner also. *Why were these men being sacrificed with the Fodhram?* The priest watched for a moment as both prisoners stood silently, swaying slightly, eyes glazed open, blissful smiles on their faces. *Go to your deaths in peace,* he thought. *Not like me!* In a trance once, he had foreseen the time of his own death, evil faces leaning over him as he fought for breath, rough hands pushing and pulling at him, dragging him down into the dark, wet abyss of death. The terror of it froze him for a moment, tightening his chest unbearably. Sometimes he saw those faces with his waking eyes.

He moved behind the next sacrifice. Obviously a Falthan, though not a Fodhram. *Falthans must die. Mother, this one is for you!* He raised his arms.

'M'*Bilou!*'

Keeping under the forest eaves, Mahnum took a moment to assess his position. He was now alone in a land he had only a vague remembrance of, and that only south of the Sagon. But he had burdened the Fodhram long enough; he only hoped they would not waste precious time looking for him.

Memories of an old trading journey came back to him. What was the name of the fortress near here? Adunlok. How could he have forgotten it? A huge maze of tunnels through a limestone bastion, with vast caverns below, all centred around a vast sink-hole that made Greenwoods Hole back home look tiny by comparison. He had posed as a southern official come to inspect Helig Holth, the Great Mouth of the Earth Mother. Standing on the lip of the chasm had been an awe-inspiring experience. They said that sometimes human sacrifices were hurled over the precipice . . .

The realisation of exactly what was in store for the captives hit him between the eyes. *The Widuz intend to feed their captives to the Earth Mother*. Mahnum knew he had to make all speed, but he felt so very tired. Gritting his teeth and ignoring the pain, he sprinted along a narrow path.

A few minutes later he heard voices, and pulled back into the forest. Two Widuz came crashing along the path, swords drawn. Mahnum waited until they were well past, then unsheathed his own steel and stole further down the dusky valley. The hilltops on either side glowed orange with the dying sun. Up ahead, Mahnum could make out the windowed wall of Adunlok, but Helig Holth itself was in shadow. *This is a place I had hoped never to see again*, he thought grimly.

A shout came to his ears. *Was that the priest?* Mahnum wondered. *Have the sacrifices already begun?* He increased his pace, knowing that he could be seen from the fortress, should any Widuz be watching. *Where are the Fodhram? Am I doing the right thing?* He thought of what he had seen all those years ago, and imagined Leith standing on the edge of Helig Holth. *I can do nothing else*.

The Warden of Withwestwa Wood had issued his instructions, his men were in position, waiting for his signal, and there was nothing else he could do. If only it were not the end of the day; if only his men were not so tired, facing a fresh enemy from the fortress ahead of them; if only they had caught the Widuz before now; if only . . .

There would be time for regrets later. If there was a later. Realistically, their chances were slim. The Widuz had arrived here at least a day earlier, and their captives might already have been sacrificed. The prudent thing would have been to pull back, putting both rescue and revenge out of their minds, and go home. But the time for prudence had long passed.

'M'*Bilou!*' came a loud cry, magnified beyond belief by the enclosed canyon, and immediately Axehaft jumped into action, leaping to the top of an adjacent knoll. He waved his hand to signal as previously agreed. Down the slope the Fodhram raced as one, axes, staves and swords at the ready, funnelling towards the shadowy scene ahead.

'*M'Bilou!*'

The cry echoed around the circular bowl of Adunlok. Down came the arms of the priest, and for a moment his hands rested on the back of the fair-haired youth, who stood unknowingly a foot from the darkness.

Out of the corner of his eye, the priest saw a sudden blur of movement to his right. Then something slammed into his chest, knocking him sideways on to the carven way.

'What—?' the priest had cried as he had been knocked to the ground. He struggled to his feet. *One of the captives! Had he not been drugged?*

For a moment all was confusion behind Leith, who stood dreamily on the very edge of destruction. The two guards rushed towards the scene, but were too far away.

'Guards!' bellowed the masked man, then the wind was knocked out of him again. He fought the captive with all his strength, realising that he was fighting for his life, and managed with a great effort to push him away.

The man facing him was thin and wiry, with wide eyes and a grim face – no sign of stupor about him. *This is the second foreigner*, thought the priest. For some reason his mind filled with the technicalities of administering the drug, something he prided himself on above all else. *The drug may not work with foreigners. But he was unconscious half an hour ago – I checked him myself!*

Then the foreigner rushed at him again, feinted to the right and thrust out a foot, tripping the priest. He fell to the ground, his momentum carrying him to the very edge of Helig Holth. Pure terror rose within him and his chest tightened unbearably, his heart seemingly exploding within. A foot came down on his head. He scrabbled for a hold, but his hands found nothing but air. He looked up and saw the round outline of Helig Holth, now above him and receding as he fell.

Not without the drug! his mind shouted. Then the evil faces came for him as the air roared past, their rough hands pushing and pulling at him, dragging him down into the dark, wet abyss. *For you, Mother!* His last cry was swallowed up in death.

Phemanderac wasted no time watching the priest fall to his doom, but rose to meet the two guards. Powerful hands groped for him, but he danced away from them along the carven way, grabbing Leith and pulling him after. The Firanese youth collapsed on the ground, made dizzy by the sudden movement, leaving Phemanderac to face the guards.

The narrowness of the carven way prevented both men coming for him at once. The bigger of the two men lunged forward, sword in his left hand, confident in his ability to dispose of this foreigner. He chopped at the thin, naked frame, but it moved sideways with remarkable agility. Again he thrust forward; again his sword bit nothing but air. Now the guard began to work himself into a rage.

The second guard watched for a moment, then turned and set off at a dead run, meaning to go right around Helig Holth on the carven way and come up behind their prey.

The burly guard grasped the broadsword in both hands and swung powerfully, but somehow each time the gaunt figure managed to avoid it. The guard moved further forward, meaning to force Phemanderac over the edge into the abyss. At that moment Leith, who had lain prone on the ground, head thick with the semi-consciousness of the drug, tried to get to his feet and succeeded only in taking the legs out from under the unwitting guard, who fell on top of him. The force of the impact knocked Leith senseless. The guard grabbed at the earth to keep from falling, but succeeded only in grasping hold of one of Leith's legs. In a moment they were both sliding towards the darkness, up from which came a wet, earthy smell.

Phemanderac snatched at one of the disappearing limbs, anything to prevent Leith from falling over the edge. For a moment he had an arm, but his grip loosened and the arm slipped away. With all his strength, he held on to the wrist. Now both figures hung part-way over the edge of the precipice, the weight of Leith and the huge guard slowly dragging Phemanderac closer to the hungry blackness. *You have to let go*, cried his mind, *or all three of you will die!*

Hold on! came a voice from somewhere deeper within. *Hold on!* For an instant, all three bodies teetered on the very edge, then Phemanderac sprang back on to the carven way as though he had been pushed. At first he thought he had let go of the others, then found he was still holding Leith, who hung over the brink. Quickly, he hauled the youth to the safety of the carven way. Leith's skin was torn where he had been held by the ankle, but there was no sign of the guard.

Phemanderac took Leith by the elbow and thrust him along the narrow path. The wide platform and the path that led away from Helig Holth were only twenty yards in front of them, but the journey seemed to take forever, with Phemanderac aware of the second guard rapidly approaching them from behind. As they finally made it to the platform, the clanging of many bells rang out from the walls and windows of Adunlok high above them.

CHAPTER 20

THE ACOLYTE

THE LOW CLOUDS LIFTED and grey skies parted as the remnants of the Company set out on the last stage of their journey to Instruere. Steffl brooded quietly as they sought a passage across the unbridged river, the scene of their battle with the Bhrudwans. A thin column of steam came from her ochre-coloured crown; otherwise there was no sign of the destructive violence she could bring to bear on the Westway – and the Fodhram inhabitants for leagues around – whenever she chose.

During their first morning on the road back towards Instruere, Kurr cast a sharp eye over his charges. Something bothered him, something about the group that he could not put a name to, though he thought long and hard about it. At the front of the Company walked Farr and Perdu, looking oddly similar with their bandaged right forearms and hands. Both held swords in their left hands, blades levelled at the back of the bound figure they had risked so much to capture. Silently, the old farmer acknowledged the bravery of these two grim-faced men, chance acquaintances found along their road.

Behind them, Indrett and Parlevaag battled their way along the narrow path. Kurr was keenly aware of how much their captivity had cost them. The woman from Loulea was hardly recognisable as the one he had seen beaming proudly on the night of the Midwinter Play. The flesh had melted away from her face, and those proud southern cheekbones now stood out from dreadfully gaunt features. The left side of her jaw had a yellow cast, as though bruised. Various pale marks spoke of further wounds still healing. But her eyes carried the most pain: black-rimmed and hollow, brimming with loss.

Beside her the Fenni woman appeared less ill-used, but she too had suffered cruelly. Though it did not show, Kurr could sense how she felt – or rather how she did not feel. That great gap, that unfillable void, left within when that which is closest to the heart is taken away, was something the old farmer did not care to dwell on.

Stella walked by herself. She had said little since the death of Wira, and her eyes were dark wells of misery in her face. Her feelings about the battle on the slopes of Steffl were locked up inside her with bonds drawn so tight that she gave Kurr the impression she could barely breathe.

Bringing up the rear came Hal, hobbling crab-like to compensate for his crippled right side, giving no ground to his able-bodied companions. The boy seemed the least affected of all the Company by what had happened. *Well, perhaps he is a little more sorrowful these days, but he ever was a serious lad.* As always he kept his own counsel, speaking seldom.

Ah, that was it. The silence that had descended on the Company – the remnants of the Company, Kurr reminded himself – was beginning to affect him. The incessant chatter of the Haufuth, Leith's questions, Wira's gentle wit and ready laughter; all were missed on their present road.

The days that followed were warm and close and a bleary heat haze, uncharacteristic of early spring, hung over Withwestwa Wood. Kurr strode ahead of the group, his keen farmer's eyes alert for any trouble, though none was expected. Many Fodhram lived between Steffl and Vindstrop House, but these peaceable people were unlikely to bother them, especially given that Leader (who had turned out to be a sort of local king, Kurr was given to understand) had supplied them with a letter of safe passage through Fodhram lands.

Eventually the Company straggled into Vindstrop House, thoroughly exhausted and bone-weary. Here they planned to pause only long enough to replenish their supplies at the Trading Post, to acquire food and summer clothing granted them from the generosity of Leader. It was partial payment, the Warden had told them, from a higher-than-expected return for the first furs of the season, and they were grateful for it.

On the morning after their arrival in the small trading settlement, Kurr, Perdu and Farr sat together sharing a thoughtful breakfast. Outside, the weather had taken a turn for the worse, as brisk winds sent rain tumbling in from the far north. It served to remind the travellers that the season of changeable weather was upon them, as hail and sleet swept across the wooden buildings huddled together against the elbow of the Mossbank River. Not a day to be travelling.

'It's not snowing, but it might as well be,' said Perdu dolefully. 'I'm surprised you coastlanders can tolerate it.'

Kurr raised his eyebrows but did not reply, choosing instead to take another sip of hot broth.

'It gets very cold in the Vinkullen Hills,' Farr replied tersely. 'Or had you forgotten, after all this time?'

The adopted Fenni sighed. 'I have forgotten a lot of things, common sense not least among them. I ought now to be on my way home to the *vidda* to see my family and my clan chief. But here I sit, in violation of my duty to the Fenni, preparing to head out into the sleet towards a city whose name I have forgotten about for many years. I am a fool.'

'Perhaps we're all fools,' the old farmer responded. 'Perhaps if we make it through the petty villages of Treika, and manage to sneak past the infamous Robbers of the Ramparts, and pick our way through the politics of Deuverre, we might make it to Instruere with our tale. But who will believe us?'

'Our pet Bhrudwan will persuade them.' Farr did not like this uncertain talk regarding their quest.

'I know about the Iron Door of the Outer Chamber,' said Kurr. 'We'll need more than a Bhrudwan to get past that. We'll need money or influence, or both, and lots of it.' He frowned as outside the hail beat even harder on the shuttered windows.

'Are you saying that we have to *pay* to deliver a warning to the Falthan council? How can this be?' Farr was incredulous.

'They won't know we have a warning for them, you see. To them we will be but one more in the long line of petitioners claiming this piece of land or part of that inheritance. Politics is the art of patience in Instruere, they say.'

'Why didn't you tell us this before?' demanded Farr, some of the old fire in his voice. 'If you are correct, what hope do we have?'

'I have contacts in the city, people who may be able to help us gain an audience with the council much more quickly than otherwise would be the case.'

'Contacts?' Perdu said, puzzled. 'Forgive me, but what contact could a farmer from the uttermost end of Faltha have with the Great City?'

For a while Kurr sat and explained about the Watchers, voicing his hope that the organisation was still strong and with influence in Instruere – but keeping his doubts and fears to himself – while outside the hail gave way to a cold rain.

They were interrupted by the two women, Indrett and Parlevaag. The woman from Loulea was noticeably pale, and Parlevaag seemed to be supporting her. They sat down heavily at the table.

'Indrett!' exclaimed Kurr. 'You look unwell! What's the matter?'

'I am unwell,' she croaked. 'Caught some sort of chill.'

'That settles it,' the farmer announced. 'We go no further until the weather clears and Indrett is feeling better. We've all been through a great deal – Indrett more than anyone – and we must take time to recover. No sense in rushing, anyway. It would be foolish to exhaust ourselves getting to Instruere and be in no state to press our request for an audience.'

'I want to wait for a few days,' Indrett said, the effort of talking stretching lines of pain across her hollow face. 'Perhaps we will hear news of Mahnum and Leith.'

Perhaps, thought Kurr. *But probably not. It was bravely but foolishly done, plunging into the heart of Widuz in pursuit of a boy who is likely to be dead. And now we struggle on without his Trader experience.* The farmer counted in his head: *Mahnum, Leith, Wira, the Haufuth. How many more will we lose?*

As Indrett sat glassy-eyed at the table, breathing thickly, Kurr reflected on the last few months. He remembered the *Iskelwen* of last autumn, and the night he had stayed with Mahnum's family as the vicious storm battered the house. How different those eyes across the table looked now – but, then again, his own were doubt-less not unchanged. For her sake, they should remain here in Vindstrop House for many weeks, resting and recovering until she was fit enough to attempt the rest of the journey, a journey fully as far as they had already travelled.

But the Company could not wait. Already it had been a year or more since Mahnum had escaped from Andratan, and who among them knew how much longer they had to mobilise the armies of the Falthan kingdoms? Did Bhrudwo stand astride The Gap already, threatening Faltha with utter annihilation? Or – and this was his deepest fear – had Mahnum merely been deluded, and were they risking everything to travel across the world for no good reason?

Three days. That was as long as Kurr was prepared to wait. If Indrett was not ready to travel by then, she would remain behind in the care of the Fodhram, and the remainder of the Company would press on. The decision made, the old farmer relaxed and finished his broth.

After a short debate over what to do with their captive, the Company agreed to Kurr's suggestion. A special arrangement was made with the proprietor of the Trading Post, and an armed Fodhram guard kept constant watch on the imprisoned Bhrudwan. The proprietor had been told that the fierce-looking captive was a Firanese criminal about whom the travellers sought judgement from the Council of Faltha. While he did not look convinced by this tale, he took their money eagerly enough.

The men spent the next three days exploring the town, while

423

the three women stayed indoors. A light northerly drizzle continued to fall, robbed of its wintry bite by miles of travel over the warmth of the forest, but incessant enough to keep all but the hardiest of Fodhram off the churned-up streets. Farr, Perdu, Kurr and Hal kept their cloaks over their heads as they went from storefront to storefront, admiring the wide range of goods available at this outpost, merchandise from the homely to the exotic.

A small grove of jack pines stood at the south end of town, beside which many of the old men spent their time watching the incoming and outgoing trade, reminiscing about the time when they ran the trapping trails or took on the forest unarmed save for a two-bladed axe. Many of the men, wizened and toothless, had tumplines attached to their waists and wore clothes suited to long overland journeys, as though they expected to be called off on a run, or were competing with each other to see who could be the most outrageous caricature of a Fodhram fur trader. Here the four men of the Company whiled away their afternoons, listening to the conversations and relaxing under the shelter of the trees. An assortment of wagons came past, most containing produce from outlying farms. The wagon drivers engaged the old men in good-natured banter, of which the Firanese understood little as it was conducted in the language of the Fodhram. But the laughter they understood, as they had sampled the humour of the Fodhram on the Southern Run.

On the afternoon of the third day, a brace of canoes pulled in to shore some distance to the left of the road, and six weary-looking Fodhram heaved their fur bales on to dry land. They sauntered over to where the old men stood, obviously pleased with themselves.

'These men think they are the first of the season to bring furs to Vindstrop House,' Farr whispered to Kurr. 'I'll place a small wager on it.' The old farmer raised his eyebrows and nodded in reply.

After a few moments' conversation the fur traders shook their heads in disbelief, and looked over towards the men of the Company when directed by hordes of gleefully pointing old men.

Clearly, they had not expected to be beaten for first furs of the season, and were not pleased. One of their number, a rangy young man with unkempt hair, came over to where the four men stood.

'I hear tell you people made the Southern Run early this spring,' he said in the common tongue, making it sound more like an accusation than a statement.

Kurr nodded in reply.

'Came across with the Warden, from what I hear.'

Kurr nodded again.

'So what's your business in the land of the Fodhram?' The question came out in a slow, lazy drawl, but carried an implicit threat.

'We have no business here,' Kurr replied amiably. 'We travelled the Westway from Firanes, seeking a path to Instruere. Our meeting with your Warden and his friends was mutually convenient, and we helped him bring his furs to Vindstrop House in exchange for free passage through his lands.' The meaning was clear: free passage had been obtained, and was not to be interfered with.

The young man was not so easily put off. 'Helped him?' he said loudly, with mock incredulity. 'Helped him? Fare-paying passengers, more like. Dead weight.'

Farr stepped forward angrily, but was restrained by Kurr's outstretched arm. 'Take it quietly,' he hissed through clenched teeth. 'He's trying to upset us.'

'He's doing a good job,' Farr hissed back.

'So how'd you get here so soon in the season?' continued their questioner, spurred on by the accumulating knots of old men looking for excitement on a dull afternoon. 'Did you tunnel through the snow, or fly over it? We were held up a week by the big white up north.'

'We ran Mossbank Cadence,' Farr snapped, before Kurr could stop him. 'Not bad for fare-paying passengers, don't you think?'

The wiry youth took a step backwards in surprise. 'Did the Warden claim Mossbank Cadence?' he asked the group of old men.

They nodded in reply.

A low whistle came from the youth; then he turned on his heel and went to help his companions unload their canoes.

One of the old men spoke up.

'Sorry about the youngster. His father was lost in Mossbank Cadence last year. Hasn't been the same since.'

Another old-timer spoke up, fingering his tumpline all the while.

'But the young'un made some fair points. What's a group of westerners doing on the Southern Run? More to the point, what was their business out near Steffl a few days ago? I hear they were out there about the time of the Widuz raid. Came back with different people than they went out with. Speak up, now. Who was the man in the grey cloak, the one you held as prisoner? Are you spies of the Widuz come to prepare for the big invasion?'

He looked at the four men with shrewd eyes, seeing that his questions had hit their mark.

'Let's get out of here,' Farr said quietly.

'No, we must clear this up,' Kurr responded. He took a deep breath. How much of the truth was it safe to tell?

'We came down the Westway into Withwestwa Wood to pursue ruffians from far away who had captured three of our friends. On the borders of Firanes, near Fort Brumal, we met up with the Warden and his three companions, who offered us passage to Vindstrop House as a shorter route than the Westway in the thaw. From there we went back to Steffl, where we ambushed the ruffians, reclaiming our friends. One of our number was killed, another was taken by the Widuz and a third went with the Warden in pursuit of them. The rest of us returned to Vindstrop House, where we recover from our ordeal with the help of generous Fodhram hospitality.'

The old farmer spread his arms wide. 'The Warden travelled with us for weeks. He was satisfied that we are what we claim to be. You might want to ask him about us when he returns.'

'Well answered!' came the reply. 'Yes, our hospitality is generous, certainly better than the weather we provide. It's a shame you did not visit in the autumn. The forest is at its best then. Such colours!'

And so the conversation drifted into a series of pleasantries, as everyone tried to avoid the tension that had been kindled.

As evening drew near and the four men made to leave, the old man with the shrewd eyes came over to them. 'You did well in a hard place,' he said. 'Though you did not lie, it was obvious you did not tell all the truth. I can see that there is some great tale behind all this, one which I would love to hear around a camp-fire under the open stars.' He laughed. 'But it is easy to see that the tale is not finished yet. I hear that you plan to go on south to Stanlow and beyond. Were you merely rescuing your friends, you would return to the west from where you came. I hope one day to hear the full story.'

Kurr did not know what to say.

The shrewd old man laughed softly. '*Fuir af Himinn!*' he said. 'Go with the blessing of the Most High!' And before they could respond, he sauntered off back to his friends.

'Well, what do you make of that?' Farr exclaimed, scratching his head as he watched the old man talking to his fellows.

'I have no idea,' Kurr replied, disquieted. 'Perhaps it is a good thing we leave tomorrow.'

It was still raining, but the rain was warm and came from the south, filtering across their path as the Company followed the right bank of the Mossbank, now a wider, more sluggish river, stained brown with leaf-tannin. Its course ran southeast from Vindstrop House down to Stanlow, a journey that would normally take two weeks, but on which Kurr judged they should spend an extra week recuperating from the rigours of the Bhrudwan pursuit.

Their captive remained silent, walking quietly among them, bloodstained grey robe and cowl masking the threat of his strength and bitter anger. His obvious ignorance of the common tongue enabled the others to talk freely, with no fear of betraying their purpose. The wrists of the Bhrudwan were bound together behind his back, and shackles had been placed around his ankles. A constant vigilance was maintained, and no concessions were made to him. Either Farr or Perdu, his two minders, would feed him and assist him to relieve himself. Otherwise, no acknowledgement was made of his existence.

The Acolyte, Mahnum had called him. Indrett mulled over this. It made him sound somehow less dangerous than the other Bhrudwans. But smaller doses of poison could still be fatal. Whether this man had yet hardened into the pitiless killer his leader had been was not the issue. He could kill with his bare hands, and he would, given the slightest opportunity. Those hands, now hidden behind his back, had helped beat her, reducing her face to a swollen, bruised coagulum. She had seen the evil in his eyes as he struck her with his fists. The day the Bhrudwans had cut down the lone rider in the Torrelstrommen valley he had been there, wielding his sword to sickening effect. She had no illusions about the hatred and anger that coursed through his veins, and the plotting and planning of escape that ran through his mind. The Company would need to keep a close watch on this beast. Travelling the Westway with the Acolyte felt like pulling a snow leopard along by its tail.

As they walked day after day through the never-ending forest, they were able to observe the woods come to life. Winter had passed, and the period of hibernation, of enforced starvation, was over. In meadows beside the Westway deer played or nursed their young, while the tracks of small animals criss-crossed the muddy path. Occasionally they caught a glimpse of the larger beasts, but never saw one clearly enough to agree on whether it was a bear, a moose or a bison.

The rain-soaked air was laden with the scent of growing things, and the musty, somewhat acrid smell of decaying timber. Ferns unfolded their delicate green fronds at the fringes of the path, interspersed with starbursts of gold, the marsh marigold. Juneberry had begun to bloom, its tiny, delicate flowers a sure sign of warmer weather. Dogwood and juniper gladly soaked up the abundance of moisture. This far south the forest itself was made up in large part of pine and spruce, with birch and white cedar competing with aspen and alder for air space between the forest giants. The smell of a grove of white cedar was unmistakable, and the Company paused more than once to crush a green frond and savour the refreshingly pungent aroma.

Around them the hauntingly bittersweet song of the whitethroat competed with the incessant drumming of grouse and the strident calls of waterfowl, now far away, now close at hand. Above them came flock after flock of birds returning to Withwestwa from their winter homes: the common ducks flying together serenely, with only the whirring of wings signalling their passage north; great V-shaped flocks of geese, honking and raising a racket; whistling swans spearing low over the swamps and copses of the Fenbeck plain; ravens rabble-rousing in the tree tops, arguing with each other with croaks that grated on the ear; and, just once, the huge and ungainly crane, mansized, ghost-coloured, with an eerie trumpet call that cut across all other sounds in the forest, even the sound of running water.

With all this rain, water was the dominant sound of the forest. It dripped off trees, off hair, off noses, cheeks and cloaks; chattered against rocks, seeking out every crevice; gathered in depressions that soon became pools; spilled and flowed into rivulets, streams and every channel, seeking the lowest place, ever falling, falling, eventually finding its way into the Mossbank River. The Westway became a small river itself – or, more correctly, a series of small rivers flowing downhill to ponds that forced the travellers to seek some dry alternative path.

Not surprisingly, they met few people. Though they were now in an area that was at least sparsely populated, those who lived in the southern margins of the great forest had the good sense to postpone all but the shortest journeys when the moisture-laden south wind blew.

Rather than turning to the north as it usually did, the wind remained in the southerly quarter day after day, sending rain sheeting down on the travellers with little or no respite. One afternoon, still at least a week northwest of Stanlow, the Company found a dry place under the shelter of the base of a huge, uprooted tree, lit a fire and tried to dry out.

'We might have been wiser to have bought a canoe and travelled the Mossbank down to Stanlow,' Kurr mused. 'We certainly would have made better time.'

'I'll not be going on one of those things again!' said Perdu. 'I still have nightmares about the Mossbank Cadence.'

'There are no rapids below Vindstrop House, according to the Fodhram.'

'Even if the water was completely calm, I would have chosen land over water,' Perdu said, only half-joking.

Farr leaned over. 'With the way the weather is, it seems as though you have no choice. There is as much water on this road as there is in the river!'

Kurr laughed. 'We could do with a canoe or two, couldn't we?'

'What we could do with is a couple of days of sun,' Farr insisted. 'I keep imagining the Vinkullen Hills in the springtime. Not a patch on Withwestwa Wood, but at least it's sunny.'

The Company huddled around the fire, waiting for its tentacles of heat to search them out. As the air about them warmed, they were able to remove their sopping cloaks. Meanwhile, Indrett and Hal prepared a hot soup.

'Can you remember what land looks like without trees?' Indrett was getting to know these people, her rescuers, and had begun to recover her effervescence.

Perdu turned to her. 'We've been in this wood for weeks now, but I still remember the *vidda*. These trees are but passing shadows; the snow lives forever.'

'But the snow melts in the spring, while the trees grow taller,' Indrett replied. 'The forest is therefore more permanent than the snow.'

'Wishful thinking,' the Fenni responded. 'Snow is the master of the north. We tell a story in the tents about the snow and the forest.'

'Well, let's hear it,' Kurr growled. 'I'm certain you have engineered this discussion to regale us with another Fenni morality tale.'

'Actually, it is much better told by an expert storyteller.' He tapped Parlevaag on the shoulder, then spoke quietly to the shy, solemn woman. She shook her head, but he persisted. Indrett smiled encouragingly at her. *Anything to bring her out of herself*, she thought.

'The great god Qali ruled the world,' she said, with Perdu interpreting, 'keeping it in subjection under snow and ice. His breath lay on the land and the inhabitants could not escape his dominion, nor had they any hope of ending it.

'One severe winter a meeting took place near Styggesbreen, the great ice tongue in the Grossbergen of the Jawbone Mountains. Many were there: representatives from the birds, the animals and the insects joined with rivers and lakes, mountains and hills to discuss doing away with their god.

'"He wants the whole world for himself," complained the brown bear. "He cares not whether we live or die."

'"Perhaps he does care," said the deer, moving back nervously under the hungry eye of the bear. "If we were all destroyed, he would have nothing to make sport of, and no one to pay him homage."

'"Even if we could shorten the length of our winter prison," burbled one of the streams, "then life for us might be more tolerable."

'And so the talk went on, each member laying out his or her complaint, but no one had a solution to the problem of the great god Qali.

'Just then, a human came rushing up to the meeting ground. "Why are you holding a meeting without inviting me?" he said.

'"We're sorry," came the reply. "We didn't know there were any humans still living in the domain of Qali."

'"Nor are there, though once there were. We have been forced southwards by successive winters. Our numbers have dwindled, until now we are forced to eke out our lives on the margin of land and sea."

'One of the birds – some say it was a pigeon, others a mallard – turned and spoke quietly to her neighbour. "Therefore the harsh winters have had one benefit! When Qali's power was not so great, humans hunted us by lake and stream. Now they leave us alone. Perhaps the winters of Qali can be endured!"

'Similar murmurs spread out across the meeting. "Perhaps Qali sends these hard winters for our protection!" said one. "If I have to choose between Qali and humans, I choose Qali," said another. "They dam us and drain us," said a third. "They tunnel us and level us," growled a fourth. "They hunt us and kill us," still another said, "and then they discard our bodies without making use of them. Death to the humans!"

'"Death to the humans!" rang out the cry.

'Seeing how the land lay, the representative of the humans tried to escape, but rough hands held him fast. Eyes filled with terror, he struggled against his captors.

'"Hunt him! Trap him! Tunnel him! Drain him!" cried the frenzied crowd. Qali was completely forgotten as the crowd descended on the unfortunate human and tore him limb from limb, scattering his bones across the valley.

'"Very good, very good!" came a deep voice from behind them, cutting across their celebrations. The inhabitants turned to see where the voice came from.

'It was Styggesbreen himself, the vast glacier of the Grossbergen, who had crept quietly down the valley to listen and to observe the meeting of those plotting against Qali, his master. "Very good, very good!" he repeated, his deep voice rumbling across the open space, loosening a few rocks and sending some of the more nervous animals skittering away. "Qali will be pleased to hear about this demonstration of loyalty. His hatred of humans exceeds even yours! Perhaps he might relent a little when he is told about the love his subjects have for him!"

'The members of the meeting were encouraged by this news, and went their separate ways filled with hope. Styggesbreen watched them go, satisfied with his work. He knew that Qali would never relent, and Styggesbreen himself, who fed on snow and ice, wanted his god to make the winters even harsher.

'That night Qali came to talk with his trusted servant, and Styggesbreen told him what had transpired. The wrath of Qali was kindled when he heard about the purpose of the meeting, and was not assuaged by news of its outcome. The two conspirators talked together far into the night, their cold breath mixing and sending a dense fog rolling down to the wide coastal plain.

'The humans awaited in vain the return of their ambassador. "What has happened?" they asked themselves. Finally they decided to send a spy to learn of his fate.

'Up through the thick fog he went, unobserved by the inhabitants of the land. Finally he arrived at the Valley of Meeting, but he could find no sign of his friend. As he was about to leave, a deep, cold voice spoke, saying: "Do you search for the human who attended the meeting here? Then search no longer; he is dead. See, here are his bones."

'The man knelt down by the bones of his friend and wept. "Who did this thing?" he asked the great ice tongue.

'"It was the inhabitants of the land," came the reply. "Their hatred of humans knows no bounds, and they seek to rid even the southern lands of your kind. Why, I heard them plotting an attack on you. They want to drive you into the sea." Styggesbreen smiled as he watched his lies take effect.

'The man thanked the glacier for the information, then scurried back to the others under cover of darkness. That night Styggesbreen reported to Qali on the success of their ruse. "With any luck the humans will do battle with the inhabitants of the land, and we will be rid of both," the ice tongue said. Qali laughed in reply.

'Indeed, the very next day, a vast army came up from the south. Rank upon rank, they marched across the treeless plains, seeking those who would plot their destruction. News of the army reached the inhabitants of the land, who sent forth spies. "They stretch from east to west, from the mountains to the sea," the spies reported. "No one can stand against them."

'The inhabitants of the land fled in fear, crying out to their god as they ran. Qali was driven to rage as he realised his plan had failed, and the land was about to be occupied by humans.

'So the great snow god summoned the north wind, laced him

with shards from the vast ice plateau of the north, and sent him south with specific instructions. And so it was that the north wind came cruelly against the vast army, and they met in the midst of the treeless plains. The men of the south resisted valiantly, but they were no match for the merciless north wind, and were frozen solid where they stood.

'Then the great god Qali appeared amongst his subjects and cried: "Behold the forest of the north!" and his laughter echoed around the valleys and hills for a day and a half, until the inhabitants of the land had to stop their ears for fear of being deafened. When the laughter had ceased they looked upon the vast army, and behold! there was indeed a huge forest where once had lain open land, each human having sprouted roots and branches. Then the inhabitants of the land rejoiced, for it seemed to them their enemy had been destroyed.

'But the power of their god, though great, was limited, and he had not succeeded in entrapping all of the human army. Many of the southernmost ranks escaped the freezing blast of the north wind, and returned to the south with their sorrowful news. A new determination was made to conquer the lands of the north, in spite of the hardships. "After all, our brothers offer us shelter from the blasts of Qali, and wood for home and hearth." So it was agreed that the next invasion would be stealthier, so as not to stir up the full wrath of the northern god.

'The inhabitants of the land explored the new forest. They found that the trees offered them shelter, and they began to multiply under the protection of the frozen army. When he heard about this, Qali was enraged beyond measure and sent his fiercest wintry blast against the forest. But the forest protected its new inhabitants, animal and human alike, and Qali could not touch them. Moreover, the warm forest breath began to loosen Qali's grip on the land. The north wind retreated, the vast ice plateau began to melt at the edges, and a great thaw set in.

'Qali raged up and down his domain looking for weapons to hurl against the new forest, but his hand found none. Then, his rage tempered with fear at the power of the humans, he retreated to his fastness at Myrvidda, which even humans had not yet succeeded in penetrating. As he retreated, the great snow god withdrew his power from the Grossbergen, seeking to punish Styggesbreen for his part in the failed plan. From that day on, the great ice tongue has been melting, shrinking up the valley towards its source in the mountains.'

That evening the Company gave voice to a number of campfire songs, and Perdu and Parlevaag essayed a few Fenni dances around the blazing fire. When the hilarity had died down along with the flames, the members of the Company settled down to a good night's sleep, the nagging fear that had been their portion since the beginning of their adventure eased a little by the story Parlevaag had told them.

The low cloud cleared and the stars came out, chased across the sky by a waxing moon. The others were all asleep, but that particular avenue of escape into forgetfulness continued to elude Indrett, so she rose and, wrapping her now-dry cloak around her, went for a walk to clear her head of ominous thoughts.

The others mourn over loved ones lost or separated, and their grief will surely pass, she thought bitterly. *But my grief is just beginning. Leith is lost, taken by a nameless enemy, and my husband is gone in pursuit of him. I wish he had stayed with me! Or that he had taken me with him! Now I have lost two of the three keepers of my heart. Oh, why, why, why do such things happen? Where have the happy times gone?* And she sat down on a rock some distance from the fallen tree and the fire, and shed bitter tears for the loss in her life.

When Indrett came to herself again, she noticed a deep red glow all about her. Standing, she saw in the northern sky her familiar friend the *Kleitaf Northr*, the Northern Lights, spread across the horizon, a shimmering, pulsating curtain of light.

'Are you my answer?' she asked the lights aloud. There came no reply, of course, but the glow deepened further and suffused the landscape with a cheering light. 'Thank you for coming to comfort me,' she said, as the lights reached their zenith and then began to fade. 'Thank you. You've never let me down.'

She thought of the time in her own childhood when her mother had died and left her in the care of her father. On many nights during that dark and wretched period of her life she had climbed up to the roof, partly to escape his attentions, partly to watch her friend the Northern Lights dance for her and warm her frightened little heart. Then her father had sent her to the Court of the Firanese King and she had not seen the lights for a long time, while her own star had risen in the Court. A thing of beauty she was then, radiating a light of her own, a brilliant but cold light that no man could be warmed by. Until a northern Trader had happened by and warmed her with his own gentle light, given freely and without fear. She had gone with him to the obscurity of a northern village, escaping the memories of her childhood in Rammr, and drawing closer to her friend the Northern Lights.

But in those years of happiness she ceased to look for the lights, content instead to gain all her light from her husband and latterly her children. For a long while this contented her, but after many years had passed she found herself looking to the mountainous northern and eastern horizons, as though expecting something. A great longing had reawakened within her and she had realised that no matter how excellent a husband she had found, he did not satisfy all her needs. For a while, she had buried her dissatisfaction under the cares of life and the demands of the moment, but her heart would not be deceived. And eventually Mahnum had noticed her discontent.

They had discussed it one day, but she had not found words sufficient to convey her need, and she was not yet able to tell him of those bleak years of her childhood. So he had been unable to help her, returning instead to the demands of his own calling. And then had come the fateful day when he was called away on the King's business, taking the light with him.

As she watched the last of *Kleitaf Northr* fade away, Indrett realised that it was not Mahnum she wanted, not really. Yes, she loved him with a comfortable familiarity, but that was not the reason she had fallen for him all those years ago. With a sick feeling that seemed to root itself within her, she admitted the truth to herself. She had seen Mahnum as a way of escape. A way to put behind her the gossip and the pity and the memory of that face and the powerlessness and the nights that would never end.

Her life had been defined by what had been done to her, she knew that. From the time she had been old enough to feel shame, Indrett had vowed never to use another person as she had been used. But the vow had not been enough; she had used the man she married merely as a way to make a fresh start. And now, as her husband sought to rescue their son, all she felt was shameful and selfish. Child of her father.

Yet the fading remnants of the Northern Lights did not judge her. She still felt their warmth.

'My friends,' she whispered, as the lights vanished, 'my true friends, goodbye. I will not forget you again.'

Pale pre-dawn fingers stretched westwards across the diamond-studded carpet of night as Indrett finally took leave of the rock where she had sat for so long. Above her, star after star was absorbed into the vast light of day, and the message was not lost on her. She rose and stretched aching muscles, rubbing away the pain from her right elbow where the Bhrudwans had struck her. *It's funny how the pain they inflicted never went below the surface*, she reflected.

There was movement back at the campsite. Indrett frowned; it was early even for Hal to get up, but someone moved quietly amongst their packs. Not Hal, there was no limp. Puzzled, she pressed forward. She was perhaps fifty yards from the campsite when the figure stood, something – a sword – in its hand. The head was turned away, but the cowling was unmistakable.

Indrett gave herself no time to become frightened. For the merest of moments she considered shouting a warning, but she held her tongue at the thought of what the alerted Bhrudwan might do to the defenceless Company as they struggled to waken. Instead, she immediately ducked out of his line of sight, thankful that the chattering sounds of running water masked her scrabbling around in the trees, looking for anything that might pass for a weapon. Rocks, branches, there were plenty of both. She grabbed a hefty stick and a particularly wicked looking rock, and looked for cover.

Ahead the grey shape continued to rummage amongst the possessions of the Company. Indrett wondered how much more time she had before the Acolyte decided to use the sword. She flitted frantically from tree to tree, trying to keep in the shadowy gloom as the forest brightened in the dawn. Now she was within ten yards of the menacing figure.

One of the prone forms stirred in its sleep, then groaned as it awakened on the hard ground. The Acolyte whipped around, a bag filled with provisions in one hand, sword in the other. Too late, Indrett darted forward from behind a tree. As she ran, she saw with horror the Acolyte raise his sword arm, then cut downwards with shocking force at the stirring shape on the ground, the sword making contact with a thud. The Bhrudwan withdrew his weapon, then turned and made to escape. A moment later Indrett burst into the camp, stick in one hand, rock in the other.

The Acolyte swung around to face her, his cowl swept back, arrogantly confident, not a single betrayal of surprise marring his hard features. With a fluid motion, he sprang forward and struck at Indrett. She twisted away and the blade struck her a sharp but glancing blow across her forearm. The frightened woman dropped the rock with a cry of pain.

Again the sword bit through the air, but this time the cry came from the Bhrudwan, a cry of anger as Indrett parried his blow with her stick. He made to strike again, but with the stirring in the camp he decided to abandon his attack. Without taking his eyes from Indrett, he stepped backwards and picked up the provisions he had let fall. Then he spun around to make his escape, but turned directly into the rock Indrett had dropped, held in the waiting hand of Farr. His hand swung swiftly, and the Bhrudwan fell to the ground unconscious from a blow to the head.

In a moment, the camp was in uproar, with Farr making good the loosened bonds on the Acolyte's wrists, while Kurr, Perdu, Parlevaag and Stella strove to clear their eyes of sleep and come to terms with events. The Fenni woman rushed over to where Indrett stood, dazed and in shock, with a profusely bleeding arm hanging limply by her side.

'Tie him tight!' Kurr barked, as together Farr and Perdu drew the cords so tight around the Bhrudwan that they cut into his flesh. The old farmer hustled over to where Indrett sat, with Parlevaag holding her arm aloft, above the level of the cut.

'Hal!' the old man cried. 'Here's one for you!' But the bundle of bedclothes where Hal lay did not move.

'He got Hal, he got Hal!' Indrett shrieked. 'Let me go to him!' With that she pulled her arm away from the Fenni woman, made to go to her son, stumbled, and fell in a heap beside the embers of the fire. The valiant Parlevaag struggled to raise her, but Indrett was unconscious, a dead weight.

'Help me!' Kurr called to the others as he leapt across to where Hal lay. There was a long gash in the bedclothes; impatiently, the farmer pulled them away from the body.

'Hal!' he cried. 'Are you all right?'

The body rolled away as Kurr removed the last of the shredded cloth, but made no other movement.

'There's no blood,' Perdu commented. 'But he looks to be hurt. What happened?'

'I have no idea,' Kurr replied, tension draining from his voice as he ascertained that the cripple was still breathing. 'Here, look: a bruise on the side of his head. He's been struck at with a sword – is that the weapon?' He pointed to a bloodied blade held by Farr.

'Thankfully it was Hal's sword, rusty and blunt. Even the Bhrudwan did not have enough strength to cut right through the bedclothes. But the force of the blow must have driven Hal's head against the ground.'

The others nodded their heads in relief.

Kurr sent Farr to fetch some fresh water, while Perdu and Parlevaag made up bandages for Hal and Indrett. Pale but determined, Indrett had regained her feet, and with her left arm she stemmed the bleeding from her right as she made her way to her son's side.

'How did this happen?' Kurr asked, his voice edged with anger.

'I don't know,' Farr replied contritely. 'We checked the bindings late in the afternoon, and they appeared to be as tight as ever. He must have loosened them somehow. They were not cut.'

'We have been very fortunate,' the old farmer continued. 'Had Indrett not disturbed him, not one of us would be alive at this moment. Do you understand? He would have killed us all.'

Farr and Perdu nodded miserably.

'I wonder if the best plan would be to kill this Bhrudwan, after all. He is much too dangerous to take with us all the way to Instruere; it is like trying to contain a forest fire within the bowl of your hands.' Kurr shook his head. 'I'll think about it later. You two go back and recheck those cords. Make them tighter still. I don't mind if you hurt him, as long as you keep him alive – for now.'

'No,' came a voice. 'Don't hurt him. If he is to be of any use, we have to win his confidence.'

Kurr turned around to see Hal, the colour already returning to his face, sitting up with a cloth held to his temple.

'What do you mean?' Kurr asked. *How did he recover so swiftly?*

'What I said. Our plan depends not only on bringing him alive to the Council of Faltha, but encouraging him to testify to them of his purposes and what he knows about the Bhrudwan plans.'

'Since when did our plans include him *speaking* to the council?' the old man spluttered. 'Surely it will be enough for them to see him? His origins will be obvious!'

'If it was enough that they see him, you would not lie awake at night worrying about how to convince the council of the peril posed to Faltha. It is our only chance. We have to win his confidence.'

'Not if I have my way,' Kurr replied angrily. 'That man is a callous killer, responsible for the deaths of many innocent people, and within moments of being responsible for mine. I refuse to take the chance. I have decided: he will be put to death.'

Hal stood on unsteady legs. 'Let me take responsibility for him,' the crippled youth said gently. 'I have seen many animals like him.

440

Cornered and frightened, lashing out at anyone, friend or foe. He is a man, not a beast, and will surely respond to trust and love more readily than do the beasts. Give him to me. Let me take care of him. Or kill him and abandon your quest.'

Kurr stood silent for a long time, weighing the alternatives. Surely there was no choice? The Bhrudwan had proved his danger to the Company, and now he waited for his inevitable death, a steely indifference in his eyes. And it was just and right that he should die, for the sake of the Company.

But what if Hal was right? What if he could be persuaded to testify to the Council of Faltha? Then surely the council would listen and take action. Hal was right in one thing: he had spent too many sleepless nights wrestling with the problem posed by the rulers of Faltha. Perhaps the Bhrudwan had to live for the sake of Faltha.

There could be no alternative. Entrust the safety of the Company to a cripple, where two able-bodied men had failed? Surely not. Yet here he was, giving Hal's suggestion serious consideration. Why, when it was so patently absurd? *Because Hal is so persuasive*, came the answer. *He can get you to consider something as ridiculous as him taking charge of the prisoner. What might he achieve with the Bhrudwan?*

I could always have a backup plan, he reasoned. *Get Farr and Perdu to keep a close eye on the Bhrudwan, and at the slightest sign of trouble – whack! In with the swords. Perhaps we can give Hal's suggestion a try, just for a few days. To see if he can talk this Bhrudwan around.*

He shook his head as if to dislodge the idea, but it remained firmly fixed in his mind. *Are you sure you were not the one knocked senseless?* he asked himself.

'All right,' he said to Hal. 'Take charge of the prisoner. But be warned. There will be no testifying before the council if we don't make it there alive.'

CHAPTER 21

THE BATTLE OF HELIG HOLTH

THE FODHRAM SPRINTED DOWN the path towards Adunlok, all attempts at stealth forgotten in the sudden need for speed. Boot-shod feet beat against the paved road; sword- and staff-wielding men fought for breath as two weeks of pursuing the Widuz culminated in this wild charge down the narrow gut of Numen Scou. Dark and ominous cliffs reared up ahead, some hundreds of yards in front of them at the head of the valley.

Axehaft knew that his small raiding force had been seen. This was confirmed emphatically when warning bells sounded from the many-eyed fortress above them. Armed warriors began pouring from holes in the walls like borers from a burning tree, then the first of them reached the open space before the Fodhram and began running across it. For a moment, the Warden caught a glimpse of two figures dashing hand in hand along a narrow path directly below the cliffs, pursued by a third figure; then he lost them in the shadows.

The two forces came together with a shattering blow. Steel flickered dully in the grey light of the day's last stand, as the short, squat men of the northern forest exchanged furious blows with the taller, more lithe men of Clovenhill. Three able captains stood with Axehaft in the vanguard of his men, swinging their staffs in a wide arc as they tried to clear a path to the fortress. Their blows stunned rather than killed, but the men behind finished off their foes with the point of a sword.

442

The Widuz, who favoured woodcrafty stealth and surprise, fought valiantly, but it soon became apparent that they could not match the Fodhram man for man, which was as it always had been. However, when one Widuz was cut down, three more took his place. Warriors continued to issue from their holes, the Warden observed ruefully, and they emitted high-pitched shouts as they came.

Beside him one of his captains fell, mortally wounded by a freakish blow from a spiked club. Axehaft turned and hacked at the huge Widuz warrior who, having spent a moment too long admiring his own skill, fell dead without knowing what had happened to him.

The open space in front of Helig Holth filled with warriors engaged in hand-to-hand combat. Gradually the field became littered with the bodies of the dead and the dying, Widuz and Fodhram both. The last direct sunlight lifted from the limestone crags above them as they fought, and twilight descended on the battleground with the result still in doubt, but with the tide turning against the northerners.

This is no good, the Fodhram leader told himself as slowly, inexorably, his small raiding party began to be forced back towards the dark forest eaves by the sheer weight of Widuz numbers. *We cannot allow ourselves to be trapped in the forest; we will become easy prey in the darkness.* Night drew near; yellow light faded from Clovenhill behind them, and still more Widuz warriors poured on to the field.

Phemanderac sped up the path towards the fortress, half pulling, half dragging Leith along behind him. Above them the bells pealed out their urgent warning. He knew he was running into danger, but the remaining guard lumbered after them only a few yards behind, gaining on them with every step.

'Come on, Leith, come on!' he cried in desperation. But Leith moved sluggishly, still under the influence of the drug. *Thus would I have been, had I not realised there was poison in the water.* Not for the first time, Phemanderac had reason to be thankful for his rigorous training.

The bells ceased their raucous clanging, but ahead, at the top of the path, the stone of the door rolled open and grim-faced warriors of Widuz began to issue from it. Behind them the guard raised his voice in a shout. The two fugitives were trapped.

At the last moment, Phemanderac threw himself off the path to the right, in the direction of Helig Holth. Above him the guard met with his fellow warriors, but his urgent shouts were ignored in the pressing need to meet the Fodhram threat in the valley below. The burly guard was swept back down the path.

Phemanderac pulled Leith close to him, trying to make both of them invisible to whatever eyes still gazed from the dark windows directly above them. They crouched on a narrow shelf some yards below the path. To their right lay the black nothingness of Mother Earth, sucking at them with her cold breath as the cooler night air rushed down the cliff face. Out of their sight now, warriors continued to run along the path, throwing themselves into the battle.

Gradually, Leith began to come to his senses. *Too soon!* Better he remain drugged than endanger their perilous position by movement or noise. The youth, however, remained perfectly still, only moving his head slightly as with wide eyes he took in their predicament. He obviously had no idea how they had arrived in this position, but he was going to do nothing to jeopardise it.

Eventually the sound of slapping feet died away, and was replaced with the noises of battle some distance behind them, groans and cries amplified in the natural amphitheatre of Adunlok.

'Now!' Phemanderac hissed. 'Are you ready?' Leith nodded, barely able to contain his fear. 'Then follow me!'

Together they scrambled up to the path. One look down to their left told them that to attempt that way would be fraught with danger; fighters stood at the bottom of the path, where it joined the carven way, and beyond them a battle was being fought, barely visible in the haze of evening.

'This way!' Phemanderac urged, and Leith followed his new friend up and to the right, still struggling to comprehend what was happening. He remembered little after the prison cell. How had they finished up outside? What was the fighting down in the valley? He sincerely hoped it was a rescue party.

Up the path they ran, bare feet on cold stone roots, unchecked by any foe. Then past the huge round stone, through the doorway, and into the fastness of Adunlok. For a moment, Phemanderac paused; then, deciding, he motioned Leith to help him roll the stone door shut behind them.

Down in the valley, the fighting was not going well for the Warden and his raiders. Seven of his band had fallen; the Fodhram were now a small wedge in a sea of at least a hundred Widuz, who jostled each other for a chance to strike at their enemy. The Widuz leaders, stationed at the back of the army to drive them on, could not believe their good fortune. Everything was so perfect! Here, in the presence of Mother Earth, they were dealing a heavy blow to the hated woodsmen of the north. The gods themselves had delivered their enemy into their hands.

From behind the Warden came a cry of surprise and pain, and a shout of warning. Though he was engaged with a broad-chested brute who flailed at him with an axe, he risked a glance behind him. *Disaster!* A number of the enemy had found their way behind the Fodhram and were attacking from the rear. In the grey murk of this moonless evening, he could make out shadows racing down the ridges on either side, closing the trap. They were surrounded.

The leaders of the Widuz shouted in fierce delight. Their entrapment had worked perfectly, and now they would finish off these foolhardy woodsmen with little further loss. Those of their men who could not join battle on the narrow field had been sent along the ridgetops, and they spilled down behind the small band of Fodhram. It was only a matter of time.

'Call out the priest!' their Chief commanded.

'The priest is gone, taken by Helig Holth, O Great One,' came the answer from beside him.

'What? How so?'

'There was a fight with one of the prisoners, my Chief, and he was lost, along with one of the guards.'

'Then get me that good-for-nothing disciple! You'll no doubt find him skulking in the living quarters. He would not be found risking his neck on a blood-night such as this! Bring him here! The slaughter cannot begin without the appropriate ceremony!'

His servant scurried away up the path. The Chief turned to his lieutenants, smiled, and said: 'This night is shaped perfectly, as one ordained by the Earth Mother herself. The death of the priest is the crowning goodness. He was old and stubborn, slow to obey me, while I have the lazy disciple in my hand.

'Now, command the warriors to encircle the Fodhram, then disengage. We will have the ceremony of sacrifice performed correctly, and then we will make an end of them.'

Mahnum had been forced to stand and watch his son and another man scurry up the path and into the fortress. Between him and Leith lay a hundred or more warriors of the Widuz, and above him still more ran along ridgetop paths. With a heavy heart, he watched the entrapment of the Fodhram, his friends from the Cloventop trail. He would not stay to see their end. But how would he gain access to the citadel?

The disciple hustled importantly out of his private rooms, determined to enjoy the first of what would be many pleasing tasks. It had been with unmasked pleasure that he had received news of the priest's untimely demise; the old fool had been a tyrant, making him do most of the work and sharing none of the rewards. But now it would be different. Now life would be sweet.

He propelled his corpulent body through the outer doorway of the second level and on to the pathway above Helig Holth. Although normally walking this path scared him witless, he was prepared to put up with the fear in exchange for the power that was now his. Puffy fingers nervously adjusted the red mask. Everything must be perfect for such an auspicious night.

As Mahnum watched from his vantage point above the battle-field, the Widuz marched ahead, forcing the Fodhram back into the clutches of their waiting fellows, leaving the area around Helig

Holth clear. The end was very near. But the Trader had eyes only for his chance. He plunged forward, down the hillside.

Halfway down the path the disciple began to feel his bravado drain away. The black nothingness to his left pulled at him with an audible sucking sound, whispering to him with a thick, wet voice. *I'm too superstitious for this calling*, he thought.

Now someone came up the path. *Worse yet*, the big man thought. *How will he pass me on this narrow way?* But the man did not want to pass. In an instant, a sword was drawn, with the razor-sharp point poised under the disciple's wobbling chins.

'Back up the path! Make no noise!' Mahnum hissed. Though the disciple did not know the common speech, he knew the intent of what had been said. Whimpering with fear, he turned and heaved himself back up the way he had come, with the sword at his back.

'This way!' Phemanderac whispered, motioning Leith to follow. There had been a choice of ways, one a corridor straight ahead and the other a stairway down and to the right. The philosopher chose the stairway, and Leith, still a little dizzy from the effects of the drug, forced himself down after him.

The fortress appeared to be completely deserted. They were apparently on the level where the Widuz lived, with small rooms – even smaller than the cells above – with four bunks to a room, either side of a central corridor. Down this corridor they raced, with Phemanderac casting swift glances in each of the rooms.

'What are you looking for?' Leith hissed in his ear.

'My harp,' came the reply.

'Your what? We're in mortal danger! Leave your harp! We must escape before the men return!'

'I'll not leave without my harp,' Phemanderac said flatly. 'There is none other like it in all of Faltha.'

Leith cried aloud with frustration, but his companion would not be dissuaded from his search. The end of the corridor reached, he turned on his heel and retraced his steps. It took at least five long minutes to search the rest of the level, without success.

'Down the stairs again! There must be a third level!'

'How do you know they didn't throw it into Helig Holth, along with your clothes?'

Phemanderac pulled up short.

'I hadn't thought of that,' he said sadly. 'And that reminds me: we've a better chance of getting past anyone remaining here if we find some Widuz raiment.'

'You mean you've only just realised?' Leith had been uncomfortably aware of his nakedness, as much for the cold as for the embarrassment. His thin companion, however, did not seem to notice such things. They rummaged among a few rooms until they found clothes of approximate fit, then dressed and scampered down the corridor to the stairway.

'Back outside?' Leith inquired.

Phemanderac strode to the nearest window. 'We cannot go back the way we came,' he reported. 'Many warriors block that path. No, we must find another way out of this place.' He sighed. His harp had been very dear to him.

Down the stairs they raced, to the third and lowest inhabited level. Here they discovered an armoury, containing nothing but a few swords and clubs. Leith grabbed a cruel-looking blade, but Phemanderac declined. 'If it comes to a fight, I'd be no use to you,' he said cheerfully. 'No use at all. The philosophers offered no swordsmanship courses.'

The door of the last room but one was locked and bolted. 'Smash it open,' Phemanderac said. 'This could be our way out.'

Leith hacked at the lock with the sword. A loud clanging rang out, echoing along the corridor, but all he succeeded in doing was notching the blade.

'Quietly!' said Phemanderac. 'You'll bring them all here with that noise!'

'I can't do this quietly!' Leith snapped, his fear threatening to overwhelm him. 'You have a try!'

Phemanderac took the sword, stared at it a moment, wedged the hilt between the bolt and the door and pulled at the blade. The lock groaned, then gave way with a loud report.

'I've cut myself!' the thin man complained.

'In here!' Leith called.

'My harp!' cried Phemanderac.

'Look at this!' gasped Leith.

In the corner of the room lay a veritable treasure trove: coins, jewels and precious stones, all items of value no doubt taken from captives over the years before their owners were given to Mother Earth. Leith was drawn to the scene like a blackbird to bread, but Phemanderac had eyes only for his harp.

'Undamaged!' he declared after a swift examination. 'The Most High be praised!'

Leith fingered a few of the largest jewels, seemingly oblivious to all else.

'Leith! We must escape!'

'What? Oh! Yes, I'm coming,' he stammered, and reluctantly turned his back on the riches that were his for the choosing. 'Where to now?'

'To the end of the corridor. Then, if there is no other way out, we take our chances out there.'

'To me! To me! Form a tight circle! Swords outwards!' The Warden knew they were overmatched, but was determined to make a worthy end of it. Though the song would not be sung, its lyrics began to form in his mind as he fought.

> In the valley long, in the valley grey,
> Did the Fodhram fight till the end of day.
> In the valley grey, in the valley long,
> They swung their swords till hope was gone.
> To the last man fought, to the last man fell,
> Now all are gone, with none to tell
> Of deeds of greatness, deeds of yore,
> Their hearty laughter heard no more.

The Fodhram Warden considered these words, then decided that the making of songs would best be left to a bard. *But there are none*

449

with us, he lamented as he hacked at a thick-necked Widuz. *I've never known a bard who has made even a passable swordsman, certainly not one with the skill needed to free us from this trap. Why did I not bring my two-bladed axe?*

This man is more of a liability than an asset, Mahnum decided. He could not communicate his wishes to his captive. It had been many years since he had traded goods in Widuz, in the more civilised south near Tolmen, and little but snippets of their hard-edged language remained in his mind. Moreover it appeared that the fortress was empty of Widuz, so he would not need this bulky man to help him. He flicked the red mask off with the tip of his sword. Behind the mask, the flabby face was pasty and sweating with fear.

I cannot let him go now, the Trader reasoned. *He would report my presence to the soldiers below.* He'd been of some help in shifting the huge stone, but since then had offered nothing more. Down the stone stairway Mahnum forced his prisoner. No sign of Leith in the upper levels. Where had he gone?

His captive beckoned him forward down the corridor. *Is this a trap, or does he have something he wants to show me?* In a moment he made up his mind: *I will not stay undiscovered in this keep forever.* He took a deep breath, then motioned the red-robed man onwards, prodding him with the tip of his sword.

A dead end! Leith and Phemanderac had reached the end of the last corridor, and like all the other corridors they had searched there was no passage, no way out of this fastness.

Think, Leith, think! 'There must be a way out!' he ground out in frustration. *To be caught like rabbits in a mesh trap; to be impaled on the end of swords or thrown into that fearsome pit: that was no way for one with a high and lofty destiny to die.*

Then for a moment his head cleared, and he thought more about the Hermit and what he had said. What was his first prophetic word? It sounded like a bell through his mind: *I saw you standing naked at the edge of a vast abyss, a captive of cruel men. Other captives stood to your left and right. Your captors threw them into the chasm, one by one. The only way out is to cling to the fire.*

His eyes widened. Why had he not remembered the words earlier? Were they any use now? He had escaped the abyss without 'clinging to the fire', whatever that meant.

But had he escaped? *The only way out is to cling to the fire.*

'Leith! Look here!' Phemanderac cried. At the very end of the corridor, etched in the limestone wall, was the outline of a door. At least ten feet high, it was perfectly circular, with the merest of cracks to tell where it lay. It flickered in the dancing light of a single torch.

'Open it!' Leith called frantically and unnecessarily, rushing over to where Phemanderac was already pushing against the outline with all his might.

'It is definitely an opening,' he reported. 'Put your face to the crack; you can feel the cold air on the other side.'

Together they thumped at the door, but it remained closed. They spread out, looking along the bare, smooth wall for a lock or handle or something with which to open it. Finding nothing, Leith beat at the door with his sword hilt in desperation. *So close!*

Then from behind them they heard the slapping sound of feet on stone, as someone came down the stairs towards the corridor. Leith and Phemanderac looked at each other in horror.

'Perhaps if we hide in one of the rooms!' Leith whispered.

'And then what? Wait for the fortress to fill up again with soldiers? We must be patient and search for the key to this door. This is our only way out.'

Our only way out, Leith thought as the feet drew closer. There was a slight curve in the passage that hid from view the stairway behind them. They pressed themselves against the inner wall, overcome with fear, hoping somehow to remain undetected. Perhaps the feet would turn the other way. Perhaps they would stop short of the end of the corridor. Leith held his sword at the ready, and cast a last look at the door outlined in the wall. *Our only way out!* The footfalls reached the base of the stairs, then turned and came slowly towards them around the curve of the fortress. More than

451

one person. A moment more and they would be discovered. *Our only way out!*

'Fool!' breathed Leith, his breath coming out with a rush. 'Our only way out is to cling to the fire!' And with that he rushed past the transfixed Phemanderac and reached up for the torch. It was just out of his grasp.

'Help me!' he hissed. Instantly, Phemanderac was at his side, realisation dawning on him. His thin, bony hands took hold of the torch and pulled it downwards. Immediately, and without a sound, the door swung open, revolving on a central axis. The two fugitives flashed through the opening and into a dimly lit cave. Leith turned and pushed the door shut; it gave way effortlessly before him, falling into place with a soft, reassuring click.

The Fodhram, numbering now no more than twenty, were completely surrounded. Men slumped forward on their swords, some searching for courage with which to face inevitable death, others too exhausted to care. Around them the many corpses of their enemies were mute testimony to the ferocity of the battle.

'What's happened?' Jackpine asked his Warden. 'Why have they withdrawn?'

The Widuz waited for something, that much was obvious. For reinforcements? Surely not! There were more than enough Widuz to finish them off. For leadership? But there were the leaders, standing in plain sight, and that man must be their chief. The order could be given at any time. Why the delay?

The Widuz Chief was furious. 'Did you deliver him my summons?'

'Yes, my lord. I told him personally.'

'And his response?'

'He said he would be down immediately he donned the sacred garments.'

'Well, where is he?'

'He should be here by now, my Chief.' The servant struggled to hide his nervousness.

'Go and find him, then! Do not return without him!'

Once again the unfortunate man made off.

The Warden watched the exchange, taking place as it did not fifty yards distant.

'Should we not attack, and make an end?' whispered Fernroot, his most able lieutenant. 'The captives will be beyond our help if we delay any longer.'

Axehaft laughed loud and long, a sound that eased his aching heart and sent the Widuz warriors reaching for their swords. 'Look around you!' he said in a steady voice. 'The captives are beyond our help already!'

'I'd love to see my beautiful Marigold one more time,' came a sorrowful voice from behind. 'Such a slender waist, such deep blue eyes. And little Brownfinch, he'll miss his father. Just one more look, that's all I ask!'

'Then close your eyes and look upon your loved ones,' the Warden answered. This waiting made their deaths all the more cruel. He could sense the courage draining from his men. *Curse you! Attack and have done with it!*

The mind of the disciple worked feverishly. *How can I save myself? For it is obvious that this man intends to do away with me.*

His best chance lay in keeping the man occupied long enough for others to come searching for their new priest. *After all, my presence is necessary in order for the consecration ceremony to proceed. There is no one else who knows the ritual. I will not be abandoned.*

But how to keep him busy? His captor was looking for something; perhaps he could be tempted with the lure of riches? He beckoned the man forward, down the stairway that separated the living quarters from the armoury.

The lowest level of Adunlok, in which the armoury was situated, was deserted as they walked along the corridor. Or was it? The disciple heard a noise ahead, just out of sight around the curve in the passageway. His captor had heard it too, brushing past the rotund Widuz in an instant. There, at the end of the corridor, was the door to the lower caverns and to the womb of the Earth Mother. It was closing.

453

Mahnum rushed towards the door, but it closed too quickly. He was about to call out, but thought better of it; what if a Widuz warrior waited on the other side?

'Is this why you brought me here?' he asked his sweating captive, who shrugged his shoulders in answer. *This man is nothing but a dead weight*, the Trader thought. *Time to get rid of him.*

But when he came to it, Mahnum could not make the swordthrust necessary. The fat man stood there in the corridor, wide-eyed and terrified, waiting for death, but Mahnum could not do it. Images of defenceless villagers dying cruelly under the hands of the Bhrudwan warriors shimmered in the air around him. *O Most High, I would rather die than become one of them. Should I kill someone merely because they are no use to me?*

Instead, he grabbed his captive by a flabby arm and pulled him into the nearest room. *The door shows signs of having recently been forced*, the Trader noted in passing. Inside, in the far corner of the room, lay riches, treasures beyond the wildest imaginings of a Trader, scattered across the floor and festooned on the walls. The sight quite took his breath away.

His captive was saying something, gesturing to the piles of valuables. *He's trying to make a bargain*, Mahnum realised. *That's why he brought me down here.* His Trader's soul was held captive by the sight: here were undoubtedly the spoils of war, the accumulations of many lifetimes. Here was the key to abundant life. Here was everything he had dreamed of. How would that necklace, for example, look upon the creamily perfect skin of his dear Indrett?

No, none of his dreams were here in this room. Leith was somewhere in this fortress, but not here. This treasure of nations could not hold the Trader. He turned and led his still gesticulating captive back into the corridor.

'The door, the door,' he said, pointing to the end of the corridor. He had decided. His boy was nowhere in this fortress, it was time to continue the search. The Widuz word came to his mind: '*Dhuir na, Dhuir na!*'

Startled at this use of the Widuz tongue, the disciple waddled towards the door under the encouragement of the sword. He could smell, almost taste, the blade a few inches from his throat. But now a new fear reached out for him.

Priests have never gone into this tunnel, he reminded himself. For good reason: it was forbidden by holy decree of the Earth Mother herself. If he were to break this prohibition, his life would be forfeit. He would lose his powers before he had truly gained them. They would feed him to her, and he would die in her ravenous belly.

I can't go through the door! his mind cried.

Behind him the sword whispered: 'You can! You can!'

He took the sword's advice and triggered the opening mechanism.

Leith followed Phemanderac down the winding tunnel, fearful of the inevitable pursuit. No light illuminated their passage, just the cold draught of stale air, the roughness of the rock on each side of them, and darkness black as pitch. *My life is in his hands*, he thought.

Under the immense limestone and marble mountain of Cloventop lay many dark and secret caverns, most unexplored by humans. Adunlok had been built atop a system of caverns, formed like Bandits' Cave far to the north by the patient action of acidic water on alkaline rock. Through this cave system a river still ran, entering the earth a league or so to the north of Adunlok at Rinnan Holth, the River Cave, a place known and venerated by the Widuz. Thereafter its paths were unknown, but it emerged in Wambakalven, the Womb Cavern, almost a thousand feet directly under the fastness of Adunlok. It wound its way through Wambakalven, passing close by the light of the sun at the bottom of Helig Holth and the unspeakable mound that had grown there over the years, then ponded up at the Womb's exit. The sombre waters of Telba Poul were continually astir as the sacred river sought various narrow pathways through the rock and into the lower caverns of Adunlok. From there the gurgling, rushing water found its way into Drozzakalven, the smallest of the caverns under the mountain. Here it rushed down the sloping floor and out through a series of rapids into Stalassokalven, the largest of them all, over fifteen hundred feet below the eyes of Adunlok. Finally, the river emerged into the light through Anukalva, a narrow grotto that opened to the sunlight, and tumbled chill and pallid into the warm waters of Brinan Scou, the Burning Stream.

The Widuz had worked tirelessly for many years to establish a path down into Wambakalven. Parad Matr, the road upon which Leith and Phemanderac ran, had taken them over a hundred years to carve out of solid rock. It took a circuitous route, following ancient fractures in the fabric of the mountain, down and through Geotakalven, a dry cave, to Wambakalven herself. From the Mother's Womb there was no escape save returning up the same pathway: the Earth Mother herself forbade further tunnelling.

After many minutes of running, during which both Leith and Phemanderac accumulated a variety of bumps and scrapes, they arrived in a place where the echo of their feet rang out loudly, and they judged they were in an open space. 'We need a torch,' Phemanderac whispered to himself; some yards behind, Leith heard him clearly.

'Slow down,' he called. 'There could be pits, cliffs, lakes, anything. Keep to the path!'

'Of course!' came the amplified answer. Phemanderac halted, then took his harp from his shoulder.

'I've always wanted to do this,' he said, and put his fingers to the harp.

Beginning on the very edge of hearing, clear liquid notes flowed back and forth across the unguessed length of the cavern. The simple melody played by skilled fingers was magnified and echoed a hundred-fold, until the blackness around them was filled with noise.

'We don't have time for this!' Leith yelled.

'Just a moment! I have to get the echo interval right.'

Then the sound changed from a solid wall of interlocking notes to the repeating of a string being plucked, as Phemanderac played his tune more slowly, in time with the echo. An ineffable sweetness permeated the sound, as deep bass notes alternated with a crisp, bright melody until Leith's ears rang with the beauty of it.

Now, as before, the notes began to run together into one sound; but this time it carried with it the sound of hope after loss, joy after sadness, laughter after pain; a sound that rang in the cavern long after Phemanderac stopped playing.

The thin foreigner hoisted his harp back on to his shoulder. 'Sounded fine once I got the echo right,' he said.

Sounded fine? I've never heard anything like it, Leith wanted to say, as he found his eyes brimming with tears at the same time as his heart wanted to leap from his chest. *I've been in the throne room of the Most High; I've heard the music of creation.* But Phemanderac was gone, invisible in front of him, his football masked by the ringing that reverberated still around the cavern. Sighing for the longing of it, Leith stepped carefully forward down Mother's Road.

Some way behind them Mahnum and the disciple froze as the sound of the harp came to their ears. But instead of the sound as it was heard in the cavern, the twists and turns of Parad Matr turned it into a frightful ululation, the death call of some departed spirit. It was all Mahnum could do to force himself on into the inky blackness and the dreadful noise. Behind him, the disciple remained rooted to the spot.

The frightened Widuz priest began to shake with terror as the sound surrounded him, coming at him from above and below, ahead and behind, settling on him like the wraith of his nightmares. He beat his arms at the air, trying to drive it away; then he lurched down the forbidden path like a drunken man, his fear of the sword, fear of discovery, fear of death itself, forgotten in the dread terror of the god he served, the god he had disobeyed. He did not realise he had entered a wide open space; for him the music remained terrible, an overbearing discord, a threat finally coming true. His unknowing feet turned off the path into the uncharted maze of blind tunnels and dead ends to the left of Parad Matr, and the sound of his vengeful god followed him.

As Mahnum ran through Geotakalven, the sound seemed to intensify, but here it was arrestingly powerful, a concordant harmony rather than the cacophony that had followed him down the tunnel. As he strode on into the blackness, his eyes picking

out the pale marble of the path in the faintest of lights – perhaps
the very glow of the rock – the chord hanging in the air ravished
him with its grandeur, bringing the spinning heavens down,
sending him soaring, bursting through the clouds like some
unshackled bird. *This can't be the same sound.* His feet slowed to a
walk; he found himself holding his breath for fear he might destroy
the bittersweet purity of the chord. Then the echoes died out and
silence fell.

'What is happening?' Mahnum cried. But there was no reply.

Wambakalven was lit with torches. Leith and Phemanderac
blinked like waking owls in the red-yellow light. Parad Matr
levelled out, snaking across the floor of the huge cavern to run
beside a dark stream. Here and there great pillars rose into the air,
reaching up to the far-off roof. A million encrusted jewels glit-
tered in the torchlight, precious gems polished on an ancient
beach, captives of the rock formed long ago when the world was
young.

'Have you ever seen anything like this?' Leith whispered. The
sound of Geotakalven still rang faintly in his ears; whether from
memory or reality he could not tell. But now his eyes were receiving
the same message.

'Never, truly never,' Phemanderac breathed. 'There is a beauty
here beyond the power of language to express. Yet I sense evil also
in these caves; not authored by the maker of beauty, but from
some other source.'

They wandered enraptured through the cavern. *If these caves
were in Firanes*, Leith thought, *we would all live underground.*

'Careful,' said Phemanderac. 'These torches have been lit by
someone. We must watch for the Widuz.'

As if to punctuate his words, a shout came from behind them.
Both men spun around. A lone Widuz guard had seen them, and
was even now rushing in their direction from the far end of the
cave.

'Come on!' Leith cried, grabbing Phemanderac by the arm.
Together they pelted along the smooth straightness of the road,

while some distance behind a second, then a third Widuz joined the first.

At that moment, Mahnum emerged from Parad Matr into the wonder of Wambakalven. For the first time since he had entered the fortress of Adunlok he caught a glimpse of Leith with another man, many yards ahead, and in between him and them ran the Widuz guards, chasing his son. They appeared to be gaining.

'Leith!' he called, but his voice was swallowed up in the dome-shaped cavern. 'Leith!' He threw himself down the path, sprinting for all he was worth, sword at the ready.

The path veered to the right, drawing Phemanderac and Leith towards a small hill on which rested a pale light. Without breaking stride, they leapt over the stream where the road forded it, past an amazed Widuz guard, and on towards the hill that now lay in front of them.

This is the source of the evil, Phemanderac decided. Leith glanced up as he ran, and instead of a roof he could see stars, small cold pricks in a black sky. Both men realised at the same moment that they were seeing Helig Holth, the bottom of the abyss; Adunlok was directly above them; and the hill the road now skirted was not made of rock at all.

Leith cried out in horror. Of all the sights he had seen since leaving Loulea, this was the worst. It was a black smear across the glory of the cavern, a deep wound in the beauty of the earth. It was a mound of the bones of the dead, the sacrifices of centuries of obeisance to the god of Helig Holth. The reek of it choked them; it fouled the stream that wound around its base. At the apex of the mound lay the broken bodies of those most recently given to Mother Earth. Phemanderac and Leith averted their eyes, held their breaths and ran past the ghastly scene.

The long weeks of deprivation began to tell on Mahnum as he hastened along the path. His breath came in short gasps, his chest tightened and his already heavy limbs cried out for relief. He was making up distance on the Widuz, but not as much as the ground the guards gained on the fugitives ahead. Unless he increased his speed still further, he would lose the race.

459

Phemanderac cast an anxious glance over his shoulder. The three Widuz sped towards them, now almost within touching distance. Without warning, the philosopher veered to the left, ducking behind a huge rock column. As he had hoped, the exhausted youth followed his lead. The Widuz clattered to a halt. For a moment, no one moved, yet Phemanderac could still hear the sound of running feet. The Widuz evidently heard them too, and all three warriors turned to look back down the road. Seeing this, Phemanderac grabbed Leith's arm and pulled him after, dashing across broken ground away from their pursuers.

The senior Widuz guard dispatched his two fellows to run after the intruders, then turned and himself faced this new menace. A quick assessment gave the veteran Widuz fighter encouragement. This was an older man – older even than him, the Widuz champion of many years – thin, wiry, with plenty of strength in the shoulders but obviously short of wind. *Take this one slowly. Defend yourself, then wear him down.*

For his part, Mahnum stood and waited for the Widuz warrior to make the first move, a necessity born of tiredness, not of tactics. It had been a long time since he had wielded a sword. *Better get on with it,* he thought. *Every moment I pause is a moment further from Leith.*

Out flashed the sword of the Widuz, far too quickly for Mahnum, whose parry merely deflected the blade on to the fleshy part of his upper arm. His grunt of pain was matched by the snort of satisfaction, of mockery, from the Widuz. *I am overmatched,* Mahnum realised. *Unless I flee, I will die here.*

Phemanderac and Leith made it to the far side of Wambakalven, shrouded in darkness, some distance from the torchlight. Here the walls were honeycombed by the black mouths of caves leading to unguessable depths of the earth. Phemanderac considered for a moment. Sure death, not refuge, waited within. Backed into some miserable corner, falling into some unmarked pit, or the lingering death of the lost, would likely be their fate. The caves were not an option.

Ahead lay a pool. Beyond that, the end of the cavern. Their

options had all but run out. Suddenly the two pursuers were upon them with a flailing of swords and grunting of breath. Phemanderac pushed off a guard, while beside him Leith swung his blade wildly.

The harp, came a clear thought to the philosopher's mind.

In instant response, Phemanderac dropped to his knees; above him a blade flashed and bit air. He took the instrument from his shoulder and struck a chord with trembling fingers.

By the path, Mahnum ducked another blow. *How do I make an attack? This man has no weakness.* He was able to counter a straight thrust, but he was tiring. *How much longer?* Bright steel flicked past an inch from his eyes. *Not much longer.* His opponent readied himself for the kill.

The music! In the great cavern it swelled, a joy cutting like a sword through the besmirching cruelty that had ruled here for centuries. Strength and hope flowed out from the music, infusing tired limbs with renewed vigour, lifting crestfallen spirits, girding Mahnum as he faced the Widuz warrior.

The noise! It shrieked through the air like a fiend, a *dybbuk* of the earth disturbed by the fighting in the sacred womb. Sheer terror ripped at the Widuz warrior like a wild wind; his sword dropped from frightened fingers, and he raised his arms as if to fend off a blow. One short thrust from Mahnum and it was over. From somewhere behind him, the Trader heard a cry. Another warrior, perhaps, shouting in dismay at the fall of the guard.

Phemanderac made his fingers fly across the strings. The melody he played was a favourite of the philosophers, but they would not have recognised it in Wambakalven, magnified a thousand-fold by the confines of the cave. Here the notes melded into a ringing that shook the ground. In Geotakalven it had been an ecstasy, in Wambakalven it was raw power.

The Widuz fought against the noise, trying to strike at their quarry. Their movements were slow and cumbersome, as though the sound was a semi-solid mass through which they had to force a path. Leith and Phemanderac backed away from the guards.

Into this chaotic scene blundered a huge figure, issuing from one of the caves in the far wall. White-faced, clothes shredded, hands over his ears, the disciple found his way into Wambakalven and the sound was waiting there for him. He shrieked with fear; the Widuz turned blindly and without thought struck at the ghostly figure, cutting him down with cruel blows.

'Now!' cried Phemanderac, hoisting the harp to its place on his shoulder. He ran to the pool and dived in. Leith followed the stranger as though in a dream. The ripples closed over them both.

A wailing arose from the guards, who had identified the one they had killed. They had taken the life of the new priest, and their own deaths were now required by law. They turned in search of the intruders, who had simply vanished. This was too much for the warriors, who threw down their weapons and fled in terror of the wrath of their gods.

Below the dark fortress of Adunlok, the two armies waited. It had been many long minutes since the Fodhram had been surrounded, yet still the Widuz had shown no sign of finishing the job. Axehaft could see the growing agitation of the captains of Adunlok. He turned to his men.

'We will not die at the leisure of these killers,' he whispered hoarsely. 'They deny us the decency of death by battle, so we will take death from them! We wait no longer! Take arms!'

His men acknowledged their leader with nods of approval, and made themselves ready without alerting their enemy.

'We will strike directly at their captains,' the Warden continued, 'craven men who refuse to fight, but who send soldiers to do the work in their place. We will teach them how to fight! Attack and make no defence!' His men were gathering behind his will, forming it into a solid fist, readying for the strike.

'Forward!' Axehaft cried, sword upraised, in a last, desperate rallying cry. 'To the victory or to the death!' And the Fodhram took up the cry – 'To the victory or to the death!' – and shouted it to the darkling heavens. They plunged forward into the surprised Widuz, whose hands lay but lightly upon their hilts, and whose minds had taken victory for granted.

'Make this a song to be sung at the Fodhram firesides!' Axehaft roared, as they clove a path through the captains of their enemy. 'For the glory of Withwestwa Wood!' His warriors picked up this chant and filled the air with it, driving the Widuz back towards Helig Holth with the power of their voices as much as the power of their arms. 'For the glory of Withwestwa Wood!' Behind them the Widuz warriors realised too late what had happened and rushed after their foe, but could not catch them.

The last captain of the Widuz melted away before them, slain by a blow from Axehaft's bitter-edged blade. The Fodhram had fought their way to the very edge of Helig Holth, and marvelled at the great chasm before them, darker and more deadly than the blackest night. Now the Widuz seized their chance and rushed at the Fodhram, who were pinned against Helig Holth. The Warden turned his men and drove them into the wave of attackers. The Fodhram vanguard burst into the fury of the Widuz, and over-topped them, sending them back on to the plain in temporary defeat.

The Widuz mounted another charge. This time Axehaft waited for them, then at the last possible moment pulled his warriors aside. The Widuz plunged ahead in the darkness, unable to arrest their charge, and many were taken by Helig Holth, screaming as they fell into the embrace of their god.

'Now it is our turn!' Axehaft cried, and led his warriors forward in a glorious charge that simply swept their enemy away. A number of the Widuz laid down their weapons and cried out for mercy; others fell beneath sword or staff; while the rest melted into the forest, lamenting the loss of their priest and fearing the wrath of the northern woodsmen.

Phemanderac's idea had been to swim underwater to the far end of the pool, surface, and find somewhere to hide until they were free to make their way out of the caves. But the pool would not allow them to follow this plan. With irresistible power it sucked them down, further and further down into its cold heart. Leith struggled to get free of the current, flailing with arms and legs, and failed. Beside him Phemanderac relaxed and rode the surge.

At least we're going somewhere, he reasoned. *As long as there are no waterfalls*.

Rock walls closed around them. Ahead, Leith could make out a narrow gap, surely far too narrow for a person to pass through. The powerful current insisted they head towards it, and Leith had no strength with which to argue, by now being wholly concerned with the lack of air. Through the opening he flashed, banging his shoulder painfully as he went; behind him Phemanderac's harp wedged fast.

There was nothing Leith could do to help his new-found friend. He turned and battled into the current but could make no headway. Roiling water took him away from Phemanderac and, after long moments of twisting and turning through water-filled tunnels, deposited him on a sandy beach. He gasped for air a few times, then passed out.

The search of the ground near Helig Holth had been going on for many precious minutes when the Fodhram of Withwestwa Wood finally found what they were searching for. 'Over here!' came the cry, and Axehaft rushed back to the brink of the abyss. A narrow path wound to the right, cut into the very rock of the cliff, and on it the remaining Fodhram captives had been discovered. In haste, they were led away from the scene, still dazed by the mind-numbing drugs they had been given.

Axehaft took stock of the situation. Nine captives had been rescued – nine out of twenty or more. Mahnum's son was not one of them, meaning that he, like the other captives, had undoubtedly been thrown down the great hole. At least fifteen of his warriors had been slain, or were so cruelly wounded they were unlikely to survive the night. *Was this good sense?* he wondered. *We have exchanged fifteen for nine. Would we have done better to remain at home?* His heart cried 'No!' in answer. *My slain warriors died in a noble cause. At least the living can live without the guilt of having abandoned the captives.*

'Shall we attack the fortress?' one beside him asked, eyes still burning with the lust of battle.

'No, lad, we have done what we came to do,' was his answer. 'Now, let us remain here no longer, leaving ourselves exposed to counterattack. Withdraw!'

At his word, the Fodhram turned as one and, taking the surviving captives of the Widuz with them, moved silently away from the blood-drenched field, some already composing lines that would be sung around campfires whenever discussion turned to the Battle of Helig Holth.

CHAPTER 22

STORM IN THE AFTERNOON

IT TOOK LEITH A long time to decide that he had awoken; then, when he realised that his eyes were open, he imagined he was lying under the countless points of light that make up the night sky. Nearby a small freshet splashed merrily, otherwise all was silent: no wind, no murmuring trees, none of the outdoor sounds that he had become familiar with on his journey from Loulea; instead an unusual hollow quietness that made him a little uneasy. He sat up and listened intently. He heard nothing but the stream for a long while, but gradually he was able to distinguish the sound of breathing from nearby.

He had grown accustomed to the sounds of his travelling companions sleeping, but could not recall this slow, rhythmical breathing. Recent memory returned: *The last I remember is the water dragging me under – through underwater caves – Phemanderac trapped – Phemanderac, you made it!* he rejoiced. *It must be you I can hear. But it is a shame about your harp. I've never heard anything like that in all my life.*

He stood up and brushed the gritty sand off the Widuz attire he wore, then groped through the darkness to the stream. *I've had nothing to drink since that jug of water in Adunlok,* he reflected as he made to drink from the gurgling waters. *The jug must have had some potion in it.*

Leith was about to plunge his face into the stream when he drew back in horror, remembering the foetid hill of the slain at the bottom of Helig Holth. Though his mind told him the water

466

was probably safe to drink, the fear of the mound of dead and decayed bodies was still on him, and he could not drink it.

'Where are we?' he muttered out loud.

From the darkness around him came the question repeated as if from a thousand querulous bystanders. Where are we? Where are we? Where are we? The sound chilled Leith to the bone: *Is this the Hall of the Dead?* For a wild moment he was convinced he had died and now awaited judgement beyond the walls of time.

'In the lower caverns,' the answer came from close beside him. 'We're out of reach of the Widuz.'

'Phemanderac!' Leith exclaimed. 'Have you died too?'

'Not to my knowledge,' came the amused reply, 'though it seemed I might back there in the river.'

'So is this another cave?'

'It must be. For a while I thought we were out in the open, but those lights above us are some kind of insect or animal, not stars.'

Of course! Leith felt so foolish for not recognising the scene above him. 'They're glow-worms. They hang their lights on long threads. I've seen them in the hills above Loulea, under banks and in caves, but never in such numbers.'

Though they could not see each other, both turned their faces upwards. The sight was peaceful somehow, these insects patiently shining their lights, prepared to wait for unseen prey, undisturbed by the evil of men. The Widuz could not reach this far under the ground. They were safe.

'The underground river has taken us deep into the earth.' Phemanderac began to review their options. 'There's no way back upstream, not against that current. We could look for tunnels – the whole hill seems to be riddled with passages – but we might end up anywhere. It seems to me that we must trust our fate to the course of this river.'

'What if there's no way out?'

'Then we'll spend our last days exploring,' came the reply.

A fierce thirst consumed Leith. Phemanderac had twice taken water from the stream, but the youth could not shift the image of

Helig Holth and the bodies of the slain from the forefront of his mind. Alongside the leaping stream they walked, arms outstretched to alert them to any obstacles in the total darkness. *We must have come half a mile from the pool and the mound; the stream will be free of the foulness by now.* It was no good: his stomach turned at the thought of the water.

The glow-worm cavern left behind, they navigated a narrow tunnel, no wider than the stream, through which they had to wade waist-deep. Ahead Phemanderac kept up a constant flow of chatter; after some time Leith realised that his companion was using his voice to determine the size of the cavern they were in. He talked about his homeland, which he described as a small island under a tall cliff at the head of a long, narrow inlet. Dhauria, he called it; Leith had never heard of such a country. At least it was not one of the Falthan countries, that much he remembered of the Haufuth's teaching.

Phemanderac talked about his occupation as a philosopher, how he had served as a student of languages at the feet of the great minds of his race, and of the *Fuirfad*, the Way of Fire. He spoke of his *dominie*, his beloved teacher Pyrinius, who had taught him a deep love of the written word, and had passed on to his pupil his ability with the harp. He described to Leith the delights of his home city, where many thousands joined together daily to offer praise to the Most High, making music far into the night.

He talked too of the politics of his homeland, describing how Dhauria had remained hidden from Faltha, taking advantage of its location on the far side of Dessica, the Great Desert, because of the fear of being contaminated by the secular Falthans, heathens who had rejected the memory of the Most High. He spoke of the difficulties this isolationism brought to his home, the hardening of habits into rigid traditions, where freedoms were imposed as laws, and his abiding frustration with them.

In truth, he conversed with himself rather than with Leith, reassembling his thoughts, contrasting what he had seen in Faltha with the way his own people lived, trying to sort out

what things he should reject and what things he should take
back to Dhauria.

His voice returned to them as a great echo; apparently they had
entered another chamber, larger even than Wambakalven if the
echoes were to be believed. Leith and Phemanderac stepped out
of the water, their exertions having warmed them in spite of the
coldness of the river.

'I'm the only Dhaurian ever to cross the Great Desert, do you
know?'

Leith was not able to read into this remark the significance its
speaker demanded, and grunted some noncommittal acknowledgement.

'Imagine if Firanes was isolated from the rest of the world.'
Phemanderac pressed on with his thoughts, obviously trying to
make a point. 'How many years would it take for the culture to
freeze into a collection of meaningless rituals?'

Leith shook his head, then realised that Phemanderac could
not see him. 'I don't know what you mean.'

'All my life I've argued with the scholars and the leaders of my
country, trying to convince them that it is time to be drawn once
again into the affairs of Faltha. We have lost something, I tell
them, by hiding away on our island. But no, the leaders are afraid
of losing their mandate, their so-called anointing from the Most
High as prophets of His word; they remain separate and so ensure
their purity – and their uselessness. Whenever I spoke to them of
this they reminded me of *Dhaur Bitan*, the story of the Destroyer
– are you familiar with it? – who sought his own paths, travelling
beyond the Vale and so becoming corrupt. "You will suffer the
same fate as he," they warned me. "But we are called to be the
prophets of Faltha," I said. "How can we prophesy to Faltha if we
never go there?" Yet this logic could not overcome their fear of
the unknown. I asked permission to travel across Dessica, the Great
Desert; they would not give it. I begged for their leave and their
blessing; I was sent away with a curse. They pronounced judgement on me, accusing me of the heresy of evangelism, seeking to
risk contamination for the sake of telling others. *Yet you are a*

prophet, the voice within said to me; *that is your mandate*. So I said goodbye to my teacher and my family, and followed the voice.

'Leith, I don't mean to belittle my countrymen and women. I wish I could describe their inner beauty, fragile like the purest crystal. They have much that Faltha needs, yet they withhold it for fear of losing it. And now I have travelled across Faltha, from Sarista to Sna Vaztha, from Nemohaim to Straux, and have seen that the descendants of the First Men have not entirely forgotten He who called them into being. From the highest to the lowest the faint aroma of holiness can still be discerned, though it has been many generations since He came to you Falthans with fire.

'And on you, my friend, there is more than a faint aroma. It is all over you. You have been marked out for some great purpose; your falling in with me is proof that the Most High orders both our lives, and that I have not fallen prey to the same temptations that assailed the Destroyer, as my leaders feared. If only I could take you back to Dhauria with me, show you to the Assembly of Scholars, and tell them that of such as you will arise the Hand of God – how could they fail to be convinced?'

Leith had no chance to reply, though questions left unanswered since his meeting with the Hermit seemed about to spill out of him. Phemanderac continued with rising vehemence.

'Yet they would not see us! I have been sent into exile, no longer welcome in my own country because of the heresy I believe. To have befriended you would be to them proof of my decadence. Oh Most High, what are we to do? The Hand of God is about to be revealed, just as Arminia prophesied all those years ago. What will he find when he comes? A people asleep, a people afraid, an enemy poised and ready to invade!' His anguished voice echoed from the cavern walls.

'Leith,' he said as the echoes died down, 'what do you think we should do?'

The youth from Loulea sat down on the sandy floor of the cavern, struggling towards an answer.

'I have no choice,' he said finally. 'My Company was charged with two tasks. We were to rescue my parents from the Bhrudwans; well, we've done that. Then we were to go on to Instruere and tell the Council of Leaders of the threatened Bhrudwan invasion. I need to get out of these endless caves, find my friends and complete the task.'

'But what about the Hand of God?'

'I know only what you have said, and what my father told us about Andratan and the questions he was asked there. There was no Hand of God in Loulea when we left. We're a simple village, farmers and artisans. Not a famous warrior among us.'

'Yet you tell me a group of "simple villagers", as you call yourselves, set out after four dread Bhrudwan warriors, servants of the Lords of Fear or maybe even Lords themselves, and succeeded in defeating them. From where I come that would be seen as proof that the Most High has indeed chosen you and equipped you beyond your knowledge for some great purpose. Tell me: would you believe a group of people from your village if they told you they had won a great victory over the most feared fighters in the world?'

'No.'

'Then perhaps you are not what you think you are. Perhaps others in your village are not what they seem. Perhaps the Hand of God has already risen; perhaps he has left Loulea already. Perhaps he is here.'

Leith could do nothing but laugh bitterly in the face of the hollow feeling that rose within him. 'Phemanderac, you don't know me. You're right; things are not what they seem. I'm not even a normal villager. The boys laugh at me; they mock my fears, my worries, my tears. I'm a crybaby. They tell me that I have to do things for them if I want to be their friend. None of the girls will be seen with me, because the others would tease them. I'm too weak, too small, I speak too much, I have a cripple for a brother.

'Then I come on this journey, and you say things about "greatness" and "purpose". Not only you. We met a hermit, a religious man, who said similar things. What am I supposed to think? I would give everything, *everything*, just to be like the others, to be

471

one of them. I don't want to be great! I don't want to be different! I – want – to – be – left – alone!'

The inner dam burst, and Leith cried bitter tears. Phemanderac stood close by, not knowing what to do.

'Listen to me,' he said finally. 'You remind me of a boy I used to know back in my homeland, one who struggled with his calling. I remember him crying out in the night, when he thought no one else could hear: "I want to be like the others!" But in His mercy the Most High did not grant his prayer.' The voice coming from the close darkness seemed strangely flat after the animation of a few moments earlier.

'One day he told his teacher about these things. I remember it clearly. "You are fighting with yourself," the teacher said, "and you cannot win. Every unique thing you succeed in locking away, out of reach of the ridicule of others, is a defeat for you and for everyone else. Your only hope is to abandon all hope of being like them, and learn who you are."

'This boy learned that his friends ridiculed what they did not understand. He learned to value his gifts. He learned to put them in the hands of the Most High. Now his life is free of that constant inner battle. Mind you,' he added with a laugh, 'his feet still get cold!'

Through his misery Leith heard Phemanderac sit down. A moment later, the soft sound of notes like liquid fire began to dance around them.

'I thought you lost that!' Leith cried, amazed.

'My friend,' came the reply, 'if I had not been able to get my harp through the underground river, I would still be under water now, trying to free it. Now be silent, and listen.'

The music that unfolded was a series of low notes with no apparent rhythm or melody, played softly; a sound that spoke of solidity, of the unchanging earth, of the undergirding arms that held them close throughout the summers and the winters. Leith was reminded somehow of a little boy lying awake in bed and listening to his father humming tunelessly as he worked late into the night; of the comfort and security that the unfailing presence

472

of his father had brought to him; of the love his family shared, a love that he had locked himself away from as a sense of betrayal had taken hold deep within him, fuelled by the absence of his father . . .

Memories came tumbling out with the music: the laughter of the children as crippled Hal walked past; his father riding away with the messengers of the King; his mother crying at night when she thought the children were asleep; a boy taunting him until he could stand it no longer and rushed him, arms flailing wildly, but was knocked down by a single blow; standing under the Common Oak waiting for a girl who never came; Stella and Wira, hand in hand; her voice as they huddled together on the ice; the voice of his father. The tears continued to come, there in the unknowing dark, beyond the gaze of those who saw fit to ridicule a boy who reacted to things differently, bittersweet tears of remorse and release that flowed as the music lanced the darkness within.

Leith awoke hours later to the sound of tranquil music. He and Phemanderac spoke little, concentrating on their downward journey following the never-ending stream. Their footfalls shushed in the sand or echoed dully on stone. Time and again they took to the stream itself as their passage was blocked by unseen pillars or walls. *I'll never again ridicule poor Augon of Spindlewood*, Leith resolved, thinking of the blind farmer who lived north of Loulea.

The cavern narrowed about them until once again it was a mere tunnel the width of the stream. The roof lowered until they were forced to stoop, and Leith soon added to his collection of bruises. Smooth walls indicated that the tunnel would be submerged in times of flood. To the left it swung, then to the right, water surging around their waists as the two men struggled onwards. Another, gentler curve to the right, with a dim glow ahead, a glow that made Leith's eyes water. Steadily it increased, shining on the green walls, dappling the surface of the water, making a silhouette of Phemanderac and his harp as he forged through the stream slightly ahead of Leith. Then suddenly they were out of the tunnel into the overwhelming light of day, the cave disgorging the stream and the two travellers, blinking owl-like, into the bottom of a bush-clad, steep-sided gorge under the morning sun.

Footsteps faded away into cold silence. Apart from two dead bodies, Mahnum was now alone in Wambakalven. He grimaced as he examined what was left of the fat man he had taken hostage. In their panic, the guards had hacked the man into a mangled, sodden mess, then had run off. What had scared them? The man had obviously been a leader, a man of importance, of some stature in the fastness of Adunlok.

He spent fruitless time in that ill-fated chamber looking for any sign that might indicate what had happened to his son. For a while he searched silently, but as his desperation increased, so his caution diminished, and near the end he found himself shouting for Leith with no regard for his own safety. However, no one came to investigate the source of the noise, or to find the dead guard and the fat man, perhaps because of the battle that no doubt still raged far above.

Finally frustration and sorrow mastered him, and he sank tiredly to his knees by the path. Leith was not in the cavern, that was obvious, so what were the logical alternatives? He forced himself to think, pushing his mind through the blackness of his despair and self-doubt. The most likely alternative seemed to be that he and his companion had escaped up one of the dark tunnels near the pool, at the lower end of the cave. Less likely, but still possible, was that they had retraced their steps and taken the wider path back up to Adunlok, pursued by the guards. Less likely because surely Mahnum would have seen them.

He would have to do something, and a desperate plan began to form in his mind. But did he remember enough of the Widuz tongue to carry it off? He doubted it, but since there seemed to be no other course of action, he shed his cloak and breeches, took the uniform from the guard he had slain and dressed himself in it, then disposed of his own clothes by throwing them on to the horrifying mound at the bottom of Helig Holth. *Take heart*, he told himself, *you've done this before, you can do it again. People don't like to ask questions. Just remain inconspicuous. If Leith has escaped up to Adunlok, you'll find him. If not . . .*

In less than thirty minutes, he stood on the far side of the hidden door. He straightened the uniform, slightly too large for him and blood-stained near his left armpit, and hoped he was presentable.

A solitary figure stood in this, the lowest passage, staring out of one of the small, round windows, but did not turn to see who had come through the door. Perhaps he did not hear the door's soft click. Mahnum brushed past him, trying to look as though he was in a hurry to go somewhere, breath held, his back prickling with nervousness.

'What are you doing here? Go down to Numen Scou and help bury our dead!' The figure turned towards Mahnum, impatience written on his face. The keys at his side rattled as he slapped his side angrily. 'I want Adunlok emptied. I want every Widuz gathered at the pyre within the hour. Go!'

Little of this was intelligible to Mahnum, but he could read the look on the face of this Widuz, and could understand the impatient gesture. He nodded noncommittally, then turned and made his way up the passage to the stairs.

The second level was empty. Mahnum hurried up the narrow stone stairway to the uppermost level. He turned to the right, hurried down the passage lit only by a flickering torch, and tried the first door. Locked. One after another proved to be locked, with thick bolts drawn across what were clearly cell doors. There was no way of ascertaining if any cells contained prisoners, let alone whether Leith was held here, without making a dangerous amount of noise. The passage ended abruptly at a cold stone wall, the final end of all hopes.

Where hope died, anger began, followed by a gamut of other emotions. Anger over the senseless way the captives of the Widuz had been slain, bitterness at the presumed defeat of the Fodhram raiders, rage over the abomination in the cavern far below, fury at the disappearance of his son. He had been held captive by the most brutal of Bhrudwans, but they had been hardly more evil than these Widuz. All excuses for their behaviour had been forgotten, all rational thought abandoned. All Mahnum wanted to do now was make them pay.

As he sat deep in thought, he heard movement in the cell nearest him. So there were prisoners still! Acting even as he thought, Mahnum launched himself along the corridor, then down the stairs to the lowest level. The figure near the hidden door remained motionless, gazing sightlessly on the battlefield below, and did not stir at the sound of footsteps on the stairs. Coldly furious, Mahnum gave no thought to his actions beyond remembering the correct word: 'Keys!' he growled in the Widuz tongue.

The man turned towards him, and Mahnum noticed with amazement that he had tears in his eyes.

'Keys?'

'Feed the prisoners,' Mahnum said awkwardly, hoping he would not notice.

'Where's the guard?' the man said wearily, but Mahnum noticed that he was removing the keyring from his belt even as he spoke.

He pointed mutely through the window, down to the battlefield. The man nodded, threw the keys to Mahnum, then turned and leaned through the window, head in his hands, paying no more attention to the man beside him.

You could push him through the window, said a voice, and the thought appealed to him. His hands tingled as he imagined the man's back against his palms, stiffening too late, then falling away from the window and tumbling helplessly down into the deadly blackness. *It would only be justice; it would help wrest power away from this foul brood*. Besides, he had been so helpless throughout this long night; here fate was offering him a chance to hit back.

Do it now! the voice urged, and Mahnum actually took a step forward – then froze as he remembered the hideous mound almost directly below. Wasn't the hill high enough? *If I was to send this man to his death, undoubtedly guilty though he is, how would I be any better than him? Leave revenge alone.*

He drew a settling breath, surely making enough noise to warn the Widuz, but the man didn't stir. Mahnum wiped nervous hands on his drab brown uniform, turned on his heel, and made his way through the impregnable fortress of Adunlok, keys gripped firmly in his hand.

It was the work of a few minutes to release the captives in the cells of the topmost level; there were fifteen men and three women in ten small cells, each with a window over Helig Holth thoughtfully provided by the Widuz for their education. But no Leith.

This is the best way to get back at them. They'll want to make sacrifices to thank their gods for their great victory. Well, they'll find no prisoners to hurl down their foul hole. His fury mounted further. *How can we be so concerned about the threat from Bhrudwo when we allow things like this to happen on the borders of our own lands? For that matter, what vile things disfigure our own cities, our own villages, our own homes – our own hearts? Are the Bhrudwans more important than our own evil?*

The newly released captives milled about in the corridor, while in Mahnum's mind a bleak picture unfolded. *So we struggle on to Instruere, and maybe even arrive there, with the loss of many innocent lives. Then perhaps we manage to sweet-talk or more likely bribe our way into the Council of Faltha, and someone among us speaks so eloquently that the Falthan kings believe us. How likely is that? And the kings are able to overcome their border squabbles and petty prejudices; and join forces in an army mighty enough to defeat – how did the Voice of Andratan put it? – 'an iron rod forged from the steel of our people, fashioned to flail the Falthan flab without a shred of mercy'. He could not imagine it. But most ironic of all, should this series of unlikely events culminate in the defeat of the Bhrudwan army, we Falthans may be the big losers: we'll be so busy congratulating ourselves, we'll have less incentive than ever to tackle the evil in our midst. We won't even see it.*

There was some sort of noise behind him, and he turned as, without warning, the prisoners jumped him. 'No, no!' Mahnum cried frantically, trying to fight them off, his vision filled with bodies and arms, fighting ineffectually but overpowering him by sheer weight of numbers. For a moment he was angry rather than fearful; after having faced and fooled the Widuz, the notion of being overcome by those he had just freed simply didn't make sense. But then his head slammed into the marble floor, dazing him, and then again, harder this time, causing blood to flow from his nose. He twisted and turned, ripping his stolen garments, tearing his skin in the grip of clasping hands, not able to evade them, not able to strike; then, inevitably, down came a heavy blow – an elbow, a knee, a foot, it didn't matter – crushing his head against the rock of Adunlok and knocking him senseless.

The problem, the Haufuth discovered, was not in crossing the unbridged, steep-sided stream themselves, even though it appeared the nearest crossing point was nearly half a mile upstream. What gave the Hermit and the Haufuth most concern was working out how to get Wisent the aurochs to the other side. There seemed no alternative to searching more widely for a passage, but as the Haufuth leaned over the edge and looked into the southern distance, he could see no break in the lava cliffs stretching away into the midday haze. Upstream was no more promising, for although the cliffs reduced in height, they had discovered dangerous lava fields through which it would likely prove impossible for Wisent to navigate.

'We're going south,' the Haufuth announced to his friend. 'We must find a way across this river.' He began hauling up the remains of the rope-and-slat bridge that hung uselessly from the top of the cliff.

'How much of a delay will it cause?' The blue-robed Hermit came up behind him, chagrin on his face and in his voice. They had made such good time since leaving Bandits' Cave, having enjoyed mainly fine weather, and having accepted hospitality (and fresh meat) from friendly travellers on the path. Wisent had attracted favourable attention and their fame had gone before them, so that families living deep in the woods came to see them pass, pointing and remarking at the huge beast they brought with them. The Hermit had harboured hopes of catching up with the Company well before Instruere, but that now seemed unlikely. And there had been no sign of the Bhrudwans' passage.

'Possibly a day, probably more. There is no path south from here, as far as I can tell. We'll need to break a path through the forest. What could possibly have happened to the bridge?'

The last of the rope appeared, and the Hermit grabbed at it, frowning.

'Many bridges in the north are destroyed by spring floods, but that was not, I think, the fate of this one. Come over here and take a close look at this rope. See here? This was cut with a sword or a knife.'

'The Bhrudwans?'

'That's my guess also. They are trying to slow down any pursuit.'

'Hopefully they rushed into the waiting ambush of the Company, though we must be nearing Vindstrop House by now. I'm worried; I thought we would have seen signs of their fate—'

'But wait!' cried the Hermit. 'Come and look at this!' He stood over dark-stained stones on the left of the path, a stain four weeks of weather had not wholly obliterated.

'Blood. Enough shed for a man to die.' Now he saw evidence of conflict, the Haufuth was less than sure he wanted to see more. 'But perhaps it was an animal,' he said doubtfully.

'And over here,' the blue-robed man called. 'Here a burning has been conducted – a funeral pyre, perhaps; look, here lie bones.' He stepped back a few feet. 'Best not to look too closely.'

'I don't have to look closely. See this?' He pointed to a sword, planted in the softer ground at the edge of the forest near the place of the burning. 'Vinkullen men use such blades. Here lies one of the Storrsen boys.'

Both men knelt there on the path, alone with their thoughts for a private moment.

'Then the Company is no more.' Sorrow filled the Hermit's voice.

'You're mistaken,' replied the Haufuth, a tear in his eye but a smile on his face. 'If indeed the Company fought the Bhrudwans in this place, there must have been survivors enough to honour the slain with a funeral. The Bhrudwans would not have done such a thing. It stands to reason, therefore, that the

Company must have been victorious – or, at least, not wholly defeated.'

'And, since we did not meet up with the remnants of the Company on their way home along the Westway, it follows that they continue on their journey to Instruere.' The Hermit became excited: 'Possibly with the Bhrudwan captive they sought.'

'Yes – if we're reading the signs with our heads, and not our hearts.'

'No. It has the ring of truth about it.' The Hermit spoke with certainty.

'You sound exactly like Hal!' The big headman laughed. 'In our village he's known as . . .' He snapped his mouth shut too late, having forgotten Hal's behaviour in Bandits' Cave. 'I'm sorry.'

'That's all right,' the Hermit replied graciously. 'I've thought about what he had to say. I can definitely sense an anointing on him, and one day he will make a prophet. But it is important to remember that he is only a youth, immature and with much to learn. Perhaps I might be able to spend some time with him in Instruere. His younger brother, now; he's a different matter altogether – don't you sense it? A great Hand is upon him, steering his life, using this journey to make him into something sharp and accurate, a mighty arrowhead in the quiver of the Most High.'

His voice rose in volume, as though through some inner sight he spoke not to a simple village headman but to the assembled emissaries of the Council of Faltha. 'Though I grew up in the favoured houses of Instruere, I have never seen one with such authority, such a cloak of leadership on his shoulders. If it is my life's destiny to prepare such a one for his time of greatness, and even if I do not see him come into his glory, I shall be content.' He paused for a moment, then laughed merrily at himself. 'Forgive me, my friend; whenever I think about that boy I can't help myself. The anointing of the Most High comes upon me and I cannot remain silent.'

The Haufuth shrugged his vast shoulders. 'Can't say that I see what you see,' he said. 'He's an ordinary village lad. A bit more sense than most, perhaps, a thinker; keeps to himself mostly. A bit sensitive, a bit delicate. Not a patch on his father. Now there's one who might have achieved greatness if he hadn't chosen the quiet life of the North March. Mahnum was a Trader, respected by all at the Firanes Court; but for some reason, one he has never shared with anyone, he retired at the height of his powers and came to Loulea. Leith has potential, perhaps, but at his age Mahnum had already travelled along the Twilight Road to Ciennan.'

'And at his age Leith is on his way to Instruere,' the Hermit reminded him gently.

'True! I had forgotten that. And at my age, so am I. It only goes to show how ridiculous life can be.'

'You're an irascible rogue,' the blue-robed Hermit pronounced, with a hint of levity to leaven his words. 'Your cynicism is a cover for disillusionment and lack of faith. What has the Most High done to offend you?'

The Haufuth squatted down on the stone path. 'Nothing,' he stated flatly. 'That's the problem: he does nothing. More than anything, I'd like to believe in a god who looked after everyone, but I can't. I look at my villagers and, in spite of all my efforts and those of many good men and women, some of them live lives of suffering and pain. As I wander around the village I find myself thinking: if there is a god, how is it that he has favourites? Why does he not do anything for those who need it most? Failing an answer, I conclude that he does not act because he does not exist. I prefer that conclusion to the alternative: that he blesses some and curses others. Were such a god to exist, I would be his enemy.'

The two men and the enormous aurochs spent the afternoon fighting through the bush along the cliff-line, until near dusk they came across a path. Though little more than an animal track, it afforded far quicker passage through the younger, thicker foliage near the riverbank. The Hermit attempted to turn their conversation to the metaphysical, having apparently taken the Haufuth's rejection of faith as a challenge, but the big headman would not discuss it any further. Instead he tried to encourage the Hermit to talk about his past life in Mercium, with an equal lack of success. For the latter part of the afternoon their journey was conducted in an uncomfortable silence, straining the tenuous bonds of friendship that had begun to develop between them.

Dusk found them looking for a place to spend the night. The path led them away from the riverbank into older, more widely spaced trees, a mature forest not so recently affected by lava and mud flows from the menacing volcano some miles behind them. As the sun sank and the shadows merged into greyness the travellers came out of the forest into a pale clearing.

'You look a lot better than when I saw you last,' came a voice from some way off to the right. Two heads jerked in the direction of the voice, where a silhouette stood outlined against the last of the light.

'And you look a lot worse,' the Hermit replied evenly. 'Where have you been, and what have you seen? Your soul is scarred.'

Leader laughed long and deeply, a rich laugh that seemed to take over his body. 'You're right, as usual,' he said. 'Come, both of you; come and share a hearth with the Fodhram, and perhaps you will hear songs and stories to ease your hearts – or perhaps to sadden them. There is much news to tell.'

'What grows in this meadow?' the Haufuth asked, as they skirted around the edge of the clearing towards a flickering fire on its far side. 'A forest of spears?'

'No, friend. What grow here are the sorrows of the Fodhram and their desire for revenge – and the difficulties of their leader, who now desires only peace and not fire or the sword. But tonight you will hear the tale of the Meadow of Spears, as it bears on the fate of certain of your Company.'

'Are they—?'

'In good time. I know how you must thirst for news, yet you must respect your hosts and allow us to tell you in our own fashion. Your thirst will be quenched. Come now; we have a fine roasted lamb, with warm beer and cool water to ease its passage.' He turned to the others gathered around the welcoming fire. 'My brothers,

482

here are two members of the Company of the West. Make them
welcome!'

Once again the magic of the Fodhram began to weave about
strangers to their land. Their open-handedness, their laughter and
their wholesome friendship drew the two weary travellers immediately into the circle, warming and filling them inside and out.
And when the feasting was over and the tales begun, their souls
soared with the singers and storytellers. They struggled to keep
their balance on an ice-covered lake that suddenly gave way; they
gripped the sides of a birch bark canoe with white-knuckled hands
as they drew ever nearer to Bircheater Teeth, menacing flint-sharp
rock shards taller than a tree, thicker than a forest; they cowered
in fear as the terrible warriors from Bhrudwo struck at them with
fiery blades, only to be felled by the bravery of a sandy-haired
mountain man who willingly gave his life that they would escape
the sword. They stood weeping amidst the forest of spears, looking
on the cruelly smoking remains of their sons and daughters; they
crouched in horror on the edge of a vast black abyss as the
screaming horde came at them again, repulsed only by the uttermost effort, while behind them the black-eyed fortress looked on
implacably. They drew breath in the forest under the stars, unsure
for a time where they were, returning slowly to a reality that was
subtly changed, enriched by the tales that still swirled around them
somehow. And then they slept, Fodhram beside Firanese beside
Mercian, each reassured that, although all was not well, not all
hope had been lost.

The Company spent a night in Stanlow, the biggest town they
had yet encountered. Arriving late in the afternoon, the travellers were indistinguishable from many other groups buying and
selling wares at the northern frontier of Treika, and found lodgings at a comfortable inn. In the morning, Kurr used the bulk of
the remaining money from the Southern Run to purchase two
horses; a bay mare on which the women could ride and recover
their strength, and a sturdy baggage pony. Neither was a shadow
of the thoroughbreds he had of necessity given to the Fenni, but

to be close again to any sort of horseflesh was a comfort to the old farmer.

Stanlow nestled into an elbow of the Sagon River, at the point where the Mossbank (known as the Fenbeck to the Treikans) disgorged its chilly northern waters into the broader, slower Sagon. A few leagues to the south the great Withwestwa Wood came to an abrupt end, giving way to cultivated fields, then to an open expanse of grassland, level country alternating with rolling hills. This country was known as the Northern Wastes, or Sheeldalian Muir in the old tongue, on which few trees grew. In late summer all this land was subject to hot winds from the southwest that roared down swiftly from the heights of Clovenhill. Such was the heat of this wind, called The Bellows by those unlucky enough to cross the Wastes in the autumn, that few crops could survive its withering blasts, and most of the land between Stanlow and Ashdown had been abandoned to the tall grasses and the wild animals.

Across this land the Westway ran straight and true, affording travellers the shortest possible route between the two towns. Its builders certainly had the interests of its users at heart. But to the members of the Company, who had passed through Breidhan Moor in winter and made the Southern Run, stories of ill-equipped or unlucky travellers suffering lingering, thirsty deaths seemed exaggerated, and they crossed this open land in four days. To the eye of the visitor the starkness of the landscape mellowed into an austere beauty, a welcome contrast to the never-ending greenery of Withwestwa Wood, and travelling was much easier. The only unhappy one was Farr, who had already begun to miss the joy of the great forest. It seemed to him he had lost both his brother and his heart in the soft light under the forest canopy, and now he was alone.

On the third morning out from Stanlow, the Company woke to a glistening, frosted landscape, and during the day hoar frost rendered the few poplars they passed delicate sculptures. The grass beside the path was brittle to the touch, and all still water froze into sheets of ice. The temperature did not rise above freezing level throughout the long, cold day and that night, after an extensive search for wood, the Company set two fires and slept between them.

The days on the Northern Wastes were days of silence. Stella was locked in her own frozen world, speaking little beyond the briefest possible responses to questions. Parlevaag seemed to Kurr to be tortured by grief, unable to find consolation in the friendship of the Company. *She needs to be among her own people*, Kurr judged. *Even Perdu cannot help her, though he speaks the language.* Farr was plainly disconsolate at having to leave his friends the Fodhram, and nothing Kurr said helped to brighten his downcast countenance. The worry of a missing husband and son was telling on brave Indrett. Though she held her head high and took upon herself a greater share of the work, there were times during the day when even she retreated to gnaw at her fears.

That left Perdu, and it was to the adopted Fenni that Kurr found himself unburdening the cares of leadership. On the third and fourth days, they walked together at the head of the Company, discussing how they might approach the Council of Faltha, debating the merits of sound argument and of bribery. Kurr discovered in the Fenni a slow but deep thinker, one who was able to reason, a practical man who had little love of argument for its own sake. He seemed to be bearing the separation from his wife and children more easily than the others bore their hurt, or perhaps he masked his pain more effectively, and talking to him allowed Kurr to avoid once again thinking about his own inner anguish.

The Company travelled of necessity as a tight group, Kurr having insisted that Farr and Perdu watch over Hal as he tried to befriend the Acolyte, as Mahnum had named him. Hal said little, as ever, to the other members of the Company, and his crippled leg obviously pained him. Quite how he was progressing with the Bhrudwan warrior none of the others could tell. To them, the Acolyte was a wild power barely restrained. They had seen what he could do. It was, frankly, a regularly recurring source of amazement that he remained their captive, that he didn't burst his bonds like some giant of legend, slay them all, then fly away on magical

485

wings. Each of them privately wondered why this man of Bhrudwo did not exercise the magical powers of which Kroptur the seer had warned them.

The bound Bhrudwan captive reminded Hal of the feral cat he'd found caught in a trap three, perhaps four years ago. It had been a huge thing, much larger than the few cats kept as pets by the villagers, and it backed away silently when he approached. Its behaviour had surprised him; he had seen cats caught before, and they were all spitting rage, claws and fangs. But not this one. It seemed to ignore its hurt, acting almost as if its pain came from the humiliation of having been caught. The youth had waited patiently most of that day, but the cat never let him approach it. Hal remembered burying the stiffening corpse later the next day.

So, with the Bhrudwan he was patient, a patience learned from many solitary times spent in the forest, and never made a move against the warrior's pride. The Acolyte did not speak any Falthan language, but then neither had any of the animals Hal had befriended. They communicated using a complex combination of gestures, words and facial expressions, which meant that the Bhrudwan warrior could not hide his thoughts from the young Falthan. But little obvious progress was made, and others in the Company counselled the abandonment of so risky an experiment, in light of what the Acolyte had so nearly done on the road south of Vindstrop House.

But Hal had been lax then, allowing the Bhrudwan access to his magic. He would not make that mistake again. Whenever he thought of the captive, he checked the barrier he had placed between the Acolyte and the source of his power.

Ashdown provided them with a soft bed and a warm night's sleep, and it wasn't until near midday that the Company left the new city on a hill above the Lavera River and passed through the ruins of Inverlaw Eich, the old waterfront town that had burned down less than fifty years before. It was said that no one survived the burning, started accidentally in a kitchen in the crowded docks, and that every house had been razed to the ground. It certainly seemed that way as the Company walked between the charred remains, old bones of a dead town slowly being reclaimed by the grasses and riverbank trees. The old town had been peopled by descendants of the original inhabitants of this wide land, so the story went, those who had escaped the atrocities of the First Men and who had not been forced to find refuge in Cloventop far to the west, but their heritage had perished with them in the ghastly fire that had swept through the town in a matter of minutes.

Yet within two years a new town had been built on a hill overlooking the old town, the markets were as busy as before, and traders haggled with each other over what each claimed were the finest goods of Faltha. But these were different people, people from the south, new people who knew little of the Widuz or the old ways. Kurr had heard the story from the innkeeper and now wished he had not; he could almost hear the screams of the dying as his eyes rested on the skeleton of Inverlaw Eich. He was glad when they had left that place of ill omen well behind.

Now the road broadened, as Laverock, the great city of the Treikans, was less than two days' march in front of them. To their left the Lavera, brown with sediment from Thuya Wood and Plutobaran, a thousand miles to the north, rolled slowly past them, sometimes hidden from view by majestic weeping willows or elegant, tall poplars. Sheep-dotted fields alternated with cultivated land, either already ploughed or about to be. Seagulls swooped behind horse and plough, farmers preparing to plant wheat, barley, oats and other crops for the markets of Laverock. Narrow paths swept back from wooden gates to houses in the distance, increasing in frequency as the Company drew closer to true civilisation.

On the last day before arriving in the Treikan capital, Kurr took Farr to buy food from a local farmer, leaving the others to sleep away the hottest part of the afternoon. Indrett found she could not relax, so she joined Parlevaag in mending the winter cloaks – though in this heat, such a contrast to the Wastes less than a hundred miles to the north, the task seemed nonsensical. But she bent her head to the task, trying not to think the thoughts that hovered like birds of prey above her vulnerable mind, picking over the bones of her loss even while she did something else. It was only when she looked up that she noticed the tears in Parlevaag's eyes.

It was as much her own need as that of her companion that caused Indrett to reach out and embrace the Fenni woman, and the common language of pain and grief superseded any barriers the spoken word presented. For the longest time, they clung to each other, sobbing out their darkness, giving voice to their sorrow, taking comfort in the closeness of another human being. Neither cared where their tears fell, nor did they notice the return of the farmer and the mountain man. It was only the stiffness of their limbs that ended the fierce embrace, and they drew away from each other, but held each other with their eyes. There was understanding there, something shared; they had been strangers, but now they were sisters.

That night the Company slept in soft beds as the inn and the whole city of Laverock was drenched by heavy rains. A storm had come up from the southwest during the hot, still afternoon and pelted the wide Treikan plains with rain and hail before dying out above the capital city. Indrett lay listening to the rain drumming on the tin roof and thought of her own tears. Nothing had changed – Mahnum and Leith were still lost – yet she saw things differently since she had shared her grief. The storm seemed to seal it somehow, as though the great outpouring had been sent to confirm she had been right to follow her instincts. Tomorrow, she knew, the air would smell clean and the city fresh. With a relieved sigh, she closed her eyes and gave in to the weariness that surrounded her.

In the depths of Adunlok, the warriors of Widuz met to gnaw the bones of their defeat. Most of their army had been lost, either to the blades of the hated northern woodsmen or to the insatiable mouth of Helig Holth. The priest and his disciple were dead. And even if they had lived, the Mother could not be fed for some time, as the remaining captives had somehow been freed.

But what galled most of all was the death of Talon, their Eldest warrior. His body now lay on a low bench in the middle of the mess hall, situated on the central level of the stone fortress. By his ever-defiant face, resisting defeat even in the grip of death, stood his younger brother, now by common assent the Eldest. His face seemed hardly less defiant than that of his older brother, and was creased by anger that mounted towards madness.

'Abjure? Concede?' the new Eldest shouted. 'Have the cowards from the north exchanged hearts with you all? How can we leave this death – these deaths,' he corrected himself, 'how can we leave them unavenged? We must strike now!'

'No.' The denial came from the Widuz Chief, under whose command the army had been destroyed. The defeat had robbed him of credibility, but his remained a voice that needed to be regarded. 'No,' he repeated, hoping that logic would suffice. 'We have been beaten once, in this holy place, where all the auguries were in our favour. How can we expect victory in a field not of our own choosing?'

With a yell, the younger brother of Talon leapt at the Widuz Chief, arms outstretched as if to strangle him; but at the last moment what sanity remained to him pulled him up short.

'What field is of our own choosing?' he cried in a voice shorn of restraint. 'What fields have we left to choose? Two thousand years ago, we tilled all the fields within a week's journey of Adunlok. Now those fields are tilled by others! Our fields! A hundred years ago, we hunted deer on the skirts of Blaenau Law. Now the arrows that fly there are not ours, and the meat does not end up on Widuz tables! Was this your choice?' He remained poised in front of the Widuz Chief.

'No, I did not choose—'

'You did! Yes, all of you chose to let our soil leak between our fingers. You do not fight for it! You let it be taken by the arrogant men of Faltha!' His voice rose almost to a shriek, and his spittle showered all within hearing. 'And now they come to the very heart of our keep and kill the best among us! Can you not see? Do you no longer have hearts? Better to die winning back what is ours than to live hiding among the rocks while the little we have left is taken from us!'

489

'You are right, Tala, but what—?'

'What? You say what? Kill them all, that is what! You've seen them die. You've seen them fall into the mouth of Helig Holth. You've seen the Mother take them. They die, just like us! This is what I intend to do. I will lead a fist of warriors, twenty, no more – and we will pursue our enemies. We will return and use them to consecrate the selection of a new priest and a new Widuz Chief. The life of the man who slew my brother is forfeit to me. When he is slain, when I send him screaming into the mouth of the Mother, only then will I be satisfied.

'Now, who will join me? Or do I have to go south to Uflok and ask the widows if they will avenge their dead?'

With a great cry, the warriors of Widuz arose as one man, and Tala the Eldest selected twenty from among them. As they left the room, he paused at the door and said: 'The Widuz Chief will guide you until I return. And then we shall see who is fit to lead our people.' Then he took his fist of men and raced towards the surface.

Mahnum woke to find he was being carried between two strong men. For a ghastly moment he thought he was still in the clutches of the Bhrudwans.

'Where are we? What is going on?' he asked through swollen lips.

'So he speaks the common tongue!' said one of his captors. 'So much the better! He can guide us through this country!'

'I'm sorry to disappoint you, but I'm no Widuz,' Mahnum replied gently. 'I'm a Trader from Firanes, trying as you are to escape.'

At this the two men let him fall to the ground. Harsh and unbelieving questions came at him from all sides, and Mahnum was hard-pressed to prove his point. 'Listen,' he said, 'have you ever heard a Widuz speak the common tongue?' Nobody had. 'Who let you out of your cells?' They had to acknowledge that he had. 'I'm wearing the uniform of a Widuz guard I slew. See this blood-caked tear? Here's where my sword went in. Do you see any wound there?' Not one of them could.

'Look, just keep an eye on me, or tie me up, or anything. I'm not going to give you away. I'm as keen as you to escape from this place.'

The knot of men and women debated for a moment, a debate cut short by a shout from their lookout. 'Behind us! They come!'

Mahnum assessed the situation with a glance. The group of escaped captives stood on a steep path near the bottom of a valley notched deep into the hills. *This must be Clovenchine*, he reasoned. Behind them, at the very top of the path, stood a number of tiny figures, picked out by the morning sun.

'Then let's get out of sight as quickly as possible!' Mahnum said forcefully, and ducked into the trees to his left. 'Come on!'

A shout, echoing faintly across the valley, told them they had been seen. Moving swiftly, the others followed him deep into the forest.

This won't do, thought the Trader. *All the Widuz need to do is to follow the path. They'll make faster time than us, and will be able to cut us off. We must find the path again!* He struck out to the right, down the hill, explaining his thinking as he went.

Two or three of the men were unhappy with the idea of this man in a Widuz uniform leading them, and said so. 'We have no time for debate!' Mahnum replied. 'Go your own way if you don't trust mine!'

So it was that he led no more than a dozen escapees through the great valley that divided Clovenhill in two. They found the path without difficulty, but were helpless to act when shouts and screams were heard from the forest some distance behind them. The five men and one woman who had not trusted him had undoubtedly been caught by the Widuz, and their shrieks gave a chilling indication of their fate.

'There is nothing we can do for them now,' the Trader said gently, exhorting his charges to make haste along the path, 'except remember what happened, and determine that we will not be taken.'

Night and day they struggled along the path, somehow keeping ahead of the pursuing Widuz. Water was taken from streams on the way, while food was stolen from whatever farms or hamlets they encountered. But always behind came the Widuz, their wrath matched by the desperation of the captives. Sometimes the captives managed to draw well in front, while at other times little more than a mile separated the two groups. On the fourth or fifth morning – Mahnum was unsure which – he spotted two figures high on a spur on the far side of the river. *Lookouts, no doubt; they will make it harder for us to escape.* As if in answer to his fear, the figures vanished from the ridge, heading east. And behind them came the Widuz, now definitely gaining ground as the captives tired.

It took five days for Leith and Phemanderac to make their way down the steep slope from the caves under Cloventop and out of the land of Widuz. The land was divided in two by Clovenchine, the gorge of the Sagon River, which flowed in a narrow floodplain over three thousand feet below the heights above, though in most places the drop was by no means sheer. The most difficult moment was the crossing of the Sagon River, which they essayed on the first day. They had to turn aside from a manned ferry at a small town directly below Cloventop, for fear the story of their escape had spread; and it was another day's march before they found an unguarded boat. There were many clearings in the wooded country on the deep valley floor, small patches where farmers fought the thin soil and the yearly floods, and from one of these farms Leith and Phemanderac stole enough food to see them safely out of Widuz.

Leith had no real idea of where they were, or in which direction they should head. His only instinct was to return to the slopes of the volcano, where surely his parents searched for him still. Phemanderac would not consider this, insisting the best plan was to make for Instruere and wait for the others to arrive – if indeed they had not arrived there already. Besides, he argued, neither of them knew the way back to the volcano, and that journey would involve travelling the length of this hostile land. It would be better simply to retrace the path Phemanderac had used to enter Widuz in the first place.

Across the Face of the World

Early on the fifth day away from Adunlok, the two men stood high on a ridge overlooking the Sagon, with a wide view to the east where a great plain stretched away to the horizon. Down in the Clovenchine, two groups of people hurried along the river-bank path that Leith and Phemanderac had abandoned the evening before.

'They're after us,' Leith said simply.

'Possibly,' the thin man agreed. 'They are certainly in a hurry. But why do two groups travel the same road? Why have they split up? Our trail should not be that hard to find!'

'I don't want to be captured. I don't want to be taken back to that fortress. I'd rather die out here in the open.'

'I'd rather live; there's still too much to see. Quickly, we must hurry. If we wish to get down to the plains ahead of them, we will have to run for it.'

The rest of the morning was a blur of uncertain footsteps, of rocks and trees rushing past, of constant pounding as they descended the slopes of the spur they had climbed. This sentinel guarded the eastern approaches to Clovenchine, and had an evil name and reputation unknown to them: Cairn Deargh, the Mountain of Dead Men's Bones. On its upper slopes a lookout was once kept, manned not by the Widuz but by the First Men, designed to keep the ferocious tribal warriors shut in. The bones of the slain were piled at the base of the lookout, and for a time the large pile bore witness to the ferocity of the war. Bones and lookout both were lost now in the regenerating forest. Leith and Phemanderac flashed through this country, scattering birds and animals before them, eyes for nothing save the uneven path below their feet.

Eventually the ground flattened out and their run slowed to a trot, then a walk, and for a few moments they stopped to rest. But the horror of Widuz was still all about them, and long before they had rested fully they were on the move again, drawing on reserves of energy they were unaware they possessed. They walked the rest of that day and well into the night, and early the next morning they came out from under the eaves of the forest and found the wide, grassy plain they had seen from the ridge the day before.

There were no paths through this land, so they struck out across country, uncertain of their exact destination. Somehow they had missed their way back on the ridge, and now they were certainly further south than Phemanderac would have liked. 'There is a road from Stanlow that runs along the Sagon River, which took me two-thirds of the way to Widuz,' he explained. 'When I didn't know better. That is the road I am looking for.'

Leith did not answer, saving his energy for a leap off a bank down into a small stream. Both men splashed noisily across it, then climbed up the far bank into a grove of trees.

'Over this way!' came a shout from somewhere to their right.

Leith froze. Beside him, Phemanderac was the first to respond, grabbing Leith's arm and pulling him to the left. 'Run! Now!'

'Flush them out!' came another voice, this time from their left and much closer. 'They can't be far ahead!'

Phemanderac spun Leith around and they moved quietly back in the direction of the creek. In a moment they stood at the top of the bank, but their escape was cut off by three men standing in the stream. One of the men looked up, saw them and gave a shout. At that moment a group of men, swords and knives drawn, emerged from the trees, surrounding them.

'I'm not going back to Adunlok. They're not throwing me down that hole,' Leith hissed in desperation.

'Well, what have we here?' one of the men said. 'Two deer, caught in our trap. But what kind of deer are these? Foolish Widuz deer, by the cut of their cloth. Don't you know it's not safe for you to browse down on the plains?' His voice had an ugly cast.

Leith could not understand the meaning of the man's words, but Phemanderac spoke up. 'We are not Widuz, although we have borrowed their uniforms. We have escaped from the grim fortress of Adunlok, and seek shelter with Treikans. What manner of men are you?'

'We are a party of Treikan hunters from Inch Chanter,' the man replied evenly. Around him the other men relaxed visibly, lowering their swords. 'We thought you were deer – noisy, foolhardy animals, to be sure – but now we see that you are neither deer nor Widuz. Escaped from Adunlok, you say? Now that would be a feat of courage!'

The raven-haired man turned and spoke for a moment to the man beside him.

'This is what we will do,' he said, turning back to the two brown-cloaked strangers. 'We were on the trail of two deer, and we must hunt them down. You will remain here, with Creen here as a guard, and we will come back for you in two hours at the most; then you may come with us to Inch Chanter and tell us your story. Agreed?'

Leith looked at Phemanderac. 'What other choice do we have?'

That afternoon Leith and Phemanderac travelled with the Treikan hunters in the second of two horse-drawn carts. The first cart was filled with the carcasses of two horned stags, great prizes this far south, apparently, and the Treikans joked of the luck the strangers had brought with them.

The air was hot and still, stifling any attempts at serious conversation. Weary beyond knowledge, Leith cast himself into the bottom of the cart and sought rest, finally being rocked to sleep by the swaying of the cart and the rhythm of the horses' hoofs.

When he awoke in the late afternoon the air was hotter still, a sweaty, breathless heat unlike any he had experienced. On the front of the cart the driver sang a lilting tune to the beat of the hoofs, while walking beside him another played a strange instrument by alternately squeezing it together and pulling it apart, as it seemed to Leith. More Treikans walked beside the carts than had been in the hunting party; it appeared that all the workers in the fields were making for the town that still lay some way ahead. For a moment Leith was puzzled; at least two hours remained before sunset, but when Phemanderac tapped him on the shoulder and pointed behind them, he understood why.

Away to the west rose a massive cloud, easily the equal of the stormcloud that had brought snow to Breidhan Moor, and as he watched it appeared to be rolling slowly towards them like a huge

495

wave. It loomed blackly over the fields, reaching out dark fingers; its base sat squarely on Clovenhill, a grey smudge on the horizon.

'Some storm!' remarked one of the men beside the cart.

'When will it arrive?' Leith wanted to know.

'Not for a while yet. Hopefully we'll be well inside Inch Chanter by then.'

A few of the hunters grunted their agreement.

'What sort of weapon is that?' asked a freckle-faced boy, pointing to Phemanderac's harp.

Phemanderac laughed. 'It's not a weapon,' he replied. 'It's a musical instrument.'

The boy's eyes widened. 'How does it work?'

'Let me show you. Just pluck the string here with your finger – like that – now run your finger along the strings . . . What do you think?' He didn't have to ask; the boy was laughing with pleasure.

Phemanderac anchored the base of the harp between his feet, then began to play in time with the clopping of hoofs on stone. Leith held his breath; but this time the sound was not magnified by the enclosed space of a cavern, and for a while he was a little disappointed. The subtlety of the rhythm crept over him, however, and he found himself beating time on the side of the cart.

Now others gathered around the cart, drawn by the music. One man began to clap his hands, and invited others to join him. A youngish woman took a long-necked stringed instrument from a pack on her back, and started strumming it. The driver of the cart kept up his song, which seemed to Leith to be a series of sounds rather than words.

As they drew near to the small hill upon which Inch Chanter was built, at least a score of people swirled around the cart as the music reached out and pulled them in. But now the storm was upon them, and a huge clap of thunder interrupted the singer. The music continued bravely for another minute, but another, louder thunderclap sent them scurrying towards the open gate of the town. A third rumble rolled across the plain, following closely behind a searing lightning bolt, and Phemanderac gave up playing. 'I can't compete with this!' he shouted.

Across the Face of the World

A strong wind began to blow, ruffling hair and bending the willows by the stream that surrounded the town. Another crack of thunder shook the earth beneath them, then rumbled on for what seemed like a minute or more. Large raindrops fell, a few at first, rapidly escalating into a downpour. By the time the carts were safely inside the gate, everyone aboard was soaked to the skin.

Out on the plains Mahnum marshalled the escapees, trying with valiant words to keep their spirits up. But they were unarmed, and the Widuz were now only a few hundred yards behind them.

'See!' one man cried, turning and pointing wildly. 'The Widuz come for us! They bring a storm with them to seal our doom!'

'Don't be foolish! It's just a spring storm!' Mahnum shouted, but his voice was lost in a clap of thunder so loud that the ground heaved under them. 'Press on! We've come this far!'

But even to his mind, practical and unencumbered by superstition, the appearance of the vast dark cloud rearing up behind their pursuers seemed a harbinger of doom, a manifestation of wrath and vengeance. The Widuz had seen it too, and it filled them with brazen courage, so that their wild shouts were borne to the ragged group of escapees on a rising wind. Around him the escaped captives slowed, exhausted, robbed of their energy by fear.

Then the full force of the storm was upon them, with lightning ripping the sky apart and thunder boiling all about them. Sheets of rain were unleashed upon them, replaced in an instant by hailstones that forced pursued and pursuer alike to seek protection under their cloaks. The chase was forgotten in the midst of this furious assault from the skies, from clouds that seemed to swirl just above them. A lone tree almost exactly between the two groups exploded as a bolt of lightning smote the earth, and terror filled all those on the plain. The hail turned to rain, then back to hail – huge stones this time – and suddenly a kind of madness descended upon them all. Mahnum's cries of frustration went unheeded as, with thought for nothing but their own safety, both groups scattered over the fields, seeking drains, ditches, or any kind of shelter.

CHAPTER 23

THE GATES OF INSTRUERE

THE NEXT FEW WEEKS forever remained a haze to Leith. Vaguely he recalled scenes of pastoral beauty, crisp, frosty mornings and balmy spring afternoons, but the necessity to press on before he had in any way recovered his strength robbed Leith of the opportunity to enjoy them. So he retreated within himself, saying little to Phemanderac, choosing instead to walk the misty paths of his mind, turning over his conversations with Stella time and again, wondering what sort of impression he had made on her. For it was towards her his thoughts had turned: had he merely imagined her favour that night on the ice? Had she simply extended a condescending kindness, a regal queen distributing largesse to a pauper at the roadside, or did she mean something deeper? Her smile was the one clear image his weary mind carried. Clean and fresh it was, like a Treikan morning after rain in the night, with wildly dancing eyes like the sun flashing in puddles on the Paludis Road, full of life and the promise of youth, and his heart ached with longing at the thought of her.

Of his parents he thought little. He had scant memories of that part of his journey, and could not remember sighting his mother or his father by the bridge in the hour of their triumph over the Bhrudwans, though surely he must have seen them, must have said something to them. Strangely, the clearest image that remained after the months of their journey was the disturbing sight of Hal, enfolded by black wings, muttering incantations as he bent over the prone body of the sleeping Hermit.

498

Across the Face of the World

Leith and Phemanderac travelled southward through the country of Old Deer, a land once the border between Treika and Widuz. Of recent times the Treikans had pushed the border further west in their search for the famed and increasingly rare antlered stag, and the newly acquired land became known as New Deer. It had been through New Deer that Leith and Phemanderac had come on their way out of Widuz, and they had encountered the Treikan hunting party on the hazy boundary between New and Old Deer. New Deer was still largely forest, though the Treikans were burning the trees at a great rate, and evidence of their depredations could be seen almost every day on the journey south to the coast. Old Deer was now pasture, apart from a few isolated copses, a land of soft greens and gentle browns. The smell of freshly tilled earth had replaced the dankness of the forest, and no one hunted there any more.

By the time the road veered to the east once again and entered a swampy, dune-scattered country, Leith was footsore beyond belief. The soles of his walking boots, picked up in the Adunlok armoury, had worn unbearably thin, and offered his feet no protection from the stones of the road. 'The Paludis Road,' Phemanderac had told him cheerfully. 'A bit light on people, but then you've probably had enough people for a while. The shortest road from Inch Chanter to Instruere, they told me, so here we are.' He appeared not to notice Leith's discomfort, and the youth was certainly not going to tell him. He needed something to help him remain angry at the world.

The Paludis was a marshland formed as water from the north became trapped in the lowlands behind a series of old dune ridges. Too wet and disease-ridden to farm, the Treikans had given it up a long time ago, seeking new lands to the west, preferring the Widuz to the mosquitoes. After a few days on the Paludis Road, Leith understood why: they seemed worse even than the black biters of the northern spring. It reminded him of something the Haufuth had said. Had it been on their journey? 'There's always a fly in the ointment,' he had grumbled. 'This is how I know there is no Most High God: for every spring there's a mosquito, in every field there are stones. What sort of cruel god would tease his people by making life so demanding that there was no time to enjoy the world he made for them?' The words had stuck in Leith's mind. *For every Stella there's a Druin, for every Leith there's a Hal.*

I wonder what answer Hal would give? Leith didn't want to know, didn't want any more correction from anyone. *I don't want to be changed*, he thought. *I want to be judged right even if I stay exactly as I am.*

As spring gave way to summer, bloom replacing blossom as blossom had replaced bud, the Company left Laverock and Treika behind and began the slow climb over the flanks of the Remparer Mountains, the barrier between western and central Faltha. The Westway regressed from paved road to narrow path, and the hordes of people living their lives on and alongside it were reduced to a trickle of hardier souls eking out a livelihood on the thin soils of the uplands. Here in ages past feudal lords had ruled over tiny kingdoms, the largest domain barely stretching out of eyesight. The depredations of bandits had reduced this fair borderland to ruin, and the wind played in empty courtyards while treeroot and ivy slowly peeled stone from stone as once-proud castles melted imperceptibly into the grass. The infamous Robbers of the Ramparts were nowhere to be seen, seeking richer pickings further north perhaps, leaving an old, tired land struggling for breath.

As Kurr took the last steps of a long, slow climb, he reflected that a few short months ago the exertion would have left him breathless. He could feel the years falling from him, though surely the burdens he carried would have weighed him down no matter how fit he had been.

But nothing could weigh down the heart that beheld such beauty, he thought, as the path began its descent. Almost directly below, at the bottom of a winding path, the town of Inverell snuggled against grassy hills. A valley of woods and fields stretched away on their right to the sea at the edge of their clear-air vision. Kurr imagined he could see farmers in their fields, people on the streets, smoke coming from the chimneys of the tiny houses. And even though he knew it was a trick of the mountain air, he fancied he could reach down and pick up the houses like toys between thumb and forefinger.

To their left lay a different kind of beauty, not unmixed with dread, for there marched the Remparer Mountains, the Ramparts of Faltha, also called Manu Irion, the Man-Eaters. Greater than the Jawbone Mountains far to the west, second in Faltha only to the mighty but remote Aldhras on the Bhrudwan border, the Man-Eaters had long been a trap for the unwary. Two thousand years after the First Men settled the land, there were still only two roads through them, the gentle Westway to the south and the terrible Whitefang Pass far to the north. Between the two passes towered the Skyvault Range, a tangle of rock and ice that suffered no path. The morning sun backlit peak after peak, a giant army marching away into the distance, reminding Kurr of the deadlier army that might already be poised at Faltha's gates. At the head of the white-tipped throng stood Drum Mountain, Druim Corrie as the mountain-dwellers called it, looming over the small town just as the Destroyer might soon loom over every town in Faltha. With these morose thoughts for company, the old farmer hurried his charges down the narrow path as a cold wind blew in from the southwest.

That night the Company found lodging at a pleasant enough inn, claiming the very last beds. As usual they kept to themselves, trying to avoid the inevitable questions. There was no way they could disguise the fact that they brought a prisoner along with them, and those who gained a closer look could tell that the man held captive was of a different race. Their story for anyone bold enough to inquire (and in every town there was always someone) was that there was a reward in Instruere for this robber, and they were taking him to face justice.

Kurr took time in every town to ask a few questions of his own, and tonight at the Wayfarers Inn he asked them again. Had other travellers from the west passed this way recently? A sandy-haired lad of about fifteen, though he looked at least two years younger, and a tall, dark-haired man about forty years of age; had anyone seen them? Tonight the answer was the same as always.

No, there had been no such travellers. With the frequency and dependability of the journey by ship, few people made long journeys on the Westway any more. The only travellers were locals and a few Treikans making the risky journey to Deuverre. Kurr sighed, and wondered whether they should have taken Farr's advice and sought ship themselves at Lavana, a week's walk south of Laverock at the mouth of the Lavera River. *We might have been in Instruere by now – at the latest within a week. But,* he reminded himself, *we might have missed Leith and Mahnum. If they are still alive . . .*

The Paludis behind them, Leith and Phemanderac began to make much better time. Hard calluses had formed on Leith's feet, and his calves had become inured to pain. His companion strode tirelessly in front of him with a mile-eating gait, and it was easy to imagine that this man had indeed travelled across the world. Such experience proved invaluable. Penniless in a strange land, they could not avail themselves of the ships that lay waiting at Lavana docks. Neither could they stay in formal lodgings in the cities and towns they passed through, but Phemanderac was adept at winning them a bed of soft straw in a barn, or occasionally even a mattress in a farmhouse. They certainly never wanted for food. The lean philosopher had learned how to live from charity without ever giving offence, more often than not playing his harp to earn their supper.

The gentle coast road took them across the Tarradale Broads, known of old as Rhinn na Torridon, and up a wooded valley to a small town nestled under a steep-sided mountain. That evening the inn was full – the first time in months, they were told – but the night was warm after a day of cool breezes at their backs, and the two companions found shelter under a high hedge a mile or so south of the town gates.

'How much further?' Leith asked Phemanderac as they prepared to leave in the pink dawn of a misty morning. 'I would really like a rest. I've forgotten what it's like to stay in one place.'

'We are closer now to Instruere than we are to Inch Chanter.

In perhaps two weeks we will cross the Longbridge and be safe behind her stout walls, where maybe you can find rest.'

Leith made to reply, but Phemanderac had already shaken out his long legs and applied them to the task of striding on to the Westway. Shaking his head, the youth stretched the kinks out of his back and hurried to follow.

Deuverre was a low-lying, densely populated land, with few of the familiar trees or plants Leith knew from the north. It seemed that nothing there was left to nature, people contriving instead to make some use of every inch of ground. Here folk were wealthier and farmed their own lands, unlike Treika where most of the land was owned by a few lords. Rather than farms clinging to the land, as they did in the highlands of the Remparers, or being interspersed with forest and mountain, as in Leith's homeland, here they dominated the landscape. Towns were larger and more frequent, but people were busier and less hospitable, and as a consequence Phemanderac was less successful in obtaining charity from them.

'Because they are wealthy,' he grumbled. 'The more they have, the more they protect it.'

'If I had been travelling alone, I would have starved to death by now.' Leith rubbed his stomach expressively. His hunger had done nothing to improve his temper, soured by weeks of foot-slogging.

Phemanderac laughed. 'They would let you work for your supper. Of course, it would then have taken you six months to reach Instruere.'

'I don't like it here.' To Leith, the people of Deuverre seemed less open than those of the north. He compared them unfavourably with his own villagers, with the Fodhram, even with the Fenni. They spoke the common tongue only when necessary, and were indifferent at best to travellers.

'Stick to the path, then, and let me do the talking, though how much use I can be is uncertain. I avoided this land on my way west, choosing instead to take the northern roads through Asgowan and Haurn, and came into Treika through Whitefang Pass.'

'I hope Instruere is not like this.'

'It's not,' said Phemanderac cryptically. 'It is quite different.'

Finally, in the last week of June, and in heat and humidity the like of which Leith had never experienced, they came to what at first appeared to be a lake, with a bridge stretching away into the hazy distance.

'The Aleinus,' Phemanderac announced. 'Another hour and we'll be there.'

'This is a river?' Leith asked, incredulous. 'Surely there cannot be this much water in all the mountains of the world!'

'Indeed it is a river; well, actually, it is *the* River. When in flood it can be many miles across, brown with silt from the upriver countries, so the locals told me when I came through here last year. Did you notice how the Westway runs along the top of an earthen bank? That arrangement keeps it above all but the largest of the floods. This was built, apparently, after the Bhrudwan invasion, when the armies of northern Faltha were cut off from Instruere by a vast flood.'

Phemanderac had stepped on to the bridge as he talked, to be interrupted by a bald-headed man who swung a wooden gate closed in front of them. 'No one crosses the Longbridge without proper authority,' he growled.

'What authority is this?' the gaunt philosopher asked, puzzled.

'If you have to ask, you obviously do not have it,' came the abrupt reply. 'Now, move on.'

'There was no gate on this bridge last year!'

'Stranger,' the man said with exaggerated patience, 'there is a gate here now. That is all that matters.'

'But we need to get to Instruere!' Leith cried.

'Then enter from Straux,' came the rumbling reply. 'There is no gate on the bridge from Straux.'

'And how, good sir, do we get to Straux,' Phemanderac responded heavily, 'when the only bridge south is this one?'

The bald man shrugged his shoulders. Behind them a line of people began to form.

'Be reasonable!' Phemanderac said, exasperated by the officiousness of the man. 'I just want to leave Deuverre and go to

504

Instruere!' But the man had turned aside and was talking to a young couple, who showed him a small yellow piece of paper. The gate swung open and they passed through, walking rapidly off into the distance.

While the two travellers watched, a succession of people showed their yellow papers and gained access to the bridge. Then one man, with a wife and several small children in tow, could not produce his paper. Even with his keen eyes, Phemanderac nearly missed the discreet exchange of money, but the gate swung open and the man and his family passed through.

Phemanderac turned to Leith. 'This is obviously another Instruian moneymaking scheme. They're famous for them. Come, we must find out where to get a piece of paper each – or, more likely, some money with which to purchase them.'

After a great deal of fruitless inquiry, in which many of the local populace appeared not to wish to discuss the subject, Phemanderac finally discovered that Instruere had imposed a tax on all Deuverrans who worked in the great city and, finding it an easy and lucrative source of revenue, had extended it to cover all travellers. The only way of avoiding the tax was to obtain an exemption from the mayor of Instruere, at whose discretion a yellow paper could be issued. At first this was limited to those who were deemed of importance to the city, but soon it became known that exemptions could be purchased from certain city officials for a fraction of the cost of the tax.

'Is there nowhere else apart from Instruere I can buy a yellow paper?' Phemanderac asked angrily.

His informant shook her head.

'So all I have to do is to go to Instruere and find the right man, and purchase from him a yellow paper. Except I need the paper to get across the bridge. Surely this is someone's idea of a joke!'

Leith spoke up. 'Perhaps we could find someone willing to sell their papers.'

'And what would we pay for them with? You forget we have no money – and the lady here tells us the papers cost the equivalent of two days' wages each.'

'Is there no other way into the city?'

'Apparently not,' the philosopher answered, but his gaze rested on the line of small fishing smacks at the water's edge.

That night they found a fisherman willing to spite the tax men in return for assistance with the evening's catch. As a result, it was two weary, tired and foul-smelling companions who clambered out of the boat on to the far shore under a half-moon, and spent a chilly few hours waiting for the sun to rise and the city gate to open.

'I'll remember this,' Phemanderac said, stretching his stiffening back. 'There is as little civility here as we found on Clovenhill.'

Leith shuddered. 'At least they've not tried to throw us down any deep holes.'

'What is bureaucracy if it is not a deep hole? There was no need for this!'

Leith shook his head. They had risked death – and at least one of their companions had died – to bring a warning to this great city, and yet at journey's end they were denied entry, having instead to sneak in like thieves. If this was how the prophecies of his greatness were to be fulfilled, he would rather turn around and make for home now. *Home*. Sheltering under the towering walls of Instruere, he could think of nothing but his rustic village. His place was the village, he realised, and he would never rise above it. Greatness was for the great. He would be happy with – what? His thoughts returned to that familiar image, that bright smile and the happiness it might bestow on the one who won its favour.

Though its buildings were the wonder of the western world, and its streets reeked of the passage of the years, Instruere was not quite the fabulous city of which its inhabitants boasted. This was due in no small part to the circumstances of its birth. When the First Men had arrived in Straux over two thousand years ago, they found a collection of mud huts at that point where the Aleinus, the father of rivers, divides into a delta. With little regard for ceremony – or for the local inhabitants – rival towns were built on the large island they found there, Inna on the northern shore,

Struere on the southern. This division reflected the contention between the First Men over the guardianship of the Jugom Ark, the Arrow of Yoke, the symbol of the favour of the Most High, and for a bitter generation those who dwelt in the two towns looked across at each other over a few hundred yards of open ground: looked, but made no contact. Finally, when the decision was made to allow Bewray to take the arrow south, an uneasy reconciliation was reached and the two towns worked together. Eventually from this coalescing union came a third town, engulfing the island in the middle of the Aleinus, and Instruere was born.

Instruere's planners sought to make it the capital of the world, building on a scale unparalleled in Faltha, even when earnings were not sufficiently large to justify it. Time and again speculators invested in grand schemes, time and again moneylenders called in their loans and the grand schemes failed, but on the ruins of such schemes the great city was built. After the speculators came the traders who claimed the western end of the island as their own, erecting on it vast warehouses and sending long wharves out into the wide blue-green waters to which came barges and scows from throughout Faltha, creating real wealth for the first time.

Centuries of trading cemented the place of Instruere as a commercial centre, and from the profits they made the masters of trade were able to patronise the arts and sciences, which flourished during the Golden Age of Faltha in the second five hundred years after the fall of Dona Mihst. The governors of Instruere constructed a Hall of Lore, modelled after that of the Vale of old; following the pattern of Dona Mihst, a tall tower was raised, a monument to their high past rather than as a place of worship. The largest and most ornate building in the city, the cavernous Hall of Meeting, was also the most expensive ever built, with carven ceilings that occupied the most talented artisans in the land for ten years. Its main hall stretched over fifteen hundred feet in length, and it stood over a hundred feet high. These buildings housed the most prized artefacts – paintings, sculptures, music – of each generation, and the Council of Faltha made its home in the Hall of Meeting.

The heavily defended city had been taken only once by an enemy, and that without a fight. The end of the Golden Age was signalled by the Bhrudwan invasion, when the armies of southern Faltha were defeated by the superior army of the Destroyer on the fields of Straux, a few leagues south of Instruere. While the south remembered only that the north did not fight with them, they forgot the storm that kept the northerners pinned in Deuverre, unable to lend assistance. The Destroyer walked unchallenged in victory into Instruere and set up a hundred years of government in the Hall of Meeting.

When eventually he was driven out – whether by sickness, as some said, or by the weakening of his forces through intermarriage, or by insurrection, as Instruians claimed – his rule was replaced by a strengthened council made up of representatives of the southern Falthan nations. This was extended to include all Falthans in NA173, when a new generation concerned itself more with the politics of trade than gnawing the bones of old grievances, and it is from this date that existence of the full Council of Faltha is reckoned. It was with this powerful, inscrutable body that the Company sought audience – if they could win their way to the city.

The day after the musician and his companion left Inch Chanter another foreigner, also dressed in the clothes of the Widuz, made his way across the fields. Behind him came the bedraggled remnants of the prisoners of Adunlok, those the foreigner had managed to regather from their hiding places in ditches and hedgerows. These prisoners were Treikans, most from Inch Chanter and the surrounding farmlands, men and women who had been mourned as dead, and the joy of the townspeople when they beheld their lost sons and daughters was without bounds. They feted this stranger, the more so when the full story was told, but the stranger wanted little of their praise or celebration. Urgently he asked after a tousle-haired youth and was astonished to find he had missed his son by less than twelve hours.

Though the storm had scattered the Widuz, it had not destroyed them. They encamped around the walled town and laid siege to it for five days, determined to avenge the death of Talon, their champion, killed in Wambakalven, the womb of Mother Earth. Farmers working their fields were prevented from returning home by the sword-wielding Widuz, and no one could leave by either of the two gates. As much as Mahnum wished to pursue his son, he could not.

'What do they want?' the elders of the town asked the stranger.

'Us,' Mahnum said. 'Myself and the other former captives.'

'What have you done that makes them so eager to get at you?'

'I killed one of their guards; that and emptying their cells of potential sacrifices undoubtedly earned their displeasure.'

'You have done a brave and noble thing,' the elders told him, 'and for the moment you are the hero of the town. But after a week or two without food or fresh water, and with many of our people left to find shelter on the open plain or in other towns, people may be less enthusiastic at your continued residence here.'

'I understand. But what is stopping us simply driving them away? At most there are two dozen Widuz outside your walls, while there must be at least a hundred able-bodied men in this town.'

'Who no doubt wish to remain able-bodied,' came the quick reply.

'Are you trying to tell me that you want me to surrender to these killers?' Mahnum looked heatedly around the sumptuously appointed room, but each one there avoided his gaze.

'So I just walk through the gate and into their sword blades?'

One man cleared his throat; still no one spoke.

Mahnum felt anger rise within him. 'Perhaps we could make it a social event! You could all watch from the walls, and I could call out so you know how I feel as they cut me down! Or would this complete the great myth of the gallant stranger who rescued townspeople from the Widuz and then gave his life for the town? Well?

'I thought it would have taken a certain amount of courage to live here, close as you are to Clovenhill, but I see I was mistaken. At least lend me a sword, so I might give a good account of myself.

509

May my death be on your conscience!' And with those words he snatched a broadsword and a jewelled scabbard from the wall, and strode towards the door.

'Not that sword!' came a plaintive cry from behind him. 'That's the sword of Jethart, the great warrior captain of Treika, and a mighty heirloom. It is worth more than all of Inch Chanter together!'

'Then may it serve me well!' Mahnum growled and, as the stunned gathering of elders looked on, he drew the sword from the scabbard and swung it in a great arc about him. 'There are none here worthy even to display it on their walls. Or does anyone want to take it from me?'

No one moved.

'I thought not. Pray for my success, or prepare to watch your precious heirloom be taken to the fastness of Adunlok!'

He slammed the door behind him, but already anger was giving way to prudence. A bold and heroic gesture his death might be, but the secrets of the Destroyer's great strategy were locked in his mind, and his death would deal a severe blow to the Falthan cause. He stormed out into the main street and through the throng of curious onlookers.

Something pulled at his sleeve, and Mahnum was about to knock it away when he saw that it was a small boy. 'What do you want?' he growled.

'Excuse me, mister,' he stammered, 'but my aulfather wants to have a word with you.'

'Couldn't he come himself? Why send a youngster? What is wrong with this town?'

'Come this way, if you please,' said the small boy politely, and tugged at Mahnum's sleeve again.

Down the main street and away from the stares of the townspeople they went, and through a maze of narrow side streets until they halted at a brown wooden door. The boy knocked and after a moment they were admitted by an old man.

'This is my aulfather,' whispered the little boy. 'You rescued his daughter from the Widuz.'

Across the Face of the World

The leathery-faced old man led him into a small sitting room, and bade him take a seat. *I could do without this right now*, Mahnum thought. *What I need is a chance to think things through.*

'You could probably do without this right now,' wheezed the old man. 'I imagine you would rather have some time to yourself. I hear that things did not go too well for you in your meeting with the elders.'

'You seem to know a surprising amount,' said Mahnum with raised eyebrows.

'I know you are thinking of behaving rashly,' the old man replied evenly. 'You rescued my daughter and gave me back my heart, and in exchange I will give you information that might save your life, and your mission.'

'What do you know of my mission?' The Firanese Trader was incredulous.

'It is vital that you escape this town before the Widuz lose patience and come for you. They have access to farmers and their families trapped in their fields, and may yet offer the elders a trade. There is a small gate in the wall, equidistant from each of the main gates and invisible to anyone from the outside, through which you might escape under cover of night. You'll have a greater chance than even Jethart's blade would give you.'

Mahnum looked gratefully into the man's clear eyes. 'How is your daughter?' he asked gently.

The old man sighed. 'She is well, and her family rejoice that she is back among them, but she will never be the same. She has seen too much. My daughter saw her friends fed to the deep hole, and she lived in terror of following them.'

'All the Treikans showed courage in our escape.'

'Not like our elders?' the old man said, again reading Mahnum's thoughts with uncanny accuracy. 'Inch Chanter was once a border village, full of hunters and warriors ready to try their strength against the feared Widuz. But now the border has been pushed westwards and our people have grown soft. All they want is to be left alone.'

'And so they shall, if you will show me the gate.'

'You don't want to spend another moment in this town,' the little boy's aulfather guessed correctly. 'However, if you try to escape before dark you will not spend many more moments on this earth. Be my guest for the evening meal.'

Mahnum laughed, his heart eased for the first time in many days. 'My son is alive, and soon I will be free to pursue him. Until then it will be an honour to sup with a man of such surprising wisdom.'

Under the cover of darkness, the old man led Mahnum to the outer wall, then along some distance to the left until he located the small wooden door.

'Goodbye, my friend,' the Trader said. 'I am in your debt.'

'I hope that soon we will all be in yours,' came the whispered reply. 'Now draw that sword, in case the Widuz are patrolling the walls. They have not done so thus far, so you should be safe, but it is best to take no chances.' He struggled with the bolt, then slid it open with effort. 'This door hasn't been used for many years, not since the days when Inch Chanter was an outpost in disputed territory. I'm surprised the bolt gave way so easily. Perhaps it has been oiled recently.' And he smiled.

'Quick. On with you. This is not the time to dally! Once you are out on the *erse*, turn to the southeast and strike out cross-country for a mile or so, until you come to a narrow lane. Follow this to a farmhouse. My youngest son and his family live there. They will give you a bed for the night, should you wish it.'

'I have slept enough. My son is five days ahead of me, and I will not rest until I have found him.'

'So be it. *Fuir af Himinn!* Go with the blessing of the Most High!'

Through the door Mahnum squeezed, then out into the open and across the fields of the *erse* he ran, stooped low to avoid detection. He ran for perhaps ten minutes, then found the lane the old man had described. He did not stop, refusing even to slow down as he ran past the farmhouse with its welcoming lights.

* * *

Mahnum found the Westway a week or so later just north of Laverock, driving himself relentlessly through the pain and into the mind-numbing repetitiveness of simply placing one foot before the other. Whenever he crossed a ridge or found himself on a piece of higher ground, he turned and searched the horizon behind him for any sign of pursuit; as the days passed, the habit was dropped as it became obvious he was not being followed.

However, the pursuit was real, and it was gaining on him. In spite of the stirring words of the old warrior Jethart, who pleaded for a few days' head start for the hero of the Adunlok escape, the elders of Inch Chanter wasted no time telling the Widuz their quarry was no longer within their walls. Immediately the warriors abandoned their siege and set off over the fields in a loping, ground-eating trot.

'How did the Widuz know to head in the same direction as your rescuer?' Jethart asked his daughter angrily. 'They virtually trod in his footsteps.'

She shook her head, tears in her eyes. 'Our leaders must have told them. What way is that to treat one who has done so much for us? We have betrayed him.'

'I fear for him,' her father rasped, his throat tight with emotion, 'but I fear for ourselves more. What future do we have if our leaders act so shamefully? How can we continue our tenuous hold on the ground of New Deer if we surrender the moral ground so easily? The elders have betrayed the man from Firanes, and they have betrayed me and all I have worked for. Only one thing gives me comfort. My blade is in the hands of one worthy of wielding it.'

The week's wait outside the walls of Inch Chanter had done nothing to ease the wrath of the Widuz. Some had suggested forcing their quarry out by executing the prisoners, or taking more captives from the surrounding farming community. The more level heads counselled prudence. While they would eventually deal with the hated foreigner who had killed their champion and emptied the cells of their sacred city, their eastern neighbours – hated descendants of the First Men though they were – held great power through superior numbers. Any action which antagonised their powerful neighbours would be regarded as treasonable by Tolmen, and would be punished accordingly. The strategy for survival remained the same: lull them to sleep, so their defences became lax and they grew vulnerable. Proof of the wisdom of this course was already visible, said Tala the brother of Talon: the rulers of the walled city of the plain were willing to surrender the fugitive to them – indeed, had sought them out, begging their favour and wishing to know how best they could assist them. In the old days, he reminded them, they would have faced fierce warriors well before they drew close to the walls.

When the fifth day passed and the fugitive still remained harboured in the town, even the moderates among the Widuz party sought to bring the matter to a swift conclusion. On the sixth morning, however, came the news that their quarry had effected an escape some time during the night, and had made off in the direction of Laverock. This news fuelled an already acrimonious discussion, with Tala leading the faction who still sought revenge. For a time, it appeared they would come to blows, a fight being averted only when the leader of the moderates announced he was returning home. 'For,' he said, 'we must be in Adunlok for the selection of our new priest: those who are absent will be under a curse. Besides, we lost more than half our number in the assault by the treacherous Tree-men. We can ill afford further losses.'

Talon's brother laughed at him and his four followers as they set out for Clovenhill, a dark smudge on the western horizon. 'There go the shattered shards of the weak, while the strong fashion themselves a cup large enough to contain their revenge. Look, my brothers! Decide in your hearts not to become as he is. Choose instead to show him the head of this foreigner! Let nothing stand in your way! Let all of single mind follow me!'

The small band kept away from the main roads, travelling cross-country by day and night, held to their hard path by the iron will of their leader. Through Laverock they sliced, turning the town inside-out but obtaining no news of their foe. Their path then took them across the Remparers by a little-known track, one used by the Widuz in days of old long before the First Men dispossessed them, and which rejoined the Westway a few miles south of Inverell.

'My ancestors lived in this valley,' Tala snarled. 'Look at the fields! More food here than in the whole of Widuz. Brothers, this will be ours – in our lifetime!'

As the party drew nearer to their prey they spread out, leaving two only to travel along the Westway itself. The others took to the open fields again as they crossed Deuverre, and the rumours of their passing struck fear into the locals. Deuverre had not seen a Widuz raiding party for many centuries, and did not like the look of this one. The raiders helped themselves to all the food they wanted, and destroyed much of what they did not eat, but still their anger was not assuaged.

The Trader crossed into Deuverre without incident, puzzled that he had not found his son, nor indeed any sign of him. *Surely he would have made for Instruere? Unless his companion had other ideas. I wish I knew who he was!* But no amount of worrying was going to get him to Instruere a moment sooner, so he dismissed the thoughts and continued his journey.

The Company were halfway across the plain, within two days of Instruere if Kurr's reckoning was correct, when they discovered a sheltered pool between two low, wooded hills. Here they took their rest, and the waters of a mineral spring eased their aches.

'Have you made further headway with the Bhrudwan?' Kurr asked Hal as the others rested their feet in the cool waters. 'Is he likely to be cooperative?'

'It is too early to say,' the cripple replied carefully. 'I have learned his name – Achtal – and think that we should use it when talking to him. He understands a smattering of the common tongue and, while he says little, he has let slip that he was born in the province of Birinjh, nearer Faltha than most other Bhrudwan lands, and that he was in the regular army for five years before being compelled to join the *Maghdi Dasht*. It seems to me that we have a chance of winning his confidence. I want to allow him to walk without restraint.'

'Of course not,' came the swift reply. 'Perhaps you want also to give him a sword, and for us to bare our necks before it? What foolishness is this?'

'The foolishness of trust,' Hal replied evenly. 'No other wisdom, however appealing, holds the key to this man's heart.'

'Are you quite sure you come from Firanes, and not a browner land?' Kurr was tired, and in that state his thoughts became words more easily. 'Are you one of us?'

Hal took no offence. 'I am as much a Firanese as you,' he said, looking directly into the rheumy eyes of the old farmer. Something passed between them then, an acknowledgement that secrets were known.

And so it was that Mahnum found them, Hal and Kurr in earnest discussion, the others – including the one he knew and loved so well – bathing in the pool.

'Is there room for me?' he asked quietly.

Indrett's head snapped round in shock, then a smile spread across her features, replaced by a frown as she saw that her husband was alone.

'No, dear one,' he said, 'I have not found him. But he is alive, of that I am sure. He passed through Widuz and escaped their snares, heading in this direction. I thought I would have found him before now, but no doubt he is but a day or two ahead of us – perhaps already safe in Instruere, the first of us to arrive there.' He broke off for a moment as his wife embraced him.

'And you,' he continued, 'are you well? You look – you look . . .' Words failed him temporarily, and the love that passed between them was a tangible thing that the rest of the Company could see.

While the couple continued to talk, Kurr climbed the leftmost of the small hills, looking for any sign of the great city in the distance. His return was swift, and he was out of breath as he spoke to the Company.

'Behind us – a group scouring the countryside – could be trouble!' he puffed.

516

'How many?' Mahnum asked.

'Maybe a dozen, maybe more.'

'How close?'

'A few miles away, but they come quickly.'

'How far have we to go, by your reckoning?'

'The Aleinus is visible on the horizon – two days. A day and a half if we hurry.'

'Then we'd better hurry,' Mahnum said urgently. 'This is what I feared: the Widuz have not given up the chase.' As they gathered their belongings and set their feet to the Westway once again, he told them the story of what had taken place since he left them on the slopes of the volcano. The telling took him the best part of an hour.

'Can we not leave the Westway and simply let them pass?' Perdu asked.

'They were spread across the plain,' Kurr insisted.

'Besides, if Leith is ahead, he might fall into their hands,' Indrett said quietly.

'Then let us turn and fight them!' Farr cried. 'We have defeated the Bhrudwan warriors, more fierce by far than these primitive *losian*. So why should we flee before them?'

'Count them!' Kurr growled. 'There are too many. Our captive might escape in the confusion, or perhaps be killed. We lost a good man when fighting four Bhrudwans. How many might we lose if we face these Widuz? We will do nothing to jeopardise our quest. We must continue to Instruere. There we will find haven.'

A while later their thoughts turned to food and shelter. 'We cannot stop,' Mahnum insisted. 'They must know they are close to me, and may travel at night as well as by day. We will eat on foot.'

'And how will we sleep?' Perdu asked.

'On foot.'

After what seemed like forever, the sun rose, the gate opened and Leith and Phemanderac followed other travellers in through Instruere's Inna Gate. As they passed under the intricately fashioned stone archway, Leith experienced a strange sense of fear, an unsettling, nagging feeling that refused to let him go throughout the day. If Phemanderac felt it, he did not say.

If the pre-dawn had taken an age, the day itself seemed to Leith to last an eternity. Phemanderac took him from place to place, trying every possible avenue first to obtain charity, then to gain work. 'We need money to rent lodgings large enough for your compatriots,' he explained. 'If the Instruian guards find you on the streets after dark they put you in prison until the next morning.'

'What sort of place is this?' Leith wanted to know. His village had never needed guards to keep order.

'The more people who live in one place, the more evil things happen. Therefore the more organised must be the enforcers of the law.'

'I don't like it here. It was foolish to think we might find help here.'

At first the Great City had simply been a melange of images so foreign his brain could make no sense of what his eyes were seeing. Gradually the shapes and colours resolved into buildings and people, far more of either than he had ever imagined could be found in one place, and much more tightly packed together. Broad thoroughfares flanked by vast ornate civic edifices gave way to narrow lanes, overflowing with pedestrians and overshadowed by tall tenement buildings, into each of which seemingly hundreds of people had been crammed. Through the centre of these cobbled lanes ran foetid open sewers choked by the spoil of the congested city, amid which children played with dogs and rats ran unchecked. Here and there a market spread, attracting Instruians like ants to honey. But ranking above the swirling colours and the pungent smells was the overwhelming noise: the sheer intensity of it seemed calculated to set a boy from a small village on edge. To his left a pack of mangy dogs barked and howled as they fought over something unspeakable; some distance ahead another market was the scene of squabbling as shrill voices competed for attention; while somewhere to his right, at the top of a building taller than the Common Oak back home, a baby screamed and screamed, almost unnoticed in the din. Leith found himself clenching his teeth and making fists as though to repel this many-pronged assault.

Instruere seemed to have the opposite effect on Phemanderac. The tension of weeks on the run drained from him, to be replaced by the excitement of the city. With the increasingly reluctant Leith in tow, he went from one market to the next, searching for some way of obtaining food and shelter for the two of them. Leith suspected that he deliberately took them to the loudest and most colourful spots, irrespective of the likelihood of getting what they needed. Phemanderac revelled in the colour and light in a way Leith could not comprehend.

Late in the afternoon, at yet another stall of still another market, the philosopher finally succeeded. An old woman who operated a shoe stall needed some assistance in tidying up her property. Apparently her husband had passed on a year ago, leaving their three-storeyed residence in some disrepair, a state which had compounded since. In exchange for restorative labour on the house, the woman (whose name was Foilzie) agreed to allow Phemanderac and Leith to live in the basement and to supply them with two meals a day.

'Only if you're in, mind,' she cautioned them. 'I'll not keep food for anyone. I didn't for old Ferdie and I won't for you. Be sure you keep the place tidy or you'll be out on your ear, no second warning.'

Their first night in the basement was a trial. The room was windowless and dank, and had been neglected for some time. Leith could hear the scuffling of some small animal – probably a rat, or more than one – and found himself unable to sleep in spite of extreme tiredness. Some time during the night he complained to Phemanderac.

'At least we're here within the walls and not still waiting on the far end of that accursed bridge,' came the weary reply. 'We'll clean up the room tomorrow. You'll see, it will be fine once we've been through it. We'll probably only be here for a few days, until the others come and we can arrange our audience with the Council of Faltha.'

It took them most of the next day to clean out the basement, hauling many seemingly useless artefacts off to the market, where Foilzie insisted they would fetch a good price. There was no sign of the rats, nor of where they might have entered.

It was the middle of the afternoon when they finished in the basement, and Phemanderac went to tour the markets. Leith tried to rest on his mattress for a while, but kept imagining he heard the sound of small animals at the far end of the room, so he gave up and headed for the city wall.

While it would be many weeks before Leith became used to the layout and the sheer size of the city, he used Instruere's geography to his advantage. Foilzie's tenement was within view of the city wall, and so he was able to find the Inna Gate by simply heading to the wall and working his way around it. Later he was to learn that he had passed through a particularly dangerous quarter of the city, but no one was bold enough to accost him in the harsh afternoon light.

Steep stairways ascended the interior of the wall at regular intervals, and Leith chose the stairway nearest the gate to gain access to the broad walk at the top of the wall. From this vantage point he was able to see all those who entered or left the city by the Inna Gate. Moreover, as the wall was very high, he could see through the hazy air above the north branch of the Aleinus River to the other end of Longbridge.

'What are you doing on the walls?' came a voice from behind him.

Leith started and spun around. There stood a man in the red-and-black livery of the Instruian Guard, hand resting easily on sword hilt, a slightly bored look on his face.

'I – I'm waiting for the rest of my party,' Leith explained, choosing the truth over any of the implausible stories that came to his mind. 'We became separated on our way here.'

The guard nodded his head, then took a closer look at him. 'Where are you from, boy? And what is your name? You don't look like you're from anywhere around these parts.'

Leith waited for a moment before answering. He was in a strange land, but what harm could there be in telling this man where he was from? 'My name is Leith, and my home is Firanes.'

The man's eyes widened. 'Firanes! What brings you this far?'

The youth cast his eyes down. 'I'm not sure,' he said eventually. 'My parents – my father is a Trader; he has some reason for coming here.'

The guard grunted, his curiosity satisfied.

Emboldened, Leith continued the conversation. 'How high is this wall? Tell me what I can see from here!'

The man paused for a moment, then began telling Leith about the wall. Built after the Bhrudwan invasion, he explained, it was sixty-five feet high and thirty feet thick, with two main gates: one here, one to the south. There were other small gates in the wall, openable only from the inside, after the fashion of all Falthan walled cities. From here one could see up and down the Aleinus, but the real sights were within the walls. There the spire of the House of Worship, the tallest building in the world; over there the bulk of the Hall of Meeting, where the Council of Faltha met, while further to the right . . .

Leith did not follow the pointing arm of the guard, choosing instead to keep his eyes on the Inna Gate. He did not turn even when the guard, understanding the anxiety of a youth who awaited his family, bade him goodbye and moved along the wall. Leith remained on the wall until sundown when, mindful of Phemanderac's warning about being on the streets after dark, he scurried back to the basement and the evening meal.

It was all he could do the next morning to stop himself stealing away to his 'place' on the city wall. What would they do, he explained to Phemanderac, if they missed seeing the Company enter the city? How would they find his friends among so many people? While the philosopher was sympathetic, he reminded Leith that they had made an agreement with Foilzie, without which they would not be able to stay in the city at all. At lunchtime Phemanderac relented, allowing Leith to go to the Inna Gate, as much because his not-unnatural preoccupation with his parents and the Company rendered him of little use in their task of cleaning and repairing the house. 'I'll finish up here,' the thin man said. 'Go on, off with you.' Before he had finished uttering the words, Leith had sprinted away round the corner and was gone.

This afternoon the usual heat haze was replaced by a cool sea breeze coming in over his left shoulder as he stood on top of the wall. Because of this, Leith found he could see much further, and more clearly, than yesterday. At first he watched every face carefully as they passed through the gate immediately below him and to his right, but he realised eventually that he would be able to detect a large group like the Company from a much greater distance, perhaps even from the far end of the bridge. He spent some time trying to trace the Westway north and west into the distance, where it eventually merged with the greys and folds of a range of low hills . . .

What was that? His eyes jerked back to a place roughly halfway between the hills and Longbridge, maybe three or four miles from where he stood. There was a group of people walking – no, running – down the Westway, catching and passing others on the road. Was this the Company? After twenty minutes, Leith decided it was not: there were far too many, perhaps twenty or thirty of them. Or was that because there were two groups?

The road made a southward turn about a mile north of the bridge. Now the people were on the final straight of the Westway. He strained his eyes. It was difficult to tell, the sun was too bright – yes, there *were* two groups, one chasing the other – and in the first group of nine, the group being chased, he could see – could he be sure? He waited for some minutes, then yes, he *was* sure. He could see Farr, and there was Kurr, and – his father and mother. He couldn't make out the others – except the limping one must be Hal. He was falling a little way behind. It was all Leith could do not to cry out from the battlements.

His eyes lifted slightly to the pursuing party, and for a moment he ceased breathing. He would never forget the uniform of the Widuz. *Why do they chase the Company? What was happening?* The sun flickered on the edges of their drawn swords; there was no doubting their murderous intent. Surely they would overtake their quarry before they got to the bridge.

At that moment, Leith felt an arm on his shoulder, forcing a frightened cry from his lips. It was Phemanderac, who said: 'What's wrong? I just came up to see if there was anything . . .' His voice tailed off as he looked out over the plain.

'Your friends?' he asked.

Leith could only nod in reply.

'We can't leave Hal behind!' Kurr cried, looking over his shoulder.

'I'll go back for him!' Mahnum said, and turned away. Kurr watched as the Trader bravely snatched his son from just in front of the pursuing warriors and dragged him forward out of their reach – for the moment.

'Achtal, Achtal!' Hal was shouting as he struggled forward, as though the pursuit had tipped him into some pit of madness. 'Let Achtal go!'

'Who's Achtal? Do you mean the Bhrudwan? Do you want us to free him? You can't be serious!'

'Yes, yes, I *am* serious! Please,' Hal begged his father as they ran, 'please untie his hands and give him a sword. Achtal could save us from these men!'

'Has he bewitched you?' Mahnum asked his son incredulously, drawing deeply on his reserves in order to speak. 'He'd likely slay anyone between him and freedom. That murdering monster must never touch a weapon again. The only time he'll ever feel a sword will be when I finally end his life – after he's spoken to the council. Hal, you weren't there. You never saw what he did to your mother!'

'There will be a price to pay for your fear,' Hal gasped out. He was completely out of breath.

'Less of a price than that we would pay for your foolishness.'

Unperturbed, unhurried, the Widuz were spreading out. Those to the right and the left of the Westway were almost level with the Company. The bridge was close now, close but too far away. Kurr bit his lip in frustration. So close! It seemed so unfair, yet there was nothing he could do. *This is all a matter of timing; if we hadn't tarried so long in Treika . . .*

'We must stand and fight!' Farr called out.

'Not far now to the bridge,' Perdu answered him. 'If we can get to the bridge, we will be safe.'

'Surely the men of the city will come to our aid!' Stella cried.

There were now perhaps fifty paces between the Company and their pursuers; both flanks were beginning to close in. Cruel smiles spread across their faces as they anticipated their moment of revenge.

Suddenly Mahnum came to a stop. 'Go on ahead!' he shouted at the rest of the Company. 'It's me they want anyway! I'll hold them here!'

'Mahnum, *no!*' Indrett cried, and made to rush to his side, but Parlevaag grabbed her arm and dragged her on towards the bridge.

Behind them the Widuz closed in more slowly now on the man they sought; warily, cautiously they approached, for they had been travelling hard on foot for many days, and each man was suddenly aware that this warrior had defeated their champion. For a moment there was a standoff; then Tala lost patience with his men and drew his sword. 'Follow me!' he cried, leaping at Mahnum. 'Make his blood flow over the cobbles of this road!'

Mahnum drew the sword of Jethart from its jewelled scabbard, and immediately felt courage flow through his veins. 'Come on then!' he challenged them. 'Come and test yourself against me!' He waved the sword in their faces.

One after another the Widuz halted in their tracks. Even Talon's brother stood still, consternation on his face. There was no doubt, they all knew that infamous sword, its deeds woven into the tales of their great defeats; the sword of Jethart, Thunderbolt of the East, the Avenger of the Plains. By some magic it had appeared again, after many years. *No wonder Talon fell to this man. Could this be Jethart? Surely not! He would be an old man by now even if he were still alive.*

Seizing on their confusion, Mahnum turned and ran towards the bridge. The spell of the sword held the warriors for a moment longer, then they gave a shout and streamed down the road after the Company, too late. By the time the Widuz came to the bridge, the Company had pushed past the frightened gatekeeper and were making their way towards the city.

Now the guards on the wall had seen the Company, and Leith's heart rose even further. Surely they would do something. *They will prepare a sortie to drive these Widuz away. It will take only a fraction of their number.* The Company would escape.

'Close the gates!' came the cry. 'Close the gates! Bring everyone inside!'

'*No!*' cried a stunned Leith. 'You can't do that! They'll be trapped between the Widuz and the wall!' But his words were lost in the sudden swell of noise and commotion as people rushed for the safety of the gate. When everyone was safely inside, the huge wooden gates were slowly drawn together, slamming shut like a hollow death-knell. Boom. With tears in his eyes, Leith watched the faces of the Company change as the realisation dawned on them that they were trapped.

'Keep going!' Kurr urged. 'Perhaps they will let us in when we are close to the gates!' But his voice carried no conviction, and all knew they had been pointlessly betrayed at the last. Now the Widuz gained on them, as despair robbed the Company of strength.

On the battlements Leith turned to the nearest guard; by chance, it was the man he had spoken to the previous afternoon. 'This is my family!' he screamed. 'Please let them in!'

The man spread his hands in a gesture of helplessness. 'I'm sorry, we've had orders. Nothing is to threaten the safety of the inhabitants of the city. If I were you, I would keep quiet about knowing them. Others, less kindly than I, might see in that sufficient reason to put you outside the gate also.'

'Now, see here—' Phemanderac began, but the guard had turned his back on them and begun to walk down the stairs. 'There are hundreds of guards in this cursed city! Why can you not rescue those trapped outside?' But he was wasting his breath.

The Company stumbled on across the bridge. With a last

supreme effort, coming at the end of weeks of exhaustion, it seemed as though they would make it to the far end before the Widuz caught them. Then it would be touch and go as to whether they could attain the gates unmolested. But the gates were closed . . .

'I can't stand it any longer!' Leith shouted, then turned and ran recklessly down the stone stairway, taking three steps at a time.

'Leith! Come back!' Phemanderac called.

Below, Mahnum heard the cry, and distinguished his son's name. He looked up to the battlements, but his son was not among the ghouls who had assembled to watch their grisly deaths. The Company clattered over the last of the wooden boards that made up Longbridge, then ran on to the grass strip between the bridge and the gate.

A hundred yards behind them, Tala the brother of Talon laughed. The gate was closed. No assistance would be coming from the cowardly city of Instruere. They could take their time, sword of Jethart or not, and make these fools pay for what had been done to his brother.

Leith rushed along the inside of the wall. *May the words of the guard be proved right!* he thought frantically. *Where are these lesser gates? This is taking too much time!*

Eventually he found one, but his heart sank when he saw a broad-shouldered guard stationed in front of it. There was no time to think. He took a water jug from the side of the narrow lane, climbed up the nearest stairway to the battlements, then positioned himself above the unfortunate guard. A second later the jug, empty but still deadly, hurtled towards its target. At the last moment the guard looked up, but could not prevent the missile crashing down on top of him.

Seconds later, Leith was working the huge bolt of the gate, then swinging it open. *I only hope no one closes it again behind me*, he thought as he stepped through into the tunnel under the wall. There was a second gate at the far end of the tunnel! For a heart-sinking moment Leith gave up hope. It was locked.

It had been a thousand years since Instruere had fallen to the

Bhrudwans and the walls had been built; in all that time, they had not had to withstand further attack from any source. Instruere's establishment as the financial and political capital of Faltha had guaranteed it a safety that no wall could enhance. Knowing this, the inhabitants of the great city had reduced their army to a largely ceremonial guard. They had also neglected the maintenance of their walls.

In frustration, Leith hurled himself at the outer gate, and was immediately rewarded when the rotten wood around the bolt cracked. He took a longer run this time; the wood split further, but the bolt held stubbornly. *Come on, I don't have time for this,* he thought desperately as his fingers worked unsuccessfully at the bolt. With a yell of frustration he flung himself at the door a third time, and it gave way before him. He landed painfully on his side, the rusted bolt underneath him.

'Let us in!' Kurr cried to those on the battlements above the gate. 'We claim sanctuary in the city of Instruere!'

There was no reply. Farr was certain he heard laughter from the walls – or perhaps the sound came from behind them. The Widuz were almost at the end of the bridge.

Then two unexpected things happened simultaneously. From the right, at the base of the city wall, came a shout. Wonder of wonders, it was Leith.

'This way!' he cried. 'This way!'

At that moment Parlevaag snatched the sword from the hand of Perdu, and sprang towards the bridge. The adopted Fenni leapt after her.

'What are you doing?' he cried.

Parlevaag ran to hold the bridge for them, having seen that the open door Leith offered them was too far away to reach without being overtaken by their enemy. Kurr grabbed Perdu's arm, crying, 'There is nothing we can do! Come quickly!'

'Come on!' Leith shouted urgently.

From his place high on the battlements, Phemanderac watched the drama unfold below him. The Company sprinted desperately towards safety; though he could not see Leith, he could hear the youth exhorting them on. But his eyes were drawn to the approaches to Longbridge, where the woman from the Company stood alone, holding the bridge against the Widuz.

The members of the Company drew up to Leith and the open gate. To Leith's relief, no one had closed the gate from the inside. 'Quickly!' he encouraged them. One after another they ran down the tunnel and into the city: Farr, Perdu, Kurr, Hal – leading a Bhrudwan warrior – Mahnum and Stella. Leith's heart lodged in his throat as she ran past, her wide scared eyes staring straight ahead.

Indrett was the last through the tunnel. At its entrance, she turned and looked back to the bridge. Above them many eyes watched along with her as Parlevaag calmly took her sword and struck at the closest of the Widuz, who went down with the blow.

'Parlevaag! This way! Quickly!' Indrett cried, but the Fenni woman did not turn. Mahnum took the hand of his wife, attempting to lead her through the tunnel, but she resisted him impatiently. At the end of the bridge, another Widuz warrior stepped up, and with a blow struck Parlevaag's sword from her hand. Still she did not flinch, even when the warrior raised his sword for a final blow. Time stood still; then the blade flashed down and Parlevaag crumpled silently to the ground.

Indrett screamed, but resisted no longer as Mahnum pulled her to safety and bolted the inner gate firmly closed behind her. Though the members of the Company had finally realised their seemingly unattainable goal of Instruere, they looked at each other not with joy but with sorrow – some stunned, some weeping openly, all exhausted beyond explanation. Indrett reached out for her son and clasped Leith to her, sobs racking her thin frame, the image of her friend and fellow-sufferer forever seared on her memory.

From the battlements Phemanderac watched the Widuz, unmolested by the cowardly guards of the city, step over Parlevaag and draw close to the walls.

'We have revenge!' Their leader spat out the words as though the common tongue were poison to him. Then, piling horror on horror, he turned and buried his sword contemptuously in the defenceless body at his feet, crying out with a fierce joy. Phemanderac could watch no longer. Incensed with the inaction of the Instruian Guard and enraged at the insult offered to the body of one so brave, he stormed down the stone stairway away from the sordid scene, and set out to find Leith and the Company.

To be continued in

Fire of Heaven: Book Two
In the Earth Abides the Flame

GLOSSARY

AS = Ancient Straux
CT = Common Tongue
FI = Firanese
FM = First Men
FN = Fenni
JS = Jasweyan
MB = Middle Bhrudwan
MT = Modern Treikan
OB = Old Bhrudwan
OF = Old Falthan
OSV = Old Sna Vazthan
OT = Old Treikan
P = Plonyan
WZ = Widuz

Achtal (Arck-tahl) aka the Acolyte: Personal name of the young
Bhrudwan acolyte, a Lord of Fear. [OB *death dealer*]
Adunlok (Ah-**doon**-lock): Fortress of the Widuz, built around a
deep sinkhole just south of Cloventop. [WZ *down look*]
Aigelstrommen (Ai-gill-**strom**-in): Tributary of the Torrelstrommen.
[FI *angel stream*]
Aldha (Ell-duh): Oldest man in Loulea Vale, passed away in the
year 1026. His name is a nickname. [CT *old*]
Aldhras Mountains (Ell-drass): High mountains on the border
between Faltha and Bhrudwo. [FM *old head*]
Aleinus (Ar-lay-**ee**-niss): Great River with headwaters in the
Aldhras Mountains, flows through Faltha. [FM *barrier*]

Alvaspan (Ell-vuh-spann): Wooden bridge over Mjolk River just west of Mjolkbridge. [FI *river span*]

Andratan Island, keep (Ann-druh-tan): Island off the coast of Bhrudwo, home of the Destroyer. [OB *dread*]

Anesel (Ar-nuh-sell): Young woman of Loulea, betrothed to Stend. [FI *sweet*]

Anoan (An-owe-in): Youth of Loulea, older brother of Druin. [FI *boy child*]

Ansula (Ann-shill-uh): Senior courtier at the Firanese Court at the time Indrett lived in Rammr. [FI *swift answer*]

Anukalva (Ar-noo-cal-vah): Narrow grotto which provides the exit to the Adunlok cave system. [WZ *anal passage*]

Arkhos (Ar-coss): Leader of a clan in the Vale of Youth; later coming to mean an ambassador to the Council of Faltha. [FM *arrow-bearer*]

Arminia Skreud (Ar-min-ee-uh **Skroyd**): Scroll of prophecies by Arminius of Dhauria. [FM *Arminius' scroll*]

Asgowan (Az-gouw-in): One of the Sixteen Kingdoms of Faltha, located north of Deuverre. [FM *horse country*]

Ashdown: Town on the banks of the Lavera River, replacing Inverlaw Eich which burned down in 979.

Aspen Grange: Small inn at Windrise, Firanes.

Aspenlimb aka Taller: From Rockford on the slopes of the Black Hills, now part of Axehaft's trading band.

Assembly of Scholars: The legislative body of Dhauria charged with making moral and theological rulings.

Astora (Ah-stor-uh): First capital city of Firanes, located in North March until it fell into the sea. [FM *northern jewel*]

Augon (Or-gone): Farmer of Loulea Vale, lives at Spindlewood Farm, but has gone blind. [FI *augury, foretelling*]

Aulfather (Orl-father): Grandfather. [FM *old father*]

Aurochs (Or-rocks): Legendary wild ox, found only on the inland moors of Firanes. [FN *urus*]

Axehaft aka Leader: The Warden of the Fodhram, from Fernthicket.

Bandits' Cave: Limestone formation in Withwestwa Wood,

formerly a base for robbers, now the abode of the Hermit.

Bellows, the: Hot autumn wind that blows across the Northern Wastes.

Bewray (Bee-**ray**): Arkhos of Saiwiz, entrusted with the Jugom Ark by the Council of Leaders. Founded Nemohaim and hid the Jugom Ark. [FM *to reveal involuntarily*]

Bhrudwo (**Brood**-woe): Continent covering the north-eastern hemisphere, a federation of provinces ruled by the Destroyer. [OB *brown land*]

Birch Hill: Fodhram village near Fernthicket in the heart of Withwestwa Wood, home of Leafholm.

Bircheater Teeth: Rocky obstacle near the end of Mossbank Cadence. It has never been negotiated.

Birinjh (Bear-**arnge**): Vast province of Bhrudwo, located in the north-western interior, a land of desert and plateau. [OB *tableland*]

Black Hills aka Beinn Dubh: Low, treeless hills in northern Treika. Said to be inhabited by the Dubhnan, a race of merciless killers.

Black Winter, the: The winter of NA1016, when the thaw in North March was delayed for three months.

Blacksod: Farm in Loulea Vale.

Bream Hill: Low hill forming the western boundary of Loulea Vale.

Breidhan Moor (**Bray**-than): Westernmost highlands of inland Firanes, considered part of the Myrvidda. [OF *white lands*]

Brethren, the: Four large hills at the eastern end of Breidhan Moor; the Westway runs between the third and fourth Brethren.

Briar and Thistle: Large inn at Windrise.

Brinan Scou (**Brin**-in **Scow**): Stream draining the valley below Adunlok. [WZ *burning stream*]

Brookside: Small hamlet at the southern end of Loulea Vale.

Brookside Road: Road connecting Loulea with Great North Road.

Brookside Valley: Small valley extending southwards from Loulea Vale.

Brownfinch: Fodhram child, son of an unnamed Fodhram warrior.

Cairn Deargh (Cairn **Dairgg**): Spur of Clovenhill, once a lookout of the First Men. [WD *bone hill*]

Capstone, the: Most northerly of the Snaerfence mountains, near confluence of Torrelstrommen and Mjolk rivers.

Chillan (chill-in): Personal bodyguards of the Fenni clan chiefs. [FN *strength*]

Chosen, the: People called by the Most High to travel to the Vale of Youth.

Chute, the: A chasm draining an unnamed lake beside the Westway near the Grossbergen Mountains.

Ciennan (See-yenn-in): Capital city and chief port of Plonya, located at the mouth of the Sagon River. [P *sea path*]

Clovenchine: Deep gorge of the Sagon, carved through Clovenhill and giving the latter its name. [FM *cloven ravine*]

Clovenhill aka Blaenau Law: Broad tableland separating Plonya and Treika, last refuge of the Widuz.

Clyma II (Cli-mah): Former king of Firanes (NA971–982), king when the black fly plague covered Firanes.

Coast Road: Alternative route south from Oln to Rammr in western Firanes.

Coastlander: Derogatory name for coastal-dwellers of northern Firanes, given by those living in the interior.

Conal Greatheart: One-time leader of the Knights of Fealty, who according to the Lay of Fealty defeated the Destroyer in single combat a thousand years ago.

Cotyledon, Lake (Cott-ee-**lee-**din): Large lake on the Mossbank River. [FD *pennywort*, sense of meaning from FD *cup-shaped depression*]

Council of Faltha: Ruling council of ambassadors from the Sixteen Kingdoms of Faltha, based in Instruere.

Council of Leaders: Ruling body in Dona Mihst, of the leaders of the clans.

Cowyn the Hunter (Couw-in): Legendary Firanese hero who fought in the first Halvoyan invasion. [FI *of the forest*]

Dammish (Dah-meesh): Young huntsman of Loulea Vale. [FI *mistwalker*]

Deorc (Dee-york): Lieutenant to the Destroyer, Keeper of Andratan. [JS *spearhead*]

Derkskogen Forest (Dirk-**skoe**-gin): Extensive coastal forest of southern Firanes. [FI *stony plain*]

Dessica (**Dess**-ih-cuh) aka the Great Desert: Desert land extending over southern Faltha. [FM *to dry out*]

Destroyer, the, aka Undying Man, Lord of Bhrudwo, Lord of Andratan, Kannwar: Rebel against the Most High, cursed with immortality and now makes his home in Bhrudwo. Rules from his fortress of Andratan.

Deuverre (Doo-**vair**): One of the Sixteen Kingdoms of Faltha, located north of Straux in central Faltha; rich, densely populated farmland. [FM *twin rivers*]

Dhaur Bitan (**Dour** Bit-**arn**) aka The Poisoning: Story of the fall of Kannwar and exile from the Vale, contained in the Domaz Skreud. [FM *death bite*]

Dhauria (Dau-ree-yah) aka the Drowned Land: Names for the Vale of Youth after it was drowned by the sea. [FM *death estuary*]

Domaz Skreud (**Doh**-marz **Scroyd**): The Scroll which recounts the rise of the Destroyer and the fall of the Vale of Youth. [FM *doom scroll*]

Dominie (**domm**-in-ee): Dhaurian name for a scholar who trains students [FM *schoolmaster*]

Dona Mihst (**Doh**-na **Mist**): City built on the site of the Rock of the Fountain in the Vale of Youth. [FM *misty down*, later corrupted to dunamis, FM *power*]

Drozzakalven (**Drohzz**-uh-cal-vin): Cavern filled with glow-worms, part of Adunlok cave system. [WZ *dazzle cavern*]

Druim Corrie (**Droo**-im **Coh-ree**) aka Drum Mountain: Broad peak at the southern end of the Remparer Mountains. [WZ *drum rock*]

Druin (**Drew**-in): Youth of Loulea, large boy who bullies others and is keen on Stella. [FI *brown*]

Dybbuk (**dibb**-ook): Small spirit said by the Widuz to inhabit the cave systems of Clovenhill. [WZ *clinging spirit*]

East Bank Road: Little-used road following Aleinus River through Piskasia.

Ehrenmal (**Air**-en-mall): Town in western Favony on the north bank of the Aleinus River. [FM *bad blood*]

Eremos (Air-ee-moss) aka the Hermit: The prescient given name of the Hermit of Bandits' Cave. [AS *solitary man*]

Erse (Erss): Treikan name for flat land, applied to any flat lowland. [OT uncertain origin – highland?]

Factor of Malayu: Chief administrator of Malayu, the largest city in Bhrudwo.

Falla (Fell-ah) aka Flowermask: Mask used in the Midwinter Play to represent spring. [of uncertain origin]

Faltha (Fal-thuh): Continent of north-western hemisphere, an alliance of sixteen independent kingdoms. [CT contraction of *Falthwaite*, itself a corruption of *Withwestwa*]

Falthwaite End (Fal-thwayte): Farm on a hillock just north of Loulea. Renowned as the northernmost point reached by the First Men. [OF *cultivated land*]

Fanajokull (Fan-ah-yock-ill): Massive ice plain to the north of the Plains of Pollerne. [FI *ice water fan*]

Fania (Far-nee-yuh): Young woman of Loulea Vale, friend of Stella. [FI *fern*]

Farr Storrsen (Far Store-sin): Older son of Storr of Vinkullen, a thin, angular man. [FI *far*]

Favony (Fah-vone-ee): One of the Sixteen Kingdoms of Faltha, located on the central Falthan plains north of Straux. [FM *hot wind*)

Fealty, Knights of: Knights said to have driven the Destroyer out of Faltha a thousand years ago, led by Conal Greatheart.

Fealty, Lay of: Verse epic recounting the story of Conal Greatheart and the Knights of Fealty.

Feerich (Fee-ritch): Young man of Loulea Vale, supposedly a dullard. [FI *foeman*]

Fells, the: Mountain range of northern Firanes, separating coastlands from harsh uplands of interior.

Fenbeck River aka Mossbank River: Tributary of the Sagon River, draining Withwestwa Wood. [FD *marsh brook*]

Fenni, the (Fen-ny): Race of *losian* dwelling on the moors of inland Firanes. [FN *ancient people*]

Ferdie (Ferr-dee): Husband of Foilzie, property owner of Instruere, recently deceased. [FM *shrewd*]

Fernthicket: Fodhram village deep in Withwestwa Wood, home of Axehaft, the Fodhram Warden.

Fiannan Road (Fee-**yarn**-in): Path connecting the Westway to Ciennan, capital city and chief port of Plonya. [P *fair path*]

Firanes (Firr-uh-**ness**): Westernmost of the Sixteen Kingdoms of Faltha. Named for the sunrise on the heights of the Jawbone Mountains. [FM *Fire Cape*]

First Men, the: Those called north from Jangela by the Most High to live in the Vale of Youth; name also applies to those exiled from the Vale who settled in Faltha, and to their descendants.

Firststep Falls: First rapid in Mossbank Cadence.

Flame of the East: Fenni name for the Destroyer.

Fodhram (**Fodd**-rum): A short-statured *losian* race dwelling in the forests of Withwestwa. [FD *woodsman*]

Foilzie (**Foyl**-zee): Widow from Instruere, tenement-owner, shoemaker and stall-holder. [FM *help mate*]

Fonndelva (Fonn-**dell**-vuh): River of inland Firanes, separating the Fells and Havanger Range. [FI *wide stream*]

Fort Brumal (**Broo**-mull): Abandoned trading post at the western terminus of the Southern Run, previously known as Fort Ermine. [FD *brumous = wintry*]

Freta (**fray**-tuh): Small denomination coin common to northern Faltha. [origin uncertain]

Fuir af Himmin (**Foo**-ir Ahf **Him**-min): Affirmation of the Watchers, used as a greeting. [FM *Fire of Heaven*]

Fuirfad (Foo-ir-**fadd**) aka Realm of Fire, Way of Fire: The lore and religion of the First Men, teachings which enabled them to follow the Most High. [FM *fire path*]

Furist (**Few**-rist): Arkhos (leader) of the House of Landam in exile, founder of Sarista. [FM *to be admired*]

Gap, the: Narrow pass between Aldhras Mountains and The Armatura, linking Faltha and Bhrudwo.

Garadh (**Garr**-ath): Man of Dona Mihst, son of Raedh, assumed leadership of Kerd clan when his father was translated. [FM *straight spear*]

Garrison Hill: Low, dome-shaped hill on southern margins of Loulea Vale.

Garth, The: Lake about two-thirds through Mossbank Cadence.

Gealla Dalen (Gay-**arla Dah**-lin) aka Vithrain Uftan, Valley of Respite: Farr's name for the Valley of Respite. [CT *spiteful valley*]

Geotakalven (Gee-**yott**-uh-cal-vin): Small cavern on Parad Matr, not naturally connected to Adunlok cave system. [WZ *earth cavern*]

Gloan (**Glow**-in): Young man of Loulea Vale, supposedly unclean. [FI *darkness*]

Gloum Stair (Gloom): Waterfall of the Torrelstrommen, separating the lower and middle valleys. [FI *gloom falls*]

Great North Woods: Boreal forest of northern Firanes, part of a much larger forest encompassing northern Faltha.

Greenwoods Hole: Sinkhole complex to the north of Watch Hill, North March.

Grossbergen (**Grohss**-berr-gin): Range of the Jawbone Monuntains, from which Styggesbreeen flows. [FM *large mountains*]

Hal Mahnumsen: Youth of Loulea, adopted older son of Mahnum and Indrett. A cripple whose name is seemingly ironic. [FI *whole, hale*]

Haldemar (**Hall**-da-marr): Fenni wife of Perdu, the adopted Fenni. [FN *wholesome*]

Hall of the Disappearing Mountain: Part of the Westway near Windrise which climbs a shingle fan, in doing so hiding the Capstone from view.

Hallowed Beach: Small beach at the end of Mossbank Cadence, where graves of those who died in the rapids are found.

Hasteval (**Haa**-steh-varl): One of the Fenni who apprehended the Company. [FN *swift brook*]

Haufuth (**How**-footh): Title of village headmen in northern Firanes. [FI *head*]

Haurn (Hown): One of the Sixteen Kingdoms of Faltha, located north of Asgowan. Annexed by Sna Vaztha in NA1006. [FM *horn*]

Hauthius (**How**-thee-yoos): Scholar of Dhauria, author of the *Sayings of Hauthius*. [FM *head scholar*]

Hayne (**Haynn**): Young man from Loulea Vale, training under Kurr to be a Watcher. [CT *grain farmer*]

Helig Holth (**Hay**-ligg **Holth**): Huge sinkhole on the edge of Clovenhill, on which the fortress of Adunlok is built. Venerated by the Widuz as the mouth of Mother Earth. [WZ *holy mouth*]

Hermesa (Her-**may**-sah): Youth of Loulea, friend of Stella. [FI *interpreter*]

Herza (**Her**-zuh): Mother of Stella, wife of Pell, woman of Loulea Vale. [FI *choice*]

High Portage: Longest portage on the Northern Run, along which Fodhram challenge themselves to carry heavy loads.

Horstaag (**Horr**-starg): Fenni hunter, husband of Parlevaag, slain by Bhrudwans. [FN *long story*]

Inch Chanter (**Inch Charn**-tuh): Treikan walled town, hunting and farming community in Old Deer. [OT *small song*]

Indrett (**Inn**-dritt): Woman of Loulea, formerly of Rammr, married to Mahnum. [FI *right hand*]

Inmennost (**In**-men-ost): Capital city of Sna Vaztha and seat of the descendants of Raupa, Arkhos of Leuktom. Greatest of the northern cities of Faltha. [of uncertain origin]

Inna (**In**-nuh): Northern of two villages founded on an island in the Aleinus River, coalescing into Instruere; also one of the three main gates to the Great City. [FM *within*]

Instruere (In-strew-**ear**) aka Great City: Largest city in Faltha and seat of the Council of Faltha. [combination of Inna and Struere, together forming the OF word meaning *to instruct*]

Intika (inn-tee-kah): Fenni name for an outcast, banished from the clan. [FN *anathema*]

Inverell (**Inn**-vuh-**rell**): Town on the Westway in the Bannire, the unclaimed lands between Treika and Deuverre. [WZ *distance between*]

Inverlaw Eich (**Inn**-vuh-lore **Aick**): Town on a terrace above the Lavera River, destroyed in NA979, replaced by Ashdown. [WZ *between hill place*]

Iron Door: Door guarding the entrance to the Outer Chamber of the Hall of Meeting in Instruere, where the Council of Faltha meet.

Iskelfjorth (Iss-kill-fiyorth): Ice-bound fiord in the remote north of Firanes, under Halvoyan control. [FI *ice fiord*]

Iskelwen (Iss-kill-**when**) aka Icewind: North wind of northern Firanes, brings storms. [CT *ice wind*]

Jawbone Mountains aka Tanthussa: Main mountain chain of Firanes (rare form Tanthussa derived from FM *teeth*)

Jethart (Jeh-thirt): Heroic figure of western Treika, hated foe of the Widuz, now an old man. [OT *bright hunter*]

Jona (Yonn-ah): Hunter from Hustad, a small hamlet near Vinkullen hills. [FI *ice-master*]

Jugom Ark (Yu-gum **Ark)** aka Arrow of Yoke: Flaming arrow loosed by Most High at Kannwar, severing his right hand and sealing his doom. Symbol of unity for Faltha. Name derives from 'yoking together' like oxen. [FM *yoke arrow*]

Jujune (djew-djew-nay): Potent drink favoured amongst ruling classes in southern Bhrudwo. [MB *spice juice*]

Kanabar (Can-a-barr): Wide inland steppes in southern Birinjh, a province of Bhrudwo. [OB *sulphur brown*]

Kannwar (Cann-wah) aka the Destroyer: Original name of Destroyer, means Guardian of Knowledge. [FM *ken-ward*]

Kauma (Cow-muh): Capital city of Sarista, seat of the descendants of Furist, Arkhos of Landam. [OF *calm*, FM *heat*]

Kaupa (Cow-puh): Man of Windrise. [FI *oppressive*]

Kerd Clan (Curd): Clan of the House of Leuktom, from which Kannwar the Destroyer sprang. [FM *cheese*]

Kilth Keening (Killth Key-ning): Upper Torrelstrommen valley, afflicted by high winds. [FI *child's cry*]

Kilthen Stair (Killth-in): Rapids of the Torrelstrommen separating the middle and upper valleys. [FI *children's falls*]

Kleitaf Northr (Clay-taff **North**-er): Northern Lights, occasionally visible over much of northern Faltha. [FM *north lights*]

Kljufa River (Clue-fah): Largest river in Firanes, carving a path through the Jawbone Mountains. [FM *to cleave*]

Kroptur (Crop-tuh): Seer and Watcher of the seventh rank, lives on Watch Hill near Vapnatak. [FM *spell-caster*]

Kurr (Cur) aka Kurrnath: Man of Loulea, formerly from the south.

Reflects ironic naming practices of Straux. [OF *ill-bred dog*, perh. from FM *grumbler*]

Landam, House of (**Lan**-dam): One of the four great houses of the First Men. [FM *house of earth*]

Lanka (**Lan**-kuh): Tall, thin youth from Brookside. Nick-name. [CT *lanky*]

Lankangas, the (Lan-**kan**-guz): Ten feudal cities of south-eastern Firanes unwilling to accept leadership of King of Firanes. [FI *long plain*]

Lavana (Lah-**var**-na): Port city of Treika, at mouth of Lavera River. [OT *jug spout*]

Lavera River (La-**ver**-uh): River of Treika, draining eastern Treika and the northlands of the Bleakness and Plutobaran. [OT *water basin*]

Laverock (**Lay**-va-rock): Capital city of Treika, largest city in western Faltha. [OT *water rock*]

Leafholm aka Scar-face: Fodhram fur trader who lives in Birch Hill, talented with the quarterstaff, part of Axehaft's trading band.

Leith Mahnumsen (Leeth): Younger son of Mahnum of Loulea and Indrett of Rammr. Name carries sense of putting aside the past. [CT *forgetful, lethargic*]

Leuktom, House of (**Luke**-tom): One of the four great houses of the First Men. [FM *house of light*]

Lime Brook: Stream draining Loulea Vale, emptying into sea at Varec Beach.

Lime Flats: Farm to the south-east of Loulea Vale, in limestone valley.

Limedale: Farm to the south-east of Loulea Vale, in limestone valley.

Little Melg River (Mellg): River of North March of Firanes, flows past Vapnatak to join with Mjolk River. [FI *milky*]

Longacre: Small coastal village a day's walk north of Loulea.

Longbridge: The mile-long bridge connecting Instruere with Deuverre. Its southern counterpart is Southbridge.

Lonie (**Low**-nee): Youth of Loulea, girl who is friend of Hermesa. [FI *a gift*]

Lore, Hall of: Centre of learning in Dona Mihst; latterly a major building in Instruere.

Losian (low-si-yin): Properly those who left the Vale of Youth before the fall, forsaking the Most High; popularly, all those races of Faltha who are not First Men. [FM *the lost*]

Loulea/Loulea Vale (Low-lee) aka Louleij: Small coastal village in North March of Firanes, set in vale of same name. [CT *low lea*]

Louthwaite Fens (Low-thwayte): Extensive marshlands near the mouth of the Mjolk River, extending well inland. [OF *poor pasture*]

Lower Cadence: Shorter but more difficult part of Mossbank Cadence, encompassing Thirdstep Falls and Bircheater Teeth.

Lower Clough (Cloff): Lower of the two deep gorges by which the Kljufa River passes through the Jawbone Mountains. [CT *ravine, steep valley*]

Maelstrom, the (Mal-strom): Whirlpool in the Lower Clough of the Kljufa River, below which the river runs underground until surfacing downstream. [FM *whirling stream*]

Maghdi Dasht (Marg-dee **Darshht**) aka Lords of Fear: One hundred and sixty-nine feared Bhrudwan warrior-wizards. [OB *Heart of the Desert*]

Mahnum (Marr-num): Trader of Loulea, son of Modahl, married to Indrett. [FI *man, human*]

Malayu (Mah-lah-you): Chief city of province of Malayu, most populous city in Bhrudwo. [OB *corruption*]

Malos (Mar-loss): Loulea villager, small in stature. [MF *gentleman*]

Manimeria (Man-ih-mare-ee-ah) aka Moonraker: Frontmost of three great peaks of Grossbergen, consisting of one tall pinnacle. [FM *moon friend*]

Manu Irion (Mar-noo **Irr**-ee-in) aka Man Eaters, Remparer Mountains: Widuz name for the Remparer Mountains, once the eastern border of their lands. [WZ *eaters of men*]

Marigold: Fodhram woman, wife of an unnamed Fodhram warrior.

Mariswan (marr-ih-swan): Huge birds now extinct. The Jugom Ark is fletched with *mariswan* feathers. [FM *majestic fowl*]

Meadow of Spears: Glade in Withwestwa Wood, some distance south of the Westway.

Meeting, Hall of: Largest building in Faltha, the place of public gatherings in Instruere; latterly the home of the Council of Faltha.

Mercium (Merr-see-um): Capital city of Straux, the second-largest city in Faltha, on the inland edge of the Aleinus Delta. [AS *merchant*]

Merin (Mair-in): Wife of the Loulea village Haufuth. [FI *laughter*]

Midrun Hut: Hut located at the midway point of the Southern Run.

Midwinter Play: The highlight of the Midwinter celebration in northern Faltha, the Play is symbolic of the defeat of winter by summer.

Midwinter Speech: Customary address to the Midwinter gathering by the oldest one present.

Midwinter's Day: Midwinter celebations, held in northern Faltha, asserting the coming of spring.

Millford Farm: Farm on Swill Down, south of Loulea Vale.

Mjolkbridge (Myoulk-bridge): Town in inland Firanes, on the southern bank of Mjolk River. Site of the last bridge across the river. [OF *milk*]

Mjolkelva (Myoulk Ell-vuh) aka Mjolk, Milk River: Largest river in northern Firanes, one of two great Firanese rivers. So called because of the milky appearance of its glacial silt. [FI *milk*]

Modahl (Mow-darl): Legendary Trader of Firanes and father of Mahnum.

Mossbank Cadence: Complex set of rapids on the Mossbank River, part of the Southern Run; considered to be impassable by canoe.

Mossbank River aka Fenbeck River: Tributary of the Sagon River, drains most of eastern Withwestwa Wood.

Most High: Supreme god of the First Men.

Mot (mott): Black emulsion worn under the eyes to prevent snow-blindness. [FN *black*]

Mudvaerks (Mud-works): Mudflats at the southern end of Iskelsee, the great bay north of North March. [FI *mud grounds*]

Mudwise Farm: Farm to the south-east of Loulea Vale.

Mul (mool): Meditation exercise practised by Bhrudwans. [OB *to reflect*]

Mulberry aka Shabby: Fodhram of Vindstrop House, where he grew up as a thief. Since taking up with Axehaft his character has improved.

Myrvidda (Mir-vid-duh): Vast interior moors of northern Firanes. [FN *swampy moor*]

NA: see New Age.

Nagorj (Nah-gorge): Southern upland province of Sna Vaztha immediately west of The Gap. [OSV *north gorge*]

Neck, the: Short name for The Necklace, a series of rapids on the upper Kljufa River, part of the Southern Run.

New Age: Calendar of Faltha, the first year of which was the Destroyer's supposed defeat by Conal Greatheart.

New Deer: Forested edge of Clovenhill, disputed by Treikans and Widuz.

Nordviken (Nord-vie-kin): Southern port of Firanes, at mouth of Kljufa River. [FI *northern raider*]

North March: Area of Firanes bounded by Iskelsee to the north, Wodhaitic Sea to the west, the Fells to the east and the Innerlie Plains to the south.

North Road, the: **aka** the Great North Road: Main highway north from Oln to the North March of Firanes.

Northern Run: Fur trapping route across Withwestwa, between the Southern and Summer Runs.

Noyan Hills (Noy-in): Hills inland from Vapnatak, part of the North March of Firanes. [CT *northwards*]

Old Deer: Strip of land near the eastern edge of Clovenhill, once forested, now clear-felled and claimed by Treika.

Oln (Oaln): Town in southern Firanes. [FI *bastion*]

Omat (oh-**mart**): Pink alchemical pain-amplifying powder designed to aid in interrogations. [OB *mushroom*]

Ostval (Aust-varl): A Fenni huntsman.

Outer Chamber: Main meeting hall in the Hall of Meeting, site of public gatherings in Instruere.

Paludis Road (Parl-oo-diss): Treikan coastal land and the road that traverses it, made up of sand dunes and swamplands. [OT *bad air*]

Parad Matr (Puh-**rad Mart**-ah): Path the Widuz use to gain entrance to the Adunlok cave system. [WZ *mother's path*]

Parlevaag (**Parl**-ih-vagg): Fenni woman captured by Bhrudwans. [FN *storyteller*]

Pell (Pell): Father of Stella, husband of Herza, member of Loulea village council. [FI *small bush*]

Pending (**pen**-ding): Medium denomination coin common to northern Faltha (twelve fretas to one pending), equivalent to a day's wages. [origin uncertain]

Perdu (**Purr**-do): Mjolkbridge hunter rescued from death by the Fenni, now serving them as interpreter. [FI *in hiding*]

Phemanderac (**Fee-man**-duh-**rack**): Scholar of Dhauria who leaves his homeland to learn the whereabouts of the Right Hand. [FM *the mandate*]

Piskasia (Pisk-**ay**-zha): One of the Sixteen Kingdoms of Faltha, located south of Sna Vaztha along the banks of the Aleinus. [FM *fish land*]

Plonya (**Plonn**-yuh): One of the Sixteen Kingdoms of Faltha, located between Firanes and the wild Widuz country. [FM *floodplain*]

Plutobaran (**Plew**-toe-**barr**-in): Unknown northern country, supposedly covered in snow all year round. [FM *empty barrens*]

Pollerne wind, plains (**Pol**-earn): Extensive lake-studded plains of northern Firanes. The spring wind from Pollerne is fiercely cold. [FI *pollen*]

Poplar Alley: Farm in Loulea Vale.

Portals, the: Two hills guarding the eastern entrance to the Kljufa River's Upper Clough.

Prester (**Pres**-tah): Farmer who lives in Longacre, a small coastal village to the north of Loulea.

Pyrinius (Pie-**rinn-ee**-yoos): Dominie (teacher) of Phemanderac, expert harpist and scholar of Dhauria. [FM *fire servant*]

Qali (**Karl**-ee): A type of snow, dry and light, and by association the name of the northern god of winter. [FN *dry snow*]

Raedh (Rayth): Leader of the Kerd clan of the House of Leuktom in the Vale of Youth, was translated rather than dying. [FM *ruddy, red*]

Rakkra (Rahh-kra) aka Land of Sour Smell, the: Fodhram name for Myrvidda. [FD *dried faeces*]

Rammr (Ram-ir): Capital city of Firanes and seat of the King. [FI *straight*]

Raupa (Rau-puh): Arkhos of the House of Leuktom in exile, founder of Sna Vaztha. [FM *royal one*]

Rauth (Rowth): Loulea village elder, red-haired. Likely a nickname. [CT *red*]

Rehtal clan (Ray-tal): Small clan of the House of Saiwiz, remained in the Vale after all others were exiled. [FM *mouse-like*]

Remparer Mountains (Remm-pa-**rair**) aka Ramparts of Faltha, Manu Irion, Man-Eaters: Continental mountain range dividing western from central Faltha. [FM *the ramparts*]

Reynir (Ree-nir): Man of the House of Wenta, exiled from the Vale. [FM *river reeds*]

Rhinn na Torridon (Rinn nar **toh**-rih-don) aka Tarradale Broads: Coastlands south of Remparer Mountains. [WZ *rack of gentle valleys*]

Ribtickler: Hal's name for the sword he was given at Mjolkbridge.

Right Hand: Mysterious weapon, person or organisation mentioned in prophecy as overcoming the Destroyer.

Rinnan Holth (Rinn-un **Holth)** aka River Cave: Underground entrance to the Adunlok cave system. [WZ *river cave*]

Robbers of the Ramparts: Loosely organised bandits inhabiting the lower slopes of the Remparer Mountains.

Rock of the Fountain: Place in the Vale of Youth where the Most High set the fountain of eternal life.

Rockford: Small village on the slopes of the Black Hills in eastern Fodhram lands, home of Aspenlimb.

Roiling Pool: Small lake at the base of Secondstep Falls, Mossbank Cadence.

Roleystone Bridge: Stone arch over the Kljufa River at the head of the Upper Clough, the only bridge north of the Trow of Kljufa.

Roofed Road: Section of the Westway carved into the side of the Lower Clough of the Kljufa River.

Rotten Lands: Fenni name for Withwestwa Wood.

Sagon River (Sarr-gone): Major river of Plonya, also draining much of northern Treika and Withwestwa Wood. [FM *serpent*]

Saiwiz, House of (**Sigh**-wizz): One of the four great houses of the First Men. [FM *house of the sea*]

Salopa (Sar-**low**-puh): Old mare kept by Loulea Village Council for children to ride on. [CT *ease*]

Saurga (**Sour**-gah): The father of Kannwar, the Destroyer, cousin to the leader of the Kerd clan of the House of Leuktom. [FM *bitterness*]

Scymria (**Sim**-ree-yah): The Hidden Kingdom, a race of *losian* living in an interior valley in Firanes with a warm microclimate. [OF *bitterness*]

Seasnow: Snow that falls near the coast, heavy and water-laden.

Seaspray Farm: Farm on Swill Down, south of Loulea Vale.

Secondstep Falls: Second rapid in Mossbank Cadence, follows immediately after Firststep Falls, leads to Roiling Pool.

Sheeldalian Muir (Sheel-**dale**-ee-yin **Mew**-uh) aka Northern Wastes: Infertile grassland country between Stanlow and Ashdown in northern Treika. [FM *stone shield moor*]

Skyvault Range: Highest part of the Remparer Mountains, dominating skyline of eastern Treika.

Sna Vaztha (Snarr **Vazz**-thuh): One of the Sixteen Kingdoms of Faltha, located to the north-east of Faltha. [FM *frozen snow*]

Snaer (Sneer) aka Snowmask: Mask used in the Midwinter Play to represent winter. [FI *snow*]

Snaerfence (Sneer-fence): Rugged barrier at west end of Breidhan Moor, separating moors from the Torrelstrommen valley. [FI *snow fence*]

Snershil (**snerr**-shill): Large shoes for walking in soft snow. [FN *snow shoe*]

Snoweater: South wind heralding spring thaw.

Southern Run: Southern fur trapping route across Withwestwa, the earliest that can be used after the spring thaw.

Spindlewood Farm: Farm in Loulea Vale, home of blind Augon.

Square of Rainbows: The centre of Dona Mihst, within which is set the Rock of the Fountain.

Stalassokalven (Stuh-**lass**-oh-**cal**-vin): Vast cavern, buttressed by pillars, part of the Adunlok cave system. [WZ *stalagmite cavern*]

Stanlow (Stan-low): Treikan trading post at the confluence of the Mossbank and Sagon Rivers, popular early in the fur season. [OT *stone wall*]

Starfjell (Star-fell): Most northerly of the mountains that make up the Fells. [CT *star rock*]

Steffl (Stef-fill) aka Meall Gorm: Active volcano in Withwestwa Wood, a well-known landmark by the Westway. [FM *the hood*]

Stella Pellwen (Stell-ah **Pell**-win): Youth of Loulea, daughter of Pell and Herza of Loulea. [CT *from the stars*]

Stend (Stennd): Young man of Loulea Vale, betrothed to Anesel. [FI *stand tall*]

Sthane (Sthayn): Leader of the smallest clan and member of the Council of Leaders in the Vale of Youth, opposes Kannwar. [FM *spine*]

Stibbourne Farm (Stib-**born**): Farm of Kurr, located on Swill Down, possibly named after corn stubble, or less likely an FM word (*stiborn*) meaning stubborn.

Stickslap: A popular two-player game in northern Firanes involving the use of twelve sticks (two strike sticks and ten hand sticks).

Storr (Store): Farmer and woodsman of Storrdal, a hamlet in the Vinkullen Hills, Firanes. [FI *gaze*]

Straux (Strouw): Most populous of the Sixteen Kingdoms of Faltha, located south of Aleinus River on the central plains. [FM *wheat field*]

Stravanter (Strah-**varnt**-ah) aka Stormbringer: One of the three great peaks of the Grossbergen, with a rounded dome. [FM *storm signal*]

Struere (Strew-**ear**): Southern and larger of two villages founded on an island in the Aleinus River, coalescing into Instruere. [FM *instruct*]

Styggesbreen: (**Stigg**-iz-breen) aka Iskelelva: Large glacier extending south-westwards from the Grossbergen. [FN *silent glacier*]

Sumar (Soo-mah) aka Sunmask: Mask used in the Midwinter Play to symbolise high summer. [FI *sun mask*]

Summer Run: Northernmost of three fur trapping routes across Withwestwa and the Vollervei. Can be used only in summer.

Swill Down: Hill forming the southern boundary of Loulea Vale.

Sword of Jethart: Feared blade of the hero of Inch Chanter, held by the elders of the town.

Tala (**Tah**-lah): Younger brother of Talon, the Eldest warrior of the Widuz. [WD *nail*]

Talon (**Tah**-lonn): Eldest (most gifted) warrior of the Widuz. [WD *claw*]

Telba Poul (**Tell**-buh **Poul**): Pool at the lowest point of Wambakalven, draining the cave. [WZ *sombre pool*]

Thirdstep Falls: Spout-like waterfall in the Lower Cadence of Mossbank Cadence.

Thraell River (**Thray**-ell): River draining the eastern part of Breidhan Moor, flowing into Kljufa River. [FM *in thrall*]

Thuya Wood (**Thoy**-ah): Extensive boreal forest of northern Treika; part of the forest that extends across northern Faltha. [OT *thicket*]

Thyrtinden Massif (**Thir**-tin-din) aka Cloudpiercer: Tallest of three great peaks of the Grossbergen, it has a triple spire. [FM *cloud peak*]

Tilthan Vale (**Till**-thin) aka Valley of Plenty: Old name for the lower Torrelstrommen valley, before Mjolkbridge invaded. [FI *tilled valley*]

Tinei (**Tin**-ay): Wife to Kurr of Loulea. [OF *twist*]

Tolmen (**Toll**-men): Largest of the Widuz towns, located on the coast at the southern extremity of Widuz lands. [WZ *standing stone*]

Toothless: Fodhram fur trader, formerly a member of Shabby's band.

Torrelstrommen River, valley (**Torr**-ill-**strom**-in): Deep river valley in northern Firanes, draining much of Breidhan Moor. [FI *torrent stream*]

Trader: Merchant who makes a living trading goods across Faltha and Bhrudwo. Many Traders serve as spies for their kings.

Translation, The: by which the First Men of the Vale of Youth might be taken to be with the Most High without dying.

Treika (**Tree**-kuh): One of the Sixteen Kingdoms of Faltha, located between Widuz lands and the Remparer Mountains. [FM *forest land*]

Trenstane (Trenn-stayne): Treikan trading post at the confluence of the Lavera and Cauda Rivers, favoured by the Fodhram. [OT *tryst stone*]

Troldale Road (**Troll**-dayle): Road connecting Troldale valley with Westway, North March, Firanes. [FI *pine tree valley*]

Twilight Road: Coastal road connecting Rammr in Firanes with Ciennan in Plonya.

Uflok (**Ouf**-lock): Widuz town on the banks of the Sagon, where the families of the warriors of Adunlok make their homes. [WD *up look*]

Under The Wood Farm: Farm to the south-east of Loulea Vale, on limestone hills.

underworlder: Derogatory name for the First Men, given by the Fenni.

Upper Cadence: Longer but easier part of Mossbank Cadence, encompassing Firststep and Secondstep Falls.

Upper Clough (Cloff): Upper of the two deep gorges by which the Kljufa River passes through the Jawbone Mountains. [CT *ravine, steep valley*]

Urus: see Aurochs.

Vale of Youth aka Vale of the Chosen: Vale in the south of Faltha to which the First Men were drawn by the Most High.

Valley of Meeting: The valley immediately below the snout of Styggesbreen, Firanes.

Vaniyo (**Var**-nee-yoh): Bhrudwan Trader. [MB *subtle hands*]

Vapnatak (**Vapp**-nuh-tack): Largest town in the North March of Firanes. Named after the annual weapontake that took place here in the years of the Halvoyan incursions. [OF *weapontake*]

Varec Beach: Fishing village on the coast of North March, Firanes. [FI *sea squid*]

Vidda (**vid**-duh): Generic name for the inland plateaus and moors of Firanes. [FN *moor*]

Vinbrenna (Vinn-**brenn**-uh): One of main peaks of Vinkullen Hills, Firanes. [FI *high bare hill*]

Vindstrop House (Vinnd-strop): Main town of the Fodhram, a trading post on the Mossbank River. [MT *wind drop*]

Vinkullen Hills (Vinn-**cull**-in): Hills to the north of Mjolkbridge, Firanes. [FI *shield hills*]

Vithrain Gloum (Vith-**rayn Gloom**) aka Valley of Gloom, Tilthan Vale: Valley of the lower Torrelstrommen. [FI *valley of gloom*]

Vithrain Uftan (Vith-**rayn Ouf**-tan) aka Valley of Respite: Middle valley of the Torrelstrommen, broad and straight. [FI *valley of ease*]

Vollervei, the (Voll-uh-vai): Wastelands east of the Jawbone Mountains; also a legendary race living in the waste. [FD *wide waste*]

Vulture's Craw: Central gorge of the Aleinus River through the Wodranian Mountains, dividing Piskasia and Redana'a.

Wacke (wakk-ee): Large rocks and boulders scattered around the upper Torrelstrommen valley. [FI *boulder*]

Wambakalven (Wumm-buh-cal-vin) aka Womb Cavern: Large cave directly below Adunlok, part of Adunlok cave system [WZ *womb cavern*]

Warden: Informal leader of the Fodhram.

Watch Hill aka Kenna Hill, Magic Mountain: Forested hill, highest point in the Loulea region, home to Kroptur the Watcher.

Watch Ridge: Spur extending northwards from Watch Hill, North March, Firanes.

Watchers, the: Secret organisation dedicated to protecting Faltha from invasion.

Waybridge Inn: Hostelry at Mjolkbridge, Firanes.

Weid (Weed): Scholar of the House of Wenta in the Vale of Youth, dominie (instructor) of Kannwar. [FM *wisdom*]

Wenta, House of (Wen-tuh): One of the four great houses of the First Men. [FM *house of wind*]

Westway, the: Former main highway east from Firanes to Instruere, now superseded.

White Forks: Farm and valley to the south-east of Loulea Vale.

Whitebirch: From Woodsmancote, the first Fodhram Warden. Led an army which laid siege to Bandits' Cave, defeated bandits at the cost of his life.

Whitefang Pass: One of only two routes through the Remparer Mountains, a dangerous pass that regularly claims lives.

Windrise: Town in inland Firanes, situated where the Westway leaves the Mjolk valley.

Windrise Manor: Old inn at Windrise, Firanes, burned down in NA1009

Wira Storrsen (**Wee**-rah **Store**-sin): Younger son of Storr of Vinkullen, a solid, blond-haired man. [FI *wiry*]

Wisent (Wih-**sent**): Name of the Fenni clan chief's own aurochs. [FN *bison*]

Wisula (**Wih**-shill-uh): Senior courtier at the Firanese Court. [FI *careful answer*]

Withwestwa Wood (With-**west**-wuh): Extensive boreal forest of northern Plonya; part of the forest that extends across northern Faltha. The name was originally given to the whole continent. [FM *westwood*, backform of Falthwaite and Faltha]

Wodhaitic Sea (Woe-day-it-ick): Western sea bordering Faltha, specifically that ocean partly enclosed by north-western and south-western Faltha. [FM *hot water*]

Wodranian Mountains (Woe-**drain**-ee-an): Large mountainous area in east central Faltha, home of the Wodrani. [FM *water men*]

Wordweave: One of the word-based powers wielded by an adept in the *Fuirfad*. The Wordweave allows the user to weave another meaning into her or his words.

Worship, House of: Tall tower of Instruere, a monument based on the Tower of Worship in Dona Mihst.

Worship, Tower of: Centre of worship in Dona Mihst.

To be continued in

IN THE EARTH ABIDES THE FLAME

Fire of Heaven Book Two

And concludes in

THE RIGHT HAND OF GOD

Fire of Heaven Book Three

www.orbitbooks.co.uk

THE DARKNESS THAT COMES BEFORE

The Prince of Nothing, Book One

R. Scott Bakker

A score of centuries has passed since the First
Apocalypse and the thoughts of men have turned,
inevitably, to more worldly concerns . . .

A veteran sorcerer and spy seeks news of an ancient
enemy. A military genius plots to conquer the known
world for his Emperor but dreams of the throne for
himself. The spiritual leader of the Thousand Temples
seeks a Holy War to cleanse the land of the infidel. An
exiled barbarian chieftain seeks vengeance against the
man who disgraced him. And into this world steps a
man like no other, seeking to bind all – man and
woman, emperor and slave – to his own mysterious ends.

But the fate of men – even great men – means little
when the world itself may soon be torn asunder. Behind the
politics, beneath the religious fervour, a dark and ancient
evil is reawakening. After two thousand years, the No-God
is returning. The Second Apocalypse is nigh. And one
cannot raise walls against what has been forgotten . . .

GEOMANCER

Volume One of The Well of Echoes

Ian Irvine

Two hundred years ago the Charon fought for their lives against the creatures of the Void. Hunted and afraid, the last of the Charon sought to cross the Forbidding and take refuge on the human world of Santhenar.

In the battle that followed the power of the Charon was broken and humanity saved – but every victory comes at a price . . . For in that battle the Forbidding was destroyed. Now the forces that slaughtered the Charon have emerged from the Void, and Santhenar's people fight a desperate battle for survival.

But there is yet hope. For in the Secret Arts there lies hidden a strength as perilous and deadly as anything the Void commands. And it is the destiny of one woman to wield that power – to become a warrior, a leader, a saviour . . . a Geomancer.

A CAVERN OF BLACK ICE

Sword of Shadows Book One

J.V. Jones

When Raif Sevrance and his brother return home to their clan as the only survivors of a vicious attack in which both their father and the clan chief were killed, it is not only grief that clouds Raif's thoughts. The new chief's reign is a brutal one, made worse by his brother's acceptance of it.

When his uncle, Angus Lok, invites Raif to accompany him to Spire Vanis, it seems that he has no choice but to leave his home. It is the start of a journey that will change his life – and the world he inhabits.

MEDALON

Book One of the Demon Child Trilogy

Jennifer Fallon

A breathtaking fantasy adventure is about to unfold.
Enter the extraordinary world of Medalon . . .

According to legend, the last king of the ancient
Harshini race sired a half-human child. Now the demon
child must be found – and it must be killed.

It is a time of upheaval among the ruling elite of
Medalon. Intrigue is rife and treachery is the only means
of political advancement. It is a time when lies conceal
more lies and the truth has been long abandoned. It is a
time when only the most ruthless survive.

It is into this world that a forgotten magic is about to be
unleashed. And it is two siblings, R'shiel and Tarja, whose
story will become one with the legends of the land.

MYRREN'S GIFT

The Quickening Book One

Fiona McIntosh

When Wyl Thirsk, General of the Morgravian Legion, is forced to watch the torture of Myrren, a young woman accused of witchcraft, it seems little enough comfort to speed her passing. But Myrren is grateful for even this small mercy and promises Wyl a gift. He thanks her but dismisses the notion – what could this poor, doomed girl have to give him?

It is only years later that Wyl, shorn of his friends and allies, betrayed by his king, and forced to make an impossible choice, remembers the dying words of the young woman about to burn for the crime of witchcraft. As his enemy's sword draws closer, Wyl finally understands the meaning of Myrren's gift, and he wonders how one act of kindness could have unleashed such evil . . .

Gripping the reader from the very first page, *Myrren's Gift* marks Fiona McIntosh as one of fantasy fiction's most gifted storytellers.

DEVICES AND DESIRES

The Engineer Trilogy Book One

K.J. Parker

When an engineer is sentenced to death for a petty
transgression of guild law, he flees the city, leaving
behind his wife and daughter. Forced into exile, he
seeks a terrible vengeance – one that will leave a trail
of death and destruction in its wake.

But he will not be able to achieve this by himself. He
must draw up his plans using the blood of others . . .

A compelling tale of intrigue and injustice, *Devices and
Desires* is the beginning of a brilliant new fantasy series from
K. J. Parker, the acclaimed author of The Fencer Trilogy.